COME TO GRIEF
&
FOR KICKS

Dick Francis has written over forty-one international best-sellers and is widely acclaimed as one of the world's finest thriller writers. His awards include the Crime Writers' Association's Cartier Diamond Dagger for his outstanding contribution to the crime genre, and an honorary Doctorate of Humane Letters from Tufts University of Boston. In 1996 Dick Francis was made a Mystery Writers of America Grand Master for a lifetime's achievement and in 2000 he received a CBE in the Queen's Birthday Honours list.

Dick Francis

COME TO GRIEF
&
FOR KICKS

PAN BOOKS

Come to Grief first published 1995 by Michael Joseph.
First published in paperback 1991 by Pan Books in association with Michael Joseph.
For Kicks first published 1965 by Michael Joseph.
First published in paperback 1967 by Pan Books in association with Michael Joseph.

This omnibus first published 2006 by Pan Books
an imprint of Pan Macmillan, a division of Macmillan Publishers Limited
Pan Macmillan, 20 New Wharf Road, London N1 9RR
Basingstoke and Oxford
Associated companies throughout the world
www.panmacmillan.com

ISBN-13: 978-0-330-44669-3
ISBN-10: 0-330-44669-X

3 5 7 9 8 6 4

A CIP catalogue record for this book is available from
the British Library.

Printed and bound in the UK by
CPI Mackays, Chatham ME5 8TD

COME TO GRIEF

In November 1994, as part of the BBC's Children in Need Appeal, Radio 2 gave an auction of opportunities 'that money can't buy'. One of the lots was 'To have one's name used as a character in Dick Francis's next book'.

The lot was secured by Mrs Patricia Huxford. It has given Dick Francis great pleasure to include her in *Come to Grief*.

CHAPTER ONE

I had this friend, you see, that everyone loved.

(My name is Sid Halley.)

I had this friend that everyone loved, and I put him in the dock.

The trouble with working as an investigator, as I had been doing for approaching five years, was that occasionally one turned up facts that surprised and appalled and smashed peaceful lives for ever.

It had taken days of inner distress for me to decide to act on what I'd learned. Miserably, by then, I'd suffered through disbelief, through denial, through anger and at length through acceptance; all the stages of grief. I grieved for the man I'd known. For the man I *thought* I'd known, who had all along been a façade. I grieved for the loss of a friendship, for a man who still looked the same but was different, alien . . . despicable. I could much more easily have grieved for him dead.

The turmoil I'd felt in private had on public disclosure become universal. The press, jumping instinctively and strongly to his defence, had given me, as his accuser, a severely rough time. On racecourses, where I chiefly worked, long-time acquaintances had turned their backs. Love, support and comfort poured out towards my friend. Disbelief and denial and anger prevailed: acceptance lay a long way ahead. Meanwhile I, not he, was seen as the target for hatred. It would pass, I knew. One had simply to endure it, and wait.

On the morning set for the opening of his trial, my friend's mother killed herself.

The news was brought to the law courts in Reading, in Berkshire, where the presiding judge, gowned, had already heard the opening statements and where I, a witness for the prosecution, waited alone in a soulless side-room to be called. One of the court officials came to give me the suicide information and to say that the judge had adjourned the proceedings for the day, and I could go home.

'Poor woman,' I exclaimed, truly horrified.

Even though he was supposed to be impartial, the official's own sympathies were still with the accused. He eyed me without favour and said I should return the following morning, ten o'clock sharp.

I left the room and walked slowly along the corridor towards the exit, fielded on the way by a senior lawyer who took me by the elbow and drew me aside.

'His mother took a room in a hotel and jumped from the sixteenth floor,' he said without preamble. 'She left a note saying she couldn't bear the future. What are your thoughts?'

I looked at the dark, intelligent, eyes of Davis Tatum, a clumsy fat man with a lean agile brain.

'You know better than I do,' I said.

'*Sid!*' A touch of exasperation. 'Tell me your thoughts.'

'Perhaps he'll change his plea.'

He relaxed and half smiled. 'You're in the wrong job.'

I wryly shook my head. 'I catch the fish. You guys gut them.'

He amiably let go of my arm and I continued to the outside world to catch a train for the thirty-minute ride to the terminus in London, flagging down a taxi for the last mile or so home.

Ginnie Quint, I thought, travelling through London. Poor, poor Ginnie Quint, choosing death in preference to the everlasting agony of her son's disgrace. A lonely slamming exit. An end to tears. An end to grief.

The taxi stopped outside the house in Pont Square (off Cadogan Square), where I currently lived on the first floor, with a balcony overlooking the central leafy railed garden. As usual, the small secluded square was quiet, with little passing traffic and only a few people on foot. A thin early October wind shook the dying leaves on the lime trees, floating a few of them sporadically to the ground like soft yellow snowflakes.

I climbed out of the cab and paid the driver through his open window, and, as I turned to cross the pavement and go up the few steps to the front door, a man who

3

was apparently quietly walking past suddenly sprang at me in fury, raising a long black metal rod with which he tried to brain me.

I sensed rather than saw the first wicked slash and moved enough to catch the weight of it on my shoulder, not my head. He was screaming at me, half demented, and I fielded a second brutal blow on a raised defensive forearm. After that I seized his wrist in a pincer grip and rolled the bulk of his body backward over the leg I pushed out rigidly behind his knees, and felled him, sprawling, iron bar and all, onto the hard ground. He yelled bitter words; cursing, half incoherent, threatening to kill.

The taxi still stood there, diesel engine running, the driver staring wide-mouthed and speechless, a state of affairs that continued while I yanked open the black rear door and stumbled in again onto the seat. My heart thudded. Well, it would.

'*Drive*,' I said urgently. 'Drive on.'

'But . . .'

'Just drive. Go *on*. Before he finds his feet and breaks your windows.'

The driver closed his mouth fast and meshed his gears, and wavered at something above running pace along the road.

'Look,' he said, protesting, half turning his head back to me, 'I didn't see nothing. You're my last fare today, I've been on the go eight hours and I'm on my way home.'

'Just drive,' I said. Too little breath. Too many jumbled feelings.

'Well . . . but, drive where *to*?'

Good question. Think.

'He didn't look like no mugger,' the taxi driver observed aggrievedly. 'But you never can tell these days. D'you want me to drop you off at the police? He hit you something shocking. You could *hear* it. Like he broke your arm.'

'Just drive, would you?'

The driver was large, fiftyish and a Londoner, but no John Bull, and I could see from his head movements and his repeated spiky glances at me in his rear-view mirror that he didn't want to get involved in my problems and couldn't wait for me to leave his cab.

Pulse eventually steadying, I could think of only one place to go. My only haven, in many past troubles.

'Paddington,' I said. 'Please.'

'St Mary's, d'you mean? The hospital?'

'No. The trains.'

'But you've just come from there!' he protested.

'Yes, but please go back.'

Cheering a little he rocked round in a U-turn and set off for the return to Paddington Station where he assured me again that he hadn't seen nothing, nor heard nothing neither, and he wasn't going to get involved, did I see?

I simply paid him and let him go, and if I memorised

his cab-licensing number it was out of habit, not expectation.

As part of normal equipment I wore a mobile phone on my belt and, walking slowly into the high airy terminus, I pressed the buttons to reach the man I trusted most in the world, my ex-wife's father, Rear Admiral Charles Roland, Royal Navy, retired, and to my distinct relief he answered at the second ring.

'Charles,' I said. My voice cracked a bit, which I hadn't meant.

A pause, then, 'Is that you, Sid?'

'May I . . . visit?'

'Of course. Where are you?'

'Paddington. I'll come by train and taxi.'

He said calmly, 'Use the side-door. It's not locked,' and put down his receiver.

I smiled, reassured as ever by his steadiness and his brevity with words. An unemotional, undemonstrative man, not paternal towards me and very far from indulgent, he gave me nevertheless a consciousness that he cared considerably about what happened to me and would proffer rocklike support if I needed it. Like I needed it at that moment, for several variously dire reasons.

Trains to Oxford being less frequent in the middle of the day, it was four in the afternoon by the time the country taxi, leaving Oxford well behind, arrived at Charles's vast old house at Aynsford and decanted me at the side-door. I paid the driver clumsily owing to

stiffening bruises, and walked with relief into the pile
I really thought of as home, the one unchanging constant in a life that had tossed me about, rather, now
and then.

Charles sat, as often, in the large leather armchair
that I found too hard for comfort but that he, in his
uncompromising way, felt appropriate to accommodate
his narrow rump. I had sometime in the past moved
one of the softer but still fairly formal old gold brocade
armchairs from the drawing-room into the smaller
room, his 'wardroom', as it was there we always sat
when the two of us were alone. It was there that he
kept his desk, his collection of flies for fishing, his
nautical books, his racks of priceless old orchestral
recordings and the gleaming marble and steel wonder
of a custom-built, frictionless turntable on which he
played them. It was there on the dark green walls
that he'd hung large photographs of the ships he'd
commanded, and smaller photos of shipmates, and
there, also, that he'd lately positioned a painting of me
as a jockey riding over a fence at Cheltenham racecourse, a picture that summed up every ounce of vigour
needed for race-riding, and which had hung for years
less conspicuously in the dining-room.

He had had a strip of lighting positioned along the
top of the heavy gold frame, and when I got there that
evening, it was lit.

He was reading. He put his book face down on his
lap when I walked in, and gave me a bland noncommittal

7

inspection. There was nothing, as usual, to be read in his eyes: I could often see quite clearly into other people's minds, but seldom his.

'Hullo,' I said.

I could hear him take a breath and trickle it out through his nose. He spent all of five seconds looking me over, then pointed to the tray of bottles and glasses which stood on the table below my picture.

'Drink,' he said briefly. An order, not invitation.

'It's only four o'clock.'

'Immaterial. What have you eaten today?'

I didn't say anything, which he took to be answer enough.

'Nothing,' he said, nodding. 'I thought so. You look thin. It's this *bloody* case. I thought you were supposed to be in court today.'

'It was adjourned until tomorrow.'

'Get a drink.'

I walked obediently over to the table and looked assessingly at the bottles. In his old-fashioned way he kept brandy and sherry in decanters. Scotch – Famous Grouse, his favourite – remained in the screw-topped bottle. I would have to have Scotch, I thought, and doubted if I could pour even that.

I glanced upwards at my picture. In those days, six years ago, I'd had two hands. In those days I'd been British steeplechasing's champion jockey: whole, healthy and, I dared say, fanatical. A nightmare fall had resulted in a horse's sharp hoof half ripping off my left hand: the end of one career and the birth, if you could call it that, of another. Slow lingering birth of a detective, while I spent two years pining for what I'd lost and drifted rudderless like a wreck that didn't quite sink but was unseaworthy, all the same. I was ashamed of those two years. At the end of them a ruthless villain had smashed beyond mending the remains of the useless hand and had galvanised me into a resurrection of the spirit and the impetus to seek what I'd had since, a myoelectric false hand that worked on nerve impulses from my truncated forearm and looked and behaved so realistically that people often didn't notice its existence.

My present problem was that I couldn't move its thumb far enough from its fingers to grasp the large heavy cut-glass brandy decanter, and my right hand wasn't working too well either. Rather than drop alcohol all over Charles's Persian rug, I gave up and sat in the gold armchair.

'What's the matter?' Charles asked abruptly. 'Why did you come? Why don't you pour a drink?'

After a moment I said dully, knowing it would hurt him, 'Ginnie Quint killed herself.'

'*What?*'

'This morning,' I said. 'She jumped from sixteen floors up.'

His fine-boned face went stiff and immediately looked much older. The bland eyes darkened, as if retreating into their sockets. Charles had known Ginnie

Quint for thirty or more years, and had been fond of her and had been a guest in her house often.

Powerful memories lived in my mind also. Memories of a friendly, rounded, motherly woman happy in her role as a big-house wife, inoffensively rich, working genuinely and generously for several charities and laughingly glowing in reflected glory from her famous, good-looking successful only child, the one that everyone loved.

Her son, Ellis, that I had put in the dock.

The last time I'd seen Ginnie she'd glared at me with incredulous contempt, demanding to know how I could *possibly* seek to destroy the golden Ellis, who counted me his friend, who liked me, who'd done me favours, who would have trusted me with his life.

I'd let her molten rage pour over me, offering no defence. I knew exactly how she felt. Disbelief and denial and anger . . . The idea of what he'd done was so sickening to her that she rejected the guilt possibility absolutely, as almost everyone else had done, though in her case with anguish.

Most people believed I had got it all wrong, and had ruined *myself*, not Ellis. Even Charles, at first, had said doubtfully, 'Sid, are you *sure*?'

I'd said I was certain. I'd hoped desperately for a way out . . . for *any* way out . . . as I knew what I'd be pulling down on myself if I went ahead. And it had been at least as bad as I'd feared, and in many ways worse. After the first bombshell solution – a proposed solution – to a crime that had had half the country baying for blood (but not *Ellis*'s blood, no *no*, it was *unthinkable*), there had been the first court appearance, the remand into custody (a *scandal*, he should of *course* be let out immediately on bail), and after that there had fallen a sudden press silence, while the *sub judice* law came into effect.

Under British *sub judice* law, no evidence might be publicly discussed between the remand and the trial. Much investigation and strategic trial planning could go on behind the scenes, but neither potential jurors nor John Smith in the street was allowed to know details. Uninformed, public opinion had consequently stuck at the 'Ellis is innocent' stage, and I'd had nearly three months, now, of obloquy.

Ellis, you see, was a Young Lochinvar, in spades. Ellis Quint, once champion amateur jump jockey, had flashed onto television screens like a comet, a brilliant, laughing, able, funny performer, the draw for millions on sports quiz programmes, the ultimate chat-show host, the model held up to children, the glittering star that regularly raised the nation's happiness level, to whom everyone, from tiara to baseball cap worn backwards, responded.

Manufacturers fell over themselves to tempt him to endorse their products, and half the kids in England strode about with machismo in glamorised jockey-type riding boots over their jeans. And it was this man, this *paragon* that I sought to eradicate.

No one seemed to blame the tabloid columnist who'd written, 'The once-revered Sid Halley, green with envy, tries to tear down a talent he hasn't a prayer of matching . . .' There had been inches about 'A spiteful little man trying to compensate for his own inadequacies.' I hadn't shown any of it to Charles, but others had.

The telephone at my waist buzzed suddenly, and I answered its summons.

'Sid . . . Sid . . .'

The woman on the other end was crying. I'd heard her crying often.

'Are you at home?' I asked.

'No . . . In the hospital.'

'Tell me the number and I'll phone straight back.'

I heard murmuring in the background; then another voice came on, efficient, controlled, reading out a number, repeating it slowly. I tapped the digits onto my mobile so that they appeared on the small display screen.

'Right,' I said, reading the number back. 'Put down your receiver.' To Charles I said, 'May I use your phone?'

He waved a hand permissively towards his desk, and I pressed the buttons on his phone to get back to where I'd been.

The efficient voice answered immediately.

'Is Mrs Ferns still there?' I said. 'It's Sid Halley.'

'Hang on.'

Linda Ferns was trying not to cry. 'Sid . . . Rachel's worse. She's asking for you. Can you come? Please.'

'How bad is she?'

'Her temperature keeps going up.' A sob stopped her. 'Talk to Sister Grant.'

I talked to the efficient voice, Sister Grant. 'How bad is Rachel?'

'She's asking for you all the time,' she said. 'How soon can you come?'

'Tomorrow.'

'Can you come this evening?'

I said, 'Is it that bad?'

I listened to a moment of silence, in which she couldn't say what she meant because Linda was beside her.

'Come this evening,' she repeated.

This evening. Dear God. Nine-year-old Rachel Ferns lay in a hospital in Kent a hundred and fifty miles away. Ill to death, this time, it sounded like.

'Promise her,' I said, 'that I'll come tomorrow.' I explained where I was. 'I have to be in court tomorrow morning, in Reading, but I'll come to see Rachel as soon as I get out. Promise her. Tell her I'm going to be there. Tell her I'll bring six wigs and an angel fish.'

The efficient voice said, 'I'll tell her,' and then added, 'Is it true that Ellis Quint's mother has killed herself? Mrs Ferns says someone heard it on the radio news and repeated it to her. She wants to know if it's true.'

'It's true.'

'Come as soon as you can,' the nurse said, and disconnected.

I put down the receiver. Charles said, 'The child?'

'It sounds as if she's dying.'

'You knew it was inevitable.'

'It doesn't make it any easier for the parents.' I sat down again slowly in the gold armchair. 'I would go tonight if it would save her life, but I . . .' I stopped, not knowing what to say, how to explain that I wouldn't go. Couldn't go. Not except to save her life, which no one could do however much they ached to.

Charles said briefly, 'You've only just got here.'

'Yeah.'

'And what else is there, that you haven't told me?'

I looked at him.

'I know you too well, Sid,' he said. 'You didn't come all this way just because of Ginnie. You could have told me about her on the telephone.' He paused. 'From the look of you, you came for the oldest of reasons.' He paused again, but I didn't say anything. 'For sanctuary,' he said.

I shifted in the chair. 'Am I so transparent?'

'Sanctuary from what?' he asked. 'What is so sudden . . . and urgent?'

I sighed. I said with as little heat as possible, 'Gordon Quint tried to kill me.'

Gordon Quint was Ginnie's husband. Ellis was their son.

It struck Charles silent, open mouthed: and it took a great deal to do that.

After a while I said, 'When they adjourned the trial I went home by train and taxi. Gordon Quint was waiting there in Pont Square for me. God knows how long he'd been there, how long he would have waited, but anyway, he was there, with an iron bar.' I swallowed. 'He aimed it at my head, but I sort of ducked, and it hit my shoulder. He tried again . . . Well, this mechanical hand has its uses. I closed it on his wrist and put into practice some of the judo I've spent so many hours learning, and I tumbled him onto his back . . . and he was screaming at me all the time that I'd killed Ginnie . . . I'd killed her.'

'*Sid.*'

'He was half mad . . . raving, really . . . He said I'd destroyed his whole family. I'd destroyed all their lives . . . he swore I would die for it . . . that he would get me . . . get me . . . I don't think he knew what he was saying, it just poured out of him.'

Charles said dazedly, 'So what did you do?'

'The taxi driver was still there, looking stunned, so . . . er . . . I got back into the taxi.'

'You got back . . .? But . . . what about Gordon?'

'I left him there. Lying on the pavement. Screaming revenge . . . starting to stand up . . . waving the iron bar. I . . . er . . . I don't think I'll go home tonight, if I can stay here.'

Charles said faintly, 'Of course you can stay. It's

15

taken for granted. You told me once that this was your home.'

'Yeah.'

'Then believe it.'

I did believe it, or I wouldn't have gone there. Charles and his certainties had in the past saved me from inner disintegration, and my reliance on him had oddly been strengthened, not evaporated, by the collapse of my marriage to his daughter Jenny, and our divorce.

Aynsford offered respite. I would go back soon enough to defuse Gordon Quint; I would swear an oath in court and tear a man to shreds; I would hug Linda Ferns and, if I were in time, make Rachel laugh; but for this one night I would sleep soundly in Charles's house in my own accustomed room – and let the dry well of mental stamina refill.

Charles said, 'Did Gordon ... er ... hurt you, with his bar?'

'A bruise or two.'

'I know your sort of bruises.'

I sighed again. 'I think ... um ... he's cracked a bone. In my arm.'

His gaze flew instantly to the left arm, the plastic job.

'No,' I said, 'the other one.'

Aghast, he said, 'Your *right* arm?'

'Well, yeah. But only the ulna, which goes from the little finger side of the wrist up to the elbow. Not the radius as well, luckily. The radius will act as a natural splint.'

'But *Sid* . . .'

'Better than my skull. I had the choice.'

'How can you *laugh* about it?'

'A bloody bore, isn't it?' I smiled without stress. 'Don't *worry* so, Charles. It'll heal. I broke the same bone worse once before, when I was racing.'

'But you had two hands then.'

'Yes, so I did. So would you mind picking up that damned heavy brandy decanter and sloshing half a pint of anaesthetic into a glass?'

Wordlessly he got to his feet and complied. I thanked him. He nodded. End of transaction.

When he was again sitting down, he said, 'So the taxi driver was a witness.'

'The taxi driver is a "don't-get-involved" man.'

'But if he *saw* . . . He must have heard . . .'

'Blind and deaf, he insisted he was.' I drank fiery neat liquid gratefully. 'Anyway, that suits me fine.'

'But, Sid . . .'

'Look,' I said reasonably, 'what would you have me do? Complain? Prosecute? Gordon Quint is normally a level-headed worthy sixty-ish citizen. He's not your average murderer. Besides, he's your own personal long-time friend, and I, too, have eaten in his house. But he already hates me for attacking Ellis, the light of his life, and he'd not long learned that Ginnie, his adored wife, had killed herself because she couldn't bear what lies ahead. So how do you think Gordon feels?' I paused. 'I'm just glad he didn't succeed in smashing my brains in. And, if you can believe it, I'm almost as glad for *his* sake that he didn't, as for my own.'

Charles shook his head resignedly.

'Grief can be dangerous,' I said.

He couldn't dispute it. Deadly revenge was as old as time.

We sat companionably in silence. I drank brandy and felt marginally saner. Knots of tension relaxed in my stomach. I made various resolutions to give up chasing the deadlier crooks – but I'd made resolutions like that before, and hadn't kept them.

I'd stopped asking myself why I did it. There were hundreds of other ways of passing the time and earning one's keep. Other ex-jockeys became trainers or commentators or worked in racing in official capacities and only I, it seemed, felt impelled to swim round the hidden fringes, attempting to sort out doubts and worries for people who for any reason didn't want to bother the police or the racing authorities.

There was a need for me and what I could do, or I would have sat around idle, twiddling my thumbs. Instead, even in the present general climate of ostracism, I had more offers of work than I could accept.

Most jobs took me less than a week, particularly those that involved looking into someone's credit and credibility rating: bookmakers asked me to do that frequently, before taking on new account customers, and trainers paid me fees to assure them that if they bought expensive two-year-olds for new owners at the Sales, they wouldn't be left with broken promises and a mountain of debt. I'd checked on all sorts of proposed business plans and saved a lot of people from confidence tricksters, and I'd uncovered absconding debtors, and thieves of all sorts, and had proved a confounded nuisance to imaginative felons.

People had sobbed on my shoulders from joy and deliverance: others had threatened and battered to make me quit: Linda Ferns would hug me and Gordon Quint hate me; and I also had two more investigations in hand that I'd spent too little time on. So why didn't I give it up and change to a life of quiet safe financial management, which I wasn't bad at either? I felt the effects of the iron bar from neck to fingers . . . and didn't know the answer.

The mobile phone on my belt buzzed and I answered it as before, finding on the line the senior lawyer I'd talked to in the corridor in the law courts.

'Sid, this is Davis Tatum. I've news for you,' he said.

'Give me your number and I'll call you back.'

'Oh? Oh, OK.' He read off his number, which I copied as before, and also as before I borrowed Charles's phone on the desk to get back to square one.

'Sid,' said Tatum, coming as usual straight to the point, 'Ellis Quint is changing his plea from not guilty to guilty by reason of diminished responsibility. It seems his mother's powerful statement of no confidence in his innocence has had a laxative effect on the bowels of the counsel for the defence.'

'Jeez,' I said.

Tatum chuckled. I imagined his double chin wobbling. He said, 'The trial will now be adjourned for a week to allow expert psychiatric witnesses to be briefed. In other words, you don't have to turn up tomorrow.'

'Good.'

'But I hope you will.'

'How do you mean?'

'There's a job for you.'

'What sort of job?'

'Investigating, of course. What else? I'd like to meet you somewhere privately.'

'All right,' I said, 'but sometime tomorrow I have to go to Kent to see the child, Rachel Ferns. She's back in hospital and it doesn't sound good.'

'Hell.'

'Yeah.'

'Where are you?' he asked. 'The Press are looking for you.'

'They can wait a day.'

'I told the people from *The Pump* that after the mauling they've given you they haven't a prayer of you talking to them.'

'I appreciate that,' I said, smiling.

He chuckled. 'About tomorrow . . .'

'I'll go to Kent in the morning,' I said. 'I don't know how long I'll stay, it depends on Rachel. How about five o'clock in London? Would that do you? The end of your business day.'

'Right. Where? Not in my office. How about your place? No, perhaps not, if *The Pump*'s after you.'

'How about, say, the bar leading to the second-floor restaurant of the Le Meridien Hotel in Piccadilly?'

'I don't know it.'

'All the better.'

'If I need to change it,' he said, 'can I still get you on your mobile phone?'

'Always.'

'Good. See you tomorrow.'

I replaced Charles's receiver and sat on the gold armchair as before. Charles looked at the mobile instrument I'd lain this time on the table beside my glass and asked the obvious question.

'Why do you ring them back? Why don't you just talk?'

'Well,' I said, 'someone is listening to this gadget.'

'*Listening?*'

I explained about the insecurity of open radio transmission, that allowed anyone clever and expert to hear what they shouldn't.

Charles said, 'How do you know someone's listening to you?'

'A lot of small things people have recently learned that I haven't told them.'

21

'Who is it?'

'I don't actually know. Someone has also accessed my computer over the phone lines. I don't know who did that, either. It's disgustingly easy nowadays – but again, only if you're expert – to suss out people's private passwords and read their secret files.'

He said with slight impatience, 'Computers are beyond me.'

'I've had to learn,' I said, grinning briefly. 'A bit different from scudding over hurdles at Plumpton on a wet day.'

'Everything you do astounds me.'

'I wish I was still racing.'

'Yes, I know. But if you were, you'd anyway be coming to the end of it soon, wouldn't you? How old are you now? Thirty-four?'

I nodded. Thirty-five loomed.

'Not many top jump jockeys go on much after that.'

'You put things so delightfully bluntly, Charles.'

'You're of more use to more people the way you are.'

Charles tended to give me pep talks when he thought I needed them. I could never work out how he knew. He'd said something once about my looking like a brick wall: that when I shut out the world and retreated into myself, things were bad. Maybe he was right. Retreat inwards meant for me not retreating outwards, and I supposed I'd learned the technique almost from birth.

Jenny, my loved and lost wife, had said she couldn't

live with it. She'd wanted me to give up race-riding and become a softer shelled person, and when I wouldn't – or couldn't – we had shaken acridly apart. She had recently remarried, and this time she'd tied herself not to a thin dark-haired risk-taking bundle of complexes, but to a man to fit her needs, a safe, greying, sweet-natured uncomplicated fellow with a knighthood. Jenny, the warring unhappy Mrs Halley, was now ser-enely Lady Wingham. A photograph of her with her handsome beaming Sir Anthony stood in a silver frame next to the telephone on Charles's desk.

'How's Jenny?' I asked politely.

'Fine,' Charles answered without expression.

'Good.'

'He's a bore, after you,' Charles observed.

'You can't say such things.'

'I can say what I bloody well like in my own house.'

In harmony and mutual regard we passed a peaceful evening, disturbed only by five more calls on my mobile phone, all demanding to know, with varying degrees of peremptoriness, where they could find Sid Halley.

I said each time, 'This is an answering service. Leave your number and we'll pass on your message.'

All of the callers, it seemed, worked for newspapers, a fact that particularly left me frowning.

'I don't know where they all got this number from,' I told Charles. 'It's not in any directory. I give it only to people I'm working for, so they can reach me day or night, and only to others whose calls I wouldn't want to miss. I tell them it's a private line for their use only. I don't hand this number out on printed cards, and I don't have it on my writing paper. Quite often I re-route calls to this phone from my phone in the flat, but I didn't today because of Gordon Quint bashing away outside and preventing me from going in. So how do half the newspapers in London know it?'

'How will you find out?' Charles asked.

'Um . . . engage Sid Halley to look into it, I dare say'.

Charles laughed. I felt uneasy, all the same. Someone had been listening on that number, and now someone had broadcast it. It wasn't that my phone conversations were excessively secret – and I'd started the semi-exclusive number anyway solely so that the machine didn't buzz unnecessarily at awkward moments – but now I had a sense that someone was deliberately crowding me. Tapping into my computer – which wouldn't get anyone far, as I knew a lot of defences. Assaulting me electronically. *Stalking*.

Enough was enough. Five newspapers were too much. Sid Halley, as I'd said, would have to investigate his own case.

Charles's long-time live-in housekeeper, Mrs Cross, all dimples and delight, cooked us a simple supper and fussed over me comfortably like a hen. I guiltily found her a bit smothering sometimes, but always sent her a card for her birthday.

I went to bed early and found that, as usual, Mrs

Cross had left warm welcoming lights on in my room and had put out fresh pyjamas and fluffy towels.

A pity the day's troubles couldn't be as easily cosseted into oblivion.

I undressed and brushed my teeth and eased off the artificial hand. My left arm ended uselessly four inches below the elbow; a familiar punctuation, but still a sort of bereavement.

My right arm now twinged violently at every use.

Damn the lot, I thought.

CHAPTER TWO

The morning brought little improvement.

I sometimes used a private chauffeur-driven car hire firm based in London to ferry around people and things I wanted to keep away from prying eyes and, consequently, waking to a couple of faulty arms, I telephoned from Charles's secure number and talked to my friends at TeleDrive.

'Bob?' I said. 'I need to get from north-west of Oxford to Kent, Canterbury. There'll be a couple of short stops on the journey. And, sometime this afternoon, a return to London. Can anyone do it at such short notice?'

'Give me the address,' he said briefly. 'We're on our way.'

I breakfasted with Charles. That is to say, we sat in the dining-room where Mrs Cross, in her old-fashioned way, had set out toast, coffee and cereals and a warming dish of scrambled eggs.

Charles thought mornings hadn't begun without scrambled eggs. He ate his on toast and eyed me drinking coffee left-handedly. From long acquaintance with my preference for no fuss, he made no comment on the consequences of iron bars.

He was reading a broad-sheet newspaper which, as he showed me, was making a good-taste meal of Ginnie Quint's death. Her pleasant, smiling face inappropriately spread across two columns. I shut out of my mind any image of what she might look like sixteen floors down.

Charles said, reading aloud, ' "Friends say she appeared depressed about her son's forthcoming trial. Her husband, Gordon, was unavailable for comment." In other words, the Press couldn't find him.'

Ordeal by newsprint, I thought; the latter-day torture.

'Seriously, Sid,' Charles said in his most calm civilised voice, 'was Gordon's rage at you transient or . . . er . . . obsessive?'

'Seriously,' I echoed him, 'I don't know.' I sighed. 'I should think it's too soon to tell. Gordon himself probably doesn't know.'

'Do take care, Sid.'

'Sure.' I sorted through the flurry of impressions I'd gathered in the brief seconds of violence in Pont Square. 'I don't know where Ginnie was when she jumped,' I said, 'but I don't think Gordon was with her. I mean, when he leaped at me he was wearing country clothes. Work-day clothes: mud on his boots, corduroy trousers, old tweed jacket, open-necked blue shirt. He hadn't been staying in any sixteen-storey hotel. And the metal bar he hit me with . . . it wasn't a smooth rod, it was a five-foot piece of angle iron, the sort you thread wire through or fencing. I saw the holes in it.'

Charles stared.

I said, 'I'd say he was at home in Berkshire when he was told about Ginnie. I think if I'd loitered around to search, I would have found Gordon's Land-Rover parked near Pont Square.'

Gordon Quint, though a landowner, was a hands-on custodian of his multiple acres. He drove tractors, scythed weeds to clear streams, worked alongside his men to repair his boundaries, re-fence his sheep fields and thin out his woodlands, enjoying both the physical labour and the satisfaction of a job most competently done.

I knew him also as self-admiring and as expecting – and receiving – deference from everyone, including Ginnie. It pleased him to be a generous host while leaving his guests in no doubt of his superior worth.

The man I'd seen in Pont Square, all 'squire' manner stripped away, had been a raw, hurt, *outraged* and oddly more genuine person than the Gordon I'd known before: but until I learned for sure which way the explosively tossed-up bricks of his nature would come down, I would keep away from fencing posts and any other agricultural hardware he might be travelling with.

I told Charles I'd engaged TeleDrive to come and pick me up. To his raised eyebrows I explained I would put the cost against expenses. Whose expenses? General running expenses, I said.

'Is Mrs Ferns paying you?' Charles neutrally asked.

'Not any more.'

'Who is, exactly?' He liked me to make a profit. I did, but he seldom believed it.

'I don't starve,' I said, drinking my coffee. 'Have you ever tried three or four eggs whipped up in mushroom soup? Instant mushroom omelette, not at all bad.'

'Disgusting,' Charles said.

'You get a different perspective, living alone.'

'You need a new wife,' Charles said. 'What about that girl who used to share a flat with Jenny in Oxford?'

'Louise McInnes?'

'Yes. I thought you and she were having an affair.'

No one had affairs any more. Charles's words were half a century out of date. But though the terms might now be different, the meaning was eternal.

'A summer picnic,' I said. 'The frosts of winter killed it off.'

'Why?'

'What she felt for me was more curiosity than love.'

He understood that completely. Jenny had talked about me so long and intimately to her friend Louise, mostly to my detriment, that I recognised – in retrospect – that the friend had chiefly been fascinated in checking out the information personally. It had been a lighthearted passage from mating to parting. Nice while it lasted, but no roots.

When the car came for me I thanked Charles for his sanctuary.

'Any time,' he said, nodding.

We parted as usual without physically touching. Eye contact said it all.

Getting the driver to thread his way back and forth through the maze of shopping dead-ends in the town of Kingston in Surrey, I acquired six dressing-up party wigs from a carnival store and an angel fish in a plastic tub from a pet shop; and, thus armed, arrived eventually at the children's cancer ward that held Rachel Ferns.

Linda greeted my arrival with glittering tears, but her daughter still lived. Indeed, in one of those unpredictable quirks that made leukaemia such a roller-coaster of hope and despair, Rachel was marginally better. She was awake, semi-sitting up in bed and pleased at my arrival.

'Did you bring the angel fish?' she demanded by way of greeting.

I held up the plastic bucket, which swung from my plastic wrist. Linda took it and removed the watertight lid, showing her daughter the shining black-and-silver fish that swam vigorously inside.

Rachel relaxed. 'I'm going to call him Sid,' she said.

She'd been a lively, blonde, pretty child once, according to her photographs: now she seemed all huge eyes in a bald head. Lassitude and anaemia had made her frighteningly frail.

When her mother had first called me in to investigate an attack on Rachel's pony, the illness had been in remission, the dragon temporarily sleeping. Rachel had become someone special to me and I'd given her a fish tank complete with lights, aeration, water plants, Gothic castle arches, sand and brilliant tropical swimming inhabitants. Linda had wept. Rachel had spent hours getting to know her new friends' habits; the ones that skulked in corners, the one who bossed all the rest. Half of the fish were called Sid.

The fish tank stood in the Ferns' sitting-room at home and it seemed uncertain now whether Rachel would see the new Sid among his mates.

It was there, in the comfortable middle-sized room furnished with unaggressively expensive modern sofas, with glass-topped end tables and stained-glass Tiffany lamps, that I had first met my clients, Linda and Rachel Ferns.

There were no books in the room, only a few magazines; dress fashions and horses. Shiny striped curtains in crimson and cream; geometrically patterned carpet in merging fawn and grey; flower prints on pale pink walls. Overall the impression was a degree of lack of coordination which probably indicated impulsive inhabitants without strongly formed characters. The Ferns weren't 'old' money, I concluded, but there appeared to be plenty of it.

Linda Ferns, on the telephone, had begged me to come. Five or six ponies in the district had been attacked by vandals, and one of the ponies belonged to her daughter, Rachel. The police hadn't found out who the vandals were and now months had gone by, and her daughter was still very distressed and would I *please*, *please*, come and see if I could help.

'I've heard you're my only hope. I'll pay you, of course. I'll pay you *anything* if you help Rachel. She has these terrible nightmares. *Please.*'

I mentioned my fee.

'Anything,' she said.

She hadn't told me, before I arrived in the far-flung village beyond Canterbury, that Rachel was ill unto death.

When I met the huge-eyed bald-headed slender child she shook hands with me gravely.

'Are you really Sid Halley?' she asked.

I nodded.

'Mum said you would come. Daddy said you didn't work for kids.'

'I do sometimes.'

'My hair is growing,' she said; and I could see the thin fine blonde fuzz just showing over the pale scalp.

'I'm glad.'

She nodded. 'Quite often I wear a wig, but they itch. Do you mind if I don't?'

'Not in the least.'

'I have leukaemia,' she said calmly.

'I see.'

She studied my face, a child old beyond her age, as I'd found all sick young people to be.

'You will find out who killed Silverboy, won't you?'

'I'll try,' I said. 'How did he die?'

'No, no,' Linda interrupted. 'Don't ask her. I'll tell you. It upsets her. Just say you'll sort them out, those *pigs*. And Rachel, you take Pegotty out into the garden and push him round so that he can see the flowers.'

Pegotty, it transpired, was a contented-looking baby strapped into a buggy. Rachel without demur pushed him out into the garden and could presently be seen through the window giving him a close-up acquaintance with an azalea.

Linda Ferns watched and wept the first of many tears.

'She needs a bone marrow transplant,' she said, trying to suppress sobs. 'You'd think it would be simple, but no one so far can find a match to her, not even in the international register set up by the Anthony Nolan Trust.'

I said inadequately, 'I'm sorry.'

'Her father and I are divorced,' Linda said. 'We divorced five years ago, and he's married again.' She spoke without bitterness. 'These things happen.'

'Yes,' I said.

I was at the Ferns' house early in a June of languorous days and sweet-smelling roses, a time for the lotus, not horrors.

33

'A bunch of vandals,' Linda said with a fury that set her whole body trembling, 'they maimed a lot of ponies in Kent... in this area particularly... so that poor loving kids went out into their paddocks and found their much loved ponies *mutilated*. What sick, sick mind would *blind* a poor inoffensive pony that had never done anyone any harm? Three ponies round here were blinded and others had had knives stuck up their back passages.' She blinked on her tears. 'Rachel was terribly upset. All the children for miles were crying inconsolably. And the police couldn't find who'd done any of it.'

'Was Silverboy blinded?' I asked.

'No... no... It was worse... For Rachel, it was worse. She found him, you see... out in the paddock...' Linda openly sobbed. 'Rachel wanted to sleep in a makeshift stable... a lean-to shed, really. She wanted to sleep there at nights with Silverboy tied up there beside her, and I wouldn't let her. She's been ill for nearly three years. It's such a *dreadful* disease, and I feel so helpless...' She wiped her eyes, plucking a tissue from a half-empty box. 'She keeps saying it wasn't my fault, but I know she thinks Silverboy would be alive if I'd let her sleep out there.'

'What happened to him?' I asked neutrally.

Linda shook her head miserably, unable still to tell me. She was a pretty woman in a conventional thirty-something way: trim figure, well-washed short fair hair, all the health and beauty magazine tips come to admirable life. Only the dullness in the eyes and the intermittent vibrations in many of her muscles spoke plainly of the long strain of emotional buffeting still assailing her.

'She went out,' she said eventually, 'even though it was bitter cold, and beginning to rain . . . February . . . she always went to see that his water trough was filled and clean and not frozen over . . . and I'd made her put on warm clothes and gloves and a scarf and a real thick woolly hat . . . and she came back running, and screaming . . . *screaming* . . .'

I waited through Linda's unbearable memories.

She said starkly, 'Rachel found his *foot*.'

There was a moment of utter stillness, an echo of the stunned disbelief of that dreadful morning.

'It was in all the papers,' Linda said,

I moved and nodded. I'd read – months ago – about the blinded Kent ponies. I'd been busy, inattentive: hadn't absorbed names or details, hadn't realised that one of the ponies had lost a foot.

'I've found out since you telephoned,' I said, 'that round the country, not just here in Kent, there have been another half a dozen or so scattered vandalising attacks on ponies and horses in fields.'

She said unhappily, 'I did see a paragraph about a horse in Lancashire, but I threw the paper away so that Rachel wouldn't read it. Every time anything reminds her of Silverboy, she has a whole week of nightmares. She wakes up sobbing. She comes into my bed, shivering, crying. Please, please find out why . . . find out *who* . . . She's so ill . . . and although she's in remission just now and able to live fairly normally, it almost certainly won't last. The doctors say she needs the transplant.'

I said, 'Does Rachel know any of the other children whose ponies were attacked?'

Linda shook her head. 'Most of them belonged to the Pony Club, I think, but Rachel didn't feel well enough to join the Club. She loved Silverboy – her father gave him to her – but all she could do was sit in the saddle while we led her round. He was a nice quiet pony, a very nice-looking grey with a darker smoky-coloured mane. Rachel called him Silverboy, but he had a long pedigree name really. She needed something to *love*, you see, and she wanted a pony so *much*.'

I asked, 'Did you keep any of the newspaper accounts of Silverboy and the other local ponies being attacked? If you did, can I see them?'

'Yes,' she answered doubtfully, 'but I don't see how they could help. They didn't help the police.'

'They'd be a start,' I said.

'All right, then.' She left the room and after a while returned with a small blue suitcase, the size for stowing under the seats of aircraft. 'Everything's in here,' she said, passing me the case, 'including a tape of a pro-gramme a television company made. Rachel and I are in it. You won't lose it, will you? We never show it, but I wouldn't want to lose it.' She blinked against tears. 'It was actually the only good thing that happened.

Ellis Quint came to see the children and he was utterly sweet with them. Rachel loved him. He was so *kind*.'

'I know him quite well,' I said. 'If anyone could comfort the children, he could.'

'A really *nice* man,' Linda said.

I took the blue suitcase with its burden of many small tragedies back with me to London and spent indignant hours reading muted accounts of a degree of vandalism that must have been mind-destroying when fresh and bloody and discovered by loving children.

The twenty-minute video tape showed Ellis Quint at his best: the gentle sympathetic healer of unbearable sorrows; the sensible, caring commentator urging the police to treat these crimes with the seriousness given to murders. How good he was, I thought, at pitching his responses exactly right. He put his arms round Rachel and talked to her without sentimentality, not mentioning, until right at the end of the programme when the children were off the screen, that for Rachel Ferns the loss of her pony was just one more intolerable blow in a life already full of burdens.

For that programme, Rachel had chosen to wear the pretty blonde wig that gave her back her pre-chemotherapy looks. Ellis, as a final dramatic impact, had shown for a few seconds a photo of Rachel bald and vulnerable: an ending poignant to devastation.

I hadn't seen the programme when it had been broadcast: from the March date on the tape, I'd been away in America trying to find an absconding owner who'd left a monstrous training account unpaid. There were, anyway, many of Ellis's programmes I hadn't seen: he presented his twenty-minute twice-weekly journalistic segments as part of an hour-long sports news medley, and was too often on the screen for any one appearance to be especially fanfared.

Meeting Ellis, as I often did at the races, I told him about Linda Ferns calling me in, and asked him if he'd learned any more on the subject of who had mutilated the Kent ponies.

'My dear old Sid,' he said, smiling, 'all of that was months ago, wasn't it?'

'The ponies were vandalised in January and February and your programme was aired in March.'

'And it's now June, right?' He shook his head, neither distressed nor surprised. 'You know what my life's like, I have *researchers* digging out stories for me. Television is insatiably hungry. Of course, if there were any more discoveries about these ponies, I would have been told, and I would have done a follow-up, but I've heard nothing.'

I said, 'Rachel Ferns, who has leukaemia, still has nightmares.'

'Poor little kid.'

'She said you were very kind.'

'Well . . .' He made a ducking, self-deprecating movement of his head, 'It isn't so very difficult. Actually that programme did marvels for my ratings.' He paused. 'Sid, do you know anything about this bookmaker kickback scandal I'm supposed to be doing an exposé on next week?'

'Nothing at all,' I regretted. 'But Ellis, going back to the mutilations, did you chase up those other scattered cases of foals and two-year-old thoroughbreds that suffered from vandalism?'

He frowned lightly, shaking his head. 'The researchers didn't think them worth more than a mention or two. It was copycat stuff. I mean, there wasn't anything as strong as that story about the children.' He grinned. 'There were no heartstrings attached to the others.'

'You're a cynic,' I said.

'Aren't we all?'

We had been close friends for years, Ellis and I. We had ridden against each other in races, he as a charismatic amateur, I as a dedicated pro, but both with the inner fire that made hurtling over large jumps on semi-wild half-ton horses at thirty miles an hour seem a wholly reasonable way of passing as many afternoons as possible.

Thinking, after three or four months of no results from the police or the Ellis Quint programme, that I would probably fail also in the search for vandals, I nevertheless did my best to earn my fee by approaching the problem crabwise, from the side, not by asking questions of the owners of the ponies, but of the newspapermen who had written the columns in the papers.

I did it methodically on the telephone, starting with

the local Kent papers, then chasing up the by-line reporters in the London dailies. Most of the replies were the same: the story had originated from a news agency that supplied all papers with condensed factual information. Follow-ups and interpretation were the business of the papers themselves.

Among the newspapers Linda Fern had given me, *The Pump* had stirred up most disgust, and after about six phone calls I ran to earth the man who'd practically burned holes in the page with the heat of his prose; Kevin Mills, *The Pump*'s chief bleeding hearts reporter.

'A jar?' he said, to my invitation. 'Don't see why not.'

He met me in a pub (nice anonymous surroundings) and he told me he'd personally been down to Kent on that story. He'd interviewed all the children and their parents and also a fierce lady who ran one of the branches of the Pony Club, and he'd pestered the police until they'd thrown him out.

'Zilch,' he said, downing a double gin and tonic. 'No one saw a thing. All those ponies were out in fields and all of them were attacked some time between sunset and dawn, which in January and February gave the vandals hours and hours to do the job and vamoose.'

'All dark, though,' I said.

He shook his head. 'They were all done over on fine nights, near the full moon in each month.'

'How many, do you remember?'

'Four altogether in January. Two of them were

blinded. Two were mares with torn knife wounds up their . . . well, *birth passages*, as our squeamish editor had me put it.'

'And February?'

'One blinded, two more chopped up mares, one cut-off foot. A poor little girl found the foot near the water trough where her pony used to drink. Ellis Quint did a brilliant TV programme about it. Didn't you see it?'

'I was in America, but I've heard about it since.'

'There were trailers of that programme all week. Almost the whole nation watched it. It made a hell of an impact. That pony was the last one in Kent, as far as I know. The police think it was a bunch of local thugs who got the wind up when there was so much fuss. And people stopped turning ponies out into unguarded fields, see?'

I ordered him another double. He was middle-aged, half bald, doing nicely as to paunch. He wiped an untidy moustache on the back of his hand and said that in his career he'd interviewed so many parents of raped and murdered girls that the ponies had been almost a relief.

I asked him about the later copycat attacks on thoroughbreds in other places, not Kent.

'Copycat?' he repeated. 'So they say.'

'But?' I prompted.

He drank, thought it over, confided.

'All the others,' he said, 'are not in bunches, like Kent. As far as I know – and there may be still others – there were about five very young horses, foals and

41

yearlings, that had things done to them, bad enough mostly for them to have to be put down, but none of them was blinded. One had his muzzle hacked off. None of them were mares. But . . .' He hesitated, sure of his facts, I thought, but not of how I would react to them.

'Go on.'

'See, three others were two-year-olds, and all of those had a foot off.'

I felt the same revulsion that I saw in his face.

'One in March,' he said. 'One in April. One last month.'

'Not,' I said slowly, 'at the full moon?'

'Not precisely. Just on moonlit nights.'

'But why haven't you written about it?'

'I get sent to major disasters,' he said patiently. 'Air crashes, multiple deaths, dozens of accidents and murders. Some nutter driving around chopping off a horse's foot now and again – it's not my absolute priority, but maybe I'll get round to it. The news agency hasn't picked up on it, but I tend to read provincial papers. Old habit. There has been just a par or two here and there about animal vandals. It's always happening. Horses, sheep, dogs – weirdos get their mucky hands on them. Come to think of it, though, if there's another one this month I'll insist on giving it the both-barrel treatment. And now don't you go feeding this to other papers. I want my scoop.'

'Silence,' I promised, 'if . . .'

He asked suspiciously 'If what?'

'If you could give me a list of the people whose thoroughbreds have been damaged.'

He said cautiously, 'It'll cost you.'

'Done,' I said, and we agreed both on a fee and on my giving him first chance at any story I might come up with.

He fulfilled his commitment that same afternoon by sending a motorbike courier bearing a sealed brown envelope containing photocopies of several inconspicuous small paragraphs culled from provincial papers in Liverpool, Reading, Shrewsbury, Manchester, Birmingham and York. All the papers gave the names and vague addresses of the owners of vandalised thoroughbreds, so I set off by car and visited them.

Four days later, when I returned to Linda Ferns' house in Kent, I had heard enough about man's inhumanity to horses to last me for life. The injuries inflicted, from the hacked-off muzzle onwards, were truly beyond comprehension but, compared with the three two-year-olds, were all random and without pattern. It was the severed feet that were connected.

'I came across his foot by the water trough in the field,' one woman said, her eyes screwing up at the memory. 'I couldn't *believe* it. Just a *foot*. Tell you the truth, I brought up my breakfast. He was a really nice two-year-old colt.' She swallowed. 'He wasn't standing anywhere near his foot. The off-fore, it was. He'd wandered away on three legs and he was eating grass. Just *eating*, as if nothing had happened. He didn't seem to feel any pain.'

'What did you do?' I asked.

'I called the vet. He came . . . He gave *me* a tranquilliser. He said I needed it more than the colt did. He looked after everything for me.'

'Was the colt insured?' I asked.

She took no offence at the question. I guessed it had been asked a dozen times already. She said there had been no insurance. They had bred the two-year-old themselves. They had been going to race him later in the year. They had been to Cheltenham races and had backed the winner of the Gold Cup, a great day, and the very next morning . . .

I asked her for the vet's name and address, and I went to see him at his home.

'How was the foot taken off?' I asked.

He wrinkled his forehead. 'I don't rightly know. It was neat. The colt had bled very little. There was a small pool of blood on the grass about a yard away from the foot, and that was all. The colt himself let me walk right up to him. He looked calm and normal, except that his off-fore ended at the fetlock.'

'Was it done with an axe?'

He hesitated. 'I'd say more like a machete. Just the one cut, fast and clean. Whoever did it knew just where to aim for, unless he was simply lucky.'

'Did you tell the police?'

'Sure. A detective sergeant came out. He vomited

too. Then I called the knackers and put the colt down. Bloody vandals! I'd like to cut off *their* foot, see if they liked life with a stump.' He remembered suddenly about my own sliced off hand, and reddened, looking confused and embarrassed. There had been a much publicised court case about my hand. Everyone knew what had happened. I had finally stopped wincing visibly when people referred to it.

'It's all right,' I said mildly.

'I'm sorry. My big mouth . . .'

'Do you think the colt's amputation was done by a vet? By any sort of surgical expert? Was it done with a scalpel? Was the colt given a local anaesthetic?'

He said, disturbed, 'I don't know the answers. I'd just say that whoever did it was used to handling horses. That colt was loose in the field, though wearing a head-collar.'

I went to see the detective sergeant, who looked as if he might throw up again at the memory.

'I see a lot of injured people. Dead bodies, too,' he said, 'but that was different. Mindless. Fair turned my stomach.'

The police had found no culprit. It had been an isolated event, not part of a pattern. The only report they'd had was of the presence of a blue Land-Rover driving away along the lane from the colt's field; and Land-Rovers were two a penny in the countryside. Case not closed, but also not being actively investigated. The colt and his hoof had long gone to the glue factory.

'Are there any photographs?' I asked.

The sergeant said that the photographs were a police matter, not open to the general public.

'I do know who you are,' he said, not abrasively, 'but to us you're the general public. Sorry.'

The colt's owner, consulted, said she had been too upset to want photographs.

I drove onwards, northwards to Lancashire, into a gale of anger. Big, blustery and impressively furious, a hard competent large-scale farmer let loose his roaring sense of injustice, yelling in my face, spraying me with spittle, jabbing the air with a rigid forefinger, pushing his chin forward in a classic animal gesture of aggression.

'Best colt I ever owned,' he bellowed. 'He cost me a packet, but he was a good 'un. Breeding, conformation, the lot. And he was *fast*, I'll tell you. He was going to Newmarket the next week.' He mentioned a prestigious trainer who I knew wouldn't have accepted rubbish. 'A good 'un,' the farmer repeated. 'And then the sodding police asked if I'd killed him for the insurance. I ask you! He wasn't insured, I told them. They said I couldn't *prove* he wasn't insured. Did you know that? Did you know you can prove something *is* insured, but you can't prove it *isn't*? Did you know that?'

I said I'd heard it was so.

'I told them to bugger off. They weren't interested in finding who took my colt's foot off, only in proving

I did it myself. They made me that *angry* . . .' His words failed him. I'd met many people unjustly accused of setting fires, battering children, stealing, and taking bribes, and by then I knew the vocal vibrations of truly outraged innocence. The angry farmer, I would have staked all on it, had not taken the foot off his own colt, and I told him so. Some of his anger abated into surprise. 'So you *believe* me?'

'I sure do,' I nodded. 'The point is, who knew you'd bought a fine fast colt that you had at your farm in a field?'

'Who knew?' He suddenly looked guilty, as if he'd already had to face an unpalatable fact. 'I'd blown my mouth off a bit. Half the country knew. And I'd been boasting about him at Aintree, the day before the Grand National. I was at one of those sponsors' lunch things – Topline Foods, it was – and the colt was fine that night. I saw him in the morning. And it was the next night, after the National, that he was got at.'

He had taken his own colour photographs (out of distrust of the police) and he showed them to me readily.

'The off-fore,' he said, pointing to a close-up of the severed foot. 'He was cut just below the fetlock. Almost through the joint. You can see the white ends of the bones.'

The photographs jolted. It didn't help that I'd seen my own left wrist in much the same condition. I said, 'What was your vet's opinion?'

'Same as mine.'

I went to see the vet. One chop, he said. Only one. No missed shots. Straight through at the leg's most vulnerable point.

'What weapon?'

He didn't know.

I pressed onwards to Yorkshire where, barely a month earlier, at the time of the York Spring Meeting, a dark brown two-year-old colt had been deprived of his off-fore foot on a moonlit night. One chop. No insurance. Sick and angry owners. No clues.

These owners were a stiff-upper-lip couple with elderly manners and ancient immutable values who were as deeply bewildered as repelled by the level of evil that would for no clear reason destroy a thing of beauty; in this case, the fluid excellence of a fleet glossy equine princeling.

'*Why?*' they asked me insistently. '*Why* would anyone do such a pointlessly wicked thing?'

I had no answer. I prompted them only to talk, to let out their pain and deprivation. I got them to talk, and I listened.

The wife said, 'We had such a lovely week. Every year we have people to stay for the York Spring Meeting . . . because, as you can see, this is quite a large house . . . so we have six or eight friends staying, and we get in extra staff and have a party – such fun, you see – and this year the weather was perfect and we all had a great time.'

'Successful, don't you know,' said her husband, nodding.

'Dear Ellis Quint was one of our guests,' smiled the hostess, 'and he lifted everyone's spirits in that easy way of his so that it seemed we spent the whole week laughing. He was filming for one of his television programmes at York races, so we were all invited behind the scenes and enjoyed it all so much. And then . . . then . . . the very night after all our guests had left . . . well . . .'

'Jenkins came and told us – Jenkins is our groom – he told us while we were sitting at breakfast, that our colt . . . our colt . . .'

'We have three brood-mares,' his wife said. 'We love to see the foals and yearlings out in the fields, running free, you know . . . and usually we sell the yearlings, but that colt was so beautiful that we kept him, and he was going into training soon . . . All our guests had admired him.'

'Jenkins had made a splendid job of breaking him in.'

'Jenkins was in *tears*,' the wife said. 'Jenkins! A tough leathery old man. In *tears*.'

The husband said with difficulty, 'Jenkins found the foot by the gate, beside the water trough.'

His wife went on. 'Jenkins told us that Ellis had done a programme a few months ago about a pony's foot being cut off and the children being so devastated. So we wrote to Ellis about our colt and Ellis telephoned at once to say how *awful* for us. He couldn't have been

49

nicer. Dear Ellis. But there wasn't anything he could do, of course, except sympathise.'

'No,' I agreed, and I felt only the faintest twitch of surprise that Ellis hadn't mentioned the York colt when I'd been talking to him less than a week earlier about Rachel Ferns.

CHAPTER THREE

Back in London I met Kevin Mills, the journalist from *The Pump*, at lunchtime in the same pub as before.

'It's time for both barrels,' I said.

He swigged his double gin. 'What have you dis-covered?'

I outlined the rest of the pattern, beyond what he'd told me about two-year-old colts on moonlit nights. One chop from something like a machete. Always the off-fore foot. Always near a water trough. No insurance. And always just after a major local race meeting: Cheltenham, the Gold Cup Festival; the Grand National at Liverpool; the Spring Meeting at York.

'And this Saturday, two days from now,' I said levelly, 'we have the Derby.'

He put his glass down slowly, and after a full silent minute said, 'What about the kid's pony?'

I shrugged resignedly. 'It was the first that we know of.'

'And it doesn't fit the pattern. Not a two-year-old colt, was he? And no major race meeting, was there?'

'The severed foot was by the water trough. The off-fore foot. Moon in the right quarter. One chop. No insurance.'

He frowned, thinking. 'Tell you what,' he said eventually, 'it's worth a *warning*. I'm not a sports writer, as you know, but I'll get the message into the paper somewhere. "Don't leave your two-year-old colts unguarded in open fields during and after the Epsom meeting." I don't think I can do more than that.'

'It might be enough.'

'Yeah. *If* all the owners of colts read *The Pump*.'

'It will be the talk of the racecourse. I'll arrange that.'

'On Derby Day?' he looked sceptical. 'Still, it will be better than nothing.' He drank again. 'What we really need to do is catch the bugger red-handed.'

We gloomily contemplated that impossibility. Roughly fifteen thousand thoroughbred foals were born each year in the British Isles. Half would be colts. Many of those at two would already be in training for Flat racing, tucked away safely in stables; but that still left a host unattended out of doors. By June, also, yearling colts, growing fast, could be mistaken at night for two-year-olds.

Nothing was safe from a determined vandal.

Kevin Mills went away to write his column and I travelled on to Kent to report to my clients.

'Have you found out *who*?' Linda demanded.

'Not yet.'

We sat by the sitting-room window again, watching Rachel push Pegotty in his buggy round the lawn, and I told her about the three colts and their shattered owners.

'Three more,' Linda repeated numbly. 'In March, April and May? And Silverboy in February?'

'That's right.'

'And what about *now*? This month . . . *June*?'

I explained about the warning to be printed in *The Pump*.

'I'm not going to tell Rachel about the other three,' Linda said. 'She wakes up screaming as it is.'

'I enquired into other injured horses all over England,' I said, 'but they were all hurt differently from each other. I think . . . well . . . that there are several different people involved. And, I don't think the thugs that blinded and cut the ponies round here had anything to do with Silverboy.'

Linda protested. 'But they must have done! There couldn't be *two* lots of vandals.'

'I think there were.'

She watched Rachel and Pegotty, the habitual tears not far away. Rachel was tickling the baby to make him laugh.

'I'd do anything to save my daughter,' Linda said. 'The doctor said that if only she'd had several sisters, one of them might have had the right tissue type. Joe

53

– Rachel's father – is half Asian. It seems harder to find a match. So I had the baby. I had Pegotty five months ago.' She wiped her eyes. 'Joe has his new wife and he wouldn't sleep with me again, not even for Rachel. So he donated sperm and I had artificial insemination, and it worked at once. It seemed an omen . . . and I had the baby . . . but he doesn't match Rachel. There was only ever one chance in four that he would have the same tissue type and antigens . . . I hoped and prayed . . . but he *doesn't*.' She gulped, her throat closing. 'So I have Pegotty . . . he's Peter, really, but we call him Pegotty . . . but Joe won't bond with him . . . and we still can't find a match anywhere for Rachel and there isn't much time for me to try with another baby . . . and Joe *won't* anyway. His wife objects . . . and he didn't want to do it the first time.'

'I'm so sorry,' I said.

'Joe's wife goes on and on about Joe having to pay child support for Pegotty . . . and now she's pregnant herself.'

Life, I thought, brought unlimited and complicated cruelties.

'Joe isn't mean,' Linda said. 'He loves Rachel and he bought her the pony and he keeps us comfortable, but his wife says I could have *six* children without getting a match . . .' Her voice wavered and stopped, and after a while she said, 'I don't know why I burdened you with all that. You're so easy to talk to.'

'And interested.'

She nodded, sniffing and blowing her nose. 'Go out and talk to Rachel. I told her you were coming back today. She liked you.'

Obediently I went out into the garden and gravely shook hands with Rachel, and we sat side by side on a garden bench like two old buddies.

Though still warm, the golden days of early June were greying and growing damp: good for roses perhaps, but not for the Derby.

I apologised that I hadn't yet found out who attacked Silverboy.

'But you will in the end, won't you?'

'I hope so,' I said.

She nodded. 'I told Daddy yesterday that I was sure you would.'

'Did you?'

'Yes. He took me out in his car. He does that sometimes, when Didi goes to London to do shopping.'

'Is Didi his wife?'

Rachel's nose wrinkled in a grimace, but she made no audible judgement. She said, 'Daddy says someone chopped your hand off, just like Silverboy.'

She regarded me gravely, awaiting confirmation.

'Er,' I said, unnerved, 'not exactly like Silverboy.'

'Daddy says the man who did it was sent to prison, but he's out again now on parole.'

'Do you know what "on parole" means?' I asked curiously

'Yes. Daddy told me.'

55

'Your daddy knows a lot.'

'Yes, but it is *true* that someone chopped your hand off?'

'Does it matter to you?'

'Yes, it does,' she said. 'I was thinking about it in bed last night. I have awful dreams. I tried to stay awake because I didn't want to go to sleep and dream about you having your hand chopped off.'

She was trying to be grown up and calm, but I could feel screaming hysteria too near the surface; so, stifling my own permanent reluctance to talk about it, I gave her an abbreviated account of what had happened.

'I was a jockey,' I began.

'Yes, I know. Daddy said you were the champion for years.'

'Well, one day my horse fell in a race, and while I was on the ground another horse landed over a jump straight onto my wrist and ... um ... tore it apart. It got stitched up, but I couldn't use my hand much. I had to stop being a jockey, and I started doing what I do now, which is finding out things, like who hurt Silverboy.'

She nodded.

'Well, I found out something that an extremely nasty man didn't want me to know, and he ... er ... he hit my bad wrist and broke it again, and that time the doctors couldn't stitch it up, so they decided that I'd be better off with a useful plastic hand instead of the useless old one.'

'So he didn't really . . . not *really* chop it off. Not like with an axe or anything?'

'No. So don't waste dreams on it.'

She smiled with quiet relief and, as she was sitting on my left, put her right hand down delicately but without hesitation on the replacement parts. She stroked the tough plastic unfeeling skin and looked up with surprise at my eyes.

'It isn't *warm*,' she said.

'Well, it isn't cold, either.'

She laughed with uncomplicated fun. 'How does it work?'

'I tell it what to do,' I said simply. 'I send a message from my brain down my arm saying open thumb from fingers, or close thumb to fingers, to grip things, and the messages reach very sensitive terminals called electrodes, which are inside the plastic and against my skin.' I paused, but she didn't say she didn't understand. I said, 'My real arm ends about there' – I pointed – 'and the plastic arm goes up round my elbow. The electrodes are up in my forearm, there, against my skin. They feel my muscles trying to move. That's how they work.'

'Is the plastic arm tied on, or anything?'

'No. It just fits tightly and stays on by itself. It was specially made to fit me.'

Like all children she took marvels for granted, although to me, even though by then I'd had the false arm for nearly three years, the concept of nerve messages moving machinery was still extraordinary.

'There are three electrodes,' I said. 'One for opening the hand, one for closing, and one for turning the wrist.'

'Do electrodes work on electricity?' It puzzled her. 'I mean, you're not plugged into the wall, or anything?'

'You're a clever girl,' I told her. 'It works on a special sort of battery which slots into the outside above where I wear my watch. I charge up the batteries on a charger which *is* plugged into the wall.'

She looked at me assessingly. 'It must be pretty useful to have that hand.'

'It's brilliant,' I agreed.

'Daddy says Ellis Quint told him that you can't tell you have a plastic hand unless you touch it.'

I asked, surprised, 'Does your daddy know Ellis Quint?'

She nodded composedly. 'They go to the same place to play squash. He helped Daddy buy Silverboy. He was really really sorry when he found out it was Silverboy himself that he was making his programme about.'

'Yes, he would be.'

'I wish . . .' she began, looking down at my hand, 'I do wish Silverboy could have had a new foot . . . with electrodes and a battery.'

I said prosaically, 'He might have been able to have a false foot fitted, but he wouldn't have been able to trot or canter, or jump. He wouldn't have been happy just limping around.'

She rubbed her own fingers over the plastic ones, not convinced.

I said, 'Where did you keep Silverboy?'

'The other side of that fence at the end of the garden.' She pointed. 'You can't see it from here because of those trees. We have to go through the house and out and down the lane.'

'Will you show me?'

There was a moment of drawing back, then she said, 'I'll take you if I can hold your hand on the way.'

'Of course.' I stood up and held out my real, warm, normal arm.

'No . . .' She shook her head, standing up also. 'I mean, can I hold this hand that you can't feel?'

It seemed to matter to her that I wasn't whole; that I would understand someone ill, without hair.

I said lightly, 'You can hold which hand you like.'

She nodded, then pushed Pegotty into the house, and matter of factly told Linda she was taking me down to the field to show me where Silverboy had lived. Linda gave me a wild look but let us go, so the bald-headed child and the one-handed man walked in odd companionship down a short lane and leaned against a five-barred gate across the end.

The field was a lush paddock of little more than an acre, the grass growing strongly, uneaten. A nearby standing pipe with an ordinary tap on it stood ready to fill an ordinary galvanised water trough. The ground round the trough was churned up, the grass growing more sparsely, as always happened round troughs in fields.

'I don't want to go in,' Rachel said, turning her head away.

'We don't need to.'

'His foot was by the trough,' she said jerkily, 'I mean . . . you could see *blood* . . . and white bones.'

'Don't talk about it.' I pulled her with me and walked back along the lane, afraid I should never have asked her to show me.

She gripped my unfeeling hand in both of hers, slowing me down.

'It's all right,' she said. 'It was a long time ago. It's all right now when I'm awake.'

'Good.'

'I don't like going to sleep.'

The desperation of that statement was an open appeal, and had to be addressed.

I stopped walking before we reached the door of the house. I said, 'I don't usually tell anyone this, but I'll tell you. I still sometimes have bad dreams about my hand. I dream I can clap with two hands. I dream I'm still a jockey. I dream about my smashed wrist. Rotten dreams can't be helped. They're awful when they happen. I don't know how to stop them. But one does wake up.'

'And then you have leukaemia . . . or a plastic arm.'

'Life's a bugger,' I said.

She put her hand over her mouth and, in a fast release of tension, she giggled. 'Mum won't let me say that.'

'Say it into your pillow.'

'Do you?'

'Pretty often.'

We went on into the house and Rachel again pushed Pegotty into the garden. I stayed in the sitting-room with Linda and watched through the window.

'Was she all right?' Linda asked anxiously.

'She's a very brave child.'

Linda wept.

I said, 'Did you hear anything at all the night Silverboy was attacked?'

'Everyone asks that. I'd have said if I had.'

'No car engines?'

'The police said they must have stopped the car in the road and walked down the lane. My bedroom window doesn't face the lane, nor does Rachel's. But that lane doesn't go anywhere except to the field. As you saw, it's only a track really, it ends at the gate.'

'Could anyone see Silverboy from the road?'

'Yes, the police asked that. You could see him come to drink. You can see the water trough from the road, if you know where to look. The police say the thugs must have been out all over this part of Kent looking for unguarded ponies like Silverboy. Whatever you say about two-year-olds, Silverboy *must* have been done by thugs. Why don't you ask the police?'

'If you wholeheartedly believed the police, you wouldn't have asked me for help.'

'Joe just telephoned,' she confessed, wailing, 'and he says that calling you in to help is a waste of money.'

'Ah.'

'I don't know what to think.'

I said, 'You're paying me by the day, plus expenses. I can stop right now, if you like.'

'No. Yes. I don't *know*.' She wiped her eyes, undecided, and said, 'Rachel dreams that Silverboy is standing in the field and he's glowing bright and beautiful in the moonlight. He's *shining*, she says. And there's a dark mass of monsters oozing down the lane . . . oozing is what she says . . . and they are shapeless and devils and they're going to kill Silverboy. She says she is trying to run fast to warn him, and she can't get through the monsters, they clutch at her like cobwebs. She can't get through them and they reach Silverboy and smother his light, and all his hair falls out, and she wakes up and screams. It's always the same nightmare. I thought if you could find out who cut the poor thing's foot off, the monsters would have names and faces and would be in the papers, and Rachel would know who they were and stop thinking they're lumps that ooze without eyes and won't let her through.'

After a pause, I said, 'Give me another week.'

She turned away from me sharply and, crossing to a desk, wrote me a cheque. 'For two weeks, one gone, one ahead.'

I looked at the amount. 'That's more than we agreed on.'

'Whatever Joe says, I want you to go on trying.'

I gave her tentatively a small kiss on the cheek. She smiled, her eyes still dark and wet. 'I'll pay anything for Rachel,' she said.

I drove slowly back to London thinking of the cynical old ex-policemen who had taught me the basics of investigation. 'There are two cardinal rules in this trade,' he said. 'One. Never believe everything a client tells you, and always believe they could have told you more if you'd asked the right questions. And two. Never, never get emotionally involved with your client.'

Which was all very well, except when your client was a bright truthful nine-year-old fighting a losing battle against a rising tide of lymphoblasts.

I bought a take-out curry on the way home and ate it before spending the evening on overdue paperwork.

I much preferred the active side of the job, but clients wanted, and deserved, and paid for, detailed accounts of what I'd done on their behalf, preferably with results they liked. With the typed recital of work done, I sent also my final bill, adding a list of itemised expenses supported by receipts. I almost always played fair, even with clients I didn't like: investigators had been known to charge for seven days' work when, with a little application, they could have finished the job in three. I didn't want that sort of reputation. Speed succeeded in my new occupation as essentially as in my old.

Besides bathroom and kitchen, my pleasant (and frankly, expensive) flat consisted of three rooms; bedroom, big sunny sitting-room and a third, smaller, room that I used as an office. I had no secretary or helper; no one read the secrets I uncovered except the client and myself, and whatever the client did with the information he'd paid for was normally his or her own business. Privacy was what drove many people to consult me, and privacy was what they got.

I listened to some unexciting messages on my answering machine, typed a report on my secure word-processor, printed it and put it ready for posting. For reports and anything personal I used a computer system that wasn't connected to any phone line. No one could in consequence tap into it and, as a precaution against thieves, I used also unbreakable passwords. It was my second system that could theoretically be accessed; the one connected by modem to the big wide world of universal information. Any snooper was welcome to anything found there.

On the subject of the management of secrecy, my cynical mentor had said, 'Never ever tell your right hand what your left hand is doing. Er . . .' he added, 'whoops. Sorry, Sid.'

'It'll cost you a pint.'

'And,' he went on later, drinking, 'keep back-up copies of completed sensitive enquiries in a bank vault, and wipe the information from any computer systems in your office. If you use random passwords, and change them weekly, you should be safe enough while you're actually working on something, but once you've finished, get the back-up to the bank and wipe the office computer, like I said.'

'All right.'

'Never forget,' he told me, 'that the people you are investigating may go to violent lengths to stop you.'

He had been right about that.

'Never forget that you don't have the same protection as the police do. You have to make your own protection. You have to be careful.'

'Maybe I should look for another job.'

'No, Sid,' he said earnestly, 'you have a gift for this. You listen to what I tell you and you'll do fine.'

He had taught me for the two years I'd spent doing little but drift in the old Radnor detection agency after the end of my racing life and, for nearly three years since, I'd lived mostly by his precepts. But he was dead now, and Radnor himself also, and I had to look inwards for wisdom, which could be a variable process, not always ultra-productive.

I could try to comfort Rachel by telling her I had bad dreams also, but I could never have told her how vivid and liquefying they could be. That night, after I'd eased off the arm and showered and gone peacefully to bed, I fell asleep thinking of her, and descended after midnight into a familiar dungeon.

It was always the same.

I dreamed I was in a big dark space, and some people were coming to cut off both my hands.

Both.

They were making me wait, but they would come. There would be agony and humiliation and helplessness . . . and no way out.

I semi-awoke in shaking, sweating heart-thudding terror and then realised with flooding relief that it wasn't true, I was safe in my own bed: and then remembered that it had already half happened in fact, and also that I'd come within a fraction once of a villain's shooting the remaining hand off. As soon as I was awake enough to be clear about the present actual not-too-bad state of affairs I slid back reassured into sleep, and that night the whole appalling nightmare cycled again . . . and again.

I forced myself to wake up properly, to sit up and get out of bed and make full consciousness take over. I stood under the shower again and let cool water run through my hair and down my body. I put on a towelling bathrobe and poured a glass of milk, and sat in an armchair in the sitting-room with all the lights on.

I looked at the space where a left hand had once been, and I looked at the strong whole right hand that held a glass, and I acknowledged that often, both waking as well as sleeping, I felt, and could not repress, stabs of savage petrifying fear that one day it would indeed be both. The trick was not to let the fear show, nor to let it conquer, nor rule my life.

It was pointless to reflect that I'd brought the terrors on myself. I had chosen to be a jockey. I had chosen to go after violent crooks. I was at that moment actively seeking out someone who knew how to cut off a horse's foot with one chop.

My own equivalent of the off-fore held a glass of milk.

I had to be mentally deranged.

But then there were people like Rachel Ferns.

In one way or another I had survived many torments, and much could have been avoided but for my own obstinate nature. I knew by then that whatever came along, I would deal with it. But that child had had her hair fall out and had found her beloved pony's foot, and none of that was her fault. No nine-year-old mind could sleep sweetly under such assaults.

Oh God, Rachel, I thought, I would dream your nightmares for you, if I could.

In the morning I made a working analysis in five columns of the Ferns pony and the three two-year-olds. The analysis took the form of a simple graph, ruled in boxes. Across the top of the page I wrote: Factors, Ferns, Cheltenham, Aintree, York, and down the left-hand column, Factors, I entered 'date', 'name of owner', 'racing programme', 'motive', and finally, 'who knew of

victim's availability?' I found that although I could
think of answers to that last question, I hadn't the wish
to write them in, and after a bit of indecision I phoned
Kevin Mills at *The Pump* and, by persistence, reached
him.

'Sid,' he said heartily, 'the warning will be in the
paper tomorrow. You've done your best. Stop agi-
tating.'

'Great,' I said, 'but could you do something else?
Something that could come innocently from *The Pump*,
but would raise all sorts of reverberations if I asked
directly myself.'

'Such as what?'

'Such as ask Topline Foods for a list of the guests
they entertained at a sponsors' lunch at Aintree the
day before the National.'

'What the *hell* for?'

'Will you do it?'

He said, 'What are you up to?'

'The scoop is still yours. Exclusive.'

'I don't know why I trust you.'

'It pays off,' I said, smiling.

'It had better.' He put down his receiver with a crash,
but I knew he would do what I asked.

It was Friday morning. At Epsom that day they
would be running the Coronation Cup and also the
Oaks, the fillies' equivalent of the Derby. It was also
lightly raining: a weak warm front, it seemed, was
slowly blighting southern England.

Racecourses still drew me as if I were tethered to them with bungy elastic, but before setting out I telephoned the woman whose colt's foot had been amputated during the night after the Cheltenham Gold Cup.

'I'm sorry to bother you again, but would you mind a few more questions?'

'Not if you can catch the bastards.'

'Well, was the two-year-old alone in his field?'

'Yes, he was. It was only a paddock. Railed, of course. We kept him in the paddock nearest to the house, that's what is so infuriating. We had two old hacks turned out in the field beyond him, but the vandals left them untouched.'

'And,' I said neutrally, 'how many people knew the colt was accessible? And how accessible was he?'

'Sid,' she exclaimed, 'don't think we haven't racked our brains. The trouble is, all our friends knew about him. We were excited about his prospects. And then, at the Cheltenham meeting, we had been talking to people about *trainers*. Old Gunners, who used to train for us in the past, has died, of course, and we don't like that uppity assistant of his that's taken over the stable, so we were asking around, you see.'

'Yeah. And did you decide on a trainer?'

'We did, but, of course . . .'

'Such a bloody shame,' I sympathised. 'Who did you decide on?'

She mentioned a first-class man. 'Several people said that with him we couldn't go wrong.'

'No.' I mentally sighed, and asked obliquely, 'What did you especially enjoy about the Festival meeting?'

'The Queen came,' she said promptly. 'I had thick warm boots on, and I nearly fell over them, curtseying.' She laughed. 'And oh, also, I suppose you do know you're in the Hall of Fame there?'

'It's an honour,' I said. 'They gave me an engraved glass goblet that I can see across the room right now from where I'm sitting.'

'Well, we were standing in front of that big exhibit they've put together of your life, and we were reading the captions, and dear Ellis Quint stopped beside us and put his arm round my shoulders and said that our Sid was a pretty great guy, all in all.'

Oh *shit*, I thought.

Her warm smile was audible down the line. 'We've known Ellis for years, of course. He used to ride our horses in amateur races. So he called in at our house for a drink on his way home after the Gold Cup. Such a *lovely* day.' She sighed. 'And then those *bastards* . . . You will catch them, won't you, Sid?'

'If I can,' I said.

I left a whole lot of the boxes empty on my chart, and drove to Epsom Downs, spirits as grey as the skies. The bars were crowded. Umbrellas dripped. The brave colours of June dresses hid under drabber raincoats, and only the geraniums looked happy.

I walked damply to the parade ring before the two-year-old colts' six-furlong race and thoughtfully watched all the off-fore feet plink down lightheartedly. The young spindly bones of those forelegs thrust 450-kilo bodies forward at sprinting speeds near forty miles an hour. I had mostly raced on the older mature horses of steeplechasing, half a ton in weight, slightly slower, capable of four miles and thirty jumps from start to finish, but still on legs scarcely thicker than a big man's wrist.

The anatomy of a horse's foreleg consisted, from the shoulder down, of forearm, knee, cannon bone, fetlock joint (also known as the ankle), pastern bone, and hoof. The angry Lancashire farmer's coloured photograph had shown the amputation to have been effected straight through the narrowest part of the whole leg, just at the base of the fetlock joint, where the pastern emerged from it. In effect, the whole pastern and the hoof had been cut off.

Horses had very fast instincts for danger and were easily scared. Young horses seldom stood still. Yet one single chop had done the job each time. *Why* had all those poor animals stood quietly while the deed was done? None of them had squealed loud enough to alert his owner.

I went up on the stands and watched the two-year-olds set off from the spur away to the left at the top of the hill; watched them swoop down like a flock of starlings round Tattenham Corner, and sort themselves out into winner and losers along the straight with its deceptively difficult camber that could tilt a horse towards the rails if his jockey were inexperienced.

I watched, and I sighed. Five long years had passed since I'd ridden my last race. Would regret, I wondered, ever fade?

'Why so pensive, Sid, lad?' asked an elderly trainer, grasping my elbow. 'A Scotch and water for your thoughts!' He steered me round towards the nearest bar and I went with him unprotestingly, as custom came my way quite often in that casual manner. He was great with horses and famously mean with his money.

'I hear you're damned expensive,' he began inoffensively, handing me a glass. 'What will you charge me for a day's work?'

I told him.

'Too damned much. Do it for nothing, for old times' sake.'

I added, smiling, 'How many horses do you train for nothing?'

'That's different.'

'How many races would you have asked me to ride for nothing?'

'Oh, all *right* then. I'll pay your damned fee. The fact is, I think I'm being *had*, and I want you to find out.'

It seemed he had received a glowing testimonial from the present employer of a chauffeur/houseman/handyman who'd applied for a job he'd advertised. He wanted to know if it was worth bringing the man up for an interview.

'She–' he said, 'his employer is a woman – I phoned her when I got the letter, to check the reference, you see. She couldn't have been more complimentary about the man if she'd tried, but . . . I don't know . . . She was *too* complimentary, if you see what I mean.'

'You mean you think she might be glad to see the back of him?'

'You don't hang about, Sid. That's exactly what I mean.'

He gave me the testimonial letter of fluorescent praise.

'No problem,' I said, reading it. 'One day's fee, plus travel expenses. I'll phone you, then send you a written report.'

'You still *look* like a jockey,' he complained. 'You're a damned sight more expensive on your feet.'

I smiled, put the letter away in a pocket, drank his Scotch and applauded the string of winners he'd had recently, cheering him up before separating him from his cash.

I drifted around pleasurably but unprofitably for the rest of the day, slept thankfully without nightmares and found on a dry and sunny Derby Day morning that my friendly *Pump* reporter had really done his stuff.

'Lock up your colts,' he directed in the paper. 'You've heard of foot-fetishists? This is one beyond belief.'

He outlined in succinct paragraphs the similarities in 'the affair of the four severed fetlocks' and pointed out that on that very night after the Derby – the biggest race of all – there would be moonlight enough at 3.00 a.m. for torches to be unnecessary. All two-year-old colts should, like Cinderella, be safe indoors by midnight. 'And if . . .' he finished with a flourish, '. . . you should spy anyone creeping through the fields armed with a machete, phone ex-jockey turned gumshoe Sid Halley, who provided the information gathered here and can be reached via *The Pump*'s special Hotline. Phone *The Pump*! Save the colts! Halley to the rescue!'

I couldn't imagine how he had got that last bit – including a telephone number – past any editor, but I needn't have worried about spreading the message on the racecourse. No one spoke to me about anything else all afternoon.

I phoned *The Pump* myself and reached someone eventually who told me that Kevin Mills had gone to a train crash; sorry.

'Damn,' I said. 'So how are you re-routing calls about colts to me? I didn't arrange this. How will it work?'

'Hold on.'

I held on. A different voice came back.

'As Kevin isn't available, we're re-routing all Halley Hotline calls to this number,' he said, and he read out my own Pont Square number.

'Where's your bloody Mills? I'll wring his neck.'

'Gone to the train crash. Before he left he gave us this number for reaching you. He said you would want to know at once about any colts.'

That was true enough – but hell's bloody bells, I thought, I could have set it up better if he'd warned me.

I watched the Derby with inattention. An outsider won.

Ellis teased me about the piece in *The Pump*.

'Hotline Halley,' he said, laughing and clapping me on the shoulder, tall and deeply friendly and wiping out in a flash the incredulous doubts I'd been having about him. 'It's an extraordinary coincidence, Sid, but I actually *saw* one of those colts. Alive, of course. I was staying with some chums for York, and after we'd gone home someone vandalised their colt. Such fun people. They didn't deserve anything like that.'

'No one does.'

'True.'

'The really puzzling thing is motive,' I said. 'I went to see all the owners. None of the colts was insured. Nor was Rachel Ferns' pony, of course.'

He said interestedly, 'Did you think it was an insurance scam?'

'It jumps to mind, doesn't it? Theoretically it's possible to insure a horse and collect the lucre without the owner knowing anything about it. It's been done. But if that's what this is all about, perhaps someone in an insurance company somewhere will see the piece in

75

The Pump and connect a couple of things. Come to think of it,' I finished slowly, 'I might send a copy to every likely insurance company's board of directors, asking, and warning them.'

'Good idea,' he said. 'Does insurance and so on really take the place of racing? It sounds a pretty dull life for you, after what we used to do.'

'Does television replace it for you?'

'Not a hope.' He laughed. 'Danger is addictive, wouldn't you say? The only dangerous job in television is reporting wars and – have you noticed – the same few war reporters get out there all the time, talking with their earnest committed faces about this or that month's little dust-up, while bullets fly and chip off bits of stone in the background to prove how brave they are.'

'You're jealous,' I smiled.

'I get sodding bored sometimes with being a chat-show celebrity, even if it's nice being liked. Don't you ache for speed?'

'Every day,' I said.

'You're about the only person who understands me. No one else can see that fame's no substitute for danger.'

'It depends what you risk.'

Hands, I thought. One could risk hands.

'Good luck, Hotline,' Ellis said.

It was the owners of two-year-old colts that had the good luck. My telephone jammed and rang non-stop all evening and all night when I got home after the Derby, but the calls were all from people enjoying their shivers and jumping at shadows. The moonlight shone on quiet fields, and no animal, whether colt or two-year-old thoroughbred or children's pony, lost a foot.

In the days that followed, interest and expectation dimmed and died. It was twelve days after the Derby, on the last night of the Royal Ascot meeting, that the screaming heeby-jeebies reawoke.

CHAPTER FOUR

On the Monday after the Derby I trailed off on the one-day dig into the overblown reference and, without talking to the lady-employer herself (which would clearly have been counter-productive) I uncovered enough to phone the tight-fisted trainer with sound advice.

'She wants to get rid of him without the risk of being accused of unfair dismissal,' I said. 'He steals small things from her house which pass through a couple of hands and turn up in the local antique shop. She can't prove they were hers. The antique shop owner is whining about his innocence. The lady has apparently said she won't try to prosecute her houseman if he gets the heck out. Her testimonial is part of the bargain. The houseman is a regular in the local betting shop, and gambles heavily on horses. Do you want to employ him?'

'Like hell.'

'The report I'll write and send to you,' I told him, 'will say only, "Work done on recruitment of staff." You can claim tax relief on it.'

He laughed dryly. 'Any time you want a reference,' he said, pleased, 'I'll write you an affidavit.'

'You never know,' I said, 'and thanks.'

I had phoned the report from the car park of a motorway service station on my way home late in the dusky evening, but it was when I reached Pont Square that the day grew doubly dark. There was a two-page fax waiting on my machine and I read it standing in the sitting-room with all thoughts of a friendly glass of Scotch evaporating into disbelief and the onset of misery.

The pages were from Kevin Mills. 'I don't know why you want this list of the great and good,' he wrote, 'but for what it's worth and because I promised, here is a list of the guests entertained by Topline Foods at lunch at Aintree on the day before the Grand National.'

The list contained the name of the angry Lancashire farmer, as was expected, but it was the top of the list that did the psychological damage.

'Guest of Honour,' it announced, 'Ellis Quint.'

All the doubts I'd banished came roaring back with double vigour. Back too came self-ridicule and every defence mechanism under the sun.

I couldn't, didn't, *couldn't* believe that Ellis could maim – and effectively kill – a child's pony and three young racehorses. Not Ellis! It was *impossible*.

There had to be *dozens* of other people who could have learned where to find all four of those vulnerable unguarded animals. It was *stupid* to give any weight to an unreliable coincidence. All the same, I pulled my box chart out of a drawer, and in very small letters, as if in that way I could physically diminish the implication, I wrote in each 'who knew of victim's availability?' space the unthinkable words, Ellis Quint.

The 'motive' boxes had also remained empty. There was no apparent rational motive. Why did people poke out the eyes of ponies? Why did they stalk strangers and write poison pen letters? Why did they torture and kill children and tape-record their screams?

I wrote 'self gratification', but it seemed too weak. Insanity? Psychosis? The irresistible primordial upsurge of a hunger for pointless, violent destruction?

It didn't fit the Ellis I knew. Not the man I'd raced against and laughed with, and had deemed a close friend for years. One couldn't know someone that well, and yet not know them at all.

Could one?

No.

Relentless thoughts kept me awake all night and in the morning I sent Linda Ferns' cheque back to her, uncashed.

'I've got no further,' I wrote. 'I'm exceedingly sorry.'

Two days later the same cheque returned.

'Dear Sid,' Linda replied, 'Keep the money. I know you'll find the thugs one day. I don't know what you said to Rachel but she's much happier and she hasn't had any bad dreams since you came last week. For that alone I would pay you double. Affectionately, Linda Ferns.'

I put the cheque in a pending file, caught up with paperwork and attended my usual judo training session.

The judo I practised was the subtle art of self-defence, the shifting of balance that used an attacker's own momentum to overcome him. Judo was rhythm, leverage and speed; a matter sometimes of applying pressure to nerves and always, in the way I learned, a quiet discipline. The yells and the kicks of karate, the arms slapped down on the padded mat to emphasise aggression, they were neither in my nature nor what I needed. I didn't seek physical domination. I didn't by choice start fights. With the built-in drawbacks of half an arm, a light frame and a height of about five feet seven, my overall requirement was survival.

I went through the routines absentmindedly. They were at best a mental crutch. A great many dangers couldn't be wiped out by an ability to throw an assailant over one's shoulder.

Ellis wouldn't leave my thoughts.

I was wrong. Of *course* I was wrong.

His face was universally known. He wouldn't risk being seen sneaking around fields at night armed with anything like a machete.

But he was bored with celebrity. Fame was no substitute for danger, he'd said. Everything he had was not enough.

All the same . . . *he couldn't.*

*

81

In the second week after the Derby I went to the four days of the Royal Ascot meeting, drifting around in a morning suit, admiring the gleaming coats of the horses and the women's extravagant hats. I should have enjoyed it, as I usually did. Instead, I felt as if the whole thing were a charade taking illusory place over an abyss.

Ellis, of course, was there every day: and, of course, he sought me out.

'How's it going, Hotline?'

'The Hotline is silent.'

'There you are, then,' Ellis said with friendly irony, 'you've frightened your foot merchant off.'

'For ever, I hope.'

'What if he can't help it?' Ellis said.

I turned my head: looked at his eyes. 'I'll catch him,' I said.

He smiled and looked away. 'Everyone knows you're a whiz at that sort of thing, but I'll bet you—'

'Don't,' I interrupted. 'Don't bet on it. It's bad luck.'

Someone came up to his other elbow, claiming his attention. He patted my shoulder, said with the usual affection, 'See you, Sid,' and was drawn away; and I couldn't believe, I *couldn't*, that he had told me *why*, even if not how.

'What if he can't help it?'

Could compulsion lead to cruel senseless acts?

No . . .

Yes, it could, and yes, it often did.

But not in Ellis. Not, *not* in Ellis.

Alibis, I thought, seeking for a rational way out. I would find out – somehow – exactly where Ellis had been on the nights the horses had been attacked. I would prove to my own satisfaction that it couldn't have been Ellis, and I would return with relief to the beginning, and admit I had no pointers at all, and would never find the thugs for Linda, and would quite happily chalk up a failure.

At five-thirty in the morning on the day after the Ascot Gold Cup, I sleepily awoke and answered my ringing telephone to hear a high agitated female voice saying, 'I want to reach Sid Halley.'

'You have,' I said, pushing myself up to sitting and squinting at the clock.

'What?'

'You are talking to Sid Halley.' I stifled a yawn. Five-bloody-thirty.

'But I phoned *The Pump* and asked for the Hotline!'

I said patiently, 'They re-route the Hotline calls direct to me. This is Sid Halley you're talking to. How can I help you?'

'Christ,' she said, sounding totally disorganised. 'We have a colt with a foot off.'

After a breath-catching second I said, 'Where are you?'

83

'At home. Oh, I see, Berkshire.'

'Where, exactly?'

'Combe Bassett, south of Hungerford.'

'And . . . um . . .' I thought of asking, 'What's the state of play?' and discarded it as less than tactful. 'What is . . . happening?'

'We're all up. Everyone's yelling and crying.'

'And the vet?'

'I just phoned him. He's coming.'

'And the police?'

'They're sending someone. Then we decided we'd better call you.'

'Yes,' I replied. 'I'll come now, if you like.'

'That's why I phoned you.'

'What's your name then? Address?'

She gave them. 'Betty Bracken, Manor House, Combe Bassett' – stumbling on the words as if she couldn't remember.

'Please,' I said, 'ask the vet not to send the colt or his foot off to the knackers until I get there.'

'I'll try,' she said jerkily. 'For God's sakes, *why*? Why our colt?'

'I'll be there in an hour,' I said.

What if he can't help it . . .

But it took such planning. Such stealth. So many crazy risks. Someone, sometime, would see him.

Let it not be Ellis, I thought. Let the compulsion be some other poor bastard's ravening subconscious. Ellis would be able to control such a vicious appetite, even if he felt it.

Let it not be Ellis.

Whoever it was, he had to be stopped: and I would stop him, if I could.

I shaved in the car (a Mercedes), clasping the battery-driven razor in the battery-driven hand, and I covered the eighty miles to south-west Berkshire in a time down the comparatively empty M4 that had the speedometer needle quivering where it had seldom been before. The radar speed traps slept. Just as well.

It was a lovely high June morning, fine and fresh. I curled through the gates of Combe Bassett Manor, cruised to a stop in the drive and at six-thirty walked into a house where open doors led to movement, loud voices and a general gnashing of teeth.

The woman who'd phoned rushed over when she saw me, her hands flapping in the air, her whole demeanour in an out-of-control state of fluster.

'Sid Halley? Thank God. Punch some sense into this lot.'

This lot consisted of two uniformed policemen and a crowd of what later proved to be family members, neighbours, ramblers and half a dozen dogs.

'Where's the colt?' I asked. 'And where's his foot?'

'Out in the field. The vet's there. I told him what you wanted but he's an opinionated Scot. God knows if he'll wait, he's a cantankerous old devil. He—'

'Show me where,' I said abruptly, cutting into the flow.

She blinked. 'What? Oh, yes. This way.'

She set off fast, leading me through big-house, unevenly painted hinterland passages reminiscent of those of Aynsford, of those of any house built with servants in mind. We passed a gun-room, flower-room, and mud-room (ranks of green wellies) and emerged at last through a rear door into a yard inhabited by dustbins. From there, through a green wooden garden door, she led the way fast down a hedge-bordered grass path and through a metal-railing gate at the far end of it. I'd begun to think we were off to limbo when suddenly, there before us, was a lane full of vehicles and about ten people leaning on paddock fencing.

My guide was tall, thin, fluttery, at a guess about fifty, dressed in old cord trousers and a drab olive sweater. Her greying hair flopped, unbrushed, over a high forehead. She had been, and still was, beyond caring how she looked, but I had a powerful impression that she was a woman to whom looks mattered little anyway.

She was deferred to. The men leaning on the paddock rails straightened and all but touched their forelocks, 'Morning, Mrs Bracken.'

She nodded automatically and ushered me through the wide metal gate that one of the men swung open for her.

Inside the field, at a distance of perhaps thirty paces,

stood two more men, also a masculine-looking woman and a passive colt with three feet. All, except the colt, showed the facial and body language of impatience.

One of the men, tall, white-haired, wearing black-rimmed glasses, took two steps forward to meet us.

'Now, Mrs Bracken, I've done what you asked, but it's past time to put your poor boy out of his misery. And you'll be Sid Halley, I suppose,' he said, peering down as from a mountain top. 'There's little you can do.' He shook hands briefly as if it were a custom he disapproved of.

He had a strong Scottish accent and the manner of one accustomed to command. The man behind him, unremarkably built, self-effacing in manner, remained throughout a silent watcher on the fringe.

I walked over to the colt and found him wearing a head-collar, with a rope halter held familiarly by the woman. The young horse watched me with calm bright eyes, unafraid. I stroked my hand down his nose, talking to him quietly. He moved his head upwards against the pressure and down again as if nodding, saying hello. I let him whiffle his black lips across my knuckles. I stroked his neck and patted him. His skin was dry: no pain, no fear, no distress.

'Is he drugged?' I asked.

'I'd have to run a blood test,' the Scotsman said.

'Which you are doing, of course?'

'Of course.'

One could tell from the faces of the other man

and the woman that no blood test had so far been considered.

I moved round the colt's head and squatted down for a close look at his off-fore, running my hand down the back of his leg, feeling only a soft area of no resistance where normally there would be the tough bowstring tautness of the leg's main tendon. Pathetically, the fetlock was tidy, not bleeding. I bent up the colt's knee and looked at the severed end. It had been done neatly, sliced through, unsplintered ends of bone showing white, the skin cleanly cut as if a practised chef had used a disjointing knife.

The colt jerked his knee, freeing himself from my grasp.

I stood up.

'Well?' the Scotsman challenged.

'Where's his foot?'

'Over yon, out of sight behind the water trough.' He paused, then as I turned away from him, suddenly added, 'It wasn't found there. I put it there, out of sight. It was they ramblers that came to it first.'

'Ramblers?'

'Aye.'

Mrs Bracken, who had joined us, explained. 'One Saturday every year in June, all the local rambling clubs turn out in force to walk the footpaths in this part of the country, to keep them legally open for the public.'

'If they'd stay on the footpaths,' the Scot said forbiddingly, 'they be within their rights.'

Mrs Bracken agreed. 'They bring their children and their dogs and their picnics, and act as if they own the place.'

'But . . . what on earth time did they find your colt's foot?'

'They set off soon after dawn,' Mrs Bracken observed morosely. 'In the middle of June, that's four-thirty in the morning, more or less. They gather before five o'clock while it is still cool, and set off across my land first, and they were hammering on my door by five-fifteen. Three of the children were in full-blown hysteria, and a man with a beard and a pony-tail was screaming that he blamed the élite. What élite? One of the ramblers phoned the Press and then someone fanatical in animal rights, and a carload of activists arrived with "ban horse racing" banners.' She rolled her eyes. 'I *despair*,' she said. 'It's bad enough losing my glorious colt. These people are turning it into a *circus*.'

Hold on to the real tragedy at the heart of the farce, I thought briefly, and walked over to the water trough to look at the foot that lay behind it. There were horse-feed nuts scattered everywhere around. Without expecting much emotion, I bent and picked the foot up.

I hadn't seen the other severed feet. I'd actually thought some of the reported reactions excessive. But the reality of that poor, unexpected, curiously lonely lump of bone, gristle and torn ends of blood vessels, that wasted miracle of anatomical elegance, moved me close to the fury and grief of all the owners.

There was a shoe on the hoof; the sort of small light shoe fitted to youngsters to protect their fore feet out in the field. There were ten small nails tacking the shoe to the hoof. The presence of the shoe brought its own powerful message: civilisation had offered care to the colt's foot, barbarity had hacked it off.

I'd loved horses always: it was hard to explain the intimacy that grew between horses and those who tended or rode them. Horses lived in a parallel world, spoke a parallel language, were a mass of instincts, lacked human perceptions of kindness or guilt, and allowed a merging on an untamed, untamable mysterious level of spirit. The Great God Pan lived in racehorses. One cut off his foot at one's peril.

On a more prosaic level I put the hoof back on the ground, unclipped the mobile phone I wore on my belt and, consulting a small diary/notebook for the number, connected myself to a veterinary friend who worked as a surgeon in an equine hospital in Lambourn.

'Bill?' I said. 'This is Sid Halley.'

'Go to sleep,' he said.

'Wake up. It's six-fifty and I'm in Berkshire with the severed off-fore hoof of a two-year-old colt.'

'Jesus.' He woke up fast.

'I want you to look at it. What do you advise?'

'How long has it been off? Any chance of sewing it back on?'

'It's been off at least three hours, I'd say. Probably more. There's no sign of the achilles tendon. It's contracted up inside the leg. The amputation is through the fetlock joint itself.'

'One blow, like the others?'

I hesitated. 'I didn't see the others.'

'But something's worrying you?'

'I want you to look at it,' I said.

Bill Ruskin and I had worked on other, earlier puzzles, and got along together in a trusting undemanding friendship that remained unaltered by periods of non-contact.

'What shape is the colt in generally?' he asked.

'Quiet. No visible pain.'

'Is the owner rich?'

'It looks like it.'

'See if he'll have the colt – and his foot, of course – shipped over here.'

'She,' I said. 'I'll ask her.'

Mrs Bracken gaped at me mesmerised when I relayed the suggestion, and said 'Yes' faintly.

Bill said, 'Find a sterile surgical dressing for the leg. Wrap the foot in another dressing and a polythene bag and pack it in a bucket of ice cubes. Is it clean?'

'Some early morning ramblers found it.'

He groaned. 'I'll send a horse ambulance,' he said. 'Where to?'

I explained where I was, and added, 'There's a Scots

91

vet here that's urging to put the colt down at once. Use honey-tongued diplomacy.'

'Put him on.'

I returned to where the colt still stood and, explaining who he would be talking to, handed my phone to the vet. The Scot scowled. Mrs Bracken said 'Anything, anything,' over and over again. Bill talked.

'Very well,' the Scot said frostily, finally, 'but you do understand, don't you, Mrs Bracken, that the colt won't be able to race, even if they do succeed in reattaching his foot, which is very, very doubtful.'

She said simply, 'I don't want to lose him. It's worth a try.'

The Scot, to give him his due, set about enclosing the raw leg efficiently in a dressing from his surgical bag and in wrapping the foot in a businesslike bundle. The row of men leaning on the fence watched with interest. The masculine-looking woman holding the head-collar wiped a few tears from her weatherbeaten cheeks while crooning to her charge, and eventually Mrs Bracken and I returned to the house, which still rang with noise. The ramblers, making the most of the drama, seemed to be rambling all over the ground floor and were to be seen assessing their chances of penetrating upstairs. Mrs Bracken clutched her head in distraction and said, 'Please will everyone leave,' but without enough volume to be heard.

I begged one of the policemen, 'Shoo the lot out, can't you?' and finally most of the crowd left, the ebb revealing a large basically formal pale green and gold drawing-room inhabited by five or six humans, three dogs and a clutter of plastic cups engraving wet rings on ancient polished surfaces. Mrs Bracken, like a somnambulist, drifted around picking up cups from one place only to put them down in another. Ever tidy-minded, I couldn't stop myself twitching up a waste-paper basket and following her, taking the cups from her fingers and collecting them all together.

She looked at me vaguely. She said, 'I paid a quarter of a million for that colt.'

'Is he insured?'

'No. I don't insure my jewellery either.'

'Or your health?'

'No, of course not.'

She looked unseeingly round the room. Five people now sat on easy chairs, offering no help or succour.

'Would someone make a cup of tea?' she asked.

No one moved.

She said to me, as if it explained everything, 'Esther doesn't start work until eight.'

'Mm,' I said. 'Well . . . er . . . who is everybody?'

'Goodness, yes. Rude of me. That's my husband.' Her gaze fell affectionately on an old bald man who looked as if he had no comprehension of anything. 'He's deaf, the dear man.'

'I see.'

'And that's my aunt, who mostly lives here.'

The aunt was also old and proved unhelpful and selfish.

'Our tenants.' Mrs Bracken indicated a stolid couple. 'They live in part of the house. And my nephew.'

Even her normal good manners couldn't keep the irritation from either her voice or her face at this last identification. The nephew was a teenager with a loose mouth and an attitude problem.

None of this hopeless bunch looked like an accomplice in a spite attack on a harmless animal, not even the unsatisfactory boy, who was staring at me intensely as if demanding to be noticed: almost, I thought fleetingly, as if he wanted to tell me something by telepathy. It was more than an interested inspection, but also held neither disapproval nor fear, as far as I could see.

I said to Mrs Bracken, 'If you tell me where the kitchen is, I'll make you some tea.'

'But you've only one hand.'

I reassured her, 'I can't climb Everest but I can sure make tea.'

A streak of humour began to banish the morning's shocks from her eyes. 'I'll come with you,' she said.

The kitchen, like the whole house, had been built on a grand scale for a cast of dozens. Without difficulties we made tea in a pot and sat at the well-scrubbed old wooden central table to drink it from mugs.

'You're not what I expected,' she said. 'You're *cosy*.'

I liked her: couldn't help it.

She went on, 'You're not like my brother said. I'm afraid I didn't explain that it is my brother who is out in the field with the vet. It was he who said I should phone you. He didn't say you were cosy, he said you were flint. I should have introduced you to him, but you can see how things are ... Anyway, I rely on him dreadfully. He lives in the next village. He came at once when I woke him.'

'Is he,' I asked neutrally, 'your nephew's father?'

'Goodness, no. My nephew ... Jonathan ...' She stopped, shaking her head. 'You don't want to hear about Jonathan.'

'Try me.'

'He's our sister's son. Fifteen. He got into trouble, expelled from school ... on probation ... his step-father can't stand him. My sister was at her wits' end so I said he could come here for a bit. It's not working out, though. I can't get through to him.' She looked suddenly aghast. 'You don't think he had anything to do with the colt?'

'No, no. What trouble did he get into? Drugs?'

She sighed, shaking her head. 'He was with two other boys. They stole a car and crashed it. Jonathan was in the back seat. The boy driving was also fifteen and broke his neck. Paralysed. Joy-riding, they called it. Some joy! Stealing, that's what it was. And Jonathan isn't repentant. Really, he can be a *pig*. But not the colt ... not that?'

'No,' I assured her, 'positively not.' I drank hot tea

and asked, 'Is it well known hereabouts that you have this great colt in that field?'

She nodded. 'Eva, who looks after him, she talks of nothing else. All the village knows. That's why there are so many people here. Half the men from the village, as well as the ramblers. Even so early in the morning.'

'And your friends?' I prompted.

She nodded gloomily. 'Everyone. I bought him at the Premium Yearling Sales last October. His breeding is a dream. He was a late foal – end of April – he's . . . he *was* going into training next week. Oh *dear*.'

'I'm so sorry,' I said. I screwed myself unhappily to ask the unavoidable question, 'Who, among your friends, came here in person to admire the colt?'

She was far from stupid, and also vehement. 'No one who came here could *possibly* have done this! People like Lord and Lady Dexter? Of course not! Gordon and Ginnie Quint, and darling Ellis? Don't be silly. Though I suppose,' she went on doubtfully, 'they could have mentioned him to other people. He wasn't a *secret*. Anyone since the Sales would know he was here, like I told you.'

'Of course,' I said.

Ellis.

We finished the tea and went back to the drawing-room. Jonathan, the nephew, stared at me again unwaveringly, and after a moment, to test my own impression, I jerked my head in the direction of the door, walking that way; and, with hardly a hesitation, he stood up and followed.

I went out of the drawing-room, across the hall and through the still wide-open front door onto the drive.

'Sid Halley,' he said behind me.

I turned. He stopped four paces away, still not wholly committed. His accent and general appearance spoke of expensive schools, money and privilege. His mouth and his manner said slob.

'What is it that you know?' I asked.

'Hey! Look here! What do you mean?'

I said without pressure, 'You want to tell me something, don't you?'

'I don't know. Why do you think so?'

I'd seen that intense bursting-at-the-seams expression too often by then to mistake it. He knew something that he ought to tell: it was only his own contrary rebelliousness that had kept him silent so far.

I made no appeal to a better nature that I wasn't sure he had.

I said, guessing, 'Were you awake before four o'clock?'

He glared, but didn't answer.

I tried again. 'You hate to be helpful, is that it? No one is going to catch you behaving well – that sort of thing? Tell me what you know. I'll give you as bad a press as you want. Your obstructive reputation will remain intact.'

'Sod you,' he said.

I waited.

'She'd kill me,' he said. 'Worse, she'd pack me off home.'

'Mrs Bracken?'

He nodded. 'My Aunt Betty.'

'What have you done?'

He used a few old Anglo-Saxon words: bluster to impress me with his virility, I supposed. Pathetic, really. Sad.

'She has these effing stupid rules,' he said. 'Be back in the house at night by eleven-thirty.'

'And last night,' I suggested, 'you weren't?'

'I got probation,' he said. 'Did she tell you?'

'Yeah.'

He took two more steps towards me, into normal talking distance.

'If she knew I went out again,' he said, 'I could get youth custody.'

'If she shopped you, you mean?'

He nodded. 'But . . . sod it . . . to cut a foot off a horse . . .'

Perhaps the better nature was somewhere there after all. Stealing cars was OK, maiming racehorses wasn't. He wouldn't have blinded those ponies: he wasn't that sort of lout.

'If I fix it with your aunt, will you tell me?' I asked.

'Make her promise not to tell Archie. He's worse.'

'Er,' I said, 'who is Archie?'

'My uncle. Aunt Betty's brother. He's Establishment, man. He's the flogging classes.'

I made no promises. I said, 'Just spill the beans.'

'In three weeks I'll be sixteen.' He looked at me intently for reaction, but all he'd caused in me was puzzlement. I thought the cut-off age for crime to be considered 'juvenile' was two years older. He wouldn't be sent to an adult jail.

Jonathan saw my lack of understanding. He said impatiently, 'You can't be under age for sex if you're a man, only if you're a girl.'

'Are you sure?'

'*She* says so.'

'Your Aunt Betty?' I felt lost.

'No, stupid. The woman in the village.'

'Oh . . . ah.'

'Her old man's a long-distance lorry driver. He's away for nights on end. He'd kill me. Youth custody would be apple-pie.'

'Difficult,' I said.

'She *wants* it, see? I'd never done it before. I bought her a gin in the pub.' Which, at fifteen, was definitely illegal to start with.

'So . . . um . . .' I said, 'last night you were coming back from the village . . . When, exactly?'

'It was dark. Just before dawn. There had been more moonlight earlier, but I'd left it late. I was *running*. She – Aunt Betty – she wakes with the cocks. She lets the dogs out before six.' His agitation, I thought, was producing what sounded like truth.

I thought, and asked, 'Did you see any ramblers?'

'No. I was earlier than them.'

I held my breath. I had to ask the next question, and dreaded the answer.

'So, who was it that you saw?'

'It wasn't a "who", it was a "what".' He paused and reassessed his position. 'I didn't go to the village.' He said, 'I'll deny it.'

I nodded. 'You were restless. Unable to sleep. You went for a walk.'

He said, 'Yeah, that's it,' with relief.

'And you saw?'

'A Land-Rover.'

Not a who. A what. I said, partly relieved, partly disappointed, 'That's not so extraordinary, in the country.'

'No, but it wasn't Aunt Betty's Land-Rover. It was much newer, and blue, not green. It was standing in the lane not far from the gate into the field. There was no one in it. I didn't think much of it. There's a path up to the house from the lane. I always go out and in that way. It's miles from Aunt Betty's bedroom.'

'Through the yard with all the dustbins?' I asked.

He was comically astounded. I didn't explain that his aunt had taken me out that way. I said, 'Couldn't it have been a rambler's Land-Rover?'

He said sullenly, 'I don't know why I bothered to tell you.'

I asked, 'What else did you notice about the Land-Rover, except for its colour?'

'Nothing. I told you, I was more interested in getting back into the house without anyone spotting me.'

I thought a bit and said, 'How close did you get to it?'

'I touched it. I didn't see it until I was almost on top of it. Like I told you, I was running along the lane. I was mostly looking at the ground, and it was still almost dark.'

'Was it facing you, or did you run into the back of it?'

'Facing. There was still enough moonlight to reflect off the windscreen. That's what I saw first, the reflection.'

'What part of it did you touch?'

'The bonnet.' Then he added as if surprised by the extent of his memory, 'It was quite hot.'

'Did you see a number plate?'

'Not a chance. I wasn't hanging about for things like that.'

'What else did you see?'

'Nothing.'

'How did you know there was no one in the cab? There might have been a couple lying in there snogging.'

'Well, there wasn't. I looked through the window.'

'Open or shut windows?'

'Open.' He surprised himself again. 'I looked in fast, on the way past. No people, just a load of machinery behind the front seats.'

'What sort of machinery?'

'How the eff do I know? It had handles sticking up. Like a lawn mower. I didn't look. I was in a hurry. I didn't want to be seen.'

'No,' I agreed. 'How about an ignition key?'

'Hey?' It was a protest of hurt feelings. 'I didn't drive it away.'

'Why not?'

'I don't take every car I see. Not alone, ever.'

'There's no fun in it if you're alone?'

'Not so much.'

'So there *was* a key in the ignition?'

'I suppose so. Yah.'

'Was there one key, or a bunch?'

'Don't know.'

'Was there a key-ring?'

'You don't ask much!'

'Think, then.'

He said unwillingly, 'See, I *notice* ignition keys.'

'Yes.'

'It was a bunch of keys, then. They had a silver horseshoe dangling from them on a little chain. A little horseshoe. Just an ordinary key-ring.'

We stared at each other briefly.

He said, 'I didn't think anything of it.'

'No,' I agreed. 'You wouldn't. Well, go back a bit. When you put your hand on the bonnet, were you looking at the windscreen?'

'I must have been.'

'What was on it?'

'Nothing. What do you mean?'

'Did it have a tax disc?'

'It must have done, mustn't it?' he said.

'Well, did it have anything else? Like, say, a sticker saying "Save the Tigers"?'

'No, it didn't.'

'Shut your eyes and think,' I urged him. 'You're running. You don't want to be seen. You nearly collide with a Land-Rover. Your face is quite near the wind-screen—'

'There was a red dragon,' he interrupted. 'A red circle with a dragon thing in it. Not very big. One of those sort of transparent transfers that stick to glass.'

'Great,' I said. 'Anything else?'

For the first time he gave it concentrated thought, but came up with nothing more.

'I'm nothing to do with the police,' I said, 'and I won't spoil your probation and I won't give you away to your aunt, but I'd like to write down what you've told me, and if you agree that I've got it right, will you sign it?'

'Hey. I don't know. I don't know why I told you.'

'It might matter a lot. It might not matter at all. But

I'd like to find this bugger . . .' God help me, I thought. I have to.

'So would I.' He meant it. Perhaps there was hope for him yet.

He turned on his heel and went rapidly alone into the house, not wanting to be seen in even semi-reputable company, I assumed. I followed more slowly. Jonathan had not returned to the drawing-room, where the tenants still sat stolidly, the difficult old aunt complained about being woken early, the deaf husband said, 'Eh?' mechanically at frequent intervals and Betty Bracken sat looking into space. Only the three dogs, now lying down and testing their heads on their front paws, seemed fully sane.

I said to Mrs Bracken, 'Do you by any chance have a typewriter?'

She said incuriously, 'There's one in the office.'

'Er . . .'

'I'll show you.' She rose and led me to a small, tidy back room containing the bones of communication but an impression of under-use.

'I don't know how anything works,' Betty Bracken said frankly. 'We have a part-time secretary, once a week. Help yourself.'

She left, nodding, and I thanked her, and I found an electric typewriter under a fitted dust-cover, plugged ready into the current.

I wrote:

Finding it difficult to sleep I went for a short walk
in the grounds of Combe Bassett Manor at about
three-thirty in the morning. [I inserted the date.] In
the lane near to the gate of the home paddock I
passed a Land-Rover that was parked there. The
vehicle was blue. I did not look at the number plate.
The engine was still hot when I touched the bonnet
in passing. There was a key in the ignition. It was
one of a bunch of keys on a key-ring which had a
silver horseshoe on a chain. There was no one in
the vehicle. There was some sort of equipment
behind the front seat, but I did not take a close look.
On the inside of the windscreen I observed a small
transfer of a red dragon in a red circle. I went past
the vehicle and returned to the house.

Under another fitted cover I located a copier, so I left
the little office with three sheets of paper and went
in search of Jonathan, running him to earth eating a
haphazard breakfast in the kitchen. He paused over his
cereal, spoon in air, while he read what I'd written.
Wordlessly, I produced a ballpoint pen and held it out
to him.

He hesitated, shrugged and signed the first of the
papers with loops and a flourish.

'Why *three*?' he asked suspiciously, pushing the
copies away.

'One for you,' I said calmly. 'One for my records.

One for the on-going file of bits and pieces which may eventually catch our villain.'

'Oh.' He considered. 'All right then.' He signed the other two sheets and I gave him one to keep. He seemed quite pleased with his civic-mindedness. He was re-reading his edited deposition over his flakes as I left.

Back in the drawing-room, looking for her, I asked where Mrs Bracken had gone. The aunt, the tenants and the deaf husband made no reply.

Negotiating the hinterland passage and the dustbin yard again, I arrived back at the field, to see Mrs Bracken herself, the fence-leaners, the Scots vet and her brother watching the horse ambulance drive into the field and draw up conveniently close to the colt.

The horse ambulance consisted of a narrow low-slung trailer pulled by a Range Rover. There was a driver and a groom used to handling sick and injured horses and, with crooning noises from the solicitous Eva, the poor young colt made a painful-looking, head-bobbing stagger up a gentle ramp into the waiting stall.

'Oh *dear*, oh *dear*,' Mrs Bracken whispered beside me. 'My dear, dear, young fellow . . . how *could* they?'

I shook my head. Rachel Ferns' pony and four prized colts . . . How could *anyone*.

The colt was shut into the trailer, the bucket containing the foot was loaded, and the pathetic twelve-mile journey to Lambourn began.

The Scots vet patted Betty Bracken sympathetically on the arm, gave her his best wishes for the colt, claimed his car from the line of vehicles in the lane and drove away.

I unclipped my mobile phone and got through to *The Pump*, who forwarded my call to an irate newspaperman at his home in Surrey.

Kevin Mills yelled, 'Where the hell are you? They say all anyone gets on the Hotline now is your answering machine, saying you'll call back. About fifty people have phoned. They're all rambling.'

'Ramblers,' I said.

'What?'

I explained.

'It's supposed to be my day off,' he grumbled. 'Can you meet me in the pub? What time? Five o'clock?'

'Make it seven,' I suggested.

'It's no longer a *Pump* exclusive, I suppose you realise?' he demanded. 'But save yourself for me alone, will you, buddy? Give me the inside edge?'

'It's yours.'

I closed my phone and warned Betty Bracken to expect the media on her doorstep.

'Oh no!'

'Your colt is one too many.'

'Archie!' She turned to her brother for help with a beseeching gesture of the hand and, as if for the thousandth time in their lives, he responded with comfort and competent solutions.

'My dear Betty,' he said, 'if you can't bear to face the Press, simply don't be here.'

'But . . .' she wavered.

'I shouldn't waste time,' I said.

The brother gave me an appraising glance. He himself was of medium height, lean of body, grey in colour, a man to get lost in a crowd. His eyes alone were notable: brown, bright and *aware*. I had an uncomfortable feeling that, far beyond having his sister phone me, he knew a good deal about me.

'We haven't actually met,' he said to me civilly. 'I'm Betty's brother. I'm Archie Kirk.'

I said, 'How do you do,' and I shook his hand.

CHAPTER FIVE

Betty Bracken, Archie Kirk and I returned to the house, again circumnavigating the dustbins. Archie Kirk's car was parked outside the Manor's front door, not far from my own.

The lady of the Manor refusing to leave without her husband, the uncomprehending old man, still saying 'Eh?', was helped with great solicitude across the hall, through the front door and into an ancient Daimler, an Establishment-type conservative-minded political statement if ever I saw one.

My own Mercedes, milk-coffee-coloured, stood beyond: and what, I thought astringently, was it saying about *me*? Rich enough, sober enough, preferring reliability to flash? All spot on, particularly the last. And speed, of course.

Betty spooned her beloved into the back seat of the Daimler and folded herself in beside him, patting him gently. Touch, I supposed, had replaced speech as their means of communication. Archie Kirk took his place behind the wheel as natural commander-in-chief, and drove away, leaving for me the single short parting remark, 'Let me know.'

I nodded automatically. Let him know *what*? Whatever I learned, I presumed.

I returned to the drawing-room. The stolid tenants, on their feet, were deciding to return to their own wing of the house. The dogs snoozed. The cross aunt crossly demanded Esther's presence. Esther, on duty at eight and not a moment before, come ramblers, police or whatever, appeared forbiddingly in the doorway, a small, frizzy-haired worker, clear about her 'rights'.

I left the two quarrelsome women pitching into each other and went in search of Jonathan. What a household! The media were welcome to it. I looked but couldn't find Jonathan, so I just had to trust that his boorishness would keep him well away from inquisitive reporters with microphones. The Land-Rover he'd seen might have brought the machete to the colt, and I wanted, if I could, to find it before its driver learned there was a need for rapid concealment.

The first thing in my mind was the colt himself. I started the car and set off north to Lambourn, driving thoughtfully, wondering what was best to do concerning the police. I had had varying experiences with the Force, some good, some rotten. They did not, in general, approve of freelance investigators like myself, and could be downright obstructive if I appeared to be working on something they felt belonged to them alone. Sometimes, though, I'd found them willing to take over if I'd come across criminal activity that couldn't go unprosecuted. I stepped gingerly round their sensitive areas, and also those of racing's own security services run by the Jockey Club and the British Horse-racing Board. I was careful always not to claim credit for clearing up three-pipe problems. Not even one-pipe problems, hardly worthy of Sherlock Holmes.

Where the Jockey Club itself was concerned, I fluctuated in their view between flavour of the month and anathema, according as to who currently reigned as Senior Steward. With the police, collaboration depended very much on which individual policeman I reached and his private-life stress level at the moment of contact.

The rules governing evidence, moreover, were growing ever stickier. Juries no longer without question believed the police. For an object to be admitted for consideration in a trial it had to be ticketed, docketed and continuously accounted for. One couldn't, for instance, flourish a machete and say, 'I found it in X's Land-Rover, therefore it was X who cut off a colt's foot.' To get even within miles of conviction one needed a specific search warrant before one could even *look* in the Land-Rover for a machete, and search warrants weren't granted to Sid Halleys, and sometimes not to the police.

The police force as a whole was divided into autonomous districts, like the Thames Valley Police, who solved crimes in their own area but might not take much notice outside. A maimed colt in Lancashire might not have been heard of in Yorkshire. Serial rapists had gone for years uncaught because of the slow flow of information. A serial horse maimer might have no central file.

Dawdling along up the last hill before Lambourn I became aware of a knocking in the car and pulled over to the side with gloomy thoughts of broken shock absorbers and misplaced trust in reliability, but after the car stopped the knocking continued. With awakening awareness, I climbed out, went round to the back and with difficulty opened the boot. There was something wrong with the lock.

Jonathan lay curled in the space for luggage. He had one shoe off, with which he was assaulting my milk-coffee bodywork. When I lifted the lid he stopped banging and looked at me challengingly.

'What the hell are you doing there?' I demanded.

Silly question. He looked at his shoe. I rephrased it. 'Get out.'

He manoeuvred himself out onto the road and calmly replaced his shoe with no attempt at apology. I slammed the boot lid shut at the second try and returned to the driver's seat. He walked to the passenger side, found the door there locked and tapped on the window to draw my attention to it. I started the engine, lowered the electrically controlled window a little, and shouted to him, 'It's only three miles to Lambourn.'

'No. Hey! You can't leave me here!'

Want to bet, I thought, and set off along the deserted downland road. I saw him, in the rear-view mirror, running after me determinedly. I drove slowly, but faster than he could run. He went on running, nevertheless.

After nearly a mile a curve in the road took me out of his sight. I braked and stopped. He came round the bend, saw my car and put on a spurt, racing this time up to the driver's side. I'd locked the door but lowered the window three or four inches.

'What's all that for?' he demanded.

'What's all what for?'

'Making me run.'

'You've broken the lock on my boot.'

'What?' He looked baffled. 'I only gave it a clout. I didn't have a key.' No key; a clout. Obvious, his manner said.

'Who's going to pay to get it mended?' I asked.

He said impatiently, as if he couldn't understand such small-mindedness, 'What's that got to do with it?'

'With what?'

'With the colt.'

Resignedly I leaned across and pulled up the locking knob on the front passenger door. He went round there and climbed in beside me. I noted with interest that he was hardly out of breath.

Jonathan's haircut, I thought as he settled into his seat and neglected to buckle the seat-belt, shouted an indication of his adolescent insecurity, of his desire to shock or at least to be *noticed*. He had, I thought, bleached inexpert haphazard streaks into his hair with a comb dipped in something like hydrogen peroxide. Straight and thick, the mop was parted in the centre with a wing each side curving down to his cheek, making a curtain beside his eye. From one ear backwards, and round to the other ear, the hair had been sliced off in a straight line. Below the line, his scalp was shaven. To my eyes it looked ugly, but then I wasn't fifteen.

Making a statement through hairstyle was universal, after all. Men with bald crowns above pigtails, men with plaited beards, women with severely scraped back pinnings, all were saying 'This is *me*, and I'm *different*.' In the days of Charles I, when long male hair was normal, rebellious sons had cut off their curls to have roundheads. Archie Kirk's grey hair had been short, neat and controlled. My own dark hair would have curled girlishly if allowed to grow. A haircut was still the most unmistakable give-away of the person inside.

Conversely, a wig could change all that.

I asked Jonathan, 'Have you remembered something else?'

'No, not really.'

'Then why did you stow away?'

'Come on, man, give me a break. What am I supposed to do all day in that graveyard of a house? The

114

aunt's whinging drives me insane and even Karl Marx would have throttled Esther.'

He did, I suppose, have a point.

I thoughtfully coasted down the last hill towards Lambourn.

'Tell me about your uncle, Archie Kirk,' I said.

'What about him?'

'You tell me. For starters, what does he do?'

'He works for the government.'

'What as?'

'Some sort of civil servant. Dead boring.'

Boring, I reflected, was the last adjective I would have applied to what I'd seen in Archie Kirk's eyes.

'Where does he live?' I asked.

'Back in Shelley Green, a couple of miles from Aunt Betty. She can't climb a ladder unless he's holding it.'

Reaching Lambourn itself I took the turn that led to the equine hospital. Slowly though I had made the journey, the horse-ambulance had been slower. They were still unloading the colt.

From Jonathan's agog expression, I guessed it was in fact the first view he'd had of a shorn-off leg, even if all he could now see was a surgical dressing.

I said to him, 'If you want to wait half an hour for me, fine. Otherwise, you're on your own. But if you try stealing a car, I'll personally see you lose your probation.'

'Hey. Give us a break.'

'You've had your share of good breaks. Half an hour. OK?'

He glowered at me without words. I went across to where Bill Ruskin, in a white coat, was watching his patient's arrival. He said, 'Hello, Sid,' absentmindedly, then collected the bucket containing the foot and, with me following, led the way into a small laboratory full of weighing and measuring equipment and microscopes.

Unwrapping the foot, he stood it on the bench and looked at it assessingly.

'A good clean job,' he said.

'There's nothing good about it.'

'Probably the colt hardly felt it.'

'How was it done?' I asked.

'Hm.' He considered. 'There's no other point on the leg that you could amputate a foot without using a saw to cut through the bone. I doubt if a single swipe with a heavy knife would achieve this precision. And achieve it several times, on different animals, right?'

I nodded.

'Yes, well, I think we might be looking at game shears.'

'*Game shears?*' I exclaimed. 'Do you mean those sort of heavy scissors that will cut up duck and pheasant?'

'Something along those lines, yes.'

'But those shears aren't anywhere near big enough for this.'

He pursed his mouth. 'How about a gralloching

knife, then? The sort used for disembowelling deer out on the mountains?'

'Jeez.'

'There are signs of *compression*, though. On balance, I'd hazard heavy game shears. How did he get the colt to stand still?'

'There were horse-nuts on the ground.'

He nodded morosely. 'Slime ball.'

'There aren't any words for it.'

He peered closely at the raw red and white end of the pastern. 'Even if I can reattach the foot, the colt will never race.'

'His owner knows that. She wants to save his life.'

'Better to collect the insurance.'

'No insurance. A quarter of a million down the drain. But it's not the money she's grieving over. What she's feeling is guilt.'

He understood. He saw it often.

Eventually he said, 'I'll give it a try. I don't hold out much hope.'

'You'll photograph this as it is?'

He looked at the foot. 'Oh, sure. Photos, X-rays, blood tests on the colt, micro-stitching, every luxury. I'll get on with anaesthetising the colt as soon as possible. The foot's been off too long . . .' He shook his head. 'I'll try.'

'Phone my mobile.' I gave him the number. 'Any time.'

'See you, Sid. And catch the bugger.'

He bustled away, taking the foot with him, and I returned to my car to find Jonathan not only still there but jogging around with excitement.

'What's up?' I asked.

'That Range Rover that pulled the trailer that brought the colt . . .'

'What about it?'

'It's got a red dragon on the windscreen!'

'What? But you said a *blue*—'

'Yeah, yeah, it wasn't the vet's Range Rover I saw in the lane, but it's got a red dragon transfer on it. Not exactly the same, I don't think, but definitely a red dragon.'

I looked round, but the horse-ambulance was no longer in sight.

'They drove it off,' Jonathan said, 'but I saw the transfer close to, and it has *letters* in it.' His voice held triumph, which I allowed was justified.

'Go on, then,' I said. 'What letters?'

'Aren't you going to say "well done"?'

'Well done. What letters?'

'E.S.M. They were cut out of the red circle. Gaps, not printed letters.' He wasn't sure I understood.

'I do see,' I assured him.

I returned to the hospital to find Bill and asked him when he'd bought his Range Rover.

'Our local garage got it for us from a firm in Oxford.'

'What does E.S.M. stand for?'

'God knows.'

118

'I can't ask God. What's the name of the Range-Rover firm in Oxford?'

He laughed and thought briefly. 'English Sporting Motors. E.S.M. Good Lord.'

'Can you give me the name of someone there? Who did you actually deal with?'

With impatience he said, 'Look, Sid, I'm trying to scrub up to see what I can do about sticking the colt's foot back on.'

'And I'm trying to catch the bugger that took it off. And it's possible he travelled in a Land-Rover sold by English Sporting Motors.'

He said 'Christ' wide-eyed and headed for what proved to be the hospital's record office, populated by filing cabinets. Without much waste of time he flourished a copy of a receipted account, but shook his head.

'Ted James in the village might help you. I paid *him*. He dealt direct with Oxford. You'd have to ask Ted James.'

I thanked him, collected Jonathan, drove into the small town of Lambourn and located Ted James, who would do a lot for a good customer like Bill Ruskin, it seemed.

'No problem,' he assured me. 'Ask for Roger Brook in Oxford. Do you want me to phone him?'

'Yes, please.'

'Right-oh.' He spoke briefly on the phone and reported back. 'He's busy. Saturday's always a busy sales day. He'll help you if it doesn't take long.'

The morning seemed to have been going on for ever, but it was still before eleven o'clock when I talked to Roger Brook, tubby, smooth and self-important in the carpeted sales office of English Sporting Motors.

Roger Brook pursed his lips and shook his head; not the firm's policy to give out information about its customers.

I said ruefully, 'I don't want to bother the police . . .'

'Well . . .'

'And, of course, there would be a fee for your trouble.'

A fee was respectable where a bribe wasn't. In the course of life I disbursed a lot of fees.

It helpfully appeared that the red-dragon transparent transfers were slightly differently designed each year: *improved* as time went on, did I see?

I fetched Jonathan in from outside for Roger Brook to show him the past and present dragon logos, and Jonathan with certainty picked the one that had been, Brook said, that of the year before last.

'Great,' I said with satisfaction. 'How many blue Land-Rovers did you sell in that year? I mean, what are the names of the actual buyers, not the middlemen like Ted James?'

An open-mouthed silence proved amenable to a larger fee. 'Our Miss Denver' helped with a computer print-out. Our Miss Denver got a kiss from me. Roger Brook with dignity took his reward in readies, and Jonathan and I returned to the Mercedes with the names and addresses of two hundred and eleven purchasers of blue Land-Rovers a little back in time.

Jonathan wanted to read the list when I'd finished. I handed it over, reckoning he'd deserved it. He looked disappointed when he reached the end, and I didn't point out to him the name that had made my gut contract.

One of the Land-Rovers had been delivered to Twyford Lower Farms Ltd.

I had been to Twyford Lower Farms to lunch. It was owned by Gordon Quint.

Noon, Saturday. I sat in my parked car outside English Sporting Motors, while Jonathan fidgeted beside me, demanding 'What next?'

I said, 'Go and eat a hamburger for your lunch and be back here in twenty minutes.'

He had no money. I gave him some. 'Twenty minutes.'

He promised nothing, but returned with three minutes to spare. I spent his absence thinking highly unwelcome thoughts and deciding what to do, and when he slid in beside me smelling of raw onions and chips I set off southwards again, on the roads back to Combe Bassett.

'Where are we going?'

'To see your Aunt Betty.'

'But hey! She's not at home. She's at Archie's.'

'Then we'll go to Archie's. You can show me the way.'

He didn't like it, but he made no attempt to jump ship when we were stopped by traffic lights three times on the way out of Oxford. We arrived together in due course outside a house an eighth the size of Combe Bassett Manor; a house, moreover, that was frankly modern and not at all what I'd expected.

I said doubtfully, 'Are you sure this is the place?'

'The lair of the wolf. No mistake. He won't want to see me.'

I got out of the car and pressed the thoroughly modern doorbell beside a glassed-in front porch. The woman who came to answer the summons was small and wrinkled like a drying apple, and wore a sleeveless sundress in blue and mauve.

'Er . . .' I said to her enquiring face, 'Archie Kirk?'

Her gaze lengthened beyond me to include Jonathan in my car, a sight that pinched her mouth and jumped her to an instant wrong conclusion. She whirled away and returned with Archie, who said repressively, 'What is *he* doing here?'

'Can you spare me half an hour?' I asked.

'What's Jonathan done?'

'He's been extraordinarily helpful. I'd like to ask your advice.'

'*Helpful!*'

'Yes. Could you hold your disapproval in abeyance for half an hour while I explain?'

He gave me an intense inspection, the brown eyes

sharp and knowing, as before. Decision arrived there plainly.

'Come in,' he said, holding his front door wide.

'Jonathan's afraid of you,' I told him. 'He wouldn't admit it but he is. Could I ask you not to give him the normal tongue-lashing? Will you invite him in and leave him alone?'

'You don't know what you're asking.'

'I do,' I said.

'No one speaks to me like this.' He was, however, only mildly affronted.

I smiled at his eyes. 'That's because they know you. But I met you only this morning.'

'And,' he said, 'I've heard about your lightning judgements.'

I felt, as on other occasions with people of his sort, a deep thrust of mental satisfaction. Also, more immediately, I knew I had come to the right place.

Archie Kirk stepped out from his door, took the three paces to my car, and said through the window, 'Jonathan, please come into the house.'

Jonathan looked past him to me. I jerked my head, as before, to suggest that he complied, and he left the safe shelter and walked to the house, even if reluctantly and frozen-faced.

Archie Kirk led the way across a modest hallway into a middle-sized sitting-room where Betty Bracken, her husband, and the small woman who'd answered my ring were sitting in armchairs drinking cups of coffee.

The room's overall impression was of old oak and books, a room for dark winter evenings and lamps and log fires, not fitted to the dazzle of June. None of the three faces turned towards us could have looked welcoming to the difficult boy.

The small woman, introducing herself as Archie's wife, stood up slowly and offered me coffee, 'And ... er ... Jonathan ... Coca-Cola?'

Jonathan, as if reprieved, followed her out to the next door kitchen, and I told Betty Bracken that her colt was at that moment being operated on, and that there should be news of him soon. She was pathetically pleased: too pleased, I was afraid.

I said casually to Archie, 'Can I talk to you in private?' and without question he said, 'This way,' and transferred us to a small adjacent room, again all dark oak and books, that he called his study.

'What is it?' he asked.

'I need a policeman,' I said.

He gave me a long level glance and waved me to one of the two hard oak chairs, himself sitting in the other, beside a paper-strewn desk.

I told him about Jonathan's night walk (harmless version) and about our tracing the Land-Rover to the suppliers at Oxford. I said that I knew where the Land-Rover might now be, but that I couldn't get a search warrant to examine it. For a successful prosecution, I mentioned, there had to be integrity of evidence; no chance of tampering or substitution. So I needed a policeman, but one that would listen and cooperate, not one that would either brush me off altogether or one that would do the police work sloppily.

'I thought you might know someone,' I finished. 'I don't know who else to ask, as at the moment this whole thing depends on crawling up to the machine-gun nest on one's belly, so to speak.'

He sat back in his chair staring at me vacantly while the data got processed.

At length he said, 'Betty called in the local police this morning early, but . . . ' he hesitated, 'they hadn't the clout you need.' He thought some more, then picked up an address book. He leafed through it for a number and made a phone call.

'Norman, this is Archie Kirk.'

Whoever Norman was, it seemed he was unwilling.

'It's extremely important,' Archie said.

Norman apparently capitulated, but with protest, giving directions.

'You had better be right,' Archie said to me, disconnecting. 'I've just called in about a dozen favours he owed me.'

'Who is he?'

'Detective Inspector Norman Picton, Thames Valley Police.'

'Brilliant,' I said.

'He's off duty. He's on the gravel pit lake. He's a clever and ambitious young man. And I,' he added with a glimmer, 'am a magistrate, and I may sign a search

warrant myself, if he can clear it with his superintendent.'

He rendered me speechless, which quietly amused
him.

'You didn't know?' he asked.

I shook my head and found my voice, 'Jonathan said
you were a civil servant.'

'That too,' he agreed. 'How did you get that boorish
young man to talk?'

'Er . . .' I said. 'What is Inspector Picton doing on
the gravel pit lake?'

'Water ski-ing,' Archie said.

There were speedboats, children, wet-suits, picnics.
There was a club house in a sea of scrubby grass and
people sliding over the shining water pulled by strings.

Archie parked his Daimler at the end of a row of
cars, and I, with Jonathan beside me, parked my Mercedes alongside. We had agreed to bring both cars so
that I could go on eventually to London, with Archie
ferrying Jonathan back to pick up the Brackens and
take them all home to Combe Bassett. Jonathan hadn't
warmed to the plan, but had ungraciously accompanied
me as being a lesser horror than spending the afternoon
mooching aimlessly round Archie's aunt-infested
house.

Having got as far as the lake, he began looking at
the harmless physical activity all around him, not with

a sneer but with something approaching interest. On the shortish journey from Archie's house he had asked three moody questions, two of which I answered.

First: 'This is the best day for a long time. How come you get so much done so quickly?'

No answer possible.

And second: 'Did you ever steal anything?'

'Chocolate bars,' I said.

And third: 'Do you mind having only one hand?'

I said coldly, 'Yes.'

He glanced with surprise at my face and I saw that he'd expected me to say no. I supposed he wasn't old enough to know it was a question one shouldn't ask; but then, perhaps he would have asked it anyway.

When we climbed out of the car at the water-ski club I said, 'Can you swim?'

'Do me a favour.'

'Then go jump in the lake.'

'Sod you,' he said, and actually laughed.

Archie had meanwhile discovered that one of the scudding figures on the water was the man we'd come to see. We waited a fair while until a large presence in a blue wet-suit with scarlet stripes down arms and legs let go of the rope pulling him and skied free and gracefully to a sloping landing place on the edge of the water. He stepped off his skis grinning, knowing he'd shown off his considerable skill, and wetly shook Archie's hand.

'Sorry to keep you waiting,' he said, 'but I reckoned once you got here I'd have had it for the day.'

His voice, with its touch of Berkshire accent, held self-confidence and easy authority.

Archie said formally, 'Norman, this is Sid Halley.'

I shook the offered hand, which was cold besides wet. I received the sort of slow searching inspection I'd had from Archie himself: and I had no idea what the policeman thought.

'Well,' he said finally, stirring, 'I'll get dressed.'

We watched him walk away, squelching, gingerly barefooted, carrying his skis. He was back within five minutes, clad now in jeans, sneakers, open-necked shirt and sweater, his dark hair still wet and spiky, uncombed.

'Right,' he said to me. 'Give.'

'Er . . .' I hesitated. 'Would it be possible for Mr Kirk's nephew, Jonathan, to go for a ride in a speedboat?'

Both he and Archie looked over to where Jonathan, not far away, lolled unprepossessingly against my car. Jonathan did himself no favours, I thought; self-destruction rampant in every bolshie tilt of the anti-authority haircut.

'He doesn't deserve any ride in a speedboat,' Archie objected.

'I don't want him to overhear what I'm saying.'

'That's different,' Norman Picton decided. 'I'll fix it.'

Jonathan ungraciously allowed himself to be driven

round the lake by Norman Picton's wife in Norman Picton's boat, accompanied by Norman Picton's son. We watched the boat race past with a roar, Jonathan's streaky mop blown back in the wind.

'He's on the fence,' I said mildly to Archie. 'There's a lot of good in him.'

'You're the only one who thinks so.'

'He's looking for a way back without losing face.'

Both men gave me the slow assessment and shook their heads.

I said, bringing Jonathan's signed statement from my pocket, 'Try this on for size.'

They both read it, Picton first, Archie after.

Archie said in disbelief, 'He never talks. He wouldn't have said all this.'

'I asked him questions,' I explained. 'Those are his answers. He came with me to the Land-Rover central dealers in Oxford who put that red dragon transfer on the windscreen of every vehicle they sell. And we wouldn't know of the Land-Rover's presence in the lane, or its probable owner and whereabouts now, except for Jonathan. So I really do think he's earned his ride on the lake.'

'What exactly do you want the search warrant *for*?' Picton asked. 'One can't get search warrants unless one can come up with a good reason – or at least a convincing possibility or probability of finding something material to a case.'

'Well,' I said, 'Jonathan put his hand on the bonnet

of the vehicle standing right beside the gate to the field where Betty Bracken's colt lost his foot. If you search a certain Land-Rover and find Jonathan's hand-print on the bonnet, would that be proof enough that you'd found the right wheels?'

Picton said, 'Yes.'

'So,' I went on without emphasis, 'if we leave Jonathan here by the lake while your people fingerprint the Land-Rover, there could be no question of his having touched it this afternoon, and not last night.'

'I've heard about you,' Picton said.

'I think,' I said, 'that it would be a good idea to fingerprint that bonnet before it rains, don't you? Or before anyone puts it through a car-wash?'

'Where is it?' Picton asked tersely.

I produced the English Sporting Motors' print-out, and pointed. 'There,' I said. 'That one.'

Picton read it silently, Archie aloud.

'But I know the place. You're quite *wrong*. I've been a guest there. They're friends of Betty's.'

'And of mine,' I said.

He listened to the bleakness I could hear in my own voice.

'Who are we talking about?' Picton asked.

'Gordon Quint,' Archie said. 'It's rubbish.'

'Who is Gordon Quint?' Picton asked again.

'The father of Ellis Quint,' Archie said. 'And you must have heard of *him*.'

Picton nodded. He had indeed.

'I suppose it's possible,' I suggested tentatively, 'that someone *borrowed* the Land-Rover for the night.'

'But you don't believe it,' Picton remarked.

'I wish I did.'

'But where's the connection?' Picton asked. 'There has to be *more*. The fact that Twyford Lower Farms Ltd owned a blue Land-Rover of the relevant year isn't enough on its own. We cannot search that vehicle for hand-prints unless we have good reason to believe that it was that one and no other that we are looking for.'

Archie said thoughtfully, 'Search warrants have been issued on flimsier grounds before now.'

He and Picton walked away from me, the professionals putting their distance between themselves and Sid Public. I thought that if they refused to follow the trail it would be a relief, on the whole. It would let me off the squirming hook. But there could be another month and another colt . . . and an obsession feeding and fattening on success.

They came back, asking why I should link the Quint name to the deed. I described my box chart. Not conclusive, Archie said judiciously, and I agreed, no.

Picton repeated what I'd just said, 'Rachel's pony was bought by her father, Joe, on the advice of Ellis Quint?'

I said, 'Ellis did a broadcast about Rachel's pony losing his foot.'

'I saw it,' Picton said.

They didn't want to believe it any more than I did. There was a fairly long indeterminate silence.

Jonathan came back looking uncomplicatedly happy from his fast laps round the lake, and Norman Picton abruptly went into the club house, returning with a can of Coke which he put into Jonathan's hands. Jonathan held it in his left hand to open it and his right hand to drink. Norman took the empty can from him casually but carefully by the rim, and asked if he would like to try the skiing itself, not just a ride in the boat.

Jonathan, on the point of enthusiastically saying, '*Yes,*' remembered his cultivated disagreeableness and said, 'I don't mind. If you insist, I suppose I'll have to.'

'That's right,' Picton said cheerfully. 'My wife will drive. My son will watch the rope. We'll find you some swimming trunks and a wet-suit.'

He led Jonathan away. Archie watched inscrutably.

'Give him a chance,' I murmured. 'Give him a challenge.'

'Pack him off to the colonies to make a man of him?'

'Scoff,' I smiled. 'But long ago it often worked. He's bright and he's bored and he's not yet a totally confirmed delinquent.'

'You'd make a soft and rotten magistrate.'

'I expect you're right.'

Picton returned, saying, 'The boy will stay here until I get back, so we'd better get started. We'll take two cars, mine and Mr Halley's. In that way he can go on to London when he wants. We'll leave your car here, Archie. Is that all right?'

Archie said he didn't trust Jonathan not to steal it.

'He doesn't think stealing's much fun without his pals,' I said.

Archie stared. 'That boy never says *anything*.'

'Find him a dangerous job.'

Picton, listening, said, 'Like what?'

'Like,' I said, unprepared, 'like . . . well . . . on an oil rig. Two years of that. Tell him to keep a diary. Tell him to write.'

'Good God,' Archie said, shaking his head, 'he'd have the place in flames.'

He locked his car and put the keys in his pocket, climbing into the front passenger seat beside me as we followed Norman Picton into Newbury, to his official place of work.

I sat in my car outside the police station while Archie and Picton, inside, arranged the back-ups: the photographer, the fingerprinter, the detective constable to be Inspector Picton's note-taking assistant.

I sat with the afternoon sun falling through the windscreen and wished I were anywhere else, engaged on any other mission.

All the villains I'd caught before hadn't been people I knew. Or people – one had to face it – people I'd thought I'd known. I'd felt mostly satisfaction, sometimes relief, occasionally even regret, but never anything approaching this intensity of entrapped despair.

Ellis was loved. I was going to be hated.

Hatred was inevitable.

Could I bear it?

There was no choice, really.

Archie and Picton came out of the police station followed by their purposeful troop.

Archie, sliding in beside me, said the search warrant was signed, the Superintendent had given the expedition his blessing, and off we could go to the Twyford Lower Farms.

I sat without moving, without starting the car.

'What's the matter?' Archie demanded, looking at my face.

I said with pain, 'Ellis is my friend.'

CHAPTER SIX

Ginnie Quint was gardening in a large straw hat, businesslike gloves and grey overall dungarees, waging a losing war on weeds in flower beds in front of the comfortable main house of Twyford Lower Farms.

'Hello, dear Sid!' She greeted me warmly, standing up, holding the dirty gloves wide and putting her soft cheek forward for a kiss of greeting. 'What a nice surprise. But Ellis isn't here, you know. He went to the races, then he was going up to the Regent's Park flat. That's where you'll find him, dear.'

She looked in perplexity over my shoulder to where the Norman Picton contingent were erupting from their transport.

Ginnie said uncertainly, 'Who are your friends, dear?' Her face cleared momentarily in relief, and she exclaimed, 'Why, it's Archie Kirk! My dear man. How nice to see you.'

Norman Picton, carrying none of Archie's or my social-history baggage, came rather brutally to the point.

'I'm Detective Inspector Picton, madam, of the Thames Valley Police. I've reason to believe you own a blue Land-Rover, and I have a warrant to inspect it.'

Ginnie said in bewilderment, 'It's no secret we have a Land-Rover. Of course we have. You'd better talk to my husband. Sid . . . Archie . . . what's all this about?'

'It's possible,' I said unhappily, 'that someone borrowed your Land-Rover last night and . . . er . . . committed a crime.'

'Could I see the Land-Rover, please, madam?' Picton insisted.

'It will be in the farmyard,' Ginnie said. 'I'll get my husband to show you.'

The scene inexorably unwound. Gordon, steaming out of the house to take charge, could do nothing but protest in the fact of a properly executed search warrant. The various policemen went about their business, photographing, fingerprinting and collecting specimens of dusty earth from the tyre treads. Every stage was carefully documented by the assisting constable.

The warrant apparently covered the machinery and anything else behind the front seat. The two sticking up handles that had looked to Jonathan like those of a lawn mower were, in fact, the handles of a lawn mower – a light electric model. There were also a dozen or so angled iron posts for fencing, also a coil of fencing wire and the tools needed for fastening the wire through the posts. There was an opened bag of horse-feed nuts. There was a rolled leather apron, like those used by farriers. There were two spades, a heavy four-pronged fork and a large knife like a machete wrapped in sacking.

The knife was clean, sharp and oiled.

Gordon, questioned, growled impatiently that a good workman looked after his tools. He picked up a rag and a can of oil, to prove his point. What was the knife for? Clearing ditches, thinning woodland, a hundred small jobs around the fields.

There was a second, longer bundle of sacking lying beneath the fencing posts. I pointed to it non-committally, and Norman Picton drew it out and unwrapped it.

Inside there were two once-varnished wooden handles a good metre in length, with, at the business end, a heavy arrangement of metal.

'Lopping shears,' Gordon pronounced. 'For lopping off small branches of trees in the woods. Have to keep young trees pruned, you know, or you get a useless tangle where nothing will grow.'

He took the shears from Picton's hands to show him how they worked. The act of parting the handles widely away from each other opened heavy metal jaws at the far end; sharp, clean and oiled jaws with an opening wide enough to grip a branch three inches thick. Gordon, with a strong quick motion, pulled the handles towards each other, and the metal jaws closed with a snap.

'Very useful,' Gordon nodded, and rewrapped the shears in their sacking.

Archie, Picton and I said nothing.

I felt faintly sick.

Archie walked away speechless and Gordon, not understanding, laid the sacking parcel back in the Land-Rover and walked after him, saying, puzzled, 'Archie! What is it?'

Picton said to me, 'Well?'

'Well,' I said, swallowing, 'what if you took those shears apart? They look clean, but in the jaws . . . in that hinge . . . just one drop of blood . . . or one hair . . . that would do, wouldn't it?'

'So these shears fit the bill?'

I nodded faintly. 'Mr Kirk saw the colt's leg, like I did. And he saw the foot.' I swallowed again. '*Lopping* shears. Oh Christ.'

'It was only a *horse*,' he protested.

'Some people love their horses like they do their children,' I said. 'Suppose someone lopped off your son's foot?'

He stared. I said wryly, 'Betty Bracken is the fifth bereaved owner I've met in the last three weeks. Their grief gets to you.'

'My son,' he said slowly, 'had a dog that got run over. He worried us sick . . . wouldn't eat properly . . .' He stopped, then said, 'You and Archie Kirk are too close to this.'

'And the Great British public,' I reminded him, 'poured their hearts out to those cavalry horses maimed by terrorists in Hyde Park.'

138

He was old enough to remember the carnage that had given rise to the daily bulletins and to medals and hero-status bestowed on Sefton, the wonderful survivor of heartless bombs set off specifically to kill harmless horses used by the army solely as a spectacle in plumed parades.

This time the Great British public would vilify the deed, but wouldn't, and couldn't, believe a national idol guilty. Terrorists, yes. Vandals, yes. Idol . . . *no*.

Picton and I walked in the wake of Archie and Gordon, returning to Ginnie in front of the house.

'I don't understand,' Ginnie was saying plaintively. 'When you say the Land-Rover may have been taken and used in a crime . . . what crime do you mean?'

Gordon jumped in without waiting for Picton to explain.

'It's always for robbery,' he said confidently. 'Where did the thieves take it?'

Instead of answering, Norman Picton asked if it was Gordon Quint's habit to leave the ignition key in the Land-Rover.

'Of course not,' Gordon said, affronted. 'Though a little thing like no ignition key never stops a practised thief.'

'If you did by any chance leave the key available – which I'm sure you didn't, sir, please don't get angry – but if anyone could have found and used your key, would it have been on a key-ring with a silver chain and a silver horseshoe?'

'Oh no,' Ginnie interrupted utterly guilelessly. 'That's Ellis's key-ring. And it's not a silver horseshoe, it's white gold. I had it made especially for him last Christmas.'

I drove Archie Kirk back to Newbury. The unmarked car ahead of us carried the four policemen and a variety of bagged, docketed, documented objects for which receipts had been given to Gordon Quint.

Lopping shears in sacking. Machete, the same. Oil rag and oil-can. Sample of horse-feed nuts. Instant photos of red-dragon logo. Careful containers of many lifted fingerprints, including one sharply defined right full hand-print from the Land-Rover's bonnet that, on first inspection, matched exactly the right hand-print from the Coke can held by Jonathan at the lake.

'There's no doubt that it was the Quint Land-Rover in my sister's lane,' Archie said. 'There's no doubt Ellis's keys were in the ignition. But there's no proof that Ellis himself was anywhere near.'

'No,' I agreed. 'No one saw him.'

'Did Norman ask you to write a report?'

'Yes.'

'He'll give your report and Jonathan's statement to the Crown Prosecution Service, along with his own findings. After that, it's up to them.'

'Mm.'

After a silence, as if searching for words of comfort, Archie said, 'You've done wonders.'

'I hate it.'

'But it doesn't stop you.'

What if he can't help it . . .? What if I couldn't help it, either?

At the police station, saying goodbye, Archie said, 'Sid . . . you don't mind if I call you Sid? And I'm Archie, of course, as you know . . . I do have some idea of what you're facing. I just wanted you to know.'

'I . . . er . . . thanks,' I said. 'If you wait a minute, I'll phone the equine hospital and find out how the colt is doing.'

His face lightened but the news was moderate.

'I've re-attached the tendon,' Bill reported. 'I grafted a couple of blood vessels so there's now an adequate blood supply to the foot. Nerves are always difficult. I've done my absolute best and, bar infection, the foot could technically stay in place. The whole leg is now in a cast. The colt is semi-conscious. We have him in slings. But you know how unpredictable this all is. Horses don't recover as easily as humans. There'll be no question of racing, of course, but breeding . . . I understand he's got the bloodlines of champions. Absolutely no promises, mind.'

'You're brilliant,' I said.

'It's nice,' he chuckled, 'to be appreciated.'

I said, 'A policeman will come and collect some of the colt's hair and blood.'

'Good. Catch the bugger,' he said.

I drove willy nilly without haste in heavy traffic to London. By the time I reached the pub I was half an hour late for my appointment with Kevin Mills of *The Pump*, and he wasn't there. No balding head, no paunch, no drooping beer-frothed moustache, no cynical world-weariness.

Without regret I mooched tiredly to the bar, bought some whisky and poured into it enough London tap water to give the distiller fits.

All I wanted was to finish my mild tranquilliser, go home, find something to eat, and sleep. Sleep, I thought, yawning, had overall priority.

A woman's voice at my side upset those plans.

'Are you Sid Halley?' it said.

I turned reluctantly. She had shining black shoulder-length hair, bright light-blue eyes and dark red lipstick, sharply edged. Naturally unblemished skin had been given a matt porcelain powdering. Black eyebrows and eyelashes gave her face strong definition, an impression her manner reinforced. She wore black clothes in June. I found it impossible to guess her age, within ten years, from her face, but her manicured red-nailed hands said no more than thirty.

'I'm from *The Pump*,' she said. 'My colleague, Kevin Mills, has been called away to a rape.'

I said, 'Oh,' vaguely.

'I'm India Cathcart,' she said.

I said 'Oh' again, just as vaguely, but I knew her by her name, by her reputation and by her writing. She was a major columnist, a ruthless interviewer, a deconstructing nemesis, a pitiless exposer of pathetic human secrets. They said she kept a penknife handy for sharpening her ballpoints. She was also funny, and I, like every *Pump* addict, avidly read her stuff and laughed even as I winced.

I did not, however, aim to be either her current or future quarry.

'I came to pick up our exclusive,' she said.

'Ah. 'Fraid there isn't one.'

'But you *said*.'

'I hoped,' I agreed.

'And you haven't answered your phone all day.'

I unclipped my mobile phone and looked at it as if puzzled, which I wasn't. I said, making a discovery, 'It's switched off.'

She said, disillusioned, 'I was warned you weren't dumb.'

There seemed to be no answer to that, so I didn't attempt one.

'We tried to reach you. Where have you been?'

'Just with friends,' I said.

'I went to Combe Bassett. What did I find? No colt,

143

with or without feet. No Sid Halley. No sobbing colt-owner. I find some batty old fusspot who says everyone went to Archie's house.'

I gazed at her with a benign expression. I could do a benign expression rather well.

'So,' continued India Cathcart with visible disgust, 'I go to the house of a Mr Archibald Kirk in the village of Shelley Green, and what do I find *there*?'

'What?'

'I find about five other newspapermen, sundry photographers, a Mrs Archibald Kirk and a deaf old gent saying "Eh?" '

'So then what?'

'Mrs Kirk is lying, all wide-eyed and helpful. She's saying she doesn't know where anyone is. After three hours of that, I went back to Combe Bassett to look for ramblers.'

'Did you find any?'

'They had rambled twenty miles and had climbed a stile into a field with a resident bull. A bunch of ramblers crashed out in panic through a hedge backwards and the rest are discussing suing the farmer for letting a dangerous animal loose near a public footpath. A man with a pony-tail says he's also suing Mrs Bracken for not keeping her colt in a stable, thus preventing an amputation that gave his daughter hysterics.'

'Life's one long farce,' I said.

A mistake. She pounced on it. 'Is that your comment on the maltreatment of animals?'

'No.'

'Your opinion of ramblers?'

'Footpaths are important,' I said.

She looked past me to the bartender. 'Sparkling mineral water, ice and lemon, please.'

She paid for her own drink as a matter of course. I wondered how much of her challenging air was unconscious and habitual, or whether she volume-adjusted it according to who she was talking to. I often learned useful things about people's characters by watching them talk to others than myself, and comparing the response.

'You're not playing fair,' she said, judging me over the wedge of lemon bestriding the rim of her glass. 'It was *The Pump*'s Hotline that sent you to Combe Bassett. Kevin says you pay your debts. So pay.'

'The Hotline was his own idea. Not a bad one, except for about a hundred false alarms. But there's nothing I can tell you this evening.'

'Not can't. Won't.'

'It's often the same thing.'

'Spare me the philosophy!'

'I enjoy reading your page every week,' I said.

'But you don't want to figure in it?'

'That's up to you.'

She raised her chin. 'Strong men *beg* me not to print what I know.'

I didn't want to antagonise her completely and I could forgo the passing pleasure of banter, so I gave her the benign expression and made no comment.

She said abruptly, 'Are you married?'

'Divorced.'

'Children?'

I shook my head. 'How about you?'

She was more used to asking questions than answering. There was perceptible hesitation before she said, 'The same.'

I drank my Scotch. I said, 'Tell Kevin I'm very sorry I can't give him his inside edge. Tell him I'll talk to him on Monday.'

'Not good enough.'

'No, well . . . I can't do more.'

'Is someone *paying* you?' she demanded. 'Another paper?'

I shook my head. 'Maybe Monday,' I said. I put my empty glass on the bar. 'Goodbye.'

'Wait!' She gave me a straight stare, not overtly or aggressively feminist, but one that saw no need to make points in a battle that had been won by the generation before her. I thought that perhaps India Cathcart wouldn't have made it a condition of continued marriage that I should give up the best skill I possessed. I'd married a loving and gentle girl and turned her bitter: the worst, the most miserable failure of my life.

India Cathcart said, 'Are you hungry? I've had nothing to eat all day. My expense account would run to two dinners.'

There were many worse fates. I did a quick survey of the possibility of being deconstructed all over page

146

fifteen, and decided as usual that playing safe had its limits. Take risks with caution: a great motto.

'Your restaurant or mine?' I said, smiling, and was warned by the merest flash of triumph in her eyes that she thought the tarpon hooked and as good as landed.

We ate in a noisy brightly lit large and crowded black-mirrored restaurant that was clearly the in-place for the in-crowd. India's choice. India's habitat. A few sycophantic hands shot out to make contact with her as we followed a lisping young greeter to a central, noteworthy table. India Cathcart acknowledged the plaudits and trailed me behind her like a comet's tail (Halley's?) while introducing me to no one.

The menu set out to amaze, but from long habit I ordered fairly simple things that could reasonably be dealt with one-handed: watercress mousse, then duck curry with sliced baked plantains. India chose baby aubergines with oil and pesto, followed by a large mound of crisped frogs' legs that she ate uninhibitedly with her fingers.

The best thing about the restaurant was that the decibel level made private conversation impossible: everything anyone said could be overheard by those at the next table.

'So,' India raised her voice, teeth gleaming over a herb-dusted *cuisse*, 'was Betty Bracken in tears?'

'I didn't see any tears.'

'How much was the colt worth?'

I ate some plantain and decided they'd overdone the caramel. 'No one knows,' I said.

'Kevin told me it cost a quarter of a million. You're simply being evasive.'

'What it cost and what it was worth are different. It might have won the Derby. It might have been worth millions. No one knows.'

'Do you always play word games?'

'Quite often,' I nodded. 'Like you do.'

'Where did you go to school?'

'Ask Kevin,' I said, smiling.

'Kevin's told me things about you that you wouldn't want me to know.'

'Like what?'

'Like it's easy to be taken in by your peaceful front. Like you having tungsten where other people have nerves. Like you being touchy about losing a hand. That's for starters.'

I would throttle Kevin, I thought. I said, 'How are the frogs' legs?'

'Muscular.'

'Never mind,' I said. 'You have sharp teeth.'

Her mind quite visibly changed gears from patronising to uncertain, and I began to like her.

Risky to like her, of course.

After the curry and the frogs we drank plain black coffee and spent a pause or two in eye-contact appraisal. I expected she saw me in terms of adjectives and paragraphs. I saw her with appeased curiosity. I now knew what the serial reputation-slasher looked like at dinner.

In the way one does, I wondered what she looked like in bed; and in the way that one doesn't cuddle up to a potential cobra, I made no flicker of an attempt to find out.

She seemed to take this passivity for granted. She paid for our meal with a *Pump* business credit card, as promised, and crisply expected I would kick in my share on Monday as an exclusive for Kevin.

I promised what I knew I wouldn't be able to deliver, and offered her a lift home.

'But you don't know where I live!'

'Wherever,' I said.

'Thanks. But there's a bus.'

I didn't press it. We parted on the pavement outside the restaurant. No kiss. No handshake. A nod from her. Then she turned and walked away, not looking back: and I had no faith at all in her mercy.

On Sunday morning I reopened the small blue suitcase Linda had lent me, and read again through all the clippings that had to do with the maimed Kent ponies.

I played again the video tape of the twenty-minute programme Ellis had made of the child owners, and watched it from a different, and sickened, perspective.

There on the screen he looked just as friendly, just as charismatic, just as expert. His arms went round

Rachel in sympathy. His good-looking face filled with compassion and outrage. Blinding ponies, cutting off a pony's foot, he said, those were crimes akin to murder.

Ellis, I thought in wretchedness, how *could* you?

What if he can't help it?

I played the tape a second time, taking in more details and attentively listening to what he had actually said.

His instinct for staging was infallible. In the shot where he'd commiserated with the children all together, he had had them sitting around on hay bales in a tack room, the children dressed in riding breeches, two or three wearing black velvet riding hats. He himself had sat on the floor among them, casual in a dark open-necked jogging suit, a peaked cap pushed back on his head, sunglasses in pocket. Several of the children had been in tears. He'd given them his handkerchief and helped them cope with grief.

There were phrases he had used when talking straight to camera that had brought the children's horrors sharply to disturbingly visual life: 'pierced empty sockets, their eyesight running down their cheeks', and 'a pure-bred silver pony proud and shining in the moonlight'.

His caring tone of voice alone had made the word-pictures bearable.

'A silver pony shining in the moonlight.' The basis of Rachel's nightmare.

'In the moonlight.' He had *seen* the pony in the moonlight.

I played the tape a third time, listening with my eyes shut, undistracted by the familiar face, or by Rachel in his comforting hug.

He said, 'A silver pony trotting trustfully across the field lured by a handful of horse-nuts.'

He shouldn't have known that.

He could have known it if any of the Ferns had suggested it.

But the Ferns themselves wouldn't have said it. They hadn't fed Silverboy on nuts. The agent of destruction that had come by night had brought the nuts.

Ellis would say, of course, that he had made it up, and the fact that it might be true was simply a coincidence. I rewound the tape and stared for a while into space. Ellis would have an answer to everything. Ellis would be believed.

In the afternoon I wrote a long, detailed report for Norman Picton: not a joyous occupation.

Early Monday morning, as he had particularly requested it, I drove to the police station in Newbury and personally delivered the package into the Detective Inspector's own hands.

'Did you talk about this to anybody?' he asked.

'No.'

'Especially not to Quint?'

'Especially not. But . . .' I hesitated, 'they're a close family. It's more than likely that on Saturday evening

151

or yesterday, Ginnie and Gordon told Ellis that you and I and Archie were sniffing round the Land-Rover and that you took away the shears. I think you must consider that Ellis knows the hunt is on.'

He nodded disgustedly. 'And as Ellis Quint officially lives in the Metropolitan area, we in the Thames Valley district cannot pursue our enquiries . . .'

'You mean, you can't haul him down to the local Regent's Park nick and ask him awkward questions, like what was he doing at 3.00 a.m. on Saturday?'

'That's right. We can't ask him ourselves.'

'I thought these divisions were being done away with.'

'Everything takes time.'

I left him to sort out his problems and set off to drive to Kent. On the way, wanting to give Rachel Ferns a cheering-up present, I detoured into the maze of Kingston and, having parked, walked around the precincts looking for inspiration in the shops.

A windowful of tumbling puppies made me pause; perhaps Rachel needed an animal to love, to replace the pony. And perhaps Linda would *not* be pleased at having to house-train a growing nuisance that moulted and chewed the furniture. I went into the pet shop, however, and that's how I came to arrive at Linda Fern's house with my car full of fish tank, water weeds, miniature ruined castle walls, electric pump, lights, fish food, instructions, and three large lidded buckets of tropical fish.

Rachel was waiting by the gate for my arrival.

'You're half an hour late,' she accused. 'You said you'd be here by twelve.'

'Have you heard of the M25?'

'*Everyone* makes that motorway an excuse.'

'Well, sorry.'

Her bald head was still a shock. Apart from that she looked well, her cheeks full and rounded by steroids. She wore a loose sundress and clumpy trainers on stick-like legs. It was crazy to love someone else's child so comprehensively, yet for the first time ever, I felt the idea of fatherhood take a grip.

Jenny had refused to have children on the grounds that any racing day could leave her a widow, and at the time I hadn't cared one way or another. If ever I married again, I thought, following Rachel into the house, I would long for a daughter.

Linda gave me a bright bright smile, a pecking kiss and the offer of a gin and tonic while she threw together some pasta for our lunch. The table was laid. She set out steaming dishes.

'Rachel was out waiting for you two hours ago!' she said. 'I don't know what you've done to the child.'

'How are things?'

'Happy.' She turned away abruptly, tears as ever near the surface. 'Have some more gin. You said you'd got news for me.'

'Later. After lunch. And I've brought Rachel a present.'

The fish tank after lunch was the ultimate success. Rachel was enthralled, Linda interested and helpful. 'Thank goodness you didn't give her a dog,' she said. 'I can't stand animals under my feet. I wouldn't let Joe give her a dog. That's why she wanted a pony.'

The vivid fish swam healthily through the Gothic ruins, the water weeds rose and swelled, the lights and bubbles did their stuff. Rachel sprinkled fish food and watched her new friends eat. The pet shop owner had persuaded me to take a bigger tank than I'd thought best, and he had undoubtedly been right. Rachel's pale face glowed. Pegotty, in a baby-bouncer, sat wide eyed and open mouthed beside the glass. Linda came with me into the garden.

'Any news about a transplant?' I asked.

'It would have been the first thing I'd told you.'

We sat on the bench. The roses bloomed. It was a beautiful day, heartbreaking.

Linda said wretchedly, 'In acute lymphoblastic leu-kaemia, which is what Rachel's got, chemotherapy causes remission almost always. More than ninety per cent of the time. In seven out of ten children, the remission lasts for ever, and after five years they can be thought of as cured for life. And girls have a better chance than boys, isn't that odd? But in thirty per cent of children, the disease comes back.'

She stopped.

'And it has come back in Rachel?'

'Oh, *Sid*!'

'Tell me.'

She tried, the tears trickling while she spoke. 'The disease came back in Rachel after less than two years, and that's not good. Her hair was beginning to grow, but it came out again with the drugs. They re-established her again in remission, and they're so good, it isn't so easy the second time. But I know from their faces – and they don't suggest transplants unless they have to, because only about half of bone marrow transplants are successful. I always talk as if a transplant will definitely save her, but it only *might*. If they found a tissue match they'd kill all her own bone marrow with radiation, which makes the children terribly nauseous and wretched, and then when the marrow's all dead they transfuse new liquid marrow into the veins and hope it will migrate into the bones and start making leukaemia-free blood there, and quite often it *works* . . . and sometimes a child can be born with one blood group and be transfused with another. It's extraordinary. Rachel now has type A blood, but she might end up with type O, or something else. They can do so *much* nowadays. One day they may cure *everybody*. But oh . . . oh . . .'

I put my arm round her shoulders while she sobbed. So many disasters were for ever. So many Edens lost.

I waited until the weeping fit had passed, and then I told her I'd discovered who had maimed and destroyed Silverboy.

'You're not going to like it,' I said, 'and it might be

best if you can prevent Rachel from finding out. Does she ever read the newspapers?'

'Only Peanuts.'

'And the television news?'

'She doesn't like news of starving children.' Linda looked at me fearfully. 'I've *wanted* her to know who killed Silverboy. That's what I'm paying you for.'

I took out of my pocket and put into her hands an envelope containing her much-travelled cheque torn now into four pieces.

'I don't like what I found, and I don't want your money. Linda . . . I'm so very sorry . . . but it was Ellis Quint himself who cut off Silverboy's foot.'

She sprang in revulsion to her feet, her immediate anger filling her, the shock hard and physical, the enormity of what I'd said making her literally shake.

I should have broken it more slowly, I thought, but the words had had to be said.

'How can you say such a thing?' she demanded. 'How *can* you? You've got it all wrong. He couldn't possibly! You're *crazy* to say such a thing.'

I stood up also. 'Linda . . .'

'Don't say anything. I won't listen. I *won't*. He is so *nice*. You're *truly* crazy. And of course I'm not going to tell Rachel what you've accused him of, because it would upset her, and you're *wrong*. And I know you've been kind to her . . . and to me . . . but I wouldn't have asked you here if I'd thought you could do so much awful harm. So please . . . *go*. Go, just *go*.'

I shrugged a fraction. Her reaction was extreme, but her emotions were always at full stretch. I understood her, but that didn't much help.

I said persuasively, 'Linda, *listen.*'

'No!'

I said, 'Ellis has been my own friend for years. This is terrible for me, too.'

She put her hands over her ears and turned her back, screaming, 'Go away. Go away.'

I said uncomfortably, 'Phone me, then,' and got no reply.

I touched her shoulder. She jerked away from me and ran a good way down the lawn, and after a minute I turned and went back into the house.

'Is Mummy crying?' Rachel asked, looking out of the window. 'I heard her shout.'

'She's upset.' I smiled, though not feeling happy. 'She'll be all right. How are the fish?'

'Cool.' She went down on her knees, peering into the wet little world.

'I have to go now,' I said.

'Goodbye.' She seemed sure I would come back. It was a temporary farewell, between friends. She looked at the fishes, not turning her head.

'Bye,' I said, and drove ruefully to London knowing that Linda's rejection was only the first: the beginning of the disbelief.

In Pont Square the telephone was ringing when I opened my front door, and continued to ring while

157

I poured water and ice from a jug in the refrigerator, and continued to ring while I drank thirstily after the hot afternoon, and continued to ring while I changed the battery in my left arm.

In the end, I picked up the receiver.

'Where the bloody hell have you *been*?'

The Berkshire voice filled my ear, delivering not contumely, but information. Norman Picton, Detective Inspector, Thames Valley Police.

'You've heard the news, of course.'

'What news?' I asked.

'Do you live with your head in the sand? Don't you own a radio?'

'What's happened?'

'Ellis Quint is in custody,' he said.

'He's *what*?'

'Yes, well, hold on, he's sort of in custody. He's in hospital, under guard.'

'Norman,' I said, disoriented. 'Start at the beginning.'

'Right.' He sounded over-patient, as if talking to a child. 'This morning two plain clothes officers of the Metropolitan Police went to Ellis Quint's flat overlooking Regent's Park intending to interview him harmlessly about his whereabouts early Saturday morning. He came out of the building before they reached the main entrance, so, knowing him by sight, they approached him, identifying themselves and showing him their badges. At which point,' Picton cleared his throat but didn't seem able to clear his account of pedestrian police phraseology, '. . . at which point Mr Ellis Quint pushed one of the officers away so forcefully that the officer overbalanced into the roadway and was struck by a passing car. Mr Quint himself then ran into the path of traffic as he attempted to cross the road to put distance between himself and the police officers. Mr Quint caused a bus to swerve. The bus struck Mr Quint a glancing blow, throwing him to the ground. Mr Quint was dazed and bruised. He was taken to hospital where he is now in a secure room while investigations proceed.'

I said, 'Are you reading that from a written account?'

'That's so.'

'How about an interpretation in your own earthy words?'

'I'm at work. I'm not alone.'

'OK,' I said. 'Did Ellis panic or did he think he was being mugged?'

Picton half laughed. 'I'd say the first. His lawyers will say the second. But, d'you know what? When they emptied his pockets at the hospital, they found a thick packet of cash – and his passport.'

'No!'

'It isn't illegal.'

'What does he say?'

'He hasn't said anything yet.'

'How's the officer he pushed?'

'Broken leg. He was lucky.'

'And . . . when Ellis's daze wears off?'

'It'll be up to the Met. They can routinely hold him for seventy-two hours while they frame a charge. I'd say that's a toss-up. With the clout he can muster, he'll be out in hours.'

'What did you do with my report?'

'It went to the proper authorities.'

Authorities was such a vague word. Whoever described their occupation as 'an authority'?

'Thanks for phoning,' I said.

'Keep in touch.' An order, it sounded like.

I put down the receiver and found a handwritten scrawl from Kevin Mills on *Pump* note-headed paper in my fax.

He'd come straight to the point.

Sid, you're a shit.

CHAPTER SEVEN

The week got worse, slightly alleviated only by a letter from Linda on Thursday morning. Variably slanting handwriting. Jerky. A personality torn this way and that.

Dear Sid,

    I'm sorry I talked to you the way I did. I still cannot believe that Ellis Quint would cut off Silverboy's foot, but I remember thinking when he came here to do the TV programme that he already knew a lot about what had happened. I mean things that hadn't been in the papers, like Silverboy liking horse-nuts, which we never gave him, so how did he know, we didn't know ourselves, and I did wonder who had told him, but of course Joe asked Ellis who to buy a pony from, so of course I thought Ellis knew things about him from way back, like Silverboy being fed on horse-nuts before he came to us.

    Anyway, I can see how you got it wrong about

161

Ellis, and it was very nice of you to bring the fish
tank for Rachel, I can't tear her away from it. She
keeps asking when you will come back and I don't
like to tell her you won't, not as things are, so if
you'll visit us again I will not say any more about
you being wrong about Ellis. I ask you for Rachel.

We are glad Ellis wasn't hurt today by that
horrid bus.

Yours sincerely,

Linda Ferns.

I wrote back thanking her for her letter, accepting her
invitation and saying I would phone her soon.

On Tuesday Ellis was charged with 'actual bodily harm'
for having inadvertently and without intention pushed
'an assailant' into the path of potential danger (under
the wheels of a speeding motor) and was set free 'pending enquiries'.

Norman Picton disillusionedly reported, 'The only
approximately good thing is that they confiscated his
passport. His lawyers are pointing their fingers up any
police nose they can confront, screeching that it's a
scandal.'

'Where's Ellis now?'

'Look to your back. Your report is with the Crown
Prosecution Service, along with mine.'

'Do you mean you don't know where he is?'

'He's probably in Britain or anywhere he can get to where he doesn't need a passport. He told the magistrates in court that he'd decided to do a sports programme in Australia, and he had to have his passport with him because he needed it to get a visa for Australia.'

'Never underestimate his wits,' I said.

'And he'd better look out for yours.'

'He and I know each other too well.'

On Wednesday afternoon Ellis turned up at his regular television studio as if life were entirely normal and, on completion of an audience-attended recording of a sports quiz, was quietly arrested by three uniformed police officers. Ellis spent the night in custody, and on Thursday morning was charged with severing the foot of a colt: to be exact, the off-fore foot of an expensive two-year-old thoroughbred owned by Mrs Elizabeth Bracken of Combe Bassett Manor, Berkshire. To the vociferous fury of most of the nation, the magistrates remanded him in custody for another seven days, a preliminary precaution usually applied to those accused of murder.

Norman Picton phoned me privately on my home number.

'I'm not telling you this,' he said. 'Understand?'

'I've got cloth ears.'

'It would mean my job.'

'I hear you,' I said. 'I won't talk.'

'No,' he said, 'that, I believe.'

'Norman?'

'Word gets around. I looked up the transcript of the trial of that man that smashed off your hand. You didn't tell *him* what he wanted to know, did you?'

'No . . . well . . . everyone's a fool sometimes.'

'Some fool. Anyway, pin back the cloth ears. The reason why Ellis Quint is remanded for seven days is because after his arrest he tried to hang himself in his cell with his tie.'

'He *didn't!*'

'No one took his belt or tie away, because of who he was. No one in the station *believed* in the charge. There's all hell going on now. The top brass are passing the parcel like a children's party. No one's telling anyone outside anything on pain of death, so Sid . . .'

'I promise,' I said.

'They'll remand him next week for another seven days, partly to stop him committing suicide and partly because . . .' He faltered on the brink of utter trust, his whole career at risk.

'I *promise*,' I said again quickly. 'And if I know what it is you want to keep quiet, then I'll know what not to guess at publicly, won't I?'

'God,' he said, half the anxiety evaporating, 'then . . . there's horse blood in the hinges of the shears, and horse blood and hairs on the oily rag, and horse blood and hairs in the sacking. They've taken samples from the colt in the hospital at Lambourn, and everything's gone away for DNA testing. The results will be back next week.'

'Does Ellis know?'

'I imagine that's why he tried the quick way out. It was an Hermès tie, incidentally, with a design of horseshoes. The simple knot he tied slid undone because the tie was pure smooth silk.'

'For God's sake . . .'

'I keep forgetting he's your friend. Anyway, his lawyers have got to him. They're six deep. He's now playing the lighthearted celebrity, and he's sorrowful about *you*, Sid, for having got him all wrong. His lawyers are demanding proof that Ellis himself was ever at Combe Bassett by night, and we are asking for proof that he wasn't. His lawyers know we would have to drop the case if they can come up with a trustable alibi for any of the other amputations, but so far they haven't managed it. It's early days, though. They'll dig and dig, you can bet on it.'

'Yeah.'

'None of the Land-Rover evidence will get into the papers because the *sub judice* rule kicked in the minute they remanded him. Mostly, that helps us but you, as Sid Halley, won't be able to justify yourself in print until after the trial.'

'Even if I can then.'

'Juries are unpredictable.'

'And the law is, frequently, an ass.'

'People in the Force are already saying you're off your rocker. They say Ellis is too well known. They say that wherever he went he would be recognised, therefore if no one recognised him, that in itself is proof he wasn't there.'

'Mm,' I said. 'I've been thinking about that. Do you have time off at the weekend?'

'Not this weekend, no. Monday do you?'

'I'll see if I can fix something up with Archie . . . and Jonathan.'

'And there's another thing,' Norman said, 'the Land-Rover's presence at Combe Bassett is solid in itself, but Jonathan, if he gets as far as the witness box, will be a *meal* for Ellis's lawyers. On probation for stealing cars! What sort of witness is that?'

'I understood the jury isn't allowed to know anything about a witness. I was at a trial once in the Central Law Courts – the Old Bailey – when a beautifully dressed and blow-dried twenty-six-year-old glamour boy gave evidence – all lies – and the jury weren't allowed to know that he was already serving a sentence for confidence tricks and had come to court straight from jail, via the barber and the wardrobe room. The jury thought him a *lovely* young man. So much for juries.'

'Don't you believe in the jury system?'

'I would believe in it if they were told more. How can a jury come to a prison-or-freedom decision if half

166

the facts are withheld? There should be *no* inadmissable evidence.'

'You're naive.'

'I'm Sid Public, remember? The law bends over backwards to give the accused the benefit of the slightest doubt. The *victim* of murder is never there to give evidence. The colt in Lambourn can't talk. It's safer to kill animals. I'm sorry, but I can't stand what Ellis has become.'

He said flatly, 'Emotion works against you in the witness box.'

'Don't worry. In court, I'm a block of ice.'

'So I've heard.'

'You've heard too damned much.'

He laughed. 'There's an old-boy internet,' he said. 'All you need is the password and a whole new world opens up.'

'What's the password?'

'I can't tell you.'

'Don't bugger me about. What's the password?'

'Archie,' he said.

I was silent for all of ten seconds, remembering Archie's eyes the first time I met him, remembering the *awareness*, the message of knowledge. Archie knew more about me than I knew about him.

I asked, 'What exactly does Archie do in the Civil Service?'

'I reckon,' Norman said, amused, 'that he's very like

you, Sid. What he don't want you to know, he don't
tell you.'

'Where can I reach you on Monday?'

'Police station. Say you're John Paul Jones.'

Kevin Mills dominated the front page of *The Pump* on
Friday – a respite from the sexual indiscretions of cabinet ministers but a demolition job on myself. '*The
Pump*', he reminded readers, 'had set up a Hotline to
Sid Halley to report attacks on colts. Owners had been
advised to lock their stable doors, and to great effect
had done so after the Derby. *The Pump* disclaims all
responsibility for Sid Halley now ludicrously fingering
Ellis Quint as the demon responsible for torturing
defenceless horses. Ellis Quint, whose devotion to
thoroughbreds stretches back to his own starry career
as the country's top amateur race-rider, the popular
hero who braved all perils in the ancient tradition of
gentlemen sportsmen . . .'

More of the same.

'See also "Analysis" on page 10, and India Cathcart,
page 15.'

I supposed one had to know the worst. I read the
leader column – 'Should an ex-jockey be allowed free
rein as pseudo sleuth? (Answer: no, of course not.)' –
and then, dredging deep for steel, I finally turned to
India Cathcart's piece.

Sid Halley, smugly accustomed to acclaim as a
champion, in short time lost his career, his wife
and his left hand, and then weakly watched his
friend soar to super-celebrity and national star
status, all the things that he considered should be
his. Who does this pathetic little man think he's
kidding? He's no Ellis Quint. He's a has-been with
an ego problem, out to ruin what he envies.

That was for starters. The next section pitilessly but not
accurately dissected the impulse that led one to com-
pete at speed (ignoring the fact that presumably Ellis
himself had felt the same power-hungry inferiority
complex).

My ruthless will to win, India Cathcart had written,
had destroyed everything good in my own life. The
same will to win now aimed to destroy my friend Ellis
Quint. This was ambition gone mad.

The Pump would not let it happen. Sid Halley was
a beetle ripe for squashing. *The Pump* would extermi-
nate. The Halley myth was curtains.

Damn and blast her, I thought and, for the first time
in eighteen years, got drunk.

On Saturday morning, groaning around the flat with a
headache, I found a message in my fax machine.

Handwritten scrawl, *Pump*-headed paper same as
before . . . Kevin Mills.

Sid, sorry, but you asked for it.

You're still a shit.

Most of Sunday I listened to voices on my answering machine delivering the same opinion.

Two calls relieved the gloom.

One from Charles Roland, my ex-father-in-law. 'Sid, if you're in trouble, there's always Aynsford,' and a second from Archie Kirk, 'I'm at home. Norman Picton says you want me.'

Two similar men, I thought gratefully. Two men with cool dispassionate minds who would listen before condemning.

I phoned back to Charles, who seemed relieved I sounded sane.

'I'm all right,' I said.

'Ellis is a knight in shining armour, though.'

'Yeah.'

'Are you *sure*, Sid?'

'Positive.'

'But Ginnie . . . and Gordon . . . they're *friends*.'

'Well,' I said, 'if *I* cut the foot off a horse, what would you do?'

'But you *wouldn't*.'

'No.'

I sighed. That was the trouble. No one could believe it of Ellis.

'Sid, come, any time,' Charles said.

170

'You're my rock,' I said, trying to make it sound light. 'I'll come if I need to.'

'Good.'

I phoned Archie and asked if Jonathan were still staying with Betty Bracken.

Archie said, 'I've been talking to Norman. Jonathan is now addicted to water ski-ing and spends every day at the lake. Betty is paying hundreds and says it's worth it to get him out of the house. He'll be at the lake tomorrow. Shall we all meet there?'

We agreed on a time, and met.

When we arrived, Jonathan was out on the water.

'That's him,' Norman said, pointing.

The flying figure in a scarlet wet-suit went up a ramp, flew, turned a somersault in the air and landed smoothly in the water on two skis.

'*That*,' Archie said in disbelief, 'is *Jonathan*?'

'He's a natural,' Norman said. 'I've been out here for a bit most days. Not only does he know his spatial balance and attitude by instinct, but he's fearless.'

Archie and I silently watched Jonathan approach the shore, drop the rope and ski confidently up the sloping landing place with almost as much panache as Norman himself.

Jonathan grinned. Jonathan's streaky hair blew wetly back from his forehead. Jonathan, changed, looked blazingly *happy*.

A good deal of the joy dimmed with apprehension as he looked at Archie's stunned and expressionless face. I took a soft sports bag out of my car and held it out to him, asking him to take it with him to the dressing-rooms.

'Hi,' he said. 'OK.' He took the grip and walked off barefooted, carrying his skis.

'Incredible,' Archie said, 'but he can't ski through life.'

'It's a start,' Norman said.

After we'd stood around for a few minutes discussing Ellis we were approached by a figure in a dark blue tracksuit, wearing also black running shoes, a navy baseball cap and sunglasses and carrying a sheet of paper. He came to within fifteen feet of us and stopped.

'Yes?' Norman asked, puzzled, as to a stranger. 'Do you want something?'

I said, 'Take off the cap and the glasses.'

He took them off. Jonathan's streaky hair shook forward into its normal startling shape and his eyes stared at my face. I gave him a slight jerk of the head, and he came the last few paces and handed the paper to Norman.

Archie for once looked wholly disconcerted. Norman read aloud what I'd written on the paper.

' "Jonathan, this is an experiment. Please put on the clothes you'll find in this bag. Put on the baseball cap, peak forward, hiding your face. Wear the sunglasses. Bring this paper. Walk towards me, stop a few feet away, and don't speak. OK. Thanks, Sid." '

Norman lowered the paper, looked at Jonathan and said blankly, 'Bloody hell.'

'Is that the lot?' Jonathan asked me.

'Brilliant,' I said.

'Shall I get dressed now?'

I nodded, and he walked nonchalantly away.

'He looked totally different,' Archie commented, still amazed. 'I didn't know him at all.'

I said to Norman, 'Did you look at the tape of Ellis's programme, that one I put in with my report?'

'The tape covered with stickers saying it was the property of Mrs Linda Ferns? Yes, I did.'

'When Ellis was sitting on the floor with those children,' I said, 'he was wearing a dark tracksuit, open at the neck. He had a peaked cap pushed back on his head. He looked young. Boyish. The children responded to him ... touched him ... *loved* him. He had a pair of sunglasses tucked into a breast pocket.'

After a silence Norman said, 'But he *wouldn't*. He wouldn't wear those clothes on television if he'd worn them to mutilate the Ferns pony.'

'Oh yes he would. It would deeply amuse him. There's nothing gives him more buzz than taking risks.'

'A baseball cap,' Archie said thoughtfully, 'entirely changes the shape of someone's head.'

I nodded. 'A baseball cap and sports clothes can reduce any man of status to anonymity.'

'We'll never prove it,' Norman said.

Jonathan slouched back in his own clothes and with

his habitual half-sneering expression firmly in place. Archie's exasperation with him sharply returned.

'This is not the road to Damascus,' I murmured.

'Damn you, Sid.' Archie glared, and then laughed.

'What are you talking about?' Norman asked.

'St Paul's conversion on the road to Damascus happened like a thunderclap,' Archie explained. 'Sid's telling me not to look for instant miracles by the gravel pit lake.'

Jonathan, now listening, handed me the grip. 'Cool idea,' he said. 'No one knew me.'

'They would, close to.'

'It was still a risk,' Norman objected.

'I told you,' I said, 'the risk is the point.'

'It doesn't make sense.'

'Cutting off a horse's foot doesn't make sense. Half of human actions don't make sense. Sense is in the eye of the beholder.'

I drove back to London.

My answer-phone had answered so many calls that it had run out of recording tape.

Among the general abuse, three separate calls were eloquent about the trouble I'd stirred up. All three of the owners of the other colt victims echoed Linda Ferns' immovable conviction.

The lady from Cheltenham: 'I can't believe you can be so misguided. Ellis is absolutely innocent. I wouldn't have thought of you as being jealous of him, but all the papers say so. I'm sorry, Sid, but you're not welcome here any more.'

The angry Lancashire farmer: 'You're a moron, do you know that? Ellis Quint! You're stupid. You were all right as a jockey. You should give up this pretence of being Sherlock Holmes. You're pitiful, lad.'

The lady from York. 'How *can* you? Dear Ellis! He's worth ten of you, I have to say.'

I switched off the critical voices, but they went on reverberating in my brain.

The Press had more or less uniformly followed *The Pump*'s lead. Pictures of Ellis at his most handsome smiled confidently from news stands everywhere. Trial by media found Ellis Quint the wronged and innocent hero, Sid Halley the twisted jealous cur snapping at his heels.

I'd known it would be bad: so why the urge to bang my head against the wall? Because I was human, and didn't have tungsten nerves, whatever anyone thought. I sat with my eyes shut, ostrich fashion.

Tuesday was much the same. I still didn't bang my head. Close run thing.

On the Wednesday Ellis appeared again before magistrates, who that time set him free on bail.

Norman phoned.

'Cloth ears?' he said. 'Same as before?'

'Deaf,' I assured him.

'It was fixed beforehand. Two minutes in court. Different time than posted. The Press arrived just after it was over. Ellis greeted them, free, smiling broadly.'

'Shit.'

Norman said, 'His lawyers have done their stuff. It's rubbish to think that the well-balanced personality intended to kill himself – his tie got caught somehow but he managed to free it. The policeman he pushed failed to identify himself adequately and is now walking about comfortably in a cast. The colt Ellis is accused of attacking is alive and recovering well. As bail is granted in cases of manslaughter, it is unnecessary to detain Ellis Quint any longer on far lesser charges. So . . . he's walked.'

'Is he still to be tried?'

'So far. His lawyers have asked for an early trial date so that he can put this unpleasantness behind him. He will plead not guilty, of course. His lawyers are already patting each other on the back. And . . . I think there's a heavyweight manoeuvring someone in this case.'

'A heavyweight? Who?'

'Don't know. It's just a feeling.'

'Could it be Ellis's father?'

'No, no. Quite different. It's just . . . since our reports, yours and mine, reached the Crown Prosecution Service, there's been a new factor. Political, perhaps. It's difficult to describe. It's not exactly a cover-up. There's already been too much publicity, it's more a sort of re-direction. Even officially, and not just to the Press, someone with muscles is trying to get you thoroughly, and I'm afraid I must say, *malignantly* discredited.'

'Thanks a bunch.'

'Sid, seriously, look out for yourself.'

I felt as prepared as one could be for some sort of catastrophic pulverisation to come my way, but in the event the process was subtler and long drawn out.

As if nothing had happened, Ellis resumed his television programme and began making jokes about Sid Halley – 'Sid Halley? That friend of mine! Have you heard that he comes from Halifax? Halley facts – he makes them up.'

And 'I like halibut – I eat it.' And the old ones that I was used to, 'Halitosis' and 'Hallelujah'.

Hilarious.

When I went to the races, which I didn't do as often as earlier, people either turned their backs or *laughed*, and I wasn't sure which I disliked more.

I took to going only to jumping meetings, knowing Ellis's style took him to the most fashionable meetings on the Flat. I acknowledged unhappily to myself that in my avoidance of him there was an element of cringe. I despised myself for it. All the same, I shrank from a confrontation with him and truly didn't know whether it was because of an ever-deepening aversion to what

177

he had done, or because of the fear – the certainty – that he would publicly mock me.

He behaved as if there were never going to be a trial; as if awkward details like Land-Rovers, lopping shears, and confirmed matching DNA tests tying the shears to the Bracken colt were never going to surface, once the *sub judice* silence ended.

Norman, Archie and also Charles Roland worried that, for all the procedural care we had taken, Ellis's lawyers would somehow get the Land-Rover disallowed. Ellis's lawyers, Norman said, backed by the heavy unseen presence that was motivating them and possibly even paying the mounting fees, now included a defence counsel whose loss rate for the previous seven years was nil.

Surprisingly, despite the continuing barrage of ignominy, I went on being offered work. True, the approach was often tentative and apologetic – 'Whether you're right or pigheaded about Ellis Quint . . .' and 'Even if you've got Ellis Quint all wrong . . .' The nitty-gritty seemed to be that they needed me and there was no one else.

Well, hooray for that. I cleaned up minor mysteries, checked credit ratings, ditto characters, found stolen horses, caught sundry thieves, all the usual stuff.

July came in with a deluge that flooded rivers and ruined the shoes of racegoers, and no colt was attacked at the time of the full moon, perhaps because the nights were wet and windy and black dark with clouds.

The Press finally lost interest in the daily trashing of Sid Halley and Ellis Quint's show wrapped up for the summer break. I went down to Kent a couple of times, taking new fish for Rachel, sitting on the floor with her, playing draughts. Neither Linda nor I mentioned Ellis. She hugged me goodbye each time and asked when I would be coming back. Rachel, she said, had had no more nightmares. They were a thing of the past.

August came quietly and left in the same manner. No colts were attacked. The Hotline went cold. India Cathcart busied herself with a cabinet member's mistress but still had a routinely vindictive jab at me each Friday. I went to America for two short weeks and rode horses up the Teton mountains in Wyoming, letting the wide skies and the forests work their peace.

In September, one dew-laden early autumn English Saturday morning after a calm moonlit night, a colt was discovered with a foot off.

Nauseated, I heard the announcement on the radio in the kitchen while I made coffee.

Listeners would remember, the cool newsreader said, that in June Ellis Quint had been notoriously accused by ex-jockey Sid Halley of a similar attack. Quint was laughing off this latest incident, affirming his total ignorance on the matter.

There were no Hotline calls from *The Pump*, but Norman Picton scorched the wires.

'Have you heard?' he demanded.

'Yes. But no details.'

179

'It was a yearling colt this time. Apparently, there aren't many two-year-olds in the fields just now, but there are hundreds of yearlings.'

'Yes,' I agreed. 'The yearling sales are starting.'

'The yearling in question belonged to some people near Northampton. They're frantic. Their vet put the colt out of his misery. But get this. Ellis Quint's lawyers have already claimed he has an alibi.'

I stood in silence in my sitting-room, looking out to the unthreatening garden.

'Sid?'

'Mm.'

'You'll have to break that alibi. Otherwise, it will break *you*.'

'Mm.'

'Say something else, dammit.'

'The police can do it. Your lot.'

'Face it. They're not going to try very hard. They're going to believe in his alibi, if it's anything like solid.'

'Do you think, do you *really* think,' I asked numbly, 'that an ultra-respected barrister would connive with his client to mutilate ... to kill ... a colt – or pay someone else to do it – to cast doubt on the prosecution's case in the matter of a *different* colt?'

'Put like that, no.'

'Nor do I.'

'So Ellis Quint has set it up himself, and what he has set up, you can knock down.'

'He's had weeks – more than two months – to plan it.'

'Sid,' he said, 'it's not like you to sound defeated.'

If he, I thought, had been on the receiving end of a long pitiless barrage of systematic denigration, he might feel as I did, which, if not comprehensively defeated, was at least battle weary before I began.

'The police at Northampton,' I said, 'are not going to welcome me with open arms.'

'That's never stopped you before.'

I sighed. 'Can you find out from the Northampton police what his alibi actually is?'

'Piece of cake. I'll phone you back.'

I put down the receiver and went over to the window. The little square looked peaceful and safe, the railed garden green and grassy, a tree-dappled haven where generations of privileged children had run and played while their nursemaids gossiped. I'd spent my own childhood in Liverpool's back streets, my father dead and my mother fighting cancer. I in no way regretted the contrast in origins. I had learned self-sufficiency and survival there. Perhaps because of the back streets I now valued the little garden more. I wondered how the children who'd grown up in that garden would deal with Ellis Quint. Perhaps I could learn from them. Ellis had been that sort of child.

Norman phoned back later in the morning.

'Your friend,' he said, 'reportedly spent the night at a private dance in Shropshire, roughly a hundred miles to the north-west of the colt. Endless friends will testify to his presence, including his hostess, a duchess. It was a dance given to celebrate the twenty-first birthday of the heir.'

'Damn.'

'He could hardly have chosen a more conspicuous or more watertight alibi.'

'And some poor bitch will swear she lay down for him at dawn.'

'Why dawn?'

'It's when it happens.'

'How do you know?'

'Never you mind,' I said.

'You're a bad boy, Sid.'

Long ago, I thought. Before Jenny. Summer dances, dew, wet grass, giggles and passion. Long ago and innocent.

Life's a bugger, I thought.

'Sid,' Norman's voice said, 'do you realise the trial is due to start two weeks on Monday?'

'I do realise.'

'Then get a move on, with this alibi.'

'Yes, sir, Detective Inspector.'

He laughed. 'Put the bugger back behind bars.'

On the Tuesday I went to see the Shropshire duchess, for whom I had ridden winners in that former life. She even had a painting of me on her favourite horse, but I was no longer her favourite jockey.

'Yes, of *course* Ellis was here all night,' she confirmed. Short, thin, and at first unwelcoming, she led me through the armour-dotted entrance hall of her draughty old house to the sitting-room where she had been watching the jump racing on television when I arrived.

Her front door had been opened to me by an arthritic old manservant who had hobbled away to see if Her Grace was in. Her Grace had come into the hall clearly anxious to get rid of me as soon as possible, and had then relented, her old kindness towards me resurfacing like a lost but familiar habit.

A three-mile steeplechase was just finishing, the jockeys kicking side by side to the finish line, the horses tired and straining, the race going in the end to the one carrying less weight.

The duchess turned down the volume, the better to talk.

'I cannot *believe*, Sid,' she said, 'that you've accused dear Ellis of something so *disgusting*. I know you and Ellis have been friends for years. Everyone knows that. I do think he's been a bit unkind about you on television, but you did *ask* for it, you know.'

'But he *was* here . . .?' I asked.

'Of course. All night. It was five or later when everyone started to leave. The band was playing still . . . we'd all had breakfast . . .'

'When did the dance start?' I asked.

'*Start?* The invitations were for ten. But you know how people are. It was eleven or midnight before most people came. We had the fireworks at three-thirty because rain was forecast for later, but it was fine all night, thank goodness.'

'Did Ellis say goodnight when he left?'

'My dear Sid, there were over three hundred people here last Friday night. A *succès fou*, if I say it myself.'

'So you don't actually remember when Ellis left?'

'The last I saw of him he was dancing an eightsome with that gawky Raven girl. Do drop it, Sid. I'm seeing you now for old times' sake, but you're not doing yourself any good, are you?'

'Probably not.'

She patted my hand. 'I'll always *know* you, at the races and so on.'

'Thank you,' I said.

'Yes. Be a dear and find your own way out. Poor old Stone has such bad arthritis these days.'

She turned up the volume in preparation for the next race, and I left.

The gawky Raven girl who had danced an eightsome reel with Ellis turned out to be the third daughter of an earl. She herself had gone off to Greece to join someone's yacht, but her sister (the second daughter) insisted that Ellis had danced with dozens of people after that, and wasn't I, Sid Halley, being a teeny weeny *twit*?

I went to see Miss Richardson and Mrs Bethany, joint owners of the Windward Stud Farm, home of the latest colt victim: and to my dismay found Ginnie Quint there as well.

All three women were in the stud farm's office, a building separate from the rambling one-storey dwelling house. A groom long-reining a yearling had directed me incuriously and I drew up outside the pinkish brick new-looking structure without relish for my mission, but not expecting a tornado.

I knocked and entered, as one does with such offices, and found myself in the normal clutter of desks, computers, copiers, wall charts and endless piles of paper.

I'd done a certain amount of homework before I went there, so it was easy to identify Miss Richardson as the tall bulky dominant figure in tweed jacket, worn cord trousers and wiry grey short cropped curls. Fifty, I thought; despises men. Mrs Bethany, a smaller, less powerful version of Miss Richardson, was reputedly the one who stayed up at night when the mares were foaling, the one on whose empathy with horses the whole enterprise floated.

The women didn't own the farm's two stallions (they belonged to syndicates) nor any of the mares: Windward Stud was a cross between a livery stable and a maternity ward. They couldn't afford the bad publicity of the victimised yearling.

Ginnie Quint, sitting behind one of the desks, leapt furiously to her feet the instant I appeared in the doorway and poured over me an accumulated concentration of verbal volcanic lava, scalding, shrivelling, sticking my feet to the ground and my tongue in dryness to the roof of my mouth.

'He *trusted* you. He would have *died* for you.'

I sensed Miss Richardson and Mrs Bethany listening in astonishment, not knowing who I was nor what I'd done to deserve such an onslaught; but I had eyes only for Ginnie, whose long fondness for me had fermented to hate.

'You're going to go into court and try to send your best friend to prison . . . to destroy him . . . pull him down . . . ruin him. You're going to *betray* him. You're not fit to live.'

Emotion twisted her gentle features into ugliness. Her words came out spitting.

It was her own son who had done this. Her golden idolised son. He had made of me finally the traitor that would deliver the kiss.

I said absolutely nothing.

I felt, more intensely than ever, the by now accustomed and bitter awareness of the futility of rebellion. Gagged by *sub judice*, I'd been unable all along to put up any defence, especially because the Press had tended to pounce on my indignant protests and label them as 'whining' and 'diddums', and 'please teacher, he hit me . . .' and 'it's not fair, I hit him first'.

A quick check with a lawyer had confirmed that though trying to sue one paper for libel might have been possible, suing the whole lot was not practical. Ellis's jokes were not actionable and, unfortunately, the fact that I was still profitably employed in my chosen occupation meant that I couldn't prove the criticism had damaged me financially.

'Grit your teeth and take it,' he'd advised cheerfully, and I'd paid him for an opinion I gave myself free every day.

As there was no hope of Ginnie's listening to anything I might say, I unhappily but pragmatically turned to retreat, intending to return another day to talk to Miss Richardson and Mrs Bethany, and found my way barred by two new burly arrivals, known already to the stud owners as policemen.

'Sergeant Smith reporting, madam,' one said to Miss Richardson.

She nodded. 'Yes, sergeant?'

'We've found an object hidden in one of the hedges round the field where your horse was done in.'

No one objected to my presence, so I remained in the office, quiet and riveted.

Sergeant Smith carried a long narrow bundle which

he laid on one of the desks. 'Could you tell us, madam, if this belongs to *you*?'

His manner was almost hostile: accusatory. He seemed to expect the answer to be yes.

'What is it?' Miss Richardson asked, very far from guilty perturbation.

'This, madam,' the sergeant said with a note of triumph, and lifted back folds of filthy cloth to reveal their contents, which were two long wooden handles topped by heavy metal clippers.

A pair of lopping shears.

Miss Richardson and Mrs Bethany stared at them unmoved. It was Ginnie Quint who turned slowly white and fainted.

CHAPTER EIGHT

So here we were in October, with the leaves weeping yellowly from the trees.

Here I was, perched on the end of Rachel Ferns' bed, wearing a huge fluffy orange clown wig and a red bulbous nose, making sick children laugh while feeling far from merry inside.

'Have you hurt your arm?' Rachel asked conversationally.

'Banged it,' I said.

She nodded. Linda looked surprised. Rachel said, 'When things hurt it shows in people's eyes.'

She knew too much about pain for a nine-year-old. I said, 'I'd better go before I tire you.'

She smiled, not demurring. She, like the children wearing the other wigs I'd brought, all had very short bursts of stamina. Visiting was down to ten minutes maximum.

I took off the clown wig and kissed Rachel's forehead. 'Bye,' I said.

'You'll come back?'

'Of course.'

She sighed contentedly, knowing I would. Linda walked with me from the ward to the hospital door.

'It's . . . *awful*,' she said, forlorn, on the exit steps. Cold air. The chill to come.

I put my arms round her. Both arms. Hugged her.

'Rachel asks for you all the time,' she said. 'Joe cuddles her, and cries. She cuddles *him*, trying to comfort him. She's her daddy's little girl. She loves him. But you . . . you're her *friend*. You make her laugh, not cry. It's you she asks for all the time – not Joe.'

'I'll always come if I can.'

She sobbed quietly on my shoulder and gulped, 'Poor Mrs Quint.'

'Mm,' I said.

'I haven't told Rachel about Ellis . . .'

'No. Don't,' I said.

'I've been beastly to you.'

'No, far from it.'

'The papers have said such *dreadful* things about you.' Linda shook in my arms. 'I knew you weren't like that . . . I told Joe I have to believe you about Ellis Quint and he thinks I'm stupid.'

'Look after Rachel, nothing else matters.'

She went back into the hospital and I rode dispiritedly back to London in the TeleDrive car.

Even though I'd returned with more than an hour to spare I decided against Pont Square and took the sharp memory of Gordon Quint's attack straight to the bar in the Piccadilly hotel where I'd agreed to meet the lawyer Davis Tatum.

With a smile worth millions, the French lady in charge of the restaurant arranged for me to have coffee and a sandwich in the tiny bar while I waited for my friend. The bar, in fact, looked as if it had been wholly designed as a meeting place for those about to lunch. There were no more than six tables, a bartender who brought drinks to one's elbow, and a calm atmosphere. The restaurant itself was full of daylight, with huge windows and green plants, and was sufficiently hidden from the busy artery of Mayfair downstairs as to give peace and privacy and no noisy passing trade.

I sat at a bar table in the corner with my back to the entrance, though in fact few were arriving: more were leaving after long hours of talk and lunch. I took some ibuprofen, and waited without impatience. I spent hours in my job, sometimes, waiting for predators to pop out of their holes.

Davis Tatum arrived late and out of breath from having apparently walked up the stairs instead of waiting for the lift. He wheezed briefly behind my back, then came round into view and lowered his six foot three inch bulk into the chair opposite.

He leaned forward and held out his hand for a shake. I gave him a limp approximation, which raised his eyebrows but no comment.

He was a case of an extremely agile mind in a totally unsuitable body. There were large cheeks, double chins, fat-lidded eyes and a small mouth. Dark smooth hair had neither receded nor greyed. He had flat ears, a neck like a weight-lifter and a charcoal pin-striped suit straining over a copious belly. He might have difficulty, I thought, in catching sight of certain parts of his own body. Except in the brain-box, nature had dealt him a sad hand.

'First of all,' he said, 'I have some bad news, and I possibly shouldn't be here talking to you at all, according to how you read *Archbold*.'

'*Archbold* being the dos and don'ts manual for trial lawyers?'

'More or less.'

'What's the bad news, then?' I asked. There hadn't been much that was good.

'Ellis Quint has retracted his "guilty" plea, and has gone back to "not guilty".'

'*Retracted?*' I exclaimed. 'How can one retract a confession?'

'Very easily.' He sighed. 'Quint says he was upset yesterday about his mother's death, and what he said about feeling guilty was misinterpreted. In other words, his lawyers have got over the shock and have had a rethink. They apparently know you have so far not been able to break Ellis Quint's alibi for the night that last colt was attacked in Northamptonshire, and they think they can therefore get the Bracken colt charge dismissed, despite the Land-Rover and circumstantial evidence, so they are aiming for a complete acquittal, not psychiatric treatment, and, I regret to tell you, they are likely to succeed.'

He didn't have to tell me that my own reputation would never recover if Ellis emerged with his intact.

'And *Archbold*?'

'If I were the crown prosecuting counsel in this case I could be struck off for talking to you, a witness. As you know, I am the senior barrister in the chambers where a colleague prosecuting Ellis Quint works. I have seen his brief and discussed the case with him. I can absolutely properly talk to you, though perhaps some people might not think it prudent.'

I smiled. 'Bye bye, then.'

'I may not discuss with you a case in which I may be examining you as a witness. But of course I will not be examining you. Also, we can talk about anything else. Like, for instance, a recent game of golf.'

'I don't play golf.'

'Don't be obtuse, my dear fellow. Your perceptions are acute.'

'Are we talking about angles?'

His eyes glimmered behind the folds of fat. 'I saw the report package that you sent to the CPS.'

'The Crown Prosecution Service?'

'The same. I happened to be talking to a friend. I said your report had surprised me, both by its thoroughness and by your deductions and conclusions. He said I shouldn't be surprised. He said you'd had the whole top echelon of the Jockey Club hanging on your every word. He said that, about a year ago, you'd cleared up two major racing messes at the same time. They've never forgotten it.'

'A year last May,' I said. 'Is that what he meant?'

'I expect so. He said you had an assistant then that isn't seen around any more. The job I'd like you to do might need an assistant for the leg-work. Don't you have your assistant nowadays?'

'Chico Barnes?'

He nodded. 'A name like that.'

'He got married,' I said briefly. 'His wife doesn't like what I do, so he's given it up. He teaches judo. I still see him – he gives me a judo lesson most weeks, but I can't ask him for any other sort of help.'

'Pity.'

'Yes. He was good. Great company and bright.'

'And he got *deterred*. That's why he gave it up.'

I went, internally, very still. I said, 'What do you mean?'

'I heard,' he said, his gaze steady on my face, 'that he got beaten with some sort of thin chain to deter him from helping you. To deter him from all detection. And it worked.'

'He got married,' I said.

David Tatum leaned back in his chair, which creaked under his weight.

'I heard,' he said, 'that the same treatment was doled out to you, and in the course of things the Jockey Club mandarins made you take your shirt off. They said they had never seen anything like it. The whole of your upper body, arms included, was black with bruising, and there were vicious red weals all over you. And with your shirt hiding all that you'd calmly explained to them how and why you'd been attacked and how one of their number, who had arranged it, was a villain. You got one of the big shots chucked out.'

'Who told you all that?'

'One hears things.'

I thought in unprintable curses. The six men who'd seen me that day with my shirt off had stated their intention of never talking about it. They'd wanted to keep to themselves the villainy I'd found within their own walls; and nothing had been more welcome to me than that silence. It had been bad enough at the time. I didn't want continually to be reminded.

'Where does one hear such things?' I asked.

'Be your age, Sid. In the clubs . . . Buck's, the Turf, the RAC, the Garrick . . . these things get mentioned.'

'How often . . . do they get mentioned? How often have you heard that story?'

He paused as if checking with an inner authority, and then said, 'Once.'

'Who told you?'

'I gave my word.'

'One of the Jockey Club?'

'I gave my word. If you'd given your word, would *you* tell *me*?'

'No.'

He nodded. 'I asked around, about you. And that's what I was told. Told in confidence. If it matters to you, I've heard it from no one else.'

'It matters.'

'It reflects to your credit,' he protested. 'It obviously didn't stop you.'

'It could give other villains ideas.'

'And do villains regularly attack you?'

'Well, no,' I said. 'Physically no one's laid a finger on me since that time.' Not until yesterday, I thought. 'If you're talking about non-physical assaults . . . Have you read the papers?'

'Scurrilous.' Davis Tatum twisted in his seat until he could call the barman. 'Tanqueray and tonic, please – and for you, Sid?'

'Scotch. A lot of water.'

The barman brought the glasses, setting them out on little round white mats.

'Health,' Davis Tatum toasted, raising his gin.

'Survival,' I responded, and drank to both.

He put down his glass and came finally to the point.

'I need someone,' he said, 'who is clever, unafraid and able to think fast in a crisis.'

'No one's like that.'

'What about you?'

I smiled. 'I'm stupid, scared silly a good deal of the time, and I have nightmares. What you think you see, is not what you get.'

'I get the man who wrote the Quint report.'

I looked benignly at my glass and not at his civilised face.

'If you're going to do something to a small child that you know he won't like,' I said, 'such as sticking a needle into him, you *first* tell him what a brave little boy he is – in the hope that he'll then let you make a pincushion of him without complaint.'

There was a palpable silence, then he chuckled, the low rich timbre filling the air. There was embarrassment in there somewhere; a ploy exposed.

I said prosaically, 'What's the job?'

He waited while four businessmen arrived, arranged their drinks and sank into monetary conversation at the table furthest from where we sat.

'Do you know who I mean by Owen Yorkshire?' Tatum asked, looking idly at the newcomers, not at me.

'Owen Yorkshire,' I rolled the name around in memory and came up with only doubts. 'Does he own a horse or two?'

'He does. He also owns Topline Foods.'

'Topline . . . as in sponsored race at Aintree? As in Ellis Quint, guest of honour at the Topline Foods lunch the day before the Grand National?'

'That's the fellow.'

'And the enquiry?'

'Find out if he's manipulating the Quint case to his own private advantage.'

I said thoughtfully, 'I did hear that there's a heavy-weight abroad.'

'Find out who it is, and why.'

'What about poor old Archbold? He'd turn in his grave.'

'So you'll do it!'

'I'll try. But why me? Why not the police? Why not the old boy internet?'

He looked at me straightly. 'Because you include silence in what you sell.'

'And I'm expensive,' I said.

'Retainer and refreshers,' he promised.

'Who's paying?'

'The fees will come through me.'

'And it's agreed,' I said, 'that the results, if any, are yours. Prosecution or otherwise will normally be your choice.'

He nodded.

'In case you're wondering,' I said, 'when it comes to Ellis Quint, I gave the client's money back, in order to be able to stop him myself. The client didn't at first believe in what he'd done. I made my own choice. I have to tell you that you'd run that risk.'

He leaned forward and extended his pudgy hand.

'We'll shake on it,' he said, and grasped my palm with a firmness that sent a shockwave fizzing clear up to my jaw.

'What's the matter?' he said, sensing it.

'Nothing.'

He wasn't getting much of a deal, I thought. I had a reputation already in tatters, a crackled ulna playing up, and the prospect of being chewed to further shreds by Ellis's defence counsel. He'd have done as well to engage my pal Jonathan of the streaky hair.

'Mr Tatum,' I began.

'Davis. My name's Davis.'

'Will you give me your *assurance* that you won't speak of that Jockey Club business around the clubs?'

'Assurance?'

'Yes.'

'But I told you . . . it's to your credit.'

'It's a private thing. I don't like *fuss*.'

He looked at me thoughtfully. He said, 'You have my assurance.' And I wanted to believe in it, but I wasn't sure that I did. He was too intensely a club man, a filler of large armchairs in dark panelled rooms full of old exploded reputations and fruitily repeated secrets. 'Won't say a word, old boy.'

'Sid.'

'Mm?'

'Whatever the papers say, where it really counts, you are respected.'

'Where's that?'

'The clubs are good for gossip, but these days that's not where the power lies.'

'Power wanders round like the magnetic North Pole.'

'Who said that?'

'I just did,' I said.

'No, I mean, did you make it up?'

'I've no idea.'

'Power, these days, is fragmented,' he said.

I added, 'And where the power is at any one time is not necessarily where one would want to be.'

He beamed proprietorially as if he'd invented me himself.

There was a quick rustle of clothes beside my ear and a drift of flowery scent, and a young woman tweaked a chair round to join our table and sat in it, looking triumphant.

'Well, well, well,' she said. 'Mr Davis Tatum and Sid Halley! What a surprise!'

I said, to Davis Tatum's mystified face, 'This is Miss India Cathcart, who writes for *The Pump*. If you say nothing you'll find yourself quoted repeating things you never thought, and if you say anything at all, you'll wish you hadn't.'

'Sid,' she said mock-sorrowfully, 'can't you take a bit of kicking around?'

Tatum opened his mouth indignantly and, as I was afraid he might try to defend me, I shook my head. He stared at me, then with a complete change of manner said in smooth lawyerly detachment, 'Miss Cathcart, why are you here?'

'Why? To see you, of course.'

'But why?'

She looked from him to me and back again, her appearance just as I remembered it: flawless porcelain skin, light-blue eyes, cleanly outlined mouth, black shining hair. She wore brown and red, with amber beads.

She said, 'Isn't it improper for a colleague of the Crown Prosecutor to be seen talking to one of the witnesses?'

'No, it isn't,' Tatum said, and asked me, 'Did you tell her we were meeting here?'

'Of course not.'

'Then how . . . why, Miss Cathcart, are you here?'

'I told you. It's a story.'

'Does *The Pump* know you're here?' I asked.

A shade crossly she said, 'I'm not a child. I'm allowed out on my own, you know. And anyway, the paper sent me.'

'*The Pump* told you we'd be here?' Tatum asked.

'My editor said to come and see you. And he was right!'

Tatum said, 'Sid?'

'Mm,' I said. 'Interesting.'

India said to me, 'Kevin says you went to school in Liverpool.'

Tatum, puzzled, asked, 'What did you say?'

She explained, 'Sid wouldn't tell me where he went to school, so I found out.' She looked at me accusingly. 'You don't sound like Liverpool.'

'Don't I?'

'You sound more like Eton. How come?'

'I'm a mimic,' I said.

If she really wanted to, she could find out also that

between the ages of sixteen and twenty-one I'd been more or less adopted by a Newmarket trainer (who *had* been to Eton) who made me into a good jockey and by his example changed my speech and taught me how to live and how to behave and how to manage the money I earned. He'd been already old then, and he died. I often thought of him. He opened doors for me still.

'Kevin told me you were a slum child,' India said.

'Slum is an attitude, not a place.'

'Prickly, are we?'

Damn, I thought. I will *not* let her goad me. I smiled, which she didn't like.

Tatum, listening with disapproval, said, 'Who is Kevin?'

'He works for *The Pump*,' I told him.

India said, 'Kevin Mills is *The Pump*'s chief reporter. He did favours for Halley and got kicked in the teeth.'

'Painful,' Tatum commented dryly.

'This conversation's getting nowhere,' I said. 'India, Mr Tatum is not the prosecutor in any case where I am a witness, and we may talk about anything we care to, including, as just now before you came, golf.'

'You can't play golf with one hand.'

It was Tatum who winced, not I. I said, 'You can watch golf on television without arms, legs or ears. Where did your editor get the idea that you might find us here?'

'He didn't say. It doesn't matter.'

'It is of the essence,' Tatum said.

'It's interesting,' I said, 'because to begin with it was *The Pump* that worked up the greatest head of steam about the ponies mutilated in Kent. That was why I got in touch with Kevin Mills. Between us we set up a Hotline, as a "Save the *Tussilago farfara*" sort of thing.'

India demanded, 'What did you say?'

'*Tussilago farfara*,' Tatum repeated, amused. 'It's the botanical name of the wildflower, coltsfoot.'

'How did you know that?' she asked me fiercely.

'I looked it up.'

'Oh.'

'Anyway, the minute I linked Ellis Quint, even tentatively, to the colts, and to Rachel Ferns' pony, *The Pump* abruptly changed direction and started tearing me apart with crusading claws. I can surely ask, India, why do you write about me so ferociously? Is it just your way? Is it that you do so many hatchet jobs that you can't do anything else? I didn't expect kindness, but you are . . . every week . . . extreme.'

She looked uncomfortable. She did what she had one week called me 'diddums' for doing: she defended herself.

'My editor gives me guidelines.' She almost tossed her head.

'You mean he tells you what to write?'

'Yes. No.'

'Which?'

She looked from me to Tatum and back.

She said, 'He subs my piece to align it with overall policy.'

I said nothing. Tatum said nothing. India, a shade desperately, said, 'Only saints get themselves burned at the stake.'

Tatum said with gravitas, 'If I read any lies or innuendoes about my having improperly talked to Sid Halley about the forthcoming Quint trial, I will sue you personally for defamation, Miss Cathcart, and I will ask for punitive damages. So choose your stake. Flames seem inevitable.'

I felt almost sorry for her. She stood up blankly, her eyes wide.

'Say we weren't here,' I said.

I couldn't read her frozen expression. She walked away from us and headed for the stairs.

'A confused young woman,' Tatum said. 'But how did she – or her paper – know we would be here?'

I asked, 'Do you feed your appointments into a computer?'

He frowned. 'I don't do it personally. My secretary does it. We have a system which can tell where all the partners are, if there's a crisis. It tells where each of us can be found. I did tell my secretary I was coming here, but not who I was going to meet. That still doesn't explain . . .'

I sighed. 'Yesterday evening you phoned my mobile number.'

'Yes, and you phoned me back.'

204

'Someone's been listening on my mobile phone's frequency. Someone heard you call me.'

'Hell! But you called me back. They heard almost nothing.'

'You gave your name . . . How secure is your office computer?'

'We change passwords every three months.'

'And you use passwords that everyone can remember easily?'

'Well . . .'

'There are people who crack passwords just for the fun of it. And others hack into secrets. You wouldn't believe how *careless* some firms are with their most private information. Someone has recently accessed my own on-line computer – during the past month. I have a detector program that tells me. Much good it will do any hacker as I never keep anything personal there. But a combination of my mobile phone and your office computer must have come up with the *possibility* that your appointment was with me. Someone in *The Pump* did it. So they sent India along to find out . . . and here we are. And because they succeeded, we now know they tried.'

'It's incredible.'

'Who runs *The Pump*? Who sets the policy?'

Tatum said thoughtfully, 'The editor is George Godbar. The proprietor's Lord Tilepit.'

'Any connection with Ellis Quint?'

He considered the question and shook his head. 'Not that I know of.'

'Does Lord Tilepit have an interest in the television company that puts on Ellis Quint's programme? I think I'd better find out.'

Davis Tatum smiled.

Reflecting that, as about thirty hours had passed since Gordon Quint had jumped me in Pont Square, he was unlikely still to be hanging about there with murderous feelings and his fencing post (not least because with Ginnie dead he would have her inquest to distract him) and also feeling that one could take self-preservation to shaming lengths, I left the Piccadilly restaurant in a taxi and got the driver to make two reconnoitring passes round the railed central garden.

All seemed quiet. I paid the driver, walked without incident up the steps to the front door, used my key, went up to the next floor and let myself into the haven of home.

No ambush. No creaks. Silence.

I retrieved a few envelopes from the wire basket clipped inside the letter box and found a page in my fax. It seemed a long time since I'd left, but it had been only the previous morning.

My cracked arm hurt. Well, it would. I'd ridden races – and winners – now and then with cracks: disguising them, of course, because the betting public deserved healthy riders to carry their money. The odd thing was that in the heat of a race one didn't feel an injury. It was in the cooler ebbing of excitement that the discomfort returned.

The best way, always, to minimise woes was to concentrate on something else. I looked up a number and phoned the handy acquaintance who had set up my computers for me.

'Doug,' I said, when his wife had fetched him in from an oil change, 'tell me about listening in to mobile phones.'

'I'm covered in grease,' he complained. 'Won't this do another time?'

'Someone is listening to my mobile.'

'Oh.' He sniffed. 'So you want to know how to stop it?'

'You're dead right.'

He sniffed again. 'I've got a cold,' he said, 'my wife's mother is coming to dinner and my sump is filthy.'

I laughed: couldn't help it. 'Please, Doug.'

He relented. 'I suppose you've got an analog mobile. They have radio signals that can be listened to. It's difficult, though. Your average bloke in the pub couldn't do it.'

'Could you?'

'I'm not your average bloke in the pub. I'm a walking mid-life crisis halfway through an oil change. I could do it if I had the right gear.'

'How do I deal with it?'

'Blindingly simple.' He sneezed and sniffed heavily. 'I need a tissue.' There was a sudden silence on the line, then the distant sound of a nose being vigorously blown, then the hoarse voice of wisdom in my ear.

'OK,' he said. 'You ditch the analog, and get a digital.'

'I do?'

'Sid, being a jockey does not equip the modern man to live in tomorrow's world.'

'I do see that.'

'Everyone,' he sniffed, 'if they had any sense, would go digital.'

'Teach me.'

'The digital system,' he said, 'is based on two numbers, nought and one. Nought and one have been with us from the dawn of computers, and no one has ever invented anything better.'

'They haven't?'

He detected my mild note of irony. 'Has anyone,' he asked, 're-invented the wheel?'

'Er, no.'

'Quite. One cannot improve on an immaculate conception.'

'That's blasphemous.' I enjoyed him always.

'Certainly not,' he said, 'Some things are perfect to begin with. $E = mc^2$, and all that.'

'I grant that. How about my mobile?'

'The signal sent to a digital telephone,' he said, 'is

not one signal, as in analog, but is eight simultaneous signals, each transmitting one eighth of what you hear.'

'Is that so?' I asked dryly.

'You may bloody snigger,' he said, 'but I'm giving you the goods. A digital phone receives eight simultaneous signals, and it is *impossible* for anyone to decode them, except the receiving mobile. Now, because the signal arrives in eight pieces, the reception isn't always perfect. You don't get the crackle or the fading in and out that you get on analog phones, but you do sometimes get bits of words missing. Still, *no one* can listen in. Even the police can never tap a digital mobile number.'

'So,' I said, fascinated, 'where do I get one?'

'Try Harrods,' he said.

'*Harrods?*'

'Harrods is just round the corner from where you live, isn't it?'

'More or less.'

'Try there, then. Or anywhere else that sells phones. You can use the same number that you have now. You just need to tell your service provider. And, of course, you'll need an SIM card. You have one, of course?'

I said meekly, 'No.'

'Sid!' he protested. He sneezed again. 'Sorry. An SIM card is a Subscribers Identity Module. You can't live without one.'

'I can't?'

'Sid, I despair of you. Wake up to technology.'

'I'm better at knowing what a horse thinks.'

Patiently he enlightened me, 'An SIM card is like a credit card. It actually *is* a credit card. Included on it are your name and mobile phone number and other details, and you can slot it into any mobile that will take it. For instance, if you are someone's guest in Athens and he has a mobile that accepts an SIM card, you can slot *your* card into *his* phone and the charge will appear on your account, not his.'

'Are you serious?' I asked.

'With my problems, would I joke?'

'Where do I get an SIM card?'

'Ask Harrods.' He sneezed. 'Ask anyone who travels for a living. Your service provider will provide.' He sniffed. 'So long, Sid.'

Amused and grateful, I opened my post and read the fax. The fax being most accessible got looked at first.

Handwritten, it scrawled simply, 'Phone me,' and gave a long number.

The writing was Kevin Mills', but the fax machine he'd sent it from was anonymously not *The Pump*'s.

I phoned the number given, which would have connected me to a mobile, and got only the infuriating instruction, 'Please try later.'

There were a dozen messages I didn't much want on my answering machine and a piece of information I *definitely* didn't want in a large brown envelope from Shropshire.

The envelope contained a copy of a glossy county magazine, one I'd sent for as I'd been told it included lengthy coverage of the heir-to-the-dukedom's coming-of-age dance. There were, indeed, four pages of pictures, mostly in colour, accompanied by prose gush about the proceedings and a complete guest list.

A spectacular burst of fireworks filled half a page, and there in a group of heaven-gazing spectators, there in white dinner jacket and all his photogenic glory, there unmistakably stood Ellis Quint.

My heart sank. The fireworks had started at three-thirty. At three-thirty, when the moon was high, Ellis had been a hundred miles north-west of the Windward Stud's yearling.

There were many pictures of the dancing, and a page of black and white shots of the guests, names attached. Ellis had been dancing. Ellis smiled twice from the guests' page, carefree, having a good time.

Damn it to hell, I thought. He had to have taken the colt's foot off early. Say by one o'clock. He could then have arrived for the fireworks by three-thirty. I'd found no one who'd seen him *arrive*, but several who swore to his presence after five-fifteen. At five-fifteen he had helped the heir to climb onto a table to make a drunken speech. The heir had poured a bottle of champagne over Ellis's head. Everyone remembered *that*. Ellis could not have driven back to Northampton before dawn.

For two whole days the previous week I'd traipsed

round Shropshire, and next door Cheshire, handed on from grand house to grander, asking much the same questions (according to sex) – did you dance with Ellis Quint or did you drink/eat with him. The answers at first had been freely given, but, as time went on, news of my mission spread before me until I was progressively met by hostile faces and frankly closed doors. Shropshire was solid Ellis country. They'd have stood on their heads to prove him unjustly accused. They were not going to say that they didn't know when he'd arrived.

In the end I returned to the duchess's front gates, and from there drove as fast as prudence allowed, to the Windward Stud Farm, timing the journey at two hours and five minutes. On empty roads at night, Northampton to the duchess might have taken ten minutes less. I'd proved nothing except that Ellis had had time.

Enough time was not enough.

As always before gathering at such dances, the guests had given and attended dinner parties both locally and further away. No one that I'd asked had entertained Ellis to dinner.

No dinner was not enough.

I went through the guest list crossing off the people I'd seen. There were still far more than half unconsulted, most of whom I'd never heard of.

Where was Chico? I needed him often. I hadn't the time, or to be frank, the appetite to locate and question all the guests, even if they would answer. There must have been people – local people – helping with the parking of cars that night. Chico would have chatted people up in the local pubs and found out if any of the car-parkers remembered Ellis's arrival. Chico was good at pubs, and I wasn't in his class.

The police might have done it, but they wouldn't. The death of a colt still didn't count like murder.

The police.

I phoned Norman Picton's police station number and gave my name as John Paul Jones.

He came on the line in a good humour and listened to me without protest.

'Let me get this straight,' he said. 'You want me to ask favours of the Northamptonshire police? What do I offer in return?'

'Blood in the hinges of lopping shears.'

'They'll have made their own tests.'

'Yes, and that Northamptonshire colt is dead and gone to the glue factory. An error, wouldn't you say? Might they not do you a favour in exchange for com-miseration?'

'You'll have my head off. What is it you actually *want*?'

'Er . . .' I began, 'I was there when the police found the lopping shears in the hedge.'

'Yes, you told me.'

'Well, I've been thinking. Those shears weren't wrap-ped in sacking, like the ones we took from the Quints.'

'No, and the shears weren't the same, either. The

213

ones at Northampton are a slightly newer model. They're on sale everywhere in garden centres. The problem is that Ellis Quint hasn't been reported as buying any, not in the Northamptonshire police district, nor ours.'

'Is there any chance,' I asked, 'of my looking again at the material used for wrapping the shears?'

'If there are horse hairs in it, there's nothing left to match them to, same as the blood.'

'All the same, the cloth might tell us where the shears came from. *Which* garden centre, do you see?'

'I'll see if they've done that already.'

'Thanks, Norman.'

'Thank Archie. He drives me to help you.'

'Does he?'

He heard my surprise. 'Archie has *influence*,' he said, 'and I do what the magistrate tells me.'

When he'd gone off the line I tried Kevin Mills again and reached the same electronic voice: 'Please try later.'

After that I sat in an armchair while the daylight faded and the lights came on in the peaceful square. We were past the equinox, back in winter thoughts, the year dying ahead. Autumn for me had for almost half my life meant the longed-for resurgence of major jump racing, the time of big winners and speed and urgency in the blood. Winter now brought only nostalgia and heating bills. At thirty-four I was growing old.

I sat thinking of Ellis and the wasteland he had made of my year. I thought of Rachel Ferns and Silverboy, and lymphoblasts. I thought of the Press, and especially *The Pump* and India Cathcart and the orchestrated months of vilification. I thought of Ellis's relentless jokes.

I thought for a long time about Archie Kirk, who had drawn me to Combe Bassett and given me Norman Picton. I wondered if it had been from Archie that Norman had developed a belief in a heavy presence behind the scenes. I wondered if it could possibly be Archie who had prompted Davis Tatum to engage me to find that heavyweight. I wondered if it could possibly have been Archie who told Davis Tatum about my run-in with the bad hat at the Jockey Club, and if so, how did *he* know?

I trusted Archie. He could pull my strings, I thought, as long as I was willing to go where he pointed, and as long as I was sure no one was pulling *his*.

I thought about Gordon Quint's uncontrollable rage, and the practical difficulties his fencing post had inflicted. I thought of Ginnie Quint and despair and sixteen floors down.

I thought of the colts and their chopped-off feet.

When I went to bed I dreamed the same old nightmare.

Agony. Humiliation. Both hands.

I awoke sweating.

Damn it all to hell.

CHAPTER NINE

In the morning, when I'd failed yet again to get an answer from Kevin Mills, I shunted by tube across central London and emerged not far from Companies House at 55 City Road, E.C.

Companies House, often my friend, contained the records of all public and private limited companies active in the United Kingdom, including the audited annual balance sheets, investment capital, fixed assets and the names of major shareholders and the directors of the boards.

Topline Foods, I soon learned, was an old company recently taken over by a few new big investors and a bustling new management. The chief shareholder and managing director was listed as Owen Cliff Yorkshire. There were fifteen non-executive directors, of whom one was Lord Tilepit.

The premises at which business was carried out were located at Frodsham in Cheshire. The registered office was at the same address.

The product of the company was foodstuffs for animals.

After Topline, I looked up Village Pump Newspapers (they'd dropped the 'Village' in about 1900, but retained the idea of a central meeting place for gossip) and found interesting items, and after Village Pump Newspapers I looked up the TV company that aired Ellis's sports programme, but found no sign of Tilepit or Owen Yorkshire in its operations.

I travelled home (safely) and phoned Archie, who was, his wife reported, at work.

'Can I reach him at work?' I asked.

'Oh no, Sid. He wouldn't like it. I'll give him a message when he gets back.'

Please try later.

I tried Kevin Mills later and this time nearly got my eardrums perforated. 'At last!'

'I've tried you a dozen times,' I said.

'I've been in an old people's home.'

'Well, bully for you.'

'A nurse hastened three harpies into the hereafter.'

'Poor old sods.'

'If you're in Pont Square,' he said, 'can I call round and see you? I'm in my car not far away.'

'I thought I was *The Pump*'s number one all-time shit.'

'Yeah. Can I come?'

'I suppose so.'

'Great.' He clicked off before I could change my mind and he was at my door in less than ten minutes.

'This is *nice*,' he said appreciatively, looking round my sitting-room. 'Not what I expected.'

There was a Sheraton writing-desk and buttoned brocade chairs and a couple of modern exotic wood inlaid tables by Mark Boddington. The overall colours were greyish blue, soft and restful. The only brash intruder was an ancient fruit machine that worked on tokens.

Kevin Mills made straight towards it, as most visitors did. I always left a few tokens haphazardly on the floor, with a bowl of them nearby on a table. Kevin picked a token from the carpet, fed it into the slot, and pulled the handle. The wheels clattered and clunked. He got two cherries and a lemon. He picked up another token and tried again.

'What wins the jackpot?' hc asked, achieving an orange, a lemon and a banana.

'Three horses with jockeys jumping fences.'

He looked at me sharply.

'It used to be the bells,' I said. 'That was boring, so I changed it.'

'And do the three horses ever come up?'

I nodded. 'You get a fountain of tokens all over the floor.'

The machine was addictive. It was my equivalent of the psychiatrist's couch. Kevin played throughout our conversation but the nearest he came was two horses and a pear.

'The trial has started, Sid,' he said, 'so give us the scoop.'

'The trial's only technically started. I can't tell you a thing. When the adjournment's over, you can go to court and listen.'

'That's not exclusive,' he complained.

'You know damned well I can't tell you.'

'I gave you the story to begin with.'

'I sought you out,' I said. 'Why did *The Pump* stop helping the colt owners and shaft me instead?'

He concentrated hard on the machine. Two bananas and a blackberry.

'Why?' I asked.

'Policy.'

'Whose policy?'

'The public wants demolition, they gobble up spite.'

'Yes, but—'

'Look, Sid, we get the word from on high. And don't ask *who* on high. I don't know. I don't like it. None of us likes it. But we have the choice, go along with overall policy or go somewhere else where we feel more in tune. And do you know where that gets you? I work for *The Pump* because it's a good paper with, on the whole, fair comment. OK, so reputations topple. Like I said, that's what Mrs Public wants. Now and then we get a *request*, such as "lean hard on Sid Halley". I did it without qualms, as you'd clammed up on me.'

He looked all the time at the machine, playing fast.

'And India Cathcart?' I asked.

He pulled the lever and waited until two lemons and a jumping horse came to rest in a row.

'India . . .' he said slowly. 'For some reason she didn't want to trash you. She said she'd enjoyed her dinner with you and you were quiet and kind. Kind! I ask you! Her editor had to squeeze the poison out of her drop by drop for that first long piece. In the end he wrote most of her page himself. She was furious the next day when she read it, but it was out on the streets by then and she couldn't do anything about it.'

I was more pleased than I would have expected, but I wasn't going to let Kevin see it. I said, 'What about the continued stab wounds almost every week?'

'I guess she goes along with the policy. Like I said, she has to eat.'

'Is it George Godbar's policy?'

'The big white chief himself? Yes, you could say the editor of the paper has the final say.'

'And Lord Tilepit?'

He gave me an amused glance. Two pears and a lemon. 'He's not a hands-on proprietor of the old school. Not a Beaverbrook or a Harmsworth. We hardly know he's alive.'

'Does he give the overall policy to George Godbar?'

'Probably.' A horse, a lemon and some cherries. 'Why do I get the idea that *you* are interviewing *me*, instead of the other way round?'

'I cannot imagine. What do you know about Owen Cliff Yorkshire?'

'Bugger all. Who is he?'

'Quite likely a friend of Lord Tilepit.'

'Sid,' he protested. 'I do my job. Rapes, murders, little old ladies smothered in their sleep. I do *not* chew off the fingernails of my pay cheque.'

He banged the fruit machine frustratedly. 'The bloody thing hates me.'

'It has no soul,' I said. I fed in a stray token myself with my plastic fingers and pulled the handle. Three horses. Fountains of love. Life's little irony.

Kevin Mills took his paunch, his moustache and his disgusted disgruntlement off to his word-processor, and I again phoned Norman as John Paul Jones.

'My colleagues now think John Paul Jones is a snitch,' he said.

'Fine.'

'What is it this time?'

'Do you still have any of those horse-nuts I collected from Betty Bracken's field, and those others we took from the Land-Rover?'

'Yes, we do. And as you know, they're identical in composition.'

'Then could you find out if they were manufactured by Topline Foods Ltd, of Frodsham in Cheshire?'

After a short silence he said cautiously, 'It could be done, but is it necessary?'

'If you could let me have some of the nuts I could do it myself.'

'I can't let you have any. They are bagged and counted.'

'Shit.' And I could so easily have kept some in my own pocket. Careless. Couldn't be helped.

'Why does it matter where they came from?' Norman asked.

'Um . . . You know you told me you thought there might be a heavyweight somewhere behind the scenes? Well, I've been asked to find out.'

'Jeez,' he said. 'Who asked you?'

'Can't tell you. Client confidentiality and all that.'

'Is it Archie Kirk?'

'Not so far as I know.'

'Huh!' He sounded unconvinced. 'I'll go this far. If you get me some authenticated Topline nuts I'll see if I can run a check on them to find out if they match the ones we have. That's the best I can do, and that's stretching it, and you wouldn't have a prayer if you hadn't been the designer of our whole prosecution – and you can *not* quote me on that.'

'I'm truly grateful. I'll get some Topline nuts, but they probably won't match the ones you have.'

'Why not?'

'The grains – the balance of ingredients – will have changed since those were manufactured. Every batch must have its own profile, so to speak.'

He well knew what I meant, as an analysis of ingredi-

222

ents could reveal their origins as reliably as grooves on a bullet.

'What interests you in Topline Foods?' Norman asked.

'My client.'

'Bugger your client. Tell me.' I didn't answer and he sighed heavily. 'All right. You can't tell me now. I hate amateur detectives. I've got you a strip off that dirty Northampton material. At least, it's promised for later today. What are you going to do about it, and have you cracked Ellis Quint's alibi yet?'

'You're *brilliant*,' I said. 'Where can I meet you? And no, I haven't cracked the alibi.'

'Try harder.'

'I'm only an amateur.'

'Yeah, yeah. Come to the lake at five o'clock. I'm picking up the boat to take it home for winter storage. OK?'

'I'll be there.'

'See you.'

I phoned the hospital in Canterbury. Rachel, the ward sister told me, was 'resting comfortably'.

'What does that mean?'

'She's no worse than yesterday, Mr Halley. When can you return?'

'Sometime soon.'

'Good.'

I spent the afternoon exchanging my old vulnerable analog mobile cellular telephone for a digital receiving eight splintered transmissions that would baffle even the Thames Valley stalwarts, let alone *The Pump*.

From my flat I then phoned Miss Richardson of Northamptonshire, who said vehemently that *no*, I certainly might *not* call on her again. Ginnie and Gordon Quint were her dear friends and it was *unthinkable* that Ellis could harm horses, and I was foul and *wicked* even to think it. Ginnie had told her about it. Ginnie had been very distressed. It was all my fault that she had killed herself.

I persevered with two questions, however, and did get answers of sorts.

'Did your vet say how long he thought the foot had been off when the colt was found at seven o'clock?'

'No, he didn't.'

'Could you give me his name and phone number?'

'No.'

As I had over the years accumulated a whole shelfful of area telephone directories, it was not so difficult, via the Northamptonshire Yellow Pages, to find and talk to Miss Richardson's vet. He would, he said, have been helpful if he could. All he could with confidence say was that neither the colt's leg nor the severed foot had shown signs of recent bleeding. Miss Richardson herself had insisted he put the colt out of his misery immediately, and, as it was also his own judgement, he had done so.

He had been unable to suggest to the police any particular time for the attack; earlier rather than later was as far as he could go. The wound had been clean: one chop. The vet said he was surprised a yearling would have stood still long enough for shears to be applied. Yes, he confirmed, the colt had been lightly shod, and yes, there had been horse-nuts scattered around, but Miss Richardson often gave her horses nuts as a supplement to grass.

He'd been helpful, but no help.

After that I had to decide how to get to the lake, as the normal taken-for-granted act of driving now had complications. I had a knob fixed on the steering wheel of my Mercedes which gave me a good grip for one-(right)handed operation. With my left unfeeling hand I shifted the automatic gear lever.

I experimentally flexed and clenched my right hand. Sharp protests. Boring. With irritation I resorted to ibuprofen and drove to the lake wishing Chico were around to do it.

Norman had winched his boat onto its trailer by the edge of the water. Big, competent and observant, he watched my slow emergence to upright and frowned.

'What hurts?' he asked.

'Self-esteem.'

He laughed. 'Give me a hand with the boat, will you? Pull when I lift.'

I looked at the job and said briefly that I couldn't.

'You only need one hand for pulling.'

I told him unemotionally that Gordon Quint had aimed for my head and done lesser but inconvenient damage. 'I'm telling you in case he tries again and succeeds. He was slightly out of his mind over Ginnie.'

Norman predictably said I should make an official complaint.

'No,' I said. 'This is unofficial, and ends right here.'

He went off to fetch a friend to help him with the boat, and then busied himself with enclosing his powerful outboard engine into a fitted zipped cover.

I said, 'What first gave you the feeling that there was some heavyweight meandering behind the scenes?'

'First?' He went on working while he thought. 'It's months ago. I talked it over with Archie. I expect it was because one minute I was putting together an ordinary case – even if Ellis Quint's fame made it newsworthy – and the next I was being leaned on by the Superintendent to find some reason to drop it, and when I showed him the strength of the evidence, he said the Chief Constable was unhappy, and the reason for the Chief Constable's unhappiness was always the same, which was political pressure from outside.'

'What sort of political?'

Norman shrugged. 'Not party politics especially. A pressure group. Lobbying. A bargain struck somewhere, along the lines of "Get the Quint prosecution aborted and such-and-such a good thing will come your way!" '

'But not a direct cash advantage?'

'Sid!'

'Well, sorry.'

'I should frigging well hope so.' He wrapped thick twine round the shrouded engine. 'I'm not asking cash for a strip of rag from Northamptonshire.'

'I grovel,' I said.

He grinned. 'That'll be the day.' He climbed into his boat and secured various bits of equipment against movement en route.

'No one has entirely given in to the pressure,' he pointed out. 'The case against Ellis Quint has not been dropped. True, it's now in a ropey state. You yourself have been relentlessly discredited to the point where you're almost a liability to the prosecution, and even though that's brutally unfair, it's a fact.'

'Mm.'

In effect, I thought, I'd been commissioned by Davis Tatum to find out who had campaigned to defeat me. It wasn't the first time I'd faced campaigns to enforce my inactivity, but it was the first time I'd been offered a fee to save myself. To save myself, in this instance, meant to defeat Ellis Quint: so I was being paid for *that*, in the first place. And for what *else*?

Norman backed his car up to the boat trailer and hitched them together. Then he leaned through the open front passenger window of the car, unlocked the glove compartment there, and drew out and handed me a plastic bag.

'One strip of dirty rag,' he said cheerfully. 'Cost to you, six grovels before breakfast for a week.'

I took the bag gratefully. Inside, the filthy strip, about

three inches wide, had been loosely folded until it was several layers thick.

'It's about a metre long,' Norman said. 'It was all they would let me have. I had to sign for it.'

'Good.'

'What are you going to do with it?'

'Clean it, for a start.'

Norman said doubtfully, 'It's got some sort of pattern in it but there wasn't any printing on the whole wrapping. Nothing to say where it came from. No garden centre name, or anything.'

'I don't have high hopes,' I said, 'but, frankly, just now every straw's worth clutching.'

Norman stood with his legs apart and his hands on his hips. He looked like a pillar of every possible police strength but what he was actually feeling turned out to be indecision.

'How far can I trust you?' he asked.

'For silence?'

He nodded.

'I thought we'd discussed this already.'

'Yes, but that was months ago.'

'Nothing's changed,' I said.

He made a decision, stuck his head into his car again and this time brought out a business-sized brown envelope which he held out to me.

'It's a copy of the analysis done on the horse-nuts,' he said. 'So read it and shred it.'

'OK. And thanks.'

I held the envelope and plastic bag together and knew I couldn't take such trust lightly. He must be very sure of me, I thought; and felt not complimented but apprehensive.

'I've been thinking,' I said, 'do you remember, way back in June, when we took those things out of Gordon Quint's Land-Rover?'

'Of course I remember.'

'There was a farrier's apron in the Land-Rover. Rolled up. We didn't take that, did we?'

He frowned. 'I don't remember it, but no, it's not among the things we took. What's significant about it?'

I said, 'I've always thought it odd that the colts should stand still long enough for the shears to close round the ankle, even with head-collars and those nuts. But horses have an acute sense of smell . . . and all those colts had shoes on – I checked with their vets – and they would have known the smell of a blacksmith's apron. I think Ellis might have worn that apron to reassure the colts. They may have thought he was the man who shod them. They would have *trusted* him. He could have lifted a fetlock and gripped it with the shears.'

He stared.

'What do you think?' I asked.

'It's you who knows horses.'

'It's how I might get a two-year-old to let me near his legs.'

'As far as I'm concerned,' he said, 'that's how it was done.'

He held out his hand automatically to say goodbye, then remembered Gordon Quint's handiwork, shrugged, grinned, and said instead, 'If there's anything interesting about that strip of rag, you'll let me know?'

'Of course.'

'See you.'

He drove off with a wave, trailing his boat, and I returned to my car, stowed away the bag and the envelope and made a short journey to Shelley Green, the home of Archie Kirk.

He had returned from work. He took me into his sitting-room while his smiling wife cooked in the kitchen.

'How's things?' Archie asked. 'Whisky?'

I nodded. 'A lot of water . . .'

He indicated chairs, and we sat. The dark room looked right in October: imitation flames burnt imitation coals in the fireplace, giving the room a life that the sun of June hadn't achieved.

I hadn't seen Archie since then. I absorbed again the probably deliberate greyness of his general appearance, and I saw again the whole internet in the dark eyes.

He said casually, 'You've been having a bit of a rough time.'

'Does it show?'

'Yes.'

'Never mind,' I said. 'Will you answer some questions?'

'It depends what they are.'

I drank some of his undistinguished whisky and let my muscles relax into the ultimate of non-aggressive, non-combative postures.

'For a start, what do you do?' I said.

'I'm a civil servant.'

'That's not . . . well . . . specific.'

'Start at the other end,' he said.

I smiled. I said, 'It's a wise man who knows who's paying him.'

He paused with his own glass halfway to his lips.

'Go on,' he said.

'Then . . . do you know Davis Tatum?'

After a pause he answered, 'Yes.'

It seemed to me he was growing wary; that he, as I did, had to sort through a minefield of facts one could not or should not reveal that one knew. The old dilemma – does he know I know he knows – sometimes seemed like child's play.

I said, 'How's Jonathan?'

He laughed. 'I hear you play chess,' he said. 'I hear you're a whiz at misdirection. Your opponents think they're winning, and then . . . wham.'

I played chess only with Charles at Aynsford, and not very often.

'Do you know my father-in-law?' I asked. 'Ex-father-in-law, Charles Roland?'

With a glimmer he said, 'I've talked to him on the telephone.'

At least he hadn't lied to me, I thought; and, if he hadn't lied he'd given me a fairly firm path to follow. I asked about Jonathan, and about his sister, Betty Bracken.

'That wretched boy is still at Combe Bassett and now that the water ski-ing season is over he is driving everyone *mad*. You are the only person who sees any good in him.'

'Norman does.'

'Norman sees a talented water-skier with criminal tendencies.'

'Has Jonathan any money?'

Archie shook his head. 'Only the very little we gave him for toothpaste and so on. He's still on probation. He's a mess.' He paused. 'Betty has been paying for the water ski-ing. She's the only one in our family with real money. She married straight out of school. Bobby's thirty years older – he was rich when they married and he's richer than ever now. As you saw, she's still devoted to him. Always has been. They had no children; she couldn't. Very sad. If Jonathan had any sense he would be *nice* to Betty.'

'I don't think he's that devious. Or not yet, anyway.'

'Do you like him?' Archie asked curiously.

'Not much, but I hate to see people go to waste.'

'Stupid boy.'

'I checked on the colt,' I said. 'The foot stayed on.'

Archie nodded. 'Betty's delighted. The colt is permanently lame, but they're going to see if, with his breeding, he's any good for stud. Betty's offering him free next year to good mares.'

Archie's sweet wife came in and asked if I would stay to dinner; she could easily cook extra. I thanked her but stood up to go. Archie shook my hand. I winced through not concentrating, but he made no comment. He came out to my car with me as the last shreds of daylight waned to dark.

He said, 'In the Civil Service, I work in a small unacknowledged off-shoot department which was set up sometime ago to foretell the probable outcome of any high political appointment. We also predict the future inevitable consequences of pieces of proposed legislation.' He paused and went on wryly, 'We call ourselves the Cassandra outfit. We see what will happen and no one believes us. We are always on the look out for exceptional independent investigators with no allegiances. They're hard to find. We think you are one.'

I stood beside my car in the dying light looking into the extraordinary eyes. An extraordinary man of unimaginable insights. I said, 'Archie, I'll work for you to the limit as long as I'm sure you're not sending me into a danger that you know exists but are not telling me about.'

He took a deep breath but gave no undertaking.

'Goodnight,' I said mildly.

'Sid.'

'I'll phone you.' It was as firm a promise, I thought, as 'let's do lunch'.

He was still standing on his gravel as I drove out through his gates. A true civil servant, I thought ruefully. No positive assurances could ever be given because the rules could at any time be changed under one's feet.

I drove north across Oxfordshire to Aynsford and rang the bell of the side entrance of Charles's house. Mrs Cross came in answer to the summons, her enquiring expression melting to welcome as she saw who had arrived.

'The Admiral's in the wardroom,' she assured me, when I asked if he were at home, and she bustled along before me to give Charles the news.

He made no reference to the fact that it was the second time in three days that I had sought his sanctuary. He merely pointed to the gold brocade chair and poured brandy into a tumbler without asking.

I sat and drank and looked gratefully at the austerity and restraint of this thin man who'd commanded ships and was now my only anchor.

'How's the arm?' he asked briefly, and I said lightly, 'Sore.'

He nodded and waited.

'Can I stay?' I said.

'Of course.'

After a longish pause, I said, 'Do you know a man called Archibald Kirk?'

'No, I don't think so.'

'He says he talked to you on the telephone. It was months ago, I think. He's a civil servant and a magistrate. He lives near Hungerford, and I've come here from his house. Can you remember? Way back. I think he may have been asking you about *me*. Like sort of checking up, like a reference. You probably told him that I play chess.'

He thought about it, searching for the memory.

'I would always give you a good reference,' he said. 'Is there any reason why you'd prefer I didn't?'

'No, definitely not.'

'I've been asked several times about your character and ability. I always say if they're looking for an investigator they couldn't do better.'

'You're . . . very kind.'

'Kind, my foot. Why do you ask about this Archibald Church?'

'Kirk.'

'Kirk, then.'

I drank some brandy and said, 'Do you remember that day you came with me to the Jockey Club? The day we got the head of the Security section sacked?'

'I could hardly forget it, could I?'

'You didn't tell Archie Kirk about it, did you?'

'Of course not. I *never* talk about it. I gave you my word I wouldn't.'

'Someone has,' I said morosely.

'The Jockey Club didn't actually swear an oath of silence.'

'I know.' I thought a bit and asked, 'Do you know a barrister called Davis Tatum? He's the head of chambers of the prosecution counsel at Ellis's trial.'

'I know *of* him. Never met him.'

'You'd like him. You'd like Archie, too.' I paused, and went on, 'They both know about that day at the Jockey Club.'

'But Sid . . . does it really matter? I mean, you did the Jockey Club a tremendous favour, getting rid of their villain.'

'Davis Tatum and, I'm sure, Archie, have engaged me to find out who is moving behind the scenes to get the Quint trial quashed. And I'm not telling you that.'

He smiled. 'Client confidentiality?'

'Right. Well, Davis Tatum made a point of telling me that he knew all about the mandarins insisting I took off my shirt, and why. I think he and Archie are trying to reassure themselves that if they ask me to do something dangerous, I'll do it.'

He gave me a long slow look, his features still and expressionless.

Finally he said, 'And will you?'

I sighed, 'Probably.'

'What sort of danger?'

'I don't think they know. But realistically, if someone has an overwhelming reason for preventing Ellis's trial

from ever starting, who is the person standing chiefly
in the way?'

'*Sid!*'

'Yes. So they're asking me to find out if anyone
might be motivated enough to ensure my permanent
removal from the scene. They want me to find out *if*
and *who* and *why*.'

'God, Sid.'

From a man who never blasphemed, those were
strong words.

'So . . .' I sighed. 'Davis Tatum gave me a name,
Owen Yorkshire, and told me he owned a firm called
Topline Foods. Now Topline Foods gave a sponsored
lunch at Aintree on the day before the Grand National.
Ellis Quint was guest of honour. Also among the guests
was a man called Lord Tilepit, who is both on the
Board of Topline Foods and the proprietor of *The
Pump*, which has been busy mocking me for months.'

He sat as if frozen.

'So,' I said, 'I'll go and see what Owen Yorkshire
and Lord Tilepit are up to, and if I don't come back
you can kick up a stink.'

When he'd organised his breath, he said, 'Don't do
it, Sid.'

'No . . . but if I don't, Ellis will walk out laughing,
and my standing in the world will be down the tubes
for ever, if you see what I mean.'

He saw.

After a while he said, 'I do vaguely remember talking to this Archie fellow. He asked about your *brains*. He said he knew about your physical resilience. Odd choice of words – I remember them. I told him you played a wily game of chess. And it's true, you do. But it was a long time ago. Before all this happened.'

I nodded. 'He already knew a lot about me when he got his sister to phone at five-thirty in the morning to tell me she had a colt with his foot off.'

'So that's who he is? Mrs Bracken's brother?'

'Yeah.' I drank brandy and said, 'If you're ever talking to Sir Thomas Ullaston, would you mind asking him – and don't make a drama of it – if he told Archie Kirk or Davis Tatum about that morning in the Jockey Club?'

Sir Thomas Ullaston had been Senior Steward at the time, and had conducted the proceedings which led to the removal of the head of the Security section who had arranged for Chico and me to be thoroughly deterred from investigating anything ever again. As far as I was concerned it was all past history, and I most emphatically wanted it to remain so.

Charles said he would ask Sir Thomas.

'Ask him not to let *The Pump* get hold of it.'

Charles contemplated that possibility with about as much horror as I did myself.

The bell of the side-door rang distantly, and Charles frowned at his watch.

'Who can that be? It's almost eight o'clock.'

We soon found out. An ultra-familiar voice called

'Daddy?' across the hall outside, and an ultra-familiar figure appeared in the doorway. Jenny ... Charles's younger daughter ... my sometime wife. My still-embittered wife, whose tongue had barbs.

Smothering piercing dismay I stood up, and Charles also.

'Jenny,' Charles said, advancing to greet her. 'What a lovely surprise.'

She turned her cheek coolly, as always, and said, 'We were passing. It seemed impossible not to call in.' She looked at me without much emotion and said, 'We didn't know *you* were here until I saw your car outside.'

I took the few steps between us and gave her the sort of cheek to cheek salutation she'd bestowed on Charles. She accepted the politeness, as always, as the civilised acknowledgement of adversaries after battle.

'You look thin,' she observed, not with concern but with criticism, from habit.

She, I thought, looked as beautiful as always, but there was nothing to be gained by saying so. I didn't want her to sneer at me. To begin with, it ruined the sweet curve of her mouth. She could hurt me with words whenever she tried, and she'd tried often. My only defence had been – and still was – silence.

Her handsome new husband had followed her into the room, shaking hands with Charles and apologising for having appeared without warning.

'My dear fellow, any time,' Charles assured him.

Anthony Wingham turned my way and with self-conscious affability said, 'Sid . . .' and held out his hand.

It was extraordinary, I thought, enduring his hearty embarrassed grasp, how often one regularly shook hands in the course of a day. I'd never really noticed it before.

Charles poured drinks and suggested dinner. Anthony Wingham waffled a grateful refusal. Jenny gave me a cool look and sat in the gold brocade chair.

Charles made small talk with Anthony until they'd exhausted the weather. I stood with them but looked at Jenny, and she at me. Into a sudden silence, she said, 'Well, Sid, I don't suppose you want me to say it, but you've got yourself into a proper mess this time.'

'No.'

'No what?'

'No, I don't want you to say it.'

'Ellis Quint! Biting off more than you can chew. And back in the summer the papers pestered me too. I suppose you know?'

I unwillingly nodded.

'That reporter from *The Pump*,' Jenny complained. 'India Cathcart, I couldn't get rid of her. She wanted to know all about you and about our divorce. Do you know what she wrote? She wrote that I'd told her that quite apart from being crippled, you weren't man enough for me.'

'I read it,' I said briefly.

'Did you? And did you like it? Did you like that, Sid?'

I didn't reply. It was Charles who fiercely protested. '*Jenny!* Don't.'

Her face suddenly softened, all the spite dissolving and revealing the gentle girl I'd married. The transformation happened in a flash, like prison bars falling away. Her liberation, I thought, had dramatically come at last.

'I didn't say that,' she told me, as if bewildered. 'I really didn't. She made it up.'

I swallowed. I found the re-emergence of the old Jenny harder to handle than her scorn.

'What *did* you say?' I said.

'Well . . . I . . . I . . .'

'*Jenny*,' Charles said again.

'I told her,' Jenny said to him, 'that I couldn't live in Sid's hard world. I told her that whatever she wrote she wouldn't smash him or disintegrate him because no one had ever managed it. I told her that he never showed his feelings and that steel was putty compared to him, and that I couldn't live with it.'

Charles and I had heard her say much the same thing before. It was Anthony who looked surprised. He inspected my harmless-looking self from his superior height and obviously thought she had got me wrong.

'India Cathcart didn't believe Jenny either,' I told him soothingly.

'*What?*'

241

'He reads minds, too,' Jenny said, putting down her glass and rising to her feet. 'Anthony, darling, we'll go now. OK?' To her father she said, 'Sorry it's such a short visit,' and to me, 'India Cathcart is a bitch.'

I kissed Jenny's cheek.

'I still love you,' I said.

She looked briefly into my eyes. 'I couldn't live with it. I told her the truth.'

'I know.'

'Don't let her break you.'

'No.'

'Well,' she said brightly, loudly, smiling. 'When birds fly out of cages they sing and rejoice. So . . . goodbye, Sid.'

She looked happy. She laughed. I ached for the days when we'd met, when she looked like that always; but one could never go back.

'Goodbye, Jenny,' I said.

Charles, uncomprehending, went with them to see them off and came back frowning.

'I simply don't understand my daughter,' he said. 'Do you?'

'Oh, yes.'

'She tears you to pieces. *I* can't stand it, even if you can. Why don't you ever fight back?'

'Look what I did to her.'

'She knew what she was marrying.'

'I don't think she did. It isn't always easy, being married to a jockey.'

242

'You forgive her too much! And then, do you know what she said just now, when she was leaving? I don't understand her. She gave me a hug – a hug – not a dutiful peck on the cheek, and she said, "Take care of Sid." '

I felt instantly liquefied inside: too close to tears.

'Sid . . .'

I shook my head, as much to retain composure as anything else.

'We've made our peace,' I said.

'When?'

'Just now. The old Jenny came back. She's free of me. She felt free quite suddenly . . . so she'll have no more need to . . . to tear me to pieces, as you put it. I think that all that destructive anger has finally gone. Like she said, she's flown out of the cage.'

He said, 'I hope so,' but looked unconvinced. 'I need a drink.'

I smiled and joined him, but I discovered, as we later ate companionably together, that even though his daughter might no longer despite or torment me, what I perversely felt wasn't relief, but loss.

CHAPTER TEN

Leaving Aynsford early I drove back to London on Thursday morning and left the car, as I normally did, in a large public underground car park near Pont Square. From there I walked to the laundry where I usually took my shirts and waited while they fed my strip of rag from Northampton twice through the dry-cleaning cycle.

What emerged was a stringy looking object, basically light turquoise in colour, with a non-geometric pattern on it of green, brown and salmon pink. There were also black irregular stains that had stayed obstinately in place.

I persuaded the cleaners to iron it, with the only result that I had a flat strip instead of a wrinkled one.

'What if I wash it with detergent and water?' I asked the burly half-interested dry cleaner.

'You couldn't exactly *harm* it,' he said sarcastically.

So I washed it and ironed it and ended as before: turquoise strip, wandering indeterminate pattern, stubborn black stain.

With the help of Yellow Pages I visited the wholesale showrooms of a well-known fabric designer. An infinitely polite old man there explained that my fabric pattern was *woven*, while theirs – the wholesaler's – was *printed*. Different market, he said. The wholesaler aimed at the upper end of the middle-class market. I, he said, needed to consult an interior decorator, and with kindness he wrote for me a short list of firms.

The first two saw no profit in answering questions. At the third address I happened on an underworked twenty-year-old who ran pale long fingers through clean shoulder-length curls while he looked with interest at my offering. He pulled out a turquoise thread and held it up to the light.

'This is silk,' he said.

'Real silk?'

'No possible doubt. This was expensive fabric. The pattern is woven in. See.' He turned the piece over to show me the back. 'This is remarkable. Where did you get it? It looks like a very old lampas. Beautiful. The colours are organic, not mineral.'

I looked at his obvious youth and asked if he could perhaps seek a second opinion.

'Because I'm straight out of design school?' he guessed without umbrage. 'But I studied *fabrics*. That's why they took me on here. I *know* them. The designers don't weave them, they use them.'

'Then tell me what I've got.'

He fingered the turquoise strip and held it to his lips

and his cheek and seemed to commune with it as if it were a crystal ball.

'It's a modern copy,' he said. 'It's very skilfully done. It is lampas, woven on a Jacquard loom. There isn't enough of it to be sure, but I think it's a copy of a silk hanging made by Philippe de Lasalle in about 1760. But the original hadn't a blue-green background, it was cream with this design of ropes and leaves in greens and red and gold.'

I was impressed. 'Are you sure?'

'I've just spent three years learning this sort of thing.'

'Well, who makes it now? Do I have to go to France?'

'You could try one or two English firms but, you know what—'

He was brusquely interrupted by a severe-looking woman in a black dress and huge Aztec-type necklace who swept in and came to rest by the counter on which lay the unprepossessing rag.

'What are you doing?' she asked. 'I asked you to catalogue the new shipment of *passementerie*.'

'Yes, Mrs Lane.'

'Then please get on with it. Run along now.'

'Yes, Mrs Lane.'

'Do you want help?' she asked me briskly.

'Only the names of some weavers.'

On his way to the *passementerie*, my source of knowledge spoke briefly over his shoulder. 'It looks like a solitary weaver, not a firm. Try Saul Marcus.'

'Where?' I called.

'London.'

'Thanks.'

He went out of sight. Under Mrs Lane's inhospitable gaze I picked up my rag, smiled placatingly and departed.

I found Saul Marcus first in the telephone directory and then in white-bearded person in an airy artist's studio near Chiswick in west London where he created fabric patterns.

He looked with interest at my rag but shook his head.

I urged him to search the far universe.

'It might be Patricia Huxford's work,' he said at length, dubiously. 'You could try her. She does – or did – work like this sometimes. I don't know of anyone else.'

'Where would I find her?'

'Surrey. Sussex. Somewhere like that.'

'Thank you very much.'

Returning to Pont Square I looked for Patricia Huxford in every phone book I possessed for Surrey and Sussex and, for good measure, the bordering southern counties of Hampshire and Kent. Of the few Huxfords listed, none turned out to be Patricia, a weaver.

I really *needed* an assistant, I thought, saying good-bye to Mrs Paul Huxford, wife of a double-glazing salesman. This sort of search could take hours. Damn Chico, and his dolly-bird protective missus.

With no easy success from the directories I started on directory enquiries, the central computerised number-finder. As always, to get a number one had to give an address, but the computer system contemptuously spat out Patricia Huxford, Surrey, as being altogether too vague.

I tried Patricia Huxford, Guildford (Guildford being Surrey's county town) but learned only of the two listed P. Huxfords that I'd already tried. Kingston, Surrey: same lack of results. I systematically tried all the other main areas: Sutton, Epsom, Leatherhead, Dorking . . . Surrey might be a small county in square-mile size, but large in population. I drew a uniform blank.

Huxfords were fortunately rare. A good job she wasn't called Smith.

Sussex, then. There was East Sussex (county town Lewes) and West Sussex (Chichester). I flipped a mental coin and chose Chichester, and could hardly believe my lucky ears.

An impersonal voice told me that the number of Patricia Huxford was ex-directory and could only be accessed by the police, in an emergency. It was not even in the C.O. grade one class of ex-directory, where one could sweet-talk the operator into phoning the number on one's behalf (C.O. stood for Calls Offered). Patricia Huxford valued absolute grade two privacy and couldn't be reached that way.

In the highest, third grade, category, there were the numbers that weren't on any list at all, that the exchanges and operators might not know even existed; numbers for government affairs, the Royal Family and spies.

I yawned, stretched and ate cornflakes for lunch.

While I was still unenthusiastically thinking of driving to Chichester, roughly seventy more miles of armache, Charles phoned from Aynsford.

'So glad to catch you in,' he said. 'I've been talking to Thomas Ullaston, I thought you'd like to know.'

'Yes,' I agreed with interest. 'What did he say?'

'You know, of course, that he's no longer Senior Steward of the Jockey Club? His term of office ended.'

'Yes, I know.'

I also regretted it. The new Senior Steward was apt to think me a light-weight nuisance. I supposed he had a point, but it never helped to be discounted by the top man if I asked for anything at all from the department heads in current power. No one was any longer thanking me for ridding them of their villain: according to them, the whole embarrassing incident was best forgotten, and with that I agreed, but I wouldn't have minded residual warmth.

'Thomas was dumbfounded by your question,' Charles said. 'He protested that he'd meant you no harm.'

'Ah!' I said.

'Yes. He didn't deny that he'd told someone about that morning, but he assured me that it had been only *one* person, that that person was someone of utterly good standing, a man of the utmost probity. I asked if it was Archibald Kirk, and he *gasped*, Sid. He said it was early in the summer when Archie Kirk sought him out to ask about you. Archie Kirk told him he'd heard you were a good investigator and he wanted to know *how* good. It seems Archie Kirk's branch of the Civil Service occasionally likes to employ independent investigators quietly, but that it's hard to find good ones they can trust. Thomas Ullaston told him to trust *you*. Archie Kirk apparently asked more and more questions, until Thomas found himself telling about that chain and those awful marks . . . I mean, sorry, Sid.'

'Yeah,' I said, 'go on.'

'Thomas told Archie Kirk that with your jockey constitution and physical resilience – he said physical resilience, Thomas did, so that's exactly where Kirk got that phrase from – with your natural inborn physical resilience you'd shaken off the whole thing as if it had never happened.'

'Yes,' I said, which wasn't entirely true. One couldn't ever forget. One could, however, ignore. And it was odd, I thought, that I never had nightmares about whippy chains.

Charles chuckled. 'Thomas said he wouldn't want young master Halley on his tail if he'd been a crook.'

Young master Halley found himself pleased.

Charles asked, 'Is there anything else I can do for you, Sid?'

'You've been great.'

'Be careful.'

I smiled as I assured him I would. Be careful was hopeless advice to a jockey, and at heart I was as much out to win as ever.

On my way to the car I bought some robust adhesive bandage and, with my right forearm firmly strapped and a sufficient application of ibuprofen, drove to Chichester in West Sussex, about seven miles inland from the coast.

It was a fine spirits-lifting afternoon. My milk-coffee Mercedes swooped over the rolling South Downs and sped the last flat mile to the cathedral city of Chichester, wheels satisfyingly fast but still not as fulfilling as a horse.

I sought out the public library and asked to see the electoral roll.

There was masses of it: all the names and addresses of registered voters in the county, divided into electoral districts.

Where was Chico, blast him?

Resigned to a long search that could take two or three hours, I found Patricia Huxford within a short fifteen minutes. A record. I hated electoral rolls: the small print made me squint.

Huxford, Patricia Helen, Bravo House, Lowell.

Hallelujah.

I followed my road map, and asked for directions in the village of Lowell, and found Bravo House, a small converted church with a herd of cars and vans outside.

It didn't look like the reclusive lair of an ex-directory hermit.

As people seemed to be walking in and out of the high heavy open west door, I walked in too. I had arrived, it was soon clear, towards the end of a photographic session for a glossy magazine.

I said to a young woman hugging a clipboard, 'Patricia Huxford?'

The young woman gave me a radiant smile. 'Isn't she *wonderful*?' she said.

I followed the direction of her gaze. A small woman in an astonishing dress was descending from a sort of throne that had been built on a platform situated where the old transepts crossed the nave. There were bright theatrical spotlights that began to be switched off, and there were photographers unscrewing and dismantling and wrapping cables into hanks. There were effusive thanks in the air and satisfied excitement and the overall glow of a job done well.

I waited, looking about me, discovering the changes from church to modern house. The window glass, high up, was clear, not coloured. The stone-flagged nave had rugs, no pews, comfortable modern sofas pushed back against the wall to accommodate the crowd, and a large-screen television set.

A white-painted partition behind the throne platform cut off the view of what had been the altar area, but nothing had been done to spoil the sweep of the vaulted ceiling, built with soaring stone arches to the glory of God.

One would have to have a very secure personality, I thought, to choose to live in that place.

The media flock drifted down the nave and left with undiminished goodwill. Patricia Huxford waved to them and closed her heavy door and, turning, was surprised to find me still inside.

'So sorry,' she said, and began to open the door again.

'I'm not with the photographers,' I said. 'I came to ask you about something else.'

'I'm tired,' she said. 'I must ask you to go.'

'You look beautiful,' I told her, 'and it will only take a minute.' I brought my scrap of rag out and showed it to her. 'If you are Patricia Huxford, did you weave this?'

'Trish,' she said absently. 'I'm called Trish.'

She looked at the strip of silk and then at my face.

'What's your name?' she asked.

'John.'

'John what?'

'John Sidney.'

John Sidney were my real two first names, the ones my young mother had habitually used. 'John Sidney, give us a kiss.' 'John Sidney, wash your face.' 'John Sidney, have you been fighting again?'

I often used John Sidney in my job: whenever, in fact, I didn't want to be known to be Sid Halley. After the past months of all-too-public drubbing I wasn't sure that Sid Halley would get me anything anywhere but a swift heave-ho.

Trish Huxford, somewhere, I would have guessed, in the middle to late forties, was pretty, blonde (natural?), small-framed and cheerful. Bright observant eyes looked over my grey business suit, white shirt, unobtrusive tie, brown shoes, dark hair, dark eyes, unthreatening manner; my usual working confidence-inspiring exterior.

She was still on a high from the photo session. She needed someone to help her unwind, and I looked – and was – safe. Thankfully I saw her relax.

The amazing dress she had worn for the photographs was utterly simple in cut, hanging heavy and straight from her shoulders, floor length and sleeveless with a soft ruffled frill round her neck. It was the cloth of the dress that staggered: it was blue and red and silver and gold, and it *shimmered*.

'Did you weave your dress?' I asked.

'Of course.'

'I've never seen anything like it.'

'No, you wouldn't, not nowadays. Can I do anything for you? Where did you come from?'

'London. Saul Marcus suggested you might know who wove my strip of silk.'

'Saul! How is he?'

'He has a white beard,' I said. 'He seemed fine.'

'I haven't seen him for years. Will you make me some tea? I don't want marks on this dress.'

I smiled. 'I'm quite good at tea.'

She led the way past the throne and round the white-painted screen. There were choir stalls beyond, old and untouched, and an altar table covered by a cloth that brought me to a halt. It was of a brilliant royal blue with shining gold Greek motifs woven into its deep hem. On the table, in the place of religious altar furniture, stood an antique spinning wheel, good enough for Sleeping Beauty. Above the table, arched clear glass windows rose to the roof.

'This way,' Patricia Huxford commanded, and, leading me past the choir stalls, turned abruptly through a narrow doorway which opened onto what could only probably have been a vestry and was now a small modern kitchen with a bathroom beside it.

'My bed is in the south transept,' she told me, 'and my looms are in the north. You might expect us to be going to drink China tea with lemon out of a silver teapot, but in fact I don't have enough time for that sort of thing, so the tea bags and mugs are on that shelf.'

I half filled her electric kettle and plugged it in, and she spent the time walking around watching the miraculous colours move and mingle in her dress.

Intrigued, waiting for the water to boil, I asked, 'What is it made of?'

'What do you think?'

'Er, it looks like . . . well . . . gold.'

She laughed. 'Quite right. Gold, silver thread, and silk.'

I rather clumsily filled the mugs.

'Milk?' she suggested.

'No, thank you.'

'That's lucky. The crowd that's just left finished it off.' She gave me a brilliant smile, picked up a mug by its handle and returned to the throne, where she sat neatly on the vast red velvet chair and rested a thin arm delicately along gilt carving. The dress fell into sculptured folds over her slender thighs.

'The photographs,' she said, 'are for a magazine about a festival of the arts that Chichester is staging all next summer.'

I stood before her like some mediaeval page: stood chiefly because there was no chair nearby to sit on.

'I suppose,' she said, 'that you think me madly eccentric?'

'Not madly.'

She grinned happily. 'Normally I wear jeans and an old smock.' She drank some tea. 'Usually I work. Today is play-acting.'

'And magnificent.'

She nodded. 'No one, these days, makes cloth of gold.'

'The Field of the Cloth of Gold,' I exclaimed.

'That's right. What do you know of it?'

'Only that phrase.'

'The field was the meeting place at Guines, France,

256

in June 1520, of Henry VIII of England and Francis I of France. They were supposed to be making peace between England and France but they hated each other and tried to outdo each other in splendour. So all their courtiers wore cloth woven out of gold and they gave each other gifts you'd never see today. And I thought it would be historic to weave some cloth of gold for the festival . . . so I did. And this dress weighs a ton, I may tell you. Today is the only time I've worn it and I can't bear to take it off.'

'It's breathtaking,' I said.

She poured out her knowledge. 'In 1476 the Duke of Burgundy left behind a hundred and sixty gold cloths when he fled from battle against the Swiss. You make gold cloth – like I made this – by supporting the soft gold on threads of silk, and you can recover the gold by burning the cloth. So when I was making this dress, that's what I did with the pieces I cut out to make the neck and armholes. I burnt them and collected the melted gold.'

'Beautiful.'

'You know something?' she said. 'You're the only person who's seen this dress who hasn't asked how much it cost.'

'I did wonder.'

'And I'm not telling. Give me your strip of silk.'

I took her empty mug and tucked it under my left arm, and in my right hand held out the rag, which she took; and I found her looking with concentration at my left hand. She raised her eyes to meet my gaze.

'Is it . . .?' she said.

'Worth its weight in gold,' I said flippantly. 'Yes.'

I carried the mugs back to the kitchen and returned to find her standing and smoothing her fingers over the piece of rag.

'An interior decorator,' I said, 'told me it was probably a modern copy of a hanging made in 1760 by . . . um . . . I think Philippe de Lasalle.'

'How clever. Yes, it is. I made quite a lot of it at one time.' She paused, then said abruptly, 'Come along,' and dived off again, leaving me to follow.

We went this time through a door in another white-painted partition and found ourselves in the north transept, her workroom.

There were three looms of varying construction, all bearing work in progress. There was also a business section with filing cabinets and a good deal of office paraphernalia, and another area devoted to measuring, cutting and packing.

'I make fabrics you can't buy anywhere else,' she said. 'Most of it goes to the Middle East.' She walked towards the largest of the three looms, a monster that rose in steps to double our height.

'This is a Jacquard loom,' she said. 'I made your sample on this.'

'I was told this piece was . . . a lampas? What's a lampas?'

She nodded. 'A lampas is a compound weave with extra warps and wefts which put patterns and colours on the face of the fabric only, and are tucked into the back.' She showed me how the design of ropes and branches of leaves gleamed on one side of the turquoise silk but hardly showed on the reverse. 'It takes ages to set up,' she said. 'Nowadays almost no one outside the Middle East thinks the beauty is worth the expense, but once I used to sell quite a lot of it to castles and great houses in England, and all sorts of private people. I only make it to order.'

I said neutrally, 'Would you know who you made this piece for?'

'My dear man. No, I can't remember. But I probably still have the records. Why do you want to know? Is it important?'

'I don't know if it is important. I was given the strip and asked to find its origin.'

She shrugged. 'Let's find it then. You never know, I might get an order for some more.'

She opened cupboard doors to reveal many ranks of box files, and ran her fingers along the labels on the spines until she came to one that her expression announced as possible. She lifted the box file from the shelf and opened it on a table.

Inside were stiff pages with samples of fabric stapled to them, with full details of fibres, dates, amount made, names of purchasers and receipts.

She turned the stiff pages slowly, holding my strip

in one hand for comparison. She came to several versions of the same design, but all in the wrong colour.

'That's it!' she exclaimed suddenly. 'That's the one. I see I wove it almost thirty years ago. How time flies. I was so young then. It was a hanging for a four-poster bed. I see I supplied it with gold tassels made of gimp.'

I asked without much expectation, 'Who to?'

'It says here a Mrs Gordon Quint.'

I said, '. . . Er . . .' meaninglessly, my breath literally taken away.

Ginnie? *Ginnie* had owned the material.

'I don't remember her or anything about it,' Trish Huxford said. 'But all the colours match. It must have been this one commission. I don't think I made these colours for anyone else.' She looked at the black stains disfiguring the strip I'd brought. 'What a pity! I think of my fabrics as going on for ever. They could easily last two hundred years. I love the idea of leaving something beautiful in the world. I expect you think I'm a sentimental old bag.'

'I think you're splendid,' I said truthfully, and asked, 'Why are you ex-directory, with a business to run?'

She laughed. 'I hate being interrupted when I'm setting up a design. It takes vast concentration. I have a mobile phone for friends – I can switch it off – and I have an agent in the Middle East who gets orders for me. Why am I telling you all this?'

'I'm interested.'

She closed the file and put it back on the shelf, asking, 'Does Mrs Quint want some more fabric to replace this damaged bit, do you think?'

Mrs Quint was sixteen floors dead.

'I don't know,' I said.

On the drive back to London I pulled off the road to phone Davis Tatum at the number he'd given me, his home.

He was in and, it seemed, glad to hear from me, wanting to know what I'd done for him so far.

'Tomorrow,' I said, 'I'll give Topline Foods a visit. Who did you get Owen Yorkshire's name from?'

He said, stalling, 'I beg your pardon?'

'Davis,' I said mildly, 'you want me to take a look at Owen Yorkshire and his company, so why? Why *him*?'

'I can't tell you.'

'Do you mean you promised not to, or you don't know?'

'I mean . . . just go and take a look.'

I said, 'Sir Thomas Ullaston, Senior Steward last year of the Jockey Club, told Archie Kirk about that little matter of the chains, and Archie Kirk told *you*. So did the name Owen Yorkshire come to you from Archie Kirk?'

'Hell,' he said.

'I like to know what I'm getting into.'

After a pause he said, 'Owen Yorkshire has been seen twice in the boardroom of *The Pump*. We don't know why.'

'Thank you,' I said.

'Is that enough?'

'To be going on with. Oh, and my mobile phone is now safe. No more leaks. See you later.'

I drove on to London, parked in the underground garage and walked along the alleyway between tall houses that led into the opposite side of the square from my flat.

I was going quietly and cautiously in any case, and came to a dead stop when I saw that the street light almost directly outside my window was not lit.

Boys sometimes threw stones at it to break the glass. Normally its darkness wouldn't have sent shudders up my spine and made my right arm remember Gordon Quint from fingers to neck. Normally I might have crossed the square figuratively whistling while intending to phone in the morning to get the light fixed.

Things were not normal.

There were two locked gates into the central garden, one opposite the path I was on, and one on the far side, opposite my house. Standing in shadow I sorted out the resident-allocated garden key, went quietly across the circling roadway and unlocked the near gate.

Nothing moved. I eased the gate open, slid through, and closed it behind me. No squeaks. I moved slowly from patch to patch of shaded cover, the half-lit tree branches moving in a light breeze, yellow leaves drifting down like ghosts.

Near the far side I stopped and waited.

There could be no one there. I was foolishly afraid over nothing.

The street light was out.

It had been out at other times . . .

I stood with my back to a tree, waiting for alarm to subside to the point where I would unlock the second gate and cross the road to my front steps. The sounds of the city were distant. No cars drove into the cul-de-sac square.

I couldn't stand there all night, I thought . . . *and then I saw him.*

He was in a car parked by one of the few meters. His head – unmistakably Gordon Quint's head – moved behind the window. He was looking straight ahead, waiting for me to arrive by road or pavement.

I stood immobile as if stuck to the tree. It had to be obsession with him, I thought. The burning fury of Monday had settled down not into grief but revenge. I hadn't been in my flat for about thirty hours. How long had he been sitting there waiting? I'd had a villain wait almost a week for me once, before I'd walked unsuspectingly into his trap.

Obsession – fixation – was the most frightening of enemies and the hardest to escape.

I retreated, frankly scared, expecting him to see my movement, but he hadn't thought of an approach by garden. From tree to tree, round the patches of open grass, I regained the far gate, eased through it, crossed the road and drifted up the alleyway, cravenly expecting a bellow and a chase and, as he was a farmer, perhaps a shotgun.

Nothing happened. My shoes, soled and heeled for silence, made no sound. I walked back to my underground car and sat in it, not exactly trembling but nonetheless stirred up. So much, I thought, for Tatum's myth of a clever, unafraid investigator.

I kept always in the car an overnight bag containing the personality-change clothes I'd got Jonathan to wear; dark two-piece tracksuit (trousers and zip-up jacket) navy blue trainers, and a baseball cap. The bag also contained a long-sleeved open-necked shirt, two or three charged-up batteries for my arm, and a battery charger, to make sure. Habitually round my waist I wore a belt with a zipped pocket big enough for a credit card and money.

I had no weapons nor defences like mace. In America I might have carried both.

I sat in the car considering the matter of distance and ulnas. It was well over two hundred miles from my London home to Liverpool, city of my birth. Frodsham, the base of Topline Foods, wasn't quite as far as Liverpool, but still over two hundred miles. I had already, that day, steered a hundred and fifty – Chichester and back. I'd never missed Chico so much.

I considered trains. Too inflexible. Airline? Ditto.

TeleDrive? I lingered over the comfort of TeleDrive but decided against, and resignedly set off northwards.

It was an easy drive normally; a journey on wide fast motorways taking at most three hours. I drove for only one hour, then stopped at a motel to eat and sleep, and at seven o'clock in the morning wheeled on again, trying to ignore both the obstinately slow-mending fracture and India Cathcart's column that I'd bought from the motel's news stand.

Friday mornings had been a trial since June. Page fifteen in *The Pump* – trial by the long knives of journalism, the blades that ripped the gut.

She hadn't mentioned at all seeing Tatum and me in the Le Meridien bar. Perhaps she'd taken my advice and pretended we hadn't been there. What her column said about me was mostly factually true but spitefully wrong. I wondered how she could do it? Had she no sense of humanity?

Most of her page concerned yet another politician caught with his trousers at half-mast, but the far-right column said:

Sid Halley, illegitimate by-blow of a nineteen-year-old window cleaner and a packer in a biscuit factory, ran amok as a brat in the slums of Liverpool. Home was a roach-infested council flat. Nothing wrong with that! But this same Sid Halley now puts on airs of middle-class gentility. A flat in Chelsea? Sheraton furniture? Posh accent? Go back to your roots, lad.

265

No wonder Ellis Quint thinks you funny. Funny pathetic!

The slum background clearly explains the Halley envy. Halley's chip on the shoulder grows more obvious every day. Now we know why!

The Halley polish is all a sham, just like his pathetic left hand.

Christ, I thought, how much more? Why did it so bloody *hurt*?

My father had been killed in a fall eight months before my birth and a few days before he was due to marry my eighteen-year-old mother. She'd done her best as a single parent in hopeless surroundings. 'Give us a kiss, John Sidney . . .'

I hadn't ever run amok. I'd been a quiet child, mostly. 'Have you been fighting again, John Sidney . . .?' She hadn't liked me fighting, though one had to sometimes, or be bullied.

And when she knew she was dying she'd taken me to Newmarket, because I'd been short for my age, and had left me with the king of trainers to be made into a jockey, as I'd always wanted.

I couldn't possibly go back to Liverpool 'roots'. I had no sense of ever having grown any there.

I had never envied Ellis Quint. I'd always liked him. I'd been a better jockey than he, and we'd both known it. If anything, the envy had been the other way round. But it was useless to protest, as it had been all along.

Protests were used regularly to prove *The Pump*'s theories of my pitiable inadequacy.

My mobile phone buzzed. I answered it.

'Kevin Mills,' a familiar voice said. 'Where are you? I tried your flat. Have you seen today's *Pump* yet?'

'Yes.'

'India didn't write it,' he said. 'I gave her the info, but she wouldn't use it. She filled that space with some parts on sexual stress and her editor rubbed them out.'

Half of my muscles unknotted, and I hadn't realised they'd been tense. I forced unconcern into my voice even as I thought of hundreds of thousands of readers sniggering about me over their breakfast toast.

'Then you wrote it yourself,' I said. 'So who's a shit now? You're the only person on *The Pump* who's seen my Sheraton desk.'

'Blast you. Where are you?'

'Going back to Liverpool. Where else?'

'Sid, look, I'm sorry.'

'Policy?'

He didn't answer.

I asked, 'Why did you phone to tell me India didn't write today's bit of demolition?'

'I'm getting soft.'

'No one's listening to this phone any more. You can say what you like.'

'Jeez.' He laughed. 'That didn't take you long.' He paused. 'You might not believe it, but most of us on

The Pump don't any more like what we've been doing to you.'

'Rise up and rebel,' I suggested dryly.

'We have to eat. And you're a tough bugger. You can take it.'

You just try it, I thought.

'Listen,' he said, 'the paper's received a lot of letters from readers complaining that we're not giving you a fair deal.'

'How many is a lot?'

'Two hundred or so. Believe me, that's a *lot*. But we're not allowed to print any.'

I said with interest, 'Who says so?'

'That's just it. The Ed, Godbar himself, says so, and he doesn't like it either, but the policy is coming from the very top.'

'Tilepit?'

'Are you *sure* this phone's not bugged?'

'You're safe.'

'You've had a bloody raw mauling, and you don't deserve it. I know that. We all know it. I'm sorry for my part in it. I'm sorry I wrote today's venom, especially that bit about your hand. Yes, it's Tilepit. The proprietor himself.'

'Well . . . thanks.'

He said, 'Did Ellis Quint *really* cut off those feet?'

I smiled ruefully. 'The jury will decide.'

'Sid, look here,' he protested, 'you *owe* me!'

'Life's a bugger,' I said.

268

CHAPTER ELEVEN

Nine o'clock Friday morning I drove into the town of Frodsham and asked for Topline Foods.

Not far from the river, I was told. Near the river; the Mersey.

The historic docks of Liverpool's Mersey waterfront had long been silent, the armies of tall cranes dismantled, the warehouses converted or pulled down. Part of the city's heart has stopped beating. There had been by-pass surgery of sorts, but past muscle would never return. The city had a vast red-brick cathedral, but faith, as in much of Britain, had dimmed.

For years I'd been to Liverpool only to ride there on Aintree racecourse. The road I'd once lived in lay somewhere under a hyper-market. Liverpool was a place, but not home.

At Frodsham there was a 'Mersey View' vantage point with, away to the distant north, some still-working docks at Runcorn on the Manchester Ship Canal. One of those docks (I'd been told earlier by telephone from the dockmaster's office) was occupied by Topline

Foods. A ship lying alongside bearing the flag and insignia of Canada had been unloading Topline grain.

I'd stopped the car from where I could see the sweep of river with the seagulls swooping and the stiff breeze tautening flags at the horizontal. I stood in the cold open air, leaning on the car, smelling the salt and the mud, and hearing the drone of traffic on the road below.

Were these roots? I'd always loved wide skies, but it was the wide sky of Newmarket Heath that I thought of as home. When I'd been a boy there'd been no wide skies, only narrow streets, the walk to school, and rain. 'John Sidney, wash your face. Give us a kiss.'

The day after my mother died I'd ridden my first winner, and that evening I'd got drunk for the first and only time until the arrest of Ellis Quint.

Soberly, realistically, in the Mersey wind I looked at the man I had become: a jumble of self-doubt, ability, fear and difficult pride. I had grown as I was from the inside out. Liverpool and Newmarket weren't to blame.

Stirring and getting back into the car I wondered where to find all those tungsten nerves I was supposed to have.

I didn't know what I was getting into. I could still at that point retreat and leave the field to Ellis. I could – and I couldn't. I would have myself to live with, if I did.

I'd better simply get on with it, I thought.

I drove down from the vantage point, located the Topline Foods factory, and passed through its twelve foot high but hospitably open wire-mesh gates. There was a guard in a gatehouse who paid me no attention.

Inside there were many cars tidily parked in ranks. I added myself to the end of one row and decided on a clothing compromise of suit trousers, zipped up tracksuit top, white shirt, no tie, ordinary shoes. I neatly combed my hair forward into a young-looking style and looked no threat to anybody.

The factory, built round three sides of a big central area, consisted of loading bays, a vast main building and a new-looking office block. Loading and unloading took place under cover, with articulated lorries backing into the bays. In the one bay I could see into clearly, the cab section had been disconnected and removed; heavy sacks that looked as if they might contain grain were being unloaded from a long container by two large men who slung the sacks onto a moving conveyor belt of rollers.

The big building had a row of windows high up: there was no chance of looking in from outside.

I ambled across to the office building and shouldered open a heavy glass door that led into a large but mostly bare entrance hall, and found there the reason for the unguarded front gates. The security arrangements were all inside.

Behind a desk sat a purposeful-looking middle-aged woman in a green jumper. Flanking her were two men in navy blue security-guard suits with Topline Foods insignia on their breast pockets.

'Name, please,' said the green jumper. 'State your business. All parcels, carriers and handbags must be left here at the desk.'

She had a distinct Liverpool accent. With the same inflection in my own voice, I told her that, as she could see, I had no bag, carrier or handbag with me.

She took the accent for granted and unsmilingly asked again for my name.

'John Sidney.'

'Business?'

'Well,' I said as if perplexed by the reception I was getting. 'I was asked to come here to see if you made some horse-nuts.' I paused. 'Like,' I lamely finished, dredging up the idiom.

'Of course we make horse-nuts. It's our business.'

'Yes,' I told her earnestly, 'but this farmer, like, he asked me to come in, as I was passing this way, to see if it was you that made some horse-nuts that someone had given him, that were very good for his young horse, like, but he was given them loose and not in a bag and all he has is a list of what's in the nuts and he wanted to know if you made them, see?' I half pulled a sheet of paper from an inside pocket and pushed it back.

She was bored by the rigmarole.

'If I could just *talk* to someone,' I pleaded. 'See, I owe this farmer a favour and it wouldn't take no more than a minute, if I could talk to someone. Because this farmer, he'll be a big customer if these are the nuts he's looking for.'

She gave in, lifted a telephone, and repeated a short-ened version of my improbable tale.

She inspected me from head to foot. 'Couldn't hurt a fly,' she reported.

I kept the suitably feeble half-anxious smile in place.

She put down the receiver. 'Miss Rowse will be down to help you. Raise your hands.'

'Eh?'

'Raise your hands . . . please.'

Surprised, I did as I was told. One of the security guards patted me all over in the classic way of their job, body and legs. He missed the false hand and the cracked bone. 'Keys and mobile phone,' he reported. 'Clean.'

Green jumper wrote 'John Sidney' onto a clip-on identity card and I clipped it dutifully on.

'Wait by the lift,' she said.

I waited.

The doors finally parted to reveal a teenage girl with wispy fair hair who said she was Miss Rowse. 'Mr Sidney? This way, please.'

I stepped into the lift with her, and rode to the third floor.

She smiled with bright inexperienced encourage-ment and led me down a newly carpeted passage to an office conspicuously labelled 'Customer Relations' on its open door.

'Come in,' Miss Rowse said proudly. 'Please sit down.'

273

I sat in a Scandinavian-inspired chair of blond wood with arms, simple lines, blue cushioning and considerable comfort.

'I'm afraid I didn't really understand your problem,' Miss Rowse said trustingly. 'If you'll explain again, I can get the right person to talk to you.'

I looked round her pleasant office, which showed almost no sign of work in progress.

'Have you been here long?' I asked. (Guileless Liverpool accent, just like hers.) 'Nice office. They must think a lot of you here.'

She was pleased, but still honest. 'I'm new this week. I started on Monday – and you're my second enquiry.'

No wonder, I thought, that she'd let me in.

I said, 'Are all the offices as plush as this?'

'Yes,' she said enthusiastically. 'Mr Yorkshire, he likes things nice.'

'Is he the boss?'

'The managing director,' she nodded. The words sounded stiff and unfamiliar, as if she'd only newly learned them.

'Nice to work for, is he?' I suggested.

She confessed, 'I haven't met him yet. I know what he looks like, of course, but ... I'm new here, like I said.'

I smiled sympathetically and asked what Owen Yorkshire looked like.

She was happy to tell me. 'He's ever so *big*. He's got a big head and a lovely lot of hair, wavy like.'

'Moustache?' I suggested. 'Beard?'

'No,' she giggled. 'And he's not *old*. Not a grandad. Everyone gets out of his way.'

Do they indeed, I thought.

She went on, 'I mean, Mrs Dove, she's my boss really, she's the office manager, she says not to make him angry, whatever I do. She says just to do my job. She has a lovely office. It used to be Mr Yorkshire's own, she says.'

Miss Rowse, shaped like a woman, chattered like a child.

'Topline Foods must be doing all right to have rich new offices like these,' I said admiringly.

'They've got the TV cameras coming tomorrow to set up for Monday. They brought dozens of potted plants round this morning. Ever so keen on publicity, Mrs Dove says, Mr Yorkshire is.'

'The plants do make it nice and homey,' I said. 'Which TV company, do you know?'

She shook her head. 'All the Liverpool big noises are coming to a huge reception on Monday. The TV cameras are going all over the factory. Of course, although they're going to have all the machines running, they won't really make any nuts on Monday. It will all be pretend.'

'Why's that?'

'Security. They have to be security mad, Mrs Dove says. Mr Yorkshire worries about people putting things in the feed, she says.'

'What things?'

'I don't know. Nails and safety-pins and such. Mrs Dove says all the searching at the entrance is Mr York-shire's idea.'

'Very sensible,' I said.

An older and more cautious woman came into the office, revealing herself to be the fount of wisdom, Mrs Dove. Middle-aged and personally secure, I thought. Status, ability and experience all combining in priceless efficiency.

'Can I help you?' she said to me civilly, and to the girl, 'Marsha dear, I thought we'd agreed you would always come to me for advice.'

'Miss Rowse has been really helpful,' I said. 'She's going to find someone to answer my question. Perhaps you could, yourself?'

Mrs Dove (grey hair pinned high under a flat black bow, high heels, customer-relations neat satin shirt, cinched waist and black tights) listened with slowly glazing eyes to my expanding tale of the nutty farmer.

'You need our Willy Parrot,' she said when she could insert a comment. 'Come with me.'

I waggled conspiratorial fingers at Marsha Rowse and followed Mrs Dove's busy backview along the expensive passage with little partitioned but mostly empty offices on each side. She continued through a thick fire-door at the end, to emerge on a gallery round an atrium in the main factory building, where the nuts came from.

Rising from the ground, level almost to the gallery, were huge mixing vats, all with paddles circulating, activated from machinery stretching down from above. The sounds were an amalgam of whirr, rattle and slurp: the air bore fine particles of cereal dust and it looked like a brewery, I thought. It smelled rather the same also, but without the fermentation.

Mrs Dove passed me thankfully on to a man in brown overalls who inspected my dark clothes and asked if I wanted to be covered in fall-out.

'Not particularly.'

He raised patient eyebrows and gestured to me to follow him, which I did, to find myself on an iron staircase descending one floor, along another gallery and ending in a much-used battered little cubby-hole of an office, with a sliding glass door that he closed behind us.

I commented on the contrast from the office building.

'Fancy fiddle-faddle,' he said. 'That's for the cameras. This is where the work is done.'

'I can see that,' I told him admiringly.

'Now, lad,' he said, looking me up and down, unimpressed, 'what is it you want?'

He wasn't going to be taken in very far by the farmer twaddle. I explained in a shorter version and produced the folded paper bearing the analysis of the nuts from the Combe Bassett and the Land-Rover, and asked if it was a Topline formula.

He read the list that by then I knew by heart.

Wheat, oatfeed, ryegrass, straw, barley, maize,
molasses, salt, linseed.
Vitamins, selenium, copper, other substances and
probably the antioxidant Ethoxyquin.

'Where did you get this?' he asked.

'From a farmer, like I told you.'

'This list isn't complete,' he said.

'No . . . but is it enough?'

'It doesn't give percentages. I can't possibly match
it to any of our products.' He folded the paper and
gave it back. 'Your cubes might be our supplement
feed for horses out at grass. Do you know anything
about horses?'

'A little.'

'Then the more oats you give them, the more energy
they expend. Racehorses need more oats. I can't tell
you for sure if these cubes were for racehorses in training unless I know the proportion of oats.'

'They weren't racehorses in training.'

'Then your farmer friend couldn't do better than our
Sweetfield mix. They do contain everything on your
list.'

'Are other people's cubes much different?'

'There aren't very many manufacturers. We're perhaps fourth on the league table but after this advertise-

ment campaign we expect that to zoom up. The new management aims for the top.'

'But . . . um . . . do you have enough space?'

'Capacity?'

I nodded.

He smiled. 'Owen Yorkshire has plans. He talks to us man to man.' His face and voice were full of approval. 'He's brought the old place back to life.'

I said inoffensively, 'Mrs Dove seems in awe of his anger.'

Willy Parrott laughed and gave me a male chauvinist-type wink. 'He has a flaming temper, has our Owen Yorkshire. And the more a man for that.'

I looked vaguely at some charts taped to a wall. 'Where does he come from?' I asked.

'Haven't a clue,' Willy told me cheerfully. 'He knows bugger all about nutrition. He's a salesman, and *that's* what we needed. We have a couple of nerds in white coats working on what we put in all the vats.'

He was scornful of scientists as well as women. I turned back from the wall charts and thanked him for his time. Very interesting job, I told him. Obviously he ran the department that mattered most.

He took the compliment as his due and saved me the trouble of asking by offering to let me tag along with him while he went to his next task, which was to check a new shipment of wheat. I accepted with an enthusiasm that pleased him. A man good at his job often enjoyed an audience, and so did Willy Parrott.

He gave me a set of over-large brown overalls and told me to clip the identity card on the outside, like his own.

'Security is vital,' he said to me. 'Owen's stepped it all up. He lectures us on not letting strangers near the mixing vats. I can't let you any nearer than this. Our competitors wouldn't be above adding foreign substances that would put us out of business.'

'D'you mean it?' I said, looking avid.

'You have to be specially careful with horse feed,' he assured me, sliding open his door when I was ready. 'You can't mix cattle food in the same vats, for instance. You can put things in cattle feed that are prohibited for racehorses. You can get traces of prohibited substances in the horse-cubes just by using the same equipment, even if you think you've cleaned everything thoroughly.'

There had been a famous example in racing of a trainer getting into trouble by unknowingly giving his runners contaminated nuts.

'Fancy,' I said.

I thought I might have overdone the impressed look I gave him, but he accepted it easily.

'We do nothing else except horse-cubes here,' Willy said. 'Owen says when we expand we'll do cattle feed and chicken pellets, and all sorts of other muck, but I'll be staying here, Owen says, in charge of the equine branch.'

'A top job,' I said with admiration.

He nodded. 'The best.'

We walked along the gallery and came to another fire-door, which he lugged open.

'All these internal doors are locked at night now, and there's a watchman with a dog. Very thorough, is Owen.' He looked back to make sure I was following, then stopped at a place from which we could see bags marked with red maple leaves travelling upwards on an endless belt of bag-sized ledges, only to be tumbled off the top and be manhandled by two smoothly swinging muscular workers.

'I expect you saw those two security men in the entrance hall?' Willy Parrott said, the question of security not yet exhausted.

'They frisked me,' I grinned. 'Going a bit far, I thought.'

'They're Owen's private bodyguards,' Willy Parrott said with a mixture of awe and approval. 'They're real hard men from Liverpool. Owen says he needs them in case the competitors try to get rid of him the old-fashioned way.'

I frowned disbelievingly. 'Competitors don't kill people.'

'Owen says he's taking no risks because he definitely is trying to put other firms out of business, if you look at it that way.'

'So you think he's right to need bodyguards?'

Willy Parrott turned to me and said, 'It's not the

world I was brought up in, lad. But we have to live in this new one, Owen says.'

'I suppose so.'

'You won't get far with that attitude, lad.' He pointed to the rising bags. 'That's this year's wheat straight from the prairie. Only the best is good enough, Owen says, in trade wars.'

He led the way down some nearby concrete stairs and through another heavy door, and I realised we were on ground level just off the central atrium. With a smile of satisfaction he pushed through one more door and we found ourselves amid the vast mixing vats, pygmies surrounded by giants.

He enjoyed my expression.

'Awesome,' I said.

'You don't need to go back upstairs to get out,' he said. 'There's a door out to the yard just down here.'

I thanked him for his advice about the nuts for the farmer, and for showing me round. I'd been with him for half an hour and couldn't reasonably stretch it further, but while I was in mid-sentence he looked over my shoulder and his face changed completely from man-in-charge to subservient subject.

I turned to see what had caused this transformation and found it not to be a Royal Person but a large man in white overalls accompanied by several anxious blue-clad attendants who were practically walking backwards.

'Morning, Willy,' said the man in white. 'Everything going well?'

'Yes, Owen. Fine.'

'Good. Has the Canadian wheat come up from the docks?'

'They're unloading it now, Owen.'

'Good. We should have a talk about future plans. Come up to my new office at four this afternoon. You know where it is? Top floor, turn right from the lift, like my old office.'

'Yes, Owen.'

'Good.'

The eyes of the businessman glanced my way briefly and incuriously, and passed on. I was wearing brown overalls and an identity card, after all, and looked an employee. Not an employee of much worth, either, with my over-big overalls wrinkling around my ankles and drooping down my arms to the fingers. Willy didn't attempt to explain my presence, for which I was grateful. Willy was almost on his knees in reverence.

Owen Yorkshire was, without doubt, impressive. Easily over six foot tall, he was simply large, but not fat. There was a lot of heavy muscle in the shoulders, and a trim, sturdy belly. Luxuriant closely-waving hair spilled over the collar, with the beginnings of grey in the lacquered wings sweeping back from above his ears. It was a hairstyle that in its way made as emphatic a statement as Jonathan's. Owen Yorkshire intended not only to rule but to be remembered.

His accent was not quite Liverpool and not at all London, but powerful and positive. His voice was unmistakably an instrument of dominance. One could imagine that his rages might in fact shake the building. One could have sympathy with his yes-men.

Willy said, 'Yes, Owen,' several more times.

The man-to-man relationship that Willy Parrott prized so much extended, I thought, not much farther than the use of first names. True, Owen Yorkshire's manner to Willy was of the 'we're all in this together' type of management technique, and seemed to be drawing the best out of a good man; but I could imagine the boss also finding ways of getting rid of his Willy Parrott, if it pleased him, with sad shrugs and 'You know how it is these days, we no longer *need* a production manager just for horse-cubes; your job is computerised and phased out. Redundancy money? Of course. See my secretary. No hard feelings.'

I hoped it wouldn't happen to Willy.

Owen Yorkshire and his satellites swept onwards. Willy Parrott looked after him with pride tinged very faintly with anxiety.

'Do you work tomorrow?' I asked. 'Is the factory open on Saturdays?'

He reluctantly removed his gaze from the Yorkshire backview and began to think I'd been there too long.

'We're opening on Saturdays from next week,' he said. 'Tomorrow they're making more advertising films. There will be cameras all over the place, and on

Monday too. We won't get anything useful done until Tuesday.' He was full of disapproval, but he would repress all that, it was clear, for man-to-man Owen. 'Off you go then, lad. Go back to the entrance and leave the overalls and identity tag there.'

I thanked him again and this time went out into the central yard which, since my own arrival, had become clogged with vans and truckloads of television and advertising people. The television contingent were from Liverpool. The advertisement makers, according to the identification on their vans, were from Intramind Imaging (Manchester) Ltd.

One of the Intramind drivers, in the unthinking way of his kind, had braked and parked at an angle to all the other vehicles. I walked across to where he still sat in his cab and asked him to straighten up his van.

'Who says so?' he demanded belligerently.

'I just work here,' I said, still in the brown overalls that, in spite of Willy Parrott's instructions, I was not going to return. 'I was sent out to ask you. Big artics have to get in here.' I pointed to the unloading bays.

The driver grunted, started his engine, straightened his vehicle, switched off and jumped down to the ground beside me.

'Will that do?' he asked sarcastically.

'You must have an exciting job,' I said enviously. 'Do you see all those film stars?'

He sneered. 'We make *advertising* films, mate. Sure,

285

sometimes we get big names, but mostly they're endorsing things.'

'What sort of things?'

'Sports gear, often. Shoes, golf clubs.'

'And horse-cubes?'

He had time to waste while others unloaded equipment. He didn't mind a bit of showing off.

He said, 'They've got a lot of top jockeys lined up to endorse the horse-nuts.'

'Have they?' I asked interestedly. 'Why not trainers?'

'It's the jockeys the public know by their faces. That's what I'm told. I'm a football man myself.'

He didn't, I was grateful to observe, even begin to recognise my own face, that in years gone by had fairly taken up space on the nation's sports pages.

Someone in the team called him away and I walked off, sliding into my own car and making an uneventful exit through the tall unchecked outward gates. Odd, I thought, that the security-paranoid Owen Yorkshire didn't have a gate bristling with electronic barriers and ominous name-gatherers; and the only reason I could think of for such laxity was that he didn't always *want* name-takers to record everyone's visits.

Blind-eye country, I thought, like the private backstairs of the great before the India Cathcarts of the world floodlit the secretive comings and goings, and rewarded promiscuity with taint.

Perhaps Owen Yorkshire's backstairs was the lift to

the fifth floor. Perhaps Mrs Green Jumper and the bouncers in blue knew who to admit without searching.

Perhaps this, perhaps that. I'd seen the general layout and been near the power running the business, but basically I'd done little there but reconnoitre.

I stopped in a public car park, took off the brown overalls and decided to go to Manchester.

The journey was quite short, but it took me almost as long again to find Intramind Imaging (Manchester) Ltd which, although in a back street, proved to be a much bigger outfit than I'd pictured; I shed the tracksuit top and the Liverpool accent and approached the reception desk in suit, tie and business aura.

'I've come from Topline Foods,' I said. 'I'd like to talk to whoever is in charge of their account.'

Did I have an appointment?

No, it was a private matter.

If one pretended sufficient authority, I'd found doors got opened, and so it was at Intramind Imaging. A Mr Gross would see me. An electric door-latch buzzed and I walked from the entrance lobby into an inner hallway, where cream paint had been used sparingly and there was no carpet underfoot. Ostentation was out.

Mr Gross was 'third door on the left'. Mr Gross's door had his name and a message on it, 'Nick Gross. What the F do you want?'

Nick Gross looked me up and down. 'Who the hell

are *you*? You're not Topline Foods top brass, and you're over-dressed.'

He himself wore a black satin shirt, long hair and a gold earring. Forty-five disintegrating to fifty, I thought, and stuck in a time warp of departing youth. Forceful, though. Strong lines in his old-young face. Authority.

'You're making advertising films for Topline,' I said.

'So what? And if you're another of their whinging accountants sent to beg for better terms, the answer is up yours, mate. It isn't our fault you haven't been able to use those films you spent millions on. They're all brilliant stuff, the best. So you creep back to your Mr Owen effing Yorkshire and tell him there's no deal. Off you trot, then. If he wants his jockey series at the same price as before he has to send us a cheque every week. *Every week* or we yank the series, got it?'

I nodded.

Nick Gross said, 'And tell him not to forget that in ads the magic is the *cutting*, and the cutting comes *last*. No cheque, no cutting. No cutting, no magic. No magic, no message. No message, we might as well stop right now. Have you got it?'

I nodded again.

'Then you scurry right back to Topline and tell them no cheque, no cutting. And that means no campaign. Got it?'

'Yes.'

'Right. Bugger off.'

I meekly removed myself but, seeing no urgent

reason to leave altogether, I turned the wrong way out of his office and walked as if I belonged there down a passage between increasingly technical departments.

I came to an open door through which one could see a screen showing startlingly familiar pieces of an ad campaign currently collecting critical acclaim as well as phenomenally boosting sales. There were burst of pictures as short as three seconds followed by longer intervals of black. Three seconds of fast action. Ten of black.

I stopped, watching, and a man walked into my sight and saw me standing there.

'Yes?' he said. 'Do you want something?'

'Is that,' I said, nodding towards the screen, 'one of the mountain bike ads?'

'It will be when I cut it together.'

'Marvellous,' I said. I took half a step unthreateningly over his threshold. 'Can I watch you for a bit?'

'Who are you exactly?'

'From Topline Foods. I came to see Nick Gross.'

'Ah.' There was a world of comprehension in the monosyllable: comprehension that I immediately aimed to transfer from his brain to mine.

He was younger than Nick Gross and not so mock-rock-star in dress. His certainty shouted from the zany speed of his three-second flashes and the wit crackling in their juxtaposition: he had no need for earrings.

I said, quoting the bike campaign's slogan, 'Every kid under fifty wants a mountain bike for Christmas.'

He fiddled with reels of film and said cheerfully, 'There'll be hell to pay if they don't.'

'Did you work on the Topline ads?' I asked neutrally.

'No, thank Christ. A colleague did. Eight months of award-worthy brilliant work sitting idle in cans on the shelves. No prizes for us, and your top man's shitting himself, isn't he? All that cabbage spent and bugger all back. And all because some twisted little pipsqueak gets the star attraction arrested for something he didn't do.'

I held my breath, but he had no flicker of an idea what the pipsqueak looked like. I said I'd better be going and he nodded vaguely without looking up from his problems.

I persevered past his domain until I came to two big doors, one saying 'Sound Stage. Keep Out' and one, opening outwards with a push-bar, marked 'Backlot'. I pushed that door half open and saw outside in the open air a huge yellow crane dangling a red sports car by a rear axle. Film cameras and crews were busy round it. Work in progress.

I retreated. No one paid me any attention on the way out. This was not, after all, a bank vault, but a dream factory. No one could steal dreams.

The reception lobby, as I hadn't noticed on my way in, bore posters round the walls of past and current purse-openers, all prestigious prize-winning campaigns. Ad campaigns, I'd heard, were now considered an OK step on the career ladder for both directors and actors.

Sell cornflakes one day, play Hamlet the next. Intra-mind Imagining could speed you on your way.

I drove into the centre of Manchester and anony-mously booked into a spacious restful room in the Crown Plaza Hotel. Davis Tatum might have a fit over the expense but if necessary I would pay for it myself. I wanted a shower, room-service and cosseting, and hang the price.

I phoned Tatum's home number and got an answer-ing machine. I asked him to call back to my mobile number and repeated it, and then sat in an armchair watching racing on television – Flat racing at Ascot.

There was no sight of Ellis on the course. The com-mentator mentioned that his 'ludicrous' trial was due to resume in three days' time, on Monday. Sid Halley, he said, was sensibly keeping his head down as half Ellis's fan club was baying for his blood.

This little tit-bit came from a commentator who'd called me a wizard and a force for good not long ago. Times changed: did they ever. There were smiling close-ups of Ellis's face, and of mine, both helmetless but in racing colours, side by side. 'They used to be the closest of friends,' said the commentator sadly. 'Now they slash and gore each other like bulls.'

Sod him, I thought.

I also hoped that none of Mrs Green Jumper, Marsha Rowse, Mrs Dove, Willy Parrott, the Intramind van driver, Nick Gross and the film cutter had switched on to watch racing at Ascot. I didn't think Owen Yorkshire's sliding glance across my overalls would have left an imprint, but the others would remember me for a day or two. It was a familiar risk, sometimes lucky, sometimes not.

When the racing ended I phoned Intramind Imaging and asked a few general questions that I hadn't thought of in my brief career on the spot as a Topline Foods employee.

Were advertising campaigns originally recorded on film or on disks or on tape, I wanted to know, and could the public buy copies. I was answered helpfully: Intramind usually used film, especially for high-budget location-based ads and no, the public could *not* buy copies. The finished film would eventually be transferred onto Broadcast Quality video tape, known as BETACAM. These tapes then belonged to the clients, who paid television companies for air time. Intramind did not act as an agent.

'Thanks very much,' I said politely, grateful always for knowledge.

Davis Tatum phoned soon after.

'Sid,' he said, 'where are you?'

'Manchester, city of rain.'

It was sunny that day.

'Er . . .' Davis said. 'Any progress?'

'Some,' I said.

'And, er . . .' he hesitated again. 'Did you read India Cathcart this morning?'

'She didn't write that she'd seen us at Le Meridien,' I said.

'No. She took your excellent advice. But as to the rest . . .!'

I said, 'Kevin Mills phoned especially to tell me that she didn't write the rest. He did it himself. Policy. Pressure from above. Same old thing.'

'But wicked.'

'He apologised. Big advance.'

'You take it so lightly,' Davis said.

I didn't disillusion him. I said, 'Tomorrow evening – would you be able to go to Archie Kirk's house?'

'I should think so, if it's important. What time?'

'Could you arrange that with him? About six o'clock, I should think. I'll arrive there sometime myself. Don't know when.'

With a touch of complaint he said, 'It sounds a bit vague.'

I thought I'd better not tell him that with burglary, times tended to be approximate.

CHAPTER TWELVE

I phoned *The Pump*, asking for India Cathcart. Silly me.

Number one, she was never in the office on Fridays.

Number two, *The Pump* never gave private numbers to unknown callers.

'Tell her Sid Halley would like to talk to her,' I said, and gave the switchboard operator my mobile number, asking him to repeat it so I could make sure he had written it down right.

No promises, he said.

I sat for a good while thinking about what I'd seen and learned, and planning what I would do the next day. Such plans got altered by events as often as not, but I'd found that no plan at all invited nil results. If all else failed try Plan B. Plan B, in my battle strategy, was to escape with skin intact. Plan B had let me down a couple of times but disasters were like falls in racing; you never thought they'd happen until you were nose down to the turf.

I had some food sent up and thought some more, and at ten-fifteen my mobile buzzed.

'Sid?' India said nervously.

'Hello.'

'Don't say anything! I'll cry if you say anything.' After a pause she said, 'Sid! Are you there?'

'Yes. But I don't want you to cry so I'm not saying anything.'

'Oh, God.' It was half a choke, half a laugh. 'How can you be so . . . so *civilised*?'

'With enormous difficulty,' I said. 'Are you busy on Sunday evening? Your restaurant or mine?'

She said disbelievingly, 'Are you asking me out to dinner?'

'Well,' I said, 'it's not a proposal of marriage. And no knife through the ribs. Just food.'

'How can you *laugh*?'

'Why are you called India?' I asked.

'I was conceived there. What has that got to do with anything?'

'I just wondered,' I said.

'Are you *drunk*?'

'Unfortunately not. I'm sitting soberly in an armchair contemplating the state of the universe, which is C minus, or thereabouts.'

'Where? I mean, where is the armchair?'

'On the floor,' I said.

'You don't trust me!'

'No,' I sighed, 'I don't. But I do want to have dinner with you.'

'Sid,' she was almost pleading, 'be sensible.'

Rotten advice, I'd always thought. But then if I'd been sensible I would have two hands and fewer scars, and I reckoned one had to be *born* sensible, which didn't seem to have happened in my case.

I said, 'Your proprietor – Lord Tilepit – have you met him?'

'Yes.' She sounded a bit bewildered. 'He comes to the office party at Christmas. He shakes everyone's hand.'

'What's he like?'

'Do you mean to look at?'

'For a start.'

'He's fairly tall. Light-brown hair.'

'That's not much,' I said, when she stopped.

'He's not part of my day-to-day life.'

'Except that he burns saints,' I said.

A brief silence, then, 'Your restaurant, this time.'

I smiled. Her quick mind could reel in a tarpon where her red mouth couldn't. 'Does Lord Tilepit,' I asked, 'wear an obvious cloak of power? Are you aware of his power when you're in a room with him?'

'Actually . . . no.'

'Is anyone . . . *could* anyone be physically in awe of him?'

'No.' It was clear from her voice that she thought the idea laughable.

'So his leverage,' I said, 'is all economic?'

'I suppose so.'

'Is there anyone that *he* is in awe of?'

'I don't know. Why do you ask?'

'That man,' I said, 'has spent four months directing his newspaper to ... well ... ruin me. You must allow, I have an interest.'

'But you aren't ruined. You don't sound in the least ruined. And anyway, your ex-wife said it was impossible.'

'She said *what* was impossible?'

'To ... to ...'

'Say it.'

'To reduce you to rubble. To make you beg.'

She silenced me.

She said, 'Your ex-wife's still in love with you.'

'No, not any more.'

'I'm an expert on ex-wives,' India said. 'Wronged wives, dumped mistresses, women curdled with spite, women angling for money. Women wanting revenge, women breaking their hearts. I know the scenery. Your Jenny said she couldn't live in your purgatory, but when I suggested you were a selfish brute she defended you like a tigress.'

Oh *God*, I thought. After nearly six years apart the same old dagger could pierce us both.

'Sid?'

'Mm.'

'Do you still love *her*?'

I found a calm voice. 'We can't go back, and we don't want to,' I said. 'I regret a lot, but it's now finally over. She has a better husband, and she's happy.'

'I met her new man,' India said. 'He's sweet.'

'Yes.' I paused. 'What about your own ex?'

'I fell for his looks. It turned out he wanted an admiration machine in an apron. End of story.'

'Is his name Cathcart?'

'No,' she said. 'Patterson.'

Smiling to myself I said, 'Will you give me your phone number?'

She said, 'Yes,' and did so.

'Kensington Place restaurant. Eight o'clock.'

'I'll be there.'

When I was alone, which was usual nowadays, since Louise McInnes and I had parted, I took off my false arm at bedtime and replaced it after a shower in the morning. I couldn't wear it in showers, as water wrecked the works. Taking it off after a long day was often a pest, as it fitted tightly and tended to cling to my skin. Putting it on was a matter of talcum powder, getting the angle right and pushing hard.

The arm might be worth its weight in gold, as I'd told Trish Huxford, but even after three years, whatever lighthearted front I might now achieve in public, in private the management of amputation still took me a positive effort of the 'get on with it' ethos. I didn't know why I continued to feel vulnerable and sensitive. Too much pride, no doubt.

I'd charged up the two batteries in the charger overnight, so I started the new day, Saturday, with a fresh battery in the arm and a spare in my pocket.

It was by then five days since Gordon Quint had cracked my ulna, and the twinges had become less acute and less frequent. Partly it was because one naturally found the least painful way of performing any action, and partly because the ends of bone were beginning to knit. Soft tissue grew on the site of the break and on the eighth day it would normally begin hardening, the whole healing process being complete within the next week. Only splintered displaced ends caused serious trouble, which hadn't occurred in this case.

When I'd been a jockey the feel of a simple fracture had been an almost twice-yearly familiarity. One tended in jump racing to fall on one's shoulder, quite often at thirty miles an hour, and in my time I'd cracked my collar bones six times each side: only once had it been distinctly bad.

Some jockeys had stronger bones than others, but I didn't know anyone who'd completed a top career unscathed. Anyway, by Saturday morning, Monday's crack was no real problem.

Into my overnight bag I packed the battery charger, washing things, pyjamas, spare shirt, business suit and shoes. I wore both pieces of the tracksuit, white shirt, no tie and the dark trainers. In my belt I carried money and a credit card, and in my pocket a bunch of six keys on a single ring, which bore also a miniature torch. Three of the keys were variously for my car and the entry doors of my flat. The other three, looking misleadingly simple, would between them open any ordinary lock, regardless of the wishes of the owners.

My old teacher had had me practise until I was quick at it. He'd shown me also how to open the simple combination locks on suitcases; the method used by airport thieves.

I checked out of the hotel and found the way back to Frodsham, parking by the kerb within sight of the Topline Foods' wire-mesh gates.

As before, the gates were wide open and, as before, no one going in and out was challenged by the gate-keeper. No one, in fact, seemed to have urgent business in either direction and there were far fewer cars in the central area than on the day before. It wasn't until nearly eleven o'clock that the promised film crews arrived in force.

When getting on for twenty assorted vans and private cars had come to a ragged halt all over the place, disgorging film cameras (Intramind Imaging), a television camera (local station) and dozens of people looking purposeful with heavy equipment and chest-hugged clipboards, I got out of my car and put on the ill-fitting brown overalls, complete with identity badge. Into the boot I locked my bag and also the mobile phone, first taking the SIM card out of it and stowing it in my belt.

300

'Get into the habit of removing the SIM card,' my supplier had advised. 'Then if someone steals your phone, too bad, they won't be able to use it.'

'Great,' I'd said.

I started the car, drove unhesitatingly through the gates, steered a course round the assorted vans and stopped just beyond them, nearest to the unloading bays. Saturday or not, a few other brown-overall hands were busy on the rollers and the shelf escalator, and I simply walked straight in past them, saying 'Morning' as if I belonged.

They didn't answer, didn't look up, took me for granted.

Inside, I walked up the stairs I'd come down with Willy Parrott and, when I reached the right level, ambled along the gallery until I came to his office.

The sliding glass door was closed and locked and there was no one inside.

The paddles were silent in the vats. None of the day before's hum and activity remained, and almost none of the smells. Instead, there were cameras being positioned below, with Owen Yorkshire himself directing the director, his authoritative voice telling the experts their job.

He was too busy to look up. I went on along the gallery, coming to the fire-door up the flight of metal stairs. The fire-doors were locked at night. Willy had said. By day, they were open. Thankful, I reached in the end the plush carpet of the offices.

There was a bunch of three media people in there, measuring angles and moving potted plants. Office work, I gathered, was due for immortality on Monday. Cursing internally at their presence, I walked on towards the lift, passing the open door of 'Customer Relations'. No Marsha Rowse.

To the right of the lift there was a door announcing 'Office Manager, A. Dove', fastened with businesslike locks.

Looking back, I saw the measuring group taking their damned time. I needed them out of there and they infuriatingly dawdled.

I didn't like to hover. I returned to the lift and, to fill in time, opened a nearby door which proved to enclose fire-stairs, as I'd hoped.

Down a floor, and through the fire-door there, I found an expanse of open space, unfurnished and undecorated, the same in area as the office suite above. Up two storeys, above the offices, there was similar quiet, undivided, clean-swept space. Owen Yorkshire had already built for expansion, I gathered.

Cautiously, I went on upwards to the fifth floor, lair of the boss.

Trusting that he was still down among the vats, I opened the fire-door enough to put my head through.

More camera people moved around. Veritable banks of potted plants blazed red and gold. To the left, open opulently-gleaming double doors led into an entertaining and boardroom area impressive enough for a major industry of self-importance. On the right, more double doors led to Yorkshire's own new office; not, from what I could see, a place of paperwork. Polished wood gleamed. Plants galore. A tray of bottles and glasses.

I retreated down the unvarnished nitty-gritty fire-stairs until I was back on the working-office floor, standing there indecisively, wondering if the measurers still barred my purpose.

I heard voices, growing louder and stopping on the other side of the door. I was prepared to go into a busy-employee routine, but it appeared they preferred the lift to the stairs. The lifting machinery whirred on the other side of the stairwell, the voices moved into the lift and diminished to zero. I couldn't tell whether they'd gone up or down, and I was concerned only that they'd *all* gone up and not left one behind.

There was no point in waiting. I opened the fire-door, stepped onto the carpet and looked left and right towards Mrs Dove's domain.

I had the whole office floor to myself.

Great.

Mrs Dove's door was locked twice: an old-looking mortise and a new knob with a keyhole in the centre. These were locks I liked. There could be no nasty surprises like bolts or chains or wedges on the inside: also the emphatic statement of *two* locks probably meant that there were things of worth to guard.

The mortise lock took a whole minute, with the ghost of my old master breathing disapprovingly down

303

my neck. The modern lock took twenty seconds of delicate probing. One had to 'feel' one's way through. False fingers for that, as for much else, were useless.

Once inside Mrs Dove's office I spent time relocking the door so that anyone outside trying it for security would find it as it should be. If anyone came in with keys, I would have warning enough to hide.

Mrs Dove's cote was large and comfortable with a wide desk, several of the Scandinavian-design armchairs and grainy blow-up black and white photographs of racing horses round the walls. Along one side there were the routine office machines – fax, copier and large print-out calculator, and, on the desk, a computer, shrouded for the weekend in a fitted cover. There were multiple filing cabinets and a tall white-painted and – as I discovered – locked cupboard.

Mrs Dove had a window with louvred blinds and a distant view of the Mersey. Mrs Dove's office was managing director stuff.

I had only a vague idea of what I was looking for. The audited accounts I'd seen in Companies House seemed not to match the actual state of affairs at Frodsham. The audit did, of course, refer to a year gone by, to the first with Owen Yorkshire in charge, but the fragile bottom-line profit, as shown, would not suggest or justify expensive publicity campaigns or televised receptions for the notables of Liverpool.

The old French adage 'look for the lady' was a century out of date, my old teacher had said. In modern times it should be 'look for the money'; and, shortly before he died, he had amended that to 'follow the paper'. Shady or doubtful transactions, he said, always left a paper trail. Even in the age of computers, he'd insisted that paper showed the way; and over and over again I'd proved him right.

The paper in Mrs Dove's office was all tidied away in the many filing cabinets, which were locked.

Most filing cabinets, like these, locked all drawers simultaneously with a notched vertical rod out of sight within the right-hand front corner, operated by a single key at the top. Turning the key raised the rod, allowing all the drawers to open. I wasn't bad at opening filing cabinets.

The trouble was that Topline Foods had little to hide, or at least not at first sight. Pounds of paper referred to orders and invoices for incoming supplies; pounds more to sales, pounds more to the expenses of running an industry, from insurance to wages, to electricity to general maintenance.

The filing cabinets took too long and were a waste of time. What they offered was the entirely respectable basis of next year's audit.

I locked them all again and, after investigating the desk drawers themselves, which held only stationery, took the cover off the computer and switched it on, pressing the buttons for 'List Files', and 'Enter'. Scrolls of file names appeared and I tried one at random: 'Aintree'.

Onto the screen came details of the lunch given the day before the Grand National, the guest list, the menu, a summary of the speeches and a list of the coverage given to the occasion in the press.

Nothing I could find seemed any more secret. I switched off, replaced the cover and turned my lock-pickers to the tall white cupboard.

The feeling of time running out, however irrational, shortened my breath and made me hurry. I always envied the supersleuths in films who put their hands on the right papers in the first ten seconds and, this time, I didn't know if the right paper even existed.

It turned out to be primarily not a paper but a second computer.

Inside the white cupboard, inside a drop-down desk arrangement in there, I came across a second keyboard and a second screen. I switched the computer on and nothing happened, which wasn't astounding as I found an electric lead lying alongside, disconnected. I plugged it into the computer and tried again, and with a grumble or two the machine became ready for business.

I pressed 'List Files' again, and this time found myself looking not at individual subjects, but at 'Direc-tories', each of which contained file names such as 'Formula A'.

What I had come across were the more private records, the electronic files, some very secret, some not.

In quick succession I highlighted the 'Directories' and brought them to the screen until one baldly listed

'Quint': but no amount of button-pressing got me any further.

Think.

The reason I couldn't get the Quint information onto the screen must be because it wasn't in the computer.

OK? OK. So where was it?

On the shelf above the computer stood a row of box-files, numbers 1 to 9, but not one labelled Quint.

I lifted down Number 1 and looked inside. There were several letters filed in there, also a blue computer floppy disk in a clear cover. According to the letters, box-file No. 1 referred to loans made to Topline Foods, loans not repaid on the due date. There was also a mention of 'sweeteners' and 'quid pro quos'. I fed the floppy disk into the drive slot in the computer body and got no further than a single unhelpful word on the screen: PASSWORD?

Password? Heaven knew. I looked into the box-files one by one and came to 'Quint' in No. 6. There were three floppies in there, not one.

I fed in the first.

PASSWORD?

Second and third disks – PASSWORD?

Bugger, I thought.

Searching for anything helpful I lifted down a heavy white cardboard box, like a double-height shoebox, that filled the rest of the box-file shelf. In there was a row of big black high-impact plastic protective coverings. I picked out one and unlatched its fastening, and found inside it a video tape, but a tape of double the ordinary width. A label on the tape said 'Broadcast Quality Videotape'. Underneath that was the single word BETACAM. Under that was the legend 'Quint series. 15 × 30 secs.'

I closed the thick black case and tried another one. Same thing. Quint series. 15 × 30 secs. All of the cases held the same.

These double-size tapes needed a special tape player not available in Mrs Dove's office. To see what was on these expensive tapes meant taking one with me.

I could, of course, simply put one of them inside my tracksuit jacket and walk out with it. I could take all the 'PASSWORD' disks. If I did I was a) stealing, b) in danger of being found carrying the goods, and c) making it impossible for any information they held to be used in any later legal enquiry. I would steal the information itself, if I could, but not the hardware.

Think.

As I'd told Charles at Aynsford, I'd had to learn a good deal about computers just to keep a grip on the accelerating world, but the future became the present so fast that I could never get ahead.

Someone tried to open the door.

There was no time to restore the room to normal. I could only speed across the carpet and stand where I would be hidden by the door when it swung inwards. Plan B meant simply running – and I was wearing running shoes.

The knob turned again and rattled, but nothing else happened. Whoever was outside had presumably been either keyless or reassured: in either case it played havoc with my breathing.

Oddly, the pumping adrenalin brought me my computer answer which was, if I couldn't bring the contents of a floppy disk to the screen, I could transfer it whole to *another* computer, one that would give me all the time I needed to crack the password, or to get help from people who could.

Alongside the unconnected electric cable there had been a telephone cable, also unattached. I snapped it into the telephone socket on the computer, thereby connecting Mrs Dove's modem to the world-wide Internet.

It needed a false start or two while I desperately tried to remember half-learned techniques, but finally I was rewarded by the screen prompting: 'Enter telephone number.'

I tapped in my own home number in the flat in Pont Square, and pressed 'Enter', and the screen announced nonchalantly 'dialling in progress', then 'call accepted', then 'transfer', and finally 'transfer complete'.

Whatever was on the first guarded 'Quint' disk was now in my own computer in London. I transferred the other two 'Quint' floppies in the same way, and then the disk from box-file No. 1, and for good measure another from Box 3, identified as 'Tilepit'.

There was no way that I knew of transferring the

BETACAM tapes. Regretfully I left them alone. I looked through the paper pages in the 'Quint' box and make a photocopy of one page – a list of unusual racecourses – folding it and hiding it within the zipped pocket of my belt.

Finally I disconnected the electric and telephone cables again, closed the computer compartment, checked that the box-files and BETACAM tapes were as they should be, relocked the white cupboard, then unlocked and gently opened the door to the passage.

Silence.

Breathing out with relief I relocked Mrs Dove's door and walked along through the row of cubby-hole offices and came to the first setback: the fire-door leading to brown-overalls territory was not merely locked but had a red light shining above it.

Shining red lights often meant alarm systems switched on with depressingly loud sirens ready to screech.

I'd been too long in Mrs Dove's office. I retreated towards her door again and went down the fire-stairs beside the lift, emerging into the ground-floor entrance hall with its glass doors to the parking area beyond.

One step into the lobby proved to be one step too far. Something hit my head rather hard and one of the beefy body-guards in blue flung a sort of strap round my body and effectively pinned my upper arms to my sides.

I plunged about a bit and got another crack on the

head which left me unable to help myself and barely able to think. I was aware of being in the lift, but wasn't quite sure how I'd got there. I was aware of having my ankles strapped together and of being dragged ignominiously over some carpet and dropped in a chair.

Regulation Scandinavian chair with wooden arms, like all the others.

'Tie him up,' a voice said, and a third strap tightened across my chest, so that when the temporary mist cleared I woke to a state of near physical immobility and a mind full of curses.

The voice belonged to Owen Yorkshire. He said, 'Right. Good. Well done. Leave the wrench on the desk. Go back downstairs and don't let anyone up here.'

'Yes, sir.'

'Wait,' Yorkshire commanded, sounding uncertain. 'Are you sure you've got the right man?'

'Yes, sir. He's wearing the identity badge we issued to him yesterday. He was supposed to return it when he left, but he didn't.'

'All right. Thanks. Off you go.'

The door closed behind the bodyguards and Owen Yorkshire plucked the identity badge from my overalls, read the name and flung it down on his desk.

We were in his fifth-floor office. The chair I sat in was surrounded by carpet. Marooned on a desert island, feeling dim and stupid.

The man-to-man all-pals-together act was in abeyance. The Owen Yorkshire confronting me was very angry, disbelieving and, I would have said, *frightened*.

'What are you doing here?' he demanded, bellowing.

His voice echoed and reverberated in the quiet room. His big body loomed over me, his big head close to mine. All his features, I thought, were slightly oversized: big nose, big eyes, wide forehead, large flat cheeks, square jaw, big mouth. The collar-length black waving hair with its grey-touched wings seemed to vibrate with vigour. I would have put his age at forty; maybe a year or two younger.

'Answer,' he yelled. 'What are you doing here?'

I didn't reply. He snatched up from his desk a heavy fifteen-inch-long silvery wrench and made as if to hit my head with it. If that was what his boys-in-blue had used on me, and I gathered it was, then connecting it again with my skull was unlikely to produce any answer at all. The same thought seemed to occur to him, because he threw the wrench down disgustedly onto the desk again, where it bounced slightly under its own weight.

The straps round my chest and ankles were the sort of fawn close-woven webbing often used round suitcases to prevent them from bursting open. There was no elasticity in them, no stretch. Several more lay on the desk.

I felt a ridiculous desire to chatter, a tendency I'd noticed in the past in mild concussion after racing falls, and sometimes on waking up from anaesthetics. I'd learned how to suppress the garrulous impulse, but it was still an effort, and in this case, essential.

Owen Yorkshire was wearing man-to-man togs; that is to say, no jacket, a man-made-fibre shirt (almost white with vertical stripes made of interlocking beige-coloured horseshoes), no tie, several buttons undone, unmissable view of manly hairy chest, gold chain and medallion.

I concentrated on the horseshoe stripes. If I could count the number of horseshoes from shoulder to waist I would not have any thoughts that might dribble out incautiously. The boss was talking. I blanked him out and counted horseshoes and managed to say nothing.

He went abruptly out of the room, leaving me sitting there looking foolish. When he returned he brought two people with him: they had been along in the reception area, it seemed, working out table placements for Monday's lunch.

They were a woman and a man; Mrs Dove and a stranger. Both exclaimed in surprise at the sight of my trussed self. I shrank into the chair and looked mostly at their waists.

'Do you know who this is?' Yorkshire demanded of them furiously.

The man shook his head, mystified. Mrs Dove, frowning, said to me, 'Weren't you here yesterday? Something about a farmer?'

'This,' Yorkshire said with scorn, 'is Sid Halley.'

The man's face stiffened, his mouth forming an O.

'*This*, Verney,' Yorkshire went on with biting sarcasm, 'is the feeble creature you've spent months thundering on about. *This!* And Ellis said he was dangerous! Just look at him! All those big guns to frighten a mouse.'

Verney *Tilepit*. I'd looked him up in *Burke's Peerage*. Verney Tilepit, 3rd Baron, aged forty-two, a director of Topline Foods, proprietor – by inheritance – of *The Pump*.

Verney Tilepit's grandfather, created a baron for devoted allegiance to the then prime minister, had been one of the old roistering, powerful opinion-makers who'd had governments dancing to their tune. The first Verney Tilepit had put his shoulder to history and given it a shove. The third had surfaced after years of quiescence, primarily, it seemed, to discredit a minor investigator. Policy! His bewildered grandfather would have been speechless.

He was fairly tall, as India had said, and he had brown hair. The flicking glance I gave him took in also a large expanse of face with small features bunched in the middle: small nose, small mouth, small sandy moustache, small eyes behind large, light-framed glasses. Nothing about him seemed physically threatening. Perhaps I felt the same disappointment in my adversary as he plainly did about me.

'How do you know he's Sid Halley?' Mrs Dove asked.

314

Owen Yorkshire said disgustedly, 'One of the TV crew knew him. He swore there was no mistake. He'd filmed him often. He *knows* him.'

Bugger, I thought.

Mrs Dove pulled up the long left sleeve of my brown overalls, and looked at my left hand. 'Yes. It must be Sid Halley. Not much of a champion now, is he?'

Owen Yorkshire picked up the telephone, pressed numbers, waited and forcefully spoke.

'Get over here quickly,' he said. 'We have a crisis. Come to my new office.' He listened briefly. 'No,' he said, 'just get over here.' He slammed down the receiver and stared at me balefully. 'What the sod are you doing here?'

The almost overwhelming urge to tell him got as far as my tongue and was only over-ridden by clamped-shut teeth. One could understand why people confessed. The itch to unburden outweighed the certainty of retribution.

'Answer,' yelled Yorkshire. He picked up the wrench again. 'Answer, you little cuss.'

I did manage an answer of sorts.

I spoke to Verney Tilepit directly in a weak, mock-respectful tone, 'I came to see you . . . sir.'

'My lord,' Yorkshire told me. 'Call him my lord.'

'My lord,' I said.

Tilepit said, 'What for?' and 'What made you think I would be here?'

'Someone told me you were a director of Topline

315

Foods, my lord, so I came here to ask you to stop and I don't know why I've been dragged up here and tied up like this.' The last twenty words just dribbled out. Be *careful*, I thought. *Shut up*.

'To stop *what*?' Tilepit demanded.

'To stop your paper telling lies about me.' Better.

Tilepit didn't know how to answer such naivety. Yorkshire properly considered it barely credible. He spoke to Mrs Dove, who was dressed for Saturday morning, not in office black and white, but in bright red with gold buttons.

'Go down and make sure he hasn't been in your office.'

'I locked it when I left last night, Owen.'

Mrs Dove's manner towards her boss was interestingly like Will Parrott's. All-equals-together; up to a point.

'Go and look,' he said. 'And check that cupboard.'

'No one's opened that cupboard since you moved offices up here this week. And you have the only key.'

'Go and check anyway,' he said.

She had no difficulty with obeying him. I remembered Marsha Rowse's ingenuous statement – 'Mrs Dove says never to make Mr Yorkshire angry.'

Mrs Dove, self-contained, confident, was taking her own advice. She was not, I saw, in love with the man, nor was she truly afraid of him. His temper, I would have thought, was to her more of a nuisance than life – or even job – threatening.

As things stood, or rather as I sat, I saw the wisdom of following Mrs Dove's example for as long as I could.

She was gone a fair time, during which I worried more and more anxiously that I'd left something slightly out of place in that office, that she would know by some sixth sense that someone had been in there, that I'd left some odour in the air despite never using after-shave, that I'd closed the filing cabinets incorrectly, that I'd left visible fingerprints on a shiny surface, that I'd done *anything* that she knew she hadn't.

I breathed slowly, trying not to sweat.

When she finally came back she said, 'The TV crews are leaving. Everything's ready for Monday. The florists are bringing the Lady Mayoress's bouquet at ten o'clock. The red-carpet people are downstairs now measuring the lobby. And, oh, the man from Intramind Imaging says they want a cheque.'

'What about the office?'

'The office? Oh, the office is all right.' She was unconcerned. 'It was all locked. Just as I left it.'

'And the cupboard?' Yorkshire insisted.

'Locked.' She thought he was over-reacting. I was concerned only to show no relief.

'What are you going to do with *him*?' she asked, indicating me. 'You can't keep him here, can you? The TV crew downstairs were talking about him being here. They want to interview him. What shall I say?'

Yorkshire with black humour said, 'Tell them he's all tied up.'

She wasn't amused. She said, 'I'll say he went out the back way. And I'll be off, too. I'll be here by eight, Monday morning.' She looked at me calmly and spoke to Yorkshire, 'Let him go,' she said unemotionally. 'What harm can he do? He's pathetic.'

Yorkshire, undecided, said, 'Pathetic? Why pathetic?'

She paused composedly halfway through the door, and dropped a pearl beyond price.

'It says so in *The Pump*.'

Neither of these two men, I thought, listening to them, was a full-blown criminal. Not yet. Yorkshire was too near the brink.

He still held the heavy adjustable wrench, slapping its head occasionally against his palm, as if it helped his thoughts.

'Please untie me,' I said. At last I found the fatal loquaciousness had abated. I no longer wanted to gabble, but just to talk my way out.

Tilepit himself might have done it. He clearly was unused to – and disturbed by – even this level of violence. His power base was his grandfather's name. His muscle was his hire-and-fire clout. There were only so many top editorships in the British Press and George Godbar, editor of *The Pump*, wasn't going to lose his hide to save mine. Matters of principle were all too often an unaffordable luxury, and I didn't believe that in George Godbar's place, or even in Kevin Mills' or India's, I would have done differently.

Yorkshire said, 'We wait.'

He opened a drawer in his desk and drew out what looked bizarrely like a jar of gherkins. Dumping the wrench temporarily, he unscrewed the lid, put the jar on the desk, pulled out a green finger and bit it, crunching it with large white teeth.

'Gherkin?' he offered Tilepit.

The third baron averted his nose.

Yorkshire, shrugging, chewed uninhibitedly and went back to slapping his palm with the wrench.

'I'll be missed,' I said mildly, 'if you keep me much longer.'

'Let him go,' Tilepit said with a touch of impatience. 'He's right, we can't keep him here indefinitely.'

'We wait,' Yorkshire said heavily, fishing out another gherkin and, to the accompaniment of noisy munching, we waited.

I could smell the vinegar.

The door opened finally behind me and both Yorkshire and Tilepit looked welcoming and relieved.

I didn't. The newcomer, who came round in front of me blankly, was Ellis Quint.

Ellis, in open-necked white shirt; Ellis, handsome, macho, vibrating with showmanship; Ellis, the nation's darling, farcically accused. I hadn't seen him since Ascot races, and none of his radiance had waned.

'What's *Halley* doing here?' he demanded, sounding alarmed. 'What has he learned?'

'He was wandering about,' Yorkshire said, pointing a gherkin at me. 'I had him brought up here. He can't have learned a thing.'

Tilepit announced, 'Halley says he came to ask me to stop *The Pump*'s campaign against him.'

Ellis said positively, 'He wouldn't have done that.'

'Why not?' Yorkshire asked. 'Look at him. He's a wimp.'

'A *wimp*!'

Despite my precarious position I smiled involuntarily at the depth of incredulity in his voice. I even grinned at him sideways from below half-lowered eyelids, and saw the same private smile on his face: the acknowledgment of brotherhood, of secrecy, of shared esoteric experience, of cold winter afternoons, perils embraced, disappointments and injuries taken lightly, of indescribable triumphs. We had hugged each other standing in our stirrups, ecstatic after winning posts. We had trusted, bonded, and twinned.

Whatever we were now, we had once been more than brothers. The past – our past – remained. The intense and mutual memories could not be erased.

The smiles died. Ellis said, 'This *wimp* comes up on your inside and beats you in the last stride. This wimp could ruin us all if we neglect our inside rail. This wimp was champion jockey for five or six years and might have been still, and we'd be fools to forget it.'

He put his face close to mine. 'Still the same old Sid, aren't you? Cunning. Nerveless. Win at all costs.'

There was nothing to say.

Yorkshire bit into a gherkin. 'What do we do with him, then?'

'First we find out why he's here.'

Tilepit said, 'He came to get *The Pump* to stop—'

'Balls,' Ellis interrupted. 'He's lying.'

'How can you tell?' Tilepit protested.

'I know him.' He said it with authority, and it was true.

'What, then?' Yorkshire asked.

Ellis said to me, 'You'll not get me into court, Sid. Not Monday. Not ever. You haven't been able to break my Shropshire alibi, and my lawyers say that without that the prosecution won't have a chance. They'll withdraw the charge. Understand? I know you *do* understand. You'll have destroyed your own reputation, not mine. What's more, my father's going to kill you.'

Yorkshire and Tilepit showed, respectively, pleasure and shock.

'Before Monday?' I asked.

The flippancy fell like lead. Ellis strode round behind me and yanked back the right front of my brown overalls, and the tracksuit beneath. He tore a couple of buttons off my shirt, pulling that back after, then he pressed down strongly with his fingers.

'Gordon says he broke your collar-bone,' he said.

'Well, he didn't.'

321

Ellis would see the remains of bruising and he could feel the bumps of callus formed by earlier breaks, but it was obvious to him that his father had been wrong.

'My father will kill you,' he repeated. 'Don't you care?'

Another unanswerable question.

It seemed to me as if the cruel hidden side of Ellis suddenly took over, banishing the friend and becoming the threatened star who had everything to lose. He roughly threw my clothes together and continued round behind me until he stood on my left side.

'You won't defeat me,' he said. 'You've cost me half a million. You've cost me lawyers. You've cost me *sleep*.'

He might insist that I couldn't defeat him, but we both knew I would in the end, if I tried, because he was guilty.

'You'll pay for it,' he said.

He put his hands on the hard shell of my left forearm and raised it until my elbow formed a right angle. The tight strap round my upper arms and chest prevented me from doing anything to stop him. Whatever strength that remained in my upper left arm (and it was, in fact, quite a lot) was held in uselessness by that strap.

Ellis peeled back the brown sleeve, and the blue one underneath. He tore open my shirt cuff and pulled that sleeve back also. He looked at the plastic skin underneath.

'I know something about that arm,' he said. 'I got a

brochure on purpose. That skin is a sort of glove, and it comes off.'

He felt up my arm until, by the elbow, he came to the top of the glove. He rolled it down as far as the wrist and then, with concentration, pulled it off finger by finger, exposing the mechanics in all their detail.

The close-fitting textured glove gave the hand an appearance of life, with knuckles, veins and shapes like finger nails. The works inside were gears, springs and wiring. The bared forearm was bright pink, hard and shiny.

Ellis smiled.

He put his own strong right hand on my electrical left and pressed and twisted with knowledge and then, when the works clicked free, unscrewed the hand round several turns until it came right off.

Ellis looked into my eyes as at a feast. 'Well?' he said.

'You *shit*.'

He smiled. He opened his fingers and let the unscrewed hand fall onto the carpet.

CHAPTER THIRTEEN

Tilepit looked shocked enough to vomit, but not Yorkshire: in fact, he laughed.

Ellis said to him sharply, 'This man is not funny.
Everything that has gone wrong is because of *him*, and
don't you forget it. It's this Sid Halley that's going to
ruin you, and if you think he doesn't care about what
I've just done' – he put his toe against the fallen hand
and moved it a few inches – 'if you think it's something
to laugh at, I'll tell you that for *him* it's almost
unbearable ... but *not* unbearable, is it, Sid?' He
turned to ask me, and told Yorkshire at the same time.
'No one yet has invented anything you've found actually unbearable, have they, Sid?'

I didn't answer.

Yorkshire protested, 'But he's only—'

'Don't say *only*,' Ellis interrupted, his voice hard and
loud. 'Don't you understand it yet? What do you think
he's doing here? How did he get here? What does he
know? He's not going to tell you. His nickname's tungsten carbide – that's the hardest of all metals and it

saws through steel. I *know* him. I've almost loved him. You have no idea what you're dealing with, and we've got to decide what to do with him. How many people know he's here?'

'My bodyguards,' Yorkshire said. 'They brought him up.'

It was Lord Tilepit who gave him the real bad news. 'It was a TV crew who told Owen that Sid Halley was in the building.'

'*A TV crew!*'

'They wanted to interview him. Mrs Dove said she would tell them he'd gone.'

'*Mrs Dove!*'

If Ellis had met Mrs Dove he would know, as I did, that she wouldn't lie for Yorkshire. Mrs Dove had seen me, and she would say so.

Ellis asked furiously, 'Did Mrs Dove see him tied in that chair?'

'Yes,' Tilepit said faintly.

'You *stupid* . . .' Words failed Ellis, but for only a few short seconds. 'Then,' he said flatly, 'you can't kill him here.'

'*Kill* him?' Tilepit couldn't believe what he'd heard. His whole large face blushed pink. 'I'm not . . . are you talking about *murder*?'

'Oh yes, my lord,' I said dryly, 'they are. They're thinking of putting your lordship behind bars as an accessory. You'll love it in the slammer.'

I'd meant only to get Tilepit to see the enormity of

what Ellis was proposing. but in doing so I'd made the mistake of unleashing Yorkshire's rage.

He took two paces and kicked my unscrewed hand with such force that it flew across the room and crashed against the wall. Then he realised the wrench was still in his hand and swung it at my head.

I saw the blow coming but couldn't get my head back far enough to avoid it altogether. The wrench's heavy screw connected with my moving cheekbone and tore the skin, but didn't this time knock me silly.

In Owen Yorkshire, the half-slipping brakes came wholly off. Perhaps the very sight of me, left-handless and bleeding and unable to retaliate, was all it took. He raised his arm and the wrench again, and I saw the spite in his face and the implacably murderous intention and I thought of nothing much at all, which afterwards seemed odd.

It was Ellis who stopped him. Ellis caught the descending arm and yanked Owen Yorkshire round sideways, so that although the heavy weapon swept on downwards, it missed me altogether.

'You're *brainless*,' Ellis shouted. 'I said *not in here*. You're a raving lunatic. Too many people know he came here. Do you want to splatter his blood and brains all over your new carpet? You might as well go and shout from the rooftops. Get a grip on that frigging temper and find a tissue.'

'A what?'

'Something to stop him bleeding. Are you terminally

insane? When he doesn't turn up wherever he's expected, you're going to get the police in here looking for him. TV crew! Mrs Dove! The whole frigging country! You get one drop of his blood on anything in here, you're looking at twenty-five years.'

Yorkshire, bewildered by Ellis's attack and turning sullen, said there weren't any tissues. Verney Tilepit tentatively produced a handkerchief; white, clean and embroidered with a coronet. Ellis snatched it from him and slapped it on my cheek, and I wondered if ever, in any circumstances, I could, to save myself, deliberately kill *him*, and didn't think so.

Ellis took the handkerchief away briefly, looked at the scarlet staining the white, and put it back, pressing.

Yorkshire strode about, waving the wrench as if jerked by strings. Tilepit looked extremely unhappy. I considered my probable future with gloom and Ellis, taking the handkerchief away again and watching my cheek critically, declared that the worst of the bleeding had stopped.

He gave the handkerchief back to Tilepit, who put it squeamishly in his pocket, and he snatched the wrench away from Yorkshire and told him to cool down and *plan*.

Planning took them both out of the office, the door closing behind them. Verney Tilepit didn't in the least appreciate being left alone with me and went to look out of the window, to look anywhere except at me.

'Untie me,' I said with force.

No chance. He didn't even show he'd heard.

I asked, 'How did you get yourself into this mess?'

No answer.

I tried again. I said, 'If I walk out of here free, I'll forget I ever saw you.'

He turned round, but he had his back to the light and I couldn't see his eyes clearly behind the spectacles.

'You really are in deep trouble,' I said.

'Nothing will happen.'

I wished I believed him. I said, 'It must have seemed pretty harmless to you, just to use your paper to ridicule someone week after week. What did Yorkshire tell you? To save Ellis at all costs. Well, it *is* going to cost you.'

'You don't understand. Ellis is blameless.'

'I understand that you're up to your noble neck in shit.'

'I can't do anything.' He was worried, unhappy and congenitally helpless.

'Untie me,' I said again, with urgency.

'It wouldn't help. I couldn't get you out.'

'Untie me,' I said. 'I'll do the rest.'

He dithered. If he had been capable of reasoned decisions he wouldn't have let himself be used by Yorkshire, but he wasn't the first or last rich man to stumble blindly into a quagmire. He couldn't make up his mind to attempt saving himself by letting me free and, inevitably, the opportunity passed.

Ellis and Yorkshire came back, and neither of them would meet my eyes.

Bad sign.

Ellis, looking at his watch, said, 'We wait.'

'What for?' Tilepit asked uncertainly.

Yorkshire answered, to Ellis's irritation, 'The TV people are on the point of leaving. Everyone will be gone in fifteen minutes.'

Tilepit looked at me, his anxieties showing plainly. 'Let Halley go,' he begged.

Ellis said comfortingly, 'Sure, in a while.'

Yorkshire smiled. His anger was preferable, on the whole.

Verney Tilepit wanted desperately to be reassured, but even he could see that if freeing me was the intention, why did we have to wait.

Ellis still held the wrench. He wouldn't get it wrong, I thought. He wouldn't spill my blood. I would probably not know much about it. I might not consciously learn the reciprocal answer to my self-searching question: could *he* personally kill *me*, to save himself? How deep did friendship go? Did it ever have absolute taboos? Had I already, by accusing him of evil, melted his innermost restraints? He wanted to get even. He would wound me any way he could. But *kill* . . . I didn't know.

He walked round behind me.

Time, in a way, stood still. It was a moment in which to plead, but I couldn't. The decision, whatever I said, would be *his*.

329

He came eventually round to my right-hand side and murmured, 'Tungsten,' under his breath.

Water, I thought, I had water in my veins.

He reached down suddenly and clamped his hand round my right wrist, pulling fiercely upwards.

I jerked my wrist out of his grasp and without warning he bashed the wrench across my knuckles. In the moment of utter numbness that resulted he slid the open jaws of the wrench onto my wrist and tightened the screw. Tightened it further, until the jaws grasped immovably, until they squeezed the upper and lower sides of my wrist together, compressing blood vessels, nerves and ligaments, bearing down on the bones inside.

The wrench was heavy. He balanced its handle on the arm of the chair I was sitting in and held it steady so that my wrist was up at the same level. He had two strong hands. He persevered with the screw.

I said, 'Ellis,' in protest, not from anger or even fear, but in disbelief that he could do what he was doing: in a lament for the old Ellis, in a sort of passionate sorrow.

For the few seconds that he looked into my face, his expression was flooded with awareness . . . and shame. Then the feelings passed, and he returned in deep concentration to an atrocious pleasure.

It was extraordinary. He seemed to go into a kind of trance, as if the office and Yorkshire and Tilepit didn't exist, as if there were only one reality, which was the clench of forged steel jaws on a wrist and the extent to which he could intensify it.

I thought: if the wrench had been lopping shears, if its jaws had been knives instead of flat steel, the whole devastating nightmare would have come true. I shut my mind to it: made it cold. Sweated, all the same.

I thought: what I see in his face is the full-blown addiction; not the cruel satisfaction he could get from unscrewing a false hand, but the sinful fulfilment of cutting off a live hoof.

I glanced very briefly at Yorkshire and Tilepit and saw their frozen bottomless astonishment, and I realised that until that moment of revelation they hadn't wholly believed in Ellis's guilt.

My wrist hurt. Somewhere up my arm the ulna grumbled.

I said, '*Ellis*,' sharply, to wake him up.

He got the screw to tighten another notch.

I yelled at him, '*Ellis*,' and again, '*Ellis*.'

He straightened, looking vaguely down at fifteen inches of heavy stainless steel wrench incongruously sticking out sideways from its task. He tied it to the arm of the chair with another strap from the desk and went over to the window, not speaking, but not rational either.

I tried to dislodge myself from the wrench but my hand was too numb and the grip too tight. I found it difficult to think. My hand was pale blue and grey. Thought was a crushed wrist and an abysmal shattering fear that if the damage went on too long, it would be permanent. Hands could be lost.

Both hands . . . Oh God. Oh *God*.

'Ellis,' I said yet again, but in a lower voice this time: a plea for him to return to the old self, that was there all the time, somewhere.

I waited. Acute discomfort and the terrible anxiety continued. Ellis's thoughts seemed far out in space. Tilepit cleared his throat in embarrassment and Yorkshire, as if in unconscious humour, crunched a gherkin.

Minutes passed.

I said, 'Ellis . . .'

I closed my eyes. Opened them again. More or less prayed.

Time and nightmare fused. One became the other. The future was a void.

Ellis left the window and crossed with bouncing steps to the chair where I sat. He looked into my face and enjoyed what he could undoubtedly see there. Then he unscrewed and untied the wrench with violent jerks and dropped the abominable ratchet from a height onto the desk.

No one said anything. Ellis seemed euphoric, high, full of good spirits, striding round the room as if unable to contain his exhilaration.

I got stabbing pins and needles in my fingers, and thanked the fates for it. My hand felt dreadful but turned slowly yellowish pink.

Thought came back from outer space and lodged again earthily in my brain.

Ellis, coming down very slightly, looked at his watch. He plucked from the desk the cosmetic glove from my false arm, came to my right side, shoved the glove inside my shirt against my chest and, with a theatrical flourish, zipped up the front of my blue tracksuit to keep his gift from falling out.

He looked at his watch again. Then he went across the room, picked up the unscrewed hand, returned to my side, and slapped the dead mechanism into my living palm. There was a powerful impression all round that he was busy making sure no trace of Sid Halley remained in the room.

He went round behind me and undid the strap fastening me into the chair. Then he undid the second strap that held my upper arms against my body.

'Screw the hand back on,' he instructed.

Perhaps because they had bent from being kicked around, or perhaps because my real hand was eighty per cent useless, the screw threads wouldn't mesh smoothly, and after three half turns they stuck. The hand looked re-attached, but wouldn't work.

'Stand up,' Ellis said.

I stood, swaying, my ankles still tied together.

'You're letting him go,' Tilepit exclaimed, with grateful relief.

'Of course,' Ellis said.

Yorkshire was smiling.

'Put your hands behind your back,' Ellis told me.

I did so, and he strapped my wrists tight together.

Last, he undid my ankles.

'This way.' He pulled me by the arm over to the door and through into the passage. My feet walked like automatons.

Looking back, I saw Yorkshire put his hand on the telephone. Beyond him, Tilepit was happy with foolish faith.

Ellis pressed the call button for the lift, and the door opened immediately.

'Get in,' he said.

I looked briefly at his now unsmiling face. Expressionless. That made two of us, I thought, two of us thinking the same thing and not saying it.

I stepped into the lift and he leaned in quickly and pressed the button for the ground floor, then jumped back. The door closed between us. The lift began its short journey down.

To tie together the wrists of a man who could unscrew one of them was an exercise in futility. All the same, the crossed threads and my fumbling fingers gave me trouble and some severe moments of panic before the hand slipped free. The lift had already reached its destination by the time I'd shed the tying strap, leaving no chance to emerge from the opening door with everything anywhere near normal.

I put the mechanical hand deep into my right-hand tracksuit trousers pocket. Surreal, I grimly thought. The long sleeve of brown overall covered the void where it belonged.

Ellis had given me a chance. Not much of one, probably, but at least I did have the answer to my question, which was no, he wouldn't personally kill me. Yorkshire definitely would.

The two blue-clad bodyguards were missing from the lobby.

The telephone on the desk was ringing, but the bodyguards were outside, busily positioning a Topline Foods van. One guard was descending from the driver's seat. The other was opening the rear doors.

A van, I understood, for abduction. For a journey to an unmarked grave. A bog job, the Irish called it. How much, I wondered, were they being paid.

Ellis's timing had given me thirty seconds. He'd sent me down too soon. In the lobby I had no future. Out in the open air . . . some.

Taking a couple of deep breaths, I shot out through the doors as fast as I could, and sprinted: and I ran out to the right towards my own car, but veered left round the van toward the open gates.

There was a shout from one of the blue figures, a yell from the second and I thought for a moment that I could avoid them, but to my dismay the gatekeeper himself came to unwelcome life, emerging from his kiosk and barring my exit. Big man in another blue uniform, over-confident.

I ran straight at him. He stood solidly, legs apart, his

weight evenly balanced. He wasn't prepared for or expecting my left foot to knock aside the inside of his knee or for my back to bend and curl like a cannon ball into his stomach: he fell over backwards and I was on my way before he struggled to his knees. The other two, though, had gained ground.

The sort of judo Chico had taught me was in part the stylised advances and throws of a regulated sport and in part an individual style for a one-handed victim. For a start, I never wore, in my private sessions with him, the loose white judogi uniform. I never fought in bare feet but always in ordinary shoes or trainers. The judo I'd learned was how to save my life, not how to earn a black belt.

Ordinary judo needed two hands. Myoelectric hands had a slow response time, a measurable pause between instruction and action. Chico and I had scrapped all grappling techniques for that hand and substituted clubbing; and I used all his lessons at Frodsham as if they were as familiar as walking.

We hadn't exactly envisaged no useful hands at all, but it was amazing what one could do if one wanted to live. It was the same as it had been in races: win now, pay later.

My opponents were straight muscle men with none of the subtlety of the Japanese understanding of lift and leverage and speed. Chico could throw me every time, but Yorkshire's watch-dogs couldn't.

The names of the movements clicked like a litany in

my brain – shintai, randori, tai-sabaki. Fighting literally to live, I stretched every technique I knew and adapted others, using falling feints that involved my twice lying on the ground and sticking a foot into a belly to fly its owner over my head. It ended with one blue uniform lying dazed on its back, one complaining I'd broken his nose, and one haring off to the office building with the bad news.

I stumbled out onto the road, feeling that if I went back for my car the two men I'd left on the ground would think of getting up again and closing the gates.

In one direction lay houses, so I staggered that way. Better cover. I needed cover before anyone chased me in the Topline Foods van.

The houses, when I reached them, were too regular, the gardens too tidy and small. I chose one house with no life showing, walked unsteadily up the garden path, kept on going, found myself in the back garden with another row of houses over the back fence.

The fence was too high to jump or vault, but there was an empty crate lying there, a gift from the gods.

No one came out of any of the houses to ask me what I thought I was doing. I emerged into the next street and began to think about where I was going and what I looked like.

Brown overalls. Yorkshire would be looking for brown overalls.

I took them off and dumped them in one of the houses' brown-looking beech hedges.

Taking off the overalls revealed the non-existence of a left hand.

Damn it, I thought astringently. Things are never easy, so *cope*.

I put the pink exposed end of arm, with its bare electrical contacts, into my left-hand jacket pocket, and walked, not ran, up the street. I wanted to run, but hadn't the strength. Weak . . . Stamina, a memory: a laugh.

There was a boy in the distance roller-blading, coming towards me and wearing not the ubiquitous baseball cap but a striped woollen hat. That would do, I thought. I fumbled some money out of the zip pocket in my belt and stood in his way.

He tried to avoid me, swerved, overbalanced and called me filthy names until his gaze fell on the money in my hand.

'Sell me your hat,' I suggested.

'Yer wha?'

'Your hat,' I said, 'for the money.'

'You've got blood on your face,' he said.

He snatched the money and aimed to roller-blade away. I stuck out a foot and knocked him off his skates. He gave me a bitter look, and a choice of swear words, but also the hat, sweeping it off and throwing it at me.

It was warm from his head and I put it on hoping he didn't have lice. I wiped my face gingerly on my sleeve and slouched along towards the road with traffic that crossed the end of the residential street ... and saw the Topline Foods van roll past.

Whatever they were looking for, it didn't seem to be a navy tracksuit with a striped woollen hat.

Plan B – run away. OK.

Plan C – where to?

I reached the end of the houses and turned left into what might once have been a shopping street, but which now seemed to offer only estate agents, building societies and banks. Marooned in this unhelpful landscape were only two possible refuges – a betting shop and a place selling ice-cream.

I chose the ice-cream. I was barely through the door when outside the window my own Mercedes went past.

Ellis was driving.

I still had its keys in my pocket. Jonathan, it seemed, wasn't alone in his car-stealing skill.

'What do you want?' a female voice said behind me.

She was asking about ice-cream: a thin young woman, bored.

'Er ... that one,' I said, pointing at random.

'Tub or cone? Large or small?'

'Cone. Small.' I felt disoriented, far from reality. I paid for the ice-cream and licked it, and it tasted of almonds.

'You've cut your face,' she said.

'I ran into a tree.'

There were four or five tables with people sitting at them, mostly adolescent groups. I sat at a table away from the window and within ten minutes saw the Top-line van pass twice more and my own car, once.

Tremors ran in my muscles. Fear, or over-exertion, or both.

There was a door marked Gents at the back of the shop. I went in there when I'd finished the ice-cream and looked at my reflection in the small mirror over the wash basin.

The cut along my left cheekbone had congealed into a blackening line, thick and all too visible. Dampening a paper towel I dabbed gently at the mess, trying to remove the clotted blood without starting new bleeding, but making only a partial improvement.

Locked in a cubicle I had another try at screwing my wandering hand into place, and this time at length got it properly aligned and fastened, but it still wouldn't work. Wretchedly depressed, I fished out the long covering glove and with difficulty, because of no talcum powder and an enfeebled right hand, pulled that too into the semblance of reality.

Damn Ellis, I thought mordantly. He'd been right about some things being near to unbearable.

Never mind. Get on with it.

I emerged from the cubicle and tried my cheek again with another paper towel, making the cut paler, fading it into skin colour.

Not too bad.

The face below the unfamiliar woollen hat looked strained. Hardly a surprise.

I went out through the ice-cream shop and walked along the street. The Topline Foods van rolled past quite slowly, driven by one of the blue guards, who was intently scanning the other side of the road. That body-guard meant, I thought, that Yorkshire himself might be out looking for me in a car I couldn't recognise.

Perhaps all I had to do was go up to some sensible-looking motorist and say, 'Excuse me, some people are trying to kill me. Please will you drive me to the police station?' And then, 'Who are these people?' 'The managing director of Topline Foods, and Ellis Quint.' 'Oh *yes*?? And *you* are . . .??'

I did go as far as asking someone the way to the police station – 'Round there, straight on, turn left – about a mile' – and for want of anything better I started walking that way; but what I came to first was a bus shelter with several people standing in a queue, waiting. I added myself to the patient half dozen and stood with my back to the road, and a woman with two children soon came up behind me, hiding me well.

Five long minutes later my Mercedes pulled up on the far side of the road with a white Rolls Royce behind it. Ellis stepped out of my car and Yorkshire out of the Rolls. They conferred together, furiously stabbing the air, pointing up and down the street while I bent my head down to the children and prayed to remain unspotted.

The bus came while the cars were still there.

Four people got off. The waiting queue, me included, surged on. I resisted the temptation to look out of the window until the bus was travelling again, and then saw with relief that the two men were still talking.

I had no idea where the bus was going.

Who cared? Distance was all I needed. I'd paid to go to the end of the line, wherever that was.

Peaceful Frodsham in Cheshire, sometime Saturday, people going shopping in the afternoon. I felt disconnected from that sort of life; and I didn't know what the time was, as the elastic metal bracelet watch I normally wore on my left wrist had come off in Yorkshire's office and was still there, I supposed.

The bus slowly filled at subsequent stops. Shopping baskets. Chatter. Where was I going?

The end of the line proved to be the railway station in Runcorn, halfway to Liverpool, going north when I needed to go south.

I got off the bus and went to the station. There was no Mercedes, no Rolls Royce, no Topline Foods van in sight, which didn't mean they wouldn't think of buses and trains eventually. Runcorn railway station didn't feel safe. There was a train to Liverpool due in four minutes, I learned, so I bought a ticket and caught it.

The feeling of unreality continued, also the familiar aversion to asking for help from the local police. They didn't approve of outside investigators. If I ever got into messes, besides, I considered it my own responsibility to get myself out. Norman Pictons were rare. In Liverpool, moreover, I was probably counted a local boy who'd been disloyal to his 'roots'.

At Liverpool station I read the well-displayed time-table for trains going south.

An express to London, I thought; then backtrack to Reading and get a taxi to Shelley Green, Archie Kirk's house.

No express for hours. What else, then?

The incredible words took a time to penetrate: Liverpool to Bournemouth, departing at 3.10 pm. A slow train, meandering southwards across England, right down to the Channel, with many stops on the way . . . and one of the stops was *Reading*.

I sprinted, using the last shreds of strength. It was already, according to the big station clock, ticking away at 3.07. Whistles were blowing when I stumbled into the last carriage in the long train. A guard helped thrust me in and close the door. The wheels rolled. I had no ticket and little breath, but a marvellous feeling of escape. That feeling lasted only until the first of the many stops, which I discovered with horror to be Runcorn.

Square one: where I'd started. All fear came flooding back. I sat stiff and immobile, as if movement itself would give me away.

Nothing happened. The train quietly rolled onwards. Out on the platform a blue-clad Topline Foods security guard was speaking into a hand-held telephone and shaking his head.

*

Crewe, Stafford, Wolverhampton, Birmingham, Coventry, Leamington Spa, Banbury, Oxford, Didcot, Reading.

It took four hours. Slowly, in that time, the screwed-tight wires of tension slackened to manageable if not to ease. At every stop, however illogical I might tell myself it was, dread resurfaced. Oversize wrenches could kill when one wasn't looking . . . Don't be a fool, I thought. I'd bought a ticket from the train conductor between Runcorn and Crewe, but every subsequent appearance of his dark uniform as he checked his customers bumped my heart muscles.

It grew dark. The train clanked and swayed into realms of night. Life felt suspended.

There were prosaically plenty of taxis at Reading. I travelled safely to Shelley Green and rang Archie Kirk's bell.

He came himself to open the door.

'Hello,' I said.

He stood there staring, then said awkwardly, 'We'd almost given you up.' He led the way into his sitting-room. 'He's here,' he said.

There were four of them. Davis Tatum, Norman Picton, Archie himself, and Charles.

I paused inside the doorway. I had no idea what I looked like, but what I saw on their faces was shock.

'Sid,' Charles said, recovering first and standing up. 'Good. Great. Come and sit down.'

The extent of his solicitude always measured the

depth of his alarm. He insisted I take his place in a comfortable chair and himself perched on a hard one. He asked Archie if he had any brandy and secured for me a half-tumblerful of a raw-tasting own-brand from a supermarket.

'Drink it,' he commanded, holding out the glass.

'Charles . . .'

'Drink it. Talk after.'

I gave in, drank a couple of mouthfuls and put the glass on a table beside me. He was a firm believer in the life-restoring properties of distilled wine and I'd proved him right oftener than enough.

I remembered that I still wore the soft stripey hat, and took it off; and its removal seemed to make my appearance more normal to them, and less disturbing.

'I went to Topline Foods,' I said.

I thought: I don't feel well; what's wrong with me?

'You've cut your face,' Norman Picton said.

I also ached more or less all over from the desperate exertions of the judo. My head felt heavy and my hand was swollen and sore from Ellis's idea of entertainment. On the bright side, I was alive and home, safe . . . and reaction was all very well but I was *not* at this point going to faint.

'Sid!' Charles said sharply, putting out a hand.

'Oh . . . yes. Well, I went to Topline Foods.'

I drank some brandy. The weak feeling of sickness abated a bit. I shifted in my chair and took a grip on things.

Archie said, 'Take your time,' but sounded as if he didn't mean it.

I smiled. I said, 'Owen Yorkshire was there. So was Lord Tilepit. So was Ellis Quint.'

'Quint!' Davis Tatum exclaimed.

'Mm. Well . . . you asked me to find out if there was a heavyweight lumbering about behind the Quint business, and the answer is yes, but it is Ellis Quint himself.'

'But he's a playboy,' Davis Tatum protested. 'What about the big man, Yorkshire?' Tatum's own bulk quivered. 'He's getting known. One hears his name.'

I nodded. 'Owen Cliff Yorkshire is a heavyweight in the making.'

'What do you mean?'

I ached. I hadn't really noticed the wear and tear until then. Win now, pay later.

'Megalomania,' I said. 'Yorkshire's on the edge. He has a violent unpredictable temper and an uncontrolled desire to be a tycoon. I'd call it incipient megalomania because he's spending far beyond sanity on self-aggrandisement. He's built an office block fit for a major industry – and it's mostly empty – before building the industry first. He's publicity mad – he's holding a reception for half of Liverpool on Monday. He has plans – a *desire* – to take over the whole horse-feed nuts industry. He employs at least two bodyguards who will murder to order because he fears his competitors will assassinate him . . . which is paranoia.'

I paused, then said, 'It's difficult to describe the impression he gives. Half the time he sounds reasonable, and half the time you can see that he will simply get rid of anyone who stands in his way. And he is desperate . . . *desperate* . . . to save Ellis Quint's reputation.'

Archie asked 'Why?' slowly.

'Because,' I said, 'he has spent a colossal amount of money on an advertising campaign featuring Ellis, and if Ellis is found guilty of cutting off a horse's foot, that campaign can't be shown.'

'But a few advertisements can't have cost that much,' Archie objected.

'With megalomania,' I said, 'you don't just make a few economically priced advertisements. You really go to town. You engage an expensive highly prestigious firm – in this case, Intramind Imaging of Manchester – and you travel the world.'

With clumsy fingers I took from my belt the folded copy of the paper in the Quint box-file in Mrs Dove's office.

'This is a list of racecourses,' I said. 'These racecourses are where they filmed the commercials. A thirty-second commercial gleaned from each place. The expense is phenomenal.'

Archie scanned the list uncomprehendingly and passed it to Charles, who read it aloud.

'Flemington, Germiston, Sha Tin, Churchill Downs, Woodbine, Longchamps, K.L., Fuchu . . .'

There were fifteen altogether. Archie looked lost.

'Flemington,' I said, 'is where they run the Melbourne Cup in Australia. Germiston is outside Johannesburg. Sha Tin is in Hong Kong. Churchill Downs is where they hold the Kentucky Derby. K.L. is Kuala Lumpur in Malaysia, Woodbine is in Canada, Longchamps is in Paris, Fuchu is where the Japan Cup is run in Tokyo.'

They all understood.

'Those commercials are reported to be brilliant,' I said, 'and Ellis himself wants them shown as much as Yorkshire does.'

'Have you seen them?' Davis asked.

I explained about the box of BETACAM tapes. 'Making those special Broadcasting Quality tapes themselves must have been fearfully expensive – and they need special playing equipment which I didn't find at Topline Foods, so no, I haven't seen them.'

Norman Picton, with his policeman's mind, asked, 'Where did you see the tapes? Where did you get that list of racecourses?'

I said without emotion, 'In an office at Topline Foods.'

He gave me a narrow inspection.

'My car,' I told him, 'is still somewhere in Frodsham. Could you get your pals up there to look out for it?' I gave him its registration number, which he wrote down.

'Why did you leave it?' he asked.

'Er . . . I was running away at the time.' For all that I tried to say it lightly, the grim reality reached them.

'Well,' I sighed, 'I'd invaded Yorkshire's territory. He found me there. It gave him the opportunity to get rid of the person most likely to send Ellis to jail. I accepted that possibility when I went there but, like you, I wanted to know what was causing terrible trouble behind the scenes. And it is the millions spent on those ads.' I paused, and went on, 'Yorkshire and Ellis set out originally, months ago, not to kill me but to discredit me so that nothing I said would get Ellis convicted. They used a figurehead, Topline Foods director Lord Tilepit, because he owned *The Pump*. They persuaded Tilepit that Ellis was innocent and that I was all that *The Pump* has maintained. I don't think Tilepit believed Ellis guilty until today. I don't think *The Pump* will say a word against me from now on.' I smiled briefly. 'Lord Tilepit was duped by Ellis, and so, also, to some extent, was Owen Yorkshire himself.'

'How, Sid?' Davis asked.

'I think Yorkshire too believed in Ellis. Ellis dazzles people. Knowing Ellis, to Yorkshire, was a step up the ladder. Today they planned together to . . . er . . . wipe me out of the way. Yorkshire would have done it himself in reckless anger. Ellis stopped him, but left it to chance that the bodyguards might do it . . . but I escaped them. Yorkshire now knows Ellis is guilty, but he doesn't care. He cares only to be able to show that brilliant ad campaign, and make himself king of the horse-nuts. And, of course, it's not just horse-nuts that it's all about. They're a stepping stone. It's about being the Big Man with the power to bring mayors to his doorstep. If Yorkshire isn't stopped you'll find him manipulating more than *The Pump*. He's the sort of man you get in the kitchens of political clout.'

After a moment, Archie asked, 'So how do we stop him?'

I shifted wearily in the chair and drank some brandy, and said, 'I can, possibly, give you the tools.'

'What tools?'

'His secret files. His financial manoeuvrings. His debts. Details of bribes, I'd guess. Bargains struck. You scratch my back, I'll scratch yours. Evidence of leverage. Details of all his dealings with Ellis, and all his dealings with Tilepit. I'll give you the files. You can take it from there.'

'But,' Archie said blankly, 'where are these files?'

'In my computer in London.'

I explained the Internet transfer and the need for password cracking. I couldn't decide whether they were gladdened or horrified by what I'd done. A bit of both, I thought.

Charles looked the most shocked, Archie the least.

Archie said, 'If I ask you, will you work for me another time?'

I looked into the knowing eyes, and smiled, and nodded.

'Good,' he said.

CHAPTER FOURTEEN

I went home to Aynsford with Charles.

It had been a long evening in Archie's house. Archie, Davis, Norman and Charles had all wanted details, which I found as intolerable to describe as to live through. I skipped a lot.

I didn't tell them about Ellis's games with my hands. I didn't know how to explain to them that, for a jockey, his hands were at the heart of his existence . . . of his skill. One knew a horse by the feel of the bit on the reins, one listened to the messages, one interpreted the vibrations, one *talked* to a horse through one's hands. Ellis understood more than most people what the loss of a hand had meant to me, and that day he'd been busy punishing me in the severest way he could think of for trying to strip him of what he himself now valued most, his universal acclaim.

I didn't know how to make them understand that to Ellis the severing of a horse's foot had become a drug more addictive than any substance invented, that the risk and the power were intoxicating; that I'd been lucky he'd had only a wrench to use on me.

I didn't know how near he had come in his own mind to irrevocably destroying the right hand. I only knew that to me it had seemed possible that he would. I couldn't tell them that I'd intensely lived my own nightmare and still shook from fear inside.

I told them only that an adjustable wrench in Yorkshire's hands had cut my face.

I told them a little about the escape by judo, and all about the boy on roller-blades and the ice-cream cone and catching the bus within sight of Yorkshire and Ellis. I made it sound almost funny.

Archie understood that there was a lot I hadn't said, but he didn't press it. Charles, puzzled, asked, 'But did they *hurt* you, Sid?' and I half laughed and told him part of the truth. 'They scared me witless.'

Davis asked about Ellis's Shropshire alibi. His colleague, the Crown Prosecutor, was increasingly concerned, he said, that Ellis's powerful lawyers would prevent the trial from resuming.

I explained that I hadn't had time to find out at what hour Ellis had arrived at the dance.

'Someone must know,' I said. 'It's a matter of asking the local people, the people who helped to park the cars.' I looked at Norman. 'Any chance of the police doing it?'

'Not much,' he said.

'Round the pubs,' I suggested.

Norman shook his head.

'There isn't much time,' Davis pointed out. 'Sid, couldn't you do it tomorrow?'

Tomorrow, Sunday. On Monday, the trial.

Archie said firmly, 'No, Sid can't. There's a limit . . . I'll try and find someone else.'

'Chico would have done it,' Charles said.

Chico had undisputedly saved my pathetic skin that day. One could hardly ask more.

Archie's wife, before she'd driven over to spend the evening with her sister-in-law Betty Bracken, had, it appeared, made a mound of sandwiches. Archie offered them diffidently. I found the tastes of cheese and of chicken strange, as if I'd come upon them new from another world. It was weird the difference that danger and the perception of mortality made to familiar things. Unreality persisted even as I accepted a paper napkin to wipe my fingers.

Archie's doorbell rang. Archie went again to the summons and came back with a pinched displeased expression, and he was followed by a boy that I saw with surprise to be Jonathan.

The rebel wings of hair were much shorter. The yellow streaks had all but grown out. There were no shaven areas of scalp.

'Hi,' he said, looking round the room and fastening his attention on my face. 'I came over to see you. The aunts said you were here. Hey, man, you look different.'

'Three months older,' I nodded, 'so do you.'

Jonathan helped himself to a sandwich, disregarding Archie's disapproval.

'Hi,' he said nonchalantly to Norman. 'How's the boat?'

'Laid up for winter storage.'

Jonathan chewed and told me, 'They won't take me on an oil-rig until I'm eighteen. They won't take me in the navy. I've got good pecs. What do I do with them?'

'Pecs?' Charles asked, mystified.

'Pectoral muscles,' Norman explained. 'He's strong from weeks of water ski-ing.'

'Oh.'

I said to Jonathan, 'How did you get here from Combe Bassett?'

'Ran.'

He'd walked into Archie's house not in the least out of breath.

'Can you ride a motor-bike,' I asked, 'now that you're sixteen?'

'Do me a favour!'

'He hasn't got one,' Archie said.

'He can hire one.'

'But . . . what for?'

'To go to Shropshire,' I said.

I was predictably drowned by protests. I explained to Jonathan what was needed. 'Find someone – anyone – who saw Ellis Quint arrive at the dance. Find the people who parked the cars.'

'He can't go round the pubs,' Norman insisted. 'He's under age.'

Jonathan gave me a dark look which I steadfastly returned. At fifteen he'd bought gin for a truck-driver's wife.

'Hey,' he said. 'Where do I go?'

I told him in detail. His uncle and everyone else disapproved. I took all the money I had left out of my belt and gave it to him. 'I want receipts,' I said. 'Bring me paper. A signed statement from a witness. It's all got to be solid.'

'Is this,' he asked slowly, 'some sort of test?'

'Yes.'

'OK.'

'Don't stay longer than a day,' I said. 'Don't forget, you may be asked to give evidence this week at the trial.'

'As if I could forget.'

He took a bunch of sandwiches, gave me a wide smile, and without more words departed.

'You *can't*,' Archie said to me emphatically.

'What do *you* propose to do with him?'

'But . . . he's . . .'

'He's bright,' I said. 'He's observant. He's athletic. Let's see how he does in Shropshire.'

'He's only *sixteen*.'

'I need a new Chico.'

'But Jonathan steals cars.'

'He hasn't stolen one all summer, has he?'

'That doesn't mean . . .'

'An ability to steal cars,' I said with humour, 'is in my eyes an asset. Let's see how he does tomorrow, with this alibi.'

Archie, still looking affronted, gave in.

'Too much depends on it,' Davis said heavily, shaking his head.

I said, 'If Jonathan learns nothing, I'll go myself on Monday.'

'That will be too late,' Davis said.

'Not if you get your colleague to ask for one more day's adjournment. Invent flu or something.'

David said doubtfully, 'Are you totally committed to this trial? *The Pump* – or Ellis Quint – they haven't got to you in any way, have they? I mean . . . the hate campaign . . . do you want to back out?'

Charles was offended on my behalf. 'Of course he doesn't,' he said.

Such faith! I said plainly to Davis, 'Don't let your colleague back down. That's the real danger. Tell him to insist on prosecuting, alibi or no alibi. Tell the prosecution service to dredge up some guts.'

'Sid!' He was taken aback. 'They're realists.'

'They're shit-scared of Ellis's lawyers. Well, I'm not. Ellis took the foot off Betty Bracken's colt. I wish like hell that he hadn't, but he did. He has no alibi for that night. You get your colleague to tell Ellis's lawyers that the Northampton colt was a copycat crime. If we can't break Ellis's alibi, copycat is our story and we're sticking to it, and if you have any influence over your colleague the prosecutor, you make sure he gives me a chance in court to say so.'

Davis said faintly, 'I must not instruct him to do anything like that.'

'Just manage to get it dripped into his mind.'

'So there you are, Davis,' Archie said dryly, 'our boy shows no sign of the hate campaign having been successful. Rather the opposite, wouldn't you say?'

'Our boy' stood up, feeling a shade fragile. It seemed to have been a long day. Archie came out into the hall with Charles and me and offered his hand in farewell. Charles shook it warmly. Archie lifted my wrist and looked at the swelling and the deep bruising that was already crimson and black.

He said, 'You've had difficulty holding your glass all evening.'

I shrugged a fraction, long resigned to occupational damage. My hand was still a hand, and that was all that mattered.

'No explanation?' Archie asked.

I shook my head.

'Stone walls tell more,' Charles informed him calmly.

Archie, releasing my wrist, said to me, 'The British Horseracing Board wants you to double-check some of their own members for loyalty. Ultra-secret digging.'

'They wouldn't ask *me*.' I shook my head. 'I'm not the new people's idea of reliable.'

357

'They asked *me*,' he said, the eyes blazing with amusement. 'I said it would be you or nobody.'

'Nobody,' I said.

He laughed. 'You start as soon as the Quint thing is over.'

The trouble, I thought, as I sat quietly beside Charles as he drove to Aynsford, was that for me the Quint thing would never be over. Ellis might or might not go to jail . . . but that wouldn't be the end for either of us. Gordon's obsession might deepen. Ellis might maim more than horses. In both of them lay a compulsive disregard of natural law.

No one could ever be comprehensively protected from obsession. One simply had to live as best one could and disregard the feral threat lying in wait: and I would somehow have to shake Gordon loose from staking out my Pont Square door.

Charles said, 'Do you consider that transferring Yorkshire's secret files to your own computer was at all immoral? Was it . . . theft?'

He spoke without censure, but censure was implied. I remembered a discussion we'd had once along the lines of what was honourable and what was not. He'd said I had a vision of honour that made my life a purgatory and I'd said he was wrong, and that purgatory was abandoning your vision of honour and knowing you'd done it. 'Only for you, Sid,' he'd said. 'The rest of the world has no difficulty at all.'

It seemed he was applying to me my own rash judgement. Was stealing knowledge ever justified, or was it not?

I said without self-excuse, 'It was theft, and dishonourable, and I would do it again.'

'And purgatory can wait?'

I said with amusement, 'Have you read *The Pump*?'

After about five miles he said, 'That's specious.'

'Mm.'

'*The Pump*'s a different story of purgatory.'

I nodded and said idly, 'The anteroom to hell.'

He frowned, glancing across in distaste. 'Has hell arrived, then?' He hated excess emotion. I cooled it.

I said, 'No. Sorry. It's been a long day.'

He drove another mile, then asked, 'How *did* you hurt your hand?'

I sighed. 'I don't want a fuss. Don't *fuss*, Charles, if I tell you.'

'No. All right. No fuss.'

'Then . . . Ellis had a go at it.'

'*Ellis?*'

'Mm. Lord Tilepit and Owen Yorkshire watched Ellis enjoy it. That's how they now know he's guilty as charged with the colts. If Ellis had had shears instead of a wrench to use on my wrist, I would now have no hands – and for God's sake, Charles, keep your eyes on the road.'

'But *Sid* . . .'

'No fuss. You promised. There'll be no lasting harm.' I paused. 'If he'd wanted to kill me today, he could

359

have done it, but instead he gave me a chance to escape. He wanted . . .' I swallowed, 'he wanted to make me pay for defeating him . . . and he did make me pay . . . and on Monday in court I'll try to disgrace him for ever . . . and I *loathe* it.'

He drove to Aynsford in a silence I understood to be at least empty of condemnation. Braking outside the door he said regretfully, 'If you and Ellis hadn't been such good friends . . . no wonder poor Ginnie couldn't stand it.'

Charles saw the muscles stiffen in my face.

'What is it, Sid?' he asked.

'I . . . I may have made a wrong assumption.'

'What assumption?'

'Mm?' I said vaguely. 'Have to think.'

'Then think in bed,' he said lightly. 'It's late.'

I thought for half the night. Ellis's revenge brutally throbbed in my fingers. Ellis had tied my wrists and given me thirty seconds . . . I would be dead, I thought, if we hadn't been friends.

At Aynsford I kept duplicates of all the things I'd lost in my car – battery charger, razor, clothes and so on – all except the mobile phone. I did have the SIM card, but nothing to use it in.

The no-car situation was solved again by TeleDrive who came to pick me up on Sunday morning.

To Charles's restrained suggestion that I pass the

day resting with him – 'A game of chess, perhaps?' – I replied that I was going to see Rachel Ferns. Charles nodded.

'Come back,' he said, 'if you need to.'

'Always.'

'Take care of yourself, Sid.'

Rachel, Linda told me on the telephone, was home from the hospital for the day.

'Oh, do come,' she begged. 'Rachel *needs* you.'

I went empty-handed with no fish or wigs, but it didn't seem to matter.

Rachel herself looked bloodless, a white wisp of a child in the foothills of a far country. In the five days since I'd seen her, the bluish shadows under her eyes had deepened, and she had lost weight so that the round cheeks of the steroids under the bald head and the big shadowed eyes gave her the look of an exotic little bird, unlike life.

Linda hugged me and cried on my shoulder in the kitchen.

'It's good news, really,' she said, sobbing. 'They've found a donor.'

'But that's *marvellous*.' Like a sunburst of hope, I thought, but Linda still wept.

'He's a Swiss,' she said. 'He's coming from Switzerland. He's coming on Wednesday. Joe is paying his air fare and the hotel bills. Joe says money's no object for his little girl.'

'Then stop crying.'

'Yes . . . but it may not work.'

'And it *may*,' I said positively. 'Where's the gin?'

She laughed shakily. She poured two glasses. I still didn't much care for gin but it was all she liked. We clinked to the future and she began talking about paella for lunch.

Rachel was half sitting, half lying, on a small sofa that had been repositioned in the sitting-room so that she could look straight and closely into the fish tank. I sat beside her and asked how she felt.

'Did my mum tell you about the transplant?' she said.

'Terrific news.'

'I might be able to run again.'

Running, it was clear from her pervading lassitude, must have seemed at that point as distant as the moon.

Rachel said, 'I begged to come home to see the fishes. I have to go back tonight, though. I hoped you would come. I begged God.'

'You knew I would come.'

'I meant *today*, while I'm home.'

'I've been busy since I saw you on Tuesday.'

'I know, Mummy said so. The nurses tell me when you phone every day.'

Pegotty was crawling all round the floor, growing in

size and agility and putting everything unsuitable in his
mouth; making his sister laugh.

'He's so *funny*,' she said. 'They won't let him come
to the hospital. I begged to see him and the fishes. They
told me the transplant is going to make me feel sick,
so I wanted to come home first.'

'Yes,' I said.

Linda produced steamy rice with bits of chicken and
shrimps in, which we all ate with spoons.

'What's wrong with your hand?' Linda asked. 'In
places it's almost black.'

'It's only a bruise. It got a bit squashed.'

'You've got sausage fingers,' Rachel said.

'They'll be all right tomorrow.'

Linda returned to the only important subject. 'The
Swiss donor,' she said, 'is older than I am! He has three
children of his own. He's a school teacher . . . he sounds
a nice man, and they say he's so pleased to be going
to give Rachel some of his bone marrow.'

Rachel said, 'I wish it had been Sid's bone
marrow.'

I'd had myself tested, right at the beginning, but I'd
been about as far from a match as one could get.
Neither Linda nor Joe had been more than fifty per
cent compatible.

'They say he's a ninety per cent match,' Linda said.
'You never get a hundred per cent, even from siblings.
Ninety per cent is great.'

She was trying hard to be positive. I didn't know

363

enough to put a bet on ninety per cent. It sounded fine to me; and no one was going to kill Rachel's own defective bone marrow if they didn't believe they could replace it.

'They're going to put me into a bubble,' Rachel said. 'It's a sort of plastic tent over my bed. I won't be able to touch the Swiss man, except through the plastic. And he doesn't speak English, even. He speaks German. *Danke schön.* I've learned that, to say to him. Thank you very much.'

'He's a lucky man,' I said.

Linda, clearing the plates and offering ice-cream for pudding, asked if I would stay with Rachel while she took Pegotty out for a short walk in fresh air.

'Of course.'

'I won't be long.'

When she'd gone, Rachel and I sat on the sofa and watched the fish.

'You see that one?' Rachel pointed. 'That's the one you brought on Tuesday. Look how fast he swims! He's faster than all the others.'

The black and silver angel fish flashed through the tank, fins waving with vigour.

'He's you,' Rachel said. 'He's Sid.'

I teased her, 'I thought half of them were Sid.'

'Sid is always the fastest one. That's Sid,' she pointed. 'The others aren't Sid any more.'

'Poor fellows.'

She giggled. 'I wish I could have the fishes in the hospital. Mummy asked, but they said no.'

'Pity.'

She sat loosely cuddled by my right arm but held my other hand, the plastic one, pulling it across towards her. That hand still wasn't working properly, though a fresh battery and a bit of tinkering had restored it to half-life.

After a long silent pause, she said, 'Are you afraid of dying?'

Another pause. 'Sometimes,' I said.

Her voice was quiet, almost murmuring. It was a conversation all in a low key, without haste.

She said, 'Daddy says when you were a jockey you were never afraid of anything.'

'Are you afraid?' I asked.

'Yes, but I can't tell Mummy. I don't like her crying.'

'Are you afraid of the transplant?'

Rachel nodded.

'You will die without it,' I said matter-of-factly. 'I know you know that.'

'What's dying like?'

'I don't know. No one knows. Like going to sleep, I should think.' If you were lucky, of course.

'It's funny to think of not being here,' Rachel said. 'I mean, to think of being a *space*.'

'The transplant will work.'

'Everyone says so.'

'Then believe it. You'll be running by Christmas.'

She smoothed her fingers over my hand. I could feel the faint vibrations distantly in my forearm. Nothing, I thought, was ever entirely lost.

She said, 'Do you know what I'll be thinking, lying there in the bubble feeling awfully sick?'

'What?'

'Life's a bugger.'

I hugged her, but gently. 'You'll do fine.'

'Yes, but tell me.'

'Tell you what?'

'How to be brave.'

What a question, I thought. I said, 'When you're feeling awfully sick, think about something you like doing. You won't feel as bad if you don't think about how bad you feel.'

She thought it over. 'Is that all?'

'It's quite a lot. Think about fishes. Think about Pegotty pulling off his socks and putting them in his mouth. Think about things you've enjoyed.'

'Is that what *you* do?'

'It's what I do if something hurts, yes. It does work.'

'What if nothing hurts yet, but you're going into something scary!'

'Well . . . it's all right to be frightened. No one can help it. You just don't have to let being frightened stop you.'

'Are you ever frightened?' she asked.

'Yes.' Too often, I thought.

She said lazily, but with certainty, 'I bet you've never

been so frightened you didn't do something. I bet you're always brave.'

I was startled. 'No . . . I'm not.'

'But Daddy said . . .'

'I wasn't afraid of riding in races,' I agreed. 'Try me in a pit full of snakes, though, and I wouldn't be so sure.'

'What about a bubble?'

'I'd go in there promising myself I'd come out running.'

She smoothed my hand. 'Will you come and see me?'

'In the bubble?' I asked. 'Yes, if you like.'

'You'll make me brave.'

I shook my head. 'It will come from inside you. You'll see.'

We went on watching the fish. My namesake flashed his fins and seemed to have endless stamina.

'I'm going into the bubble tomorrow,' Rachel murmured. 'I don't want to cry when they put me in there.'

'Courage is lonely,' I said.

She looked up into my face. 'What does that mean?'

It was too strong a concept, I saw, for someone of nine. I tried to make things simpler.

'You'll be alone in the bubble,' I said. 'So make it your own palace. The bubble is to keep you safe from infection – safe from dragons. You won't cry.'

She snuggled against me; happier, I hoped. I loved

her incredibly. The transplant had a fifty-fifty chance of success. Rachel would run again. She *had* to.

Linda and Pegotty came back laughing from their walk and Linda built towers of bright plastic building blocks for Pegotty to knock down, a game of endless enjoyment for the baby. Rachel and I sat on the floor, playing draughts.

'You always let me be white,' Rachel complained, 'and then you sneak up with the black counters when I'm not looking.'

'You can play black, then.'

'It's disgusting,' she said, five minutes later. 'You're cheating.'

Linda looked up and said, astounded, 'Are you two *quarrelling*?'

'He always wins,' Rachel objected.

'Then don't play with him,' Linda said reasonably.

Rachel set up the white pieces as her own. I neglected to take one of them halfway through the game and with glee she huffed me, and won.

'Did you *let* me win?' she demanded.

'Winning's more fun.'

'I hate you.' She swept all the pieces petulantly from the board and Pegotty put two of them in his mouth.

Rachel, laughing, picked them out again and dried them and set up the board again, with herself again as white, and peacefully we achieved a couple of close finishes until, suddenly as usual, she tired.

Linda produced tiny chocolate cakes for tea and

talked happily of the Swiss donor and how everything was going to be *all right*. Rachel was convinced, I was convinced, Pegotty smeared chocolate all over his face. Whatever the next week might bring to all of us, I thought, that afternoon of hope and ordinariness was an anchor in reality, an affirmation that small lives mattered.

It wasn't until after she'd fastened both children into the back of her car to drive to the hospital that Linda mentioned Ellis Quint.

'That trial is on again tomorrow, isn't it?' she asked.

We stood in the chilly air a few paces from her car. I nodded. 'Don't let Rachel know.'

'She doesn't. It hasn't been hard to keep it all away from her. She never talks about Silverboy any more. Being so ill . . . she hasn't much interest in anything else.'

'She's terrific.'

'Will Ellis Quint go to prison?'

How could I say 'I hope so'? And *did* I hope so? Yet I had to stop him, to goad him, to make him fundamentally wake up.

I said, dodging it, 'It will be for the judge to decide.'

Linda hugged me. No tears. 'Come and see Rachel in her bubble?'

'You couldn't keep me away.'

'God . . . I hope . . .'

'She'll be all right,' I said. 'So will you.'

*

Patient TeleDrive took me back to London and, because of the fixed hour of Linda's departure to the hospital, I again had time to spare before meeting India for dinner.

I again ducked being dropped in Pont Square in the dark evening, and damned Gordon for his vigilance. He had to sleep *sometime* . . . but when?

The restaurant called Kensington Place was near the northern end of Church Street, the famous road of endless antique shops, stretching from Kensington High Street in the south, up to Notting Hill Gate, north. Teledrive left me and my overnight bag on the north-west corner of Church Street where I dawdled a while looking in the brightly lit windows of Waterstone's bookshop, wondering if Rachel would be able to hear the store's advertised children's audio tapes in her bubble. She enjoyed the subversive *Just William* stories. Pegotty, she thought, would grow up to be like him.

A large number of young Japanese people were milling around on the corner, all armed with cameras, taking flash pictures of each other. I paid not much attention beyond noticing that they all had straight black hair, short padded jackets, and jeans. As far as one could tell, they were happy. They also surged between me and Waterstone's windows.

They bowed to me politely, I bowed unenthusiastically in return.

They seemed to be waiting, as I was, for some pre-arranged event to occur. I gradually realised from their quiet chatter, of which I understood not a word, that half of them were men, and half young women.

We all waited. They bowed some more. At length, one of the young women shyly produced a photograph that she held out to me. I took it politely and found I was looking at a wedding. At a mass wedding of about ten happy couples wearing formal suits and western wedding dresses. Raising my head from the photo I was met by twenty smiles.

I smiled back. The shy young woman retrieved her photo, nodded her head towards her companions and clearly told me that they were all on their honeymoon. More smiles all round. More bows. One of the men held out his camera to me and asked – I gathered – if I would photograph them all as a group.

I took the camera and put my bag at my feet, and they arranged themselves in pairs neatly, as if they were used to it.

Click. Flash. The film wound on, quietly whirring.

All the newly-weds beamed.

I was presented, one by one, with nine more cameras. Nine more bows. I took nine more photos. Flash. Flash. Group euphoria.

What was it about me, I wondered, that encouraged such trust? Even without language there seemed to be no doubt on their part of my willingness to give pleasure. I mentally shrugged. I had the time, so what the hell. I took their pictures and bowed, and waited for eight o'clock.

I left the happy couples on Waterstone's corner and, carrying my bag, walked fifty yards down Church Street towards the restaurant. There was a narrow side street beside it, and opposite, on the other side of Church Street, one of those quirks of London life, a small recessed area of pavement with a patch of scrubby grass and a park bench, installed by philanthropists for the comfort of footsore shoppers and other vagrants. I would sit there, I decided, and watch for India. The restaurant doors were straight opposite the bench. A green-painted bench made of horizontal slats.

I crossed Church Street to reach it. The traffic on Sunday evening was sporadic to non-existent. I could see a brass plate on the back of the bench: the name of the benefactor who'd paid for it.

I was turning to sit when at the same time I heard a bang and felt a searing flash of pain across my back and into my right upper arm. The impact knocked me over and round so that I ended sprawling on the bench, half lying, half sitting, facing the road.

I thought incredulously, I've been *shot*.

I'd been shot once before. I couldn't mistake the *thud*. Also I couldn't mistake the shudder of outrage that my invaded body produced. Also . . . there was a great deal of blood.

I'd been shot by Gordon Quint.

He walked out of the shadows of the side street opposite and came towards me across Church Street. He carried a hand-gun with its black round mouth pointing my way. He was coming inexorably to finish what he'd started, and he appeared not to care if anyone saw him.

I didn't seem to have the strength to get up and run away.

There was nowhere to run to.

Gordon looked like a farmer from Berkshire, not an obsessed murderer. He wore a checked shirt and a tie and a tweed jacket. He was a middle-aged pillar of the community, a judge and jury and a hangman ... a raw, primitive walking act of revenge.

There was none of the screaming out-of-control obscenity with which he'd attacked me the previous Monday. This killer was cold and determined and *reckless*.

He stopped in front of me and aimed at my chest.

'This is for Ginnie,' he said.

I don't know what he expected. He seemed to be waiting for something. For me to protest, perhaps. To plead.

His voice was hoarse.

'For Ginnie,' he repeated.

I was silent. I wanted to stand. Couldn't manage it.

'Say something!' He shouted in sudden fury. The gun wavered in his hand, but he was too close to miss. 'Don't you *understand*?'

I looked not at his gun but at his eyes. Not the best view, I thought inconsequentially, for my last on earth.

Gordon's purpose didn't waver. I might deny him

any enjoyment of my fear, but that wasn't going to stop him. He stared at my face. He didn't blink. No hesitancy there. No withdrawal or doubt. None.

Now, I thought frozenly. It's going to be *now*.

A voice was shouting in the road, urgent, frantic, coming nearer, far too late.

The voice shouted one despairing word.

'*Dad*.'

Ellis . . . *Ellis* . . . Running across the road waving a five-foot piece of black angled iron fencing and shouting in frenzy at his father, '*Dad* . . . Dad . . . Don't . . . Don't do it.'

I could see him running. Nothing seemed very clear. Gordon could hear Ellis shouting but it wasn't going to stop him. The demented hatred simply hardened in his face. His arm straightened until his gun was a bare yard from my chest.

Perhaps I won't feel it, I thought.

Ellis swung the iron fencing post with two hands and all his strength and *hit his father on the side of the head*.

The gun went off. The bullet hissed past my ear and slammed into a shop window behind me. There were razor splinters of glass and flashes of light and shouting and confusion everywhere.

Gordon fell silently unconscious face down on the scrubby patch of grass, his right hand with the gun underneath him. My blood ran into a scarlet and widening pool below the slats of the bench. Ellis stood for an eternity of seconds holding the fencing post and staring at my eyes as if he could see into my soul, as if he would show me his.

For an unmeasurable hiatus blink of time it seemed there was between us a fusing of psyche, an insight of total understanding. It could have been a hallucination, a result of too much stress, but it was unmistakably the same for him.

Then he dropped the fencing post beside his father, and turned, and went away at a slow run, across Church Street and down the side road, loping, not sprinting, until he was swallowed by shadow.

I was suddenly surrounded by Japanese faces all asking unintelligible questions. They had worried eyes. They watched me bleed.

The gunshots brought more people, but cautiously. Gordon's attack, that to me had seemed to happen in slow motion, had in reality passed to others with bewildering speed. No one had tried to stop Ellis. People thought he was going to bring help.

I lost further account of time. A police car arrived busily, lights flashing, the first manifestation of all that I most detested – questions, hospitals, forms, noise, bright lights in my eyes, clanging and banging and being shoved around. There wasn't a hope of being quietly stitched up and left alone.

I told a policeman that Gordon, though unconscious at present, was lying over a loaded gun.

He wanted to know if Gordon had fired the shots in self-defence.

I couldn't be bothered to answer.

The crowd grew bigger and an ambulance made an entrance.

A young woman pushed the uniforms aside, yelling that she was from the Press. India . . . India . . . come to dinner.

'Sorry,' I said.

'*Sid* . . .' Horror in her voice and a sort of despair.

'Tell Kevin Mills . . .' I said. My mouth was dry from loss of blood. I tried again. She bent her head down to mine to hear above the hubbub.

With humour I said, 'Those Japanese people took a load of photos . . . I saw the flashes . . . so tell Kevin to get moving. Get those photos . . . and he can have . . . his exclusive.'

CHAPTER FIFTEEN

India wasn't a newspaperwoman for nothing. The front page of Monday's *Pump* bore the moderately accurate headline '*Shot in the Back*', with, underneath, a picture taken of Gordon Quint aiming his gun unequivocally at my heart.

Gordon's half-backview was slightly out of focus. My own face was sharp and clear with an expression that looked rather like polite interest, not the fatalistic terror I'd actually felt.

Kevin and *The Pump* had gone to town. *The Pump* acknowledged that its long campaign of denigration of Sid Halley had been a mistake.

Policy, I saw cynically, had done a one-eighty U-turn. Lord Tilepit had come to such senses as he possessed and was putting what distance he could between himself and Ellis Quint.

There had been twenty eyewitnesses to the shooting of J. S. Halley. Kevin, arming himself with a Japanese interpreter, had listened intently, sorted out what he'd been told, and got it right. Throughout his piece there was an undercurrent of awe that no one was going to be able to dispute the facts. He hadn't once said 'It is *alleged*.'

Gordon Quint, though still unconscious, would in due course be 'helping the police with their enquiries'. Kevin observed that Ellis Quint's whereabouts were unknown.

Inside the paper there were more pictures. One showed Ellis Quint, arms and fence post raised, on the point of striking his father. The Japanese collectively, and that one photographer in particular, had not known who Ellis Quint was. Ellis didn't appear on the TV screens in Japan.

Why had there been so much photo coverage? Because Mr Halley, Kevin said, had been kind to the honeymooners, and many of them had been watching him as he walked away down Church Street.

I read *The Pump* while sitting upright in a high bed in a small white side-room in Hammersmith Hospital, thankfully alone except for a constant stream of doctors, nurses, policemen and people with clipboards.

The surgeon who'd dealt with my punctures came to see me at nine in the morning, before he went off duty for the day. He looked a lot worse for wear by then than I did, I thought.

'How are you doing?' he asked, coming in wearily in a sweat-stained green gown.

'As you see . . . fine, thanks to you.'

He looked at the newspaper lying on the bed. 'Your

bullet,' he said, 'ploughed along a rib and in and out of your arm. It tore a hole in the brachial artery, which is why you bled so much. We repaired that and transfused you with three units of blood and saline, though you may need more later. We'll see how you go. There's some muscle damage but with physiotherapy you should be almost as good as new. You seem to have been sideways on, when he shot you.'

'I was turning. I was lucky.'

'You could put it like that,' he said dryly. 'I suppose you do know you've also got a half-mended fracture of the forearm? And some fairly deep trauma to the wrist?'

I nodded.

'And we've put a few stitches in your face.'

'Great.'

'I watched you race,' he said. 'I know how fast jockeys heal. Ex-jockeys too, no doubt. You can leave here when you feel ready.'

I said, 'Thanks,' sincerely, and he smiled exhaustedly and went away.

I could definitely move the fingers of my right hand, even though only marginally at present. There had been a private moment of sheer cowardice in the night when I'd woken gradually from anaesthesia and been unable to feel anything in my arm from the shoulder down. I didn't care to confess or remember the abject dread in which I'd forced myself to *look*. I'd awoken once before to a stump. This time the recurrent nightmare of help-

lessness and humiliation and no hands had drifted hor-
rifyingly in and out, but when I did finally look, there
was no spirit-pulverising void but a long white-wrapped
bundle that discernibly ended in fingernails. Even so,
they didn't seem to be connected to me. I had lain for
a grim while trying to consider paralysis, and when at
length pain had roared back it had been an enormous
relief: only whole healthy nerves felt that like. I had an
arm . . . and a hand . . . and a life.

Given those, nothing else mattered.

In the afternoon Archie Kirk and Norman Picton
argued themselves past the NO VISITORS sign on the door
and sat in a couple of chairs bringing good news and
bad.

'The Frodsham police found your car,' Norman said,
'but I'm afraid it's been stripped. It's up on bricks – no
wheels.'

'Contents?' I asked resignedly.

'No. Nothing.'

'Engine?'

'Most of it's there. No battery, of course. Everything
movable's missing.'

Poor old car. It had been insured though, for a
fortune.

Archie said, 'Charles sends his regards.'

'Tell him thanks.'

'He said you would be looking as though nothing
much had happened. I didn't believe him. Why aren't
you lying down?'

'It's more comfortable sitting up.'

Archie frowned.

I amplified mildly. 'There's a bullet burn across somewhere below my shoulder blade.'

Archie said, 'Oh.'

They both looked at the tall contraption standing beside the bed with a tube leading from a high bag to my elbow. I explained that too.

'It's one of those "painkiller on demand" things,' I said. 'If I get a twinge I press a button, and bingo, it goes away.'

Archie picked up the copy of *The Pump*. 'All of a sudden,' he commented, 'you're Saint Sid who can do no wrong.'

I said, 'It's enough to make Ellis's lawyers weep.'

'But you don't think, do you,' Archie said doubtfully, 'that Ellis's lawyers *connived* at the hate-Halley campaign?'

'Because they are ethical people?' I asked.

'Yes.'

I shrugged and left it.

'Is there any news of Ellis?' I asked. 'Or of Gordon?'

'Gordon Quint,' Norman said in a policeman's voice, 'was, as of an hour ago, still unconscious in a secure police facility and suffering from a depressed skull fracture. He is to have an operation to relieve the pressure on his brain. No one is predicting when he'll wake up or what mental state he'll be in, but as soon as he can understand, he'll be formally charged with attempted

381

murder. As you know, there's a whole flock of eye-witnesses.'

'And Ellis?' I asked.

Archie said, 'No one knows where he is.'

'It's very difficult,' I said, 'for him to go anywhere without being recognised.'

Norman nodded. 'Someone may be sheltering him. But we'll find him, don't worry.'

'What happened this morning,' I asked, 'about the trial?'

'Adjourned. Ellis Quint's bail is rescinded as he didn't turn up, and also he'll be charged with grievous bodily harm to his father. A warrant for his arrest has been issued.'

'He wanted to prevent his father from murdering,' I said. 'He can't have meant to hurt him seriously.'

Archie nodded. 'It's a tangle.'

'And Jonathan,' I asked, 'did he go to Shropshire?'

Both of them looked depressed.

'Well,' I said, 'didn't he go?'

'Oh yes, he went,' Norman said heavily. 'And he found the car-parkers.'

'Good boy,' I said.

'It's *not* so good.' Archie, like a proper civil servant, had brought with him a briefcase, from which he now produced a paper that he brought over to the bed. I pinned it down with the weight of my still-sluggish left hand and took in its general meaning.

The car-parkers had signed a statement saying that

Ellis Quint had dined with media colleagues and had brought several of them with him to the dance at about eleven-thirty. The parkers remembered him – of course – not only because of who he was (there had been plenty of other well-known people at the party, starting with members of the Royal Family) but chiefly because he had given them a tip and offered them his autograph. They knew it was before midnight, because their employment as car-parkers had ended then. People who arrived later had found only one car-parker – a friend of those who'd gone off duty.

Media colleagues! Damn it, I thought. I hadn't checked those with the duchess.

'It's an unbreakably solid alibi,' Norman observed gloomily. 'He was in Shropshire when the yearling was attacked.'

'Mm.'

'You don't seem disappointed, Sid,' Archie said, puzzled.

'No.'

'But why not?'

'I think,' I said, 'that you should phone Davis Tatum. Will he be in his office right now?'

'He might be. What do you want him for?'

'I want him to make sure the prosecutors don't give up on the trial.'

'You told him that on Saturday.' He was humouring me, I thought.

'I'm not light-headed from bullets, Archie, if that's

what you think. Since Saturday I've worked a few things out, and they are not as they may seem.'

'What things?'

'Ellis's alibi, for one.'

'But Sid—'

'Listen,' I said. 'This isn't all that easy to say, so don't look at me, look at your hands or something.' They showed no sign of doing so, so I looked at my own instead. I said, 'I have to explain that *I* am not as I seem. When people in general look at me they see a harmless person, youngish, not big, not tall, no threat to anyone. Self-effacing. I'm not complaining about that. In fact, I choose to be like that because people then *talk* to me, which is necessary in my job. They tend to think I'm cosy, as your sister Betty told me, Archie. Owen Yorkshire considers me a wimp. He said so. Only . . . I'm not really like that.'

'A *wimp*!' Archie exclaimed.

'I can look it, that's the point. But Ellis knows me better. Ellis calls me cunning and ruthless, and I probably am. It was he who years ago gave me the nickname of tungsten carbide because I wasn't easy to . . . er . . . intimidate. He thinks I can't be terrified, either, though he's wrong about that. But I don't mind him thinking it. Anyway, unlikely though it may seem, all this past summer, Ellis has been afraid of me. That's why he made jokes about me on television and got Tilepit to set his paper onto me. He wanted to defeat me by ridicule.'

384

I paused. Neither of them said a word.

I went on. 'Ellis is not what he seems, either. Davis Tatum thinks him a playboy. Ellis is tall, good-looking, outgoing, charming and *loved*. Everyone thinks him a delightful entertainer with a knack for television. But he's not only that. He's a strong, purposeful and power-ful man with enormous skills of manipulation. People underestimate both of us for various and different reasons – I look weak and he looks frivolous – but we don't underestimate each other. On the surface, the easy surface, we've been friends for years. But in our time we rode dozens of races against each other, and racing, believe me, strips your soul bare. Ellis and I know each other's minds on a deep level that has nothing to do with afternoon banter or chit-chat. We've been friends on that level too. You and Davis can't believe that it is Ellis himself who is the heavyweight, not Yorkshire, but Ellis and I both know it. Ellis has manipulated everyone – Yorkshire, Tilepit, *The Pump*, public opinion, and also those so-smart lawyers of his who think they're dictating the pace.'

'And you, Sid?' Norman asked. 'Has he pulled your strings too?'

I smiled ruefully, not looking at him. 'He's had a go.'

'I'd think it was impossible,' Archie said. 'He would have to put you underground to stop you.'

'You've learned a lot more about me, Archie,' I said lazily. 'I do like to win.'

He said, 'So why aren't you disappointed that Ellis's Shropshire alibi can't be broken?'

'Because Ellis set it up that way.'

'How do you mean?'

'Ever since the Northampton yearling was attacked, Ellis's lawyers have been putting it about that if Ellis had an unbreakable alibi for that night, which I bet he assured them he had, it would invalidate the whole Combe Bassett case. They put pressure on the Crown Prosecution Service to withdraw, which they've been tottering on the brink of doing. Never mind that the two attacks were separate, the strong supposition arose that if Ellis couldn't have done one, then he hadn't done the other.'

'Of course,' Norman said.

'No,' I contradicted. 'He made for himself a positively unbreakable alibi in Shropshire, and he got someone else to go to Northampton.'

'But no one *would*.'

'One person would. And did.'

'But *who*, Sid?' Archie asked.

'Gordon. His father.'

Archie and Norman both stiffened as if turned to pillars of salt.

The nerves in my right arm woke up. I pressed the magic button and they went slowly back to sleep. Brilliant. A lot better than in days gone by.

'He *couldn't* have done,' Archie said in revulsion.

'He did.'

'You're just *guessing*. And you're *wrong*.'

'No.'

'But *Sid* . . .'

'I know,' I sighed. 'You, Charles and I have all been guests in his house. But he shot me last night. See it in *The Pump*.'

Archie said weakly, 'But that doesn't mean . . .'

'I'll explain,' I said. 'Give me a moment.'

My skin was sweating. It came and went a bit, now and then. An affronted body, letting me know.

'A moment?'

'I'm not made of iron.'

Archie breathed on a smile. 'I thought it was tungsten?'

'Mm.'

They waited. I said, 'Gordon and Ginnie Quint gloried in their wonderful son, their only child. I accused him of a crime that revolted them. Ginnie steadfastly believed in his innocence; an act of faith. Gordon, however reluctantly, faced with all the evidence we gathered from his Land-Rover, must have come to acknowledge to himself that the unthinkable was true.'

Archie nodded.

I went on, 'Ellis's wretched persecution of me didn't really work. Sure, I hated it, but I was still *there*, and meanwhile the time of the trial was drawing nearer and nearer. Whatever odium I drew onto myself by doing it, I was going to describe in court, with all the Press and public listening, just how Ellis could have cut off the foot of Betty's colt. The outcome of the trial – whether or not the jury found Ellis guilty, and whether or not the judge sent him to jail – that wasn't the prime point. The trial itself, and all that evidence, would have convinced enough of the population of his guilt to destroy for ever the shining-knight persona. Topline Foods couldn't have – and, in fact, won't be able to – use those diamond-plated round-the-world ads.'

I took a deep couple of lungfuls of air. I was talking too much. Not enough oxygen, not enough blood.

I said, 'The idea of the Shropshire alibi probably came about gradually, and heaven knows to which of them first. Ellis received an invitation to the dance. The plan must have started from that. They saw it as the one effective way to stop the trial from taking place.'

Hell, I thought, I don't feel well. I'm getting old.

I said, 'You have to remember that Gordon is a farmer. He's used to the idea of the death of animals being profitable. I dare say that the death of one insignificant yearling was as nothing to him when set beside the saving of his son. And he knew where to find such a victim. He would have to have long replaced the shears taken by the police. It must have seemed quite easy, and in fact he carried out the plan without difficulty.'

Archie and Norman listened as if not breathing.

I started again. 'Ellis is many things, but he's not a murderer. If he had been, perhaps he would have been a serial killer of humans, not horses. That urge to do evil – I don't understand it, but it *happens*. Wings off butterflies and so on.' I swallowed. 'Ellis has given me a hard time, but in spite of several opportunities he hasn't let me be killed. He stopped Yorkshire doing it. He stopped his father last night.'

'People can hate until they make themselves ill,' Archie nodded. 'Very few actually murder.'

'Gordon Quint tried it,' Norman pointed out, 'and all but succeeded.'

'Yes,' I agreed, 'but that wasn't to help Ellis.'

'What was it, then?'

'Have to go back a bit.'

I'm too tired, I thought, but I'd better finish it.

I said to Norman, 'You remember that piece of rag you gave me?'

'Yes. Did you do anything with it?'

I nodded.

'What rag?' Archie asked.

Norman outlined for him the discovery at Northampton of the lopping shears wrapped in dirty material.

'The local police found the shears hidden in a hedge,' I said, 'and they brought them into the stud farm's office while I was there. The stud farm's owners, Miss Richardson and Mrs Bethany, were there, and so was Ginnie Quint, who was a friend of theirs and who had gone there to comfort them and sympathise. Ginnie forcibly said how much she despised me for falsely accusing her paragon of a son. For accusing my *friend*. She more or less called me Judas.'

'Sid!'

'Well, that's how it seemed. Then she watched the policeman unwrap the shears that had cut off the yearling's foot and, quite slowly, she went white . . . and fainted.'

'The sight of the shears,' Norman said, nodding.

'It was much more than that. It was the sight of the *material*.'

'How do you mean?'

'I spent a whole day . . . last Thursday, it seems a lifetime away . . . I chased all over London with that little piece of cloth, and I finished up in a village near Chichester.'

'Why Chichester?' Archie asked.

'Because that filthy old cloth had once been part of some bed hangings. They were woven as a special order by a Mrs Patricia Huxford, who's a doll of the first rank. She has looms in Lowell, near Chichester. She looked up her records and found that that fabric had been made nearly thirty years ago especially – and exclusively – for a Mrs Gordon Quint.'

Archie and Norman both stared.

'Ginnie recognised the material,' I said. 'She'd just been giving me the most frightful tongue-lashing for believing Ellis capable of maiming horses, and she suddenly saw, because that material was wrapped round shears, that I'd been right. Not only that, she knew that Ellis had been in Shropshire the night Miss Richardson's colt was done. She knew the importance of his alibi . . . and she saw – she understood – that the only other person who could or would have wrapped lopping shears in that unique fabric was Gordon. Gordon wouldn't have thought twice about snatching up any old rag to wrap his shears in – and I'd guess he decided to dump them because we might have checked Quint shears again for horse DNA if he'd taken them home. Ginnie saw that *Gordon* had maimed the yearling. It was too big a shock . . . and she fainted.'

Archie and Norman, too, looked shocked.

I sighed. 'I didn't understand that then, of course. I didn't understand it until the night before last, when everything sort of *clicked*. But now . . . I think it wasn't just because of Ellis's terrible guilt that Ginnie killed herself last Monday, but because it was Gordon's guilt and reputation as well . . . and then the trial was starting in spite of everything . . . and it was all too much . . . too much to bear.'

I paused briefly and went on, 'Ginnie's suicide sent Gordon berserk. He'd set out to help his son. He'd caused his wife's death. He blamed me for it, for having destroyed his family. He tried to smash my brains in, the morning she'd died. He lay in wait for me outside my flat . . . he was screaming that I'd killed her. Then, last night, in the actual moment that the picture in *The Pump* was taken, he was telling me the bullets were for Ginnie . . . it was my life for hers. He meant . . . he meant to do it.'

I stopped talking.

The white room was silent.

Later in the day I phoned the hospital in Canterbury and spoke to the ward sister.

'How is Rachel?' I asked.

'Mr Halley! But I thought . . . I mean, we've all read *The Pump*.'

'But you didn't tell Rachel, did you?' I asked anxiously.

'No . . . Linda – Mrs Ferns – said not to.'

'Good.'

'But are you—'

'I'm absolutely OK,' I assured her. 'I'm in Hammersmith Hospital. Du Cane Road.'

'The best!' she exclaimed.

'I won't argue. How's Rachel?'

'You know that she's a very sick little girl, but we're all hopeful of the transplant.'

'Did she go into the bubble?'

'Yes, very bravely. She says it's her palace and she's its queen.'

'Give her my love.'

'How soon . . . oh dear, I shouldn't ask.'

'I'll make it by Thursday.'

'I'll tell her.'

*

Kevin Mills and India came to visit before ten o'clock the following morning, on their way to work.

I was again sitting up in the high bed but by then felt much healthier. In spite of my protests my shot and mending arm was still held immobile in a swaddle of splint and bandages. Give it another day's rest, I'd been told, and just practise wiggling your fingers: which was all very well, except that the nurses had been too busy with an emergency that morning to reunite me with my left hand, which lay on the locker beside me. For all that it didn't work properly, I felt naked without it, and could do nothing for myself, not even scratch my nose.

Kevin and India both came in looking embarrassed by life in general and said far too brightly how glad they were to see me awake and recovering.

I smiled at their feelings. 'My dear children,' I said, 'I'm not a complete fool.'

'Look, mate . . .' Kevin's voice faded. He wouldn't meet my eyes.

I said, 'Who told Gordon Quint where to find me?'

Neither of them answered.

'India,' I pointed out, 'you were the only person who knew I would turn up at Kensington Place at eight o'clock on Sunday evening.'

'Sid!' She was anguished, as she had been in Church Street when she'd found me shot; and she wouldn't look at my face, either.

Kevin smoothed his moustache. 'It wasn't her fault.'

'Yours, then?'

'You're right about your not being a fool,' Kevin said. 'You've guessed what happened, otherwise you'd be flinging us out of here right now.'

'Correct.'

'The turmoil started Saturday evening,' Kevin said, feeling secure enough to sit down. 'Of course, as there's no daily *Pump* on Sundays there was hardly anyone in the office. George Godbar wasn't. No one was. Saturday is our night off. The shit really hit the fan on Sunday morning at the editorial meeting. You know editorial meetings ... well, perhaps you don't. All the department editors – news, sport, gossip, features, whatever, and the senior reporters – meet to decide what stories will be run in the next day's paper, and there was George Godbar in a positive *lather* about reversing policy on S. Halley. I mean, Sid mate, you should've heard him swear. I never knew so many orifices and sphincters existed.'

'The boss had leaned on him?'

'*Leaned!* There was a panic. Our lord the proprietor wanted you *bought off.*'

'How nice,' I said.

'He'd suggested ten thousand smackers, George said. Try ten million, I said. George called for copies for everyone of the complete file of everything *The Pump* has published about you since June, nearly all of it in India's column on Fridays. I suppose you've kept all those pieces?'

I hadn't. I didn't say so.

'Such *poison*,' Kevin said. 'Seeing it all together like that. I mean, it silenced the whole meeting, and it takes a lot to do that.'

'I wasn't there,' India said. 'I don't go to those meetings.'

'Be fair to India,' Kevin told me, 'she didn't write most of it. I wrote some. You know I did. Six different people wrote it.'

India still wouldn't meet my eyes and still wouldn't sit in the one empty chair. I knew about 'policy' and being burned at the stake and all that, yet week after week I'd dreaded her by-line. Try as I would, I still felt sore from that savaging.

'Sit down,' I said mildly.

She perched uneasily.

'If we make another dinner date,' I said, 'don't tell anyone.'

'Oh, Sid.'

'She didn't mean to get you *shot*, for Chrissakes,' Kevin protested. 'The Tilepit wanted you found. Wanted! He was shitting himself, George said. *The Pump*'s lawyer had passed each piece week by week as being just on the safe side of actionable, but at the meeting, when he read the whole file at once, he was *sweating*, Sid. He says *The Pump* should settle out of court for whatever you ask.'

'And I suppose you're not supposed to be telling me that?'

'No,' Kevin confessed, 'but you did give me the exclusive of the decade.'

'How did Gordon Quint find me?' I asked again.

'George said our noble lord was babbling on about you promising not to send him to jail if you walked out free from somewhere or other, and you *had* walked out free, and he wanted to keep you to your promise. George didn't know what he was talking about, but Tilepit made it crystal that George's job depended on finding you within the next five minutes, if not sooner. So George begged us all to find you, to say *The Pump* would confer sainthood immediately and fatten your bank balance, and I phoned India on the off-chance, and she said not to worry, she would tell you herself . . . and I asked her how . . . and where. There didn't seem to be any harm in it.'

'And you told George Godbar?' I said.

Kevin nodded.

'And he,' I said, 'told Lord Tilepit? And *he* told Ellis, I suppose . . . because Ellis turned up too.'

'George Godbar phoned Ellis's father's house, looking for Ellis. He got an answering machine telling him to try a mobile number, and he reached Gordon Quint in a car somewhere . . . and he told Gordon where you would be, if Ellis wanted to find you.'

Round and round in circles, and the bullets come out *here*.

I sighed again. I was lucky to be alive. I would settle for that. I also wondered how much I would screw out of *The Pump*. Only enough, I decided, to keep his lordship grateful.

Kevin, the confession over, got restlessly to his feet and walked round the room, stopping when he reached the locker on my left side.

He looked a little blankly at the prosthesis lying there and, after a moment, picked it up. I wished he wouldn't.

He said, surprised, 'It's bigger than I pictured. And heavier. And *hard*.'

'All the better to club you with,' I said.

'Really?' he asked interestedly. 'Straight up?'

'It's been known,' I said, and after a moment he put the arm down.

'It's true what they say of you, isn't it? You may not look it, but you're one tough bugger, Sid, mate, like I told you before.'

I said, 'Not many people look the way they are inside.'

India said, 'I'll write a piece about that.'

'There you are then, Sid.' Kevin was ready to go. 'I've got a rape waiting. Thanks for those Japs. Makes us even, right?'

'Even,' I nodded.

India stood up as if to follow him. 'Stay a bit,' I suggested.

She hesitated. Kevin said, 'Stay and hold his bloody hand. Oh shit. Well . . . sorry, mate. *Sorry*.'

'Get out of here,' I said.

India watched him go.

'I'm really sorry,' she said helplessly, 'about getting you shot.'

'I'm alive,' I pointed out, 'so forget it.'

Her face looked softer. At that hour in the morning she hadn't yet put on the sharply outlined lipstick nor the matt porcelain make-up. Her eyebrows were as dark and positive, and her eyes as light blue and clear, but this was the essential India I was seeing, not the worldly package. How different, I wondered, was the inner spirit from the cutting brain of her column.

She too, as if compelled, came over to my left side and looked at the plastic arm.

'How does it work?' she asked.

I explained about the electrodes, as I had for Rachel.

She picked up the arm and put her fingers inside, touching the electrodes. Nothing happened. No movement in the thumb.

I swallowed. I said, 'It probably needs a fresh battery.'

'Battery?'

'It clips into the side. That box-like thing...' I nodded towards the locker. '... that's a battery charger. There's a recharged battery in there. Change them over.'

She did so, but slowly, because of the unfamiliarity. When she touched the electrodes again, the hand obeyed the signals.

'Oh,' she said.

She put the hand down and looked at me.

'Do you,' she said, 'have a steel rod up your back-bone? I've never seen anyone more tense. And your forehead's sweating.'

She picked up the box of tissues lying beside the battery charger and offered it to me.

I shook my head. She looked at the immobilised right arm and at the left one on the locker, and a wave of understanding seemed to leave her without breath.

I said nothing. She pulled a tissue out of the box and jerkily dabbed at a dribble of sweat that ran down my temple.

'Why don't you put this arm on?' she demanded. 'You'd be better with it on, obviously.'

'A nurse will do it.' I explained about the emergency. 'She'll come when she can.'

'Let *me* do it,' India said.

'No.'

'Why not?'

'Because.'

'Because you're too bloody *proud*.'

Because it's too private, I thought.

I was wearing one of those dreadful hospital gowns like a barber's smock that fastened at the back of the neck and shapelessly covered the body. A white flap covered my left shoulder, upper arm, elbow, and what remained below. Tentatively India lifted and turned back the flap so that we both could see my elbow and the short piece of forearm.

'You hate it, don't you?' India said.

'Yes.'

'I would hate it, too.'

I can't bear this, I thought. I can bear Ellis unscrewing my hand and mocking me. I can't bear love.

India picked up the electric arm.

'What do I do?' she asked.

I said with difficulty, nodding again at the locker, 'Talcum powder.'

'Oh.' She picked up the prosaic white tinful of comfort for babies. 'In the arm, or on you?'

'On me.'

She sprinkled powder on my forearm. 'Is this right? More?'

'Mm.'

She smoothed the powder all over my skin. Her touch sent a shiver right down to my toes.

'And now?'

'Now hold it so that I can put my arm into it.'

She concentrated. I put my forearm into the socket, but the angle was wrong.

'What do I do?' she asked anxiously.

'Turn the thumb towards you a bit. Not too far. That's right. Now push up while I push down. That top bit will slide over my elbow and grip – and keep the hand on.'

'Like that?' She was trembling.

'Like that,' I said. The arm gripped where it was designed to.

I sent the messages. We both watched the hand open and close.

India abruptly left my side and walked over to where she'd left her handbag, picking it up and crossing to the door.

'Don't go,' I said.

'If I don't go, I'll cry.'

I thought that might make two of us. The touch of her fingers on the skin of my forearm had been a caress more intimate than any act of sex. I felt shaky. I felt more moved than ever in my life.

'Come back,' I said.

'I'm supposed to be in the office.'

'India,' I said, 'please . . .' Why was it always so impossible to plead? 'Please . . .' I looked down at my left hand. 'Please don't *write* about this.'

'Don't *write* about it?'

'No.'

'Well, I won't, but why not?'

'Because I don't like pity.'

She came halfway back to my side with tears in her eyes.

'Your Jenny,' she said, 'told me that you were so afraid of being pitied that you would never ask for help.'

'She told you too much.'

'Pity,' India said, coming a step nearer, 'is actually about as far from what I feel for you as it's possible to get.'

I stretched out my left arm and fastened the hand on her wrist.

She looked at it. I tugged, and she took the last step to my side.

'You're strong,' she said, surprised.

'Usually.'

I pulled her nearer. She saw quite clearly what I intended, and bent her head and put her mouth on mine as if it were not the first time, as if it were natural.

A pact, I thought.

A beginning.

Time drifted when she'd gone.

Time drifted to the midday news.

A nurse burst into my quiet room. 'Don't you have your television on? You're on it.'

She switched on knobs, and there was my face on the screen, with a newsreader's unemotional voice saying, 'Sid Halley is recovering in hospital.' There was a widening picture of me looking young and in racing colours: a piece of old film taken years ago of me weighing-in after winning the Grand National. I was holding my saddle in two hands and my eyes were full of the mystical wonder of having been presented with the equivalent of the Holy Grail.

The news slid to drought and intractable famine.

The nurse said 'Wait,' and twiddled more knobs,

and another channel opened with the news item and covered the story in its entirety.

A woman announcer whose lugubrious voice I had long disliked put on her portentous-solemn face and intoned:

'Police today found the body of Ellis Quint in his car deep in the New Forest in Hampshire . . .'

Frozen, I heard her saying, as if from a distance, 'Foul play is not suspected. It is understood that the popular broadcaster left a note for his father, still unconscious after an accidental blow to the head on Sunday night. Now over to our reporter in Hampshire, Buddy Bowes.'

Buddy Bowes, microphone in hand, filled the foreground of the screen with, slightly out of focus in the distance behind him, woodland and activity and a rear view of a white car.

'This is a sad ending,' Buddy Bowes said, appearing at least to show genuine regret, 'to a fairytale life. Ellis Quint, thirty-eight, who gave pleasure to millions with his appearances on television, will also be remembered as the dashing champion amateur steeplechase jockey whose courage and gallantry inspired a whole generation to get out there and *achieve*. In recent months he has been troubled by accusations of cruelty to animals from his longtime colleague and supposed friend, Sid Halley, ex-professional top jockey. Quint was due to appear in court yesterday to refute those charges . . .'

There was a montage of Ellis winning races, striding

403

about in macho riding boots, wowing a chat-show audience, looking glowingly alive and handsome.

'Ellis will be mourned by millions,' Buddy Bowes finished. 'And now back to the studio . . .'

The nurse indignantly switched off the set. 'They didn't say anything about you being shot.'

'Never mind.'

She went away crossly. The reputation Ellis had manufactured for me couldn't be reversed in a night, whatever *The Pump* might now say. Slowly perhaps. Perhaps never.

Ellis was dead.

I sat in the quiet white room.

Ellis was *dead*.

An hour later a hospital porter brought me a letter that he said had been left by hand on the counter of the hospital's main reception desk and overlooked until now.

'Overlooked since when?'

Since yesterday, he thought.

When he'd gone I held the envelope in the pincer fingers and tore it open with my teeth.

The two-page letter was from Ellis, his handwriting strong with life.

It said:

Sid, I know where you are. I followed the
ambulance. If you are reading this, you are alive
and I am dead. I didn't think you would catch me.
I should have known you would.

If you're wondering why I cut off those feet,
don't *you* ever want to break out? I was tired of
goody goody. I wanted the dark side. I wanted to
smash. To explode. To mutilate. I wanted to laugh
at the fools who fawned on me. I hugged myself. I
mocked the proles.

And that *scrunch*.

I did that old pony to make a good programme.
The kid had leukaemia. Sob-stuff story, terrific. I
needed a good one. My ratings were slipping.

Then I lusted to do it again. The danger. The
risk, the difficulty. And that *scrunch*. I can't
describe it. It gives me an ecstasy like nothing else.
Cocaine is for kids. Sex is nothing. I've had every
woman I ever wanted. The scrunch of bones is a
million-volt orgasm.

And then there's you. The only one I've ever
envied. I wanted to corrupt you too. No one
should be unbendable.

I know all you fear is helplessness. I know you.
I wanted to make you helpless in Owen Yorkshire's
office but all you did was sit there watching your
hand turn blue. I could feel you willing me to be
my real self but my real self wanted to hear your
wrist bones *crunch* to dust. I wanted to prove that

no one was good. I wanted you to crumble. To be like me.

And then, you'll think I'm crazy, I was suddenly glad you weren't sobbing and whining and I was proud of you that you really were how you are, and I felt happy and higher than a kite. And I didn't want you to die, not like that, not for anything. Not because of me.

I see now what I've done. What infinite damage.

My father did that last colt. I talked him into it.

It's cost my mother's life. If my father lives they'll lock him up for trying to kill you. They should have let me hang, back in June, when I tried with my tie.

They say people want to be caught. They go on and on sinning until someone stops them.

The letter ended there except for three words much lower down the page:

You win, Sid.

The two sheets of paper lay on the white bedclothes. No one else would see them, I thought.

I remembered Rachel saying how odd it would be to be dead. To be a *space*.

The whole white room was space.

Good and evil, he had been my friend. An enemy: but finally a friend.

The sour, cruel, underside of him receded.

I had the win, but there was no one standing in the stirrups to share it with.

Regret, loss, acceptance and relief; I felt them all.

I grieved for Ellis Quint.

FOR KICKS

CHAPTER ONE

The Earl of October drove into my life in a pale blue Holden which had seen better days, and danger and death tagged along for the ride.

I noticed the car turn in through the gateposts as I walked across the little paddock towards the house, and I watched its progress up our short private road with a jaundiced eye. Salesmen, I thought, I can do without. The blue car rolled to a gentle halt between me and my own front door.

The man who climbed out looked about forty-five and was of medium height and solid build, with a large well-shaped head and smoothly brushed brown hair. He wore grey trousers, a fine wool shirt, and a dark, discreet tie, and he carried the inevitable briefcase. I sighed, bent through the paddock rails, and went over to send him packing.

'Where can I find Mr Daniel Roke?' he asked. An English voice, which even to my untuned ear evoked expensive public schools; and he had a subtle air of authority inconsistent with the opening patter of representatives. I looked at him more attentively, and decided after all not to say I was out. He might even, in spite of the car, be a prospective customer.

'I,' I said, without too much joy in the announcement, 'am Daniel Roke.'

His eyelids flickered in surprise.

'Oh,' he said blankly.

I was used to this reaction. I was no one's idea of the owner of a prosperous stud-farm. I looked, for a start, too young, though I didn't feel it; and my sister Belinda says you don't often meet a business man you can mistake for an Italian peasant. Sweet girl, my sister. It is only that my skin is sallow and tans easily, and I have black hair and brown eyes. Also I was that day wearing the oldest, most tattered pair of jeans I possessed, with unpolished jodhpur boots, and nothing else.

I had been helping a mare who always had difficulty in foaling: a messy job, and I had dressed for it. The result of my – and the mare's – labours was a weedy filly with a contracted tendon in the near fore and a suspicion of one in the off fore too, which meant an operation, and more expense than she was likely to be worth.

My visitor stood for a while looking about him at the neat white-railed paddocks, the L-shaped stable yard away ahead, and the row of cedar-shingled foaling boxes off to the right, where my poor little newcomer lay in the straw. The whole spread looked substantial and well maintained, which it was; I worked very hard to keep it that way, so that I could reasonably ask good prices for my horses.

The visitor turned to gaze at the big blue-green lagoon to the left, with the snow-capped mountains rising steeply in rocky beauty along the far side of it. Puffs of cloud like plumes crowned the peaks. Grand and glorious scenery it was, to his fresh eyes.

But to me, walls.

'Breathtaking,' he said appreciatively. Then turning to me briskly, but with some hesitation in his speech, he said, 'I . . . er . . . I heard in Perlooma that you have . . . er . . . an English stable hand who . . . er . . . wants to go back home . . .' He broke off, and started again. 'I suppose it may sound surprising, but in certain circumstances, and if he is suitable, I am willing to pay his fare and give him a job at the other end . . .' He tailed off again.

There couldn't, I thought, be such an acute shortage of stable boys in England that they needed to be recruited from Australia.

'Will you come into the house?' I said. 'And explain?'

I led the way into the living-room, and heard his exclamation as he stepped behind me. All our visitors were impressed by the room. Across the far end a great expanse of window framed the most spectacular part of the lagoon and mountains, making them seem even closer and, to me, more overwhelming than ever. I sat down in an old bent-wood rocker with my back to

3

them, and gestured him into a comfortable armchair facing the view.

'Now, Mr . . . er?' I began.

'October,' he said easily. 'Not Mister. Earl.'

'October . . . as the month?' It was October at the time.

'As the month,' he assented.

I looked at him curiously. He was not my idea of an earl. He looked like a hard-headed company chairman on holiday. Then it occurred to me that there was no bar to an earl being a company chairman as well, and that quite probably some of them needed to be.

'I have acted on impulse, coming here,' he said more coherently. 'And I am not sure that it is ever a good thing to do.' He paused, took out a machine-turned gold cigarette case, and gained time for thought while he flicked his lighter. I waited.

He smiled briefly. 'Perhaps I had better start by saying that I am in Australia on business – I have interests in Sydney – but that I came down here to the Snowies as the last part of a private tour I have been making of your main racing and breeding centres. I am a member of the body which governs National Hunt racing – that is to say, steeplechasing, jump racing – in England, and naturally your horses interest me enormously . . . Well, I was lunching in Perlooma,' he went on, referring to our nearest township, fifteen miles away, 'and I got talking to a man who remarked on my English accent and said that the only other Pommie he

4

knew was a stable hand here who was fool enough to want to go back home.'

'Yes,' I agreed. 'Simmons.'

'Arthur Simmons,' he said, nodding. 'What sort of man is he?'

'Very good with horses,' I said. 'But he only wants to go back to England when he's drunk. And he only gets drunk in Perlooma. Never here.'

'Oh,' he said. 'Then wouldn't he go, if he were given the chance?'

'I don't know. It depends what you want him for.'

He drew on his cigarette, and tapped the ash off, and looked out of the window.

'A year or two ago we had a great deal of trouble with the doping of racehorses,' he said abruptly. 'A very great deal of trouble. There were trials and prison sentences, and stringent all-round tightening of stable security, and a stepping-up of regular saliva and urine tests. We began to test the first four horses in many races, to stop doping-to-win, and we tested every suspiciously beaten favourite for doping-to-lose. Nearly all the results since the new regulations came into force have been negative.'

'How satisfactory,' I said, not desperately interested.

'No. It isn't. Someone has discovered a drug which our analysts cannot identify.'

'That doesn't sound possible,' I said politely. The afternoon was slipping away unprofitably, I felt, and I still had a lot to do.

He sensed my lack of enthusiasm. 'There have been ten cases, all winners. Ten that we are sure of. The horses apparently look conspicuously stimulated – I haven't myself actually seen one – but nothing shows up in the tests.' He paused. 'Doping is nearly always an inside job,' he said, transferring his gaze back to me. 'That is to say, stable lads are nearly always involved somehow, even if it is only to point out to someone else which horse is in which box.' I nodded. Australia had had her troubles, too.

'We, that is to say, the other two Stewards of the National Hunt Committee, and myself, have once or twice discussed trying to find out about the doping from the inside, so to speak . . .'

'By getting a stable lad to spy for you?' I said.

He winced slightly. 'You Australians are so direct,' he murmured. 'But that was the general idea, yes. We didn't do anything more than talk about it, though, because there are many difficulties to such a plan and frankly we didn't see how we could positively guarantee that any lad we approached was not already working for . . . er . . . the other side.'

I grinned. 'And Arthur Simmons has that guarantee?'

'Yes. And as he's English, he would fade indistinguishably into the racing scene. It occurred to me as I was paying my bill after lunch. So I asked the way here and drove straight up, to see what he was like.'

'You can talk to him, certainly,' I said, standing up. 'But I don't think it will be any good.'

'He would be paid far in excess of the normal rate,' he said, misunderstanding me.

'I didn't mean that he couldn't be tempted to go,' I said, 'but he just hasn't the brain for anything like that.'

He followed me back out into the spring sunshine. The air at that altitude was still chilly and I saw him shiver as he left the warmth of the house. He glanced appraisingly at my still bare chest.

'If you'll wait a moment, I'll fetch him,' I said, and walking round the corner of the house, whistled shrilly with my fingers in my teeth towards the small bunkhouse across the yard. A head poked inquiringly out of a window, and I shouted, 'I want Arthur.'

The head nodded, withdrew, and presently Arthur Simmons, elderly, small, bow-legged, and of an endearing simplicity of mind, made his crab-like way towards me. I left him and Lord October together, and went over to see if the new filly had taken a firm hold on life. She had, though her efforts to stand on her poor misshapen foreleg were pathetic to see.

I left her with her mother, and went back towards Lord October, watching him from a distance taking a note from his wallet and offering it to Arthur. Arthur wouldn't accept it, even though he was English. He's been here so long, I thought, that he's as Australian as anyone. He'd hate to go back to Britain, whatever he says when he's drunk.

'You were right,' October said. 'He's a splendid chap, but no good for what I want. I didn't even suggest it.'

'Isn't it expecting a great deal of any stable lad, however bright, to uncover something which has got men like you up a gum-tree?'

He grimaced. 'Yes. That is one of the difficulties I mentioned. We're scraping the bottom of the barrel, though. Any idea is worth trying. Any. You can't realize how serious the situation is.'

We walked over to his car, and he opened the door.

'Well, thank you for your patience, Mr Roke. As I said, it was an impulse, coming here. I hope I haven't wasted too much of your afternoon?' He smiled, still looking slightly hesitant and disconcerted.

I shook my head and smiled back and he started the car, turned it, and drove off down the road. He was out of my thoughts before he was through the gateposts.

Out of my thoughts; but not by a long way out of my life.

He came back again the next afternoon at sundown. I found him sitting patiently smoking in the small blue car, having no doubt discovered that there was no one in the house. I walked back towards him from the stable block where I had been doing my share of the evening's chores, and reflected idly that he had again caught me at my dirtiest.

8

He got out of the car when he saw me coming, and stamped on his cigarette.

'Mr Roke.' He held out his hand, and I shook it.

This time he made no attempt to rush into speech. This time he had not come on impulse. There was absolutely no hesitation in his manner: instead, his natural air of authority was much more pronounced, and it struck me that it was with this power that he set out to persuade a boardroom full of hard directors to agree to an unpopular proposal.

I knew instantly, then, why he had come back.

I looked at him warily for a moment: then gestured towards the house and led him again into the living-room.

'A drink?' I asked. 'Whisky?'

'Thank you.' He took the glass.

'If you don't mind,' I said, 'I will go and change.' And think, I added privately.

Alone in my room I showered and put on some decent trousers, socks, and house-shoes, and a white poplin shirt with a navy blue silk tie. I brushed back my damp hair carefully in front of the mirror, and made sure my nails were clean. There was no point in entering an argument at a social disadvantage. Particularly with an earl as determined as this.

He stood up when I went back, and took in my changed appearance with one smooth glance.

I smiled fleetingly, and poured myself a drink, and another for him.

'I think,' he said, 'that you may have guessed why I am here.'

'Perhaps.'

'To persuade you to take a job I had in mind for Simmons,' he said without preamble, and without haste.

'Yes,' I said. I sipped my drink. 'And I can't do it.'

We stood there eyeing each other. I knew that what he was seeing was a good deal different from the Daniel Roke he had met before. More substantial. More the sort of person he would have expected to find, perhaps. Clothes maketh man, I thought wryly.

The day was fading, and I switched on the lights. The mountains outside the window retreated into darkness; just as well, as I judged I would need all my resolution, and they were both literally and figuratively ranged behind October. The trouble was, of course, that with more than half my mind I wanted to take a crack at his fantastic job. And I knew it was madness. I couldn't afford it, for one thing.

'I've learned a good deal about you now,' he said slowly. 'On my way from here yesterday it crossed my mind that it was a pity you were not Arthur Simmons; you would have been perfect. You did, if you will forgive me saying so, look the part.' He sounded apologetic.

'But not now?'

'You know you don't. You changed so that you wouldn't, I imagine. But you could again. Oh, I've no doubt that if I'd met you yesterday inside this house

10

looking as civilized as you do at this moment, the thought would never have occurred to me. But when I saw you first, walking across the paddock very tattered and half bare and looking like a gipsy, I did in fact take you for the hired help . . . I'm sorry.'

I grinned faintly. 'It happens often, and I don't mind.'

'And there's your voice,' he said. 'That Australian accent of yours . . . I know it's not as strong as many I've heard, but it's as near to cockney as dammit, and I expect you could broaden it a bit. You see,' he went on firmly, as he saw I was about to interrupt, 'if you put an educated Englishman into a stable as a lad, the chances are the others would know at once by his voice that he wasn't genuine. But they couldn't tell, with you. You look right, and you sound right. You seem to me the perfect answer to all our problems. A better answer than I could have dreamt of finding.'

'Physically,' I commented dryly.

He drank, and looked at me thoughtfully.

'In every way. You forget, I told you I know a good deal about you. By the time I reached Perlooma yesterday afternoon I had decided to . . . er . . . investigate you, one might say, to find out what sort of man you really were . . . to see if there were the slightest chance of your being attracted by such a . . . a job.' He drank again, and paused, waiting.

'I can't take on anything like that,' I said. 'I have enough to do here.' The understatement of the month, I thought.

11

'Could you take on twenty thousand pounds?' He said it casually, conversationally.

The short answer to that was 'Yes'; but instead, after a moment's stillness, I said 'Australian, or English?'

His mouth curled down at the corners and his eyes narrowed. He was amused.

'English. Of course,' he said ironically.

I said nothing. I simply looked at him. As if reading my thoughts he sat down in an armchair, crossed his legs comfortably, and said, 'I'll tell you what you would do with it, if you like. You would pay the fees of the medical school your sister Belinda has set her heart on. You would send your younger sister Helen to art school, as she wants. You would put enough aside for your thirteen-year-old brother Philip to become a lawyer, if he is still of the same mind when he grows up. You could employ more labour here, instead of working yourself into an early grave feeding, clothing, and paying school fees for your family.'

I suppose I should have been prepared for him to be thorough, but I felt a surge of anger that he should have pried so very intimately into my affairs. However, since the time when an angry retort had cost me the sale of a yearling who broke his leg the following week, I had learned to keep my tongue still whatever the provocation.

'I also have had two girls and a boy to educate,' he said. 'I know what it is costing you. My elder daughter

12

is at university, and the twin boy and girl have recently left school.'

When I again said nothing, he continued, 'You were born in England, and were brought to Australia when you were a child. Your father, Howard Roke, was a barrister, a good one. He and your mother were drowned together in a sailing accident when you were eighteen. Since then you have supported yourself and your sisters and brother by horse dealing and breeding. I understand that you had intended to follow your father into the law, but instead used the money he left to set up business here, in what had been your holiday house. You have done well at it. The horses you sell have a reputation for being well broken in and beauti-fully mannered. You are thorough, and you are respected.'

He looked up at me, smiling. I stood stiffly. I could see there was still more to come.

He said 'Your headmaster at Geelong says you had a brain and are wasting it. Your bank manager says you spend little on yourself. Your doctor says you haven't had a holiday since you settled here nine years ago except for a month you spent in hospital once with a broken leg. Your pastor says you never go to church, and he takes a poor view of it.' He drank slowly.

Many doors, it seemed, were open to determined earls.

'And finally,' he added, with a lop-sided smile, 'the bar keeper of the Golden Platypus in Perlooma says

13

he'd trust you with his sister, in spite of your good looks.'

'And what were your conclusions, after all that?' I asked, my resentment a little better under control.

'That you are a dull, laborious prig,' he said pleasantly.

I relaxed at that, and laughed, and sat down.

'Quite right,' I agreed.

'On the other hand, everyone says you do keep on with something once you start it, and you are used to hard physical work. You know so much about horses that you could do a stable lad's job with your eyes shut standing on your head.'

'The whole idea is screwy,' I said, sighing. 'It wouldn't work, not with me, or Arthur Simmons, or anybody. It just isn't feasible. There are hundreds of training stables in Britain, aren't there? You could live in them for months and hear nothing, while the dopers got strenuously to work all around you.'

He shook his head. 'I don't think so. There are surprisingly few dishonest lads, far fewer than you or most people would imagine. A lad known to be corruptible would attract all sorts of crooks like an unguarded goldmine. All our man would have to do would be to make sure that the word was well spread that he was open to offers. He'd get them, no doubt of it.'

'But would he get the ones you want? I very much doubt it.'

'To me it seems a good enough chance to be worth

taking. Frankly, any chance is worth taking, the way things are. We have tried everything else. And we have failed. We have failed in spite of exhaustive questioning of everyone connected with the affected horses. The police say they cannot help us. As we cannot analyse the drug being used, we can give them nothing to work on. We employed a firm of private investigators. They got nowhere at all. Direct action has achieved absolutely nothing. Indirect action cannot achieve less. I am willing to gamble twenty thousand pounds that with you it can achieve more. Will you do it?'

'I don't know,' I said, and cursed my weakness. I should have said, 'No, certainly not.'

He pounced on it, leaning forward and talking more rapidly, every word full of passionate conviction. 'Can I make you understand how concerned my colleagues and I are over these undetectable cases of doping? I own several racehorses – mostly steeplechasers – and my family for generations have been lovers and supporters of racing . . . The health of the sport means more to me, and people like me, than I can possibly say . . . and for the second time in three years it is being seriously threatened. During the last big wave of doping there were satirical jokes in the papers and on television, and we simply cannot afford to have it happen again. So far we have been able to stifle comment because the cases are still fairly widely spaced – it is well over a year since the first – and if anyone inquires we merely report that the tests were negative.

But we *must* identify this new dope before there is a widespread increase in its use. Otherwise it will become a worse menace to racing than anything which has happened before. If dozens of undetectably doped winners start turning up, public faith will be destroyed altogether, and steeplechasing will suffer damage which it will take years to recover from, if it ever does. There is much more at stake than a pleasant pastime. Racing is an industry employing thousands of people . . . and not the least of them are stud owners like you. The collapse of public support would mean a great deal of hardship.

'You may think that I have offered you an extraordinarily large sum of money to come over and see if you can help us, but I am a rich man, and, believe me, the continuance of racing is worth a great deal more than that to me. My horses won nearly that amount in prize money last season, and if it can buy a chance of wiping out this threat I will spend it gladly.'

'You are much more vehement today,' I said slowly, 'than you were yesterday.'

He sat back. 'Yesterday I didn't need to convince you. But I felt just the same.'

'There must be someone in England who can dig out the information you want,' I protested. 'People who know the ins and outs of your racing. I know nothing at all. I left your country when I was nine. I'd be useless. It's impossible.'

That's better, I approved myself. That's much firmer.

He looked down at his glass, and spoke as if with reluctance. 'Well . . . we did approach someone in England . . . A racing journalist, actually. Very good nose for news; very discreet, too; we thought he was just the chap. Unfortunately he dug away without success for some weeks. And then he was killed in a car crash, poor fellow.'

'Why not try someone else?' I persisted.

'It was only in June that he died, during steeplechasing's summer recess. The new season started in August and it was not until after that that we thought of the stable lad idea, with all its difficulties.'

'Try a farmer's son,' I suggested. 'Country accent, knowledge of horses . . . the lot.'

He shook his head. 'England is too small. Send a farmer's son to walk a horse round the parade ring at the races, and what he was doing would soon be no secret. Too many people would recognize him, and ask questions.'

'A farm worker's son, then, with a high IQ.'

'Do we hold an exam?' he said sourly.

There was a pause, and he looked up from his glass. His face was solemn, almost severe.

'Well?' he said.

I meant to say 'No', firmly. What I actually said was again 'I don't know.'

'What can I say to persuade you?'

'Nothing,' I said. 'I'll think about it. I'll let you know tomorrow.'

'Very well.' He stood up, declined my offer of a meal, and went away as he had come, the strength of his personality flowing out of him like heat. The house felt empty when I went back from seeing him off.

The full moon blazed in the black sky, and through a gap in the hills behind me Mount Kosciusko distantly stretched its blunt snow-capped summit into the light. I sat on a rock high up on the mountain, looking down on my home.

There lay the lagoon, the big pasture paddocks stretching away to the bush, the tidy white-railed small paddocks near the house, the silvery roof of the foaling boxes, the solid bulk of the stable block, the bunk-house, the long low graceful shape of the dwelling house with a glitter of moonlight in the big window at the end.

There lay my prison.

It hadn't been bad at first. There were no relations to take care of us, and I had found it satisfying to disappoint the people who said I couldn't earn enough to keep three small children, Belinda and Helen and Philip, with me. I liked horses, I always had, and from the beginning the business went fairly well. We all ate, anyway, and I even convinced myself that the law was not really my vocation after all.

My parents had planned to send Belinda and Helen to Frensham, and when the time came, they went. I dare say I could have found a cheaper school, but I had to try to give them what I had had . . . and that was why Philip was away at Geelong. The business had grown progressively, but so had the school fees and the men's wages and the maintenance costs. I was caught in a sort of upward spiral, and too much depended on my being able to keep on going. The leg I had broken in a steeplechase when I was twenty-two had caused the worst financial crisis of the whole nine years: and I had had no choice but to give up doing anything so risky.

I didn't grudge the unending labour. I was very fond of my sisters and brother. I had no regrets at all that I had done what I had. But the feeling that I had built a prosperous trap for myself had slowly eaten away the earlier contentment I had found in providing for them.

In another eight or ten years they would all be grown, educated, and married, and my job would be done. In another ten years I would be thirty-seven. Perhaps I too would be married by then, and have some children of my own, and send them to Frensham and Geelong . . . For more than four years I had done my best to stifle a longing to escape. It was easier when they were at home in the holidays, with the house ringing with their noise and Philip's carpentry all over the place and the girls' frillies hanging to dry in the bathroom. In the summer we rode or swam in the lagoon (the lake, as my English parents called it) and in the winter we ski-ed in the mountains. They were very good company and never took anything they had for

19

granted. Nor, now that they were growing up, did they seem to be suffering from any form of teenage rebellions. They were, in fact, thoroughly rewarding.

It usually hit me about a week after they had gone back to school, this fierce aching desperation to be free. Free for a good long while: to go farther than the round of horse sales, farther than the occasional quick trip to Sidney or Melbourne or Cooma.

To have something else to remember but the procession of profitable days, something else to see besides the beauty with which I was surrounded. I had been so busy stuffing worms down my fellow nestlings' throats that I had never stretched my wings.

Telling myself that these thoughts were useless, that they were self-pity, that my unhappiness was unreasonable, did no good at all. I continued at night to sink into head-holding miseries of depression, and kept these moods out of my days – and my balance sheets – only by working to my limit.

When Lord October came the children had been back at school for eleven days, and I was sleeping badly. That may be why I was sitting on a mountainside at four o'clock in the morning trying to decide whether or not to take a peculiar job as a stable lad on the other side of the world. The door of the cage had been opened for me, all right. But the tit-bit that had been dangled to tempt me out seemed suspiciously large.

Twenty thousand English pounds . . . A great deal of money. But then he couldn't know of my restless state of mind, and he might think that a smaller sum would make no impression. (What, I wondered, had he been prepared to pay Arthur?)

On the other hand, there was the racing journalist who had died in a car crash ... If October or his colleagues had the slightest doubt it was an accident, that too would explain the size of his offer, as conscience money. Throughout my youth, owing to my father's profession, I had learned a good deal about crime and criminals, and I knew too much to dismiss the idea of an organized accident as fantastic nonsense.

I had inherited my father's bent for orderliness and truth and had grown up appreciating the logic of his mind, though I had often thought him too ruthless with innocent witnesses in court. My own view had always been that justice should be done and that my father did the world no good by getting the guilty acquitted. I would never make a barrister, he said, if I thought like that. I'd better be a policeman, instead.

England, I thought. Twenty thousand pounds. Detection. To be honest, the urgency with which October viewed the situation had not infected me. English racing was on the other side of the world. I knew no one engaged in it. I cared frankly little whether it had a good or a bad reputation. If I went it would be no altruistic crusade: I would be going only because the adventure appealed to me, because it looked amusing and a challenge, because it beckoned me like a siren to fling responsibility to the wind and cut the self-imposed shackles off my wilting spirit.

Common sense said that the whole idea was crazy, that the Earl of October was an irresponsible nut, that I hadn't any right to leave my family to fend for themselves while I went gallivanting round the world, and that the only possible course open to me was to stay where I was, and learn to be content.

Common sense lost.

CHAPTER TWO

Nine days later I flew to England in a Boeing 707.

I slept soundly for most of the thirty-six hours from Sydney to Darwin, from Darwin to Singapore, Rangoon, and Calcutta, from Calcutta to Karachi and Damascus, and from Damascus to Düsseldorf and London Airport.

Behind me I left a crowded week into which I had packed months of paper-work and a host of practical arrangements. Part of the difficulty was that I didn't know how long I would be away, but I reckoned that if I hadn't done the job in six months I wouldn't be able to do it at all, and made that a basis for my plans.

The head stud-groom was to have full charge of the training and sale of the horses already on the place, but not to buy or breed any more. A firm of contractors agreed to see to the general maintenance of the land and buildings. The woman currently cooking for the lads who lived in the bunk-house assured me that she would look after the family when they came back for the long Christmas summer holiday from December to February.

23

I arranged with the bank manager that I should send post-dated cheques for the next term's school fees and for the fodder and tack for the horses, and I wrote a pile for the head groom to cash one at a time for the men's food, and wages. October assured me that 'my fee' would be transferred to my account without delay.

'If I don't succeed, you shall have your money back, less what it has cost me to be away,' I told him.

He shook his head, but I insisted; and in the end we compromised. I was to have ten thousand outright, and the other half if my mission were successful.

I took October to my solicitors and had the rather unusual appointment shaped into a dryly-worded legal contract, to which, with a wry smile, he put his signature alongside mine.

His amusement, however, disappeared abruptly when, as we left, I asked him to insure my life.

'I don't think I can,' he said, frowning.

'Because I would be . . . uninsurable?' I asked.

He didn't answer.

'I have signed a contract,' I pointed out. 'Do you think I did it with my eyes shut?'

'It was your idea.' He looked troubled. 'I won't hold you to it.'

'What really happened to the journalist?' I asked.

He shook his head and didn't meet my eyes. 'I don't know. It looked like an accident. It almost certainly *was* an accident. He went off the road at night on a bend on the Yorkshire moors. The car caught fire as it rolled down into the valley. He hadn't a hope. He was a nice chap . . .'

'It won't deter me if you have any reason for thinking it was not an accident,' I said seriously, 'but you must be frank. If it was not an accident, he must have made a lot of progress . . . he must have found out something pretty vital . . . it would be important to me to know where he had gone and what he had been doing during the days before he died.'

'Did you think about all this before you agreed to accept my proposition?'

'Yes, of course.'

He smiled as if a load had been lifted from him. 'By God, Mr Roke, the more I see of you the more thankful I am I stopped for lunch in Perlooma and went to look for Arthur Simmons. Well . . . Tommy Stapleton – the journalist – was a good driver, but I suppose accidents can happen to anyone. It was a Sunday early in June. Monday, really. He died about two o'clock at night. A local man said the road was normal in appearance at one-thirty, and at two-thirty a couple going home from a party saw the broken railings on the bend and stopped to look. The car was still smouldering: they could see the red glow of it in the valley, and they drove on into the nearest town to report it.

'The police think Stapleton went to sleep at the wheel. Easy enough to do. But they couldn't find out where he had been between leaving the house of some friends at five o'clock, and arriving on the Yorkshire

25

moors. The journey would have taken him only about an hour, which left eight hours unaccounted for. No one ever came forward to say he'd spent the evening with them, though the story was in most of the papers. I believe it was suggested he could have been with another man's wife . . . someone who had a good reason for keeping quiet. Anyway, the whole thing was treated as a straightforward accident.

'As to where he had been during the days before . . . we did find out, discreetly. He'd done nothing and been nowhere that he didn't normally do in the course of his job. He'd come up from the London offices of his newspaper on the Thursday, gone to Bogside races on the Friday and Saturday, stayed with friends near Hexham, Northumberland, over the weekend, and, as I said, left them at five on Sunday, to drive back to London. They said he had been his normal charming self the whole time.

'We – that is, the other two Stewards and I – asked the Yorkshire police to let us see anything they salvaged from the car, but there was nothing of any interest to us. His leather briefcase was found undamaged halfway down the hillside, near one of the rear doors which had been wrenched off during the somersaulting, but there was nothing in it besides the usual form books and racing papers. We looked carefully. He lived with his mother and sister – he was unmarried – and they let us search their house for anything he might have written down for us. There was nothing. We also contacted the sports editor of his paper and asked to see any possessions he had left in his office. There were only a few personal oddments and an envelope containing some press cuttings about doping. We kept that. You can see them when you get to England. But I'm afraid they will be no use to you. They were very fragmentary.'

'I see,' I said. We walked along the street to where our two cars were parked, his hired blue Holden, and my white utility. Standing beside the two dusty vehicles I remarked, 'You want to believe it was an accident . . . I think you want to believe it very much.'

He nodded soberly. 'It is appallingly disturbing to think anything else. If it weren't for those eight missing hours one would have no doubt at all.'

I shrugged. 'He could have spent them in dozens of harmless ways. In a bar. Having dinner. In a cinema. Picking up a girl.'

'Yes, he could,' he said. But the doubt remained, both in his mind and mine.

He was to drive the hired Holden back to Sydney the following day and fly to England. He shook hands with me in the street and gave me his address in London, where I was to meet him again. With the door open and with one foot in the car he said, 'I suppose it would be part of your . . . er . . . procedure . . . to appear as a slightly, shall we say, unreliable type of stable lad, so that the crooked element would take to you?'

'Definitely,' I grinned.

'Then, if I might suggest it, it would be a good idea

for you to grow a couple of sideburns. It's surprising what a lot of distrust can be caused by an inch of extra hair in front of the ears!'

I laughed. 'A good idea.'

'And don't bring many clothes,' he added. 'I'll fix you up with British stuff suitable for your new character.'

'All right.'

He slid down behind the wheel.

'Au revoir, then, Mr Roke.'

'Au revoir, Lord October,' I said.

After he had gone, and with his persuasive force at my elbow, what I was planning to do seemed less sensible than ever. But then I was tired to death of being sensible. I went on working from dawn to midnight to clear the decks, and found myself waking each morning with impatience to be on my way.

Two days before I was due to leave I flew down to Geelong to say goodbye to Philip and explain to his headmaster that I was going to Europe for a while; I didn't know exactly how long. I came back via Frensham to see my sisters, both of whom exclaimed at once over the dark patches of stubble which were already giving my face the required 'unreliable' appearance.

'For heaven's sake shave them off,' said Belinda. 'They're far too sexy. Most of the seniors are crazy about you already and if they see you like that you'll be mobbed.'

'That sounds delicious,' I said, grinning at them affectionately.

Helen, nearly sixteen, was fair and gentle and as graceful as the flowers she liked to draw. She was the most dependent of the three, and had suffered worst from not having a mother.

'Do you mean,' she said anxiously, 'that you will be away the whole summer?' She looked as if Mount Kosciusko had crumbled.

'You'll be all right. You're nearly grown up now,' I teased her.

'But the holidays will be so dull.'

'Ask some friends to stay, then.'

'Oh!' Her face cleared. 'Can we? Yes. That would be fun.'

She kissed me more happily goodbye, and went back to her lessons.

My eldest sister and I understood each other very well, and to her alone, knowing I owed it to her, I told the real purpose of my 'holiday'. She was upset, which I had not expected.

'Dearest Dan,' she said, twining her arm in mine and sniffling to stop herself crying, 'I know that bringing us up has been a grind for you, and if for once you want to do something for your own sake, we ought to be glad, only please do be careful. We do . . . we do want you back.'

'I'll come back,' I promised helplessly, lending her my handkerchief. 'I'll come back.'

*

The taxi from the air terminal brought me through a tree-filled square to the Earl of October's London home in a grey drizzle which in no way matched my spirits. Light-hearted, that was me. Springs in my heels.

In answer to my ring the elegant black door was opened by a friendly faced manservant who took my grip from my hand and said that as his lordship was expecting me he would take me up at once. 'Up' turned out to be a crimson-walled drawing-room on the first floor where round an electric heater in an Adam fireplace three men stood with glasses in their hands. Three men standing easily, their heads turned towards the opening door. Three men radiating as one the authority I had been aware of in October. They were the ruling triumvirate of National Hunt racing. Big guns. Established and entrenched behind a hundred years of traditional power. They weren't taking the affair as effervescently as I was.

'Mr Roke, my lord,' said the manservant, showing me in.

October came across the room to me and shook hands.

'Good trip?'

'Yes, thank you.'

He turned towards the other men. 'My two co-Stewards arranged to be here to welcome you.'

'My name is Macclesfield,' said the taller of them, an elderly stooping man with riotous white hair. He leaned forward and held out a sinewy hand. 'I am most interested to meet you, Mr Roke.' He had a hawk-eyed piercing stare.

'And this is Colonel Beckett.' He gestured to the third man, a slender ill-looking person who shook hands also, but with a weak limp grasp. All three of them paused and looked at me as if I had come from outer space.

'I am at your disposal,' I said politely.

'Yes . . . well, we may as well get straight down to business,' said October, directing me to a hide-covered armchair. 'But a drink first?'

'Thank you.'

He gave me a glass of the smoothest whisky I'd ever tasted, and they all sat down.

'My horses,' October began, speaking easily, conversationally, 'are trained in the stable block adjoining my house in Yorkshire. I do not train them myself, because I am away too often on business. A man named Inskip holds the licence – a public licence – and apart from my own horses he trains several for my friends. At present there are about thirty-five horses in the yard, of which eleven are my own. We think it would be best if you started work as a lad in my stable, and then you can move on somewhere else when you think it is necessary. Clear so far?'

I nodded.

He went on, 'Inskip is an honest man, but unfortunately he's also a bit of a talker, and we consider it essential for your success that he should not have any

31

reason to chatter about the way you joined the stable. The hiring of lads is always left to him, so it will have to be he, not I, who hires you.

'In order to make certain that we are short-handed – so that your application for work will be immediately accepted – Colonel Beckett and Sir Stuart Macclesfield are each sending three young horses to the stables two days from now. The horses are no good, I may say, but they're the best we could do in the time.'

They all smiled. And well they might. I began to admire their staff work.

'In four days, when everyone is beginning to feel overworked, you will arrive in the yard and offer your services. All right?'

'Yes.'

'Here is a reference.' He handed me an envelope. 'It is from a woman cousin of mine in Cornwall who keeps a couple of hunters. I have arranged that if Inskip checks with her she will give you a clean bill. You can't appear too doubtful in character to begin with, you see, or Inskip will not employ you.'

'I understand,' I said.

'Inskip will ask you for your insurance card and an income tax form which you would normally have brought on from your last job. Here they are.' He gave them to me. 'The insurance card is stamped up to date and is no problem as it will not be queried in any way until next May, by which time we hope there will be no more need for it. The income tax situation is more difficult, but we have constructed the form so that the address on the part which Inskip has to send off to the Inland Revenue people when he engages you is illegible. Any amount of natural-looking confusion should arise from that; and the fact that you were not working in Cornwall should be safely concealed.'

'I see,' I said. And I was impressed, as well.

Sir Stuart Macclesfield cleared his throat and Colonel Beckett pinched the bridge of his nose between thumb and forefinger.

'About this dope,' I said, 'you told me your analysts couldn't identify it, but you didn't give me any details. What is it that makes you positive it is being used?'

October glanced at Macclesfield, who said in his slow, rasping, elderly voice, 'When a horse comes in from a race frothing at the mouth with his eyes popping out and his body drenched in sweat, one naturally suspects that he has been given a stimulant of some kind. Dopers usually run into trouble with stimulants, since it is difficult to judge the dosage needed to get a horse to win without arousing suspicion. If you had seen any of these particular horses we have tested, you would have sworn that they had been given a big overdose. But the test results were always negative.'

'What do your pharmacists say?' I asked.

Beckett said sardonically, 'Word for word? It's blasphemous.'

I grinned. 'The gist.'

Beckett said, 'They simply say there isn't a dope they can't identify.'

'How about adrenalin?' I asked.

The Stewards exchanged glances, and Beckett said, 'Most of the horses concerned did have a fairly high adrenalin count, but you can't tell from one analysis whether that is normal for that particular horse or not. Horses vary tremendously in the amount of adrenalin they produce naturally, and you would have to test them before and after several races to establish their normal output, and also at various stages of their training. Only when you know their normal levels could you say whether any extra had been pumped into them. From the practical point of view . . . adrenalin can't be given by mouth, as I expect you know. It has to be injected, and it works instantaneously. These horses were all calm and cool when they went to the starting gate. Horses which have been stimulated with adrenalin are pepped up at that point. In addition to that, a horse often shows at once that he has had a subcutaneous adrenalin injection because the hairs for some way round the site of the puncture stand up on end and give the game away. Only an injection straight into the jugular vein is really foolproof; but it is a very tricky process, and we are quite certain that it was not done in these cases.'

'The lab chaps,' said October, 'told us to look out for something mechanical. All sorts of things have been tried in the past, you see. Electric shocks, for instance.

Jockeys used to have saddles or whips made with batteries concealed in them so that they could run bursts of current into the horses they were riding and galvanize them into winning. The horses' own sweat acted as a splendid conductor. We went into all that sort of thing very thoroughly indeed, and we are firmly of the opinion that none of the jockeys involved carried anything out of the ordinary in any of their equipment.'

'We have collected all our notes, all the lab notes, dozens of press cuttings, and anything else we thought could be of the slightest help,' said Macclesfield, pointing to three boxes of files which lay in a pile on a table by my elbow.

'And you have four days to read them and think about them,' added October, smiling faintly. 'There is a room ready for you here, and my man will look after you. I am sorry I cannot be with you, but I have to return to Yorkshire tonight.'

Beckett looked at his watch and rose slowly. 'I must be going, Edward.' To me, with a glance as alive and shrewd as his physique was failing, he said, 'You'll do. And make it fairly snappy, will you? Time's against us.'

I thought October looked relieved. I was sure of it when Macclesfield shook my hand again and rasped, 'Now that you're actually here the whole scheme suddenly seems more possible . . . Mr Roke, I sincerely wish you every success.'

October went down to the street door with them,

and came back and looked at me across the crimson room.

'They are sold on you, Mr Roke, I am glad to say.'

Upstairs in the luxurious deep-green carpeted, brass bedsteaded guest room where I slept for the next four nights I found the manservant had unpacked the few clothes I had brought with me and put them tidily on the shelves of a heavy Edwardian wardrobe. On the floor beside my own canvas and leather grip stood a cheap fibre suitcase with rust-marked locks. Amused, I explored its contents. On top there was a thick sealed envelope with my name on it. I slit it open and found it was packed with five-pound notes; forty of them, and an accompanying slip which read 'Bread for throwing on waters'. I laughed aloud.

Under the envelope October had provided everything from under-clothes to washing things, jodhpur boots to rainproof, jeans to pyjamas.

Another note from him was tucked into the neck of a black leather jacket.

'This jacket completes what sideburns begin. Wearing both, you won't have any character to speak of. They are regulation dress for delinquents! Good luck.'

I eyed the jodhpur boots. They were second-hand and needed polishing, but to my surprise, when I slid my feet into them, they were a good fit. I took them off and tried on a violently pointed pair of black walking shoes. Horrible, but they fitted comfortably also, and I kept them on to get my feet (and eyes) used to them.

The three box files, which I had carried up with me after October had left for Yorkshire, were stacked on a low table next to a small armchair, and with a feeling that there was no more time to waste I sat down, opened the first of them, and began to read.

Because I went painstakingly slowly through every word, it took me two days to finish all the papers in those boxes. And at the end of it found myself staring at the carpet without a helpful idea in my head. There were accounts, some in typescript, some in longhand, of interviews the Stewards had held with the trainers, jockeys, head travelling-lads, stable lads, blacksmiths, and veterinary surgeons connected with the eleven horses suspected of being doped. There was a lengthy report from a firm of private investigators who had interviewed dozens of stable lads in 'places of refreshment', and got nowhere. A memo ten pages long from a bookmaker went into copious details of the market which had been made on the horses concerned: but the last sentence summed it up: 'We can trace no one person or syndicate which has won consistently on these horses, and therefore conclude that if any one person or syndicate is involved, their betting was done on the Tote.' Farther down the box I found a letter from Tote Investors Ltd., saying that not one of their credit clients had backed all the horses concerned, but that of course they had no check on cash betting at race-courses.

The second box contained eleven laboratory reports of analyses made on urine and saliva samples. The first report referred to a horse called Charcoal and was dated eighteen months earlier. The last gave details of tests made on a horse called Rudyard as recently as September, when October was in Australia.

The word 'negative' had been written in a neat hand at the end of each report.

The press had had a lot of trouble dodging the laws of libel. The clippings from daily papers in the third box contained such sentences as 'Charcoal displayed a totally uncharacteristic turn of foot', and 'In the unsaddling enclosure Rudyard appeared to be considerably excited by his success'.

There were fewer references to Charcoal and the following three horses, but at that point someone had employed a news-gathering agency: the last seven cases were documented by clippings from several daily, evening, local, and sporting papers.

At the bottom of the clippings I came across a medium-sized manila envelope. On it was written 'Received from Sports Editor, Daily Scope, June 10th'. This, I realized, was the packet of cuttings collected by Stapleton, the unfortunate journalist, and I opened the envelope with much curiosity. But to my great disappointment, because I badly needed some help, all the clippings except three were duplicates of those I had already read.

Of these three, one was a personality piece on the woman owner of Charcoal, one was an account of a horse (not one of the eleven) going berserk and killing a woman on June 3rd in the paddock at Cartmel, Lancashire, and the third was a long article from a racing weekly discussing famous cases of doping, how they had been discovered and how dealt with. I read this attentively, with minimum results.

After all this unfruitful concentration I spent the whole of the next day wandering round London, breathing in the city's fumes with a heady feeling of liberation, asking the way frequently and listening carefully to the voices which replied.

In the matter of my accent I thought October had been too hopeful, because two people, before midday, commented on my being Australian. My parents had retained their Englishness until their deaths, but at nine I had found it prudent not to be 'different' at school, and had adopted the speech of my new country from that age. I could no longer shed it, even if I had wanted to, but if it was to sound like cockney English, it would clearly have to be modified.

I drifted eastwards, walking, asking, listening. Gradually I came to the conclusion that if I knocked off the aitches and didn't clip the ends of my words, I might get by. I practised that all afternoon, and finally managed to alter a few vowel sounds as well. No one asked me where I came from, which I took as a sign of success, and when I asked the last man, a barrow-boy, where I could catch a bus back to the West, I could no longer detect much difference between my question and his answer.

I made one purchase, a zip-pocketed money belt made of strong canvas webbing. It buckled flat round my waist under my shirt, and into it I packed the two hundred pounds: wherever I was going I thought I might be glad to have that money readily available.

In the evening, refreshed, I tried to approach the doping problem from another angle, by seeing if the horses had had anything in common.

Apparently they hadn't. All were trained by different trainers. All were owned by different owners: and all had been ridden by different jockeys. The only thing they all had in common was that they had nothing in common.

I sighed, and went to bed.

Terence, the manservant, with whom I had reached a reserved but definite friendship, woke me on the fourth morning by coming into my room with a laden breakfast tray.

'The condemned man ate hearty,' he observed, lifting a silver cover and allowing me a glimpse and a sniff of a plateful of eggs and bacon.

'What do you mean?' I said, yawning contentedly.

'I don't know what you and his Lordship are up to, sir, but wherever you are going it is different from what you are used to. That suit of yours, for instance, didn't come from the same sort of place as this little lot.'

He picked up the fibre suitcase, put it on a stool, and opened the locks. Carefully, as if they had been silk, he laid out on a chair some cotton pants and a checked cotton shirt, followed by a tan-coloured ribbed pull-over, some drain-pipe charcoal trousers, and black socks. With a look of disgust he picked up the black leather jacket and draped it over the chair back, and neatly arranged the pointed shoes.

'His Lordship said I was to make certain that you left behind everything you came with, and took only these things with you,' he said regretfully.

'Did you buy them?' I asked, amused, 'or was it Lord October?'

'His Lordship bought them.' He smiled suddenly as he went over to the door. 'I'd love to have seen him pushing around in that chain store among all those bustling women.'

I finished my breakfast, bathed, shaved, and dressed from head to foot in the new clothes, putting the black jacket on top and zipping up the front. Then I brushed the hair on top of my head forwards instead of back, so that the short black ends curved on to my forehead.

Terence came back for the empty tray and found me standing looking at myself in a full-length mirror. Instead of grinning at him as usual I turned slowly

41

round on my heel and treated him to a hard, narrow-eyed stare.

'Holy hell!' he said explosively.

'Good,' I said cheerfully. 'You wouldn't trust me then?'

'Not as far as I could throw that wardrobe.'

'What other impressions do I make on you? Would you give me a job?'

'You wouldn't get through the front door here, for a start. Basement entrance, if any. I'd check your references carefully before I took you on; and I don't think I'd have you at all if I wasn't desperate. You look shifty . . . and a bit . . . well . . . almost dangerous.'

I unzipped the leather jacket and let it flap open, showing the checked shirt collar and tan pullover underneath. The effect was altogether sloppier.

'How about now?' I asked.

He put his head on one side, considering. 'Yes, I might give you a job now. You look much more ordinary. Not much more honest, but less hard to handle.'

'Thank you, Terence. That's exactly the note, I think. Ordinary but dishonest.' I smiled with pleasure. 'I'd better be on my way.'

'You haven't got anything of your own with you?'

'Only my watch,' I assured him.

'Fine,' he said.

I noticed with interest that for the first time in four days he had failed to punctuate any sentence with an easy, automatic 'sir', and when I picked up the cheap suitcase he made no move to take it from me and carry it himself, as he had done with my grip when I arrived.

We went downstairs to the street door where I shook hands with him and thanked him for looking after me so well, and gave him a five-pound note. One of October's. He took it with a smile and stood with it in his hand, looking at me in my new character.

I grinned at him widely.

'Goodbye Terence.'

'Goodbye, and thank you ... sir,' he said; and I walked off leaving him laughing.

The next intimation I had that my change of clothes meant a violent drop in status came from the taxi driver I hailed at the bottom of the square. He refused to take me to King's Cross station until I had shown him that I had enough money to pay his fare. I caught the noon train to Harrogate and intercepted several disapproving glances from a prim middle-aged man with frayed cuffs sitting opposite me. This was all satisfactory, I thought, looking out at the damp autumn countryside flying past; this assures me that I do immediately make a dubious impression. It was rather a lop-sided thing to be pleased about.

From Harrogate I caught a country bus to the small village of Slaw, and having asked the way walked the last two miles to October's place, arriving just before six o'clock, the best time of day for seeking work in a stable.

Sure enough, they were rushed off their feet: I asked for the head lad, and he took me with him to Inskip, who was doing his evening round of inspection.

Inskip looked me over and pursed his lips. He was a stingy, youngish man with spectacles, sparse sandy hair, and a sloppy-looking mouth.

'References?' In contrast, his voice was sharp and authoritative.

I took the letter from October's Cornish cousin out of my pocket and gave it to him. He opened the letter, read it, and put it away in his own pocket.

'You haven't been with racehorses before, then?'

'No.'

'When could you start?'

'Now.' I indicated my suitcase.

He hesitated, but not for long. 'As it happens, we are short-handed. We'll give you a try. Wally, arrange a bed for him with Mrs Allnut, and he can start in the morning. Usual wages,' he added to me, 'eleven pounds a week, and three pounds of that goes to Mrs Allnut for your keep. You can give me your cards tomorrow. Right?'

'Yes,' I said: and I was in.

CHAPTER THREE

I edged gently into the life of the yard like a heretic into heaven, trying not to be discovered and flung out before I became part of the scenery. On my first evening I spoke almost entirely in monosyllables, because I didn't trust my new accent, but I slowly found out that the lads talked with such a variety of regional accents themselves that my cockney-Australian passed without comment.

Wally, the head lad, a wiry short man with ill-fitting dentures, said I was to sleep in the cottage where about a dozen unmarried lads lived, beside the gate into the yard. I was shown into a small crowded upstairs room containing six beds, a wardrobe, two chests of drawers, and four bedside chairs; which left roughly two square yards of clear space in the centre. Thin flowered curtains hung at the window, and there was polished linoleum on the floor.

My bed proved to have developed a deep sag in the centre over the years, but it was comfortable enough, and was made up freshly with white sheets and grey blankets. Mrs Allnut, who took me in without a second glance, was a round, cheerful little person with hair fastened in a twist on top of her head. She kept the cottage spotless and stood over the lads to make sure they washed. She cooked well, and the food was plain but plentiful. All in all, it was a good billet.

I walked a bit warily to start with, but it was easier to be accepted and to fade into the background than I had imagined.

Once or twice during the first few days I stopped myself just in time from absent-mindedly telling another lad what to do; nine years' habit died hard. And I was surprised, and a bit dismayed, by the subservient attitude everyone had to Inskip, at least to his face: my own men treated me at home with far more familiarity. The fact that I paid and they earned gave me no rights over them as men, and this we all clearly understood. But at Inskip's, and throughout all England, I gradually realized, there was far less of the almost aggressive egalitarianism of Australia. The lads, on the whole, seemed to accept that in the eyes of the world they were of secondary importance as human beings to Inskip and October. I thought this extraordinary, undignified, and shameful. And I kept my thoughts to myself.

Wally, scandalized by the casual way I had spoken on my arrival, told me to call Inskip 'Sir' and October 'My lord' – and said that if I was a ruddy Communist I could clear off at once: so I quickly exhibited what he called a proper respect for my betters.

On the other hand it was precisely because the relationship between me and my own men was so free and easy that I found no difficulty in becoming a lad among lads. I felt no constraint on their part and, once the matter of accents had been settled, no self-consciousness on mine. But I did come to realize that what October had implied was undoubtedly true: had I stayed in England and gone to Eton (instead of its equivalent, Geelong) I could not have fitted so readily into his stable.

Inskip allotted me to three newly arrived horses, which was not very good from my point of view as it meant that I could not expect to be sent to a race meeting with them. They were neither fit nor entered for races, and it would be weeks before they were ready to run, even if they proved to be good enough. I pondered the problem while I carried their hay and water and cleaned their boxes and rode them out at morning exercise with the string.

On my second evening October came round at six with a party of house guests. Inskip, knowing in advance, had had everyone running to be finished in good time and walked round himself first, to make sure that all was in order.

Each lad stood with whichever of his horses was nearest the end from which the inspection was started. October and his friends, accompanied by Inskip and

Wally, moved along from box to box, chatting, laughing, discussing each horse as they went.

When they came to me October flicked me a glance, and said, 'You're new, aren't you?'

'Yes, my lord.'

He took no further notice of me then, but when I had bolted the first horse in for the night and waited farther down the yard with the second one, he came over to pat my charge and feel his legs; and as he straightened up he gave me a mischievous wink. With difficulty, since I was facing the other men, I kept a dead-pan face. He blew his nose to stop himself laughing. We were neither of us very professional at this cloak and dagger stuff.

When they had gone, and after I had eaten the evening meal with the other lads, I walked down to the Slaw pub with two of them. Halfway through the first drinks I left them and went and telephoned October.

'Who is speaking?' a man's voice inquired.

I was stumped for a second: then I said 'Perlooma', knowing that that would fetch him.

He came on the line. 'Anything wrong?'

'No,' I said. 'Does anyone at the local exchange listen to your calls?'

'I wouldn't bet on it.' He hesitated. 'Where are you?'

'Slaw, in the phone box at your end of the village.'

'I have guests for dinner; will tomorrow do?'

'Yes.'

48

He paused for thought. 'Can you tell me what you want?'

'Yes,' I said. 'The form books for the last seven or eight seasons, and every scrap of information you can possibly dig up about the eleven . . . subjects.'

'What are you looking for?'

'I don't know yet,' I said.

'Do you want anything else?'

'Yes, but it needs discussion.'

He thought. 'Behind the stable yard there is a stream which comes down from the moors. Walk up beside it tomorrow, after lunch.'

'Right.'

I hung up, and went back to my interrupted drink in the pub.

'You've been a long time,' said Paddy, one of the lads I had come with. 'We're one ahead of you. What have you been doing – reading the walls in the Gents?'

'There's some remarks on them walls,' mused the other lad, a gawky boy of eighteen, 'that I haven't fathomed yet.'

'Nor you don't want to,' said Paddy approvingly. At forty he acted as unofficial father to many of the younger lads.

They slept one each side of me, Paddy and Grits, in the little dormitory. Paddy, as sharp as Grits was slow, was a tough little Irishman with eyes that never missed a trick. From the first minute I hoisted my suitcase on to the bed and unpacked my night things under his inquisitive gaze I had been glad that October had been so insistent about a complete change of clothes.

'How about another drink?'

'One more, then,' assented Paddy. 'I can just about run to it, I reckon.'

I took the glasses to the bar and bought refills: there was a pause while Paddy and Grits dug into their pockets and repaid me elevenpence each. The beer, which to me tasted strong and bitter, was not, I thought, worth four miles' walk, but many of the lads, it appeared, had bicycles or rickety cars and made the trek on several evenings a week.

'Nothing much doing, tonight,' observed Grits gloomily. He brightened. 'Pay day tomorrow.'

'It'll be full here tomorrow, and that's a fact,' agreed Paddy. 'With Soupy and that lot from Granger's and all.'

'Granger's?' I asked.

'Sure, don't you know nothing?' said Grits with mild contempt. 'Granger's stable, over t'other side of the hill.'

'Where have you been all your life?' said Paddy.

'He's new to racing, mind you,' said Grits, being fair.

'Yes, but all the same!' Paddy drank past the halfway mark, and wiped his mouth on the back of his hand.

Grits finished his beer and sighed. 'That's it, then. Better be getting back, I suppose.'

We walked back to the stables, talking as always about horses.

*

The following afternoon I wandered casually out of the stables and started up the stream, picking up stones as I went and throwing them in, as if to enjoy the splash. Some of the lads were punting a football about in the paddock behind the yard, but none of them paid any attention to me. A good long way up the hill, where the stream ran through a steep, grass-sided gully, I came across October sitting on a boulder smoking a cigarette. He was accompanied by a black retriever, and a gun and a full game bag lay on the ground beside him.

'Dr Livingstone, I presume,' he said, smiling.

'Quite right, Mr Stanley. How did you guess?' I perched on a boulder near to him.

He kicked the game bag. 'The form books are in here, and a notebook with all that Beckett and I could rake up at such short notice about those eleven horses. But surely the reports in the files you read would be of more use than the odd snippets we can supply?'

'Anything may be useful . . . you never know. There was one clipping in that packet of Stapleton's which was interesting. It was about historic dope cases. It said that certain horses apparently turned harmless food into something that showed a positive dope reaction, just through chemical changes in their body. I suppose it isn't possible that the reverse could occur? I mean, could some horses break down any sort of dope into harmless substances, so that no positive reaction showed in the test?'

'I'll find out.'

'There's only one other thing,' I said. 'I have been assigned to three of those useless brutes you filled the yard up with, and that means no trips to racecourses. I was wondering if perhaps you could sell one of them again, and then I'd have a chance of mixing with lads from several stables at the sales. Three other men are doing three horses each here, so I shouldn't find myself redundant, and I might well be given a raceable horse to look after.'

'I will sell one,' he said, 'but if it goes for auction it will take time. The application forms have to go to the auctioneer nearly a month before the sale date.'

I nodded. 'It's utterly frustrating. I wish I could think of a way of getting myself transferred to a horse which is due to race shortly. Preferably one going to a far distant course, because an overnight stop would be ideal.'

'Lads don't change their horses in mid-stream,' he said rubbing his chin.

'So I've been told. It's the luck of the draw. You get them when they come and you're stuck with them until they leave. If they turn out useless, it's just too bad.'

We stood up. The retriever, who had lain quiet all this time with his muzzle resting on his paws, got to his feet also and stretched himself, and wagging his tail slowly from side to side looked up trustingly at his master. October bent down, gave the dog an affectionate slap, and picked up the gun. I picked up the game bag and swung it over my shoulder.

We shook hands, and October said, smiling, 'You may like to know that Inskip thinks you ride extraordinarily well for a stable lad. His exact words were that he didn't really trust men with your sort of looks, but that you'd the hands of an angel. You'd better watch that.'

'Hell,' I said, 'I hadn't given it a thought.'

He grinned and went off up the hill, and I turned downwards along the stream, gradually becoming ruefully aware that however much of a lark I might find it to put on wolf's clothing, it was going to hurt my pride if I had to hash up my riding as well.

The pub in Slaw was crowded that evening and the wage packets took a hiding. About half the strength from October's stable was there – one of them had given me a lift down in his car – and also a group of Granger's lads, including three lasses, who took a good deal of double-meaning teasing and thoroughly enjoyed it. Most of the talk was friendly bragging that each lad's horses were better than those of anyone else.

'My bugger'll beat yours with his eyes shut on Wednesday.'

'You've got a ruddy hope . . .'

'. . . Yours couldn't run a snail to a close finish.'

'. . . The jockey made a right muck of the start and never got in touch . . .'

'. . . Fat as a pig and bloody obstinate as well.'

The easy chat ebbed and flowed while the air grew thick with cigarette smoke and the warmth of too many

53

lungs breathing the same box of air. A game of darts between some inaccurate players was in progress in one corner, and the balls of bar billiards clicked in another. I lolled on a hard chair with my arm hooked over the back and watched Paddy and one of Granger's lads engaged in a needle match of dominoes. Horses, cars, football, boxing, films, the last local dance, and back to horses, always back to horses. I listened to it all and learned nothing except that these lads were mostly content with their lives, mostly good natured, mostly observant, and mostly harmless.

'You're new, aren't you?' said a challenging voice in my ear.

I turned my head and looked up at him. 'Yeah,' I said languidly.

These were the only eyes I had seen in Yorkshire which held anything of the sort of guile I was looking for. I gave him back his stare until his lips curled in recognition that I was one of his kind.

'What's your name?'

'Dan,' I said, 'and yours?'

'Thomas Nathaniel Tarleton.' He waited for some reaction, but I didn't know what it ought to be.

'T.N.T.,' said Paddy obligingly, looking up from his dominoes. 'Soupy.' His quick gaze flickered over both of us.

'The high explosive kid himself,' I murmured.

Soupy Tarleton smiled a small, carefully dangerous smile: to impress me, I gathered. He was about my own age and build, but much fairer, with the reddish skin which I had noticed so many Englishmen had. His light hazel eyes protruded slightly in their sockets, and he had grown a narrow moustache on the upper lip of his full, moist-looking mouth. On the little finger of his right hand he wore a heavy gold ring, and on his left wrist, an expensive wrist watch. His clothes were of good material, though distinctly sharp in cut, and the enviable fleece-lined quilted jacket he carried over his arm would have cost him three weeks' pay.

He showed no signs of wanting to be friendly. After looking me over as thoroughly as I had him, he merely nodded, said 'See you', and detached himself to go over and watch the bar billiards.

Grits brought a fresh half pint from the bar and settled himself on the bench next to Paddy.

'You don't want to trust Soupy,' he told me confidentially, his raw boned unintelligent face full of kindness.

Paddy put down a double three, and looking round at us gave me a long, unsmiling scrutiny.

'There's no need to worry about Dan, Grits,' he said. 'He and Soupy, they're alike. They'd go well in double harness. Birds of a feather, that's what they are.'

'But you said I wasn't to trust Soupy,' objected Grits, looking from one to the other of us with troubled eyes.

'That's right,' said Paddy flatly. He put down a three-four and concentrated on his game.

Grits shifted six inches towards Paddy and gave me

one puzzled, embarrassed glance. Then he found the inside of his beer mug suddenly intensely interesting and didn't raise his eyes to mine again.

I think it was at that exact moment that the charade began to lose its light-heartedness. I liked Paddy and Grits, and for three days they had accepted me with casual good humour. I was not prepared for Paddy's instant recognition that it was with Soupy that my real interest lay, nor for his immediate rejection of me on that account. It was a shock which I ought to have foreseen, and hadn't: and it should have warned me what to expect in the future, but it didn't.

Colonel Beckett's staff work continued to be of the highest possible kind. Having committed himself to the offensive, he was prepared to back the attack with massive and immediate reinforcements: which is to say that as soon as he had heard from October that I was immobilized in the stable with three useless horses, he set about liberating me.

On Tuesday afternoon, when I had been with the stable for a week, Wally, the head lad, stopped me as I carried two buckets of water across the yard.

'That horse of yours in number seventeen is going tomorrow,' he said. 'You'll have to look sharp in the morning with your work, because you are to be ready to go with it at twelve-thirty. The horse box will take you to another racing stables, down near Nottingham.

You are to leave this horse there and bring a new one back. Right?'

'Right,' I said. Wally's manner was cool with me; but over the weekend I had made myself be reconciled to the knowledge that I had to go on inspiring a faint mistrust all round, even if I no longer much liked it when I succeeded.

Most of Sunday I had spent reading the form books, which the others in the cottage regarded as a perfectly natural activity; and in the evening, when they all went down to the pub, I did some pretty concentrated work with a pencil, making analyses of the eleven horses and their assisted wins. It was true, as I had discovered from the newspaper cuttings in London, that they all had different owners, trainers, and jockeys: but it was not true that they had absolutely nothing in common. By the time I had sealed my notes into an envelope and put it with October's notebook into the game bag under some form books, away from the inquiring gaze of the beer-happy returning lads, I was in possession of four unhelpful points of similarity.

First, the horses had all won selling 'chases – races where the winner was subsequently put up for auction. In the auctions three horses had been bought back by their owners, and the rest had been sold for modest sums.

Second, in all their racing lives all the horses had proved themselves to be capable of making a show in a race, but had either no strength or no guts when it came to a finish.

Third, none of them had won any races except the ones for which they were doped, though they had occasionally been placed on other occasions.

Fourth, none of them had won at odds of less than ten to one.

I learned both from October's notes and from the form books that several of the horses had changed trainers more than once, but they were such moderate, unrewarding animals that this was only to be expected. I was also in possession of the useless information that the horses were all by different sires out of different dams, that they varied in age from five to eleven, and that they were not all of the same colour. Neither had they all won on the same course, though in this case they had not all won on different courses either; and geographically I had a vague idea that the courses concerned were all in the northern half of the country – Kelso, Haydock, Sedgefield, Stafford, and Ludlow. I decided to check them on a map, to see if this was right, but there wasn't one to be found chez Mrs Allnut.

I went to bed in the crowded little dormitory with the other lads' beery breaths gradually overwhelming the usual mixed clean smells of boot polish and hair oil, and lost an argument about having the small sash window open more than four inches at the top. The lads all seemed to take their cue from Paddy, who was undoubtedly the most aware of them, and if Paddy declined to treat me as a friend, so would they: I realized that if I had insisted on having the window tight shut they would probably have opened it wide and given me all the air I wanted. Grinning ruefully in the dark I listened to the squeaking bed springs and their sleepy, gossiping giggles as they thumbed over the evening's talk; and as I shifted to find a comfortable spot on the lumpy mattress I began to wonder what life was really like from the inside for the hands who lived in my own bunk-house, back home.

Wednesday morning gave me my first taste of the biting Yorkshire wind, and one of the lads, as we scurried round the yard with shaking hands and running noses, cheerfully assured me that it could blow for six months solid, if it tried. I did my three horses at the double, but by the time the horse box took me and one of them out of the yard at twelve-thirty I had decided that if the gaps in my wardrobe were anything to go by, October's big square house up the drive must have very efficient central heating.

About four miles up the road I pressed the bell which in most horse boxes connects the back compartment to the cab. The driver stopped obediently, and looked inquiringly at me when I walked along and climbed up into the cab beside him.

'The horse is quiet,' I said, 'and it's warmer here.'

He grinned and started off again, shouting over the noise of the engine. 'I didn't have you figured for the conscientious type, and I was damn right. That horse is going to be sold and has got to arrive in good condition . . . the boss would have a fit if he knew you were up in front.'

I had a pretty good idea the boss, meaning Inskip, wouldn't be at all surprised; bosses, judging by myself, weren't as naïve as all that.

'The boss can stuff himself,' I said unpleasantly.

I got a sidelong glance for that, and reflected that it was dead easy to give oneself a bad character if one put one's mind to it. Horse-box drivers went to race meetings in droves, and had no duties when they got there. They had time to gossip in the canteen, time all afternoon to wander about and wag their tongues. There was no telling what ears might hear that there was a possible chink in the honesty of the Inskip lads.

We stopped once on the way to eat in a transport café, and again a little farther on for me to buy myself a couple of woollen shirts, a black sweater, some thick socks, woollen gloves, and a knitted yachting cap like those the other lads had worn that bitter morning. The box driver, coming into the shop with me to buy some socks for himself, eyed my purchases and remarked that I seemed to have plenty of money. I grinned knowingly, and said it was easy to come by if you knew how; and I could see his doubts of me growing.

In mid-afternoon we rolled in to a racing stable in Leicestershire, and it was here that the scope of Beckett's staff work became apparent. The horse I was to take back and subsequently care for was a useful hurdler just about to start his career as a novice 'chaser, and he had been sold to Colonel Beckett complete with all engagements. This meant, I learned from his former lad, who handed him over to me with considerable bitterness, that he could run in all the races for which his ex-owner had already entered him.

'Where is he entered?' I asked.

'Oh, dozens of places, I think – Newbury, Cheltenham, Sandown, and so on, and he was going to start next week at Bristol.' The lad's face twisted with regret as he passed the halter rope into my hand. 'I can't think what on earth persuaded the Old Man to part with him. He's a real daisy, and if I ever see him at the races not looking as good and well cared for as he does now, I'll find you and beat the living daylights out of you, I will straight.'

I had already discovered how deeply attached racing lads became to the horses they looked after, and I understood that he meant what he said.

'What's his name?' I asked.

'Sparking Plug . . . God awful name, he's no plug . . . Hey, Sparks, old boy . . . hey, boy . . . hey, old fellow . . .' He fondled the horse's muzzle affectionately.

We loaded him into the horse box and this time I did stay where I ought to be, in the back, looking after him. If Beckett were prepared to give a fortune for the cause, as I guessed he must have done to get hold of such an ideal horse in so few days, I was going to take good care of it.

Before we started back I took a look at the road map in the cab, and found to my satisfaction that all the race courses in the country had been marked in on it in Indian ink. I borrowed it at once, and spent the journey studying it. The courses where Sparking Plug's lad had said he was entered were nearly all in the south. Overnight stops, as requested. I grinned.

The five racecourses where the eleven horses had won were not, I found, all as far north as I had imagined. Ludlow and Stafford, in fact, could almost be considered southern, especially as I found I instinctively based my view of the whole country from Harrogate. The five courses seemed to bear no relation to each other on the map: far from presenting a tidy circle from which a centre might be deduced, they were all more or less in a curve from northeast to southwest, and I could find no significance in their location.

I spent the rest of the journey back as I spent most of my working hours, letting my mind drift over what I knew of the eleven horses, waiting for an idea to swim to the surface like a fish in a pool, waiting for the disconnected facts to sort themselves into a pattern. But I didn't really expect this to happen yet, as I knew I had barely started, and even electronic computers won't produce answers if they are not fed enough information.

*

On Friday night I went down to the pub in Slaw and beat Soupy at darts. He grunted, gestured to the bar billiards, and took an easy revenge. We then drank a half pint together, eyeing each other. Conversation between us was almost non-existent, nor was it necessary: and shortly I wandered back to watch the darts players. They were no better than the week before.

'You beat Soupy, didn't you Dan?' one of them said.

I nodded, and immediately found a bunch of darts thrust into my hand.

'If you can beat Soupy you must be in the team.'

'What team?' I asked.

'The stable darts team. We play other stables, and have a sort of Yorkshire League. Sometimes we go to Middleham or Wetherby or Richmond or sometimes they come here. Soupy's the best player in Granger's team. Could you beat him again, do you think, or was it a fluke?'

I threw three darts at the board. They all landed in the twenty. For some unknown reason I had always been able to throw straight.

'Cor,' said the lads. 'Go on.'

I threw three more: the twenty section got rather crowded.

'You're in the team, mate, and no nonsense,' they said.

'When's the next match?' I asked.

'We had one here a fortnight ago. Next one's next

Sunday at Burndale, after the football. You can't play football as well as darts, I suppose?'

I shook my head. 'Only darts.'

I looked at the one dart still left in my hand. I could hit a scuttling rat with a stone; I had done it often when the men had found one round the corn bins and chased it out. I saw no reason why I couldn't hit a galloping horse with a dart: it was a much bigger target.

'Put that one in the bull,' urged the lad beside me.

I put it in the bull. The lads yelled with glee.

'We'll win the league this season,' they grinned. Grits grinned too. But Paddy didn't.

CHAPTER FOUR

October's son and daughters came home for the weekend, the elder girl in a scarlet TR4 which I grew to
know well by sight as she drove in and out past the
stables, and the twins more sedately, with their father.
As all three were in the habit of riding out when they
were at home, Wally told me to saddle up two of my
horses to go out with the first string on Saturday, Sparking Plug for me and the other for Lady Patricia Tarren.

Lady Patricia Tarren, as I discovered when I led out
the horse in the half light of early dawn and held it for
her to mount, was a raving beauty with a pale pink
mouth and thick curly eyelashes which she knew very
well how to use. She had tied a green head-scarf over
her chestnut hair, and she wore a black and white harle-
quined ski-ing jacket to keep out the cold. She was
carrying some bright green woollen gloves.

'You're new,' she observed, looking up at me through
the eyelashes. 'What's your name?'

'Dan . . . miss,' I said. I realized I hadn't the faintest
idea what form of address an earl's daughter was accus-

65

tomed to. Wally's instructions hadn't stretched that far.

'Well . . . give me a leg up, then.'

I stood beside her obediently, but as I leaned forward to help her she ran her bare hand over my head and around my neck, and took the lobe of my right ear between her fingers. She had sharp nails, and she dug them in. Her eyes were wide with challenge. I looked straight back. When I didn't move or say anything she presently giggled and let go and calmly put on her gloves. I gave her a leg up into the saddle and she bent down to gather the reins, and fluttered the fluffy lashes close to my face.

'You're quite a dish, aren't you, Danny boy,' she said, 'with those googoo dark eyes.'

I couldn't think of any answer to her which was at all consistent with my position. She laughed, nudged the horse's flanks, and walked off down the yard. Her sister, mounting a horse held by Grits, looked from twenty yards away in the dim light to be much fairer in colouring and very nearly as beautiful. Heaven help October, I thought, with two like that to keep an eye on.

I turned to go and fetch Sparking Plug and found October's eighteen-year-old son at my elbow. He was very like his father, but not yet as thick in body or as easily powerful in manner.

'I shouldn't pay too much attention to my twin sister,' he said in a cool, bored voice, looking me up and down, 'she is apt to tease.' He nodded and strolled over to where his horse was waiting for him; and I gathered that what I had received was a warning off. If his sister behaved as provocatively with every male she met, he must have been used to delivering them.

Amused, I fetched Sparking Plug, mounted, and followed all the other horses out of the yard, up the lane, and on to the edge of the moor. As usual on a fine morning the air and the view were exhilarating. The sun was no more than a promise on the far distant horizon and there was a beginning-of-the-world quality in the light. I watched the shadowy shapes of the horses ahead of me curving round the hill with white plumes streaming from their nostrils in the frosty air. As the glittering rim of the sun expanded into full light the colours sprang out bright and clear, the browns of the jogging horses topped with the bright stripes of the lads' ear-warming knitted caps and the jolly garments of October's daughters.

October himself, accompanied by his retriever, came up on the moor in a Land Rover to see the horses work. Saturday morning, I had found, was the busiest training day of the week as far as gallops were concerned, and as he was usually in Yorkshire at the weekend he made a point of coming out to watch.

Inskip had us circling round at the top of the hill while he paired off the horses and told their riders what to do.

To me he said, 'Dan; three-quarter speed gallop. Your horse is running on Wednesday. Don't over-do him but we want to see how he goes.' He directed one of the stable's most distinguished animals to accompany me.

When he had finished giving his orders he cantered off along the broad sweep of green turf which stretched through the moorland scrub, and October drove slowly in his wake. We continued circling until the two men reached the other end of the gallops about a mile and a half away up the gently curved, gently rising track.

'OK,' said Wally to the first pair. 'Off you go.'

The two horses set off together, fairly steadily at first and then at an increasing pace until they had passed Inskip and October, when they slowed and pulled up.

'Next two,' Wally called.

We were ready, and set off without more ado. I had bred, broken, and rebroken uncountable racehorses in Australia, but Sparking Plug was the only good one I had so far ridden in England, and I was interested to see how he compared. Of course he was a hurdler, while I was more used to flat racers, but this made no difference, I found; and he had a bad mouth which I itched to do something about, but there was nothing wrong with his action. Balanced and collected, he sped smoothly up the gallop, keeping pace effortlessly with the star performer beside him, and though, as ordered, we went only three-quarters speed at our fastest, it was quite clear that Sparking Plug was fit and ready for his approaching race.

I was so interested in what I was doing that it was not until I had reined in – not too easy with that mouth

– and began to walk back, that I realized I had forgotten all about messing up the way I rode. I groaned inwardly, exasperated with myself: I would never do what I had come to England for if I could so little keep my mind on the job.

I stopped with the horse who had accompanied Sparking Plug in front of October and Inskip, for them to have a look at the horses and see how much they were blowing. Sparking Plug's ribs moved easily: he was scarcely out of breath. The two men nodded, and I and the other lad slid off the horses and began walking them around while they cooled down.

Up from the far end of the gallop came the other horses, pair by pair, and finally a bunch of those who were not due to gallop but only to canter. When everyone had worked, most of the lads remounted and we all began to walk back down the gallop towards the track to the stable. Leading my horse on foot I set off last in the string, with October's eldest daughter riding immediately in front of me and effectively cutting me off from the chat of the lads ahead. She was looking about her at the rolling vistas of moor, and not bothering to keep her animal close on the heels of the one in front, so that by the time we entered the track there was a ten-yard gap ahead of her.

As she passed a scrubby gorse bush a bird flew out of it with a squawk and flapping wings, and the girl's horse whipped round and up in alarm. She stayed on with a remarkable effort of balance, pulling herself back up into the saddle from somewhere below the horse's right ear, but under her thrust the stirrup leather broke apart at the bottom, and the stirrup iron itself clanged to the ground.

I stopped and picked up the iron, but it was impossible to put it back on the broken leather.

'Thank you,' she said. 'What a nuisance.'

She slid off her horse. 'I might as well walk the rest of the way.'

I took her rein and began to lead both of the horses, but she stopped me, and took her own back again.

'It's very kind of you,' she said, 'but I can quite well lead him myself.' The track was wide at that point, and she began to walk down the hill beside me.

On closer inspection she was not a bit like her sister Patricia. She had smooth silver-blonde hair under a blue head-scarf, fair eyelashes, direct grey eyes, a firm friendly mouth, and a composure which gave her an air of graceful reserve. We walked in easy silence for some way.

'Isn't it a gorgeous morning,' she said eventually.

'Gorgeous,' I agreed, 'but cold.' The English always talk about the weather, I thought: and a fine day in November is so rare as to be remarked on. It would be hotting up for summer, at home . . .

'Have you been with the stable long?' she asked, a little farther on.

'Only about ten days.'

'And do you like it here?'

'Oh, yes. It's a well-run stable . . .'

'Mr Inskip would be delighted to hear you say so,' she said in a dry voice.

I glanced at her, but she was looking ahead down the track, and smiling.

After another hundred yards she said, 'What horse is that that you were riding? I don't think that I have seen him before, either.'

'He only came on Wednesday . . .' I told her the little I knew about Sparking Plug's history, capabilities, and prospects.

She nodded. 'It will be nice for you if he can win some races. Rewarding, after your work for him here.'

'Yes,' I agreed, surprised that she should think like that.

We reached the last stretch to the stable.

'I am so sorry,' she said pleasantly, 'but I don't know your name.'

'Daniel Roke,' I said: and I wondered why to her alone of all the people who had asked me that question in the last ten days it had seemed proper to give a whole answer.

'Thank you,' she paused: then having thought, continued in a calm voice which I realized with wry pleasure was designed to put me at my ease, 'Lord October is my father. I'm Elinor Tarren.'

We had reached the stable gate. I stood back to let her go first, which she acknowledged with a friendly but impersonal smile, and she led her horse away across the yard towards its own box. A thoroughly nice girl, I thought briefly, buckling down to the task of brushing the sweat off Sparking Plug, washing his feet, brushing out his mane and tail, sponging out his eyes and mouth, putting his straw bed straight, fetching his hay and water, and then repeating the whole process with the horse that Patricia had ridden. Patricia, I thought, grinning, was not a nice girl at all.

When I went in to breakfast in the cottage Mrs Allnut gave me a letter which had just arrived for me. The envelope, postmarked in London the day before, contained a sheet of plain paper with a single sentence typed on it.

'Mr Stanley will be at Victoria Falls three p.m. Sunday.'

I stuffed the letter into my pocket, laughing into my porridge.

There was a heavy drizzle falling when I walked up beside the stream the following afternoon. I reached the gully before October, and waited for him with the rain drops finding ways to trickle down my neck. He came down the hill with his dog as before, telling me that his car was parked above us on the little used road.

'But we'd better talk here, if you can stand the wet,' he finished, 'in case anyone saw us together in the car, and wondered.'

'I can stand the wet,' I assured him, smiling.

'Good . . . well, how have you been getting on?'

I told him how well I thought of Beckett's new horse and the opportunities it would give me.

He nodded, 'Roddy Beckett was famous in the war for the speed and accuracy with which he got supplies moved about. No one ever got the wrong ammunition or all left boots when he was in charge.'

I said 'I've sown a few seeds of doubts about my honesty, here and there, but I'll be able to do more of that this week at Bristol, and also next weekend, at Burndale. I'm going there on Sunday to play in a darts match.'

'They've had several cases of doping in that village in the past,' he said thoughtfully. 'You might get a nibble, there.'

'It would be useful . . .'

'Have you found the form books helpful?' he asked. 'Have you given those eleven horses any more thought?'

'I've thought of little else,' I said, 'and it seems just possible, perhaps it's only a slight chance, but it does just seem possible that you might be able to make a dope test on the next horse in the sequence *before* he runs in a race. That is to say, always providing that there is going to be another horse in the sequence . . . and I don't see why not, as the people responsible have got away with it for so long.'

He looked at me with some excitement, the rain dripping off the down-turned brim of his hat.

'You've found something?'

'No, not really. It's only a statistical indication. But it's more than even money, I think, that the next horse will win a selling 'chase at Kelso, Sedgefield, Ludlow, Stafford, or Haydock.' I explained my reasons for expecting this, and went on, 'It should be possible to arrange for wholesale saliva samples to be taken before all the selling 'chases on those particular tracks – it can't be more than one race at each two-day meeting – and they can throw the samples away without going to the expense of testing them if no . . . er . . . joker turns up in the pack.'

'It's a tall order,' he said slowly, 'but I don't see why it shouldn't be done, if it will prove anything.'

'The analysts might find something useful in the results.'

'Yes. And I suppose even if they didn't, it would be a great step forward for us to be able to be on the lookout for a joker, instead of just being mystified when one appeared. Why on earth,' he shook his head in exasperation, 'didn't we think of this months ago? It seems such an obvious way to approach the problem, now that you have done it.'

'I expect it is because I am the first person really to be given all the collected information all at once, and deliberately search for a connecting factor. All the other investigations seemed to have been done from the other end, so to speak, by trying to find out in each case separately who had access to the horse, who fed him, who saddled him, and so on.'

He nodded gloomily.

'There's one other thing,' I said. 'The lab chaps told you that as they couldn't find a dope you should look for something mechanical . . . do you know whether the horses' skins were investigated as closely as the jockeys and their kit? It occurred to me the other evening that I could throw a dart with an absolute certainty of hitting a horse's flank, and any good shot could plant a pellet in the same place. Things like that would sting like a hornet . . . enough to make any horse shift along faster.'

'As far as I know, none of the horses showed any signs of that sort of thing, but I'll make sure. And by the way, I asked the analysts whether horses' bodies could break drugs down into harmless substances, and they said it was impossible.'

'Well, that clears the decks a bit, if nothing else.'

'Yes.' He whistled to his dog, who was quartering the far side of the gully. 'After next week, when you'll be away at Burndale, we had better meet here at this time every Sunday afternoon to discuss progress. You will know if I'm away, because I won't be here for the Saturday gallops. Incidentally, your horsemanship stuck out a mile on Sparking Plug yesterday. And I thought we agreed that you had better not make too good an impression. On top of which,' he added, smiling faintly, 'Inskip says you are a quick and conscientious worker.'

'Heck . . . I'll be getting a good reference if I don't watch out.'

'Too right you will,' he agreed, copying my accent sardonically. 'How do you like being a stable lad?'

'It has its moments . . . Your daughters are very beautiful.'

He grinned, 'Yes: and thank you for helping Elinor. She told me you were most obliging.'

'I did nothing.'

'Patty is a bit of a handful,' he said, reflectively, 'I wish she'd decide what sort of a job she'd like to do. She knows I don't want her to go on as she has during her season, never-ending parties and staying out till dawn . . . well, that's not your worry, Mr Roke.'

We shook hands as usual, and he trudged off up the hill. It was still drizzling mournfully as I went down.

Sparking Plug duly made the 250-mile journey south to Bristol, and I went with him. The racecourse was some way out of the city, and the horse-box driver told me, when we stopped for a meal on the way, that the whole of the stable block had been newly rebuilt there after the fire had gutted it.

Certainly the loose boxes were clean and snug, but it was the new sleeping quarters that the lads were in ecstasies about. The hostel was a surprise to me too. It consisted mainly of a recreation room and two long dormitories with about thirty beds in each, made up with clean sheets and fluffy blue blankets. There was a wall light over each bed, polyvinyl-tiled flooring, under-floor heating, modern showers in the washroom and a hot room for drying wet clothes. The whole place was warm and light, with colour schemes which were clearly the work of a professional.

'Ye gods, we're in the ruddy Hilton,' said one cheerful boy, coming to a halt beside me just through the dormitory door and slinging his canvas grip on to an unoccupied bed.

'You haven't seen the half of it,' said a bony long-wristed boy in a shrunken blue jersey, 'up that end of the passage there's a ruddy great canteen with decent chairs and a telly and a ping-pong table and all.'

Other voices joined in.

'It's as good as Newbury.'

'Easily.'

'Better than Ascot, I'd say.'

Heads nodded.

'They have bunk beds at Ascot, not singles, like this.'

The hostels at Newbury and Ascot were, it appeared, the most comfortable in the country.

'Anyone would think the bosses had suddenly cottoned on to the fact that we're human,' said a sharp-faced lad, in a belligerent, rabble-raising voice.

'It's a far cry from the bug-ridden doss houses of the old days,' nodded a desiccated, elderly little man with a face like a shrunken apple. 'But a fellow told me the lads have it good like this in America all the time.'

'They know if they don't start treating us decent they

soon won't get anyone to do the dirty work,' said the rabble-raiser. 'Things are changing.'

'They treat us decent enough where I come from,' I said, putting my things on an empty bed next to his and nerving myself to be natural, casual, unremarkable. I felt much more self-conscious than I had at Slaw, where at least I knew the job inside out and had been able to feel my way cautiously into a normal relationship with the other lads. But here I had only two nights, and if I were to do any good at all I had got to direct the talk towards what I wanted to hear.

The form books were by now as clear to me as a primer, and for a fortnight I had listened acutely and concentrated on soaking in as much racing jargon as I could, but I was still doubtful whether I would understand everything I heard at Bristol and also afraid that I would make some utterly incongruous impossible mistake in what I said myself.

'And where do you come from?' asked the cheerful boy, giving me a cursory looking over.

'Lord October's,' I said.

'Oh yes, Inskip's, you mean? You're a long way from home . . .'

'Inskip's may be all right,' said the rabble-raiser, as if he regretted it. 'But there are some places where they still treat us like mats to wipe their feet on, and don't reckon that we've got a right to a bit of sun, same as everyone else.'

'Yeah,' said the raw-boned boy seriously. 'I heard

that at one place they practically starve the lads and knock them about if they don't work hard enough, and they all have to do about four or five horses each because they can't keep anyone in the yard for more than five minutes!'

I said idly, 'Where's that, just so I know where to avoid, if I ever move on from Inskip's?'

'Up your part of the country . . .' he said doubtfully. 'I think.'

'No, farther north, in Durham . . .' another boy chimed in, a slender, pretty boy with soft down still growing on his cheeks.

'You know about it too, then?'

He nodded. 'Not that it matters, only a raving nit would take a job there. It's a blooming sweat shop, a hundred years out of date. All they get are riff-raff that no one else will have.'

'It wants exposing,' said the rabble-raiser belligerently. 'Who runs this place?'

'Bloke called Humber,' said the pretty boy, 'he couldn't train ivy up a wall . . . and he has about as many winners as tits on a billiard ball . . . You see his head travelling-lad at the meetings sometimes, trying to pressgang people to go and work there, and getting the brush off, right and proper.'

'Someone ought to do something,' said the rabble-raiser automatically: and I guessed that this was his usual refrain: 'someone ought to do something'; but not, when it came to the point, himself.

There was a general drift into the canteen, where the food proved to be good, unlimited, and free. A proposal to move on to a pub came to nothing when it was discovered that the nearest was nearly two (busless) miles away and that the bright warm canteen had some crates of beer under its counter.

It was easy enough to get the lads started on the subject of doping, and they seemed prepared to discuss it endlessly. None of the twenty odd there had ever, as far as they would admit, given 'anything' to a horse, but they all knew someone who knew someone who had. I drank my beer and listened and looked interested, which I was.

'. . . nobbled him with a squirt of acid as he walked out of the bleeding paddock . . .'

'. . . gave him such a whacking dollop of stopping powder that he died in his box in the morning . . .'

'Seven rubber bands came out in the droppings . . .'

'. . . overdosed him so much that he never even tried to jump the first fence: blind, he was, stone blind . . .'

'. . . gave him a bloody great bucketful of water half an hour before the race, and didn't need any dope to stop him with all that sloshing about inside his gut.'

'Poured half a bottle of whisky down his throat.'

'. . . used to tube horses which couldn't breathe properly on the morning of the race until they found it wasn't the extra fresh air that was making the horses win but the cocaine they stuffed them full of for the operation . . .'

'They caught him with a hollow apple packed with sleeping pills . . .'

'. . . dropped a syringe right in front of an effing steward.'

'I wonder if there's anything which hasn't been tried yet?' I said.

'Black magic. Not much else left,' said the pretty boy. They all laughed.

'Someone might find something so good,' I pointed out casually, 'that it couldn't be detected, so the people who thought of it could go on with it for ever and never be found out.'

'Blimey,' exclaimed the cheerful lad, 'you're a comfort, aren't you? God help racing, if that happened. You'd never know where you were. The bookies would all be climbing the walls.' He grinned hugely.

The elderly little man was not so amused.

'It's been going on for years and years,' he said, nodding solemnly. 'Some trainers have got it to a fine art, you mark my words. Some trainers have been doping their horses regular, for years and years.'

But the other lads didn't agree. The dope tests had done for the dope-minded trainers of the past; they had lost their licences, and gone out of racing. The old rule had been a bit unfair on some, they allowed, when a trainer had been automatically disqualified if one of his horses had been doped. It wasn't always the trainer's fault, especially if the horse had been doped to lose. What trainer, they asked, would nobble a horse he'd spent months training to win? But they thought there was probably *more* doping since that rule was changed, not less.

'Stands to reason, a doper knows now he isn't ruining the trainer for life, just one horse for one race. Makes it sort of easier on his conscience, see? More lads, maybe, would take fifty quid for popping the odd aspirin into the feed if they knew the stable wouldn't be shut down and their jobs gone for a burton very soon afterwards.'

They talked on, thoughtful and ribald; but it was clear that they didn't know anything about the eleven horses I was concerned with. None of them, I knew, came from any of the stables involved, and obviously they had not read the speculative reports in the papers, or if they had, had read them separately over a period of eighteen months, and not in one solid, collected, intense bunch, as I had done.

The talk faltered and died into yawns, and we went chatting to bed, I sighing to myself with relief that I had gone through the evening without much notice having been taken of me.

By watching carefully what the other lads did, I survived the next day also without any curious stares. In the early afternoon I took Sparking Plug from the stables into the paddock, walked him round the parade ring, stood holding his head while he was saddled, led him round the parade ring again, held him while the jockey mounted, led him out on to the course, and went up into the little stand by the gate with the other lads to watch the race.

Sparking Plug won. I was delighted. I met him again at the gate and led him into the spacious winner's unsaddling enclosure.

Colonel Beckett was there, waiting, leaning on a stick. He patted the horse, congratulated the jockey, who unbuckled his saddle and departed into the weighing room, and said to me sardonically, 'That's a fraction of his purchase price back, anyway.'

'He's a good horse, and absolutely perfect for his purpose.'

'Good. Do you need anything else?'

'Yes. A lot more details about those eleven horses . . . where they were bred, what they ate, whether they had had any illnesses, what cafés their box drivers used, who made their bridles, whether they had racing plates fitted at the meetings, and by which blacksmiths . . . anything and everything.'

'Are you serious?'

'Yes.'

'But they had nothing in common except that they were doped.'

'As I see it, the question really is what was it that they had in common that made it *possible* for them to be doped.' I smoothed Sparking Plug's nose. He was restive and excited after his victory. Colonel Beckett looked at me with sober eyes.

'Mr Roke, you shall have your information.'

I grinned at him. 'Thank you; and I'll take good care of Sparking Plug . . . he'll win you all the purchase price, before he's finished.'

'Horses away,' called an official: and with a weak-looking gesture of farewell from Colonel Beckett's limp hand, I took Sparking Plug back to the racecourse stables and walked him round until he had cooled off.

There were far more lads in the hostel that evening as it was the middle night of the two-day meeting, and this time, besides getting the talk around again to doping and listening attentively to everything that was said, I also tried to give the impression that I didn't think taking fifty quid to point out a certain horse's box in his home stable to anyone prepared to pay that much for the information was a proposition I could be relied on to turn down. I earned a good few disapproving looks for this, and also one sharply interested glance from a very short lad whose outsize nose sniffed monotonously.

In the washroom in the morning he used the basin next to me, and said out of the side of his mouth, 'Did you mean it, last night, that you'd take fifty quid to point out a box?'

I shrugged. 'I don't see why not.'

He looked round furtively. It made me want to laugh. 'I might be able to put you in touch with some-one who'd be interested to hear that – for a fifty per cent cut.'

'You've got another think coming,' I said offensively.

'Fifty per cent . . . what the hell do you think I am?'

'Well . . . a fiver, then,' he sniffed, climbing down.

'I dunno . . .'

'I can't say fairer than that,' he muttered.

'It's a wicked thing, to point out a box,' I said virtuously, drying my face on a towel.

He stared at me in astonishment.

'And I couldn't do it for less than sixty, if you are taking a fiver out of it.'

He didn't know whether to laugh or spit. I left him to his indecision, and went off grinning to escort Sparking Plug back to Yorkshire.

CHAPTER FIVE

Again on Friday evening I went down to the Slaw pub and exchanged bug-eyed looks with Soupy across the room.

On the Sunday half the lads had the afternoon off to go to Burndale for the football and darts matches, and we won both, which made for a certain amount of back slapping and beer drinking. But beyond remarking that I was new, and a blight on their chances in the darts league, the Burndale lads paid me little attention. There was no one like Soupy among them in spite of what October had said about the cases of doping in the village, and no one, as far as I could see, who cared if I were as crooked as a cork-screw.

During the next week I did my three horses, and read the form books, and thought: and got nowhere. Paddy remained cool and so did Wally, to whom Paddy had obviously reported my affinity with Soupy. Wally showed his disapproval by giving me more than my share of the afternoon jobs, so that every day, instead of relaxing in the usual free time between lunch and evening stables at four o'clock, I found myself bidden to sweep the yard, clean the tack, crush the oats, cut the chaff, wash Inskip's car or clean the windows of the loose boxes. I did it all without comment, reflecting that if I needed an excuse for a quick row and walked out later on I could reasonably, at eleven hours a day, complain of overwork.

However, at Friday midday I set off again with Sparking Plug, this time to Cheltenham, and this time accompanied not only by the box driver but by Grits and his horse, and the head travelling-lad as well.

Once in the racecourse stables I learned that this was the night of the dinner given to the previous season's champion jockey, and all the lads who were staying there overnight proposed to celebrate by attending a dance in the town. Grits and I, therefore, having bedded down our horses, eaten our meal, and smartened ourselves up, caught a bus down the hill and paid our entrance money to the hop. It was a big hall and the band was loud and hot, but not many people were yet dancing. The girls were standing about in little groups eyeing larger groups of young men, and I bit back just in time a remark on how odd I found it; Grits would expect me to think it normal. I took him off into the bar where there were already groups of lads from the racecourse mingled with the local inhabitants, and bought him a beer, regretting that he was with me to see what use I intended to make of the evening. Poor Grits, he was torn between loyalty to Paddy and an apparent liking for me, and I was about to disillusion him thoroughly. I wished I could explain. I was tempted to spend the evening harmlessly. But how could I justify passing over an unrepeatable opportunity just to keep temporarily the regard of one slow-witted stable lad, however much I might like him? I was committed to earning ten thousand pounds.

'Grits, go and find a girl to dance with.'

He gave me a slow grin. 'I don't know any.'

'It doesn't matter. Any of them would be glad to dance with a nice chap like you. Go and ask one.'

'No. I'd rather stay with you.'

'All right, then. Have another drink.'

'I haven't finished this.'

I turned round to the bar, which we had been leaning against, and banged my barely touched half pint down on the counter. 'I'm fed up with this pap,' I said violently. 'Hey, you, barman, give me a double whisky.'

'Dan!' Grits was upset at my tone, which was a measure of its success. The barman poured the whisky and took my money.

'Don't go away,' I said to him in a loud voice. 'Give me another while you're at it.'

I felt rather than saw the group of lads farther up the bar turn round and take a look, so I picked up the glass and swallowed all the whisky in two gulps and wiped my mouth on the back of my hand. I pushed the empty glass across to the barman and paid for the second drink.

'Dan,' Grits tugged my sleeve, 'do you think you should?'

'Yes,' I said, scowling. 'Go and find a girl to dance with.'

But he didn't go. He watched me drink the second whisky and order a third. His eyes were troubled.

The bunch of lads edged towards us along the bar.

'Hey, fella, you're knocking it back a bit,' observed one, a tallish man of my own age in a flashy bright blue suit.

'Mind your own ruddy business,' I said rudely.

'Aren't you from Inskip's?' he asked.

'Yea . . . Inskip's . . . bloody Inskip's . . .' I picked up the third glass. I had a hard head for whisky, which was going down on top of a deliberately heavy meal. I reckoned I could stay sober a long time after I would be expected to be drunk; but the act had to be put on early, while the audience were still sober enough themselves to remember it clearly afterwards.

'Eleven sodding quid,' I told them savagely, 'that's all you get for sweating your guts out seven days a week.'

It struck a note with some of them, but Blue-suit said, 'Then why spend it on whisky?'

'Why bloody not? It's great stuff – gives you a kick. And, by God, you need something in this job.'

Blue-suit said to Grits, 'Your mate's got an outsized gripe.'

'Well . . .' said Grits, his face anxious, 'I suppose he

has had a lot of extra jobs this week, come to think . . .'

'You're looking after horses they pay thousands for and you know damn well that the way you ride and groom them and look after them makes a hell of a lot of difference to whether they win or not, and they grudge you a decent wage . . .' I finished the third whisky, hiccupped and said, 'It's bloody unfair.'

The bar was filling up, and from the sight of them and from what I could catch of their greetings to each other, at least half the customers were in some way connected with racing. Bookmakers' clerks and touts as well as stable lads – the town was stuffed with them, and the dance had been put on to attract them. A large amount of liquor began disappearing down their collective throats, and I had to catch the barman on the wing to serve my fourth double whisky in fifteen minutes.

I stood facing a widening circle with the glass in my hand, and rocked slightly on my feet.

'I want,' I began. What on earth did I want? I searched for the right phrases. 'I want . . . a motor-bike. I want to show a bird a good time. And go abroad for a holiday . . . and stay in a swank hotel and have them running about at my beck and call . . . and drink what I like . . . and maybe one day put a deposit on a house . . . and what chance do I have of any of these? I'll tell you. Not a snowball's hope in hell. You know what I got in my pay packet this morning . . .? Seven pounds and fourpence . . .'

I went on and on grousing and complaining, and the

evening wore slowly away. The audience drifted and changed, and I kept it up until I was fairly sure that all the racing people there knew there was a lad of Inskip's who yearned for more money, preferably in large amounts. But even Grits, who hovered about with an unhappy air throughout it all and remained cold sober himself, didn't seem to notice that I got progressively drunker in my actions while making each drink last longer than the one before.

Eventually, after I had achieved an artistic lurch and clutch at one of the pillars, Grits said loudly in my ear, 'Dan, I'm going now and you'd better go too, or you'll miss the last bus, and I shouldn't think you could walk back, like you are.'

'Huh?' I squinted at him. Blue-suit had come back and was standing just behind him.

'Want any help getting him out?' he asked Grits.

Grits looked at me disgustedly, and I fell against him, putting my arm round his shoulders: I definitely did not want the sort of help Blue-suit looked as though he might give.

'Grits, me old pal, if you say go, we go.'

We set off for the door, followed by Blue-suit, me staggering so heavily that I pushed Grits sideways. There were by this time a lot of others having difficulty in walking a straight line, and the queue of lads which waited at the bus stop undulated slightly like an ocean swell on a calm day. I grinned in the safe darkness and looked up at the sky, and thought that if the seeds I had sown in all directions bore no fruit there was little doping going on in British racing.

I may not have been drunk, but I woke the next morning with a shattering headache, just the same: all in a good cause, I thought, trying to ignore the blacksmith behind my eyes.

Sparking Plug ran in his race and lost by half a length. I took the opportunity of saying aloud on the lads' stand that there was the rest of my week's pay gone down the bloody drain.

Colonel Beckett patted his horse's neck in the cramped unsaddling enclosure and said casually to me, 'Better luck next time, eh? I've sent you what you wanted, in a parcel.' He turned away and resumed talking to Inskip and his jockey about the race.

We all went back to Yorkshire that night, with Grits and me sleeping most of the way on the benches in the back of the horse box.

He said reproachfully as he lay down, 'I didn't know you hated it at Inskip's . . . and I haven't seen you drunk before either.'

'It isn't the work, Grits, it's the pay.' I had to keep it up.

'Still there are some who are married and have kids to keep on what you were bleating about.' He sounded disapproving, and indeed my behaviour must have affected him deeply, because he seldom spoke to me after that night.

There was nothing of interest to report to October the following afternoon, and our meeting in the gully was brief. He told me, however, that the information then in the post from Beckett had been collected by eleven keen young officer cadets from Aldershot who had been given the task as an initiative exercise, and told they were in competition with each other to see which of them could produce the most comprehensive report of the life of his allotted horse. A certain number of questions – those I had suggested – were outlined for them. The rest had been left to their own imagination and detective ability, and October said Beckett had told him they had used them to the full.

I returned down the hill more impressed than ever with the Colonel's staff work, but not as staggered as when the parcel arrived the following day. Wally again found some wretched job for me to do in the afternoon, so that it was not until after the evening meal, when half the lads had gone down to Slaw, that I had an opportunity of taking the package up to the dormitory and opening it. It contained 237 numbered typewritten pages bound into a cardboard folder, like the manuscript of a book, and its production in the space of one week must have meant a prodigious effort not only from the young men themselves, but from the typists as well. The information was given in note form for the most part, and no space had anywhere been wasted in flowing prose: it was solid detail from cover to cover.

Mrs Allnut's voice floated up the stairs. 'Dan, come down and fetch me a bucket of coal, will you please?'

I thrust the typescript down inside my bed between the sheets, and went back to the warm, communal kitchen-living-room where we ate and spent most of our spare time. It was impossible to read anything private there, and my life was very much supervised from dawn to bedtime; and the only place I could think of where I could concentrate uninterruptedly on the typescript was the bathroom. Accordingly that night I waited until all the lads were asleep, and then went along the passage and locked myself in, ready to report an upset stomach if anyone should be curious.

It was slow going: after four hours I had read only half. I got up stiffly, stretched, yawned, and went back to bed. Nobody stirred. The following night, as I lay waiting for the others to go to sleep so that I could get back to my task, I listened to them discussing the evening that four of them had spent in Slaw.

'Who's that fellow who was with Soupy?' asked Grits. 'I haven't seen him around before.'

'He was there last night too,' said one of the others. 'Queer sort of bloke.'

'What was queer about him?' asked the boy who had stayed behind, he watching the television while I in an armchair caught up on some sleep.

'I dunno,' said Grits. 'His eyes didn't stay still, like.'

'Sort of as if he was looking for someone,' added another voice.

Paddy said firmly from the wall on my right, 'You just all keep clear of that chap, and Soupy too. I'm telling you. People like them are no good.'

'But that chap, that one with that smashing gold tie, he bought us a round, you know he did. He can't be too bad if he bought us a round . . .'

Paddy sighed with exasperation that anyone could be so simple. 'If you'd have been Eve, you'd have eaten the apple as soon as look at it. You wouldn't have needed a serpent.'

'Oh well,' yawned Grits. 'I don't suppose he'll be there tomorrow. I heard him say something to Soupy about time getting short.'

They muttered and murmured and went to sleep, and I lay awake in the dark thinking that perhaps I had just heard something very interesting indeed. Certainly a trip down to the pub was indicated for the following evening.

With a wrench I stopped my eyes from shutting, got out of my warm bed, repaired again to the bathroom, and read for another four hours until I had finished the typescript. I sat on the bathroom floor with my back against the wall and stared sightlessly at the fixtures and fittings. There was nothing, not one single factor, that occurred in the life histories of all of the eleven microscopically investigated horses. No common denominator at all. There were quite a few things which were common to four or five – but not often the same four or five – like the make of saddles their jockeys used, the horse cube nuts they were fed with, or the auction rings they had been sold in: but the hopes I had had of finding a sizeable clue in those packages had altogether evaporated. Cold, stiff, and depressed, I crept back to bed.

The next evening at eight I walked alone down to Slaw, all the other lads saying they were skint until payday and that in any case they wanted to watch *Z Cars* on television.

'I thought you lost all your cash on Sparks at Cheltenham,' observed Grits.

'I've about two bob left,' I said, producing some pennies. 'Enough for a pint.'

The pub, as often on Wednesdays, was empty. There was no sign of Soupy or his mysterious friend, and having bought some beer I amused myself at the dart board, throwing one-to-twenty sequences, and trying to make a complete ring in the trebles. Eventually I pulled the darts out of the board, looked at my watch, and decided I had wasted the walk; and it was at that moment that a man appeared in the doorway, not from the street, but from the saloon bar next door. He held a glass of gently fizzing amber liquid and a slim cigar in his left hand and pushed open the door with his right. Looking me up and down, he said, 'Are you a stable lad?'

'Yes.'

'Granger's or Inskip's?'

'Inskip's.'

'Hmm.' He came farther into the room and let the door swing shut behind him. 'There's ten bob for you if you can get one of your lads down here tomorrow night . . . and as much beer as you can both drink.'

I looked interested. 'Which lad?' I asked. 'Any special one? Lots of them will be down here on Friday.'

'Well, now, it had better be tomorrow, I think. Sooner the better, I always say. And as for which lad . . . er . . . you tell me their names and I'll pick one of them . . . how's that?'

I thought it was damn stupid, and also that he wished to avoid asking too directly, too memorably for . . . well . . . for me?

'OK. Paddy, Grits, Wally, Steve, Ron . . .' I paused.

'Go on,' he said.

'Reg, Norman, Dave, Jeff, Dan, Mike . . .'

His eyes brightened. 'Dan,' he said. 'That's a sensible sort of name. Bring Dan.'

'I am Dan,' I said.

There was an instant in which his balding scalp contracted and his eyes narrowed in annoyance.

'Stop playing games,' he said sharply.

'It was you,' I pointed out gently, 'who began it.'

He sat down on one of the benches and carefully put his drink down on the table in front of him.

'Why did you come here tonight, alone?' he asked.

'I was thirsty.'

There was a brief silence while he mentally drew up a plan of campaign. He was a short stocky man in a dark suit a size too small, the jacket hanging open to reveal a monogrammed cream shirt and golden silk tie. His fingers were fat and short, and a roll of flesh overhung his coat collar at the back, but there was nothing soft in the way he looked at me.

At length he said, 'I believe there is a horse in your stable called Sparking Plug?'

'Yes.'

'And he runs at Leicester on Monday?'

'As far as I know.'

'What do you think his chances are?' he asked.

'Look, do you want a tip, mister, is that what it is? Well, I do Sparking Plug myself and I'm telling you there isn't an animal in next Monday's race to touch him.'

'So you expect him to win?'

'Yes, I told you.'

'And you'll bet on him I suppose.'

'Of course.'

'With half your pay? Four pounds, perhaps?'

'Maybe.'

'But he'll be favourite. Sure to be. And at best you'll probably only get even money. Another four quid. That doesn't sound much, does it, when I could perhaps put you in the way of winning . . . a hundred?'

'You're barmy,' I said, but with a sideways leer that told him that I wanted to hear more.

He leaned forward with confidence. 'Now you can

say no if you want to. You can say no, and I'll go away, and no one will be any the wiser, but if you play your cards right I could do you a good turn.'

'What would I have to do for a hundred quid?' I asked flatly.

He looked round cautiously, and lowered his voice still farther. 'Just add a little something to Sparking Plug's feed on Sunday night. Nothing to it, you see? Dead easy.'

'Dead easy,' I repeated: and so it was.

'You're on, then?' he looked eager.

'I don't know your name,' I said.

'Never you mind.' He shook his head with finality.

'Are you a bookmaker?'

'No,' he said. 'I'm not. And that's enough with the questions. Are you on?'

'If you're not a bookmaker,' I said slowly, thinking my way, 'and you are willing to pay a hundred pounds to make sure a certain favourite doesn't win, I'd guess that you didn't want just to make money backing all the other runners, but that you intend to tip off a few bookmakers that the race is fixed, and they'll be so grateful they'll pay you say, fifty quid each, at the very least. There are about eleven thousand bookmakers in Britain. A nice big market. But I expect you go to the same ones over and over again. Sure of your welcome, I should think.'

His face was a study of consternation and disbelief, and I realized I had hit the target, bang on.

'Who told you . . .' he began weakly.

'I wasn't born yesterday,' I said with a nasty grin. 'Relax. No one told me.' I paused. 'I'll give Sparking Plug his extra nosh, but I want more for it. Two hundred.'

'No. The deal's off.' He mopped his forehead.

'All right.' I shrugged.

'A hundred and fifty then,' he said grudgingly.

'A hundred and fifty,' I agreed. 'Before I do it.'

'Half before, half after,' he said automatically. It was by no means the first time he had done this sort of deal.

I agreed to that. He said if I came down to the pub on Saturday evening I would be given a packet for Sparking Plug and seventy-five pounds for myself, and I nodded and went away, leaving him staring moodily into his glass.

On my way back up the hill I crossed Soupy off my list of potentially useful contacts. Certainly he had procured me for a doping job, but I had been asked to stop a favourite in a novice 'chase, not to accelerate a dim long priced selling plater. It was extremely unlikely that both types of fraud were the work of one set of people.

Unwilling to abandon Colonel Beckett's typescript I spent chunks of that night and the following two nights in the bathroom, carefully re-reading it. The only noticeable result was that during the day I found the endless stable work irksome because for five nights in a row I had had only three hours' sleep. But I frankly dreaded having to tell October on Sunday that the eleven young men had made their mammoth investigation to no avail, and I had an unreasonable feeling that if I hammered away long enough I could still wring some useful message from those densely packed pages.

On Saturday morning, though it was bleak, bitter, and windy, October's daughters rode out with the first string. Elinor only came near enough to exchange polite good mornings, but Patty, who was again riding one of my horses, made my giving her a leg up a moment of eyelash-fluttering intimacy, deliberately and unnecessarily rubbing her body against mine.

'You weren't here last week, Danny boy,' she said, putting her feet in the irons. 'Where were you?'

'At Cheltenham . . . miss.'

'Oh. And next Saturday?'

'I'll be here.'

She said, with intentional insolence, 'Then kindly remember next Saturday to shorten the leathers on the saddle before I mount. These are far too long.'

She made no move to shorten them herself, but gestured for me to do it for her. She watched me steadily, enjoying herself. While I was fastening the second buckle she rubbed her knee forwards over my hands and kicked me none too gently in the ribs.

'I wonder you stand me teasing you, Danny boy,' she

said softly, bending down, 'a dishy guy like you should answer back more. Why don't you?'

'I don't want the sack,' I said, with a dead straight face.

'A coward, too,' she said sardonically, and twitched her horse away.

And she'll get into bad trouble one day, if she keeps on like that, I thought. She was too provocative. Stunningly pretty of course, but that was only the beginning; and her hurtful little tricks were merely annoying. It was the latent invitation which disturbed and aroused.

I shrugged her out of my mind, fetched Sparking Plug, sprang up on to his back and moved out of the yard and up to the moor for the routine working gallops.

The weather that day got steadily worse until while we were out with the second string it began to rain heavily in fierce slashing gusts, and we struggled miserably back against it with stinging faces and sodden clothes. Perhaps because it went on raining, or possibly because it was, after all, Saturday, Wally for once refrained from making me work all afternoon, and I spent the three hours sitting with about nine other lads in the kitchen of the cottage, listening to the wind shrieking round the corners outside and watching Chepstow races on television, while our damp jerseys, breeches, and socks steamed gently round the fire.

I put the previous season's form book on the kitchen table and sat over it with my head propped on the knuckles of my left hand idly turning the pages with my right. Depressed by my utter lack of success with the eleven horses' dossiers, by the antipathy I had to arouse in the lads, and also, I think, by the absence of the hot sunshine I usually lived in at that time of the year, I began to feel that the whole masquerade had been from the start a ghastly mistake. And the trouble was that having taken October's money I couldn't back out; not for months. This thought depressed me further still. I sat slumped in unrelieved gloom, wasting my much needed free time.

I think now that it must have been the sense that I was failing in what I had set out to do, more than mere tiredness, which beset me that afternoon, because although later on I encountered worse things it was only for that short while that I ever truly regretted having listened to October, and unreservedly wished myself back in my comfortable Australian cage.

The lads watching the television were making disparaging remarks about the jockeys and striking private bets against each other on the outcome of the races.

'The uphill finish will sort 'em out as usual,' Paddy was saying. 'It's a long way from the last . . . Aladdin's the only one who's got the stamina for the job.'

'No,' contradicted Grits. 'Lobster Cocktail's a flyer . . .'

Morosely I riffled the pages of the form book, aimlessly looking through them for the hundredth time, and came by chance on the map of Chepstow racecourse in the general information section at the beginning of the book. There were diagrammatic maps of all the main courses showing the shape of the tracks and the positioning of fences, stands, starting gates, and winning posts, and I had looked before at those for Ludlow, Stafford, and Haydock, without results. There was no map of Kelso or Sedgefield. Next to the map section were a few pages of information about the courses, the lengths of their circuits, the names and addresses of the officials, the record times for the races, and so on.

For something to do, I turned to Chepstow's paragraph. Paddy's 'long way from the last' was detailed there: two hundred and fifty yards. I looked up Kelso, Sedgefield, Ludlow, Stafford, and Haydock. They had much longer run-ins than Chepstow. I looked up the run-ins of all the courses in the book. The Aintree Grand National run-in was the second longest. The longest of all was Sedgefield, and in third, fourth, fifth, and sixth positions came Ludlow, Haydock, Kelso, and Stafford. All had run-ins of over four hundred yards.

Geography had nothing to do with it: those five courses had almost certainly been chosen by the dopers because in each case it was about a quarter of a mile from the last fence to the winning post.

It was an advance, even if a small one, to have made at least some pattern out of the chaos. In a slightly less abysmal frame of mind I shut the form book and at four o'clock followed the other lads out into the unwelcome rainswept yard to spend an hour with each of my three charges, grooming them thoroughly to give their coats a clean healthy shine, tossing and tidying their straw beds, fetching their water, holding their heads while Inskip walked round, rugging them up comfortably for the night, and finally fetching their evening feed. As usual it was seven before we had all finished, and eight before we had eaten and changed and were bumping down the hill to Slaw, seven of us sardined into a rickety old Austin.

Bar billiards, darts, dominoes, the endless friendly bragging, the ingredients as before. Patiently, I sat and waited. It was nearly ten, the hour when the lads began to empty their glasses and think about having to get up the next morning, when Soupy strolled across the room towards the door, and, seeing my eyes on him, jerked his head for me to follow him. I got up and went out after him, and found him in the lavatories.

'This is for you. The rest on Tuesday,' he said economically; and treating me to a curled lip and stony stare to impress me with his toughness, he handed me a thick brown envelope. I put it in the inside pocket of my black leather jacket, and nodded to him. Still without speaking, without smiling, hard-eyed to match, I turned on my heel and went back into the bar: and after a while, casually, he followed.

So I crammed into the Austin and was driven up the hill, back to bed in the little dormitory, with seventy-five pounds and a packet of white powder sitting snugly over my heart.

CHAPTER SIX

October dipped his finger in the powder and tasted it.

'I don't know what it is either,' he said, shaking his head. 'I'll get it analysed.'

I bent down and patted his dog, and fondled his ears.

He said 'You do realize what a risk you'll be running if you take his money and don't give the dope to the horse?'

I grinned up at him.

'It's no laughing matter,' he said seriously. 'They can be pretty free with their boots, these people, and it would be no help to us if you get your ribs kicked in . . .'

'Actually,' I said, straightening up, 'I do think it might be best if Sparking Plug didn't win . . . I could hardly hope to attract custom from the dopers we are really after if they heard I had double-crossed anyone before.'

'You're quite right.' He sounded relieved. 'Sparking Plug must lose; but Inskip . . . how on earth can I tell him that the jockey must pull back?'

'You can't,' I said. 'You don't want them getting into trouble. But it won't matter much if I do. The horse won't win if I keep him thirsty tomorrow morning and give him a bucketful of water just before the race.'

He looked at me with amusement. 'I see you've learned a thing or two.'

'It'd make your hair stand on end, what I've learned.'

He smiled back. 'All right then. I suppose it's the only thing to do. I wonder what the National Hunt Committee would think of a Steward conspiring with one of his own stable lads to stop a favourite?' He laughed. 'I'll tell Roddy Beckett what to expect . . . though it won't be so funny for Inskip, nor for the lads here, if they back the horse, nor for the general public, who'll lose their money.'

'No,' I agreed.

He folded the packet of white powder and tucked it back into the envelope with the money. The seventy-five pounds had foolishly been paid in a bundle of new fivers with consecutive numbers: and we had agreed that October would take them and try to discover to whom they had been issued.

I told him about the long run-ins on all of the courses where the eleven horses had won.

'It almost sounds as if they might have been using vitamins after all,' he said thoughtfully. 'You can't detect them in dope tests because technically they are not dope at all, but food. The whole question of vit-amins is very difficult.'

'They increase stamina?' I asked.

'Yes, quite considerably. Horses which "die" in the

last half mile – and as you pointed out, all eleven are that type – would be ideal subjects. But vitamins were among the first things we considered, and we had to eliminate them. They can help horses to win, if they are injected in massive doses into the bloodstream, and they are undetectable in analysis because they are used up in the winning, but they are undetectable in other ways too. They don't excite, they don't bring a horse back from a race looking as though Benzedrine were coming out of his ears.' He sighed. 'I don't know . . .'

With regret I made my confession that I had learned nothing from Beckett's typescript.

'Neither Beckett nor I expected as much from it as you did,' he said. 'I've been talking to him a lot this week, and we think that although all those extensive inquiries were made at the time, you might find something that was overlooked if you moved to one of the stables where those eleven horses were trained when they were doped. Of course, eight of the horses were sold and have changed stables, which is a pity, but three are still with their original trainers, and it might be best if you could get a job with one of those.'

'Yes,' I said. 'All right. I'll try all three trainers and see if one of them will take me on. But the trail is very cold by now . . . and joker number twelve will turn up in a different stable altogether. There was nothing, I suppose, at Haydock this week?'

'No. Saliva samples were taken from all the runners before the selling 'chase, but the favourite won, quite normally, and we didn't have the samples analysed. But now that you've spotted that those five courses must have been chosen deliberately for their long finishing straights we will keep stricter watches there than ever. Especially if one of those eleven horses runs there again.'

'You could check with the racing calendar to see if any has been entered,' I agreed. 'But so far none of them has been doped twice, and I can't see why the pattern should change.'

A gust of bitter wind blew down the gully, and he shivered. The little stream, swollen with yesterday's rains, tumbled busily over its rocky bed. October whistled to his dog, who was sniffing along its banks.

'By the way,' he said, shaking hands, 'the vets are of the opinion that the horses were not helped on their way by pellets or darts, or anything shot or thrown. But they can't be a hundred per cent certain. They didn't at the time examine all the horses very closely. But if we get another one I'll see they go over every inch looking for punctures.'

'Fine.' We smiled at each other and turned away. I liked him. He was imaginative and had a sense of humour to leaven the formidable big-business-executive power of his speech and manner. A tough man, I thought appreciatively: tough in mind, muscular in body, unswerving in purpose: a man of the kind to have earned an earldom, if he hadn't inherited it.

Sparking Plug had to do without his bucket of water

that night and again the following morning. The box driver set off to Leicester with a pocketful of hard-earned money from the lads and their instructions to back the horse to win; and I felt a traitor.

Inskip's other horse, which had come in the box too, was engaged in the third race, but the novice 'chase was not until the fifth race on the card, which left me free to watch the first two races as well as Sparks' own. I bought a race card and found a space on the parade ring rails, and watched the horses for the first race being led round. Although from the form books I knew the names of a great many trainers they were still unknown to me by sight; and accordingly, when they stood chatting with their jockeys in the ring, I tried, for interest, to identify some of them. There were only seven of them engaged in the first race: Owen, Cundell, Beeby, Cazalet, Humber . . . Humber? What was it that I had heard about Humber? I couldn't remember. Nothing very important, I thought.

Humber's horse looked the least well of the lot, and the lad leading him round wore unpolished shoes, a dirty raincoat, and an air of not caring to improve matters. The jockey's jersey, when he took his coat off, could be seen to be still grubby with mud from a former outing, and the trainer who had failed to provide clean colours or to care about stable smartness was a large, bad-tempered looking man leaning on a thick, knobbed walking stick.

As it happened, Humber's lad stood beside me on the stand to watch the race.

'Got much chance?' I asked idly.

'Waste of time running him,' he said, his lip curling. 'I'm fed to the back molars with the sod.'

'Oh. Perhaps your other horse is better, though?' I murmured, watching the runners line up for the start.

'My other horse?' He laughed without mirth. 'Three others, would you believe it? I'm fed up with the whole sodding set up. I'm packing it in at the end of the week, pay or no pay.'

I suddenly remembered what I had heard about Humber. The worst stable in the country to work for, the boy in the Bristol hostel had said: they starved the lads and knocked them about and could only get riff-raff to work there.

'How do you mean, pay or no pay?' I asked.

'Humber pays sixteen quid a week, instead of eleven,' he said, 'but it's not bloody worth it. I've had a bellyful of bloody Humber. I'm getting out.'

The race started, and we watched Humber's horse finish last. The lad disappeared, muttering, to lead him away.

I smiled, followed him down the stairs, and forgot him, because waiting near the bottom step was a seedy, black-moustached man whom I instantly recognized as having been in the bar at the Cheltenham dance.

I walked slowly away to lean over the parade ring rail, and he inconspicuously followed. He stopped beside me, and with his eyes on the one horse already in the ring, he said, 'I hear that you are hard up.'

'Not after today, I'm not,' I said, looking him up and down.

He glanced at me briefly. 'Oh. Are you so sure of Sparking Plug?'

'Yeah,' I said with an unpleasant smirk. 'Certain.' Someone, I reflected, had been kind enough to tell him which horse I looked after: which meant he had been checking up on me. I trusted he had learned nothing to my advantage.

'Hmm.'

A whole minute passed. Then he said casually, 'Have you ever thought of changing your job... going to another stable?'

'I've thought of it,' I admitted, shrugging. 'Who hasn't?'

'There's always a market for good lads,' he pointed out, 'and I've heard you're a dab hand at the mucking out. With a reference from Inskip you could get in anywhere, if you told them you were prepared to wait for a vacancy.'

'Where?' I asked; but he wasn't to be hurried. After another minute he said, still conversationally, 'It can be very... er... lucrative... working for some stables.'

'Oh?'

'That is,' he coughed discreetly, 'if you are ready to do a bit more than the stable tells you to.'

'Such as?'

'Oh . . . general duties,' he said vaguely. 'It varies. Anything helpful to, er, the person who is prepared to supplement your income.'

'And who's that?'

He smiled thinly. 'Look upon me as his agent. How about it? His terms are a regular fiver a week for information about the results of training gallops and things like that, and a good bonus for occasional special jobs of a more, er, risky nature.'

'It don't sound bad,' I said slowly, sucking in my lower lip. 'Can't I do it at Inskip's?'

'Inskip's is not a betting stable,' he said. 'The horses always run to win. We do not need a permanent employee in that sort of place. There are however at present two betting stables without a man of ours in them, and you would be useful in either.'

He named two leading trainers, neither of whom was one of the three people I had already planned to apply to. I would have to decide whether it would not be more useful to join what was clearly a well-organized spy system, than to work with a once-doped horse who would almost certainly not be doped again.

'I'll think it over,' I said. 'Where can I get in touch with you?'

'Until you're on the pay roll, you can't,' he said simply. 'Sparking Plug's in the fifth, I see. Well, you can give me your answer after that race. I'll be somewhere on your way back to the stables. Just nod if you agree, and shake your head if you don't. But I can't see you passing up a chance like this, not one of your sort.' There was a sly contempt in the smile he gave me that made me unexpectedly wince inwardly.

He turned away and walked a few steps, and then came back.

'Should I have a big bet on Sparking Plug, then?' he asked.

'Oh ... er. ... well ... if I were you I'd save your money.'

He looked surprised, and then suspicious, and then knowing. 'So that's how the land lies,' he said. 'Well, well, well.' He laughed, looking at me as if I'd crawled out from under a stone. He was a man who despised his tools. 'I can see you're going to be very useful to us. Very useful indeed.'

I watched him go. It wasn't from kind-heartedness that I had stopped him backing Sparking Plug, but because it was the only way to retain and strengthen his confidence. When he was fifty yards away, I followed him. He made straight for the bookmakers in Tattersalls and strolled along the rows, looking at the odds displayed by each firm; but as far as I could see he was in fact innocently planning to bet on the next race, and not reporting to anyone the outcome of his talk with me. Sighing, I put ten shillings on an outsider and went back to watch the horses go out for the race.

*

Sparking Plug thirstily drank two full buckets of water, stumbled over the second last fence, and cantered tiredly in behind the other seven runners to the accompaniment of boos from the cheaper enclosures. I watched him with regret. It was a thankless way to treat a great-hearted horse.

The seedy, black-moustached man was waiting when I led the horse away to the stables. I nodded to him, and he sneered knowingly back.

'You'll hear from us,' he said.

There was gloom in the box going home and in the yard the next day over Sparking Plug's unexplainable defeat, and I went alone to Slaw on Tuesday evening, when Soupy duly handed over another seventy-five pounds. I checked it. Another fifteen new fivers, consecutive to the first fifteen.

'Ta,' I said. 'What do you get out of this yourself?'

Soupy's full mouth curled. 'I do all right. You mugs take the risks, I get a cut for setting you up. Fair enough, eh?'

'Fair enough. How often do you do this sort of thing?' I tucked the envelope of money into my pocket.

He shrugged, looking pleased with himself. 'I can spot blokes like you a mile off. Inskip must be slipping, though. First time I've known him pick a bent penny, like. But those darts matches come in very handy . . . I'm good, see. I'm always in the team. And there's a lot of stables in Yorkshire . . . with a lot of beaten favourites for people to scratch their heads over.'

'You're very clever,' I said.

He smirked. He agreed.

I walked up the hill planning to light a fuse under T.N.T., the high explosive kid.

In view of the black-moustached man's offer I decided to read through Beckett's typescript yet again, to see if the eleven dopings could have been the result of systematic spying. Looking at things from a fresh angle might produce results, I thought, and also might help me make up my mind whether or not to back out of the spying job and go to one of the doped horse's yards as arranged.

Locked in the bathroom I began again at page one. On page sixty-seven, fairly early in the life history of the fifth of the horses, I read 'Bought at Ascot Sales, by D. L. Mentiff, Esq., of York for four hundred and twenty guineas, passed on for five hundred pounds to H. Humber of Posset, County Durham, remained three months, ran twice unplaced in maiden hurdles, subsequently sold again, at Doncaster, being bought for six hundred guineas by N. W. Davies, Esq., of Leeds. Sent by him to L. Peterson's training stables at Mars Edge, Staffs, remained eighteen months, ran in four maiden hurdles, five novice 'chases, all without being placed. Races listed below.' Three months at Humber's. I smiled. It appeared that horses didn't stay with him any longer than lads. I ploughed on through the details, page after solid page.

On page ninety-four I came across the following: 'Alamo was then offered for public auction at Kelso, and a Mr John Arbuthnot, living in Berwickshire, paid three hundred guineas for him. He sent him to be trained by H. Humber at Posset, County Durham, but he was not entered for any races, and Mr Arbuthnot sold him to Humber for the same sum. A few weeks later he was sent for resale at Kelso. This time Alamo was bought for three hundred and seventy-five guineas by a Mr Clement Smithson, living at Nantwich, Cheshire, who kept him at home for the summer and then sent him to a trainer called Samuel Martin at Malton, Yorkshire, where he ran unplaced in four maiden hurdles before Christmas (see list attached).'

I massaged my stiff neck. Humber again.

I read on.

On page one hundred and eighty, I read, 'Ridgeway was then acquired as a yearling by a farmer, James Green, of Home Farm, Crayford, Surrey, in settlement of a bad debt. Mr Green put him out to grass for two years, and had him broken in, hoping he would be a good hunter. However, a Mr Taplow of Pewsey, Wilts, said he would like to buy him and put him in training for racing. Ridgeway was trained for flat races by Ronald Streat of Pewsey, but was unplaced in all his four races that summer. Mr Taplow then sold Ridgeway privately to Albert George, farmer, of Bridge Lewes,

Shropshire, who tried to train him himself but said he found he didn't have time to do it properly, so he sold him to a man a cousin of his knew near Durham, a trainer called Hedley Humber. Humber apparently thought the horse was no good, and Ridgeway went up for auction at Newmarket in November, fetching two hundred and ninety guineas and being bought by Mr P. J. Brewer, of The Manor, Witherby, Lancs . . .'

I ploughed right on to the end of the typescript, threading my way through the welter of names, but Humber was not mentioned anywhere again.

Three of the eleven horses had been in Humber's yard for a brief spell at some distant time in their careers. That was all it amounted to.

I rubbed my eyes, which were gritty from lack of sleep, and an alarm clock rang suddenly, clamorously, in the silent cottage. I looked at my watch in surprise. It was already half past six. Standing up and stretching, I made use of the bathroom facilities, thrust the type-script up under my pyjama jacket and the jersey I wore on top and shuffled back yawning to the dormitory, where the others were already up and struggling puffy-eyed into their clothes.

Down in the yard it was so cold that everything one touched seemed to suck the heat out of one's fingers, leaving them numb and fumbling, and the air was as intense an internal shaft to the chest as iced coffee sliding down the oesophagus. Muck out the boxes, saddle up, ride up to the moor, canter, walk, ride down again, brush the sweat off, make the horse comfortable, give him food and water, and go in to breakfast. Repeat for the second horse, repeat for the third, and go in to lunch.

While we were eating Wally came in and told two others and me to go and clean the tack, and when we had finished our tinned plums and custard we went along to the tack room and started on the saddles and bridles. It was warm there from the stove, and I put my head back on a saddle and went solidly asleep.

One of the others jogged my legs and said, 'Wake up Dan, there's a lot to do,' and I drifted to the surface again. But before I opened my eyes the other lad said, 'Oh, leave him, he does his share,' and with blessings on his head I sank back into blackness. Four o'clock came too soon, and with it the three hours of evening stables: then supper at seven and another day nearly done.

For most of the time I thought about Humber's name cropping up three times in the typescript. I couldn't really see that it was of more significance than that four of the eleven horses had been fed on horse cubes at the time of their doping. What was disturbing was that I should have missed it entirely on my first two readings. I realized that I had had no reason to notice the name Humber before seeing him and his horse and talking to his lad at Leicester, but if I had missed one name occurring three times, I could have missed others as well. The thing to do would be to make lists of every single name mentioned in the typescript, and see if any other turned up in association with several of the horses. An electronic computer could have done it in seconds. For me, it looked like another night in the bathroom.

There were more than a thousand names in the typescript. I listed half of them on the Wednesday night, and slept a bit, and finished them on Thursday night, and slept some more.

On Friday the sun shone for a change, and the morning was beautiful on the moor. I trotted Sparking Plug along the track somewhere in the middle of the string and thought about the lists. No names except Humber's and one other occurred in connection with more than two of the horses. But the one other was a certain Paul J. Adams, and he had at one time or another owned six of them. Six out of eleven. It couldn't be a coincidence. The odds against it were phenomenal. I was certain I had made my first really useful discovery, yet I couldn't see why the fact that P. J. Adams, Esq., had owned a horse for a few months once should enable it to be doped a year or two later. I puzzled over it all morning without a vestige of understanding.

As it was a fine day, Wally said, it was a good time for me to scrub some rugs. This meant laying the rugs the horses wore to keep them warm in their boxes flat on the concrete in the yard, soaking them with the aid of a hose pipe, scrubbing them with a long-handled broom and detergent, hosing them off again, and hanging the wet rugs on the fence to drip before they were transferred to the warm tack room to finish drying thoroughly. It was an unpopular job, and Wally, who had treated me even more coldly since Sparking Plug's disgrace (though he had not gone so far as to accuse me of engineering it), could hardly conceal his dislike when he told me that it was my turn to do it.

However, I reflected, as I laid out five rugs after lunch and thoroughly soaked them with water, I had two hours to be alone and think. And as so often happens, I was wrong.

At three o'clock, when the horses were dozing and the lads were either copying them or had made quick trips to Harrogate with their new pay packets; when stable life was at its siesta and only I with my broom showed signs of reluctant activity, Patty Tarren walked in through the gate, across the tarmac, and slowed to a halt a few feet away.

She was wearing a straightish dress of soft looking knobbly green tweed with a row of silver buttons from throat to hem. Her chestnut hair hung in a clean shining bob on her shoulders and was held back from her forehead by a wide green band, and with her fluffy eyelashes and pale pink mouth she looked about as enticing an interruption as a hard-worked stable hand could ask for.

'Hullo, Danny boy,' she said.

'Good afternoon, miss.'

'I saw you from my window,' she said.

I turned in surprise, because I had thought October's house entirely hidden by trees, but sure enough, up the slope, one stone corner and a window could be seen through a gap in the leafless boughs. It was, however, a long way off. If Patty had recognized me from that distance she had been using binoculars.

'You looked a bit lonely, so I came down to talk to you.'

'Thank you, miss.'

'As a matter of fact,' she said, lowering the eyelashes, 'the rest of the family don't get here until this evening, and I had nothing to do in that barn of a place all by myself, and I was bored. So I thought I'd come down and talk to you.'

'I see.' I leant on the broom, looking at her lovely face and thinking that there was an expression in her eyes too old for her years.

'It's rather cold out here, don't you think? I want to talk to you about something . . . don't you think we could stand in the shelter of that doorway?' Without waiting for an answer she walked towards the doorway in question, which was that of the hay barn, and went inside. I followed her, resting the broom against the doorpost on the way.

'Yes, miss?' I said. The light was dim in the barn.

It appeared that talking was not her main object after all.

She put her hands round the back of my neck and offered her mouth for a kiss. I bent my head and kissed her. She was no virgin, October's daughter. She kissed with her tongue and with her teeth, and she moved her stomach rhythmically against mine. My muscles turned to knots. She smelled sweetly of fresh soap, more innocent than her behaviour.

'Well . . . that's all right, then,' she said with a giggle, disengaging herself and heading for the bulk of the bales of hay which half filled the barn.

'Come on,' she said over her shoulder, and climbed up the bales to the flat level at the top. I followed her slowly. When I got to the top I sat looking at the hay barn floor with the broom, the bucket, and the rug touched with sunshine through the doorway. On top of the hay had been Philip's favourite play place for years when he was little . . . and this is a fine time to think of my family, I thought.

Patty was lying on her back three feet away from me. Her eyes were wide and glistening, and her mouth curved open in an odd little smile. Slowly, holding my gaze, she undid all the silver buttons down the front of her dress to a point well below her waist. Then she gave a little shake so that the edges of the dress fell apart.

She had absolutely nothing on underneath.

I looked at her body, which was pearl pink and slender, and very desirable; and she gave a little rippling shiver of anticipation.

I looked back at her face. Her eyes were big and dark, and the odd way in which she was smiling suddenly struck me as being half furtive, half greedy; and wholly sinful. I had an abrupt vision of myself as she must see me, as I had seen myself in the long mirror in

October's London house, a dark, flashy looking stable boy with an air of deceitfulness and an acquaintance with dirt.

I understood her smile, then.

I turned round where I sat until I had my back to her, and felt a flush of anger and shame spread all over my body.

'Do your dress up,' I said.

'Why? Are you impotent after all, Danny boy?'

'Do your dress up,' I repeated. 'The party's over.'

I slid down the hay, walked across the floor, and out of the door without looking back. Twitching up the broom and cursing under my breath I let out my fury against myself by scrubbing the rug until my arms ached.

After a while I saw her (green dress rebuttoned) come slowly out of the hay barn, look around her, and go across to a muddy puddle on the edge of the tarmac. She dirtied her shoes thoroughly in it, then childishly walked on to the rug I had just cleaned, and wiped all the mud off carefully in the centre.

Her eyes were wide and her face expressionless as she looked at me.

'You'll be sorry, Danny boy,' she said simply, and without haste strolled away down the yard, the chestnut hair swinging gently on the green tweed dress.

I scrubbed the rug again. Why had I kissed her? Why, after knowing about her from that kiss, had I followed her up into the hay? Why had I been such a

stupid, easily roused, lusting fool? I was filled with useless dismay.

One didn't have to accept an invitation to dinner,
even if the appetizer made one hungry. But having
accepted, one should not so brutally reject what was
offered. She had every right to be angry.

And I had every reason to be confused. I had been
for nine years a father to two girls, one of whom was
nearly Patty's age. I had taught them when they were
little not to take lifts from strangers and when they
were bigger how to avoid more subtle snares. And here
I was, indisputably on the other side of the parental
fence.

I felt an atrocious sense of guilt towards October,
for I had had the intention, and there was no denying
it, of doing what Patty wanted.

CHAPTER SEVEN

It was Elinor who rode out on my horse the following morning, and Patty, having obviously got her to change mounts, studiously refused to look at me at all.

Elinor, a dark scarf protecting most of the silver-blonde hair, accepted a leg up with impersonal grace, gave me a warm smile of thanks and rode away at the head of the string with her sister. When we got back after the gallops, however, she led the horse into his box and did half of the jobs for him while I was attending to Sparking Plug. I didn't know what she was doing until I walked down the yard, and was surprised to find her there, having grown used to Patty's habit of bolting the horse into the box still complete with saddle, bridle, and mud.

'You go and get the hay and water,' she said. 'I'll finish getting the dirt off, now I've started.'

I carried away the saddle and bridle to the tack room, and took back the hay and water. Elinor gave the horse's mane a few final strokes with the brush, and I put on his rug and buckled the roller round his belly. She watched while I tossed the straw over the floor to make a comfortable bed, and waited until I had bolted the door.

'Thank you,' I said. 'Thank you very much.'

She smiled faintly, 'It's a pleasure. It really is. I like horses. Especially racehorses. Lean and fast and exciting.'

'Yes,' I agreed. We walked down the yard together, she to go to the gate and I to the cottage which stood beside it.

'They are so different from what I do all the week,' she said.

'What do you do all the week?'

'Oh . . . study. I'm at Durham University.' There was a sudden, private, recollecting grin. Not for me. On level terms, I thought, one might find more in Elinor than good manners.

'It's really extraordinary how well you ride,' she said suddenly. 'I heard Mr Inskip telling Father this morning that it would be worth getting a licence for you. Have you ever thought of racing?'

'I wish I could,' I said fervently, without thinking.

'Well, why not?'

'Oh . . . I might be leaving soon.'

'What a pity.' It was polite; nothing more.

We reached the cottage. She gave me a friendly smile and walked straight on, out of the yard, out of sight. I may not ever see her again, I thought; and was mildly sorry.

*

When the horse box came back from a day's racing (with a winner, a third, and an also-ran) I climbed up into the cab and borrowed the map again. I wanted to discover the location of the village where Mr Paul Adams lived, and after some searching I found it. As its significance sank in I began to smile with astonishment. There was, it seemed, yet another place where I could apply for a job.

I went back into the cottage, into Mrs Allnut's cosy kitchen, and ate Mrs Allnut's delicious egg and chips and bread and butter and fruit cake, and later slept dreamlessly on Mrs Allnut's lumpy mattress, and in the morning bathed luxuriously in Mrs Allnut's shining bathroom. And in the afternoon I went up beside the stream with at last something worthwhile to tell October.

He met me with a face of granite, and before I could say a word he hit me hard and squarely across the mouth. It was a back-handed expert blow which started from the waist, and I didn't see it coming until far too late.

'What the hell's that for?' I said, running my tongue round my teeth and being pleased to find that none of them were broken off.

He glared at me. 'Patty told me . . .' He stopped as if it were too difficult to go on.

'Oh,' I said blankly.

'Yes, oh,' he mimicked savagely. He was breathing deeply and I thought he was going to hit me again. I thrust my hands into my pockets and his stayed where they were, down by his sides, clenching and unclenching.

'What did Patty tell you?'

'She told me everything.' His anger was almost tangible. 'She came to me this morning in tears . . . she told me how you made her go into the hay barn . . . and held her there until she was worn out with struggling to get away . . . she told the . . . the disgusting things you did to her with your hands . . . and then how you forced her . . . forced her to . . .' He couldn't say it.

I was appalled. 'I didn't,' I said vehemently. 'I didn't do anything like that. I kissed her . . . and that's all. She's making it up.'

'She couldn't possibly have made it up. It was too detailed . . . She couldn't know such things unless they had happened to her.'

I opened my mouth and shut it again. They had happened to her, right enough; somewhere, with someone else, more than once, and certainly also with her willing co-operation. And I could see that to some extent at least she was going to get away with her horrible revenge, because there are some things you can't say about a girl to her father, especially if you like him.

October said scathingly, 'I have never been so mistaken in a man before. I thought you were responsible . . . or at least able to control yourself. Not a cheap lecherous jackanapes who would take my money – and my regard – and amuse yourself behind my back, debauching my daughter.'

There was enough truth in that to hurt, and the guilt I felt over my stupid behaviour didn't help. But I had to put up some kind of defence, because I would never have harmed Patty in any way, and there was still the investigation into the doping to be carried on. Now I had got so far, I did not want to be packed off home in disgrace.

I said slowly, 'I did go with Patty into the hay barn. I did kiss her. Once. Only once. After that I didn't touch her. I literally didn't touch any part of her, not her hand, not her dress . . . nothing.'

He looked at me steadily for a long time while the fury slowly died out of him and a sort of weariness took its place.

At length he said, almost calmly, 'One of you is lying. And I have to believe my daughter.' There was an unexpected flicker of entreaty in his voice.

'Yes,' I said. I looked away, up the gully. 'Well . . . this solves one problem, anyway.'

'What problem?'

'How to leave here with the ignominious sack and without a reference.'

It was so far away from what he was thinking about that it was several moments before he showed any reaction at all, and then he gave me an attentive, narrow-eyed stare which I did not try to avoid.

'You intend to go on with the investigation, then?'

'If you are willing.'

'Yes,' he said heavily, at length. 'Especially as you are moving on and will have no more opportunities of seeing Patty. In spite of what I personally think of you, you do still represent our best hope of success, and I suppose I must put the good of racing first.'

He fell silent. I contemplated the rather grim prospect of continuing to do that sort of work for a man who hated me. Yet the thought of giving up was worse. And that was odd.

Eventually he said, 'Why do you want to leave without a reference? You won't get a job in any of these three stables without a reference.'

'The only reference I need to get a job in the stable I am going to is no reference at all.'

'Whose stable?'

'Hedley Humber's.'

'Humber!' He was sombrely incredulous. 'But why? He's a very poor trainer and he didn't train any of the doped horses. What's the point of going there?'

'He didn't train any of the horses when they won,' I agreed, 'but he had three of them through his hands earlier in their careers. There is also a man called P. J. Adams who at one time or another owned six more of them. Adams lives, according to the map, less than ten miles from Humber. Humber lives at Posset, in Durham, and Adams at Tellbridge, just over the Northumberland border. That means that nine of the eleven horses spent some time in that one small area of the

British Isles. None of them stayed long. The dossiers of Transistor and Rudyard are much less detailed than the others on the subject of their earlier life, and I have now no doubt that checking would show that they too, for a short while, came under the care of either Adams or Humber.'

'But how could the horses having spent some time with Adams or Hunter possibly affect their speed months or years later?'

'I don't know,' I said. 'But I'll go and find out.'

There was a pause.

'Very well,' he said heavily. 'I'll tell Inskip that you are dismissed. And I'll tell him it is because you pestered Patricia.'

'Right.'

He looked at me coldly. 'You can write me reports. I don't want to see you again.'

I watched him walk away strongly up the gully. I didn't know whether or not he really believed any more that I had done what Patty said; but I did know that he needed to believe it. The alternative, the truth, was so much worse. What father wants to discover that his beautiful eighteen-year-old daughter is a lying slut?

And as for me, I thought that on the whole I had got off lightly; if I had found that anyone had assaulted Belinda or Helen I'd have half killed him.

After second exercise the following day Inskip told

me exactly what he thought of me, and I didn't particularly enjoy it.

After giving me a public dressing down in the centre of the tarmac (with the lads grinning in sly amusement as they carried their buckets and hay nets with both ears flapping) he handed back the insurance card and income tax form – there was still a useful muddle going on over the illegible Cornish address on the one October had originally provided me with – and told me to pack my bags and get out of the yard at once. It would be no use my giving his name as a reference he said, because Lord October had expressly forbidden him to vouch for my character, and it was a decision with which he thoroughly agreed. He gave me a week's wages in lieu of notice, less Mrs Allnut's share, and that was that.

I packed my things in the little dormitory, patted goodbye to the bed I had slept in for six weeks, and went down to the kitchen where the lads were having their midday meal. Eleven pairs of eyes swivelled in my direction. Some were contemptuous, some were surprised, one or two thought it funny. None of them looked sorry to see me go. Mrs Allnut gave me a thick cheese sandwich, and I ate it walking down the hill to Slaw to catch the two o'clock bus to Harrogate.

And from Harrogate, where?

No lad in his senses would go straight from a prosperous place like Inskip's to ask for a job at

Humber's, however abruptly he had been thrown out; there had to be a period of some gentle sliding downhill if it were to look unsuspicious. In fact, I decided, it would be altogether much better if it were Humber's head travelling-lad who offered me work, and not I who asked for it. It should not be too difficult. I could turn up at every course where Humber had a runner, looking seedier and seedier and more and more ready to take any job at all, and one day the lad-hungry stable would take the bait.

Meanwhile I needed somewhere to live. The bus trundled down to Harrogate while I thought it out. Somewhere in the northeast, to be near Humber's local meetings. A big town, so that I could be anonymous in it. An alive town, so that I could find ways of passing the time between race meetings. With the help of maps and guide books in Harrogate public library I settled on Newcastle, and with the help of a couple of tolerant lorry drivers I arrived there late that afternoon and found myself a room in a back-street hotel.

It was a terrible room with peeling, coffee-coloured walls, tatty printed linoleum wearing out on the floor, a narrow, hard divan bed, and some scratched furniture made out of stained plywood. Only its unexpected cleanliness and a shiny new washbasin in one corner made it bearable, but it did, I had to admit, suit my appearance and purpose admirably.

I dined in a fish and chip shop for three and six, and went to a cinema, and enjoyed not having to groom three horses or think twice about every word I said. My spirits rose several points at being free again and I succeeded in forgetting the trouble I was in with October.

In the morning I sent off to him in a registered package the second seventy-five pounds, which I had not given him in the gully on Sunday, together with a short formal note explaining why there would have to be a delay before I engaged myself to Humber.

From the post office I went to a betting shop and from their calendar copied down all the racing fixtures for the next month. It was the beginning of December, and I found there were very few meetings in the north before the first week in January; which was, from my point of view, a waste of time and a nuisance. After the following Saturday's programme at Newcastle itself there was no racing north of Nottinghamshire until Boxing Day, more than a fortnight later.

Pondering this set-back I next went in search of a serviceable second-hand motor-cycle. It took me until late afternoon to find exactly what I wanted, a souped-up 500 cc Norton, four years old and the ex-property of a now one-legged young man who had done the ton once too often on the Great North Road. The salesman gave me these details with relish as he took my money and assured me that the bike would still do a hundred at a push. I thanked him politely and left the machine with him to have a new silencer fitted, along with some new hand grips, brake cables, and tyres.

Lack of private transport at Slaw had not been a tremendous drawback, and I would not have been concerned about my mobility at Posset were it not for the one obtrusive thought that I might at some time find it advisable to depart in a hurry. I could not forget the journalist, Tommy Stapleton. Between Hexham and Yorkshire he had lost eight hours, and turned up dead. Between Hexham and Yorkshire lay Posset.

The first person I saw at Newcastle races four days later was the man with the black moustache who had offered me steady employment as a stable spy. He was standing in an unobtrusive corner near the entrance, talking to a big-eared boy whom I later saw leading round a horse from one of the best-known gambling stables in the country.

From some distance away I watched him pass to the boy a white envelope and receive a brown envelope in return. Money for information, I thought, and so openly done as to appear innocent.

I strolled along behind Black Moustache when he finished his transaction and made his way to the bookmakers' stands in Tattersalls. As before he appeared to be doing nothing but examining the prices offered on the first race: and as before I staked a few shillings on the favourite in case I should be seen to be following him. In spite of his survey he placed no bets at all, but strolled down to the rails which separated the enclosure from the course itself. There he came to an unplanned-looking halt beside an artificial red-head wearing a yellowish leopard skin jacket over a dark grey skirt.

She turned her head towards him, and they spoke. Presently he took the brown envelope from his breast pocket and slipped it into his race card: and after a few moments he and the woman unobtrusively exchanged race cards. He wandered away from the rails, while she put the card containing the envelope into a large shiny black handbag and snapped it shut. From the shelter of the last row of bookies I watched her walk to the entrance into the Club and pass through on to the Members' lawn. I could not follow her there, but I went up on to the stands and watched her walk across the next-door enclosure. She appeared to be well-known. She stopped and spoke to several people . . . a bent old man with a big floppy hat, an obese young man who patted her arm repeatedly, a pair of women in mink cocoons, a group of three men who laughed loudly and hid her from my view so that I could not see if she had given any one of them the envelope from her handbag.

The horses cantered down the course and the crowds moved up on to the stands to watch the race. The red-head disappeared among the throng on the Members' stand, leaving me frustrated at losing her. The race was run, and the favourite cantered in by ten lengths. The crowd roared with approval. I stood where I was while people round me flowed down from the stands, waiting without too much hope to see if the leopard-skin red-head would reappear.

Obligingly, she did. She was carrying her handbag in one hand and her race card in the other. Pausing to talk again, this time to a very short fat man, she eventually made her way over to the bookmakers who stood along the rails separating Tattersalls from the Club and stopped in front of one nearest the stands, and nearest to me. For the first time I could see her face clearly: she was younger than I had thought and plainer of feature, with gaps between her top teeth.

She said in a piercing, tinny voice, 'I'll settle my account, Bimmo dear,' and opening her handbag took out a brown envelope and gave it to a small man in spectacles, who stood on a box beside a board bearing the words Bimmo Bognor (est. 1920), Manchester and London.

Mr Bimmo Bognor took the envelope and put it in his jacket pocket, and his hearty 'Ta, love,' floated up to my attentive ears.

I went down from the stands and collected my small winnings, thinking that while the brown envelope that the red-head had given to Bimmo Bognor *looked* like the envelope that the big-eared lad had given to Black Moustache, I could not be a hundred per cent sure of it. She might have given the lad's envelope to any one of the people I had watched her talk to, or to anyone on the stands while she was out of my sight: and she might then have gone quite honestly to pay her bookmaker.

If I wanted to be certain of the chain, perhaps I could send an urgent message along it, a message so urgent that there would be no wandering among the crowds, but an unconcealed direct line between a and b, and b and c. The urgent message, since Sparking Plug was a runner in the fifth race, presented no difficulty at all; but being able to locate Black Moustache at exactly the right moment entailed keeping him in sight all the afternoon.

He was a creature of habit, which helped. He always watched the races from the same corner of the stand, patronized the same bar between times, and stood inconspicuously near the gate on the course when the horses were led out of the parade ring. He did not bet.

Humber had two horses at the meeting, one in the third race and one in the last; and although it meant leaving my main purpose untouched until late in the afternoon, I let the third race go by without making any attempt to find his head travelling-lad. I padded slowly along behind Black Moustache instead.

After the fourth race I followed him into the bar and jogged his arm violently as he began to drink. Half of his beer splashed over his hand and ran down his sleeve, and he swung round cursing, to find my face nine inches from his own.

'Sorry,' I said. 'Oh, it's you.' I put as much surprise into my voice as I could.

His eyes narrowed. 'What are you doing here? Sparking Plug runs in this race.'

I scowled. 'I've left Inskip's.'

'Have you got one of the jobs I suggested? Good.'

'Not yet. There might be a bit of a delay there, like.'

'Why? No vacancies?'

'They don't seem all that keen to have me since I got chucked out of Inskip's.'

'You got what?' he said sharply.

'Chucked out of Inskip's,' I repeated.

'Why?'

'They said something about Sparking Plug losing last week on the day you spoke to me . . . said they could prove nothing but they didn't want me around no more, and to get out.'

'That's too bad,' he said, edging away.

'But I got the last laugh,' I said, sniggering and holding on to his arm. 'I'll tell you straight, I got the bloody last laugh.'

'What do you mean?' He didn't try to keep the contempt out of his voice, but there was interest in his eyes.

'Sparking Plug won't win today neither,' I stated. 'He won't win because he'll feel bad in his stomach.'

'How do you know?'

'I soaked his salt-lick with liquid paraffin,' I said. 'Every day since I left on Monday he's been rubbing his tongue on a laxative. He won't be feeling like racing. He won't bloody win, he won't.' I laughed.

Black Moustache gave me a sickened look, prised

my fingers off his arm, and hurried out of the bar. I followed him carefully. He almost ran down into Tattersalls, and began frantically looking around. The red-headed woman was nowhere to be seen, but she must have been watching, because presently I saw her walking briskly down the rails, to the same spot where they had met before. And there, with a rush, she was joined by Black Moustache. He talked vehemently. She listened and nodded. He then turned away more calmly, and walked away out of Tattersalls and back to the parade ring. The woman waited until he was out of sight: then she walked firmly into the Members' enclosure and along the rails until she came to Bimmo Bognor. The little man leant forward over the rails as she spoke earnestly into his ear. He nodded several times and she began to smile, and when he turned round to talk to his clerks I saw that he was smiling broadly too.

Unhurriedly I walked along the rows of bookmakers, studying the odds they offered. Sparking Plug was not favourite, owing to his waterlogged defeat last time out, but no one would chance more than five to one. At that price I staked forty pounds – my entire earnings at Inskip's – on my old charge, choosing a prosperous, jolly-looking bookmaker in the back row.

Hovering within earshot of Mr Bimmo Bognor a few minutes later I heard him offer seven to one against Sparking Plug to a stream of clients, and watched him rake in their money, confident that he would not have to pay them out.

Smiling contentedly I climbed to the top of the stands and watched Sparking Plug make mincemeat of his opponents over the fences and streak insultingly home by twenty lengths. It was a pity, I reflected, that I was too far away to hear Mr Bognor's opinion of the result.

My jolly bookmaker handed me two hundred and forty pounds in fivers without a second glance. To avoid Black Moustache and any reprisals he might be thinking of organizing, I then went over to the cheap enclosure in the centre of the course for twenty boring minutes; returning through the horse gate when the runners were down at the start for the last race, and slipping up the stairs to the stand used by the lads.

Humber's head travelling-lad was standing near the top of the stands. I pushed roughly past him and tripped heavily over his feet.

'Look where you're bloody going,' he said crossly, focusing a pair of shoe-button eyes on my face.

'Sorry mate. Got corns, have you?'

'None of your bloody business,' he said, looking at me sourly. He would know me again, I thought.

I bit my thumb nail. 'Do you know which of this lot is Martin Davies' head travelling-lad?' I asked.

He said, 'That chap over there with the red scarf. Why?'

'I need a job,' I said: and before he could say anything I left him and pushed along the row to the man in the red scarf. His stable had one horse in the race. I asked him quietly if they ran two, and he shook his head and said no.

Out of the corner of my eye I noticed that this negative answer had not been wasted on Humber's head lad. He thought, as I had hoped, that I had asked for work, and had been refused. Satisfied that the seed was planted, I watched the race (Humber's horse finished last) and slipped quietly away from the racecourse via the paddock rails and the Members' car park, without any interception of Black Moustache or a vengeful Bimmo Bognor.

A Sunday endured half in my dreary room and half walking round the empty streets was enough to convince me that I could not drag through the next fortnight in Newcastle doing nothing, and the thought of a solitary Christmas spent staring at coffee-coloured peeling paint was unattractive. Moreover I had two hundred pounds of bookmakers' money packed into my belt alongside what was left of October's: and Humber had no horses entered before the Stafford meeting on Boxing Day. It took me only ten minutes to decide what to do with the time between.

On Sunday evening I wrote to October a report on Bimmo Bognor's intelligence service, and at one in the morning I caught the express to London. I spent

Monday shopping and on Tuesday evening, looking civilized in some decent new clothes and equipped with an extravagant pair of Kastle skis I signed the register of a comfortable, bright little hotel in a snow-covered village in the Dolomites.

The fortnight I spent in Italy made no difference one way or another to the result of my work for October, but it made a great deal of difference to me. It was the first real holiday I had had since my parents died, the first utterly carefree, purposeless, self-indulgent break for nine years.

I grew younger. Fast strenuous days on the snow slopes and a succession of evenings dancing with my ski-ing companions peeled away the years of responsibility like skins, until at last I felt twenty-seven instead of fifty, a young man instead of a father; until the unburdening process, begun when I left Australia and slowly fermenting through the weeks at Inskip's, suddenly seemed complete.

There was also a bonus in the shape of one of the receptionists, a rounded glowing girl whose dark eyes lit up the minute she saw me and who, after a minimum of persuasion, uninhibitedly spent a proportion of her nights in my bed. She called me her Christmas box of chocolates. She said I was the happiest lover she had had for a long time, and that I pleased her. She was probably doubly as promiscuous as Patty but she was much more wholesome; and she made me feel terrific instead of ashamed.

On the day I left, when I gave her a gold bracelet, she kissed me and told me not to come back, as things were never as good the second time. She was God's gift to bachelors, that girl.

I flew back to England on Christmas night feeling as physically and mentally fit as I had ever been in my life, and ready to take on the worst that Humber could dish out. Which, as it happened, was just as well.

CHAPTER EIGHT

At Stafford on Boxing Day one of the runners in the first race, the selling 'chase, threw off his jockey a stride after landing in fourth place over the last fence, crashed through the rails, and bolted away across the rough grass in the centre of the course.

A lad standing near me on the draughty steps behind the weighing room ran off cursing to catch him; but as the horse galloped crazily from one end of the course to the other it took the lad, the trainer, and about ten assorted helpers a quarter of an hour to lay their hands on his bridle. I watched them as with worried faces they led the horse, an undistinguished bay, off the course and past me towards the racecourse stables.

The wretched animal was white and dripping with sweat and in obvious distress; foam covered his nostrils and muzzle, and his eyes rolled wildly in their sockets. His flesh was quivering, his ears lay flat back on his head, and he was inclined to lash out at anyone who came near him.

His name, I saw from the race card, was Superman.

He was not one of the eleven horses I had been investigating: but his hotted up appearance and frantic behaviour, coupled with the fact that he had met trouble at Stafford in a selling 'chase, convinced me that he was the twelfth of the series. The twelfth; and he had come unstuck. There was, as Beckett had said, no mistaking the effect of whatever had pepped him up. I had never before seen a horse in such a state, which seemed to me much worse than the descriptions of 'excited winners' I had read in the press cuttings: and I came to the conclusion that Superman was either suffering from an overdose, or had reacted excessively to whatever the others had been given.

Neither October nor Beckett nor Macclesfield had come to Stafford. I could only hope that the precautions October had promised had been put into operation in spite of its being Boxing Day, because I could not, without blowing open my role, ask any of the officials if the pre-race dope tests had been made or other precautions taken, nor insist that the jockey be asked at once for his impressions, that unusual bets should be investigated, and that the horse be thoroughly examined for punctures.

The fact that Superman had safely negotiated all the fences inclined me more and more to believe that he could not have been affected by the stimulant until he was approaching, crossing, or landing over the last. It was there that he had gone wild and, instead of winning, thrown his jockey and decamped. It was there that he had been given the power to sprint the four hundred yards, that long run-in which gave him time and room to overhaul the leading horses.

The only person on the racecourse to whom I could safely talk was Superman's lad, but because of the state of his horse it was bound to be some time before he came out of the stables. Meanwhile there were more steps to be taken towards getting myself a job with Humber.

I had gone to the meeting with my hair unbrushed, pointed shoes unpolished, leather collar turned up, hands in pockets, sullen expression in place. I looked, and felt, a disgrace.

Changing back that morning into stable lad clothes had not been a pleasant experience. The sweaters stank of horses, the narrow cheap trousers looked scruffy, the under-clothes were grey from insufficient washing, and the jeans were still filthy with mud and muck. Because of the difficulty of getting them back on Christmas night I had decided against sending the whole lot to the laundry while I was away, and in spite of my distaste in putting them on again, I didn't regret it. I looked all the more on the way to being down and out.

I changed and shaved in the cloakroom at the West Kensington Air Terminal, parked my skis and grip of ski clothes in the Left Luggage department on Euston Station, slept uneasily on a hard seat for an hour or two, breakfasted on sandwiches and coffee from the auto-buffet, and caught the race train to Stafford. At this rate, I thought wryly, I would have bundles of

148

belongings scattered all over London; because neither on the outward nor return journeys had I cared to go to October's London house to make use of the clothes I had left with Terence. I did not want to meet October. I liked him, and saw no joy in facing his bitter resentment again unless I absolutely had to.

Humber had only one runner on Boxing Day, a weedy looking hurdler in the fourth race. I hung over the rails by the saddling boxes and watched his head travelling-lad saddle up, while Humber himself leant on his knobbed walking stick and gave directions. I had come for a good close look at him, and what I saw was both encouraging from the angle that one could believe him capable of any evil, and discouraging from the angle that I was going to have to obey him.

His large body was encased in a beautifully cut short camel-hair overcoat, below which protruded dark trousers and impeccable shoes. On his head he wore a bowler, set very straight, and on his hands some pale unsoiled pig skin gloves. His face was large, not fat, but hard. Unsmiling eyes, a grim trap of a mouth, and deep lines running from the corners of his nose to his chin gave his expression a look of cold wilfulness.

He stood quite still, making no unnecessary fussy movements, the complete opposite of Inskip, who was for ever walking busily from side to side of his horse, checking straps and buckles, patting and pulling at the saddle, running his hand down legs, nervously making sure over and over that everything was in order.

In Humber's case it was the boy who held the horse's head who was nervous. Frightened, I thought, was hardly too strong a word for it. He kept giving wary, startled-animal glances at Humber, and stayed out of his sight on the far side of the horse as much as possible. He was a thin, ragged-looking boy of about sixteen, and not far, I judged, from being mentally deficient.

The head travelling-lad, middle-aged, with a big nose and an unfriendly air, unhurriedly adjusted the saddle and nodded to the lad to lead the horse off into the parade ring. Humber followed. He walked with a slight limp, more or less disguised by the use of the walking stick, and he proceeded in a straight line like a tank, expecting everyone else to get out of his way.

I transferred myself to the parade ring rails in his wake and watched him give instructions to his jockey, an allowance-claimer who regarded his mount with justified disillusion. It was the head travelling-lad, not Humber, who gave the jockey a leg up, and who picked up and carried off with him the horse's rug. Round at the lads' stand I carefully stood directly in front of the head travelling-lad and in the lull before the race started I turned sideways and tried to borrow some money from the lad standing next to me, whom I didn't know. Not unexpectedly, but to my relief, the lad refused indignantly and more than loudly enough for Humber's head lad to hear. I hunched my shoulders and resisted the temptation to look round and see if the message had reached its destination.

Humber's horse ran out of energy in the straight and finished second to last. No one was surprised.

After that I stationed myself outside the stable gate to wait for Superman's lad, but he didn't come out for another half an hour, until after the fifth race. I fell into step beside him as if by accident, saying 'Rather you than me, chum, with one like that to look after.' He asked me who I worked for; I said Inskip, and he loosened up and agreed that a cup of char and a wad would go down a treat, after all that caper.

'Is he always that het up after a race?' I said, halfway through the cheese sandwiches.

'No. Usually, he's dog-tired. There's been all hell breaking loose this time, I can tell you.'

'How do you mean?'

'Well, first they came and took some tests on all the runners before the race. Now I ask you, why before? It's not the thing, is it? Not before. You ever had one done before?'

I shook my head.

'Then, see, old Super, he was putting up the same sort of job he always does, looking as if he is going to come on into a place at least and then packing it in going to the last. Stupid basket. No guts, I reckon. They had his heart tested, but it ticks OK. So it's no guts, sure enough. Anyway, then at the last he suddenly kicks up his heels and bolts off as if the devil was after him. I don't suppose you saw him? He's a nervy customer always, really, but he was climbing the wall when we finally caught him. The old man was dead worried. Well, the horse looked as though he had been got at, and he wanted to stick his oar in first and get a dope test done so that the Stewards shouldn't accuse him of using a booster and take away his ruddy licence. They had a couple of vets fussing over him taking things to be analysed . . . dead funny it was, because old Super was trying to pitch them over the stable walls . . . and in the end they gave him a jab of something to quieten him down. But how we're going to get him home I don't know.'

'Have you looked after him long?' I asked sympathetically.

'Since the beginning of the season. About four months, I suppose. He's a jumpy customer, as I said, but before this I had just about got him to like me. Gawd, I hope he calms down proper before the jabs wear off, I do straight.'

'Who had him before you?' I asked casually.

'Last year he was in a little stable in Devon with a private trainer called Beaney, I think. Yes, Beaney, that's where he started, but he didn't do any good there.'

'I expect they made him nervous there, breaking him in,' I said.

'No, now that's a funny thing, I said that to one of Beaney's lads when we were down in Devon for one of the August meetings, and he said I must be talking about the wrong horse because Superman was a placid old thing and no trouble. He said if Superman was nervous it must have been on account of something that had happened during the summer after he left their place and before he came to us.'

'Where did he go for the summer?' I asked, picking up the cup of orange-coloured tea.

'Search me. The old man bought him at Ascot sales, I think, for a cheap horse. I should think he will shuffle him off again after this if he can get more than knacker's price for him. Poor old Super. Silly nit.' The lad stared gloomily into his tea.

'You don't think he went off his rocker today because he was doped then?'

'I think he just went bonkers,' he said. 'Stark, staring, raving bonkers. I mean, no one had a chance to dope him, except me and the old man and Chalky, and I didn't, and the old man didn't, because he's not the sort, and you wouldn't think Chalky would either, he's so darn proud being promoted head travelling-lad only last month . . .'

We finished our tea and went round to watch the sixth race still talking about Superman, but his lad knew nothing else which was of help to me.

After the race I walked the half mile into the centre of Stafford, and from a telephone box sent two identical telegrams to October, one to London and one to Slaw, as I did not know where he was. They read, 'Request urgent information re Superman, specifically where did he go from Beaney, permit holder, Devon, last May

153

approximately. Answer care Post Restante, Newcastle-upon-Tyne.'

I spent the evening, incredibly distant from the gaiety of the day before, watching a dreary musical in a three-quarters empty cinema, and slept that night in a dingy bed-and-breakfast hotel where they looked me up and down and asked for their money in advance. I paid, wondering if I would ever get used to being treated like dirt. I felt a fresh shock every time. I supposed I had been too accustomed to the respect I was offered in Australia even to notice it, far less appreciate it. I would appreciate some of it now, I ruefully thought, following the landlady into an unwelcoming little room and listening to her suspicious lecture on no cooking, no hot water after eleven, and no girls.

The following afternoon I conspicuously mooched around in front of Humber's head travelling-lad with a hang-dog and worried expression, and after the races went back by bus and train to Newcastle for the night. In the morning I collected the motor-cycle, fitted with the new silencer and other parts, and called at the post office to see if there was a reply from October.

The clerk handed me a letter. Inside, without salutation or signature, there was a single sheet of typescript, which read: 'Superman was born and bred in Ireland. Changed hands twice before reaching John Beaney in Devon. He was then sold by Beaney to H. Humber, Esq., of Posset, Co. Durham, on May 3rd.

Humber sent him to Ascot sales in July, where he was bought by his present trainer for two hundred and sixty guineas.

'Investigations re Superman at Stafford yesterday are all so far uninformative; dope analyses have still to be completed but there is little hope they will show anything. The veterinary surgeon at the course was as convinced as you apparently were that this is another "joker", and made a thorough examination of the horse's skin. There were no visible punctures except the ones he made himself giving the horse sedation.

'Superman was apparently in a normal condition before the race. His jockey reports all normal until the last fence, when the horse seemed to suffer a sort of convulsion, and ejected him from the saddle.

'Further enquiries re Rudyard revealed he was bought four winters ago by P. J. Adams of Tellbridge, Northumberland, and sold again within a short time at Ascot. Transistor was bought by Adams at Doncaster three years ago, sold Newmarket Dispersal Sales three months later.

'Enquiries re thirty consecutive five pound notes reveal they were issued by Barclays Bank, Birmingham New Street branch, to a man called Lewis Greenfield, who corresponds exactly to your description of the man who approached you in Slaw. Proceedings against Greenfield and T. N. Tarleton are in hand, but will be held in abeyance until after your main task is completed.

'Your report on Bimmo Bognor is noted, but as you say, the buying of stable information is not a punishable offence in law. No proceedings are at present contemplated, but warning that a spy system is in operation will be given privately to certain trainers.'

I tore the page up and scattered it in the litter basket, then went back to the motor-cycle and put it through its paces down the A1 to Catterick. It handled well, and I enjoyed the speed and found it quite true that it would still do a hundred.

At Catterick that Saturday Humber's head travelling-lad rose like a trout to the fly.

Inskip had sent two runners, one of which was looked after by Paddy; and up on the lads' stand before the second race I saw the sharp little Irishman and Humber's head lad talking earnestly together. I was afraid that Paddy might relent towards me enough to say something in my favour, but I needn't have worried. He put my mind at rest himself.

'You're a bloody young fool,' he said, looking me over from my unkempt head to my grubby toes. 'And you've only got what you deserve. That man of Humber's was asking me about you, why you got the kick from Inskip's, and I told him the real reason, not all that eye-wash about messing about with his nibs' daughter.'

'What real reason?' I asked, surprised.

His mouth twisted in contempt. 'People talk, you know. You don't think they keep their traps shut, when there's a good bit of gossip going round? You don't

156

think that Grits didn't tell me how you got drunk at Cheltenham and blew your mouth off about Inskip's? And what you said at Bristol about being willing to put the finger on a horse's box in the yard, well, that got round to me too. And thick as thieves with that crook Soupy, you were, as well. And there was that time when we all put our wages on Sparking Plug and he didn't go a yard . . . I'd lay any money that was your doing. So I told Humber's man he would be a fool to take you on. You're poison, Dan, and I reckon any stable is better off without you, and I told him so.'

'Thanks.'

'You can ride,' said Paddy disgustedly, 'I'll say that for you. And it's an utter bloody waste. You'll never get a job with a decent stable again, it would be like putting a rotten apple into a box of good ones.'

'Did you say all that to Humber's man?'

'I told him no decent stable would take you on,' he nodded. 'And if you ask me it bloody well serves you right.' He turned his back on me and walked away.

I sighed, and told myself I should be pleased that Paddy believed me such a black character.

Humber's head travelling-lad spoke to me in the paddock between the last two races.

'Hey, you,' he said, catching my arm. 'I hear you're looking for a job.'

'That's right.'

'I might be able to put you in the way of something. Good pay, better than most.'

'Whose stable?' I asked. 'And how much?'

'Sixteen quid a week.'

'Sounds good,' I admitted. 'Where?'

'Where I work. For Mr Humber. Up in Durham.'

'Humber,' I repeated sourly.

'Well, you want a job, don't you? Of course if you are so well off you can do without a job, that's different.' He sneered at my unprosperous appearance.

'I need a job,' I muttered.

'Well, then?'

'He might not have me,' I said bitterly. 'Like some others I could mention.'

'He will if I put in a word for you, we're short of a lad just now. There's another meeting here next Wednesday. I'll put in a word for you before that and if it is OK you can see Mr Humber on Wednesday and he'll tell you whether he'll have you or not.'

'Why not ask him now?' I said.

'No. You wait till Wednesday.'

'All right,' I said grudgingly. 'If I've got to.'

I could almost see him thinking that by Wednesday I would be just that much hungrier, just that much more anxious to take any job that was offered and less likely to be frightened off by rumours of bad conditions.

I had spent all the bookmaker's two hundred, as well as half of the money I had earned at Inskip's, on my Italian jaunt (of which I regretted not one penny), and after paying for the motor-cycle and the succession of dingy lodgings I had almost nothing left of October's original two hundred. He had not suggested giving me any more for expenses, and I was not going to ask him for any: but I judged that the other half of my Inskip pay could be spent how I liked, and I dispatched nearly all of it in the following three days on a motor-cycle trip to Edinburgh, walking round and enjoying the city and thinking myself the oddest tourist in Scotland.

On Tuesday evening, when Hogmanay was in full swing, I braved the head waiter of L'Aperitif, who to his eternal credit treated me with beautifully self-controlled politeness, but quite reasonably checked, before he gave me a little table in a corner, that I had enough money to pay the bill. Impervious to scandalized looks from better dressed diners, I slowly ate, with Humber's establishment in mind, a perfect and enormous dinner of lobster, duck bigarade, lemon soufflé, and brie, and drank most of a bottle of Château Leauville Lescases 1948.

With which extravagant farewell to being my own master I rode down the A1 to Catterick on New Year's Day and in good spirits engaged myself to the worst stable in the country.

CHAPTER NINE

Rumour had hardly done Hedley Humber justice. The discomfort in which the lads were expected to live was so methodically devised that I had been there only one day before I came to the conclusion that its sole purpose was to discourage anyone from staying too long. I discovered that only the head lad and the head travelling-lad, who both lived out in Posset, had worked in the yard for more than three months, and that the average time it took for an ordinary lad to decide that sixteen pounds a week was not enough was eight to ten weeks.

This meant that none of the stable hands except the two head lads knew what had happened to Superman the previous summer, because none of them had been there at the time. And caution told me that the only reason the two top men stayed was because they knew what was going on, and that if I asked *them* about Superman I might find myself following smartly in Tommy Stapleton's footsteps.

I had heard all about the squalor of the living quarters at some stables, and I was aware also that some lads deserved no better – some I knew of had broken up and burned their chairs rather than go outside and fetch coal, and others had stacked their dirty dishes in the lavatory and pulled the chain to do the washing up. But even granted that Humber only employed the dregs, his arrangements were very nearly inhuman.

The dormitory was a narrow hayloft over the horses. One could hear every bang of their hooves and the rattle of chains, and through cracks in the plank floor one could see straight down into the boxes. Upwards through the cracks rose a smell of dirty straw and an icy draught. There was no ceiling to the hayloft except the rafters and the tiles of the roof, and no way up into it except a ladder through a hole in the floor. In the one small window a broken pane of glass had been pasted over with brown paper, which shut out the light and let in the cold.

The seven beds, which were all the hayloft held in the way of furniture, were stark, basic affairs made of a piece of canvas stretched tautly on to a tubular metal frame. On each bed there was supposed to be one pillow and two grey blankets, but I had to struggle to get mine back because they had been appropriated by others as soon as my predecessor left. The pillow had no cover, there were no sheets, and there were no mattresses. Everyone went to bed fully dressed to keep warm, and on my third day there it started snowing.

The kitchen at the bottom of the ladder, the only

other room available to the lads, was nothing more than the last loose box along one side of the yard. So little had been done to make it habitable as to leave a powerful suggestion that its inmates were to be thought of, and treated, as animals. The bars were still in place over the small window, and there were still bolts on the outside of the split stable door. The floor was still of bare concrete criss-crossed with drainage grooves; one side wall was of rough boards with kick marks still in them and the other three were of bare bricks. The room was chronically cold and damp and dirty; and although it may have been big enough as a home for one horse, it was uncomfortably cramped for seven men.

The minimal furniture consisted of rough benches around two walls, a wooden table, a badly chipped electric cooker, a shelf for crockery, and an old marble wash stand bearing a metal jug and a metal basin, which was all there was in the way of a bathroom. Other needs were catered for in a wooden hut beside the muck heap.

The food, prepared by a slatternly woman perpetually in curlers, was not up to the standard of the accommodation.

Humber, who had engaged me with an indifferent glance and a nod, directed me with equal lack of interest, when I arrived in the yard, to look after four horses, and told me the numbers of their boxes. Neither he nor anyone else told me their names. The head lad, who did one horse himself, appeared to have very little authority, contrary to the practice in most other training stables, and it was Humber himself who gave the orders and who made sure they were carried out.

He was a tyrant, not so much in the quality of the work he demanded, as in the quantity. There were some thirty horses in the yard. The head lad cared for one horse, and the head travelling-lad, who also drove the horse box, did none at all. That left twenty-nine horses for seven lads, who were also expected to keep the gallops in order and do all the cleaning and mainten-ance work of the whole place. On racing days, when one or two lads were away, those remaining often had six horses to see to. It made my stint at Inskip's seem like a rest cure.

At the slightest sign of shirking Humber would dish out irritating little punishments and roar in an acid voice that he paid extra wages for extra work, and anyone who didn't like it could leave. As everyone was there because better stables would not risk employing them, leaving Humber's automatically meant leaving racing altogether. And taking whatever they knew about the place with them. It was very very neat.

My companions in this hell hole were neither friendly nor likeable. The best of them was the nearly half-witted boy I had seen at Stafford on Boxing Day. His name was Jerry, and he came in for a lot of physical abuse because he was slower and more stupid than anyone else.

Two of the others had been to prison and their out-look on life made Soupy Tarleton look like a Sunday-school favourite. It was from one of these, Jimmy, that I had had to wrench my blankets and from the other, a thick-set tough called Charlie, my pillow. They were the two bullies of the bunch, and in addition to the free use they made of their boots, they could always be relied upon to tell lying tales and wriggle themselves out of trouble, seeing to it that someone else was punished in their stead.

Reggie was a food stealer. Thin, white faced, and with a twitch in his left eyelid, he had long prehensile hands which could whisk the bread off your plate faster than the eye could follow. I lost a lot of my meagre rations to him before I caught him at it, and it always remained a mystery why, when he managed to eat more than anyone else, he stayed the thinnest.

One of the lads was deaf. He told me phlegmatically in a toneless mumble that his dad had done it when he was little, giving him a few clips too many over the earholes. His name was Bert, and as he occasionally wet himself in bed, he smelled appalling.

The seventh, Geoff, had been there longest, and even after ten weeks never spoke of leaving. He had a habit of looking furtively over his shoulder, and any mention by Jimmy or Charlie about their prison experiences brought him close to tears, so that I came to the conclusion that he had committed some crime and was terrified of being found out. I supposed ten weeks at Humber's might be preferable to jail, but it was debatable.

They knew all about me from the head travelling-lad, Jud Wilson. My general dishonesty they took entirely for granted, but they thought I was lucky to have got off without going inside if it was true about October's daughter, and they sniggered about it unendingly, and made merciless obscene jibes that hit their target all too often.

I found their constant closeness a trial, the food disgusting, the work exhausting, the beds relentless, and the cold unspeakable. All of which rather roughly taught me that my life in Australia had been soft and easy, even when I thought it most demanding.

Before I went to Humber's I had wondered why anyone should be foolish enough to pay training fees to a patently unsuccessful trainer, but I gradually found out. The yard itself, for one thing, was a surprise. From the appearance of the horses at race meetings one would have expected their home surroundings to be weedy gravel, broken-hinged boxes, and flaked-off paint: but in fact the yard was trim and prosperous looking, and was kept that way by the lads, who never had time off in the afternoons. This glossy window-dressing cost Humber nothing but an occasional gallon of paint and a certain amount of slave driving.

His manner with the owners who sometimes arrived for a look round was authoritative and persuasive, and his fees, I later discovered, were lower than anyone else's, which attracted more custom than he would otherwise have had. In addition some of the horses in the yard were not racehorses at all, but hunters at livery, for whose board, lodging, and exercise he received substantial sums without the responsibility of having to train them.

I learned from the other lads that only seven of the stable's inmates had raced at all that season, but that those seven had been hard worked, with an average of a race each every ten days. There had been one winner, two seconds, and a third, among them.

None of those seven was in my care. I had been allotted to a quartet consisting of two racehorses which belonged, as far as I could make out, to Humber himself, and two hunters. The two racehorses were bays, about seven years old; one of them had a sweet mouth and no speed and the other a useful sprint over schooling fences but a churlish nature. I pressed Cass, the head lad, to tell me their names, and he said they were Dobbin and Sooty. These unraceman-like names were not to be found in the form book, nor in Humber's list in 'Horses in Training'; and it seemed to me highly probable that Rudyard, Superman, Charcoal, and the rest had all spent their short periods in the yard under similar uninformative pseudonyms.

A lad who had gone out of racing would never connect the Dobbin or Sooty he had once looked after with the Rudyard who won a race for another trainer two years later.

But why, *why* did he win two years later? About that, I was as ignorant as ever.

The cold weather came and gripped, and stayed. But nothing, the other lads said, could be as bad as the fearsome winter before; and I reflected that in that January and February I had been sweltering under the mid-summer sun. I wondered how Belinda and Helen and Philip were enjoying their long vacation, and what they would think if they could see me in my dirty down-trodden sub-existence, and what the men would think, to see their employer brought so low. It amused me a good deal to imagine it: and it not only helped the tedious hours to pass more quickly, but kept me from losing my own inner identity.

As the days of drudgery mounted up I began to wonder if anyone who embarked on so radical a masquerade really knew what he was doing.

Expression, speech, and movement had to be unremittingly schooled into a convincing show of uncouth dullness. I worked in a slovenly fashion and rode, with a pang, like a mutton-fisted clod; but as time passed all these deceptions became easier. If one pretended long enough to be a wreck, did one finally become one, I wondered. And if one stripped oneself continuously of all human dignity would one in the end be unaware of its absence? I hoped the question would remain academic: and as long as I could have a quiet laugh at myself now and then, I supposed I was safe enough.

My belief that after three months in the yard a lad was given every encouragement to leave was amply borne out by what happened to Geoff Smith.

Humber never rode out to exercise with his horses, but drove in a van to the gallops to watch them work, and returned to the yard while they were still walking back to have a poke round to see what had been done and not done.

One morning, when we went in with the second lot, Humber was standing in the centre of the yard radiating his frequent displeasure.

'You, Smith, and you, Roke, put those horses in their boxes and come here.'

We did so.

'Roke.'

'Sir.'

'The mangers of all your four horses are in a disgusting state. Clean them up.'

'Yes, sir.'

'And to teach you to be more thorough in future you will get up at five-thirty for the next week.'

'Sir.'

I sighed inwardly, but this was to me one of his more acceptable forms of pinprick punishment, since I didn't particularly mind getting up early. It entailed merely standing in the middle of the yard for over an hour, doing nothing. Dark, cold, and boring. I don't think he slept much himself. His bedroom window faced down the yard, and he always knew if one were not standing outside by twenty to six, and shining a torch to prove it.

'And as for you.' He looked at Geoff with calculation. 'The floor of number seven is caked with dirt.

You'll clean out the straw and scrub the floor with disinfectant before you get your dinner.'

'But sir,' protested Geoff incautiously, 'if I don't go in for dinner with the others, they won't leave me any.'

'You should have thought of that before, and done your work properly in the first place. I pay half as much again as any other trainer would, and I expect value for it. You will do as you are told.'

'But, sir,' whined Geoff, knowing that if he missed his main meal he would go very hungry, 'can't I do it this afternoon?'

Humber casually slid his walking stick through his hand until he was holding it at the bottom. Then he swung his arm and savagely cracked the knobbed handle across Geoff's thigh.

Geoff yelped and rubbed his leg.

'Before dinner,' remarked Humber: and walked away, leaning on his stick.

Geoff missed his share of the watery half-stewed lumps of mutton, and came in panting to see the last of the bread-and-suet pudding spooned into Charlie's trap-like mouth.

'You bloody sods,' he yelled miserably. 'You bloody lot of sods.'

He stuck it for a whole week. He stood six more heavy blows on various parts of his body, and missed his dinner three more times, and his breakfast twice, and his supper once. Long before the end of it he was in tears, but he didn't want to leave.

After five days Cass came into the kitchen at break-fast and told Geoff, 'The boss has taken against you, I'm afraid. You won't ever do anything right for him again from now on. Best thing you can do, and I'm telling you for your own good, mind, is to find a job somewhere else. The boss gets these fits now and then when one of the lads can't do anything right, and no one can change him when he gets going. You can work until you're blue in the face, but he won't take to you any more. You don't want to get yourself bashed up any more, now do you? All I'm telling you is that if you stay here you'll find that what has happened so far is only the beginning. See? I'm only telling you for your own good.'

Even so, it was two more days before Geoff painfully packed his old army kit bag and sniffed his way off the premises.

A weedy boy arrived the next morning as a replace-ment, but he only stayed three days as Jimmy stole his blankets before he came and he was not strong enough to get them back. He moaned piteously through two freezing nights, and was gone before the third.

The next morning, before breakfast, it was Jimmy himself who collected a crack from the stick.

He came in late and cursing and snatched a chunk of bread out of Jerry's hand.

'Where's my bloody breakfast?'

We had eaten it, of course.

'Well,' he said, glaring at us, 'you can do my ruddy

horses, as well. I'm off. I'm not bloody well staying here. This is worse than doing bird. You won't catch me staying here to be swiped at, I'll tell you that.'

Reggie said, 'Why don't you complain?'

'Who to?'

'Well . . . the bluebottles.'

'Are you out of your mind?' said Jimmy in amazement. 'You're a bloody nit, that's what you are. Can you see me, with my form, going into the cop house and saying I got a complaint to make about my employer, he hit me with his walking stick? For a start, they'd laugh. They'd laugh their bleeding heads off. And then what? Supposing they come here and asked Cass if he's seen anyone getting the rough end of it? Well, I'll tell you, that Cass wants to keep his cushy job. Oh no, he'd say, I ain't seen nothing. Mr Humber, he's a nice kind gentleman with a heart of gold, and what can you expect from an ex-con but a pack of bull? Don't ruddy well make me laugh. I'm off, and if the rest of you've got any sense, you'll be out of it too.'

No one, however, took his advice.

I found out from Charlie that Jimmy had been there two weeks longer than he, which made it, he thought, about eleven weeks.

As Jimmy strode defiantly out of the yard I went rather thoughtfully about my business. Eleven weeks, twelve at the most, before Humber's arm started swinging. I had been there already three which left me a maximum of nine more in which to discover how he

171

managed the doping. It wasn't that I couldn't probably last out as long as Geoff if it came to the point, but that if I hadn't uncovered Humber's method before he focused his attention on getting rid of me, I had very little chance of doing it afterwards.

Three weeks, I thought, and I had found out nothing at all except that I wanted to leave as soon as possible.

Two lads came to take Geoff's and Jimmy's places, a tall boy called Lenny who had been to Borstal and was proud of it, and Cecil, a far-gone alcoholic of about thirty-five. He had, he told us, been kicked out of half the stables in England because he couldn't keep his hands off the bottle. I don't know where he got the liquor from or how he managed to hide it, but he was certainly three parts drunk every day by four o'clock, and snored in a paralytic stupor every night.

Life, if you could call it that, went on.

All the lads seemed to have a good reason for having to earn the extra wages Humber paid. Lenny was repaying some money he had stolen from another employer, Charlie had a wife somewhere drawing maintenance, Cecil drank, Reggie was a compulsive saver, and Humber sent Jerry's money straight off to his parents. Jerry was proud of being able to help them.

I had let Jud Wilson and Cass know that I badly needed to earn sixteen pounds a week because I had fallen behind on hire purchase payments on the motorcycle, and this also gave me an obvious reason for need-

ing to spend some time in the Posset post office on
Saturday afternoons.

Public transport from the stables to Posset, a large
village a mile and a half away, did not exist. Cass and
Jud Wilson both had cars, but would give no lifts. My
motor-cycle was the only other transport available, but
to the lads' fluently expressed disgust I refused to use it
on the frosty snow-strewn roads for trips down to the
pub in the evenings. As a result we hardly ever went to
Posset except on the two hours we had off on Saturday
afternoons, and also on Sunday evenings, when after a
slightly less relentless day's work everyone had enough
energy left to walk for their beer.

On Saturdays I unwrapped the motor-cycle from its
thick plastic cocoon and set off to Posset with Jerry
perched ecstatically on the pillion. I always took poor
simple-minded Jerry because he got the worst of everything throughout the week; and we quickly fell into a
routine. First we went to the post office for me to post
off my imaginary hire purchase. Instead, leaning on the
shelf among the telegram forms and scraps of pink blot-
ting paper, I wrote each week a report to October,
making sure that no one from the stables looked over
my shoulder. Replies, if any, I collected, read, and tore
up over the litter basket.

Jerry accepted without question that I would be at
least a quarter of an hour in the post office, and spent
the time unsuspiciously at the other end of the shop
inspecting the stock in the toy department. Twice he

bought a big friction-drive car and played with it, until it broke, on the dormitory floor: and every week he bought a children's fourpenny comic, over whose picture strips he giggled contentedly for the next few days. He couldn't read a word, and often asked me to explain the captions, so that I became intimately acquainted with the doings of Micky the Monkey and Flip McCoy.

Leaving the post office we climbed back on to the motor-cycle and rode two hundred yards down the street to have tea. This ritual took place in a square bare café with margarine coloured walls, cold lighting, and messy table tops. For decoration there were Pepsi-Cola advertisements, and for service a bored looking girl with no stockings and mousy hair piled into a matted, wispy mountain on top of her head.

None of this mattered. Jerry and I ordered and ate with indescribable enjoyment a heap of lamb chops, fried eggs, flabby chips, and bright green peas. Charlie and the others were to be seen doing the same at adjoining tables. The girl knew where we came from, and looked down on us, as her father owned the café.

On our way out Jerry and I packed our pockets with bars of chocolate to supplement Humber's food, a hoard which lasted each week exactly as long as it took Reggie to find it.

By five o'clock we were back in the yard, the motor-cycle wrapped up again, the week's highlight nothing but a memory and a belch, the next seven days stretching drearily ahead.

There were hours, in that life, in which to think. Hours of trotting the horses round and round a straw track in a frozen field, hours brushing the dust out of their coats, hours cleaning the muck out of their boxes and carrying their water and hay, hours lying awake at night listening to the stamp of the horses below and the snores and mumblings from the row of beds.

Over and over again I thought my way through all I had seen or read or heard since I came to England: and what emerged as most significant was the performance of Superman at Stafford. He had been doped: he was the twelfth of the series: but he had not won.

Eventually I changed the order of these thoughts. He had been doped, and he had not won; but was he, after all, the twelfth of the series? He might be the thirteenth, the fourteenth ... there might have been others who had come to grief.

On my third Saturday, when I had been at Humber's just over a fortnight, I wrote asking October to look out the newspaper cutting which Tommy Stapleton had kept, about a horse going berserk and killing a woman in the paddock at Cartmel races. I asked him to check the horse's history.

A week later I read his typewritten reply.

'Old Etonian, destroyed at Cartmel, Lancashire, at Whitsun last year, spent the previous November and December in Humber's yard. Humber claimed him in a selling race, and sold him again at Leicester sales seven weeks later.

'*But*: Old Etonian went berserk in the parade ring *before* the race; he was due to run in a handicap, not a seller; and the run-in at Cartmel is short. None of these facts conform to the pattern of the others.

'Dope tests were made on Old Etonian, but proved negative.

'No one could explain why he behaved as he did.'

Tommy Stapleton, I thought, must have had an idea, or he would not have cut out the report, yet he could not have been sure enough to act on it without checking up. And checking up had killed him. There could be no more doubt of it.

I tore up the paper and took Jerry along to the café, more conscious than usual of the danger breathing down my neck. It didn't, however, spoil my appetite for the only edible meal of the week.

At supper a few days later, in the lull before Charlie turned on his transistor radio for the usual evening of pops from Luxemburg (which I had grown to enjoy) I steered the conversation round to Cartmel races. What, I wanted to know, were they like?

Only Cecil, the drunk, had ever been there.

'It's not like it used to be in the old days,' he said owlishly, not noticing Reggie filch a hunk of his bread and margarine.

Cecil's eyes had a glazed, liquid look, but I had luckily asked my question at exactly the right moment, in the loquacious half-hour between the silent bleariness of the afternoon's liquor and his disappearance to tank up for the night.

'What was it like in the old days?' I prompted.

'They had a fair there.' He hiccupped. 'A fair with roundabouts and swings and side-shows and all. Bank Holiday, see? Whitsun and all that. Only place outside the Derby you could go on the swings at the races. Course, they stopped it now. Don't like no one to have a good time, they don't. It weren't doing no harm, it weren't, the fair.'

'Fairs,' said Reggie scornfully, his eyes flicking to the crust Jerry held loosely in his hand.

'Good for dipping,' commented Lenny, with superiority.

'Yeah,' agreed Charlie, who hadn't yet decided if Borstal qualified Lenny as a fit companion for one from the higher school.

'Eh?' said Cecil, lost.

'Dipping. Working the pockets,' Lenny said.

'Oh. Well, it can't have been that with the hound trails and they stopped them too. They were good sport, they were. Bloody good day out, it used to be, at Cartmel, but now it's the same as any other ruddy place. You might as well be at Newton Abbot or somewhere. Nothing but ordinary racing like any other day of the week.' He belched.

'What were the hound trails?' I asked.

'Dog races,' he said, smiling foolishly. 'Bloody dog races. They used to have one before the horse races, and one afterwards, but they've ruddy well stopped it now. Bloody killjoys, that's all they are. Still,' he leered triumphantly, 'if you know what's what you can still have a bet on the dogs. They have the hound trail in the morning now, on the other side of the village from the racetrack, but if you get your horse bedded down quick enough you can get there in time for a bet.'

'Dog races?' said Lenny disbelievingly. 'Dogs won't race round no horse track. There ain't no bloody electric hare, for a start.'

Cecil swivelled his head unsteadily in his direction.

'You don't have a track for hound trails,' he said earnestly, in his slurred voice. 'It's a *trail*, see? Some bloke sets off with a bag full of aniseed and paraffin, or something like that, and drags it for miles and miles round the hills and such. Then they let all the dogs loose and the first one to follow all round the trail and get back quickest is the winner. Year before last someone shot at the bloody favourite half a mile from home and there was a bleeding riot. They missed him, though. They hit the one just behind, some ruddy outsider with no chance.'

'Reggie's ate my crust,' said Jerry sadly.

'Did you go to Cartmel last year too?' I asked.

'No,' Cecil said regretfully. 'Can't say I did. A woman got killed there, and all.'

'How?' asked Lenny, looking avid.

'Some bloody horse bolted in the paddock, and jumped the rails of the parade ring and landed on some poor bloody woman who was just having a nice day out. She backed a loser all right, she did that day. I heard she was cut to bits, time that crazy animal trampled all over her trying to get out through the crowd. He didn't get far, but he kicked out all over the place and broke another man's leg before they got the vet to him and shot him. Mad, they said he was. A mate of mine was there, see, leading one round in the same race, and he said it was something awful, that poor woman all cut up and bleeding to death in front of his eyes.'

The others looked suitably impressed at this horrific story, all except Bert, who couldn't hear it.

'Well,' said Cecil, getting up, 'it's time for my little walk.'

He went out for his little walk, which was presumably to wherever he had hidden his alcohol, because as usual he came back less than an hour later and stumbled up the ladder to his customary oblivion.

CHAPTER TEN

Towards the end of my fourth week Reggie left (complaining of hunger) and in a day or two was duly replaced by a boy with a soft face who said in a high pitched voice that his name was Kenneth.

To Humber I clearly remained one insignificant face in this endless procession of human flotsam; and as I could safely operate only as long as that state of affairs continued I did as little as possible to attract his attention. He gave me orders, and I obeyed them: and he cursed me and punished me, but not more than anyone else, for the things I left undone.

I grew to recognize his moods at a glance. There were days when he glowered silently all through first and second exercise and turned out again to make sure that no one skimped the third, and on these occasions even Cass walked warily and only spoke if he were spoken to. There were days when he talked a great deal but always in sarcasm, and his tongue was so rough that everyone preferred the silence. There were occasional days when he wore an abstracted air and overlooked our faults, and even rarer days when he looked fairly pleased with life.

At all times he was impeccably turned out, as if to emphasize the difference between his state and ours. His clothes, I judged, were his main personal vanity, but his wealth was also evident in his car, the latest type of Cunard-sized Bentley. It was fitted with back-seat television, plush carpets, radio telephone, fur rugs, air conditioning, and a built-in drinks cabinet holding in racks six bottles, twelve glasses, and a glittering array of chromiumed cork-screws, ice-picks, and miscellaneous objects like swizzle sticks.

I knew the car well, because I had to clean it every Monday afternoon. Bert had to clean it on Fridays. Humber was proud of his car.

He was chauffeured on long journeys in this above-his-status symbol by Jud Wilson's sister Grace, a hard-faced amazon of a woman who handled the huge car with practised ease but was not expected to maintain it. I never once spoke to her: she bicycled in from wher-ever she lived, drove as necessary, and bicycled away again. Frequently the car had not been cleaned to her satisfaction, but her remarks were relayed to Bert and me by Jud.

I looked into every cranny every time while cleaning the inside, but Humber was neither so obliging nor so careless as to leave hypodermic syringes or phials of stimulants lying about in the glove pockets.

All through my first month there the freezing weather was not only a discomfort but also a tiresome delay. While racing was suspended Humber could dope no horses, and there was no opportunity for me to see what difference it made to his routine when the racing was scheduled for any of the five courses with long run-ins.

On top of that, he and Jud Wilson and Cass were always about in the stables. I wanted to have a look round inside Humber's office, a brick hut standing across the top end of the yard, but I could not risk a search when any one of them might come in and find me at it. With Humber and Jud Wilson away at the races, though, and with Cass gone home to his midday meal, I reckoned I could go into the office to search while the rest of the lads were eating.

Cass had a key to the office, and it was he who unlocked the door in the morning and locked it again at night. As far as I could see he did not bother to lock up when he went home for lunch, and the office was normally left open all day, except on Sunday. This might mean, I thought, that Humber kept nothing there which could possibly be incriminating: but on the other hand he could perhaps keep something there which was apparently innocent but would be incriminating if one understood its significance.

However, the likelihood of solving the whole mystery by a quick look round an unlocked stable office was so doubtful that it was not worth risking discovery, and I judged it better to wait with what patience I could until the odds were in my favour.

There was also Humber's house, a whitewashed converted farm house adjoining the yard. A couple of stealthy surveys, made on afternoons when I was bidden to sweep snow from his garden path, showed that this was an ultra-neat soulless establishment like a series of rooms in shop windows, impersonal and unlived-in. Humber was not married, and downstairs at least there seemed to be nowhere at all snug for him to spend his evenings.

Through the windows I saw no desk to investigate and no safe in which to lock away secrets: all the same I decided it would be less than fair to ignore his home, and if I both drew a blank and got away with an entry into the office, I would pay the house a visit at the first opportunity.

At last it began to thaw on a Wednesday night and continued fast all day Thursday and Friday, so that by Saturday morning the thin slush was disintegrating into puddles, and the stables stirred with the reawakening of hunting and racing.

Cass told me on Friday night that the man who owned the hunters I looked after required them both to be ready for him on Saturday, and after second exercise I led them out and loaded them into the horse box which had come for them.

Their owner stood leaning against the front wing of a well polished Jaguar. His hunting boots shone like glass, his cream breeches were perfection, his pink coat fitted without a wrinkle, his stock was smooth and snowy. He held a sensible leather covered riding stick in his hand and he slapped it against his boot. He was tall, broad, and bare-headed, about forty years old, and, from across the yard, handsome. It was only when one was close to him that one could see the dissatisfied look on his face and the evidence of dissipation in his skin.

'You,' he said, pointing at me with his stick. 'Come here.'

I went. He had heavy lidded eyes and a few purple thread veins on his nose and cheeks. He looked at me with superior bored disdain. I am five feet nine inches tall; he was four inches taller, and he made the most of it.

'You'll pay for it if those horses of mine don't last the day. I ride them hard. They need to be fit.'

His voice had the same expensive timbre as October's.

'They're as fit as the snow would allow,' I said calmly.

He raised his eyebrows.

'Sir,' I added.

'Insolence,' he said, 'will get you nowhere.'

'I am sorry, sir, I didn't mean to be insolent.'

He laughed unpleasantly. 'I'll bet you didn't. It's not so easy to get another job, is it? You'll watch your tongue when you speak to me in future, if you know what's good for you.'

'Yes, sir.'

'And if those horses of mine aren't fit, you'll wish you'd never been born.'

Cass appeared at my left elbow, looking anxious.

'Is everything all right, sir?' he asked. 'Has Roke done anything wrong, Mr Adams?'

How I managed not to jump out of my skin I am not quite sure. Mr Adams. Paul James Adams, sometime owner of seven subsequently doped horses?

'Is this bloody gipsy doing my horses any good?' said Adams offensively.

'He's no worse than any of the other lads,' said Cass soothingly.

'And that's saying precious little.' He gave me a mean stare. 'You've had it easy during the freeze. Too damned easy. You'll have to wake your ideas up now hunting has started again. You won't find me as soft as your master, I can tell you that.'

I said nothing. He slapped his stick sharply against his boot.

'Do you hear what I say? You'll find me harder to please.'

'Yes, sir,' I muttered.

He opened his fingers and let his stick fall at his feet.

'Pick it up,' he said.

As I bent to pick it up, he put his booted foot on my shoulder and gave me a heavy, over-balancing shove, so that I fell sprawling on to the soaking, muddy ground.

He smiled with malicious enjoyment.

'Get up, you clumsy lout, and do as you are told. Pick up my stick.'

I got to my feet, picked up his stick, and held it out to him. He twitched it out of my hand, and looking at Cass said, 'You've got to show them you won't stand any nonsense. Stamp on them whenever you can. This one,' he looked me coldly up and down, 'needs to be taught a lesson. What do you suggest?'

Cass looked at me doubtfully. I glanced at Adams. This, I thought, was not funny. His greyish blue eyes were curiously opaque, as if he were drunk: but he was plainly sober. I had seen that look before, in the eyes of a stable hand I had once, for a short time, employed, and I knew what it could mean. I had got to guess at once, and guess right, whether he preferred bullying the weak or the strong. From instinct, perhaps because of his size and evident worldliness, I guessed that crushing the weak would be too tame for him. In which case it was definitely not the moment for any show of strength. I drooped in as cowed and unresisting a manner as I could devise.

'God,' said Adams in disgust. 'Just look at him. Scared out of his bloody wits.' He shrugged impatiently. 'Well Cass, just find him some stinking useless occupation like scrubbing the paths and put him to work. There's no sport for me here. No backbone for me to break. Give me a fox any day, at least they've got some cunning and some guts.'

His gaze strayed sideways to where Humber was

crossing the far end of the yard. He said to Cass, 'Tell Mr Humber I'd like to have a word with him,' and when Cass had gone he turned back to me.

'Where did you work before this?'

'At Mr Inskip's, sir.'

'And he kicked you out?'

'Yes, sir.'

'Why?'

'I . . . er . . .' I stuck. It was incredibly galling to have to lay oneself open to such a man; but if I gave him answers he could check in small things he might believe the whopping lies without question.

'When I ask a question, you will answer it,' said Adams coldly. 'Why did Mr Inskip get rid of you?'

I swallowed. 'I got the sack for er . . . for messing about with the boss's daughter.'

'For messing about . . .' he repeated. 'Good God.' With lewd pleasure he said something which was utterly obscene, and which struck clear home. He saw me wince and laughed at my discomfiture. Cass and Humber returned. Adams turned to Humber, still laughing, and said, 'Do you know why this cockerel got chucked out of Inskip's?'

'Yes,' said Humber flatly. 'He seduced October's daughter.' He wasn't interested. 'And there was also the matter of a favourite that came in last. He looked after it.'

'October's daughter!' said Adams, surprised, his eyes narrowing. 'I thought he meant Inskip's daughter.' He casually dealt me a sharp clip on the ear. 'Don't try lying to me.'

'Mr Inskip hasn't got a daughter,' I protested.

'And don't answer back.' His hand flicked out again. He was rather adept at it. He must have indulged in a lot of practice.

'Hedley,' he said to Humber, who had impassively watched this one-sided exchange, 'I'll give you a lift to Nottingham races on Monday if you like. I'll pick you up at ten.'

'Right,' agreed Humber.

Adams turned to Cass. 'Don't forget that lesson for this lily-livered Romeo. Cool his ardour a bit.'

Cass sniggered sycophantically and raised goose pimples on my neck.

Adams climbed coolly into his Jaguar, started it up, and followed the horse box containing his two hunters out of the yard.

Humber said, 'I don't want Roke out of action, Cass. You've got to leave him fit for work. Use some sense this time.' He limped away to continue his inspection of the boxes.

Cass looked at me, and I looked steadily down at my damp, muddy clothes, very conscious that the head lad counted among the enemy, and not wanting to risk his seeing that there was anything but submissiveness in my face.

He said, 'Mr Adams don't like to be crossed.'

'I didn't cross him.'

'Nor he don't like to be answered back to. You mind your lip.'

'Has he any more horses here?' I asked.

'Yes,' said Cass, 'and it's none of your business. Now, he told me to punish you, and he won't forget. He'll check up later.'

'I've done nothing wrong,' I said sullenly, still looking down. What on earth would my foreman say about this, I thought; and nearly smiled at the picture.

'You don't need to have done nothing wrong,' said Cass. 'With Mr Adams it is a case of punish first so that you won't do anything wrong after. Sense, in a way.' He gave a snort of laughter. 'Saves trouble, see?'

'Are his horses all hunters?' I asked.

'No,' said Cass, 'but the two you've got are, and don't you forget it. He rides those himself, and he'll notice how you look after every hair on their hides.'

'Does he treat the lads who look after his other horses so shockingly unfair?'

'I've never heard Jerry complaining. And Mr Adams won't treat you too bad if you mind your p's and q's. Now that lesson he suggested . . .'

I had hoped he had forgotten it.

'You can get down on your knees and scrub the concrete paths round the yard. Start now. You can break for dinner, and then go on until evening stables.'

I went on standing in a rag-doll attitude of dejectedness, looking at the ground, but fighting an unexpectedly strong feeling of rebellion. What the hell, I thought, did October expect of me? Just how much was I to take? Was there any point at which, if he were there, he would say 'Stop; all right; that's enough. That's too much. Give it up.' But remembering how he felt about me, I supposed not!

Cass said, 'There's a scrubbing brush in the cupboard in the tack room. Get on with it.' He walked away.

The concrete pathways were six feet wide and ran round all sides of the yard in front of the boxes. They had been scraped clear of snow throughout the month I had been there so that the feed trolley could make its usual smooth journey from horse to horse, and as in most modern stables, including Inskip's and my own, they would always be kept clean of straw and excessive dust. But scrubbing them on one's knees for nearly four hours on a slushy day at the end of January was a miserable, back-breaking, insane waste of time. Ludicrous, besides.

I had a clear choice of scrubbing the paths or getting on the motor-cycle and going. Thinking firmly that I was being paid at least ten thousand pounds for doing it, I scrubbed; and Cass hung around the yard all day to watch that I didn't rest.

The lads, who had spent much of the afternoon amusing themselves by jeering at my plight as they set off for and returned from the café in Posset, made quite sure during evening stables that the concrete paths ended the day even dirtier than they had begun. I didn't care a damn about that; but Adams had sent his hunters back caked with mud and sweat and it took me two hours to clean them because by the end of that day many of my muscles were trembling with fatigue.

Then, to crown it all, Adams came back. He drove his Jaguar into the yard, climbed out, and after having talked to Cass, who nodded and gestured round the paths, he walked without haste towards the box where I was still struggling with his black horse.

He stood in the doorway and looked down his nose at me; and I looked back. He was superbly elegant in a dark blue pin-striped suit with a white shirt and a silver-grey tie. His skin looked fresh, his hair well brushed, his hands clean and pale. I imagined he had gone home after hunting and enjoyed a deep hot bath, a change of clothes, a drink . . . I hadn't had a bath for a month and was unlikely to get one as long as I stayed at Humber's. I was filthy and hungry and extremely tired. I wished he would go away and leave me alone.

No such luck.

He took a step into the box and surveyed the mud still caked solid on the horse's hind legs.

'You're slow,' he remarked.

'Yes, sir.'

'This horse must have been back here three hours ago. What have you been doing?'

'My three other horses, sir.'

'You should do mine first.'

'I had to wait for the mud to dry, sir. You can't brush it out while it's still wet.'

'I told you this morning not to answer back.' His hand lashed out across the ear he had hit before. He was smiling slightly. Enjoying himself. Which was more than could be said for me.

Having, so to speak, tasted blood, he suddenly took hold of the front of my jersey, pushed me back against the wall, and slapped me twice in the face, forehand and backhand. Still smiling.

What I wanted to do was to jab my knee into his groin and my fist into his stomach; and refraining wasn't easy. For the sake of realism I knew I should have cried out loudly and begged him to stop, but when it came to the point I couldn't do it. However, one could act what one couldn't say, so I lifted both arms and folded them defensively round my head.

He laughed and let go, and I slid down on to one knee and cowered against the wall.

'You're a proper little rabbit, aren't you, for all your fancy looks.'

I stayed where I was, in silence. As suddenly as he had begun, he lost interest in ill-treating me.

'Get up, get up,' he said irritably. 'I didn't hurt you. You're not worth hurting. Get up and finish this horse. And make sure it is done properly or you'll find yourself scrubbing again.'

He walked out of the box and away across the yard. I stood up, leaned against the doorpost, and with uncharitable feelings watched him go up the path to Humber's house. To a good dinner, no doubt. An armchair. A fire. A glass of brandy. A friend to talk to. Sighing in depression, I went back to the tiresome job of brushing off the mud.

Shortly after a supper of dry bread and cheese, eaten to the accompaniment of crude jokes about my day's occupation and detailed descriptions of the meals which had been enjoyed in Posset, I had had quite enough of my fellow workers. I climbed the ladder and sat on my bed. It was cold upstairs. I had had quite enough of Humber's yard. I had had more than enough of being kicked around. All I had to do, as I had been tempted to do that morning, was to go outside, unwrap the motor-cycle, and make tracks for civilization. I could stifle my conscience by paying most of the money back to October and pointing out that I had done at least half of the job.

I went on sitting on the bed and thinking about riding away on the motor-bike. I went on sitting on the bed. And not riding away on the motor-bike.

Presently I found myself sighing. I knew very well I had never had any real doubts about staying, even if it meant scrubbing those dreadful paths every day of the week. Quite apart from not finding myself good company in future if I ran away because of a little bit of eccentric charring, there was the certainty that it was specifically in Mr P. J. Adams' ruthless hands that the good repute of British racing was in danger of being cracked to bits. It was he that I had come to defeat. It was no good decamping because the first taste of him was unpleasant.

His name typed on paper had come alive as a worse menace than Humber himself had ever seemed. Humber was merely harsh, greedy, bad-tempered, and vain, and he beat his lads for the sole purpose of making them leave. But Adams seemed to enjoy hurting for its own sake. Beneath that glossy crust of sophistication, and not far beneath, one glimpsed an irresponsible savage. Humber was forceful; but Adams, it now seemed to me, was the brains of the partnership. He was a more complex man and a far more fearsome adversary. I had felt equal to Humber. Adams dismayed me.

Someone started to come up the ladder. I thought it would be Cecil, reeling from his Saturday night orgy, but it was Jerry. He came and sat on the bed next to mine. He looked downcast.

'Dan?'

'Yes.'

'It weren't . . . it weren't no good in Posset today, without you being there.'

'Wasn't it?'

'No.' He brightened. 'I bought my comic though. Will you read it to me?'

'Tomorrow,' I said tiredly.

There was a short silence while he struggled to organize his thoughts.

'Dan.'

194

'Mm?'

'I'm sorry, like.'

'What for?'

'Well, for laughing at you, like, this afternoon. It wasn't right ... not when you've took me on your motor-bike and all. I do ever so like going on your bike.'

'It's all right, Jerry.'

'The others were ribbing you, see, and it seemed the thing, like, to do what they done. So they would ... would let me go with them, see?'

'Yes, Jerry, I see. It doesn't matter, really it doesn't.'

'You never ribbed me, when I done wrong.'

'Forget it.'

'I've been thinking,' he said, wrinkling his forehead, 'about me mam. She tried scrubbing some floors once. In some office, it was. She came home fair whacked, she did. She said scrubbing floors was wicked. It made your back ache something chronic, she said, as I remember.'

'Did she?'

'Does your back ache, Dan?'

'Yes, a bit.'

He nodded, pleased. 'She knows a thing or two, does my mam.' He lapsed into one of his mindless silences, rocking himself gently backwards and forwards on the creaking bed.

I was touched by his apology.

'I'll read your comic for you,' I said.

'You ain't too whacked?' he asked eagerly.

I shook my head.

He fetched the comic from the cardboard box in which he kept his few belongings and sat beside me while I read him the captions of Mickey the Monkey, Beryl and Peril, Julius Cheeser, the Bustom Boys, and all the rest. We went through the whole thing at least twice, with him laughing contentedly and repeating the words after me. By the end of the week he would know most of them by heart.

At length I took the comic out of his hands and put it down on the bed.

'Jerry,' I said, 'which of the horses you look after belongs to Mr Adams?'

'Mr Adams?'

'The man whose hunters I've got. The man who was here this morning, with a grey Jaguar, and a scarlet coat.'

'Oh, that Mr Adams.'

'Why, is there another one?'

'No, that's Mr Adams, all right.' Jerry shuddered.

'What do you know about him?' I asked.

'The chap what was here before you came, Dennis, his name was, Mr Adams didn't like him, see? He cheeked Mr Adams, he did.'

'Oh,' I said. I wasn't sure I wanted to hear what had happened to Dennis.

'He weren't here above three weeks,' said Jerry reflectively. 'The last couple of days, he kept on falling down. Funny, it was, really.'

I cut him short. 'Which of your horses belongs to Mr Adams?' I repeated.

'None of them do,' he said positively.

'Cass said so.'

He looked surprised, and also scared. 'No, Dan, I don't want none of Mr Adams' horses.'

'Well, who do your horses belong to?'

'I don't rightly know. Except of course Pageant. He belongs to Mr Byrd.'

'That's the one you take to the races?'

'Uh huh, that's the one.'

'How about the others?'

'Well, Mickey . . .' His brow furrowed.

'Mickey is the horse in the box next to Mr Adams' black hunter, which I do?'

'Yeah.' He smiled brilliantly, as if I had made a point.

'Who does Mickey belong to?'

'I dunno.'

'Hasn't his owner ever been to see him?'

He shook his head doubtfully. I wasn't sure whether or not he would remember if an owner had in fact called.

'How about your other horse?' Jerry had only three horses to do, as he was slower than everyone else.

'That's Champ,' said Jerry triumphantly.

'Who owns him?'

'He's a hunter.'

'Yes, but who owns him?'

'Some fellow.' He was trying hard. 'A fat fellow. With sort of sticking out ears.' He pulled his own ears forward to show me.

197

'You know him well?'

He smiled widely. 'He gave me ten bob for Christmas.'

So it was Mickey, I thought, who belonged to Adams, but neither Adams nor Humber nor Cass had let Jerry know it. It looked as though Cass had let it slip out by mistake.

I said, 'How long have you worked here, Jerry?'

'How long?' he echoed vaguely.

'How many weeks were you here before Christmas?'

He put his head on one side and thought. He brightened. 'I came on the day after the Rovers beat the Gunners. My dad took me to the match, see? Near our house, the Rovers' ground is.'

I asked him more questions, but he had no clearer idea than that about when he had come to Humber's.

'Well,' I said, 'was Mickey here already, when you came?'

'I've never done no other horses since I've been here,' he said. When I asked him no more questions he placidly picked up the comic again and began to look at the pictures. Watching him, I wondered what it was like to have a mind like his, a brain like cotton wool upon which the accumulated learning of the world could make no dent, in which reason, memory, and awareness were blanketed almost out of existence.

He smiled happily at the comic strips. He was, I reflected, none the worse off for being simple-minded. He was good at heart, and what he did not understand could not hurt him. There was a lot to be said for life on that level. If one didn't realize one was an object of calculated humiliations, there would be no need to try to make oneself be insensitive to them. If I had his simplicity, I thought, I would find life at Humber's very much easier.

He looked up suddenly and saw me watching him, and gave me a warm, contented, trusting smile.

'I like you,' he said; and turned his attention back to the paper.

There was a raucous noise from downstairs and the other lads erupted up the ladder, pushing Cecil among them as he was practically unable to walk. Jerry scuttled back to his own bed and put his comic carefully away; and I, like all the rest, wrapped myself in two grey blankets and lay down, boots and all, on the inhospitable canvas. I tried to find a comfortable position for my excessively weary limbs, but unfortunately failed.

CHAPTER ELEVEN

The office was as cold and unwelcoming as Humber's personality, with none of the ostentation of his car. It consisted of a long narrow room with the door and the single smallish window both in the long wall facing down the yard. At the far end, away to the left as one entered, there was a door which opened into a washroom: this was whitewashed and lit by three slit-like, frosted glass windows, and led through an inner door into a lavatory. In the washroom itself there was a sink, a plastic topped table, a refrigerator, and two wall cupboards. The first of these on investigation proved to hold all the bandages, liniments, and medicines in common use with horses.

Careful not to move anything from its original position I looked at every bottle, packet, and tin. As far as I could see there was nothing of a stimulating nature among them.

The second cupboard however held plenty of stimulant in the shape of alcohol for human consumption, an impressive collection of bottles with a well stocked shelf of glasses above them. For the entertainment of owners, not the quickening of their horses. I shut the door.

There was nothing in the refrigerator except four bottles of beer, some milk, and a couple of trays of ice cubes.

I went back into the office.

Humber's desk stood under the window, so that when he was sitting at it he could look straight out down the yard. It was a heavy flat-topped knee-hole desk with drawers at each side, and it was almost aggressively tidy. Granted Humber was away at Nottingham races and had not spent long in the office in the morning, but the tidiness was basic, not temporary. None of the drawers was locked, and their contents (stationery, tax tables, and so on) could be seen at a glance. On top of the desk there was only a telephone, an adjustable reading lamp, a tray of pens and pencils, and a green glass paper weight the size of a cricket ball. Trapped air bubbles rose in a frozen spray in its depths.

The single sheet of paper which it held down bore only a list of duties for the day and had clearly been drawn up for Cass to work from. I saw disconsolately that I would be cleaning tack that afternoon with baby-voiced Kenneth, who never stopped talking, and doing five horses at evening stables, this last because the horses normally done by Bert, who had gone racing, had to be shared out among those left behind.

Apart from the desk the office contained a large floor-to-ceiling cupboard in which form books and racing colours were kept; too few of those for the space available. Three dark green filing cabinets, two leather armchairs, and an upright wooden chair with a leather seat stood round the walls.

I opened the unlocked drawers of the filing cabinets one by one and searched quickly through the contents. They contained racing calendars, old accounts, receipts, press cuttings, photographs, papers to do with the horses currently in training, analyses of forms, letters from owners, records of saddlery and fodder trans-actions; everything that could be found in the office of nearly every trainer in the country.

I looked at my watch. Cass usually took an hour off for lunch. I had waited five minutes after he had driven out of the yard, and I intended to be out of the office ten minutes before he could be expected back. This had given me a working time of three-quarters of an hour, of which nearly half had already gone.

Borrowing a pencil from the desk and taking a sheet of writing paper from a drawer, I applied myself to the drawer full of current accounts. For each of seventeen racehorses there was a separate hard-covered blue ledger, in which was listed every major and minor expense incurred in its training. I wrote a list of their names, few of which were familiar to me, together with their owners and the dates when they had come into the yard. Some had been there for years, but three had arrived during the past three months, and it was only these, I thought, which were of any real interest. None of the horses who had been doped had stayed at Humber's longer than four months.

The names of the three newest horses were Chin-Chin, Kandersteg, and Starlamp. The first was owned by Humber himself and the other two by Adams.

I put the account books back where I had found them and looked at my watch. Seventeen minutes left. Putting the pencil back on the desk I folded the list of horses and stowed it away in my money belt. The webbing pockets were filling up again with fivers, as I had spent little of my pay, but the belt still lay flat and invisible below my waist under my jeans: and I had been careful not to let any of the lads know it was there, so as not to be robbed.

I riffled quickly through the drawers of press cuttings and photographs, but found no reference to the eleven horses or their successes. The racing calendars bore more fruit in the shape of a pencilled cross against the name of Superman in the Boxing Day selling 'chase, but there was no mark against the selling 'chase scheduled for a coming meeting at Sedgefield.

It was at the back of the receipts drawer that I struck most gold. There was another blue accounts ledger there, with a double page devoted to each of the eleven horses. Among these eleven were interspersed nine others who had in various ways failed in their purpose. One of these was Superman and another Old Etonian.

In the left-hand page of each double spread had been recorded the entire racing career of the horse in question, and on the right-hand pages of my eleven old friends were details of the race they each won with assistance. Beneath were sums of money which I judged must be Humber's winnings on them. His winnings had run into thousands on every successful race. On Superman's page he had written 'Lost: three hundred pounds.' On Old Etonian's right-hand page there was no race record: only the single word 'Destroyed.'

A cross-out line had been drawn diagonally across all the pages except those concerning a horse called Six-Ply; and two new double pages had been prepared at the end, one for Kandersteg, and one for Starlamp. The left-hand pages for these three horses were written up: the right-hand pages were blank.

I shut the book and put it back. It was high time to go, and with a last look round to make sure that everything was exactly as it had been when I came in, I let myself quietly, unnoticed, out of the door, and went back to the kitchen to see if by some miracle the lads had left me any crumbs of lunch. Naturally, they had not.

The next morning Jerry's horse Mickey disappeared from the yard while we were out at second exercise, but Cass told him Jud had run him down to a friend of Humber's on the coast, for Mickey to paddle in the sea water to strengthen his legs, and that he would be back that evening. But the evening came, and Mickey did not.

On Wednesday Humber ran another horse, and I

missed my lunch to have a look inside his house while he was away. Entry was easy through an open ventilator, but I could find nothing whatever to give me any clue as to how the doping was carried out.

All day Thursday I fretted about Mickey being still away at the coast. It sounded perfectly reasonable. It was what a trainer about twelve miles from the sea could be expected to arrange. Sea water was good for horses' legs. But something happened to horses sometimes at Humber's which made it possible for them to be doped later, and I had a deeply disturbing suspicion that whatever it was was happening to Mickey at this moment, and that I was missing my only chance of finding it out.

According to the accounts books Adams owned four of the racehorses in the yard, in addition to his two hunters. None of his racehorses was known in the yard by its real name: therefore Mickey could be any one of the four. He could in fact be Kandersteg or Starlamp. It was an even chance that he was one or the other, and was due to follow in Superman's footsteps. So I fretted.

On Friday morning a hired box took the stable runner to Haydock races, and Jud and Humber's own box remained in the yard until lunch time. This was a definite departure from normal; and I took the opportunity of noting the mileage on the speedometer.

Jud drove the box out of the yard while we were still eating the midday sludge, and we didn't see him come back as we were all out on the gallop farthest away from the stables sticking back into place the divots kicked out of the soft earth that week by the various training activities; but when we returned for evening stables at four, Mickey was back in his own quarters.

I climbed up into the cab of the horse box and looked at the mileage indicator. Jud had driven exactly sixteen and a half miles. He had not, in fact, been as far as the coast. I thought some very bitter thoughts.

When I had finished doing my two racehorses I carried the brushes and pitchforks along to see to Adams' black hunter, and found Jerry leaning against the wall outside Mickey's next door box with tears running down his cheeks.

'What's the matter?' I said, putting down my stuff.

'Mickey . . . bit me,' he said. He was shaking with pain and fright.

'Let's see.'

I helped him slide his left arm out of his jersey, and took a look at the damage. There was a fierce red and purple circular weal on the fleshy part of his upper arm near the shoulder. It had been a hard, savage bite.

Cass came over.

'What's going on here?'

But he saw Jerry's arm, and didn't need to be told. He looked over the bottom half of the door into Mickey's box, then turned to Jerry and said, 'His legs were too far gone for the sea water to cure them. The vet said he would have to put on a blister, and he did it this afternoon when Mickey got back. That's what's the matter with him. Feels a bit off colour, he does, and so would you if someone slapped a flaming plaster on your legs. Now you just stop this stupid blubbing and get right back in there and see to him. And you, Dan, get on with that hunter and mind your own bloody business.' He went off along the row.

'I can't,' whispered Jerry, more to himself than to me.

'You'll manage it,' I said cheerfully.

He turned to me a stricken face. 'He'll bite me again.'

'I'm sure he won't.'

'He tried lots of times. And he's kicking out something terrible. I daren't go into his box . . .' He stood stiffly, shivering with fright, and I realized that it really was beyond him to go back.

'All right,' I said, 'I'll do Mickey and you do my hunter. Only do him well, Jerry, very well. Mr Adams is coming to ride him again tomorrow and I don't want to spend another Saturday on my knees.'

He looked dazed. 'Ain't no one done nothing like that for me before.'

'It's a swop,' I said brusquely. 'You mess up my hunter and I'll bite you worse than Mickey did.'

He stopped shivering and began to grin, which I had intended, and slipping his arm painfully back inside his jersey he picked up my brushes and opened the hunter's door.

'You won't tell Cass?' he asked anxiously.

207

'No,' I reassured him; and unbolted Mickey's box door.

The horse was tied up safely enough, and wore on his neck a long wooden-barred collar, called a cradle, which prevented his bending his head down to bite the bandages off his fore legs. Under the bandages, according to Cass, Mickey's legs were plastered with 'blister', a sort of caustic paste used to contract and strengthen the tendons. Blistering was a normal treatment for dicky tendons. The only trouble was that Mickey's legs had not needed treatment. They had been, to my eyes, as sound as rocks. But now, however, they were definitely paining him; at least as much as with a blister, and possibly more.

As Jerry had indicated, Mickey was distinctly upset. He could not be soothed by hand or voice, but lashed forwards with his hind feet whenever he thought I was in range, and made equal use of his teeth. I was careful not to walk behind him, though he did his best to turn his quarters in my direction while I was banking up his straw bed round the back of the box. I fetched him hay and water, but he was not interested, and changed his rug, as the one he wore was soaked with sweat and would give him a chill during the night. Changing his rug was a bit of an obstacle race, but by warding off his attacks with the pitchfork I got it done unscathed.

I took Jerry with me to the feed bins where Cass was doling out the right food for each horse, and when we got back to the boxes we solemnly exchanged bowls.

Jerry grinned happily. It was infectious. I grinned back.

Mickey didn't want food either, not, that is, except lumps of me. He didn't get any. I left him tied up for the night and took myself and Jerry's sack of brushes to safety on the far side of the door. Mickey would, I hoped, have calmed down considerably by the morning.

Jerry was grooming the black hunter practically hair by hair, humming tonelessly under his breath.

'Are you done?' I said.

'Is he all right?' he asked anxiously.

I went in to have a look.

'Perfect,' I said truthfully. Jerry was better at strapping a horse than at most things; and the next day, to my considerable relief, Adams passed both hunters without remark and spoke hardly a word to me. He was in a hurry to be off to a distant meet, but all the same it seemed I had succeeded in appearing too spineless to be worth tormenting.

Mickey was a good deal worse, that morning. When Adams had gone I stood with Jerry looking over the half-door of Mickey's box. The poor animal had managed to rip one of the bandages off in spite of the cradle, and we could see a big raw area over his tendon.

Mickey looked round at us with baleful eyes and flat ears, his neck stretched forward aggressively. Muscles quivered violently in his shoulders and hind quarters. I had never seen a horse behave like that except when fighting; and he was, I thought, dangerous.

'He's off his head,' whispered Jerry, awestruck.

'Poor thing.'

'You ain't going in?' he said. 'He looks like he'd kill you.'

'Go and get Cass,' I said. 'No, I'm not going in, not without Cass knowing how things are, and Humber too. You go and tell Cass that Mickey's gone mad. That ought to fetch him to have a look.'

Jerry trotted off and returned with Cass, who seemed to be alternating between anxiety and scorn as he came within earshot. At the sight of Mickey anxiety abruptly took over, and he went to fetch Humber, telling Jerry on no account to open Mickey's door.

Humber came hurriedly across the yard leaning on his stick, with Cass, who was a short man, trotting along at his side. Humber looked at Mickey for a good long time. Then he shifted his gaze to Jerry, who was standing there shaking again at the thought of having to deal with a horse in such a state, and then further along to me, where I stood at the door of the next box.

'That's Mr Adams' hunter's box,' he said to me.

'Yes, sir, he went with Mr Adams just now, sir.'

He looked me up and down, and then Jerry the same, and finally said to Cass, 'Roke and Webber had better change horses. I know they haven't an ounce of guts between them, but Roke is much bigger, stronger, and older.' And also, I thought with a flash of insight, Jerry has a father and mother to make a fuss if he gets hurt, whereas against Roke in the next-of-kin line was the single word 'none'.

'I'm not going in there alone, sir,' I said. 'Cass will have to hold him off with a pitchfork while I muck him out.' And even then, I thought, we'd both be lucky to get out without being kicked.

Cass, to my amusement, hurriedly started telling Humber that if I was too scared to do it on my own he would get one of the other lads to help me. Humber however took no notice of either of us, but went back to staring sombrely at Mickey.

Finally, he turned to me and said, 'Fetch a bucket and come over to the office.'

'An empty bucket, sir?'

'Yes,' he said impatiently, 'an empty bucket.' He turned and gently limped over to the long brick hut. I took the bucket out of the hunter's box, followed him, and waited by the door.

He came out with a small labelled glass-stoppered chemist's jar in one hand and a teaspoon in the other. The jar was three-quarters full of white powder. He gestured to me to hold out the bucket, then he put half a teaspoon of the powder into it.

'Fill the bucket only a third full of water,' he said. 'And put it in Mickey's manger, so that he can't kick it over. It will quieten him down, once he drinks it.'

He took the jar and spoon back inside the office, and I picked a good pinch of the white powder out of the bottom of the bucket and dropped it down inside the list of Humber's horses in my money belt. I licked my fingers and thumb afterwards; the particles of powder clinging there had a faintly bitter taste. The jar, which I had seen in the cupboard in the washroom, was labelled 'Soluble phenobarbitone', and the only surprising factor was the amount of it that Humber kept available.

I ran water into the bucket, stirred it with my hand, and went back to Mickey's box. Cass had vanished. Jerry was across the yard seeing to his third horse. I looked round for someone to ask for help, but everyone was carefully keeping out of sight. I cursed. I was not going into Mickey alone: it was just plain stupid to try it.

Humber came back across the yard.

'Get on in,' he said.

'I'd spill the water dodging him, sir.'

'Huh.'

Mickey's hoofs thudded viciously against the wall.

'You mean you haven't got the guts.'

'You'd need to be a fool to go in there alone, sir,' I said sullenly.

He glared at me, but he must have seen it was no use insisting. He suddenly picked up the pitchfork from where it stood against the wall and transferred it to his right hand and the walking stick to his left.

'Get on with it then,' he said harshly. 'And don't waste time.'

He looked incongruous, brandishing his two unconventional weapons while dressed like an advertisement for *Country Life*. I hoped he was going to be as resolute as he sounded.

I unbolted Mickey's door and we went in. It had been an injustice to think Humber might turn tail and leave me there alone; he behaved as coldly as ever, as if fear were quite beyond his imagination. Efficiently he kept Mickey penned first to one side of the box and then to the other while I mucked out and put down fresh straw, remaining steadfastly at his post while I cleaned the uneaten food out of the manger and wedged the bucket of doped water in place. Mickey didn't make it easy for him, either. The teeth and hooves were busier and more dangerous than the night before.

It was especially aggravating in the face of Humber's coolness to have to remember to behave like a bit of a coward myself, though I minded less than if he had been Adams.

When I had finished the jobs Humber told me to go out first, and he retreated in good order after me, his well-pressed suit scarcely rumpled from his exertions.

I shut the door and bolted out, and did my best to look thoroughly frightened. Humber looked me over with disgust.

'Roke,' he said sarcastically, 'I hope you will feel capable of dealing with Mickey when he is half asleep with drugs?'

'Yes, sir,' I muttered.

'Then in order not to strain your feeble stock of courage I suggest we keep him drugged for some days. Every time you fetch him a bucket of water you can get Cass or me to put some sedative in it. Understand?'

'Yes sir.'

I carried the sack of dirty straw round to the muck heap, and there took a close look at the bandage which Mickey had dislodged. Blister is a red paste. I had looked in vain for red paste on Mickey's raw leg; and there was not a smear of it on the bandage. Yet from the size and severity of the wound there should have been half a cupful.

I took Jerry down to Posset on the motor-cycle again that afternoon and watched him start to browse contentedly in the toy department of the post office.

There was a letter for me from October.

'Why did we receive no report from you last week? It is your duty to keep us informed of the position.'

I tore the page up, my mouth twisting. Duty. That was just about enough to make me lose my temper. It was not from any sense of duty that I stayed at Humber's to endure a minor version of slavery. It was because I was obstinate, and liked to finish what I started, and although it sounded a bit grandiose, it was because I really wanted, if I could, to remove British steeplechasing from Adams' clutches. If it had been only a matter of duty I would have repaid October his money and cleared out.

'It is your duty to keep us informed of the position.'

He was still angry with me about Patty, I thought morosely, and he wrote that sentence only because he knew I wouldn't like it.

I composed my report.

'Your humble and obedient servant regrets that he was unable to carry out his duty last week by keeping you informed of the position.

'The position is still far from clear, but a useful fact has been ascertained. None of the original eleven horses will be doped again: but a horse called Six-Ply is lined up to be the next winner. He is now owned by Mr Henry Waddington, of Lewes, Sussex.

'May I please have the answers to the following questions:

'1. Is the powder in the enclosed twist of paper soluble phenobarbitone?

'2. What are in detail the registered physical characteristics of the racehorses Chin-Chin, Kandersteg, and Starlamp?

'3. On what date did Blackburn, playing at home, beat Arsenal?'

And that, I thought, sticking down the envelope and grinning to myself, that will fix him and his duty.

Jerry and I gorged ourselves at the café. I had been

at Humber's for five weeks and two days, and my clothes were getting looser.

When we could eat no more I went back to the post office and bought a large-scale hiker's map of the surrounding district, and a cheap pair of compasses. Jerry spent fifteen shillings on a toy tank which he had resisted before, and, after checking to see if my goodwill extended so far, a second comic for me to read to him. And we went back to Humber's.

Days passed. Mickey's drugged water acted satisfactorily, and I was able to clean his box and look after him without much trouble. Cass took the second bandage off, revealing an equal absence of red paste. However, the wounds gradually started healing.

As Mickey could not be ridden and showed great distress if one tried to lead him out along the road, he had to be walked round the yard for an hour each day, which exercised me more than him, but gave me time to think some very fruitful thoughts.

Humber's stick landed with a resounding thump across Charlie's shoulders on Tuesday morning, and for a second it looked as though Charlie would hit him back. But Humber coldly stared him down, and the next morning delivered an even harder blow in the same place. Charlie's bed was empty that night. He was the fourth lad to leave in the six weeks I had been there (not counting the boy who stayed only three days) and of my original half dozen dormitory companions, only Bert and Jerry remained. The time was getting perceptibly closer when I would find myself at the top of the queue for walking the plank.

Adams came with Humber when he made his usual rounds on Thursday evening. They stopped outside Mickey's box but contented themselves with looking over the half-door.

'Don't go in, Paul,' said Humber warningly. 'He's still very unpredictable, in spite of drugs.'

Adams looked at me where I stood by Mickey's head.

'Why is the gipsy doing this horse? I thought it was the moron's job.' He sounded angry and alarmed.

Humber explained that as Mickey had bitten Jerry, he had made me change places with him. Adams still didn't like it, but looked as if he would save his comments until he wouldn't be overheard.

He said, 'What is the gipsy's name?'

'Roke,' said Humber.

'Well, Roke, come here, out of that box.'

Humber said anxiously, 'Paul, don't forget we're one lad short already.'

These were not particularly reassuring words to hear. I walked across the box, keeping a wary eye on Mickey, let myself out through the door, and stood beside it, drooping and looking at the ground.

'Roke,' said Adams in a pleasant sounding voice, 'what do you spend your wages on?'

'The never-never on my motor-bike, sir.'

'The never-never? Oh, yes. And how many instalments have you still to pay?'

'About – er – fifteen, sir.'

'And you don't want to leave here until you've finished paying them off?'

'No, sir.'

'Will they take your motor-cycle away if you stop paying?'

'Yes sir, they might do.'

'So, Mr Humber doesn't need to worry about you leaving him?'

I said slowly, unwillingly, but as it happened, truthfully, 'No, sir.'

'Good,' he said briskly. 'Then that clears the air, doesn't it. And now you can tell me where you find the guts to deal with an unstable, half-mad horse.'

'He's drugged, sir.'

'You and I both know, Roke, that a drugged horse is not necessarily a safe horse.'

I said nothing. If there was ever a time when I needed an inspiration, this was it: and my mind was a blank.

'I don't think, Roke,' he said softly, 'that you are as feeble as you make out. I think there is a lot more stuffing in you than you would have us believe.'

'No, sir,' I said helplessly.

'Let's find out, shall we?'

He stretched out his hand to Humber, and Humber

gave him his walking stick. Adams drew back his arm and hit me fairly smartly across the thigh.

If I were to stay in the yard I had got to stop him. This time the begging simply had to be done. I slid down the door, gasping, and sat on the ground.

'No sir, don't,' I shouted. 'I got some pills. I was dead scared of Mickey, and I asked the chemist in Posset on Saturday if he had any pills to make me brave, and he sold me some, and I've been taking them regular ever since.'

'What pills?' said Adams disbelievingly.

'Tranquil something he said. I didn't rightly catch the word.'

'Tranquillizers.'

'Yes, that's it, tranquillizers. Don't hit me any more sir, please sir. It was just that I was so dead scared of Mickey. Don't hit me any more, sir.'

'Well I'm damned,' Adams began to laugh. 'Well I'm damned. What will they think of next?' He gave the stick back to Humber, and the two of them walked casually away along to the next box.

'Take tranquillizers to help you out of a blue funk. Well, why not?' Still laughing, they went in to see the next horse.

I got up slowly and brushed the dirt off the seat of my pants. Damn it, I thought miserably, what else could I have done? Why was pride so important, and abandoning it so bitter?

It was more clear than ever that weakness was my

only asset. Adams had this fearful kink of seeing any show of spirit as a personal challenge to his ability to crush it. He dominated Humber, and exacted instant obedience from Cass, and they were his allies. If I stood up to him even mildly I would get nothing but a lot of bruises and he would start wondering why I stayed to collect still more. The more tenaciously I stayed, the more incredible he would find it. Hire purchase on the motor-bike wouldn't convince him for long. He was quick. He knew, if he began to think about it, that I had come from October's stables. He must know that October was a Steward and therefore his natural enemy. He would remember Tommy Stapleton. The hyper-sensitivity of the hunted to danger would stir the roots of his hair. He could check and find out from the post office that I did not send money away each week, and discover that the chemist had sold me no tranquillizers. He was in too deep to risk my being a follow-up to Stapleton; and at the very least, once he was suspicious of me, my detecting days would be over.

Whereas if he continued to be sure of my utter spine-lessness he wouldn't bother about me, and I could if necessary stay in the yard up to five or six weeks more. And heaven forbid, I thought, that I would have to.

Adams, although it had been instinct with him, not reason, was quite right to be alarmed that it was I and not Jerry who was now looking after Mickey.

In the hours I had spent close to the horse I had come to understand what was really the matter with him, and all my accumulated knowledge about the affected horses, and about all horses in general, had gradually shaken into place. I did by that day know in outline how Adams and Humber had made their winners win.

I knew in outline, but not in detail. A theory, but no proof. For detail and proof I still needed more time, and if the only way I could buy time was to sit on the ground and implore Adams not to beat me, then it had to be done. But it was pretty awful, just the same.

CHAPTER TWELVE

October's reply was unrelenting.

'Six-Ply, according to his present owner, is not going to be entered in any selling races. Does this mean that he will not be doped?

'The answers to your questions are as follows:

'1. The powder is soluble phenobarbitone.

'2. The physical characteristics of Chin-Chin are: bay gelding, white blaze down nose, white sock, off-fore. Kandersteg: gelding, washy chestnut, three white socks, both fore-legs and near hind. Starlamp: brown gelding, near hind white heel.

'3. Blackburn beat Arsenal on November 30th.

'I do not appreciate your flippancy. Does your irresponsibility now extend to the investigation?'

Irresponsibility. Duty. He could really pick his words.

I read the descriptions of the horses again. They told me that Starlamp was Mickey. Chin-Chin was Dobbin, one of the two racehorses I did which belonged to

Humber. Kandersteg was a pale shambling creature looked after by Bert, and known in the yard as Flash.

If Blackburn beat Arsenal on November 30th, Jerry had been at Humber's eleven weeks already.

I tore up October's letter and wrote back.

'Six-Ply may now be vulnerable whatever race he runs in, as he is the only shot left in the locker since Old Etonian and Superman both misfired.

'In case I fall on my nut out riding, or get knocked over by a passing car, I think I had better tell you that I have this week realized how the scheme works, even though I am as yet ignorant of most of the details.'

I told October that the stimulant Adams and Humber used was in fact adrenalin; and I told him how I believed it was introduced into the blood stream.

'As you can see, there are two prime facts which must be established before Adams and Humber can be prosecuted. I will do my best to finish the job properly, but I can't guarantee it, as the time factor is a nuisance.'

Then, because I felt very alone, I added impulsively, jerkily, a postscript.

'Believe me. Please believe me. I did nothing to Patty.'

When I had written it, I looked at this *cri de coeur* in disgust. I am getting as soft as I pretend, I thought. I tore the bottom off the sheet of paper and threw the pitiful words away, and posted my letter in the box.

Thinking it wise actually to buy some tranquillizers in case anyone checked, I stopped at the chemist's and asked for some. The chemist refused to sell me any, as they could only be had on a doctor's prescription. How long would it be, I wondered ruefully, before Adams or Humber discovered this awkward fact.

Jerry was disappointed when I ate my meal in the café very fast, and left him alone to finish and walk back from Posset, but I assured him that I had jobs to do. It was high time I took a look at the surrounding countryside.

I rode out of Posset and, stopping the motor-cycle in a lay-by, got out the map over which I had pored intermittently during the week. I had drawn on it with pencil and compasses two concentric circles: the outer circle had a radius of eight miles from Humber's stables, and the inner circle a radius of five miles. If Jud had driven straight there and back when he had gone to fetch Mickey, the place he had fetched him from would lie in the area between the circles.

Some directions from Humber's were unsuitable because of open-cast coalmines: and eight miles to the southeast lay the outskirts of the sprawling mining town called Clavering. All round the north and west sides, however, there was little but moorland interspersed with small valleys like the ones in which Humber's stable lay, small fertile pockets in miles and miles of stark windswept heath.

Tellbridge, the village where Adams lived, lay outside the outer circle by two miles, and because of this I did not think Mickey could have been lodged there during his absence from Humber's. But all the same the area on a line from Humber's yard to Adams' village seemed the most sensible to take a look at first.

As I did not wish Adams to find me spying out the land round his house, I fastened on my crash helmet, which I had not worn since the trip to Edinburgh, and pulled up over my eyes a large pair of goggles, under which even my sisters wouldn't have recognized me. I didn't, as it happened, see Adams on my travels; but I did see his house, which was a square, cream-coloured Georgian pile with gargoyle heads adorning the gate-posts. It was the largest, most imposing building in the tiny group of a church, a shop, two pubs, and a gaggle of cottages which made up Tellbridge.

I talked about Adams to the boy who filled my petrol tank in the Tellbridge garage.

'Mr Adams? Yes, he bought old Sir Lucas' place three-four years ago. After the old man died. There weren't no family to keep it on.'

'And Mrs Adams?' I suggested.

'Blimey, there isn't any Mrs Adams,' he said, laughing and pushing his fair hair out of his eyes with the back of his wrist. 'But a lot of birds, he has there sometimes. Often got a houseful there, he has. Nobs, now, don't get me wrong. Never has anyone but nobs in his house, doesn't Mr Adams. And anything he wants, he gets, and quick. Never mind anyone else. He woke the whole village up at two in the morning last Friday because he got it into his head that he'd like to ring the church bells. He smashed a window to get in . . . I ask you! Of course, no one says much, because he spends such a lot of money in the village. Food and drink and wages, and so on. Everyone's better off, since he came.'

'Does he often do things like that – ringing the church bells?'

'Well, not exactly, but other things, yes. I shouldn't think you could believe all you hear. But they say he pays up handsome if he does any damage, and everyone just puts up with it. High spirits, that's what they say it is.'

But Adams was too old for high spirits of that sort.

'Does he buy his petrol here?' I asked idly, fishing in my pocket for some money.

'Not often he doesn't, he has his own tank.' The smile died out of the boy's open face. 'In fact, I only served him once, when his supplies had run out.'

'What happened?'

'Well, he trod on my foot. In his hunting boots, too. I couldn't make out if he did it on purpose, because it seemed like that really, but why would he do something like that?'

'I can't imagine.'

He shook his head wondering. 'He must have thought I'd moved out of his way, I suppose. Put his heel right on top of my foot, he did, and leaned back. I only had sneakers on. Darn nearly broke my bones, he did. He must weigh getting on for sixteen stone, I shouldn't wonder.' He sighed and counted my change into my palm, and I thanked him and went on my way thinking that it was extraordinary how much a psychopath could get away with if he was big enough and clever and well-born.

It was a cold afternoon, and cloudy, but I enjoyed it. Stopping on the highest point of a shoulder of moorland I sat straddling the bike and looking round at rolling distances of bare bleak hills and at the tall chimneys of Clavering pointing up on the horizon. I took off my helmet and goggles and pushed my fingers through my hair to let the cold wind in to my scalp. It was invigorating.

There was almost no chance, I knew, of my finding where Mickey had been kept. It could be anywhere, in any barn, outhouse, or shed. It didn't have to be a stable, and quite likely was not a stable: and indeed all I was sure of was that it would be somewhere tucked away out of sight and sound of any neighbours. The trouble was that in that part of Durham, with its widely scattered villages, its sudden valleys, and its miles of open heath, I found there were dozens of places tucked away out of sight and sound of neighbours.

Shrugging, I put my helmet and goggles on again, and spent what little was left of my free time finding two vantage points on high ground, from one of which one could see straight down the valley into Humber's yard, and from the other a main cross roads on the way from Humber's to Tellbridge, together with good stretches of road in all directions from it.

Kandersteg's name being entered in Humber's special hidden ledger, it was all Durham to a doughnut that one day he would take the same trail that Mickey-Starlamp had done. It was quite likely that I would still be unable to find out where he went, but there was no harm in getting the lie of the land clear in my head.

At four o'clock I rolled back into Humber's yard with the usual lack of enthusiasm, and began my evening's work.

Sunday passed, and Monday. Mickey got no better; the wounds on his legs were healing but he was still a risky prospect, in spite of the drugs, and he was beginning to lose flesh. Although I had never seen or had to deal with a horse in this state before, I gradually grew certain that he would not recover, and that Adams and Humber had another misfire on their hands.

Neither Humber nor Cass liked the look of him either, though Humber seemed more annoyed than anxious, as time went on. Adams came one morning, and from across the yard in Dobbin's box I watched the three of them standing looking in at Mickey. Presently Cass went into the box for a moment or two, and came out shaking his head. Adams looked furious. He took Humber by the arm and the two of them walked across to the office in what looked like an argument. I would have given much to have overheard them. A pity I couldn't lip-read, I thought, and that I hadn't come equipped with one of those long-range listening devices. As a spy, I was really a dead loss.

On Tuesday morning at breakfast there was a letter for me, post-marked Durham, and I looked at it curiously because there were so few people who either knew where I was or would bother to write to me. I put it in my pocket until I could open it in private and I was glad I had, for to my astonishment it was from October's elder daughter.

She had written from her university address, and said briefly:

Dear Daniel Roke,
    I would be glad if you could call to see me for a few moments sometime this week. There is a matter I must discuss with you.
                                                    Yours sincerely,
                                                        Elinor Tarren.

October, I thought, must have given her a message for me, or something he wanted me to see, or perhaps he intended to be there to meet me himself, and had not risked writing to me direct. Puzzled, I asked Cass for an afternoon off, and was refused. Only Saturday, he said, and Saturday only if I behaved myself.

I thought Saturday might be too late, or that she would have gone to Yorkshire for the weekend, but I wrote to her that I could come only on that day, and walked into Posset after the evening meal on Tuesday to post the letter.

Her reply came on Friday, brief again and to the point, with still no hint of why I was to go.

'Saturday afternoon will do very well. I will tell the porter you are coming: go to the side door of the college (this is the door used by students and their visitors) and ask to be shown to my room.'

She enclosed a pencilled sketch to show me where to find the college, and that was all.

On Saturday morning I had six horses to do, because there was still no replacement for Charlie, and Jerry had gone with Pageant to the races. Adams came as usual to talk to Humber and to supervise the loading up of his hunters, but wasted no attention or energy on me, for which I was thankful. He spent half of the twenty minutes he was in the yard looking into Mickey's box with a scowl on his handsome face.

Cass himself was not always unkind, and because he knew I particularly wanted the afternoon free he even went so far as to help me get finished before the midday meal. I thanked him, surprised, and he remarked that he knew there had been a lot extra for everyone (except himself incidentally) to do, as we were still a lad short, and that I hadn't complained about it as much as most of the others. And that, I thought, was a mistake I would not have to make too often.

I washed as well as the conditions would allow; one had to heat all washing water in a kettle on the stove and pour it into the basin on the marble washstand; and shaved more carefully than usual, looking into the six-by-eight-inch flyblown bit of looking glass, jostled by the other lads who wanted to be on their way to Posset.

None of the clothes I had were fit for visiting a women's college. With a sigh I settled for the black sweater, which had a high collar, the charcoal drainpipe trousers, and the black leather jacket. No shirt, because I had no tie. I eyed the sharp-pointed shoes, but I had not been able to overcome my loathing for them, so I scrubbed my jodhpur boots under the tap in the yard, and wore those. Everything else I was wearing needed cleaning, and I supposed I smelled of horses, though I was too used to it to notice.

I shrugged. There was nothing to be done about it. I unwrapped the motor-bike and made tracks for Durham.

CHAPTER THIRTEEN

Elinor's college stood in a tree-lined road along with other sturdy and learned looking buildings. It had an imposing front entrance and a less-imposing tarmacked drive entrance along to the right. I wheeled the motor-cycle down there and parked it beside the long row of bicycles. Beyond the bicycles stood six or seven small cars, one of which was Elinor's little scarlet two-seater.

Two steps led up to a large oak door embellished with the single word 'Students'. I went in. There was a porter's desk just inside on the right, with a mournful looking middle-aged man sitting behind it looking at a list.

'Excuse me,' I said, 'could you tell me where to find Lady Elinor Tarren?'

He looked up and said. 'You visiting? You expected?'

'I think so,' I said.

He asked my name, and thumbed down the list painstakingly. 'Daniel Roke to visit Miss Tarren, please show him her room. Yes, that's right. Come on, then.'

He got down off his stool, came round from behind his desk, and breathing noisily began to lead me deeper into the building.

There were several twists in the corridors and I could see why it was necessary to have a guide. On every hand were doors with the occupant or purpose written up on small cards let into metal slots. After going up two flights of stairs and round a few more corners, the porter halted outside one more door just like the rest.

'Here you are,' he said unemotionally. 'This is Miss Tarren's room.' He turned away and started to shuffle back to his post.

The card on the door said Miss E. C. Tarren. I knocked. Miss E. C. Tarren opened it.

'Come in,' she said. No smile.

I went in. She shut the door behind me. I stood still, looking at her room. I was so accustomed to the starkness of the accommodation at Humber's that it was an odd, strange sensation to find myself again in a room with curtains, carpet, sprung chairs, cushions, and flowers. The colours were mostly blues and greens, mixed and blending, with a bowl of daffodils and red tulips blazing against them.

There was a big desk with books and papers scattered on it; a bookshelf, a bed with a blue cover, a wardrobe, a tall built-in cupboard, and two easy chairs. It looked warm and friendly. A very good room for working in. If I had had more than a moment to stand and think about it, I knew I would be envious: this was what my father and mother's death had robbed me of, the time and liberty to study.

'Please sit down.' She indicated one of the easy chairs.

'Thank you.' I sat, and she sat down opposite me, but looking at the floor, not at me. She was solemn and frowning, and I rather gloomily wondered if what October wanted her to say to me meant more trouble.

'I asked you to come here,' she started. 'I asked you to come here because . . .' She stopped and stood up abruptly, and walked round behind me and tried again.

'I asked you to come,' she said to the back of my head, 'because I have to apologize to you, and I'm not finding it very easy.'

'Apologize?' I said, astonished. 'What for?'

'For my sister.'

I stood up and turned towards her. 'Don't,' I said vehemently. I had been too much humbled myself in the past weeks to want to see anyone else in the same position.

She shook her head. 'I'm afraid,' she swallowed, 'I'm afraid that my family has treated you very badly.'

The silver-blonde hair shimmered like a halo against the pale sunshine which slanted sideways through the window behind her. She was wearing a scarlet jersey under a sleeveless dark green dress. The whole effect was colourful and gorgeous, but it was clearly not going to help her if I went on looking at her. I sat down again in the chair and said with some lightheartedness, as it appeared October had not after all dispatched a dressing-down, 'Please don't worry about it.'

'Worry,' she exclaimed. 'What else can I do? I knew of course why you were dismissed, and I've said several times to Father that he ought to have had you sent to prison, and now I find none of it is true at all. How can you say there is nothing to worry about when everyone thinks you are guilty of some dreadful crime, and you aren't?'

Her voice was full of concern. She really minded that anyone in her family should have behaved as unfairly as Patty had. She felt guilty just because she was her sister. I liked her for it: but then I already knew she was a thoroughly nice girl.

'How did you find out?' I asked.

'Patty told me last weekend. We were just gossiping together, as we often do. She had always refused to talk about you, but this time she laughed, and told me quite casually, as if it didn't matter any more. Of course I know she's . . . well . . . used to men. She's just built that way. But this . . . I was so shocked. I couldn't believe her at first.'

'What exactly did she tell you?'

There was a pause behind me, then her voice went on, a little shakily. 'She said she tried to make you make love to her, but you wouldn't. She said . . . she said she showed you her body, and all you did was to tell her to cover herself up. She said she was so flaming angry about that that she thought all next day about what revenge she would have on you, and on Sunday morning she worked herself up into floods of tears, and went and told Father . . . told Father . . .'

'Well,' I said good humouredly, 'yes, that is, I suppose, a slightly more accurate picture of what took place.' I laughed.

'It isn't funny,' she protested.

'No. It's relief.'

She came round in front of me and sat down and looked at me.

'You did mind, then, didn't you?'

My distaste must have shown. 'Yes. I minded.'

'I told Father she had lied about you. I've never told him before about her love affairs, but this was different . . . anyway, I told him on Sunday after lunch.' She stopped, hesitating. I waited. At last she went on, 'It was very odd. He didn't seem surprised, really. Not utterly overthrown, like I was. He just seemed to get very tired, suddenly, as if he had heard bad news. As if a friend had died after a long illness, that sort of sadness. I didn't understand it. And when I said that of course the only fair thing to do would be to offer you your job back, he utterly refused. I argued, but I'm afraid he is adamant. He also refuses to tell Mr Inskip that you shouldn't have had to leave, and he made me promise not to repeat to him or anyone what Patty had said. It is so unfair,' she concluded passionately, 'and I felt that even if no one else is to know, at least you should. I don't suppose it makes it any better for you that my father and I have at last found out what really happened, but I wanted you to know that I am sorry, very, very sorry for what my sister did.'

I smiled at her. It wasn't difficult. Her colouring was so blazingly fair that it didn't matter if her nose wasn't entirely straight. Her direct grey eyes were full of genuine, earnest regret, and I knew she felt Patty's misbehaviour all the more keenly because she thought it had affected a stable lad who had no means of defending himself. This also made it difficult to know what to say in reply.

I understood, of course, that October couldn't declare me an injured innocent, even if he wanted to, which I doubted, without a risk of it reaching Humber's ears, and that the last thing that either of us wanted was for him to have to offer to take me back at Inskip's. No one in their right mind would stay at Humber's if they could go to Inskip's.

'If you knew,' I said slowly, 'how much I have wanted your father to believe that I didn't harm your sister, you would realize that what you have just said is worth a dozen jobs to me. I like your father. I respect him. And he is quite right. He cannot possibly give me my old job back, because it would be as good as saying publicly that his daughter is at least a liar, if not more. You can't ask him to do that. You can't expect it. I don't. Things are best left as they are.'

She looked at me for some time without speaking. It

seemed to me that there was relief in her expression, and surprise, and finally puzzlement.

'Don't you want *any* compensation?'

'No.'

'I don't understand you.'

'Look,' I said, getting up, away from her inquiring gaze. 'I'm not as blameless as the snow. I did kiss your sister. I suppose I led her on a bit. And then I was ashamed of myself and backed out, and that's the truth of it. It wasn't all her fault. I did behave very badly. So please . . . please don't feel so much guilt on my account.' I reached the window and looked out.

'People shouldn't be hung for murders they decide not to commit,' she said dryly. 'You are being very generous, and I didn't expect it.'

'Then you shouldn't have asked me here,' I said idly. 'You were taking too big a risk.' The window looked down on to a quadrangle, a neat square of grass surrounded by broad paths, peaceful and empty in the early spring sunshine.

'Risk . . . of what?' she said.

'Risk that I would raise a stink. Dishonour to the family. Tarnish to the Tarrens. That sort of thing. Lots of dirty linen and Sunday newspapers and your father losing face among his business associates.'

She looked startled, but also determined. 'All the same, a wrong has been done, and it had to be put right.'

'And damn the consequences?'

'And damn the consequences,' she repeated faintly.

I grinned. She was a girl after my own heart. I had been damning a few consequences too.

'Well,' I said reluctantly, 'I'd better be off. Thank you for asking me to come. I do understand that you have had a horrible week screwing yourself up for this, and I appreciate it more than I can possibly say.'

She looked at her watch and hesitated. 'I know it's an odd time of day, but would you like some coffee? I mean, you've come quite a long way . . .'

'I'd like some very much,' I said.

'Well . . . sit down, and I'll get it.'

I sat down. She opened the built-in cupboard, which proved to hold a wash basin and mirror on one side and a gas ring and shelves for crockery on the other. She filled a kettle, lit the gas, and put some cups and saucers on the low table between the two chairs, moving economically and gracefully. Unselfconscious, I thought. Sure enough of herself to drop her title in a place where brains mattered more than birth. Sure enough of herself to have a man who looked like I did brought to her bed-sitting-room, and to ask him to stay for coffee when it was not necessary, but only polite.

I asked her what subject she was reading, and she said English. She assembled some milk, sugar, and biscuits on the table.

'May I look at your books?' I asked.

'Go ahead,' she said amiably.

I got up and looked along her bookshelves. There

were the language text books – Ancient Icelandic, Anglo Saxon, and Middle English – and a comprehensive sweep of English writings from Alfred the Great's Chronicles to John Betjeman's unattainable amazons.

'What do you think of my books?' she asked curiously.

I didn't know how to answer. The masquerade was damnably unfair to her.

'Very learned,' I said lamely.

I turned away from the bookshelves, and came suddenly face to face with my full-length reflection in the mirror door of her wardrobe.

I looked at myself moodily. It was the first comprehensive view of Roke the stable lad that I had had since leaving October's London house months before, and time had not improved things.

My hair was too long, and the sideburns flourished nearly down to the lobes of my ears. My skin was a sort of pale yellow now that the suntan had all faded. There was a tautness in the face and a wary expression in the eyes which had not been there before: and in my black clothes I looked disreputable and a menace to society.

Her reflection moved behind mine in the mirror, and I met her eyes and found her watching me.

'You look as if you don't like what you see,' she said.

I turned round. 'No,' I said wryly. 'Would anyone?'

'Well . . .' Incredibly she smiled mischievously. 'I wouldn't like to set you loose in this college, for instance. If you don't realize, though, the effect which you . . . you may have a few rough edges, but I do now see why Patty tried . . . er . . . I mean . . .' Her voice tailed off in the first confusion she had shown.

'The kettle's boiling,' I said helpfully.

Relieved, she turned her back on me and made the coffee. I went to the window and looked down into the deserted quad, resting my forehead on the cold glass.

It still happened, I thought. In spite of those terrible clothes, in spite of the aura of shadiness, it could still happen. What accident, I wondered for the thousandth time in my life, decided that one should be born with bones of a certain design? I couldn't help the shape of my face and head. They were a legacy from a pair of neat featured parents: their doing, not mine. Like Elinor's hair, I thought. Born in you. Nothing to be proud of. An accident, like a birth mark or a squint. Something I habitually forgot, and found disconcerting when anyone mentioned it. And it had been expensive, moreover. I had lost at least two prospective customers because they hadn't liked the way their wives looked at me instead of my horses.

With Elinor, I thought, it was a momentary attraction which wouldn't last. She was surely too sensible to allow herself to get tangled up with one of her father's ex-stable lads. And as for me, it was strictly hands off the Tarren sisters, both of them. If I was out of the frying-pan with one, I was not jumping into the fire with

241

the other. It was a pity, all the same. I liked Elinor rather a lot.

'The coffee's ready,' she said.

I turned and went back to the table. She had herself very well controlled again. There was no mischievous revealing light in her face any more, and she looked almost severe, as if she very much regretted what she had said and was going to make quite certain I didn't take advantage of it.

She handed me a cup and offered the biscuits, which I ate because the lunch at Humber's had consisted of bread, margarine, and hard tasteless cheese, and the supper would be the same. It nearly always was, on Saturdays, because Humber knew we ate in Posset.

We talked sedately about her father's horses. I asked how Sparking Plug was getting on, and she told me, very well, thank you.

'I've a newspaper cutting about him, if you'd like to see it?' she said.

'Yes, I'd like to.'

I followed her to her desk while she looked for it. She shifted some papers to search underneath, and the top one fell on to the floor. I picked it up, put it back on the desk, and looked down at it. It seemed to be some sort of quiz.

'Thank you,' she said. 'I mustn't lose that, it's the Literary Society's competition, and I've only one more answer to find. Now where did I put that cutting?'

The competition consisted of a number of quotations

to which one had to ascribe the authors. I picked up the paper and began reading.

'That top one's a brute,' she said over her shoulder. 'No one's got it yet, I don't think.'

'How do you win the competition?' I asked.

'Get a complete, correct set of answers in first.'

'And what's the prize?'

'A book. But prestige, mostly. We only have one competition a term, and it's difficult.' She opened a drawer full of papers and oddments. 'I know I put that cutting somewhere.' She began shovelling things about out on to the top of the desk.

'Please don't bother any more,' I said politely.

'No, I want to find it.' A handful of small objects clattered on to the desk.

Among them was a small chromium-plated tube about three inches long with a loop of chain running from one end to the other. I had seen something like it before, I thought idly. I had seen it quite often. It had something to do with drinks.

'What's that?' I asked, pointing.

'That? Oh, that's a silent whistle.' She went on rummaging. 'For dogs,' she explained.

I picked it up. A silent dog whistle. Why then did I think it was connected with bottles and glasses and . . . the world stopped.

With an almost physical sensation, my mind leaped towards its prey. I held Adams and Humber in my hand at last. I could feel my pulse racing.

So simple. So very simple. The tube pulled apart in the middle to reveal that one end was a thin whistle, and the other its cap. A whistle joined to its cap by a little length of chain. I put the tiny mouthpiece to my lips and blew. Only a thread of sound came out.

'You can't hear it very well,' Elinor said, 'but of course a dog can. And you can adjust that whistle to make it sound louder to human ears, too.' She took it out of my hand and unscrewed part of the whistle itself. 'Now blow.' She gave it back.

I blew again. It sounded much more like an ordinary whistle.

'Do you think I could possibly borrow this for a little while?' I asked. 'If you're not using it? I . . . I want to try an experiment.'

'Yes, I should think so. My dear old sheepdog had to be put down last spring, and I haven't used it since. But you will let me have it back? I am getting a puppy in the long vac; and I want to use it for his training.'

'Yes, of course.'

'All right, then. Oh, here's that cutting, at last.'

I took the strip of newsprint, but I couldn't concentrate on it. All I could see was the drinks compartment in Humber's monster car, with the rack of ice-picks, tongs, and little miscellaneous chromium-plated objects. I had never given them more than a cursory glance; but one of them was a small tube with a loop of chain from end to end. One of them was a silent whistle for dogs.

I made an effort, and read about Sparking Plug, and thanked her for finding the cutting.

I stowed her whistle in my money belt and looked at my watch. It was already after half past three. I was going to be somewhat late back at work.

She had cleared me with October and shown me the whistle: two enormous favours. I wanted to repay her, and could think of only one way of doing it.

' "Nowhere either with more quiet or more freedom from trouble does a man retire than into his own soul . . ." ' I quoted.

She looked up at me, startled. 'That's the beginning of the competition.'

'Yes. Are you allowed help?'

'Yes. Anything. But . . .'

'It's Marcus Aurelius.'

'Who?' She was staggered.

'Marcus Aurelius Antoninus. Roman Emperor, 121 to 180 AD . . .'

'The Meditations?' I nodded.

'What language was it originally written in? We have to put that too. Latin, I suppose.'

'Greek.'

'This is fantastic . . . just where did you go to school?'

'I went to a village school in Oxfordshire.' So I had, for two years, until I was eight. 'And we had a master who perpetually crammed Marcus Aurelius down our throats.' But that master had been at Geelong.

I had been tempted to tell her the truth about myself

245

all afternoon, but never more than at that moment. I found it impossible to be anything but my own self in her company, and even at Slaw I had spoken to her more or less in my natural accent. I hated having to pretend to her at all. But I didn't tell her where I had come from and why, because October hadn't, and I thought he ought to know his daughter better than I did. There were her cosy chats with Patty . . . whose tongue could not be relied on; and perhaps he thought it was a risk to his investigations. I didn't know. And I didn't tell her.

'Are you really sure it's Marcus Aurelius?' she said doubtfully. 'We only get one shot. If it's wrong, you don't get another.'

'I should check it then. It comes in a section about learning to be content with your lot. I suppose I remember it because it is good advice and I've seldom been able to follow it.' I grinned.

'You know,' she said tentatively, 'it's none of my business, but I would have thought you could have got on a bit in the world. You seem . . . you seem decidedly intelligent. Why do you work in a stable?'

'I work in a stable,' I told her with perfect, ironic truth, 'because it's the only thing I know how to do.'

'Will you do it for the rest of your life?'

'I expect so.'

'And will it content you?'

'It will have to.'

'I didn't expect this afternoon to turn out like this at

all,' she said. 'To be frank, I was dreading it. And you have made it easy.'

'That's all right, then,' I said cheerfully.

She smiled. I went to the door and opened it, and she said, 'I'd better see you out. This building must have been the work of a maze-crazy architect. Visitors have been found wandering about the upper reaches dying of thirst days after they were supposed to have left.'

I laughed. She walked beside me back along the twisting corridors, down the stairs, and right back to the outside door, talking easily about her life in college, talking to me freely, as an equal. She told me that Durham was the oldest English university after Oxford and Cambridge, and that it was the only place in Britain which offered a course in Geophysics. She was indeed, a very nice girl.

She shook hands with me on the step.

'Goodbye,' she said. 'I'm sorry Patty was so beastly.'

'I'm not. If she hadn't been, I wouldn't have been here this afternoon.'

She laughed. 'But what a price to pay.'

'Worth it.'

Her grey eyes had darker grey flecks in them, I noticed. She watched me go over and sit on the motorcycle and fasten on the helmet. Then she waved her hand briefly, and went back through the door. It closed with finality behind her.

CHAPTER FOURTEEN

I stopped in Posset on the return journey to see if there were any comment from October on the theory I had sent him the previous week, but there was no letter for me at all.

Although I was already late for evening stables, I stopped longer to write to him. I couldn't get Tommy Stapleton out of my head: he had died without passing on what he knew. I didn't want to make the same mistake. Or to die either, if it came to that. I scribbled fast.

'I think the trigger is a silent whistle, the sort used for dogs. Humber keeps one in the drinks compartment of his car. Remember Old Etonian? They hold hound trails at Cartmel, on the morning of the races.'

Having posted that, I bought a large slab of chocolate for food, and also Jerry's comic, and slid as quietly as I could back into the yard. Cass caught me, however, and said sourly that I'd be lucky to get Saturday off next week as he would be reporting me to Humber. I sighed resignedly, started the load of evening chores, and felt the cold, dingy, sub-violent atmosphere of the place seep back into my bones.

But there was a difference now. The whistle lay like a bomb in my money belt. A death sentence, if they found me with it. Or so I believed. There remained the matter of making sure that I had not leaped to the wrong conclusion.

Tommy Stapleton had probably suspected what was going on and had walked straight into Humber's yard to tax him with it. He couldn't have known that the men he was dealing with were prepared to kill. But, because he had died, I did know. I had lived under their noses for seven weeks, and I had been careful: and because I intended to remain undetected to the end I spent a long time on Sunday wondering how I could conduct my experiment and get away with it.

On Sunday evening, at about five o'clock, Adams drove into the yard in his shining grey Jaguar. As usual at the sight of him, my heart sank. He walked round the yard with Humber when he made his normal tour of inspection and stopped for a long time looking over the door at Mickey. Neither he nor Humber came in. Humber had been into Mickey's box several times since the day he helped me take in the first lot of drugged water, but Adams had not been in at all.

Adams said, 'What do you think, Hedley?'

Humber shrugged, 'There's no change.'

'Write him off?'

'I suppose so.' Humber sounded depressed.

'It's a bloody nuisance,' said Adams violently. He looked at me. 'Still bolstering yourself up with tranquillizers?'

'Yes, sir.'

He laughed rudely. He thought it very funny. Then his face changed to a scowl, and he said savagely to Humber, 'It's useless, I can see that. Give him the chop, then.'

Humber turned away, and said, 'Right, I'll get it done tomorrow.'

Their footsteps moved off to the next box. I looked at Mickey. I had done my best for him, but he was too far gone, and had been from the beginning. After a fortnight, what with his mental chaos, his continual state of druggedness, and his persistent refusal to eat, Mickey's condition was pitiable, and anyone less stony than Humber would have had him put down long ago.

I made him comfortable for his last night and evaded yet another slash from his teeth. I couldn't say I was sorry not to have to deal with him any more, as a fortnight of looking after an unhinged horse would be enough for anyone; but the fact that he was to be put down the next day meant that I would have to perform my experiment without delay.

I didn't feel ready to do it. Thinking about it, as I put away my brushes for the night and walked across the yard towards the kitchen, I tried to find one good reason for putting it off.

The alacrity with which a good excuse for not doing

it presented itself led me to the unwelcome, swingeing realization that for the first time since my childhood, I was thoroughly afraid.

I could get October to make the experiment, I thought, on Six-Ply. Or on any of the other horses. I hadn't got to do it myself. It would be definitely more prudent not to do it myself. October could do it with absolute safety, but if Humber found me out I was as good as dead: therefore I should leave it to October.

That was when I knew I was afraid, and I didn't like it. It took me most of the evening to decide to do the experiment myself. On Mickey. The next morning. Shuffling it off on to October doubtless would have been more prudent, but I had myself to live with afterwards. What had I really wanted to leave home for, if not to find out what I could or couldn't do?

When I took the bucket to the office door in the morning for Mickey's last dose of phenobarbitone, there was only a little left in the jar. Cass tipped the glass container upside down and tapped it on the bucket so that the last grains of white powder should not be wasted.

'That's his lot, poor bastard,' he observed, putting the stopper back in the empty jar. 'Pity there isn't a bit more left, we could have given him a double dose, just this once. Well, get on with it,' he added sharply. 'Don't hang about looking mournful. It's not you that's going to be shot this afternoon.'

Well, I hoped not.

I turned away, went along to the tap, splashed in a little water, swilled round in it the instantly dissolved phenobarbitone, and poured it away down the drain. Then I filled the bucket with clean water and took it along for Mickey to drink.

He was dying on his feet. The bones stuck out more sharply under his skin and his head hung down below his shoulders. There was still a disorientated wildness in his eye, but he was going downhill so fast that he had little strength left for attacking anyone. For once he made no attempt to bite me when I put the bucket down at his head, but lowered his mouth into it and took a few half-hearted swallows.

Leaving him, I went along to the tack room and took a new head collar out of the basket of stores. This was strictly against the rules: only Cass was supposed to issue new tack. I took the head collar along to Mickey's box and fitted it on to him, removing the one he had weakened by constant fretting during his fortnight's illness and hiding it under a pile of straw. I unclipped the tethering chain from the old collar and clipped it on to the ring of the new one. I patted Mickey's neck, which he didn't like, walked out of his box, and shut and bolted only the bottom half of the door.

We rode out the first lot, and the second lot; and by then, I judged, Mickey's brain, without its morning dose, would be coming out of its sedation.

Leading Dobbin, the horse I had just returned on, I went to look at Mickey over the stable door. His head was weaving weakly from side to side, and he seemed very restless. Poor creature, I thought. Poor creature. And for a few seconds I was going to make him suffer more.

Humber stood at his office door, talking to Cass. The lads were bustling in and out looking after their horses, buckets were clattering, voices calling to each other: routine stable noise. I was never going to have a better opportunity.

I began to lead Dobbin across the yard to his box. Halfway there I took the whistle out of my belt and pulled off its cap: then, looking round to make sure that no one was watching, I turned my head over my shoulder, put the tiny mouthpiece to my lips, and blew hard. Only a thread of sound came out, so high that I could hardly hear it above the clatter of Dobbin's feet on the ground.

The result was instantaneous and hideous.

Mickey screamed with terror.

His hooves threshed wildly against the floor and walls, and the chain which held him rattled as he jerked against it.

I walked Dobbin quickly the few remaining yards into his stall, clipped his chain on, zipped the whistle back into my belt, and ran across towards Mickey's box. Everyone else was doing the same. Humber was limping swiftly down the yard.

Mickey was still screaming and crashing his hooves against the wall as I looked into his box over the shoulders of Cecil and Lenny. The poor animal was on his hind legs, seemingly trying to beat his way through the bricks in front of him. Then suddenly, with all his ebbing strength, he dropped his forelegs to the ground and charged backwards.

'Look out,' shouted Cecil, instinctively retreating from the frantically bunching hind-quarters, although he was safely outside a solid door.

Mickey's tethering chain was not very long. There was a sickening snap as he reached the end of it and his backwards momentum was joltingly, appallingly stopped. His hind legs slid forward under his belly and he fell with a crash on to his side. His legs jerked stiffly. His head, still secured in the strong new head collar, was held awkwardly off the ground by the taut chain, and by its unnatural angle told its own tale. He had broken his neck. As indeed, to put him quickly out of his frenzy, I had hoped he might.

Everyone in the yard had gathered outside Mickey's box. Humber, having glanced perfunctorily over the door at the dead horse, turned and looked broodingly at his six ragged stable lads. The narrow-eyed harshness of his expression stopped anyone asking him questions. There was a short silence.

'Stand in line,' he said suddenly.

The lads looked surprised, but did as he said.

'Turn out your pockets,' said Humber.

Mystified, the lads obeyed. Cass went down the line, looking at what was produced and pulling the pockets out like wings to make sure they were empty. When he came to me I showed him a dirty handkerchief, a pen-knife, a few coins, and pulled my pockets inside out. He took the handkerchief from my hand, shook it out, and gave it back. The whistle at my waist was only an inch from his fingers.

I felt Humber's searching gaze on me from six feet away, but as I studied to keep my face vacantly relaxed and vaguely puzzled I was astonished to find that I was neither sweating nor tensing my muscles to make a run for it. In an odd way the nearness of the danger made me cool and clear headed. I didn't understand it, but it certainly helped.

'Back pocket?' asked Cass.

'Nothing in it,' I said casually, turning half round to show him.

'All right. Now you, Kenneth.'

I pushed my pockets in again, and replaced their contents. My hands were steady. Extraordinary, I thought.

Humber watched and waited until Kenneth's pockets had been innocently emptied: then he looked at Cass and jerked his head towards the loose boxes. Cass rooted around in the boxes of the horses we had just exercised. He finished the last, came back, and shook his head. Humber pointed silently towards the garage which sheltered his Bentley. Cass disappeared, reappeared, and again unexcitedly shook his head. In silence Humber limped away to his office, leaning on his heavy stick.

He couldn't have heard the whistle, and he didn't suspect that any of us had blown one for the sole purpose of watching its effect on Mickey, because if he had he would have had us stripped and searched from head to foot. He was still thinking along the lines of Mickey's death being an accident: and having found no whistle in any of the lads' pockets or in their horses' boxes he would conclude, I hoped, that it was none of that downtrodden bunch who had caused Mickey's brainstorm. If only Adams would agree with him, I was clear.

It was my afternoon for washing the car. Humber's own whistle was still there, tucked neatly into a leather retaining strap between a cork-screw and a pair of ice tongs. I looked and left it where it was.

Adams came the next day.

Mickey had gone to the dog-meat man, who had grumbled about his thinness, and I had unobtrusively returned the new head collar to the store basket, leaving the old one dangling as usual from the tethering chain. Even Cass had not noticed the substitution.

Adams and Humber strolled along to Mickey's empty box and leaned on the half door, talking. Jerry poked his head out of the box next door, saw them standing there, and hurriedly disappeared again. I went normally about my business, fetching hay and water for Dobbin and carting away the muck sack.

'Roke,' shouted Humber, 'come over here. At the double.'

I hurried over. 'Sir?'

'You haven't cleaned out this box.'

'I'm sorry sir. I'll do it this afternoon.'

'You will do it,' he said deliberately, 'before you have your dinner.'

He knew very well that this meant having no dinner at all. I glanced at his face. He was looking at me with calculation, his eyes narrowed and his lips pursed.

I looked down. 'Yes, sir,' I said meekly. Damn it, I thought furiously; this was too soon. I had been there not quite eight weeks, and I ought to have been able to count on at least three more. If he were already intent on making me leave, I was not going to be able to finish the job.

'For a start,' said Adams, 'you can fetch out that bucket and put it away.'

I looked into the box. Mickey's bucket still stood by the manger. I opened the door, walked over, picked it up, turned round to go back, and stopped dead.

Adams had come into the box after me. He held Humber's walking stick in his hand, and he was smiling.

I dropped the bucket and backed into a corner. He laughed.

'No tranquillizers today, eh, Roke?'

I didn't answer.

He swung his arm and the knobbed end of the stick landed on my ribs. It was hard enough, in all conscience. When he lifted his arm again I ducked under it and bolted out through the door. His roar of laughter floated after me.

I went on running until I was out of sight, and then walked and rubbed my chest. It was going to be a fair-sized bruise, and I wasn't too keen on collecting many more. I supposed I should be thankful at least that they proposed to rid themselves of me in the ordinary way, and not over a hillside in a burning car.

All through that long, hungry afternoon I tried to decide what was best to do. To go at once, resigned to the fact that I couldn't finish the job, or to stay the few days I safely could without arousing Adams' suspicions. But what, I depressedly wondered, could I discover in three or four days that I had been unable to discover in eight weeks.

It was Jerry, of all people, who decided for me.

After supper (baked beans on bread, and not enough of it) we sat at the table with Jerry's comic spread open. Since Charlie had left no one had a radio, and the evenings were more boring than ever. Lenny and Kenneth were playing dice on the floor. Cecil was out getting drunk. Bert sat in his silent world on the bench on the other side of Jerry, watching the dice roll across the concrete.

The oven door was open, and all the switches on the electric stove were turned on as high as they would go.

This was Lenny's bright idea for supplementing the small heat thrown out by the paraffin stove Humber had grudgingly provided. It wouldn't last longer than the arrival of the electricity bill, but it was warm meanwhile.

The dirty dishes were stacked in the sink. Cobwebs hung like a cornice where the walls met the ceiling. A naked light bulb lit the brick-walled room. Someone had spilled tea on the table, and the corner of Jerry's comic had soaked it up.

I sighed. To think that I wasn't happy to be about to leave this squalid existence, now that I was being given no choice!

Jerry looked up from his comic, keeping his place with his finger.

'Dan?'

'Mmm?'

'Did Mr Adams bash you?'

'Yes.'

'I thought he did.' He nodded several times, and went back to his comic.

I suddenly remembered his having looked out of the box next to Mickey's before Adams and Humber had called me over.

'Jerry,' I said slowly, 'did you hear Mr Adams and Mr Humber talking, while you were in the box with Mr Adams' black hunter?'

'Yes,' he said, without looking up.

'What did they say?'

'When you ran away Mr Adams laughed and told the boss you wouldn't stand it long. Stand it long,' he repeated vaguely, like a refrain, 'stand it long.'

'Did you hear what they said before that? When they first got there, and you looked out and saw them?'

This troubled him. He sat up and forgot to keep his place.

'I didn't want the boss to know I was still there, see? I ought to have finished that hunter a good bit before then.'

'Yes. Well, you're all right. They didn't catch you.'

He grinned and shook his head.

'What did they say?' I prompted.

'They were cross about Mickey. They said they would get on with the next one at once.'

'The next what?'

'I don't know.'

'Did they say anything else?'

He screwed up his thin little face. He wanted to please me, and I knew this expression meant he was thinking his hardest.

'Mr Adams said you had been with Mickey too long, and the boss said yes it was a bad ... a bad ... um ... oh, yes ... risk, and you had better leave, and Mr Adams said yes, get on with that as quick as you can and we'll do the next one as soon as he's gone.' He opened his eyes wide in triumph at this sustained effort.

'Say that again,' I said. 'The last bit, that's all.'

One thing Jerry could do, from long practice with the comics, was to learn by heart through his ears.

260

Obediently he repeated, 'Mr Adams said get on with that as quick as you can and we'll do the next one as soon as he's gone.'

'What do you want most on earth?' I asked.

He looked surprised and thoughtful, and finally a dreamy look spread over his face.

'Well?'

'A train,' he said. 'One you wind up. You know. And rails and things. And a signal.' He fell silent in rapture.

'You shall have them,' I said. 'As soon as I can get them.'

His mouth opened.

I said, 'Jerry, I'm leaving here. You can't stay when Mr Adams starts bashing you, can you? So I'll have to go. But I'll send you the train. I won't forget, I promise.'

The evening dragged away as so many others had done, and we climbed the ladder to our unyielding beds, where I lay on my back in the dark with my hands laced behind my head and thought about Humber's stick crashing down somewhere on my body in the morning. Rather like going to the dentist for a drilling, I thought ruefully: the anticipation was worse than the event. I sighed, and went to sleep.

Operation Eviction continued as much as expected, the next day.

When I was unsaddling Dobbin after the second exercise Humber walked into the box behind me and his stick landed with a thud across my back.

I let go of the saddle – which fell on a pile of fresh droppings – and swung round.

'What did I do wrong, sir?' I said, in an aggrieved voice. I thought I might as well make it difficult for him, but he had an answer ready.

'Cass tells me you were late back at work last Saturday afternoon. And pick up that saddle. What do you think you're doing, dropping it in that dirt?'

He stood with his legs planted firmly apart, his eyes judging his distance.

Well, all right, I thought. One more, and that's enough.

I turned round and picked up the saddle. I already had it in my arms and was straightening up when he hit me again, more or less in the same place, but much harder. The breath hissed through my teeth.

I threw the saddle down again in the dirt and shouted at him. 'I'm leaving. I'm off. Right now.'

'Very well,' he said coldly, with perceptible satisfaction. 'Go and pack. Your cards will be waiting for you in the office.' He turned on his heel and slowly limped away, his purpose successfully concluded.

How frigid he was, I thought. Unemotional, sexless, and calculating. Impossible to think of him loving, or being loved, or feeling pity, or grief, or any sort of fear.

I arched my back, grimacing, and decided to leave Dobbin's saddle where it was, in the dirt. A nice touch, I thought. In character, to the bitter end.

CHAPTER FIFTEEN

I took the polythene sheeting off the motor-cycle and coasted gently out of the yard. All the lads were out exercising the third lot, with yet more to be ridden when they got back; and even while I was wondering how five of them were possibly going to cope with thirty horses, I met a shifty-looking boy trudging slowly up the road to Humber's with a kit bag slung over his shoulder. More flotsam. If he had known what he was going to, he would have walked more slowly still.

I biked to Clavering, a dreary mining town of mean back-to-back terraced streets jazzed up with chromium and glass in the shopping centre, and telephoned to October's London house.

Terence answered. Lord October, he said, was in Germany, where his firm were opening a new factory.

'When will he be back?'

'Saturday morning, I think. He went last Sunday, for a week.'

'Is he going to Slaw for the weekend?'

'I think so. He said something about flying back to

Manchester, and he's given me no instructions for anything here.'

'Can you find the addresses and telephone numbers of Colonel Beckett and Sir Stuart Macclesfield for me?'

'Hang on a moment.' There was a fluttering of pages, and Terence told me the numbers and addresses. I wrote them down and thanked him.

'Your clothes are still here, sir,' he said.

'I know,' I grinned. 'I'll be along to collect them quite soon, I think.'

We rang off, and I tried Beckett's number. A dry, precise voice told me that Colonel Beckett was out, but that he would be dining at his Club at nine, and could be reached then. Sir Stuart Macclesfield, it transpired, was in a nursing home recovering from pneumonia. I had hoped to be able to summon some help in keeping a watch on Humber's yard so that when the horse-box left with Kandersteg on board it could be followed. It looked, however, as though I would have to do it myself, as I could visualize the local police neither believing my story nor providing anyone to assist me.

Armed with a rug and a pair of good binoculars bought in a pawn shop, and also with a pork pie, slabs of chocolate, a bottle of Vichy water, and some sheets of foolscap paper, I rode the motor-cycle back through Posset and out along the road which crossed the top of the valley in which Humber's stables lay. Stopping at the point I had marked on my previous excursion, I wheeled the cycle a few yards down into the scrubby heathland, and found a position where I was off the sky line, more or less out of sight from passing cars, and also looking down into Humber's yard through the binoculars. It was one o'clock, and there was nothing happening there.

I unbuckled the suitcase from the carrier and used it as a seat, settling myself to stay there for a long time. Even if I could reach Beckett on the telephone at nine, he wouldn't be able to rustle up reinforcements much before the next morning.

There was, meanwhile, a report to make, a fuller, more formal, more explanatory affair than the notes scribbled in Posset's post office. I took out the foolscap paper and wrote, on and off, for most of the afternoon, punctuating my work by frequent glances through the binoculars. But nothing took place down at Humber's except the normal routine of the stable.

I began . . .

To The Earl of October.

    Sir Stuart Macclesfield.

    Colonel Roderick Beckett.

Sirs,

    The following is a summary of the facts which have so far come to light during my investigations on your behalf, together with some deductions which it seems reasonable to make from them.

    Paul James Adams and Hedley Humber started collaborating in a scheme for ensuring winners about four years ago, when Adams bought the Manor House and came to live at Tellbridge, Northumberland.

Adams (in my admittedly untrained opinion) has a psychopathic personality, in that he impulsively gives himself pleasure and pursues his own ends without any consideration for other people or much apparent anxiety about the consequences to himself. His intelligence seems to be above average, and it is he who gives the orders. I believe it is fairly common for psychopaths to be aggressive swindlers: it might be enlightening to dig up his life history.

Humber, though dominated by Adams, is not as irresponsible. He is cold and controlled at all times. I have never seen him genuinely angry (he uses anger as a weapon) and everything he does seems to be thought out and calculated. Whereas Adams may be mentally abnormal, Humber seems to be simply wicked. His comparative sanity may act as a brake on Adams, and have prevented their discovery before this.

Jud Wilson, the head travelling-lad, and Cass, the head lad, are both involved, but only to the extent of being hired subordinates. Neither of them does as much stable work as their jobs would normally entail, but they are well paid. Both own big cars of less than a year old.

Adams' and Humber's scheme is based on the

fact that horses learn by association and connect noises to events. Like Pavlov's dogs who would come to the sound of a bell because they had been taught it meant feeding time, horses hearing the feed trolley rattling across a stable yard know very well that their food is on the way.

If a horse is accustomed to a certain consequence following closely on a certain noise, he automatically *expects* the consequence whenever he hears the noise. He reacts to the noise in anticipation of what is to come.

If something frightening were substituted – if, for instance, the rattle of the feed trolley were followed always by a thrashing and no food – the horse would soon begin to fear the noise, because of what it portended.

Fear is the stimulant which Adams and Humber have used. The appearance of all the apparently 'doped' horses after they had won – the staring, rolling eyes and the heavy sweat – was consistent with their having been in a state of terror.

Fear strongly stimulates the adrenal glands, so that they flood the bloodstream with adrenalin: and the effect of extra adrenalin, as of course you know, is to release the upsurge of energy needed to deal with the situation, either by fighting back or by running away. Running, in this case. At top speed, in panic.

The laboratory reports stated that the samples taken from all the original eleven horses showed a high adrenalin content, but this was not significant because horses vary enormously, some always producing more adrenalin than others. I, however, think that it *was* significant that the adrenalin counts of those eleven horses were uniformly higher than average.

The noise which triggered off their fear is the high note of the sort of silent whistle normally used for training dogs. Horses can hear it well, though to human ears it is faint: this fact makes it ideal for the purpose, as a more obtrusive sound (a football rattle, for instance) would soon have been spotted. Humber keeps a dog whistle in the drinks compartment of his Bentley.

I do not yet know for sure how Adams and Humber frighten the horses, but I can make a guess.

For a fortnight I looked after a horse known in the yard as Mickey (registered name, Starlamp) who had been given the treatment. In Mickey's case, it was a disaster. He returned from three days' absence with large raw patches on his fore legs and in a completely unhinged mental state.

The wounds on his legs were explained by the head lad as having been caused by the application of a blister. But there was no blister paste to be seen, and I think they were ordinary burns caused by some sort of naked flame. Horses are more afraid of fire than of anything else, and it seems probable to me that it is expectation of being burnt that Adams and Humber have harnessed to the sound of a dog whistle.

I blew a dog whistle to discover its effect on Mickey. It was less than three weeks after the association had been planted, and he reacted violently and unmistakably. If you care to, you can repeat this trial on Six-Ply; but give him room to bolt in safety.

Adams and Humber chose horses which looked promising throughout their racing careers but had never won on account of running out of steam or guts at the last fence; and there are of course any number of horses like this. They bought them cheaply one at a time from auction sales or out of selling races, instilled into them a noise-fear association, and quietly sold them again. Often, far from losing on the deal, they made a profit (c.f. past histories of horses collected by officer cadets).

Having sold a horse with such a built-in accelerator, Adams and Humber then waited for it to run in a selling 'chase at one of five courses: Sedgefield, Haydock, Ludlow, Kelso, and Stafford. They seem to have been prepared to wait indefinitely for this combination of place and event to occur, and in fact it has only occurred twelve times (eleven winners and Superman) since the first case twenty months ago.

These courses were chosen, I imagine, because their extra long run-in gave the most room for the panic to take effect. The horses were often lying fourth or fifth when landing over the last fence, and needed time to overhaul the leaders. If a horse was left too hopelessly behind, Adams and Humber could just have left the whistle unblown, forfeited their stake money, and waited for another day.

Selling 'chases were preferred, I think, because horses are less likely to fall in them, and because of the good possibility of the winners changing hands yet again immediately afterwards.

At first sight it looks as if it would have been safer to have applied this scheme to Flat racing: but Flat racers do not seem to change hands so often, which would lessen the confusion. Then again Humber has never held a Flat licence, and probably can't get one.

None of the horses has been galvanized twice, the reason probably being that having once discovered they were not burnt after hearing the whistle they would be less likely to expect to be again. Their reaction would no longer be reliable enough to gamble on.

All the eleven horses won at very long odds, varying from 10–1 to 50–1, and Adams and Humber must have spread their bets thinly enough to raise no comment. I do not know how much Adams won on each race, but the least Humber made was seventeen hundred pounds, and the most was four thousand five hundred.

Details of all the processed horses, successful and unsuccessful, are recorded in a blue ledger at present to be found at the back of the third drawer down in the centre one of three green filing cabinets in Humber's stable office.

Basically, as you see, it is a simple plan. All they do is make a horse associate fire with a dog whistle, and then blow a whistle as he lands over the last fence.

No drugs, no mechanical contrivances, no help needed from owner, trainer, or jockey. There was only a slight risk of Adams and Humber being found out, because their connection with the horses was so obscure and distant.

Stapleton, however, suspected them, and I am certain in my own mind that they killed him, although there is no supporting evidence.

They believe now that they are safe and undetected: and they intend, during the next

few days, to plant fear in a horse called
Kandersteg. I have left Humber's employ and
am writing this while keeping a watch on the
yard. I propose to follow the horse box when
Kandersteg leaves in it, and discover where and
how the heat is applied.

I stopped writing and picked up the binoculars. The
lads were bustling about doing evening stables and I
enjoyed not being down there among them.

It was too soon, I thought, to expect Humber to start
on Kandersteg, however much of a hurry he and Adams
were in. They couldn't have known for certain that I
would depart before lunch, or even that day, and they
were bound to let my dust settle before making a move.
On the other hand I couldn't risk missing them. Even
the two miles to the telephone in Posset made ringing
up Beckett a worrying prospect. It would take no
longer for Kandersteg to be loaded up and carted off
than for me to locate Beckett in his Club. Mickey-Starlamp had been both removed and brought back in daylight, and it might be that Humber never moved any
horses about by night. But I couldn't be sure. I bit the
end of my pen in indecision. Finally, deciding not to
telephone, I added a postscript to the report.

I would very much appreciate some help in this
watch, because if it continues for several days I
could easily miss the horse box through falling

asleep. I can be found two miles out of Posset on the Hexham road, at the head of the valley which Humber's stables lie in.

I added the time, the date, and signed my name. Then I folded the report into an envelope, and addressed it to Colonel Beckett.

I raced down to Posset to put the letter in the box outside the post office. Four miles. I was away for just under six minutes. It was lucky, I think, that I met no traffic on either part of the trip. I skidded to a worried halt at the top of the hill, but all appeared normal down in the stables. I wheeled the motor-cycle off the road again, down to where I had been before, and took a long look through the binoculars.

It was beginning to get dark and lights were on in nearly all the boxes, shining out into the yard. The dark looming bulk of Humber's house, which lay nearest to me, shut off from my sight his brick office and all the top end of the yard, but I had a sideways view of the closed doors of the horse boxes, of which the fourth from the left was occupied by Kandersteg.

And there he was, a pale washy chestnut, moving across and catching the light as Bert tossed his straw to make him comfortable for the night. I sighed with relief, and sat down again to watch.

The routine work went on, untroubled, unchanged. I watched Humber, leaning on his stick, make his slow inspection round the yard, and absent-mindedly rubbed the bruises he had given me that morning. One by one the doors were shut and the lights went out until only a single window glowed yellow, the last window along the right-hand row of boxes, the window of the lads' kitchen. I put down the binoculars, and got to my feet and stretched.

As always on the moors the air was on the move. It wasn't a wind, scarcely a breeze, more like a cold current flowing round whatever it found in its path. To break its chilling persistence on my back I constructed a rough barricade of the motor-cycle with a bank of brushwood on its roadward, moorward side. In the lee of this shelter I sat on the suitcase, wrapped myself in the rug, and was tolerably warm and comfortable.

I looked at my watch. Almost eight o'clock. It was a fine, clear night, and the sky was luminous with the white blaze of the stars. I still hadn't learned the northern hemisphere patterns except for the Great Bear and Pole Star. And there was Venus dazzling away to the west-south-west. A pity that I hadn't thought of buying an astral map to pass the time.

Down in the yard the kitchen door opened, spilling out an oblong of light. Cecil's figure stayed there for a few seconds silhouetted; then he came out and shut the door, and I couldn't see him in the dark. Off to his bottle, no doubt.

I ate some pie, and a while later, a bar of chocolate.

Time passed. Nothing happened down in Humber's yard. Occasionally a car sped along the road behind me, but none stopped. Nine o'clock came and went. Colonel Beckett would be dining at his Club, and I could after all have gone safely down to ring him up. I shrugged in the darkness. He would get my letter in the morning, anyway.

The kitchen door opened again, and two or three lads came out, picking their way with a torch round to the elementary sanitation. Upstairs in the hayloft a light showed dimly through that half of the window not pasted over with brown paper. Bedtime. Cecil reeled in, clutching the doorpost to stop himself from falling. The downstairs light went out, and finally the upper one as well.

The night deepened. The hours passed. The moon rose and shone brightly. I gazed out over the primeval rolling moors and thought some unoriginal thoughts, such as how beautiful the earth was, and how vicious the ape creature who inhabited it. Greedy, destructive, unkind, power-hungry old homo sapiens. Sapiens meaning wise, discreet, judicious. What a laugh. So fair a planet should have evolved a sweeter-natured, saner race. Nothing that produced people like Adams and Humber could be termed a roaring success.

At four o'clock I ate some more chocolate and drank some water, and for some time thought about my stud farm sweltering in the afternoon sun twelve thousand miles away. A sensible, orderly life waiting for me when I had finished sitting on wintry hillsides in the middle of the night.

Cold crept through the blanket as time wore on, but it was no worse than the temperature in Humber's dormitory. I yawned and rubbed my eyes, and began to work out how many seconds had to pass before dawn. If the sun rose (as expected) at ten to seven, that would be a hundred and thirteen times sixty seconds, which made it six thousand seven hundred and eighty ticks to Thursday. And how many to Friday? I gave up. It was quite likely I would still be sitting on the hillside, but with a little luck there would be a Beckett-sent companion to give me a pinch when things started moving.

At six fifteen the light went on again in the lads' quarters, and the stable woke up. Half an hour later the first string of six horses wound its way out of the yard and down the road to Posset. No gallops on the moors on Thursday. Road work day.

Almost before they were out of sight Jud Wilson drove into the yard in his substantial Ford and parked it beside the horse box shed. Cass walked across the yard to meet him, and the two of them stood talking together for a few minutes. Then through the binoculars I watched Jud Wilson go back to the shed and open its big double doors, while Cass made straight for Kandersteg's box, the fourth door from the end.

They were off.

And they were off very slickly. Jud Wilson backed the box into the centre of the yard and let down the ramp. Cass led the horse straight across and into the horse box, and within a minute was out helping to raise and fasten the ramp again. There was a fractional pause while they stood looking towards the house, from where almost instantly the limping back-view of Humber appeared.

Cass stood watching while Humber and Jud Wilson climbed up into the cab. The horse box rolled forward out of the yard. The loading up had taken barely five minutes from start to finish.

During this time I dropped the rug over the suitcase and kicked the brushwood away from the bike. The binoculars I slung round my neck and zipped inside the leather jacket. I put on my crash helmet, goggles, and gloves.

In spite of my belief that it would be to the north or the west that Kandersteg would be taken, I was relieved when this proved to be the case. The horse box turned sharply west and trundled up the far side of the valley along the road which crossed the one I was stationed on.

I wheeled the bike on to the road, started it, and abandoning (this time with pleasure) my third clump of clothes, rode with some dispatch towards the cross-roads. There from a safe quarter of a mile away I watched the horse box slow down, turn right, north-wards, and accelerate.

CHAPTER SIXTEEN

I crouched in a ditch all day and watched Adams, Humber, and Jud Wilson scare Kandersteg into a lathering frenzy.

It was wicked.

The means they used were as simple in essence as the scheme, and consisted mainly in the special lay-out of a small two-acre field.

The thin high hedge round the whole field was laced with wire to about shoulder height, strong, but without barbs. About fifteen feet inside this there was a second fence, solidly made of posts and rails which had weathered to a pleasant greyish-brown.

At first glance it looked like the arrangement found at many stud farms, where young stock are kept from damaging themselves on wire by a wooden protective inner fence. But the corners of this inner ring had been rounded, so that what in effect had been formed was a miniature race track between the outer and inner fences.

It all looked harmless. A field for young stock, a

training place for racehorses, a show ring . . . take your pick. With a shed for storing equipment, just outside the gate at one corner. Sensible. Ordinary.

I half-knelt, half-lay in the drainage ditch which ran along behind the hedge, near the end of one long side of the field, with the shed little more than a hundred yards away in the far opposite corner, to my left. The bottom of the hedge had been cut and laid, which afforded good camouflage for my head, but from about a foot above the ground the leafless hawthorn grew straight up, tall and weedy; as concealing as a sieve. But as long as I kept absolutely still, I judged I was unlikely to be spotted. At any rate, although I was really too close for safety, too close even to need to use the binoculars, there was nowhere else which gave much cover at all.

Bare hillsides sloped up beyond the far fence and along the end of the field to my right; behind me lay a large open pasture of at least thirty acres; and the top end, which was screened from the road by a wedge of conifers, was directly under Adams' and Humber's eyes.

Getting to the ditch had entailed leaving the inade-quate shelter of the last flattening shoulder of the hill-side and crossing fifteen yards of bare turf when none of the men was in sight. But retreating was going to be less pulse quickening, since I had only to wait for the dark.

The horse box was parked beside the shed, and

almost as soon as I had worked my way round the hill to my present position there was a clattering of hooves on the ramp as Kandersteg was unloaded. Jud Wilson led him round through the gate and on to the grassy track. Adams, following, shut the gate and then unlatched a swinging section of the inner fence and fastened it across the track, making a barrier. Walking past Jud and the horse he did the same with another section a few yards further on, with the result that Jud and Kandersteg were now standing in a small pen in the corner. A pen with three ways out; the gate out of the field, and the rails which swung across like level crossing gates on either side.

Jud let go of the horse, which quietly began to eat the grass, and he and Adams let themselves out and disappeared into the shed to join Humber. The shed, made out of weathered wood, was built like a single loose box, with a window and split door, and I imagined it was there that Mickey had spent much of the three days he had been away.

There was a certain amount of clattering and banging in the shed, which went on for some time, but as I had only a side-ways view of the door I could see nothing of what was happening.

Presently all three of them came out. Adams walked round behind the shed and reappeared beyond the field, walking up the hillside. He went at a good pace right to the top, and stood gazing about him at the countryside.

Humber and Wilson came through the gate into the field, carrying between them an apparatus which looked like a vacuum cleaner, a cylindrical tank with a hose attached to one end. They put the tank down in the corner, and Wilson held the hose. Kandersteg, quietly cropping the grass close beside them, lifted his head and looked at them, incurious and trusting. He bent down again to eat.

Humber walked the few steps along to where the swinging rail was fastened to the hedge, seemed to be checking something, and then went back to stand beside Wilson, who was looking up towards Adams.

On top of the hill, Adams casually waved his hand.

Down in one corner of the field Humber had his hand to his mouth . . . I was too far away to see with the naked eye if what he held there was a whistle, and too close to risk getting out the glasses for a better look. But even though try as I might I could hear no noise, there wasn't much room for doubt. Kandersteg raised his head, pricked his ears, and looked at Humber.

Flame suddenly roared from the hose in Wilson's hand. It was directed behind the horse, but it frightened him badly, all the same. He sat back on his haunches, his ears flattening. Then Humber's arm moved, and the swinging barrier, released by some sort of catch, sprang back to let the horse out onto the track. He needed no telling.

He stampeded round the field, skidding at the corners, lurching against the inner wooden rail, thundering past ten feet from my head. Wilson opened the second barrier, and he and Humber retired through the gate. Kandersteg made two complete circuits at high speed before his stretched neck relaxed to a more normal angle and his wildly thrusting hind quarters settled down to a more natural gallop.

Humber and Wilson stood and watched him, and Adams strolled down the hill to join them at the gate.

They let the horse slow down and stop of his own accord, which he did away to my right, after about three and a half circuits. Then Jud Wilson unhurriedly swung one of the barriers back across the track, and waving a stick in one hand and a hunting whip in the other, began to walk round to drive the horse in front of him along into the corner. Kandersteg trotted warily ahead, unsettled, sweating, not wanting to be caught.

Jud Wilson swung his stick and his whip and trudged steadily on. Kandersteg trotted softly past where I lay, his hooves swishing through the short grass: but I was no longer watching. My face was buried in the roots of the hedge, and I ached with the effort of keeping still. Seconds passed like hours.

There was a rustle of trouser leg brushing against trouser leg, a faint clump of boots on turf, a crack of the long thong of the whip . . . and no outraged yell of discovery. He went past, and on up the field.

The muscles which had been ready to expel me out of the ditch and away towards the hidden motor-cycle gradually relaxed. I opened my eyes and looked at leaf mould close to my face, and worked some saliva into my mouth. Cautiously, inch by inch, I raised my head and looked across the field.

The horse had reached the barrier and Wilson was unhooking and swinging the other one shut behind him, so that he was again penned into the small enclosure. There, for about half an hour, the three men left him. They themselves walked back into the shed, where I could not see them, and I could do nothing but wait for them to appear again.

It was a fine, clear, quiet morning, but a bit cold for lying in ditches, especially damp ones. Exercise, however, beyond curling and uncurling my toes and fingers, was a bigger risk than pneumonia; so I lay still, taking heart from the thought that I was dressed from head to foot in black, and had a mop of black hair as well, and was crouched in blackish brown rotting dead leaves. It was because of the protective colouring it offered that I had chosen the ditch in preference to a shallow dip in the hillside, and I was glad I had, because it was fairly certain that Adams from his look-out point would at once have spotted a dark intruder on the pale green hill.

I didn't notice Jud Wilson walk out of the shed, but I heard the click of the gate, and there he was, going into the little enclosure and laying his hand on Kandersteg's bridle, for all the world as if he were consoling him. But how could anyone who liked horses set about them with a flame thrower? And Jud, it was clear, was going to do it again. He left the horse, went over to the corner, picked up the hose, and stood adjusting its nozzle.

Presently Adams appeared and climbed the hill, and then Humber, limping on his stick, joined Jud in the field.

There was a long wait before Adams waved his hand, during which three cars passed along the lonely moorland road. Eventually Adams was satisfied. His arm languidly rose and fell.

Humber's hand went immediately to his mouth.

Kandersteg already knew what it meant. He was running back on his haunches in fear before the flame shot out behind him and stopped him dead.

This time there was a fiercer, longer, closer burst of fire, and Kandersteg erupted in greater terror. He came scorching round the track . . . and round again . . . it was like waiting for the ball to settle in roulette with too much staked. But he stopped this time at the top end of the field, well away from my hiding place.

Jud walked across the middle of the field to come up behind him, not round the whole track. I sighed deeply with heartfelt relief.

I had folded my limbs originally into comfortable angles, but they were beginning to ache with inactivity, and I had cramp in the calf of my right leg, but I still didn't dare move while all three men were in my sight and I in theirs.

They shut Kandersteg into his little pen and strolled

away into the field and cautiously, as quietly as I could in the rotting leaves, I flexed my arms and legs, got rid of the cramp, and discovered pins and needles instead. Ah well . . . it couldn't go on for ever.

They were, however, plainly going to repeat the process yet again. The flame thrower still lay by the hedge.

The sun was high in the sky by this time, and I looked at the gleam it raised on the leather sleeve of my left arm, close to my head. It was too shiny. Hedges and ditches held nothing as light-reflecting as black leather. Could Wilson possibly, *possibly* walk a second time within feet of me without coming close enough to the hedge to see a shimmer which shouldn't be there?

Adams and Humber came out of the shed and leaned over the gate, looking at Kandersteg. Presently they lit cigarettes and were clearly talking. They were in no hurry. They finished the cigarettes, threw them away, and stayed where they were for another ten minutes. Then Adams walked over to his car and returned with a bottle and some glasses. Wilson came out of the shed to join them and the three of them stood there in the sun, quietly drinking and gossiping in the most commonplace way.

What they were doing was, of course, routine to them. They had done it at least twenty times before. Their latest victim stood warily in his pen, unmoving, frightened, far too upset to eat.

Watching them drink made me thirsty, but that was

among the least of my troubles. Staying still was becoming more and more difficult. Painful, almost.

At long last they broke it up. Adams put the bottle and glasses away and strolled off up the hill, Humber checked the quick release on the swinging barrier, and Jud adjusted the nozzle of the hose.

Adams waved. Humber blew.

This time the figure of Kandersteg was sharply, terrifyingly silhouetted against a sheet of flame. Wilson swayed his body, and the brilliant, spreading jet flattened and momentarily swept under the horse's belly and among his legs.

I nearly cried out, as if it were I that were being burned, not the horse. And for one sickening moment it looked as if Kandersteg were too terrified to escape.

Then, squealing, he was down the track like a meteor, fleeing from fire, from pain, from a dog whistle . . .

He was going too fast to turn the corner. He crashed into the hedge, bounced off, stumbled and fell. Eyes starting out of his head, lips retracted from his teeth, he scrambled frantically to his feet and bolted on, past my head, up the field, round again, and round again.

He came to a jolting halt barely twenty yards away from me. He stood stock-still with sweat dripping from his neck and down his legs. His flesh quivered convulsively.

Jud Wilson, whip and stick in hand, started on his walk round the track. Slowly I put my face down among the roots and tried to draw some comfort from the fact that if he saw me there was still a heavily wired fence between us, and I should get some sort of start in running away. But the motor-cycle was hidden on rough ground two hundred yards behind me, and the curving road lay at least as far beyond that again, and Adams' grey Jaguar was parked on the far side of the horse box. Successful flight wasn't something I'd have liked to bet on.

Kandersteg was too frightened to move. I heard Wilson shouting at him and cracking the whip, but it was a full minute before the hooves came stumbling jerkily, in bursts and stamps, past my head.

In spite of the cold, I was sweating. Dear heavens, I thought, there was as much adrenalin pouring into my blood-stream as into the horse's; and I realized that from the time Wilson started his methodical walk round the track I had been able to hear my own heart thudding.

Jud Wilson yelled at Kandersteg so close to my ear that it felt like a blow. The whip cracked.

'Get on, get on, get on there.'

He was standing within feet of my head. Kandersteg wouldn't move. The whip cracked again. Jud shouted at the horse, stamping his boot on the ground in encouragement. The faint tremor came to me through the earth. He was a yard away, perhaps, with his eyes on the horse. He had only to turn his head . . . I began to think that anything, even discovery, was preferable to the terrible strain of keeping still.

Then, suddenly, it was over.

Kandersteg skittered away and bumped into the rails, and took a few more uneven steps back towards the top of the field. Jud Wilson moved away after him.

I continued to behave like a log, feeling exhausted. Slowly my heart subsided. I started breathing again . . . and unclamped my fingers from handfuls of leaf mould.

Step by reluctant step Jud forced Kandersteg round to the corner enclosure, where he swung the rails across and penned the horse in again. Then he picked up the flame thrower and took it with him through the gate. The job was done. Adams, Humber, and Wilson stood in a row and contemplated their handiwork.

The pale coat of the horse was blotched with huge dark patches where the sweat had broken out, and he stood stiff legged, stiff necked, in the centre of the small enclosure. Whenever any of the three men moved he jumped nervously and then stood rigidly still again: and it was clearly going to be some long time before he had unwound enough to be loaded up and taken back to Posset.

Mickey had been away three days, but that, I judged, was only because his legs had been badly burned by mistake. As Kandersteg's indoctrination appeared to have gone without a hitch, he should be back in his own stable fairly soon.

It couldn't be too soon for me and my static joints. I

watched the three men potter about in the sunlight, wandering between car and shed, shed and horse box, aimlessly passing the morning and managing never to be all safely out of sight at the same time. I cursed under my breath and resisted a temptation to scratch my nose.

At long last they made a move. Adams and Humber folded themselves into the Jaguar and drove off in the direction of Tellbridge. But Jud Wilson reached into the cab of the horse box, pulled out a paper bag, and proceeded to eat his lunch sitting on the gate. Kandersteg remained immobile in his little enclosure and I did the same in my ditch.

Jud Wilson finished his lunch, rolled the paper bag into a ball, yawned, and lit a cigarette. Kandersteg continued to sweat, and I to ache. Everything was very quiet. Time passed.

Jud Wilson finished his cigarette, threw the stub away, and yawned again. Then slowly, slowly, he climbed down from the gate, picked up the flame thrower, and took it into the shed.

He was scarcely through the door before I was slithering down into the shallow ditch, lying full length along it on my side, not caring about the dampness but thankfully, slowly, painfully, straightening one by one my cramped arms and legs.

The time, when I looked at my watch, was two o'clock. I felt hungry, and regretted that I hadn't had enough sense to bring some of the chocolate.

I lay in the ditch all afternoon, hearing nothing, but waiting for the horse box to start up and drive away. After a while in spite of the cold and the presence of Jud Wilson, I had great difficulty in keeping awake; a ridiculous state of affairs which could only be remedied by action. Accordingly I rolled over on my stomach and inch by careful inch raised my head high enough to see across to Kandersteg and the shed.

Jud Wilson was again sitting on the gate. He must have seen my movements out of the corner of his eye, because he looked away from Kandersteg, who stood in front of him, and turned his head in my direction. For a fleeting second it seemed that he was looking straight into my eyes: then his gaze swept on past me, and presently, unsuspiciously, returned to Kandersteg.

I let my held breath trickle out slowly, fighting down a cough.

The horse was still sweating, the dark patches showing up starkly, but there was a less fixed look about him, and while I watched he swished his tail and restlessly shook his neck. He was over the hump.

More cautiously still, I lowered my head and chest down again on to my folded arms, and waited some more.

Soon after four Adams and Humber came back in the Jaguar, and again, like a rabbit out of its burrow, I edged up for a look.

They decided to take the horse home. Jud Wilson backed the horse box to the gate and let down the ramp, and Kandersteg, sticking in his feet at every step, was eventually pulled and prodded into it. The poor beast's distress was all too evident, even from across the field. I liked horses. I found I was wholly satisfied that because of me Adams and Humber and Wilson were going to be out of business.

Gently I lay down again and after a short while I heard both engines – first the Jaguar's and then the horse box's – start up and drive off, back towards Posset.

When the sound of them had died away I stood up, stretched, brushed the leaf mould from my clothes, and walked round the field to look at the shed.

It was fastened shut with a complicated looking padlock, but through the window I could see it held little besides the flame thrower, some cans presumably holding fuel, a large tin funnel, and three garden chairs folded and stacked against one wall. There seemed little point in breaking in, though it would have been simple enough since the padlock fittings had been screwed straight on the surface of the door and its surround. The screwdriver blade of my penknife could have removed the whole thing, fussy padlock intact. Crooks, I reflected, could be as fantastically dim in some ways as they were imaginative in others.

I went through the gate into Kandersteg's little enclosure. The grass where he had stood was scorched. The inside surfaces of the rails had been painted white, so that they resembled racecourse rails. I stood for a

while looking at them, feeling a second-hand echo of
the misery the horse had endured in that harmless looking place, and then let myself out and walked away,
round past my hiding place in the ditch and off towards
the motor-cycle. I picked it up, hooked the crash helmet
on to the handle bars, and started the engine.

So that was the lot, I thought. My job was done.
Safely, quietly, satisfactorily done. As it should be.
Nothing remained but to complete yesterday's report
and put the final facts at the Stewards' disposal.

I coasted back to the place from where I had kept a
watch on Humber's yard, but there was no one there.
Either Beckett had not got my letter or had not been
able to send any help, or the help, if it had arrived, had
got tired of waiting and departed. The rug, suitcase, and
remains of food lay where I had left them, undisturbed.

On an impulse, before packing up and leaving the
area, I unzipped my jacket and took out the binoculars
to have a last look down into the yard.

What I saw demolished flat my complacent feeling
of safety and completion.

A scarlet sports car was turning into the yard. It
stopped beside Adams' grey Jaguar, a door opened, and
a girl got out. I was too far away to distinguish her
features but there was no mistaking that familiar car
and that dazzling silver-blonde hair. She slammed the
car door and walked hesitantly towards the office, out
of my sight.

I swore aloud. Of all the damnable, unforeseeable,

dangerous things to happen! I hadn't told Elinor anything. She thought I was an ordinary stable lad. I had
borrowed a dog whistle from her. And she was October's daughter. What were the chances, I wondered
numbly, of her keeping quiet on the last two counts and
not giving Adams the idea that she was a threat to him.

She ought to be safe enough, I thought. Reasonably,
she ought to be safe as long as she made it clear that it
was I who knew the significance of dog whistles, and
not her.

But supposing she didn't make it clear? Adams
never behaved reasonably, to start with. His standards
were not normal. He was psychopathic. He could
impulsively kill a journalist who seemed to be getting
too nosy. What was to stop him killing again, if he got it
into his head that it was necessary?

I would give her three minutes, I thought. If she
asked for me, and was told I had left, and went straight
away again, everything would be all right.

I willed her to return from the office and drive away
in her car. I doubted whether in any case if Adams were
planning to harm her I could get her out safely, since
the odds against, in the shape of Adams, Humber,
Wilson and Cass, were too great for common sense. I
wasn't too keen on having to try. But three minutes
went past, and the red car stood empty in the yard.

She had stayed to talk and she had no notion that
there was anything which should not be said. If I had
done as I wanted and told her why I was at Humber's,

she would not have come at all. It was my fault she was there. I had clearly got to do my best to see she left again in mint condition. There was no choice.

I put the binoculars in the suitcase and left it and the rug where it was. Then, zipping up the jacket and fastening on the crash helmet, I restarted the bike and rode it down and round and in through Humber's gate.

I left the bike near the gate and walked across towards the yard, passing the shed where the horse box was kept. The doors were shut, and there was no sign of Jud Wilson. Perhaps he had already gone home, and I hoped so. I went into the yard at the top end beside the wall of the office, and saw Cass at the opposite end looking over the door of the fourth box from the left. Kandersteg was home.

Adams' Jaguar and Elinor's TR4 stood side by side in the centre of the yard. Lads were hustling over their evening jobs, and everything looked normal and quiet.

I opened the office door, and walked in.

CHAPTER SEVENTEEN

So much for my fears, I thought. So much for my melo-dramatic imagination. She was perfectly safe. She held a half empty glass of pink liquid in her hand, having a friendly drink with Adams and Humber, and she was smiling.

Humber's face looked anxious, but Adams was laughing and enjoying himself. It was a picture which printed itself clearly on my mind before they all three turned and looked at me.

'Daniel!' Elinor exclaimed. 'Mr Adams said you had gone.'

'Yes. I left something behind. I came back for it.'

'Lady Elinor Tarren,' said Adams with deliberation, coming round behind me, closing the door and leaning against it, 'came to see if you had conducted the experi-ment she lent you her dog whistle for.'

It was just as well, after all, that I had gone back.

'Oh, surely I didn't say that,' she protested. 'I just came to get the whistle, if Daniel had finished with it. I mean, I was passing, and I thought I could save him the trouble of sending it . . .'

I turned to him. 'Lady Elinor Tarren,' I said with equal deliberation, 'does not know what I borrowed her whistle for. I didn't tell her. She knows nothing about it.'

His eyes narrowed and then opened into a fixed stare. His jaw bunched. He took in the way I had spoken to him, the way I looked at him. It was not what he was used to from me. He transferred his stare to Elinor.

'Leave her alone,' I said. 'She doesn't know.'

'What on earth are you talking about?' said Elinor, smiling. 'What was this mysterious experiment, anyway?'

'It wasn't important,' I said. 'There's . . . er . . . there's a deaf lad here, and we wanted to know if he could hear high pitched noises, that's all.'

'Oh,' she said, 'and could he?'

I shook my head. 'I'm afraid not.'

'What a pity.' She took a drink, and ice tinkled against the glass. 'Well, if you've no more use for it, do you think I could have my whistle back?'

'Of course.' I dug into my money belt, brought out the whistle, and gave it to her. I saw Humber's astonishment and Adams' spasm of fury that Humber's search had missed so elementary a hiding place.

'Thank you,' she said, putting the whistle in her pocket. 'What are your plans now? Another stable job?

You know,' she said to Humber, smiling, 'I'm surprised you let him go. He rode better than any lad we've ever had in Father's stables. You were lucky to have him.'

I had not ridden well for Humber. He began to say heavily, 'He's not all that good . . .' when Adams smoothly interrupted him.

'I think we have underestimated Roke, Hedley. Lady Elinor, I am sure Mr Humber will take him back on your recommendation, and never let him go again.'

'Splendid,' she said warmly.

Adams was looking at me with his hooded gaze to make sure I had appreciated his little joke. I didn't think it very funny.

'Take your helmet off,' he said. 'You're indoors and in front of a lady. Take it off.'

'I think I'll keep it on,' I said equably. And I could have done with a full suit of armour to go with it. Adams was not used to me contradicting him, and he shut his mouth with a snap.

Humber said, puzzled, 'I don't understand why you bother with Roke, Lady Elinor. I thought your father got rid of him for . . . well . . . molesting you.'

'Oh no,' she laughed. 'That was my sister. But it wasn't true, you know. It was all made up.' She swallowed the last of her drink and with the best will in the world put the finishing touches to throwing me to the wolves. 'Father made me promise not to tell anyone that it was all a story, but as you're Daniel's employer you really ought to know that he isn't anything like as bad as he lets everyone believe.'

There was a short, deep silence. Then I said, smiling, 'That's the nicest reference I've ever had . . . you're very kind.'

'Oh dear,' she laughed. 'You know what I mean . . . and I can't think why you don't stick up for yourself more.'

'It isn't always advisable,' I said, and raised an eyebrow at Adams. He showed signs of not appreciating my jokes either. He took Elinor's empty glass.

'Another gin and Campari?' he suggested.

'No thank you, I must be going.'

He put her glass down on the desk with his own, and said, 'Do you think Roke would be the sort of man who'd need to swallow tranquillizers before he found the nerve to look after a difficult horse?'

'Tranquillizers? *Tranquillizers?* Of course not. I shouldn't think he ever took a tranquillizer in his life. Did you?' she said, turning to me and beginning to look puzzled.

'No,' I said. I was very anxious for her to be on her way before her puzzlement grew any deeper. Only while she suspected nothing and learned nothing was she safe enough.

'But you said . . .' began Humber, who was still unenlightened.

'It was a joke. Only a joke,' I told him. 'Mr Adams laughed about it quite a lot, if you remember.'

'That's true. I laughed,' said Adams sombrely. At least he seemed willing for her ignorance to remain undisturbed, and to let her go.

'Oh,' Elinor's face cleared. 'Well . . . I suppose I'd better be getting back to college. I'm going to Slaw tomorrow for the weekend . . . do you have any message for my father, Daniel?'

It was a casual, social remark, but I saw Adams stiffen.

I shook my head.

'Well . . . it's been very pleasant, Mr Humber. Thank you so much for the drink. I hope I haven't taken too much of your time.'

She shook Humber's hand, and Adams', and finally mine.

'How lucky you came back for something. I thought I'd missed you . . . and that I could whistle for my whistle.' She grinned.

I laughed. 'Yes, it was lucky.'

'Goodbye then. Goodbye Mr Humber,' she said, as Adams opened the door for her. She said goodbye to him on the doorstep, where he remained, and over Humber's shoulder I watched through the window as she walked across to her car. She climbed in, started the engine, waved gaily to Adams, and drove out of the yard. My relief at seeing her go was even greater than my anxiety about getting out myself.

Adams stepped inside, shut the door, locked it, and

299

put the key in his pocket. Humber was surprised. He still did not understand.

He said, staring at me, 'You know, Roke doesn't seem the same. And his voice is different.'

'Roke, damn him to hell, is God knows what.'

The only good thing in the situation that I could see was that I no longer had to cringe when he spoke to me. It was quite a relief to be able to stand up straight for a change. Even if it didn't last long.

'Do you mean it is Roke, and not Elinor Tarren after all, who knows about the whistle?'

'Of course,' said Adams impatiently. 'For Christ's sake, don't you understand anything? It looks as though October planted him on us, though how in hell he knew . . .'

'But Roke is only a stable lad.'

'Only,' said Adams savagely. 'But that doesn't make it any better. Stable lads have tongues, don't they? And eyes? And look at him. He's not the stupid worm he's always seemed.'

'No one would take his word against yours,' said Humber.

'No one is going to take his word at all.'

'What do you mean?'

'I'm going to kill him,' said Adams.

'I suppose that might be more satisfactory.' Humber sounded as if he were discussing putting down a horse.

'It won't help you,' I said. 'I've already sent a report to the Stewards.'

'We were told that once before,' said Humber, 'but it wasn't true.'

'It is, this time.'

Adams said violently, 'Report or no report, I'm going to kill him. There are other reasons . . .' He broke off, glared at me, and said, 'You fooled me. *Me*. How?'

I didn't reply. It hardly seemed a good time for light conversation.

'This one,' said Humber reflectively, 'has a motor-cycle.'

I remembered that the windows in the office's wash room were all too small to escape through. The door to the yard was locked, and Humber stood in front of his desk, between me and the window. Yelling could only bring Cass, not the poor rabble of lads who didn't even know I was there, and wouldn't bother to help me in any case. Both Adams and Humber were taller and heavier than I was, Adams a good deal so. Humber had his stick and I didn't know what weapon Adams proposed to use; and I had never been in a serious fight in my life. The next few minutes were not too delightful a prospect.

On the other hand I was younger than they, and, thanks to the hard work they had exacted, as fit as an athlete. Also I had the crash helmet. And I could throw things . . . perhaps the odds weren't impossible, after all.

A polished wooden chair with a leather seat stood by the wall near the door. Adams picked it up and walked towards me. Humber, remaining still, slid his stick through his hands and held it ready.

I felt appallingly vulnerable.

Adams' eyes were more opaque than I had ever seen them, and the smile which was growing on his mouth didn't reach them. He said loudly, 'We might as well enjoy it. They won't look too closely at a burnt-out smash.'

He swung the chair. I dodged it all right but in doing so got within range of Humber, whose stick landed heavily on top of my shoulder, an inch from my ear. I stumbled and fell, and rolled: and stood up just in time to avoid the chair as Adams crashed it down. One of the legs broke off as it hit the floor, and Adams bent down and picked it up. A solid, straight, square-edged chair leg with a nasty sharp point where it had broken from the seat.

Adams smiled more, and kicked the remains of the chair into a corner.

'Now,' he said, 'we'll have some sport.'

If you could call it sport, I suppose they had it.

Certainly after a short space of time they were still relatively unscathed, while I added some more bruises to my collection, together with a fast bleeding cut on the forehead from the sharp end of Adams' chair leg. But the crash helmet hampered their style considerably, and I discovered a useful talent for dodging. I also kicked.

Humber, being a slow mover, stayed at his post

guarding the window and slashed at me whenever I came within his reach. As the office was not large this happened too often. I tried from the beginning either to catch hold of one of the sticks, or to pick up the broken chair, or to find something to throw, but all that happened was that my hands fared badly, and Adams guessed my intentions regarding the chair and made sure I couldn't get hold of it. As for throwing things the only suitable objects in that bare office were on Humber's desk, behind Humber.

Because of the cold night on the hillside I was wearing two jerseys under my jacket, and they did act as some sort of cushion: but Adams particularly hit very hard, and I literally shuddered whenever he managed to connect. I had had some idea of crashing out through the window, glass and all, but they gave me no chance to get there, and there was a limit to the time I could spend trying.

In desperation I stopped dodging and flung myself at Humber. Ignoring Adams, who promptly scored two fearful direct hits, I grasped my ex-employer by the lapels, and with one foot on the desk for leverage, swung him round and threw him across the narrow room. He landed with a crash against the filing cabinets.

There on the desk was the green glass paper weight. The size of a cricket ball. It slid smoothly into my hand, and in one unbroken movement I picked it up, pivoted on my toes, and flung it straight at Humber where he sprawled off-balance barely ten feet away.

It took him centrally between the eyes. A sweet shot. It knocked him unconscious. He fell without a sound.

I was across the room before he hit the floor, my hand stretching out for the green glass ball which was a better weapon to me than any stick or broken chair. But Adams understood too quickly. His arm went up.

I made the mistake of thinking that one more blow would make no real difference and didn't draw back from trying to reach the paper weight even when I knew Adams' chair leg was on its way down. But this time, because I had my head down, the crash helmet didn't save me. Adams hit me below the rim of the helmet, behind the ear.

Dizzily twisting, I fell against the wall and ended up lying with my shoulders propped against it and one leg doubled underneath me. I tried to stand up, but there seemed to be no strength left in me anywhere. My head was floating. I couldn't see very well. There was a noise inside my ears.

Adams leaned over me, unsnapped the strap of my crash helmet, and pulled it off my head. That meant something, I thought groggily. I looked up. He was standing there smiling, swinging the chair leg. Enjoying himself.

In the last possible second my brain cleared a little and I knew that if I didn't do something about it, this blow was going to be the last. There was no time to dodge. I flung up my right arm to shield my undefended head, and the savagely descending piece of wood crashed into it.

It felt like an explosion. My hand fell numb and useless by my side.

What was left? Ten seconds. Perhaps less. I was furious. I particularly didn't want Adams to have the pleasure of killing me. He was still smiling. Watching to see how I would take it, he slowly raised his arm for the *coup de grâce*.

No, I thought, no. There was nothing wrong with my legs. What on earth was I thinking of, lying there waiting to be blacked out when I still had two good legs? He was standing on my right. My left leg was bent under me and he took no special notice when I disentangled it and crossed it over in front of him. I lifted both my legs off the ground, one in front and one behind his ankles, then I kicked across with my right leg, locked my feet tight together and rolled my whole body over as suddenly and strongly as I could.

Adams was taken completely by surprise. He overbalanced with wildly swinging arms and fell with a crash on his back. His own weight made the fall more effective from my point of view, because he was winded and slow to get up. I couldn't throw any longer with my numb right hand. Staggering to my feet, I picked the green glass ball up in my left and smashed it against Adams' head while he was still on his knees. It seemed to have no effect. He continued to get up. He was grunting.

Desperately I swung my arm and hit him again, low down on the back of the head. And that time he did go down; and stayed down.

I half fell beside him, dizzy and feeling sick, with pain waking up viciously all over my body and blood from the cut on my forehead dripping slowly on to the floor.

I don't know how long I stayed like that, gasping to get some breath back, trying to find the strength to get up and leave the place, but it can't really have been very long. And it was the thought of Cass, in the end, which got me to my feet. By that stage I would have been a pushover for a toddler, let alone the wiry little head lad.

Both of the men lay in heaps on the ground, not stirring. Adams was breathing very heavily; snoring, almost. Humber's chest scarcely moved.

I passed my left hand over my face and it came away covered with blood. There must be blood all over my face, I thought. I couldn't go riding along the road covered in blood. I staggered into the washroom to rinse it off.

There were some half melted ice cubes in the sink. Ice. I looked at it dizzily. Ice in the refrigerator. Ice clinking in the drinks. Ice in the sink. Good for stopping bleeding. I picked up a lump of it and looked in the mirror. A gory sight. I held the lump of ice on the cut and tried, in the classic phrase, to pull myself together. With little success.

After a while I splashed some water into the sink and rinsed all the blood off my face. The cut was then revealed as being only a couple of inches long and not serious, though still obstinately oozing. I looked round vaguely for a towel.

On the table by the medicine cupboard stood a glass jar with the stopper off and a teaspoon beside it. My glance flickered over it, looking for a towel, and then back, puzzled. I took three shaky steps across the room. There was something the jar should be telling me, I thought, but I wasn't grasping things very clearly.

A bottle of phenobarbitone in powder form, like the stuff I'd given Mickey every day for a fortnight. Only phenobarbitone, that was all. I sighed.

Then it struck me that Mickey had had the last dose in the bottle. The bottle should be empty. Tipped out. Not full. Not a new bottle full to the bottom of the neck, with the pieces of wax from the seal still lying in crumbs on the table beside it. Someone had just opened a new bottle of soluble phenobarbitone and used a couple of spoonfuls.

Of course. For Kandersteg.

I found a towel and wiped my face. Then I went back into the office and knelt down beside Adams to get the door key out of his pocket. He had stopped snoring.

I rolled him over.

There isn't a pretty way of saying it. He was dead.

Small trickles of blood had seeped out of his ears, eyes, nose, and mouth. I felt his head where I had hit him, and the dented bones moved under my fingers.

Aghast and shaking, I searched in his pockets and found the key. Then I stood up and went slowly over to the desk to telephone to the police.

The telephone had been knocked on to the floor, where it lay with the receiver off. I bent down and picked it up clumsily left handed, and my head swam with dizziness. I wished I didn't feel so ill. Straightening up with an effort I put the telephone back on the desk. Blood started trickling again past my eyebrow. I hadn't the energy to wash it off again.

Out in the yard one or two lights were on, including the one in Kandersteg's box. His door was wide open and the horse himself, tied up by the head, was lashing out furiously in a series of kicks. He didn't look in the least sedated.

I stopped with my fingers in the dial of the telephone, and felt myself go cold. My brain cleared with a click.

Kandersteg was not sedated. They wouldn't want his memory lulled. The opposite, in fact. Mickey had not been given any phenobarbitone until he was clearly deranged.

I didn't want to believe what my mind told me; that one or more teaspoonfuls of soluble phenobarbitone in a large gin and Campari would be almost certainly fatal.

Sharply I remembered the scene I had found in the office, the drinks, the anxiety on Humber's face, the enjoyment on Adams'. It matched the enjoyment I had seen there when he thought he was killing me. He enjoyed killing. He had thought from what she had said that Elinor had guessed the purpose of the whistle, and he had wasted no time in getting rid of her.

No wonder he had raised no objections to her leaving. She would drive back to college and die in her room miles away, a silly girl who had taken an overdose. No possible connection with Adams or Humber.

And no wonder he had been so determined to kill me: not only because of what I knew about his horses, or because I had fooled him, but because I had seen Elinor drink her gin.

It didn't need too much imagination to picture the scene before I had arrived. Adams was saying smoothly, 'So you came to see if Roke had used the whistle?'

'Yes.'

'And does your father know you're here? Does he know about the whistle?'

'Oh no, I only came on impulse. Of course he doesn't know.'

He must have thought her a fool, blundering in like that: but probably he was the sort of man who thought all women were fools anyway.

'You'd like some ice in your drink? I'll get some. No bother. Just next door. Here you are, my dear, a strong gin and phenobarbitone and a quick trip to heaven.'

He had taken the same reckless risk of killing Stapleton, and it had worked. And who was to say that if I had been found in the next county over some precipice, smashed up in the ruins of a motor-cycle, and Elinor died in her college, that he wouldn't have got away with two more murders?

If Elinor died.

My finger was still in the telephone dial. I turned it three times, nine, nine, nine. There was no answer. I rattled the button, and tried again. Nothing. It was dead, the whole telephone was dead. Everything was dead, Mickey was dead, Stapleton was dead, Adams was dead, Elinor . . . stop it, stop it. I dragged my scattering wits together. If the telephone wouldn't work, someone would have to go to Elinor's college and prevent her dying.

My first thought was that I couldn't do it. But who else? If I were right, she needed a doctor urgently, and any time I wasted on bumbling about finding another telephone or another person to go in my stead was just diminishing her chances. I could reach her in less than twenty minutes. By telephoning in Posset I could hardly get help for her any quicker.

It took me three shots to get the key in the keyhole. I couldn't hold the key at all in my right hand, and the left one was shaking. I took a deep breath, unlocked the door, walked out, and shut it behind me.

No one noticed me as I went out of the yard the way I had come and went back to the motor-bike. But it didn't fire properly the first time I kicked the starter, and Cass came round the end of the row of boxes to investigate.

'Who's that?' he called. 'Is that you, Dan? What are you doing back here?' He began to come towards me.

I stamped on the starter fiercely. The engine spluttered, coughed, and roared. I squeezed the clutch and kicked the bike into gear.

'Come back,' yelled Cass. But I turned away from his hurrying figure, out of the gate and down the road to Posset, with gravel spurting under the tyres.

The throttle was incorporated into the hand grip of the right hand handle-bar. One merely twisted it towards one to accelerate and away to slow down. Twisting the hand grip was normally easy. It was not easy that evening because once I had managed to grip it hard enough to turn it the numbness disappeared from my arm with a vengeance. I damned nearly fell off before I was through the gate.

It was ten miles northeast to Durham. One and a half downhill to Posset, seven and a half across the moors on a fairly straight and unfrequented secondary road, one mile through the outskirts of the city. The last part, with turns and traffic and too much change of pace, would be the most difficult.

Only the knowledge that Elinor would probably die if I came off kept me on the motor-bike at all, and altogether it was a ride I would not care to repeat. I didn't know how many times I had been hit, but I didn't think a carpet had much to tell me. I tried to ignore it and concentrate on the matter in hand.

Elinor, if she had driven straight back to college,

could not have been there long before she began to feel sleepy. As far as I could remember, never having taken much notice, barbiturates took anything up to an hour to work. But barbiturate dissolved in alcohol was a different matter. Quicker. Twenty minutes to half an hour, perhaps. I didn't know. Twenty minutes from the time she left the yard was easily enough for her to drive back safely. Then what? She would go up to her room: feel tired: lie down: and go to sleep.

During the time I had been fighting with Adams and Humber she had been on her way to Durham. I wasn't sure how long I had wasted dithering about in the washroom in a daze, but she couldn't have been back to college much before I started after her. I wondered whether she would have felt ill enough to tell a friend, to ask for help: but even if she had, neither she nor anyone else would know what was the matter with her.

I reached Durham: made the turns: even stopped briefly for a red traffic light in a busy street: and fought down an inclination to go the last half mile at walking pace in order to avoid having to hold the throttle any more. But my ignorance of the time it would take for the poison to do irreparable damage added wings to my anxiety.

CHAPTER EIGHTEEN

It was getting dark when I swung into the college entrance, switched off the engine, and hurried up the steps to the door. There was no one at the porter's desk and the whole place was very quiet. I ran down the corridors, trying to remember the turns, found the stairs, went up two flights. And it was then that I got lost. I had suddenly no idea which way to turn to find Elinor's room.

A thin elderly woman with pince nez was walking towards me carrying a sheaf of papers and a thick book on her arm. One of the staff, I thought.

'Please,' I said, 'which is Miss Tarren's room?'

She came close to me and looked at me. She did not approve of what she saw. What would I give, I thought, for a respectable appearance at this moment.

'Please,' I repeated. 'She may be ill. Which is her room?'

'You have blood on your face,' she observed.

'It's only a cut . . . please tell me . . .' I gripped her arm. 'Look, show me her room, then if she's all right and perfectly healthy I will go away without any trouble. But I think she may need help very badly. Please believe me . . .'

'Very well,' she said reluctantly. 'We will go and see. It is just round here . . . and round here.'

We arrived at Elinor's door. I knocked hard. There was no answer. I bent down to the low keyhole. The key was in the lock on her side, and I could not see in.

'Open it,' I urged the woman, who was still eyeing me dubiously. 'Open it, and see if she's all right.'

She put her hand on the knob and turned. But the door didn't budge. It was locked.

I banged on the door again. There was no reply.

'Now please listen,' I said urgently. 'As the door is locked on the inside, Elinor Tarren is in there. She doesn't answer because she can't. She needs a doctor very urgently indeed. Can you get hold of one at once?'

The woman nodded, looking at me gravely through the pince nez. I wasn't sure that she believed me, but apparently she did.

'Tell the doctor she has been poisoned with pheno-barbitone and gin. About forty minutes ago. And please, please hurry. Are there any more keys to this door?'

'You can't push out the key that's already there. We've tried on other doors, on other occasions. You will have to break the lock. I will go and telephone.' She retreated sedately along the corridor, still breath-takingly calm in the face of a wild looking man with blood on his forehead and the news that one of her students was halfway to the coroner. A tough-minded university lecturer.

The Victorians who had built the place had not intended importunate men friends to batter down the girls' doors. They were a solid job. But in view of the thin woman's calm assumption that breaking in was within my powers, I didn't care to fail. I broke the lock with my heel, in the end. The wood gave way on the jamb inside the room, and the door opened with a crash.

In spite of the noise I had made, no students had appeared in the corridor. There was still no one about. I went into Elinor's room, switched on the light, and swung the door back into its frame behind me.

She was lying sprawled on top of her blue bedspread fast asleep, the silver hair falling in a smooth swathe beside her head. She looked peaceful and beautiful. She had begun to undress, which was why, I supposed, she had locked her door, and she was wearing only a bra and briefs under a simple slip. All these garments were white with pink rosebuds and ribbons. Pretty. Belinda would have liked them. But in these circumstances they were too poignant, too defenceless. They increased my grinding worry.

The suit which Elinor had worn at Humber's had been dropped in two places on the floor. One stocking hung over the back of a chair: the other was on the floor just beneath her slack hand. A clean pair of stockings lay on the dressing table, and a blue woollen dress on a hanger was hooked on to the outside of the ward-robe. She had been changing for the evening.

If she hadn't heard me kicking the door in she wouldn't wake by being touched, but I tried. I shook her arm. She didn't stir. Her pulse was normal, her breathing regular, her face as delicately coloured as always. Nothing looked wrong with her. I found it frightening.

How much longer, I wondered anxiously, was the doctor going to be? The door had been stubborn – or I had been weak, whichever way you looked at it – and it must have been more than ten minutes since the thin woman had gone to telephone.

As if on cue the door swung open and a tidy solid-looking middle-aged man in a grey suit stood there taking in the scene. He was alone. He carried a suitcase in one hand and a fire hatchet in the other. Coming in, he looked at the splintered wood, pushed the door shut, and put the axe down on Elinor's desk.

'That's saved time, anyway,' he said briskly. He looked me up and down without enthusiasm and gestured to me to get out of the way. Then he cast a closer glance at Elinor with her rucked up slip and her long bare legs, and said to me sharply, suspiciously, 'Did you touch her clothes?'

'No,' I said bitterly. 'I shook her arm. And felt her pulse. She was lying like that when I came in.'

Something, perhaps it was only my obvious weari-ness, made him give me a suddenly professional, impartial survey. 'All right,' he said, and bent down to Elinor.

I waited behind him while he examined her, and when he turned round I noticed he had decorously pulled down her rumpled slip so that it reached smoothly to her knees.

'Phenobarbitone and gin,' he said. 'Are you sure?'

'Yes.'

'Self-administered?' He started opening his case.

'No. Definitely not.'

'This place is usually teeming with women,' he said inconsequentially. 'But apparently they're all at some meeting or another.' He gave me another intent look. 'Are you fit to help?'

'Yes.'

He hesitated. 'Are you sure?'

'Tell me what to do.'

'Very well. Find me a good-sized jug and a bucket or large basin. I'll get her started first, and you can tell me how this happened later.'

He took a hypodermic syringe from his case, filled it, and gave Elinor an injection into the vein on the inside of her elbow. I found a jug and a basin in the built-in fitment.

'You've been here before,' he observed, eyes again suspicious.

'Once,' I said: and for Elinor's sake added, 'I am employed by her father. It's nothing personal.'

'Oh. All right then.' He withdrew the needle, dismantled the syringe, and quickly washed his hands.

'How many tablets did she take, do you know?'

'It wasn't tablets. Powder. A teaspoonful, at least. Maybe more.'

He looked alarmed, but said, 'That much would be bitter. She'd taste it.'

'Gin and Campari . . . it's bitter anyway.'

'Yes. All right. I'm going to wash out her stomach. Most of the drug must have been absorbed already, but if she had as much as that . . . well, it's still worth trying.'

He directed me to fill the jug with tepid water, while he carefully slid a thickish tube down inside Elinor's throat. He surprised me by putting his ear to the long protruding end of it when it was in position, and he explained briefly that with an unconscious patient who couldn't swallow one had to make sure the tube had gone into the stomach and not into the lungs. 'If you can hear them breathe, you're in the wrong place,' he said.

He put a funnel in the end of the tube, held out his hand for the jug, and carefully poured in the water. When what seemed to me a fantastic amount had disappeared down the tube he stopped pouring, passed me the jug to put down, and directed me to push the basin near his foot. Then, removing the funnel, he suddenly lowered the end of the tube over the side of the bed and into the basin. The water flowed out again, together with all the contents of Elinor's stomach.

'Hm,' he said calmly. 'She had something to eat first. Cake, I should say. That helps.'

I couldn't match his detachment.

'Will she be all right?' My voice sounded strained.

He looked at me briefly and slid the tube out.

'She drank the stuff less than an hour before I got here?'

'About fifty minutes, I think.'

'And she'd eaten . . . Yes, she'll be all right. Healthy girl. The injection I gave her – megimide – is an effective antidote. She'll probably wake up in an hour or so. A night in hospital, and it will be out of her system. She'll be as good as new.'

I rubbed my hand over my face.

'Time makes a lot of difference,' he said calmly. 'If she'd lain here many hours . . . a teaspoonful; that might be thirty grains or more.' He shook his head. 'She could have died.'

He took a sample of the contents of the basin for analysis, and covered the rest with a hand towel.

'How did you cut your head?' he said suddenly.

'In a fight.'

'It needs stitching. Do you want me to do it?'

'Yes. Thank you.'

'I'll do it after Miss Tarren has gone to hospital. Dr Pritchard said she would ring for an ambulance. They should be here soon.'

'Dr Pritchard?'

'The lecturer who fetched me in. My surgery is only round the corner. She telephoned and said a violent blood-stained youth was insisting that Miss Tarren was

319

poisoned, and that I'd better come and see.' He smiled briefly. 'You haven't told me how all this happened.'

'Oh . . . it's such a long story,' I said tiredly.

'You'll have to tell the police,' he pointed out.

I nodded. There was too much I would have to tell the police. I wasn't looking forward to it. The doctor took out pen and paper and wrote a letter to go with Elinor to the hospital.

There was a sudden eruption of girls' voices down the passage, and a tramp of many scholarly feet, and the opening and shutting of doors. The students were back from their meeting: from Elinor's point of view, too soon, as they would now see her being carried out.

Heavier footsteps came right up to her room and knuckles rapped. Two men in ambulance uniform had arrived with a stretcher, and with economy of movement and time they lifted Elinor between them, tucked her into blankets, and bore her away. She left a wake of pretty voices raised in sympathy and speculation.

The doctor swung the door shut behind the ambulance men and without more ado took from his case a needle and thread to sew up my forehead. I sat on Elinor's bed while he fiddled around with disinfectant and the stitching.

'What did you fight about?' he asked, tying knots.

'Because I was attacked,' I said.

'Oh?' He shifted his feet to sew from a different angle, and put his hand on my shoulder to steady himself. He felt me withdraw from the pressure and looked at me quizzically.

'So you got the worst of it?'

'No,' I said slowly. 'I won.'

He finished the stitching and gave a final snip with the scissors.

'There you are, then. It won't leave much of a scar.'

'Thank you.' It sounded a bit weak.

'Do you feel all right?' he said abruptly. 'Or is pale fawn tinged with grey your normal colouring?'

'Pale fawn is normal. Grey just about describes how I feel.' I smiled faintly. 'I got a bang on the back of the head, too.'

He explored the bump behind the ear and said I would live. He was asking me how many other tender spots I had about me when another heavy tramp of footsteps could be heard coming up the corridor, and presently the door was pushed open with a crash.

Two broad-shouldered businesslike policemen stepped into the room.

They knew the doctor. It appeared that he did a good deal of police work in Durham. They greeted each other politely and the doctor started to say that Miss Tarren was on her way to hospital. They interrupted him.

'We've come for him, sir,' said the taller one of them, pointing at me. 'Stable lad, name of Daniel Roke.'

'Yes, he reported Miss Tarren's illness . . .'

'No, sir, it's nothing to do with a Miss Tarren or

her illness. We want him for questioning on another matter.'

The doctor said, 'He's not in very good shape. I think you had better go easy. Can't you leave it until later?'

'I'm afraid that's impossible, sir.'

They both came purposefully over to where I sat. The one who had done the talking was a red-headed man about my own age with an unsmiling wary face. His companion was slightly shorter, brown eyed, and just as much on guard. They looked as if they were afraid I was going to leap up and strangle them.

With precision they leaned down and clamped hard hands round my forearms. The red-head, who was on my right, dragged a pair of handcuffs from his pocket, and between them they fastened them on my wrists.

'Better take it quietly, chum,' advised the red-head, evidently mistaking my attempt to wrench my arm free of his agonizing grip as a desire to escape in general.

'Let . . . go,' I said. 'I'm not . . . running anywhere.'

They did let go, and stepped back a pace, looking down at me. Most of the wariness had faded from their faces, and I gathered that they really had been afraid I would attack them. It was unnerving. I took two deep breaths to control the soreness of my arm.

'He won't give us much trouble,' said the dark one. 'He looks like death.'

'He was in a fight,' remarked the doctor.

'Is that what he told you, sir?' The dark one laughed. I looked down at the handcuffs locked round my wrists: they were, I discovered, as uncomfortable as they were humiliating.

'What did he do?' asked the doctor.

The red-head answered, 'He . . . er . . . he'll be helping in inquiries into an attack on a racehorse trainer he worked for and who is still unconscious, and on another man who had his skull bust right in.'

'Dead?'

'So we are told, sir. We haven't actually been to the stables, though they say it's a shambles. We two were sent up from Clavering to fetch him in, and that's where we're taking him back to, the stables being in our area you see.'

'You caught up with him very quickly,' commented the doctor.

'Yes,' said the red-head with satisfaction. 'It was a nice bit of work by some of the lads. A lady here telephoned to the police in Durham about half an hour ago and described *him*, and when they got the general call from Clavering about the job at the stables someone connected the two descriptions and told us about it. So we were sent up to see, and bingo . . . there was his motor-bike, right number plate and all, standing outside the college door.'

I lifted my head. The doctor looked down at me. He was disillusioned, disenchanted. He shrugged his shoulders and said in a tired voice, 'You never know with them, do you? He seemed . . . well . . . not quite the usual sort of tearaway. And now this.' He turned away and picked up his bag.

It was suddenly too much. I had let too many people despise me and done nothing about it. This was one too many.

'I fought because they attacked me,' I said.

The doctor half turned round. I didn't know why I thought it was important to convince him, but it seemed so at the time.

The dark policeman raised an eyebrow and said to the doctor, 'The trainer was his employer, sir, and I understand the man who died is a rich gentleman whose horses were trained there. The head lad reported the killing. He saw Roke belting off on his motor-bike and thought it was strange, because Roke had been sacked the day before, and he went to tell the trainer about it, and found him unconscious and the other man dead.'

The doctor had heard enough. He walked out of the room without looking back. What was the use of trying? Better just do what the red-head said, and take it quietly, bitterness and all.

'Let's be going, chum,' said the dark one. They stood there, tense again, with watchful eyes and hostile faces.

I got slowly to my feet. Slowly, because I was perilously near to not being able to stand up at all, and I didn't want to seem to be asking for a sympathy I was clearly not going to get. But it was all right: once upright I felt better; which was psychological as much as physical because they were then not two huge threatening policemen but two quite ordinary young men of my own height doing their duty, and very concerned not to make any mistakes.

It worked the other way with them, of course. I think they had subconsciously expected a stable lad to be very short, and they were taken aback to discover I wasn't. They became visibly more aggressive: and I realized in the circumstances, and in those black clothes, I probably seemed to them, as Terence had once put it, a bit dangerous and hard to handle.

I didn't see any sense in getting roughed up any more, especially by the law, if it could be avoided.

'Look,' I sighed, 'like you said, I won't give you any trouble.'

But I suppose they had been told to bring in someone who had gone berserk and smashed a man's head in, and they were taking no chances. Red-head took a fierce grip of my right arm above the elbow and shoved me over to the door, and once outside in the passage the dark one took a similar grip on the left.

The corridor was lined with girls standing in little gossiping groups. I stopped dead. The two policemen pushed me on. And the girls stared.

That old saying about wishing the floor would open and swallow one up suddenly took on a fresh personal meaning. What little was left of my sense of dignity revolted totally against being exhibited as a prisoner in front of so many intelligent and personable young women. They were the wrong age. The wrong sex. I could have stood it better if they had been men.

But there was no easy exit. It was a good long way from Elinor's room to the outside door, along those twisting corridors and down two flights of stairs, and every single step was watched by interested female eyes.

This was the sort of thing one wouldn't be able to forget. It went too deep. Or perhaps, I thought miserably, one could even get accustomed to being hauled around in handcuffs if it happened often enough. If one were used to it, perhaps one wouldn't care ... which would be peaceful.

I did at least manage not to stumble, not even on the stairs, so to that extent something was saved from the wreck. The police car however, into which I was presently thrust, seemed a perfect haven in contrast.

I sat in front, between them. The dark one drove.

'Phew,' he said, pushing his cap back an inch. 'All those girls.' He had blushed under their scrutiny and there was a dew of sweat on his forehead.

'He's a tough boy, is this,' said Red-head, mopping his neck with a white handkerchief as he sat sideways against the door and stared at me. 'He didn't turn a hair.'

I looked straight ahead through the windscreen as the lights of Durham began to slide past and thought how little could be told from a face. That walk had been a torture. If I hadn't shown it, it was probably only because I had by then had months of practice in hiding my feelings and thoughts, and the habit was strong. I guessed – correctly – that it was a habit I would find strength in clinging to for some time to come.

I spent the rest of the journey reflecting that I had got myself into a proper mess and that I was going to have a very unpleasant time getting out. I had indeed killed Adams. There was no denying or ducking that. And I was not going to be listened to as a respectable solid citizen but as a murdering villain trying every dodge to escape the consequences. I was going to be taken at my face value, which was very low indeed. That couldn't be helped. I had, after all, survived eight weeks at Humber's only because I looked like dregs. The appearance which had deceived Adams was going to be just as convincing to the police, and proof that in fact it already was sat on either side of me in the car, watchful and antagonistic.

Red-head's eyes never left my face.

'He doesn't talk much,' he observed, after a long silence.

'Got a lot on his mind,' agreed the dark one with sarcasm.

The damage Adams and Humber had done gave me no respite. I shifted uncomfortably in my seat, and the handcuffs clinked. The light-heartedness with which I had gone in my new clothes to Slaw seemed a long long time ago.

The lights of Clavering lay ahead. The dark one gave

me a look of subtle enjoyment. A capture made. His purpose fulfilled. Red-head broke another long silence, his voice full of the same sort of satisfaction.

'He'll be a lot older when he gets out,' he said.

I emphatically hoped not: but I was all too aware that the length of time I remained in custody depended solely on how conclusively I could show that I had killed in self-defence. I wasn't a lawyer's son for nothing.

The next hours were abysmal. The Clavering police force were collectively a hardened cynical bunch suppressing as best they could a vigorous crime wave in a mining area with a high unemployment percentage. Kid gloves did not figure in their book. Individually they may have loved their wives and been nice to their children, but if so they kept their humour and humanity strictly for leisure.

They were busy. The building was full of bustle and hurrying voices. They shoved me still handcuffed from room to room under escort and barked out intermittent questions. 'Later,' they said. 'Deal with that one later. We've got all night for him.'

I thought with longing of a hot bath, a soft bed, and a handful of aspirins. I didn't get any of them.

At some point late in the evening they gave me a chair in a bare brightly lit little room, and I told them what I had been doing at Humber's and how I had come to kill Adams. I told them everything which had happened that day. They didn't believe me, for which one couldn't blame them. They immediately, as a matter of form, charged me with murder. I protested. Uselessly.

They asked me a lot of questions. I answered them. They asked them again. I answered. They asked the questions like a relay team, one of them taking over presently from another, so that they all appeared to remain full of fresh energy while I grew more and more tired. I was glad I did not have to maintain a series of lies in that state of continuing discomfort and growing fatigue, as it was hard to keep a clear head, even for the truth, and they were waiting for me to make a mistake.

'Now tell us what really happened.'

'I've told you.'

'Not all that cloak and dagger stuff.'

'Cable to Australia for a copy of the contract I signed when I took on the job.' For the fourth time I repeated my solicitor's address, and for the fourth time they didn't write it down.

'Who did you say engaged you?'

'The Earl of October.'

'And no doubt we can check with him too?'

'He's in Germany until Saturday.'

'Too bad.' They smiled nastily. They knew from Cass that I had worked in October's stable. Cass had told them I was a slovenly stable lad, dishonest, easily frightened, and not very bright. As he believed what he said, he had carried conviction.

'You got into trouble with his Lordship's daughter, didn't you?'

Damn Cass, I thought bitterly, damn Cass and his chattering tongue.

'Getting your own back on him for sacking you, aren't you, by dragging his name into this?'

'Like you got your own back on Mr Humber for sacking you yesterday?'

'No. I left because I had finished my job there.'

'For beating you, then?'

'No.'

'The head lad said you deserved it.'

'Adams and Humber were running a crooked racing scheme. I found them out, and they tried to kill me.' It seemed to me it was the tenth time that I had said that without making the slightest impression.

'You resented being beaten. You went back to get even . . . It's a common enough pattern.'

'No.'

'You brooded over it and went back and attacked them. It was a shambles. Blood all over the place.'

'It was my blood.'

'We can group it.'

'Do that. It's my blood.'

'From that little cut? Don't be so stupid.'

'It's been stitched.'

'Ah yes, that brings us back to Lady Elinor Tarren. Lord October's daughter. Got her into trouble, did you?'

330

'No.'

'In the family way . . .'

'No. Check with the doctor.'

'So she took sleeping pills . . .'

'No. Adams poisoned her.' I had told them twice about the bottle of phenobarbitone, and they must have found it when they had been at the stables, but they wouldn't admit it.

'You got the sack from her father for seducing her. She couldn't stand the disgrace. She took sleeping pills.'

'She had no reason to feel disgraced. It was not she, but her sister Patricia, who accused me of seducing her. Adams poisoned Elinor in gin and Campari. There are gin and Campari and phenobarbitone in the office and also in the sample from her stomach.'

They took no notice. 'She found you had deserted her on top of everything else. Mr Humber consoled her with a drink, but she went back to college and took sleeping pills.'

'No.'

They were sceptical, to put it mildly, about Adams' use of the flame thrower.

'You'll find it in the shed.'

'This shed, yes. Where did you say it was?'

I told them again, exactly. 'The field probably belongs to Adams. You could find out.'

'It only exists in your imagination.'

'Look and you'll find it, and the flame thrower.'

'That's likely to be used for burning off the heath. Lots of farmers have them, round here.'

They had let me make two telephone calls to try to find Colonel Beckett. His manservant in London said he had gone to stay with friends in Berkshire for Newbury races. The little local exchange in Berkshire was out of action, the operator said, because a water main had burst and flooded a cable. Engineers were working on it.

Didn't my wanting to talk to one of the top brass of steeple-chasing convince them, I wanted to know?

'Remember that chap we had in here once who'd strangled his wife? Nutty as a fruit cake. Insisted on ringing up Lord Bertrand Russell, didn't he, to tell him he'd struck a blow for peace.'

At around midnight one of them pointed out that even if (and, mind you, he didn't himself believe it) even if all I had said about being employed to find out about Adams and Humber were against all probability true, that still didn't give me the right to kill them.

'Humber isn't dead,' I said.

'Not yet.'

My heart lurched. Dear God, I thought, not Humber too. Not Humber too.

'You clubbed Adams with the walking stick then?'

'No, I told you, with a green glass ball. I had it in my left hand and I hit him as hard as I could. I didn't mean to kill him, just knock him out. I'm right handed . . . I couldn't judge very well how hard I was hitting with my left.'

'Why did you use your left hand then?'

'I told you.'

'Tell us again.'

I told them again.

'And after your right arm was put out of action you got on a motor-cycle and rode ten miles to Durham? What sort of fools do you take us for?'

'The fingerprints of both my hands are on that paper-weight. The right ones from when I threw it at Humber, and the left ones on top, from where I hit Adams. You have only to check.'

'Fingerprints, now,' they said sarcastically.

'And while you're on the subject, you'll also find the fingerprints of my left hand on the telephone. I tried to call you from the office. My left hand prints are on the tap in the washroom . . . and on the key, and on the door handle, both inside and out. Or at least, they were . . .'

'All the same, you rode that motor-bike.'

'The numbness had gone by then.'

'And now?'

'It isn't numb now either.'

One of them came round beside me, picked up my right wrist, and pulled my arm up high. The handcuffs jerked and lifted my left arm as well. The bruises had all stiffened and were very sore. The policeman put my arm down again. There was a short silence.

333

'That hurt,' one of them said at last, grudgingly.

'He's putting it on.'

'Maybe . . .'

They had been drinking endless cups of tea all evening and had not given me any. I asked if I could have some then, and got it; only to find that the difficulty I had in lifting the cup was hardly worth it.

They began again.

'Granted Adams struck your arm, but he did it in self-defence. He saw you throw the paper weight at your employer and realized you were going to attack him next. He was warding you off.'

'He had already cut my forehead open . . . and hit me several times on the body, and once on the head.'

'Most of that was yesterday, according to the head lad. That's why you went back and attacked Mr Humber.'

'Humber hit me only twice yesterday. I didn't particularly resent it. The rest was today, and it was mostly done by Adams.' I remembered something. 'He took my crash helmet off when he had knocked me dizzy. His fingerprints must be on it.'

'Fingerprints again.'

'They spell it out,' I said.

'Let's begin at the beginning. How can we believe a yob like you?'

Yob. One of the leather boys. Tearaway. Rocker. I knew all the words. I knew what I looked like. What a millstone of a handicap.

I said despairingly, 'There's no point in pretending to be a disreputable, dishonest lad if you don't look the part.'

'You look the part all right,' they said offensively. 'Born to it, you were.'

I looked at their stony faces, their hard, unimpressed eyes. Tough efficient policemen who were not going to be conned. I could read their thoughts like glass: if I convinced them and they later found out it was all a pack of lies, they'd never live it down. Their instincts were all dead against having to believe. My bad luck.

The room grew stuffy and full of cigarette smoke and I became too hot in my jerseys and jacket. I knew they took the sweat on my forehead to be guilt, not heat, not pain.

I went on answering all their questions. They covered the ground twice more with undiminished zeal, setting traps, sometimes shouting, walking round me, never touching me again, but springing the questions from all directions. I was really much too tired for that sort of thing because apart from the wearing-out effect of the injuries I had not slept for the whole of the previous night. Towards two o'clock I could hardly speak from exhaustion, and after they had woken me from a sort of dazed sleep three times in half an hour, they gave it up.

From the beginning I had known that there was only one logical end to that evening, and I had tried to shut it out of my mind, because I dreaded it. But there you are, you set off on a primrose path and if it leads to hell that's just too bad.

Two uniformed policemen, a sergeant and a constable, were detailed to put me away for the night, which I found involved a form of accommodation to make Humber's dormitory seem a paradise.

The cell was cubic, eight feet by eight by eight, built of glazed bricks, brown to shoulder height and white above that. There was a small barred window too high to see out of, a narrow slab of concrete for a bed, a bucket with a lid on it in a corner, and a printed list of regulations on one wall. Nothing else. Bleak enough to shrink the guts; and I had never much cared for small enclosed spaces.

The two policemen brusquely told me to sit on the concrete. They removed my boots and the belt from my jeans, and also found and unbuckled the money belt underneath. They took off the handcuffs. Then they went out, shut the door with a clang, and locked me in.

The rest of that night was in every way rock bottom.

CHAPTER NINETEEN

It was cool and quiet in the corridors of Whitehall. A superbly mannered young man deferentially showed me the way and opened a mahogany door into an empty office.

'Colonel Beckett will not be long, sir. He has just gone to consult a colleague. He said I was to apologize if you arrived before he came back, and to ask if you would like a drink. And cigarettes are in this box, sir.'

'Thank you,' I smiled. 'Would coffee be a nuisance?'

'By no means. I'll have some sent in straight away. If you'll excuse me?' He went out and quietly closed the door.

It rather amused me to be called 'sir' again, especially by smooth civil servants barely younger than myself. Grinning, I sat down in the leather chair facing Beckett's desk, crossed my elegantly trousered legs, and lazily settled to wait for him.

I was in no hurry. It was eleven o'clock on Tuesday morning, and I had all day and nothing to do but buy a clockwork train for Jerry and book an air ticket back to Australia.

No noise filtered into Beckett's office. The room was square and high, and was painted a restful pale greenish grey colour, walls, door, and ceiling alike. I supposed that here the furnishings went with rank; but if one were an outsider one would not know how much to be impressed by a large but threadbare carpet, an obviously personal lamp-shade, or leather, brass-studded chairs. One had to belong, for these things to matter.

I wondered about Colonel Beckett's job. He had given me the impression that he was retired, probably on a full disability pension since he looked so frail in health, yet here he was with a well established niche at the Ministry of Defence.

October had told me that in the war Beckett had been the sort of supply officer who never sent all left boots or the wrong ammunition. Supply Officer. He had supplied me with Sparking Plug and the raw material containing the pointers to Adams and Humber. He'd had enough pull with the Army to dispatch in a hurry eleven young officer cadets to dig up the past history of obscure steeplechasers. What, I wondered, did he supply nowadays, in the normal course of events?

I suddenly remembered October saying, 'We thought of planting a stable lad . . .' not 'I thought', but 'We'. And for some reason I was now sure that it had been Beckett, not October, who had originally suggested the plan; and that explained why October had been relieved when Beckett approved me at our first meeting.

Unexcitedly turning these random thoughts over in my mind I watched two pigeons fluttering round the window sill and tranquilly waited to say goodbye to the man whose staff work had ensured the success of the idea.

A pretty young woman knocked and came in with a tray on which stood a coffee pot, cream jug, and pale green cup and saucer. She smiled, asked if I needed anything else, and when I said not, gracefully went away.

I was getting quite good at left-handedness. I poured the coffee and drank it black, and enjoyed the taste.

Snatches of the past few days drifted idly in and out of my thoughts . . .

Four nights and three days in a police cell trying to come to terms with the fact that I had killed Adams. It was odd, but although I had often considered the possibility of being killed, I had never once thought that I myself might kill. For that, as for so much else, I had been utterly unprepared; and to have caused another man's death, however much he might have asked for it, needed a bit of getting over.

Four nights and three days of gradually finding that even the various ignominies of being locked up were bearable if one took them quietly, and feeling almost like thanking Red-head for his advice.

On the first morning, after a magistrate had agreed

that I should stay where I was for seven days, a police doctor came and told me to strip. I couldn't, and he had to help. He looked impassively at Adams' and Humber's wide-spread handiwork, asked a few questions, and examined my right arm, which was black from the wrist to well above the elbow. In spite of the protection of two jerseys and a leather jacket, the skin was broken where the chair leg had landed. The doctor helped me dress again and impersonally departed. I didn't ask him for his opinion, and he didn't give it.

For most of the four nights and three days I just waited, hour after silent hour. Thinking about Adams: Adams alive and Adams dead. Worrying about Humber. Thinking of how I could have done things differently. Facing the thought that I might not get out without a trial . . . or not get out at all. Waiting for the soreness to fade from the bruises and failing to find a comfortable way of sleeping on concrete. Counting the number of bricks from the floor to the ceiling and multiplying by the length of the walls (subtract the door and window). Thinking about my stud farm and my sisters and brother, and about the rest of my life.

On Monday morning there was the by then familiar scrape of the door being unlocked, but when it opened it was not as usual a policeman in uniform, but October.

I was standing up, leaning against the wall. I had not seen him for three months. He stared at me for a long minute, taking in with obvious shock my extremely dishevelled appearance.

'Daniel,' he said. His voice was low and thick.

I didn't think I needed any sympathy. I hooked my left thumb into my pocket, struck a faint attitude, and raised a grin.

'Hullo, Edward.'

His face lightened, and he laughed.

'You're so bloody tough,' he said. Well . . . let him think so.

I said, 'Could you possibly use your influence to get me a bath?'

'You can have whatever you like as soon as you are out.'

'Out? For good?'

'For good,' he nodded. 'They are dropping the charge.'

I couldn't disguise my relief.

He smiled sardonically. 'They don't think it would be worth wasting public funds on trying you. You'd be certain of getting an absolute discharge. Justifiable homicide, quite legitimate.'

'I didn't think they believed me.'

'They've done a lot of checking up. Everything you told them on Thursday is now the official version.'

'Is Humber . . . all right?'

'He regained consciousness yesterday, I believe. But I understand he isn't lucid enough yet to answer questions. Didn't the police tell you that he was out of danger?'

I shook my head. 'They aren't a very chatty lot, here. How is Elinor?'

'She's well. A bit weak, that's all.'

'I'm sorry she got caught up in things. It was my fault.'

'My dear chap, it was her own,' he protested. 'And Daniel . . . about Patty . . . and the things I said . . .'

'Oh, nuts to that,' I interrupted. 'It was a long time ago. When you said "Out" did you mean "out" now, this minute?'

He nodded. 'That's right.'

'Then let's not hang around in here any more, shall we? If you don't mind?'

He looked about him and involuntarily shivered. Meeting my eyes he said apologetically, 'I didn't foresee anything like this.'

I grinned faintly. 'Nor did I.'

We went to London, by car up to Newcastle, and then by train. Owing to some delay at the police station discussing the details of my return to attend Adams' inquest, any cleaning up processes would have meant our missing the seats October had reserved on the non-stop Flying Scotsman, so I caught it as I was.

October led the way into the dining car, but as I was about to sit down opposite him a waiter caught hold of my elbow.

'Here you,' he said roughly, 'clear out. This is first-class only.'

'I've got a first-class ticket,' I said mildly.

'Oh yes? Let's see it, then.'

I produced from my pocket the piece of white cardboard.

He sniffed and gestured with his head towards the seat opposite October. 'All right then.' To October he said, 'If he makes a nuisance of himself, just tell me, sir, and I'll have him chucked out, ticket or no ticket.' He went off, swaying to the motion of the accelerating train.

Needless to say, everyone in the dining car had turned round to have a good view of the rumpus.

Grinning, I sat down opposite October. He looked exceedingly embarrassed.

'Don't worry on my account,' I said, 'I'm used to it.' And I realized that I was indeed used to it at last and that no amount of such treatment would ever trouble me again. 'But if you would rather pretend you don't know me, go ahead.' I picked up the menu.

'You are insulting.'

I smiled at him over the menu. 'Good.'

'For deviousness, Daniel, you are unsurpassed. Except possibly by Roddy Beckett.'

'My dear Edward . . . have some bread.'

He laughed, and we travelled amicably to London together, as ill-assorted looking a pair as ever rested heads on British Railways' starched white antimacassars.

I poured some more coffee and looked at my watch. Colonel Beckett was twenty minutes late. The pigeons sat peacefully on the window sill and I shifted gently in my chair, but with patience, not boredom, and thought about my visit to October's barber, and the pleasure with which I had had my hair cut short and sideburns shaved off. The barber himself (who had asked me to pay in advance) was surprised, he said, at the results.

'We look a lot more like a gentleman, don't we? But might I suggest . . . a shampoo?'

Grinning, I agreed to a shampoo, which left a high water mark of cleanliness about midway down my neck. Then, at October's house, there was the fantastic luxury of stepping out of my filthy disguise into a deep hot bath, and the strangeness with which I afterwards put on my own clothes. When I had finished dressing I took another look in the same long mirror. There was the man who had come from Australia four months ago, a man in a good dark grey suit, a white shirt, and a navy blue silk tie: there was his shell anyway. Inside I wasn't the same man, nor ever would be again.

I went down to the crimson drawing-room where October walked solemnly all round me, gave me a glass of bone dry sherry and said, 'It is utterly unbelievable that you are the young tyke who just came down with me on the train.'

'I am,' I said dryly, and he laughed.

He gave me a chair with its back to the door, where I drank some sherry and listened to him making social chit-chat about his horses. He was hovering round the fireplace not entirely at ease, and I wondered what he was up to.

I soon found out. The door opened and he looked over my shoulder and smiled.

'I want you both to meet someone,' he said.

I stood up and turned round.

Patty and Elinor were there, side by side.

They didn't know me at first. Patty held out her hand politely and said, 'How do you do?' clearly waiting for her father to introduce us.

I took her hand in my left one and guided her to a chair.

'Sit down,' I suggested. 'You're in for a shock.'

She hadn't seen me for three months, but it was only four days since Elinor had made her disastrous visit to Humber's. She said hesitantly, 'You don't look the same . . . but you're Daniel.' I nodded, and she blushed painfully.

Patty's bright eyes looked straight into mine, and her pink mouth parted.

'You . . . are you really? Danny boy?'

'Yes.'

'Oh.' A blush as deep as her sister's spread up from her neck, and for Patty that was shame indeed.

October watched their discomfiture. 'It serves them right,' he said, 'for all the trouble they have caused.'

'Oh no,' I exclaimed, 'it's too hard on them . . . and you still haven't told them anything about me, have you?'

'No,' he agreed uncertainly, beginning to suspect there was more for his daughters to blush over than he knew, and that his surprise meeting was not an unqualified success.

'Then tell them now, while I go and talk to Terence . . . and Patty . . . Elinor . . .' They looked surprised at my use of their first names and I smiled briefly, 'I have a very short and defective memory.'

They both looked subdued when I went back, and October was watching them uneasily. Fathers, I reflected, could be very unkind to their daughters without intending it.

'Cheer up,' I said. 'I'd have had a dull time in England without you two.'

'You were a beast,' said Patty emphatically, sticking to her guns.

'Yes . . . I'm sorry.'

'You might have told us,' said Elinor in a low voice.

'Nonsense,' said October. 'He couldn't trust Patty's tongue.'

'I see,' said Elinor, slowly. She looked at me tentatively. 'I haven't thanked you, for . . . for saving me. The doctor told me . . . all about it.' She blushed again.

'Sleeping beauty,' I smiled. 'You looked like my sister.'

'You have a sister?'

'Two,' I said. 'Sixteen and seventeen.'

'Oh,' she said, and looked comforted.

October flicked me a glance. 'You are far too kind to

them, Daniel. One of them made me loathe you and the other nearly killed you, and you don't seem to care.'

I smiled at him. 'No. I don't. I really don't. Let's just forget it.'

So in spite of a most unpromising start it developed into a good evening, the girls gradually losing their embarrassment and even, by the end, being able to meet my eyes without blushing.

When they had gone to bed October put two fingers into an inner pocket, drew out a slip of paper, and handed it to me without a word. I unfolded it. It was a cheque for ten thousand pounds. A lot of noughts. I looked at them in silence. Then, slowly, I tore the fortune in half and put the pieces in an ashtray.

'Thank you very much,' I said. 'But I can't take it.'

'You did the job. Why not accept the pay?'

'Because . . .' I stopped. Because what? I was not sure I could put it into words. It had something to do with having learned more than I had bargained for. With diving too deep. With having killed. All I was sure of was that I could no longer bear the thought of receiving money for it.

'You must have a reason,' said October, with a touch of irritation.

'Well, I didn't really do it for the money, to start with, and I can't take that sort of sum from you. In fact, when I get back I am going to repay you all that is left of the first ten thousand.'

347

'No,' he protested. 'You've earned it. Keep it. You need it for your family.'

'What I need for my family, I'll earn by selling horses.'

He stubbed out his cigar. 'You're so infuriatingly independent that I don't know how you could face being a stable lad. If it wasn't for the money, why did you do it?'

I moved in my chair. The bruises still felt like bruises. I smiled faintly, enjoying the pun.

'For kicks, I suppose.'

The door of the office opened, and Beckett unhurriedly came in. I stood up. He held out his hand, and remembering the weakness of his grasp I put out my own. He squeezed gently and let go.

'It's been a long time, Mr Roke.'

'More than three months,' I agreed.

'And you completed the course.'

I shook my head, smiling. 'Fell at the last fence, I'm afraid.'

He took off his overcoat and hung it on a knobbed hat rack, and unwound a grey woollen scarf from his neck. His suit was nearly black, a colour which only enhanced his extreme pallor and emphasized his thinness: but his eyes were as alive as ever in the gaunt shadowed sockets. He gave me a long observant scrutiny.

'Sit down,' he said. 'I'm sorry to have kept you waiting. I see they've looked after you all right.'

'Yes, thank you.' I sat down again in the leather chair, and he walked round and sank carefully into the one behind his desk. His chair had a high back and arms, and he used them to support his head and elbows.

'I didn't get your report until I came back to London from Newbury on Sunday morning,' he said. 'It took two days to come from Posset and didn't reach my house until Friday. When I had read it I telephoned to Edward at Slaw and found he had just been rung up by the police at Clavering. I then telephoned to Clavering myself. I spent a good chunk of Sunday hurrying things up for you in various conversations with ever higher ranks, and early on Monday it was decided finally in the office of the Director of Public Prosecutions that there was no charge for you to answer.'

'Thank you very much,' I said.

He paused, considering me. 'You did more towards extricating yourself than Edward or I did. We only confirmed what you had said and had you freed a day or two sooner than you might have been. But it appeared that the Clavering police had already discovered from a thorough examination of the stable office that everything you had told them was borne out by the facts. They had also talked to the doctor who had attended Elinor, and to Elinor herself, and taken a look at the shed with the flame thrower, and cabled your solicitor for a summary of the contract you signed with Edward.

By the time I spoke to them they were taking the truth of your story for granted, and were agreeing that you had undoubtedly killed Adams in self-defence.

'Their own doctor – the one who examined you – had told them straight away that the amount of crushing your right forearm had sustained was entirely consistent with its having been struck by a force strong enough to have smashed in your skull. He was of the opinion that the blow had landed more or less along the inside of your arm, not straight across it, thus causing extensive damage to muscles and blood vessels, but no bone fracture; and he told them that it was perfectly possible for you to have ridden a motor-bike a quarter of an hour later if you had wanted to enough.'

'You know,' I said, 'I didn't think they had taken any notice of a single word I said.'

'Mmm. Well, I spoke to one of the CID men who questioned you last Thursday evening. He said they brought you in as a foregone conclusion, and that you looked terrible. You told them a rigmarole which they thought was nonsense, so they asked a lot of questions to trip you up. They thought it would be easy. The CID man said it was like trying to dig a hole in a rock with your finger nails. They all ended up by believing you, much to their own surprise.'

'I wish they'd told me,' I sighed.

'Not their way. They sounded a tough bunch.'

'They seemed it, too.'

'However, you survived.'

'Oh yes.'

Beckett looked at his watch. 'Are you in a hurry?'

'No.' I shook my head.

'Good . . . I've rather a lot to say to you. Can you lunch?'

'Yes. I'd like to.'

'Fine. Now, this report of yours.' He dug the hand-written foolscap pages out of his inside breast pocket and laid them on the table. 'What I'd like you to do now is to lop off the bit asking for reinforcements and substitute a description of the flame-thrower operation. Right? There's a table and chair over there. Get to work, and when it's done I'll have it typed.'

When I had finished the report he spent some time outlining and discussing the proceedings which were to be taken against Humber, Cass, and Jud Wilson, and also against Soupy Tarleton and his friend Lewis Greenfield. He then looked at his watch again and decided it was time to go out for lunch. He took me to his Club, which seemed to me to be dark brown throughout, and we ate steak, kidney, and mushroom pie which I chose because I could manage it unobtrusively with a fork. He noticed though.

'That arm still troubling you?'

'It's much better.'

He nodded and made no further comment. Instead, he told me of a visit he had paid the day before to an elderly uncle of Adams, whom he had discovered living in bachelor splendour in Piccadilly.

'Young Paul Adams, according to his uncle, was the sort of child who would have been sent to an approved school if he hadn't had rich parents. He was sacked from Eton for forging cheques and from his next school for persistent gambling. His parents bought him out of scrape after scrape and were told by a psychiatrist that he would never change, or at least not until late middle age. He was their only child. It must have been terrible for them. The father died when Adams was twenty-five, and his mother struggled on, trying to keep him out of too disastrous trouble. About five years ago she had to pay out a fortune to hush up a scandal in which Adams had apparently broken a youth's arm for no reason at all, and she threatened to have him certified if he did anything like that again. And a few days later she fell out of her bedroom window and died. The uncle, her brother, says he has always thought that Adams pushed her.'

'Very likely, I should think,' I agreed.

'So you were right about him being psychopathic.'

'Well, it was pretty obvious.'

'From the way he behaved to you personally?'

'Yes.'

We had finished the pie and were on to cheese. Beckett looked at me curiously and said, 'What sort of life did you really have at Humber's stable?'

'Oh,' I grinned. 'You could hardly call it a holiday camp.'

He waited for me to go on and when I didn't, he said, 'Is that all you've got to say about it?'

'Yes, I think so. This is very good cheese.'

We drank our coffee and a glass of brandy out of a bottle with Beckett's name on it, and eventually walked slowly back to his office.

As before he sank gratefully into his chair and rested his head and arms, and I as before sat down opposite him on the other side of his desk.

'You are going back to Australia soon, I believe?' he said.

'Yes.'

'I expect you are looking forward to getting back into harness.'

I looked at him. His eyes stared straight back, steady and grave. He waited for an answer.

'Not altogether.'

'Why not?'

I shrugged; grinned. 'Who likes harness?'

There was no point, I thought, in making too much of it.

'You are going back to prosperity, good food, sunshine, your family, a beautiful house, and a job you do well . . . isn't that right?'

I nodded. It wasn't reasonable not to want to go to all that.

'Tell me the truth,' he said abruptly. 'The unvarnished honest truth. What's wrong?'

'I'm a discontented idiot, that's all,' I said lightly.

'Mr Roke.' He sat up slightly in the chair. 'I have a good reason for asking these questions. Please give me truthful answers. What is wrong with your life in Australia?'

There was a pause, while I thought and he waited. When at last I answered, I was aware that whatever his good reason was it would do no harm to speak plainly.

'I do a job which I ought to find satisfying, and it leaves me bored and empty.'

'A diet of milk and honey, when you have teeth,' he observed.

I laughed. 'A taste for salt, perhaps.'

'What would you have been had your parents not died and left you with three children to bring up?'

'A lawyer, I think, though possibly . . .' I hesitated.

'Possibly what?'

'Well . . . it sounds a bit odd, especially after the last few days . . . a policeman.'

'Ah,' he said softly, 'that figures.' He leant his head back again and smiled.

'Marriage might help you feel more settled,' he suggested.

'More ties,' I said. 'Another family to provide for. The rut for ever.'

'So that's how you look at it. How about Elinor?'

'She's a nice girl.'

'But not for keeps?'

I shook my head.

'You went to a great deal of trouble to save her life,' he pointed out.

'It was only because of me that she got into danger at all.'

'You couldn't know that she would be so strongly attracted to you and find you so . . . er . . . irresistible that she would drive out to take another look at you. When you went back to Humber's to extricate her, you had already finished the investigation, tidily, quietly, and undiscovered. Isn't that right?'

'I suppose so. Yes.'

'Did you enjoy it?'

'Enjoy it?' I repeated, surprised.

'Oh, I don't mean the fracas at the end, or the hours of honest toil you had to put in.' He smiled briefly. 'But the . . . shall we say, the chase?'

'Am I, in fact, a hunter by nature?'

'Are you?'

'Yes.'

There was a silence. My unadorned affirmative hung in the air, bald and revealing.

'Were you afraid at all?' His voice was matter of fact.

'Yes.'

'To the point of incapacity?'

I shook my head.

'You knew Adams and Humber would kill you if they found you out. What effect did living in perpetual danger have on you?' His voice was so clinical that I answered with similar detachment.

'It made me careful.'

'Is that all?'

'Well, if you mean was I in a constant state of nervous tension, then no, I wasn't.'

'I see.' Another of his small pauses. Then he said, 'What did you find hardest to do?'

I blinked, grinned, and lied. 'Wearing those loathsome pointed shoes.'

He nodded as if I had told him a satisfying truth. I probably had. The pointed shoes had hurt my pride, not my toes.

And pride had got the better of me properly when I visited Elinor in her college and hadn't been strong enough to play an oaf in her company. All that stuff about Marcus Aurelius was sheer showing off, and the consequences had been appalling. It didn't bear thinking of, let alone confessing.

Beckett said idly, 'Would you ever consider doing something similar again?'

'I should think so. Yes. But not like that.'

'How do you mean?'

'Well . . . I didn't know enough, for one thing. For example, it was just luck that Humber always left his office unlocked, because I couldn't have got in if he hadn't. I don't know how to open doors without keys. I would have found a camera useful . . . I could have taken films of the blue ledger in Humber's office, and so on, but my knowledge of photography is almost nil. I'd have got the exposures wrong. Then I had never fought anyone in my life before. If I'd known anything at all about unarmed combat I probably wouldn't have killed Adams or been so much battered myself. Apart from all that there was nowhere where I could send you or Edward a message and be sure you would receive it quickly. Communications, in fact, were pretty hopeless.'

'Yes. I see. All the same, you did finish the job in spite of those disadvantages.'

'It was luck. You couldn't count on being lucky twice.'

'I suppose not.' He smiled.'What do you plan to do with your twenty thousand pounds?'

'I . . . er . . . plan to let Edward keep most of it.'

'What do you mean?'

'I can't take that sort of money. All I ever wanted was to get away for a bit. It was he who suggested such a large sum, not me. I don't think he thought I would take on the job for less, but he was wrong . . . I'd have done it for nothing if I could. All I'll accept from him is the amount it has cost for me to be away. He knows, I told him last night.'

There was a long pause. Finally Beckett sat up and picked up a telephone. He dialled and waited.

'This is Beckett,' he said. 'It's about Daniel Roke . . . yes, he's here.' He took a postcard out of an inner pocket. 'Those points we were discussing this morning . . . I have had a talk with him. You have your card?'

He listened for a moment, and leaned back again in

357

his chair. His eyes were steady on my face.

'Right?' He spoke into the telephone. 'Numbers one to four can all have an affirmative. Number five is satisfactory. Number six, his weakest spot ... he didn't maintain his role in front of Elinor Tarren. She said he was good mannered and intelligent. No one else thought so ... yes, I should say so, sexual pride ... apparently only because Elinor is clever as well as pretty, since he kept it up all right with her younger sister ... yes ... oh undoubtedly it was his intellect as much as his physical appearance which attracted her ... yes, very good looking: I believe you sometimes find that useful ... no, he doesn't. He didn't look in the mirror in the washroom at the Club or in the one on the wall here ... no, he didn't admit it today, but I'd say he is well aware he failed on that point ... yes, rather a harsh lesson ... it may still be a risk, or it may have been sheer unprofessionalism ... your Miss Jones could find out, yes.'

I didn't particularly care for this dispassionate vivisection, but short of walking out there seemed to be no way of avoiding it. His eyes still looked at me expressionlessly.

'Number seven ... normal reaction. Eight, slightly obsessive, but that's all the better from your point of view.' He glanced momentarily down at the card he held in his hand. 'Nine ... well, although he is British by birth and spent his childhood here, he is Australian by inclination, and I doubt whether subservience comes easily . . . I don't know, he wouldn't talk about it . . . no, I wouldn't say he had a vestige of a martyr complex, he's clear on that . . . Of course you never get a perfect one . . . it's entirely up to you . . . Number ten? The three B's. I should say definitely not the first two, much too proud. As for the third, he's the type to shout for help. Yes, he's still here. Hasn't moved a muscle . . . yes, I do think so . . . all right . . . I'll ring you again later.'

He put down the receiver. I waited. He took his time and I refrained consciously from fidgeting under his gaze.

'Well?' he said at last.

'If you're going to ask what I think, the answer is no.'

'Because you don't want to, or because of your sisters and brother?'

'Philip is still only thirteen.'

'I see.' He made a weak-looking gesture with his hand. 'All the same, I'd better make sure you know what you are turning down. The colleague who kept me late this morning, and to whom I was talking just now, runs one of the counter-espionage departments – not only political but scientific and industrial, and anything else which crops up. His section are rather good at doing what you have done – becoming an inconspicuous part of the background. It's amazing how little notice even agents take of servants and workmen . . . and his lot have had some spectacular results. They are often used to check on suspected immigrants and political refugees who may not be all they seem, not by watching from afar, but by working for or near them day by day. And recently, for instance, several of the section have been employed as labourers on top-secret construction sites . . . there have been some disturbing leaks of security; complete site plans of secret installations have been sold abroad; and it was found that a commercial espionage firm was getting information through operatives actually putting brick on brick and photographing the buildings at each stage.'

'Philip,' I said, 'is only thirteen.'

'You wouldn't be expected to plunge straight into such a life. As you yourself pointed out, you are untrained. There would be at least a year's instruction in various techniques before you were given a job.'

'I can't,' I said.

'Between jobs all his people are given leave. If a job takes as long as four months, like the one you have just done, they get about six weeks off. They never work more than nine months in a year, if it can be helped. You could often be home in the school holidays.'

'If I'm not there all the time, there won't be enough money for fees and there won't be any home.'

'It is true that the British Government wouldn't pay you as much as you earn now,' he said mildly, 'but there are such things as full-time stud managers.'

I opened my mouth and shut it again.

'Think about it,' he said gently. 'I've another colleague to see . . . I'll be back in an hour.'

He levered himself out of the chair and slowly walked out of the room.

The pigeons fluttered peaceably on the window sill. I thought of the years I had spent building up the stud-farm, and what I had achieved there. In spite of my comparative youth the business was a solid success, and by the time I was fifty I could, with a bit of luck, put it among the top studs in Australia and enjoy a respected, comfortably-off, influential middle age.

What Beckett was offering was a lonely life of unprivileged jobs and dreary lodgings, a life of perpetual risk which could very well end with a bullet in the head.

Rationally, there was no choice. Belinda and Helen and Philip still needed a secure home with the best I could do for them as a father substitute. And no sensible person would hand over to a manager a prosperous business and become instead a sort of sweeper-up of some of the world's smaller messes . . . one couldn't put the job any higher than that.

But irrationally . . . With very little persuasion I had already left my family to fend for themselves, for as Beckett said, I wasn't the stuff of martyrs; and the prosperous business had already driven me once into the pit of depression.

I knew now clearly what I was, and what I could do.

I remembered the times when I had been tempted to give up and hadn't. I remembered the moment when I held Elinor's dog whistle in my hand and my mind made an almost muscular leap at the truth. I remembered the satisfaction I felt in Kandersteg's scorched enclosure, knowing I had finally uncovered and defeated Adams and Humber. No sale of any horse had ever brought so quiet and complete a fulfilment.

The hour passed. The pigeons defecated on the window and flew away. Colonel Beckett came back.

'Well?' he said. 'Yes or no?'

'Yes.'

He laughed aloud. 'Just like that? No questions or reservations?'

'No reservations. But I will need time to arrange things at home.'

'Of course.' He picked up the telephone receiver. 'My colleague will wish you to see him before you go back.' He rested his fingers on the dial. 'I'll make an appointment.'

'And one question.'

'Yes?'

'What are the three B's of number ten?'

He smiled secretly, and I knew he had intended that I should ask: which meant that he wanted me to know the answer. Devious, indeed. My nostrils twitched as if at the scent of a whole new world. A world where I belonged.

'Whether you could be bribed or bludgeoned or blackmailed,' he said casually, 'into changing sides.'

He dialled the number, and altered my life.

extracts reading groups
competitions books new
discounts extracts events
competitions extracts
books new discounts
new books reading groups
events extracts
extracts new titles reading groups
interviews
events extracts events
discounts books
new books events
events new events
discounts extracts discounts books
www.panmacmillan.com
extracts events reading groups
competitions books extracts new